THE DCI JACK LOGAN COLLECTION

BOOKS 4-6

JD KIRK

ZERTEX CRIME

THE DCI JACK LOGAN COLLECTION VOLUME 2
ISBN: 978-1-912767-45-8

Published worldwide by Zertex Media Ltd.
This edition published in 2020.

www.jdkirk.com
www.zertexmedia.com

BOOKS BY J.D. KIRK

A Litter of Bones

Thicker Than Water

The Killing Code

Blood & Treachery

The Last Bloody Straw

A Whisper of Sorrows

The Big Man Upstairs

A Death Most Monumental

A Snowball's Chance in Hell

Ahead of the Game

An Isolated Incident

WRITING AS BARRY J. HUTCHISON

Space Team

Dan Deadman: Space Detective

The Sidekicks Initiative

BLOOD AND TREACHERY

DCI JACK LOGAN BOOK FOUR

CHAPTER ONE

THE CALL HAD COME IN THE NIGHT BEFORE, JUST AS FULTON HAD BEEN settling down to read Carrie her bedtime story. The book was some nonsense about a magnetic cow, but she loved the pictures, and they'd always take time to point out all her favourite bits whenever she came to stay over.

Truth be told, he probably looked forward to it more than she did.

It had been years since they'd had a wee one in the house, and while he hadn't been expecting to become a grandfather quite so soon, there was no denying that the adorable wee bugger had been a blessing. She'd fairly put the bounce back into his wife's step, and had been just the kick up the backside he'd needed to avoid sliding gracelessly into a late middle-aged spread.

They'd just brushed her teeth, given Granny a kiss, and were heading up the stairs when the call came. Missing climber. Helicopter en route. All hands on deck.

That had been... what? Fourteen hours ago? He was sure they'd have found him by now, but no such luck. Still no sign.

From the car park, he could see most of the summit of Buachaille Etive Mor, aside from a few areas where the cloud clung to the peak like a wrap of cotton wool. There were two teams engaged in the search—Glencoe Mountain Rescue, and their neighbours from Lochaber—and he occasionally caught glimpses of them as they crisscrossed over the Buachaille, searching for the missing man.

The Coastguard chopper had been forced to return to Inverness for refuelling a few hours back, and some sort of collision in the Moray Firth was going to keep it busy for the foreseeable, which meant the only way they were finding the guy was on foot.

Even assuming all the information on his location was correct, it was a big mountain to cover. If he'd changed his mind and ventured elsewhere—one of the Three Sisters, maybe—then their chances of finding him were virtually non-existent.

Fulton wasn't thinking about any of that, right at that moment, though. He was thinking about his stomach, which was loudly rumbling, and felt like it was twisting itself in knots.

He unwrapped the porridge oats bar he kept in his kit and took a bite. It had the same amount of oats as a bowl of porridge, apparently. Pity it tasted like a lump of lightly-sugared cardboard.

His radio *squawked* at him, forcing him to chew faster. The dry, grainy oats put up a good fight, but he was eventually able to swallow the claggy lump down.

"Aye, go ahead," he said, using a pinkie to fish a stray wad of porridge out from between his teeth and gums. "Any sign?"

The voice on the other end belonged to Gary Rigg. He was one of the younger members of the team, though more experienced than many. His exhaustion weighed down his words as they tumbled from the radio.

They'd been up there for hours now, battling the cold, the rain, and the mountain itself. It had been dark for most of it, and Fulton knew from experience how effectively that particular combination of factors could strip away all your energy, taking most of your optimism with it. Lose that hope, and the drive to push through the pain all-but evaporated.

They were good lads, though. They'd keep going for as long as they had to. They always did.

"Any word on the chopper coming back?" Gary asked. "We could do with the support."

"Not yet. It won't be any time soon," Fulton told him. There was no point sugar-coating it. None of them would thank him for it. "We're on our own for now."

There was some swearing. Mostly good-natured, but not exclusively.

"Aye. Fine," Gary responded. "I've sent Chris back down. His knee's giving him gyp. Thought you could check him out."

Fulton winced. "He'll no' be happy about that. What way's he coming?"

"Your way. Down past the SMC hut. You'll probably see him soon."

Fulton's gaze flicked across to the white stone building with its roof of local Ballachulish Slate. Sure enough, he could just make out a figure limping forlornly down the slope behind and to the right of it. He'd known Chris long enough to judge his body language, and as a result, could well imagine the *actual* language currently coming out of his mouth.

Chris was one of the old guard. He'd have wanted to see it through, and would not take well to being benched.

"Aye, I've got him," Fulton said. "I'll let you know if I hear more about air support. Stay safe and keep in touch."

Gary grunted a sign-off, and Fulton watched Chris make his way closer. He was still a good few hundred yards away, just approaching the footbridge that crossed the River Coupall.

Chris had just stepped onto the bridge when he stopped, turned, and back-tracked. He took half a dozen paces to the left, squatted down, and peered at something on the ground.

Fulton watched him, his tongue exploring inside his mouth for any last crumbs of the porridge bar. His stomach grumbled in complaint when no hidden caches were discovered between his teeth.

Over by the bridge, Chris knelt down and brushed at the ground in front of him. His movements were slow and wary, like he was clearing away a large cobweb and was worried something eight-legged and angry might pounce on him at any moment.

"OK..." Fulton muttered, still watching. He leaned forward and squinted, trying to get a better view.

Chris's next movement was sharp and sudden. He sprang to his feet, his age and all concern for his long-suffering knees forgotten. His retreat was a series of hops, one hand held in front of him as if for protection from whatever he'd seen.

Fulton saw the older man grasp for his radio. His voice came out as a thin crackle through the speaker. He almost sounded calm, and had Fulton not just watched his performance, he might even have fallen for it.

"Hello? Fulton? I've found something."

"Aye. I noticed," Fulton replied. He swallowed, his mouth suddenly dry. "What is it?"

There was a pause. Not a long one, but long enough to disguise an unwelcome shake in a voice.

"It's a body," Chris said.

Fulton heard him exhale. At the same time, he saw him look up, and both men locked eyes from opposite sides of the river.

"But I don't think it's the fella we're looking for."

CHAPTER TWO

An hour or so before the body was found, and a hundred-odd miles away, DCI Jack Logan sat face to face with a monster.

There had been a change of staff at Carstairs State Hospital since he'd last been in. This wasn't any great surprise. It wasn't the sort of place that people settled into for the long haul. Admin staff, in particular, came and went so quickly they were given stickers instead of name badges, their tenure at the hospital often as temporary as the adhesive on the back.

Still, his warrant card, a few white lies, and what could generously be described as some 'persuasive charm' had got him through security. Had got him here. Now.

With him.

Owen Petrie, the man behind the 'Mister Whisper' child murders of over a decade ago, sat back in the padded chair beside his bed, directly across from the Detective Chief Inspector. A vague, half-there sort of smile tugged idly at the corners of his mouth, and he hummed quietly but tunelessly, as if trying to remember a song he'd once known.

He looked healthier than the last time Logan had seen him, which was a bit of a kick in the teeth. In all the years he'd been coming to visit Petrie, Logan had taken a perverse pleasure in watching the bastard getting smaller and more shrivelled, like the life was being drained out of him drop by filthy drop.

Today, though, he looked stronger. Younger, even. Someone had given him a shave recently, so only a suggestion of stubble shaded his chin. His hair, too, had been trimmed and combed down the left side of his head. Anyone standing on that side of him would have seen the profile of a respectable-looking older guy. A bit glassy-eyed, maybe, but normal enough.

From the other side, it was a different story. The fall Petrie had sustained while being brought to justice had caved in part of his skull, and caused the brain damage that had left him in a state just a couple of steps above 'vegetable'.

At least, that's what he wanted everyone to believe. Logan, unlike everyone else, hadn't fallen for it.

From his temple to up past his ear was a mess of ridges, dents, and scar tissue. The odd clump of hair sprouted here and there like bushes in the desert, but otherwise, the damage was laid bare for all to see.

"You're looking well, Owen," Logan told him. "Feeling better, are we?"

Petrie's smile broadened. He shuffled in his chair, adjusting himself, but said nothing.

"Sorry I've not been in to see you for a while, Owen," Logan continued. "Truth be told, I don't really waste much time thinking about you these days."

That was a lie, of course. A big one. No way was he letting the bastard know that, though.

"Have you missed me?" he pressed. "You missed our wee chats?"

Logan's own chair creaked as he shifted his not-inconsiderable weight forward in it. "Is that why you've been phoning me?"

He watched for the reaction on Petrie's face. Scrutinised it, searching for some minute change in expression that would give him away. There was nothing, though. Just that same empty stare, and the same half-aware smirk as always.

"Because it is you, isn't it, Owen?" Logan said. "I know it's you. You've been the one calling me."

This time, the change on Petrie's face was almost immediate. His brow twitched. His eyes tightened focus a little, like he was now looking at the DCI rather than through him.

"On... the phone?" he asked, struggling to form the words.

"Aye."

"I've n-not got a ph-phone."

"See, I think you have, Owen," Logan said. "I think you do have a phone, and I think that—for whatever reason—you've been using it to call me."

Logan stood up suddenly, and the man in the chair flinched, drawing back. That seemed to shrink him again, and the detective took a moment to savour Petrie's panicked expression before pulling open the plastic drawers of the room's one and only storage unit.

"N-no, don't," Petrie pleaded.

The drawer was filled with socks and underwear. Logan rummaged through it, ignoring the stammered objections from the monster in the corner.

Fishing down at the bottom of the drawer, he found something wrapped in a plastic bag.

"Oh-ho, what do we have here, Owen?" he asked, shooting a look in Petrie's direction.

The bag came out with a couple of firm yanks, ejecting a few black socks and several pairs of baggy off-white underwear onto the floor.

Petrie squirmed in his chair, his face a rictus of horror, his voice deserting him. He looked away as Logan unwrapped the bag and peered inside.

It wasn't a phone. Far from it. Sitting at the bottom of the bag was an open pack of incontinence pads, half of the contents gone.

Reaching into the bag, Logan gave the packaging a squeeze, still hoping he'd find a handset tucked away in there. No such luck.

In his chair, Petrie's cheeks burned red. His eyes were down, his fingers knotting and twisting together. One leg bounced, shaking the floor beneath Logan's feet.

Tossing the bag onto the floor, Logan went back to rummaging through the drawer again, pulling out underwear by the handful and casting it aside.

"Where is it?" he demanded. "I know you've got a phone here somewhere, Owen. So where the hell—"

"What on Earth is going on?"

Logan recognised the voice without turning. That doctor. The new one who'd started a few months back. Logan had crossed swords with him on his last couple of visits. What was the name again?

"D-doctor Ramesh," Petrie said, and the relief in his voice was palpable. "Doctor Ramesh."

"It's OK, Owen. Nothing to worry about," the doctor said, stepping into the room.

He was shorter than Logan, but held himself with a level of authority that added a couple of inches. There was a suggestion of an Indian accent right at the edges of his voice when he spoke, but only if you were looking for it. Mostly, he sounded what Logan always thought of as 'rich English'—a sort of generic, upper-middle-class brogue that had been sandpapered smooth through years of expensive private education.

"Well, Mr..." Ramesh waved a hand vaguely. "Logan, isn't it? I asked you a question. What on Earth do you think you're doing?"

"I'm conducting an interview," Logan told him, although the handful of y-fronts he held in each hand didn't really lend any weight to the statement. "I have reason to believe that Owen here has been—"

"Frankly, I couldn't care less what you have 'reason to believe,' Mr Logan," the doctor snapped. "You have no permission to be here. None. You are endangering the health of my patient, not to mention intimidating and harassing him unlawfully."

Logan deposited the underwear back in the drawer and turned to Ramesh, using his height advantage to loom over the smaller man. Ramesh, to his credit, didn't miss a step.

"You will leave the premises now. Either of your own free will, or I can have security escort you. That's your decision, but you *are* leaving," the doctor said. "And I'll be reporting this immediately to your superiors. If they won't take action, I'll escalate to the press, if I have to."

Logan snorted. "Oh, aye. That'll be a scoop. 'Police question convicted child murderer.' Imagine the scandal."

"'Police illegally threaten man with mental disability,' would be how I'd frame it, personally," Ramesh said. He reached into his coat pocket and produced a phone. "Now, are you leaving, or am I having you thrown out?"

For a moment, it looked like Logan might go for the second option. But then, he jabbed a finger in Petrie's direction, muttered a warning about how this wasn't over, before barging past Ramesh and out into the corridor.

By the time Logan was passing reception, he could hear Petrie humming.

By the time he was halfway across the car park, his phone was ringing.

He glanced at the screen, grunted, then looked back at the building as he pressed the handset to his ear. "Christ, have you got a camera on this place or something?" he asked. "That's twice you've phoned me at this exact spot."

"What the hell do you think you're playing at?" spat the voice on the other end.

Detective Superintendent Gordon Mackenzie—known as 'the Gozer' to most of the Scottish constabulary—rarely sounded happy. In grumpy-old-bastard terms, Logan's former superior was second only to his present superior, Detective Superintendent Bob Hoon, who had successfully turned contempt into a legitimate art form.

Today, though, the Gozer sounded like he might be angling to take Hoon's title from him.

"I've just had a phone call, Jack," the Gozer barked. "Do you want to guess who from?"

"Postcode Lottery?" Logan guessed. He winced, instantly regretting the smart-arsed remark.

He took the phone away from his ear while he tapped the button on the door of his Volvo and climbed inside. By the time the phone had connected to Bluetooth and started playing through the car's speakers, the Gozer's angry outburst was on the wane.

"—I'll fucking 'Postcode Lottery' ye!" he bellowed. "You know full well who it was from. You've been in seeing him again, haven't you? Petrie."

"Aye," Logan admitted, figuring there was no point in trying to conceal the truth.

"And what the hell did you do that for? I thought you were done with him.

In fact, what are you even doing down here? You moved! I thought we got rid of you!"

Logan pushed down on the clutch and tapped the button that started the engine. "I have reason to believe that Owen Petrie has been calling me from Carstairs," he said.

He practically heard the sneer of ridicule down the phone. "Oh, aye? And what reason's that, Jack? Paranoid Schizophrenia?" the Gozer asked. "The man's a bloody cabbage. He's no' phoning anyone."

The dash display finished its animated boot-up sequence and settled on the map screen. It showed a little triangle inside the big grey square that represented the hospital's car park. Logan's eyes drifted idly to the clock in the top right-hand corner while he considered his reply to the Gozer's rant.

He opened his mouth to speak, then hesitated. His gaze flicked from the clock to the watch on his wrist.

"Shite," he muttered, giving his wrist a shake. The second hand ticked on a few notches, then stopped again. "Shite!"

"What's the problem now?" the Gozer demanded.

Logan grabbed for his belt, snatched up his phone, and hovered his thumb over the screen as he wrestled the strap across his chest.

"Sorry, sir, we'll have to continue this another time," he said.

"*What*?!" the Gozer hissed. "We'll talk about it now, Jack. Not when you decide. We'll talk about it—"

Logan tapped the red phone icon on the screen, then tossed the handset into one of the Volvo's storage dookets.

A moment later, he picked it back up again, dialled another number, and listened to the ringing tone come *burring* out through the speakers.

"Come on, come on," he whispered.

There was a click from the earpiece. He sat up straight, watching the screen like he might be able to see the person on the other end of the line. "Hello?" he said, then he tutted when a synthesised computer voice replied.

"The number you have called cannot be reached at the moment..."

Another thumb-jab aborted the call. He wasted a few seconds typing out a text message—'On my way'—then chucked the phone, checked his mirrors and, with a roar of an engine and a spinning of wheels, went racing out of the car park.

CHAPTER THREE

SHE HAD LEFT BY THE TIME HE ARRIVED, AN EMPTY COFFEE CUP, COLD TO the touch, the only indication that she'd ever been there.

"Bollocks," Logan declared, drawing a few raised eyebrows and worried looks from the Kelvinside pan-loafers sitting sipping their Lady Greys around the neighbouring tables.

The tea room's clientele had looked alarmed enough when he'd come stumbling in through the front door, out of breath, sweat sticking the shirt to his back. Now that he'd started ejecting random obscenities at an empty table, some of them looked like they might be heading for an attack of the vapours.

"Can I help you, sir?"

Logan turned to find a young man in a black shirt and white apron eyeing him apprehensively, a tray of assorted scones balanced expertly on one raised hand.

"Aye. Maybe. There was a girl... A woman here. Short brown hair. About your height."

"Maddie. Yes," the waiter said. "She left."

"Well, I can see that. When?"

"Twenty minutes ago, maybe." The waiter's gaze gave Logan a quick once over, while his free hand went into the pocket of his apron. "She asked me to give you this."

Logan accepted the crisply folded napkin he was offered. He could feel all eyes in the place on him as he opened it up and read the short message scribbled just under the cafe's printed logo.

Thanks a fucking bunch, Dad.

Refolding the napkin, Logan pulled together some semblance of a smile. "Thanks," he told the waiter.

He looked around at the Kelvinside hoi polloi, with their flared nostrils and their judgemental looks. For a moment, he wanted to shout, to lash out, to punish them for his own bloody stupidity.

Instead, he said, "Sorry to have bothered you," and marched out the door without another word.

SHE ANSWERED on his third try, the phone having been diverted to voicemail twice, and the three text messages he'd sent having gone unanswered. Her voice barked at him through the speaker of the Volvo, amplified by the echo of the car's interior.

"What?"

Logan flinched. It was just a single word, yet it had sounded dangerous. Locked and loaded, like a bomb that might blow up in his face if he prodded it in the wrong place.

"Maddie. It's me."

"I know who it is. Your name comes up. *What*?"

"Look, I'm sorry, sweetheart," Logan told her. "My watch stopped. I lost track of time."

"Your watch stopped?" Maddie shot back. Her pitch went up half an octave. *Tick-tick-tick went the bomb.* "Seriously? Is that the best you can do?"

"Seriously, aye. I know it sounds... Well, I know how it sounds, but I'm telling the truth. It must need a new battery or something. I can send you a photo. I thought I had plenty of time, but then I realised, and..." He sighed. "Look, where are you? Why don't you come back?"

There was no response. That was promising. Maybe he'd be able to avoid an explosion, after all.

"Or, I could come to you. We could go somewhere else."

Somewhere that's no' full of stuck up arseholes, he added in his head.

"I'm supposed to be heading into work," she replied.

Not a 'yes,' but not a 'no,' either. It was time for his big play. He was cutting the red wire.

"You can spare your old man half an hour, surely?" Logan urged.

He stopped talking, left the silence hanging there for her to fill.

"Twenty minutes," she countered.

"Deal," Logan said, not daring to push his luck. "I'd make it this end of town, though. Getting across the M8 was a nightmare on the way in from Carluke."

He regretted it the moment the words left his lips.

There was another silence. This one felt heavier, more oppressive than before.

"Carluke?"

Tick-tick-tick.

Shite.

"You were in Carluke?" she asked.

"Aye," Logan said. "I was... It was a work thing."

"You were in seeing *him*, weren't you?" Maddison asked. There was no detonation. No big bang. She didn't even sound angry. He almost wished she did.

"It was—"

She sighed. It was sad, disappointed, and weary all at once.

"I should've known. God. You'd think, after all these years, I'd have remembered."

"What are you talking about, sweetheart? Remembered what?"

Her voice cracked, just a fraction. If he didn't know her, he wouldn't even have picked up on it.

"Who comes first."

"Hey, come on. What's that supposed to mean?" Logan protested. "You know that's not—"

"Listen, Dad, I better get to work."

"No, but I thought—"

She cut him off. Her voice was rock-solid now. She sounded like her mother.

"Safe trip up the road."

There was no point trying to convince her. Nothing he could do would change her mind. He'd blown it, good and proper.

"Right. Aye. Well, maybe I can give you a shout next time I'm down?"

"Aye," she said. "Maybe."

And then, the low electronic buzz that had accompanied the call stopped, and her name disappeared from the screen in the Volvo's dash.

Logan bumped his head against the padded headrest and gripped the steering wheel, his fingers tightening as if he could strangle the thing. Or better, strangle the whole bloody world.

Petrie. This was Petrie's fault, he told himself. And, not for the first time, he almost managed to believe it.

The phone rang again, blasting out of the stereo system. The surge of hope he felt faded as soon as he saw the name on the display. Ben Forde.

Logan sighed, took a moment to compose himself, then tapped one of the buttons on the underside of the steering wheel. "Ben. What's up?"

"Alright, Jack? How are things going down there?"

"Fucking awful," Logan replied. He had known the Detective Inspector too long to bother mincing his words.

"The usual, then," Ben replied. "You still heading back up the road today?"

"Aye. Shortly. Why?" Logan asked, although he could hazard a pretty good guess.

"You're going to have to make a stop in Glen Coe on the way. We'll meet you there," Ben told him. "Something's come up."

To his shame, Logan felt a moment of something not a million miles away from elation. Relief, maybe. This, he could deal with. This, he could do.

He pulled on his belt. With a jab of a button, the Volvo's engine purred into life.

"Text me the details," he instructed. "I'm on my way."

CHAPTER FOUR

There had been a bit of snarl-up of traffic on the approach to the car park, mostly caused by drivers craning their necks to try to see what all the flashing lights and fuss were about.

A couple of Uniforms had moved to intercept the Volvo as it had rumbled up the uneven track leading to the cordon, then had waved and stepped aside when he'd given them a flash of the blues.

A helicopter was circling overhead when Logan stepped out of the SUV, low enough that the *whumming* of its rotors kept altering the pressure in his ears. There were three polis cars and a van in the car park, as well as a few civilian vehicles and a Land Rover with Mountain Rescue livery on the side.

Near the Land Rover, a couple of guys in outdoor gear were sharing their flasks with three officers in high-vis jackets. The younger of the men said something into a radio and the chopper began to climb, then banked in the direction of the mountain that loomed over the scene.

The lightest suggestion of drizzle whispered through the air, the drops not so much falling as floating on the breeze, never quite reaching the ground. Logan had been living in the Highlands for a good few months now, and had been constantly surprised by the sheer range of precipitation the place had to offer. He'd encountered at least twenty distinct varieties of rain, from *misty haze* to *pishin' doon*. Often all in the same day.

A uniformed sergeant got out of the van and started making his way over to Logan, feet alternating between crunching and squelching on the uneven ground. Logan dug his warrant card from his pocket and offered it up as the sergeant drew closer.

"DCI Jack Logan. MIT."

"Aye, I know, sir," the sergeant replied. "We met briefly before. On the missing boy case. Connor Reid."

He offered a hand. "Sergeant Jaffray. Greig."

Logan tried to feign recognition, but clearly didn't do a very good job of it.

"At the initial scene. You... you asked me to get rid of a sheep."

"Christ. Aye," Logan said. "They made you a sergeant?"

He hadn't intended to sound quite so surprised, it just sort of happened. Here was the man, after all, who had tried to *physically pick up* a sheep in order to remove it from a crime scene. The man who Logan had accused of winning his job in a raffle.

A sergeant. A bloody sergeant.

What was the world coming to?

"They did, sir," Greig confirmed. If he'd picked up on the DCI's shock, he wasn't showing it. "Been... what? Three weeks now, is it?"

"Are you asking me or telling me?"

Greig smiled awkwardly. "Ha. Telling you, sir. It's been about three weeks."

"Right. Well, good. Well done," Logan said. He gestured to the tent that had been erected on the opposite side of the river that ran along the car park's edge. It sat like a tumour on the otherwise unspoiled wilderness. "What have we got?"

"Oh. Aye. Sorry," Greig said. "It's a body, sir."

Logan eyed him expectantly.

"A... a dead one."

A sergeant. God help them.

"Right. And?"

Greig's gaze tick-tocked between the DCI and the tent. "Well, I don't really know, sir. Mountain Rescue called it in. One of their boys found it, half-buried."

"An accident, then? Hill-walker?" Logan asked.

"No, he doesn't think so. I didn't get too good a look, myself. We were told just to protect the scene and wait for the cavalry. I'm guessing that's you."

"Looks like it," Logan conceded. "CID not been round?"

"They're on a training course," Greig said. "In Elgin, I think."

"Right."

"Nice place, Elgin," the sergeant continued, almost absent-mindedly. "They've got the cathedral."

Logan pursed his lips and raised his eyebrows. He kept his face that way until the message got through.

Sergeant Jaffray cleared his throat. "Anyway, they've said to keep them posted, but reckoned it was more of an MIT thing, so Jinkies... Uh, I mean, Chief Inspector Pickering, got in touch with Inverness, and..."

Logan's expression still hadn't changed. Greig cleared his throat for a second time, and had another go.

"Do you... Do you want to take a look at the body?"

"Aye," Logan said, already striding past the uniformed officer. "I mean, I did come all this way. Be a shame not to."

Greig watched the DCI go marching across the car park in the direction of the Land Rover. "It's, uh, the body's over that way, sir," he called, indicating the white canvas structure that had been erected by the footbridge. "In the tent."

Logan stopped and turned. "Right. Maybe you could keep an eye on it, Sergeant, while I go talk to the Mountain Rescue guys. Could you do that for me?"

"Keep an eye on the tent?"

"Exactly. Make sure nobody goes in."

Greig glanced around at the empty wilderness, then he straightened, stopping just short of firing off a salute. "Right you are, sir. I'm on it."

"Good lad," Logan told him.

Then, with a turn on his heel and a roll of his eyes, he continued on over to the knot of men gathered by the Land Rover. Hands were shaken, introductions were made, and an offer of tea was politely declined.

"There's going to be an accident on that road if people don't quit their rubbernecking," Logan told the Uniforms, indicating the snarl-up of slow-moving traffic on the bend approaching the car park. "Go and sort it out, will you?"

"Yes, sir."

"On it, sir."

Logan waited until they'd scurried off, then got down to business with the two members of the rescue team. One of them, who'd introduced himself as Fulton Randall, did most of the talking. He was in his late-forties, Logan guessed, and had the same no-nonsense air about him as most of the mountain rescue guys the DCI had met.

Aye, sure, they were usually up for a laugh, and most of them could've drunk him under the table, even during his worst pre-teetotal days, but when it got down to the subject of life and death, they were the type of lads you wanted on your side.

The other man was older and less forthcoming. Chris O'Hare. He'd been the one who had found the body, and the only one of the two to have actually seen it.

"Once Chris realised what we were dealing with, we thought it best not to go trampling all over the place and compromise the scene," Fulton explained.

"Aye. Good," said Logan. He shot a look in the direction of Sergeant Jaffray. "I'm sure my lot could manage that all by themselves."

"It was a bit of a pantomime watching them put up the tent, right enough," Fulton said. "Thought they were going to take off at one point."

"Great. The Scene of Crime boys will be delighted to hear that," Logan said.

He looked up at the helicopter. It was currently buzzing around the top of the closest mountain, like a bee sniffing eagerly around a flower.

From the road, the mountain had looked big. Here, closer to where it rose steeply up from the ground, it was a giant of a thing, imposing itself against the mottled grey sky.

And to think, people climbed the things for fun.

"Someone lost, I take it?" Logan asked.

Fulton nodded. "Call came in via you guys last night. No sign of him, though. We're actually starting to think it might've been a hoax. Some of the details they gave on the phone don't really stack up. The number they left goes nowhere. Most likely someone on the wind-up." He puffed out his cheeks and shrugged. "Still, got to check, haven't you?"

"Bastards," Logan said, which was about as close to a show of empathy as he was likely to get. "But aye. I suppose you do."

"Anyway, Chris was coming back down. Knackered knee. He's not as young as he used to be," Fulton said.

"Oi. Fucking watch it," Chris warned. His accent was from Northern Ireland, but mellowed by a bit of a Highland lilt. Not a born and bred local, then, but he'd been here a while.

Fulton smiled, but ignored him. "He was about to cross... Why am I telling him? Chris. You saw it."

Logan's gaze shifted to the older man. He squirmed a little, his eyes darting away. Either he wasn't one for speaking up around strangers, or he had something he was hiding.

"You were coming down the hill," Logan prompted, leaving the rest of the sentence hanging for Chris to complete.

"Mountain," Chris corrected. "It's not a hill."

"Mountain. Sorry," Logan said, although he didn't really see what difference it made. "What then?"

"Well, like this shitebag was saying, I'd just got to the bridge and something caught my eye. Like, I didn't see anything, as such. Not the body, anyway. But the way the ground had been messed with, I thought there was something buried under there."

He shot a look in the direction of the tent, and the lines of his face grew thin and tight. "I thought maybe it was a Geocache, or whatever. You know, the boxes folk hide for other people to find?"

Logan had absolutely no idea what the man was talking about, but it didn't feel important, so he nodded. "Sure."

"So, over I goes to check it out. I brush some of the dirt away, and that's when I sees it," Chris continued, his voice dropping to a whisper like he was telling a ghost story around a campfire. "An *ear*."

A crease formed on Logan's forehead. "An ear? What, on its own?"

"No. Attached to a head, like," Chris clarified. "I mean, I didn't know that right away. I just saw the ear at first, but then I clocked the rest of him. Poor bastard."

"Male, then?" Logan asked, taking out his notepad.

Chris nodded.

"Age?"

"Well, I don't know. Sure, I didn't ask to see his driver's licence."

"Approximately," Logan urged.

Chris shrugged, glanced shiftily between both men, then shrugged for a second time. "Twenties, maybe. I'm not sure. I didn't exactly get a good look at him, what with him being ninety-percent underground and everything."

"Right. Fair enough," Logan conceded.

"Based on what I did see, though, I reckon he's only been there a few days," Chris said. He offered up an answer to Logan's next question before he could ask it. "You do this job long enough, you get to see a whole lot of dead people in all kinds of states. You ask me, this one hadn't been kicking around too long. Of course, Fulton would know better than me."

Logan raised an inquisitive eyebrow in the other man's direction.

"Oh. GP. Or, I was. Retired now. Had enough of the budget cuts," Fulton said.

An upbeat Salsa number began to play from one of the pockets of his bright red jacket.

"Sorry," he said, peeling back the Velcro and unfastening the zip. He glanced at his phone screen for a second, frowned briefly, then put the phone to his ear and turned away from the other two men. "Hello? Hannah? Can you...?"

He shot the screen another quick look, then tried angling himself in another direction. "Hello? Yes. Got you. Aye. What's—"

Although he was a few feet away, Logan heard the panic in the voice on the other end of the line. He couldn't make out the words that made up the long garble that followed, but this Hannah, whoever she was, was worried.

"Whoa, whoa. Slow down, Han... You're breaking up. I can't... Hello? Hello?"

Fulton checked the screen again, then cursed under his breath.

"Everything alright?" Logan asked.

"Hmm? Oh, aye. It's nothing. It's my daughter's boyfriend. Fiancé, sorry.

He's been away for work for most of the week and was supposed to come home last night. We had the wee one staying over."

"And he didn't turn up?"

Fulton shook his head and checked his phone again, but the signal had died away to nothing. "No. She can't get hold of him on the phone, either. She hasn't heard from him in..."

He stopped talking then, the words shrivelling and dying somewhere at the back of his throat. His gaze fell on the tent, and his feet started shuffling him forward as if of their own free will.

"Oh no. No," he whispered. "Please God, no."

Logan was too slow to react. His hand brushed against the sleeve of Fulton's jacket, but the Gortex material slipped through his fingers as Fulton set off at a lumbering sprint.

"Oi! Wait!" Logan spat, giving chase. The ground was equal parts uneven and slippery, though, and his shoes were far from ideal.

With his well-worn walking boots, Fulton was off like a shot, clattering across the bridge before Logan could build up any sort of momentum.

"Wait! Stop right there!" he bellowed, slipping and sliding on the muddy ground.

Fulton was having none of it. Logan could only watch, helpless and slightly off-balance, as the mountain rescue man pulled open the flap of the tent. He had the sense not to dive inside. That was something, at least. Instead, he just stood there, one hand on his mouth, the other leaning on the tent's frame for support.

One of the Uniforms came clumping up at Logan's back. "Want me to get him, sir?"

Logan nodded and waved the officer ahead. "Aye, go," he wheezed. "Go."

He watched the officer go scurrying across the bridge. Over by the tent, Fulton took a few stumbled steps back and sunk to his knees, his legs no longer able or willing to support him. He buried his face in his hands, and even at that distance, with the chopper churning the sky overhead, Logan heard the sob.

"Ah," he muttered to nobody in particular. "Shite."

CHAPTER FIVE

"You're back, then."

Moira Corson stood behind the front desk of Fort William police station with a look on her face that suggested someone had just trodden dog shit into the carpets. She peered at Logan over the top of her narrow glasses, clearly waiting for some sort of response.

"Aye. Well spotted," Logan said, not bothering to hide the sarcasm. Good enough for the old cow. He pulled on the handle of the door that led through from reception into the station proper. The door *thunked* against the frame, but otherwise didn't budge.

With a sigh, Logan shot Moira an expectant look. "Well? Are you going to let me in?"

"I'll need to see your ID first," Moira told him.

"Bollocks you do. You know full well who I am. Open the door."

Moira flipped up the rectangular hatch at the bottom of the glass screen that separated them. "ID," she reiterated. "It's procedure. You might have no regard for the rules, but some of us still do."

Muttering, Logan fished in his pocket, then slapped the wallet containing his warrant card down on the counter. Moira regarded it with a slight flaring of her nostrils. "You have to—"

Snatching the wallet back up, Logan wrestled the card out of the holder and slid that through the gap on its own. "There. Happy?"

Without a word, Moira took the identification, held it up to the light, and spent several long seconds scrutinising it. Logan tried very hard not to look annoyed. He wasn't going to give her the satisfaction.

The trip she made to the photocopier to run off a copy of the card almost pushed him over the edge, granted, but he held his tongue until she finally slid the card back through the slot, and he manhandled it back into its tight plastic covering.

"Right, is that us? Can I go through now?" Logan asked.

Before Moira could answer, the door was opened from the other side, and a cheerful-looking older man with thinning hair and a firmly established paunch made a beckoning motion in Logan's direction.

"There you are," said Detective Inspector Ben Forde. "We thought you'd got lost."

The Incident Room hadn't changed much since the team had last set up shop there, and it quickly began to feel familiar as Logan watched DS McQuarrie set up the Big Board. Caitlyn had a real knack for keeping the board—and, by extension the team—fully organised and up-to-date, and it only took her a few minutes to pull together all the information they currently had.

Mind you, all the information they currently had consisted of a name, a photograph, and a very brief statement, so it wasn't exactly a big ask to gather it all in one place.

Something wasn't quite the same as last time, though, Logan thought. Something about the whole thing was just ever so slightly different.

It took him several seconds before he could pinpoint what it was.

"Are you singing?"

Caitlyn, who had most definitely been singing quietly below her breath, stopped immediately and turned from the board.

"Uh, no. I mean, aye. Sorry, sir."

Logan shook his head. "I mean, it's fine. If you want to sing, you go ahead and sing. It's just..."

"You're usually such a crabbit bastard," DI Forde concluded. Caitlyn smiled briefly, then turned back to the board as Ben handed Logan a mug of hot tea. "We could've met you down there. At the scene."

Logan accepted the mug, set it down on a desk, then shrugged off his coat.

"Tyler was quite excited about it. He's never seen Glen Coe. Have you, Tyler?"

At a neighbouring desk, Detective Constable Tyler Neish looked up from his phone, hastily tapped a button on the side, then shoved it in his pocket. "Boss?"

"I was telling Jack. You've never seen Glen Coe."

"How can you have never seen Glen Coe? Weren't you brought up about sixty miles away?"

"Aye, but we always did the A9, boss. When we were going anywhere. Glasgow, or whatever," Tyler explained. "Down the A9, onto the M9 at Stirling, M80 turnoff—"

"Alright, alright. I wasn't asking for your travel diaries," Logan told him. "Don't worry, there'll be plenty of opportunity for us to get down there. Scene of Crime are giving it a going over now, and we can go take a look when they're done. I've asked them not to move the body until we get a look at it."

"Nice one!" Tyler beamed. He caught the looks from the others. "About seeing Glen Coe, I mean. Not... Not the body part."

"What body part?" asked DC Khaled, appearing in the doorway of the office at the back of the room. "Someone hacking them up again?"

"Not *body part* as in parts of a body," Tyler began to explain, but then he gave a shake of his head. "Forget it. It's nothing."

Hamza appeared completely nonplussed by this, but then shrugged and indicated the office behind him with a tilt of his head. "Fine. Router's working again, by the way. Just needed a reboot."

"Good work there from the I.T. Bitch," said DC Neish, firing Hamza a thumbs-up.

"I've changed the password to 'Tyler is a fanny,' all lowercase," Hamza countered. "I'm assuming everyone's fine with that?"

"I might use that for all my passwords going forward," said Ben. "Nice and easy to remember."

"Right, we're ready, sir," DS McQuarrie volunteered. "Floor's all yours."

"Thanks, Caitlyn," Logan said. He gulped down a quick mouthful of tea before approaching the board and tilting his mug to indicate the headshot the DS had pinned up. "Brodie Welsh. Age twenty-two. Local lad. Found dead this morning at the foot of..."

He pointed to Ben.

"Buachaille Etive Mor," Ben said.

"Aye. There," Logan continued.

"At the foot? So, what? Did he fall?" asked Hamza.

"Had a helluva nasty landing, if he did," Logan said. "I couldn't see much, but from what I could tell, his teeth have been knocked out."

"Could've happened in a fall," Tyler suggested.

"Possible," Logan conceded. "Less likely he'd bother to bury himself afterwards."

"You think the teeth were done on purpose? Someone didn't want him identified?" Caitlyn asked.

"Aye, maybe. We'll see how he's doing finger-wise. Either way, it didn't work. Unfortunately for whoever killed him, his fiancée's father was part of the mountain rescue team that found the body. Fulton Randall. He recognised him right away. Poor bastard."

"Which one?" Ben asked.

"Take your pick," Logan said with a shrug. "He didn't take it well when he saw the body."

"Considering some of the sights those guys see..." Caitlyn said.

"Aye. And he's a doctor, too. Retired. Still, different when it's someone close to you," Logan pointed out. "Fulton and his wife had been looking after their granddaughter the night before."

"The victim's daughter?" Ben asked.

"Aye. She's still there now. I had someone take Fulton home. He's going to talk to the wife, then they're going to go break the news to the daughter. I offered to do it, but he thinks it'll be better coming from them. I've asked to be there, though. Framed it as me being on hand to offer support."

"But you want to see her reaction," Ben finished.

"Thought it wouldn't hurt," Logan said. "Although, given the condition and remote location of the body, unless she's built like a brick shithouse, I doubt she's involved."

He motioned to Hamza. "Check them both out, though. See if either of them has any previous."

"Worth looking for any domestic violence reports, too," Caitlyn added, and Hamza scribbled down a couple of notes on the brand-new desk pad he'd sourced from the stationery cupboard in the small office while he'd waited for the router to reboot.

He had a bit of a thing for stationery—there was little better than an unused notebook and a new pen—and the cupboard had turned out to be a bit of a goldmine.

"How long has he been in the ground for?" Ben asked.

Logan made a non-committal sort of grunt at the back of his throat. "We'll know more once forensics are done and pathology has had a look."

"The body'll have to go to Inverness. There's nobody local at the moment," Ben said.

"Aye, fine," said Logan. It was an inconvenience, but one he could cope with. He knew he could count on Shona Maguire up at Raigmore to do a thorough job. "Fulton's already provided a visual ID. Just as well, if my theory's right about the killer trying to hide the ID."

"I don't get it, boss," Tyler said.

"Surprise, surprise," Ben remarked, but Tyler pressed on.

"If someone was trying to hide his identity, why dump him just up the road? Why not put him somewhere else? Further away, like."

"I've been wondering the same thing," Logan said. "Shallow grave, not far from a public footpath. It was only a matter of time before someone found him."

"Inept, maybe," Hamza said.

Logan considered this for half a second, then shrugged. "Aye. Maybe. We'll see."

He checked his watch, then drained the last of the tea from his mug.

"Right. I need to head and talk to the victim's wife. She lives in... Kinloch something?"

"Leven, maybe? Kinlochleven," Ben said.

"Aye, that sounds about right," Logan confirmed, reaching for his coat. "Far?"

"Twenty-five miles, thereabouts," Ben told him. "Feels like longer, mind you. Horrible winding bastard of a road once you take the turn-off."

"Great," Logan grumbled. "I'll swing by the scene after I've spoken to her, and find out where we are with forensics."

"You should take Tyler," Ben suggested.

At the mention of his name, DC Neish sat up straight. He looked irritatingly eager, which always rubbed Logan up the wrong way for some reason.

"Why would I want to do that?" the DCI asked.

"Well, so..." Ben sucked in his bottom lip, trying to come up with a legitimate reason. "Just so I don't have to put up with him," was the best he could do. "I've had him all week. It must be someone else's turn by now."

Logan let out an exaggerated sigh that was solely for DC Neish's benefit. "Fine. Tyler, on your feet, you're with me."

"Nice one, boss! You won't even know I'm there," Tyler promised.

"Aye, well," said Logan, pulling open the door and ushering the younger detective out. "I'll believe that when I see it."

CHAPTER SIX

Ben Forde had not been exaggerating about the route. After turning off the A82, the road leading to Kinlochleven became twisting and narrow, meandering down along the side of a loch one minute—Loch Leven, Logan assumed, given the name of the place they were headed to—then snaking through woodland the next.

With its traction control, the Volvo was equipped to handle all the twists and turns. DC Neish, on the other hand, was not.

"Jesus," he muttered, gripping the handle above the side window and locking his eyes on the road dead ahead. "I think I left my stomach on that last bend, boss."

Logan shot Tyler a sideways look. Almost all the colour had drained from his face, leaving only the faintest tinge of green.

"Don't you throw up in my car," the DCI warned.

"I won't. I'm not going to—"

Tyler clenched a fist and held it against his mouth for a few seconds, before continuing.

"I'm not going to throw up," he said. "I'm just a bit—"

The road banked up, then sharply down again. For a moment, the Volvo seemed to be suspended in mid-air.

"Christ!" Tyler grimaced, clutching his stomach. "Are you doing this on purpose?"

"Oh, aye. Because that's just what I want. You chucking your guts up all over my nice new car," Logan snapped. He eased off the accelerator pedal and the Volvo dropped to a more sedate pace. "There. That better?"

Tyler swallowed a couple of times, then risked a nod. "Aye. Cheers, boss."

They continued on for a mile or two in silence, Logan lost in his own thoughts, Tyler trying to keep the contents of his stomach in place using sheer willpower alone. It was only when Logan heard the younger man give a groan and shift uncomfortably in his seat that he decided to deploy distraction tactics.

"How's Sinead doing? After everything that happened?"

PC Bell was made of stern stuff, Logan knew. After what she'd gone through recently, though, she was bound to be feeling it. He'd been through similar situations himself over the years, and it always left a mark. Like it or not, put on as brave a face as you wanted, it always left a mark.

"Aye. She's not bad, all things considered," Tyler said. "She was signed off for a couple of weeks, but she's just itching to get back, really."

"She needs to take her time," Logan said. "No point rushing back in until she's ready."

"She says she is ready."

Logan gripped the wheel and gazed ahead. "Of course she does. But she isn't. She won't be. Not yet."

"Maybe you should tell her that, boss. You'd probably have more luck convincing her than I—*Fuck!*"

The car zig-zagged along a series of sharp bends, then swung a right until it was curving alongside the loch. Despite them crawling along at thirty, the series of sudden movements were enough to test even Logan's normally rock-solid constitution, and there was a *hwurk* as Tyler threw up in his mouth.

"Don't you bloody dare!" Logan warned, stomping on the brake and swinging the Volvo onto the shallow embankment at the side of the road.

Tyler had his seatbelt off before the car had fully stopped. He fumbled with the door, leaned out, and everything he'd eaten that morning was hastily ejected onto the damp grass.

The smell billowed back up into the car. Scowling, Logan tapped a button on his door and his window rolled all the way to the bottom. Beside him, Tyler heaved again, giving the grass a generous second helping.

Another car passed at speed, the driver's stomach evidently conditioned to handle the twists and turns. The wind from it gave the Volvo a shake, eliciting another spectacular response from DC Neish's gag reflex.

And then, with some groaning, mumbling, and a fair amount of spitting, Tyler gingerly eased himself back into a sitting position and pulled the door closed. He placed the back of his head against the headrest and closed his eyes, pulling himself together.

"Better?" Logan asked him.

Tyler swallowed. "Aye. Bit better. Sorry."

"Happens to the best of us, son," Logan said. The moment of empathy was so unexpected that Tyler opened his eyes and looked over at the DCI.

"Cheers, boss."

"No problem," Logan said, clicking on the indicator. "But just so you know, if any of it has landed in the car, I'll be wiping it up with your face."

THE HOUSE that Brodie Welsh had shared with his fiancée was a decent enough looking semi-detached just a couple of minutes walk from the local school. Logan had been given the impression that the area was pretty rough, but he'd seen nothing yet to back that up. The neighbouring houses had all been painted in the last couple of years, and while none of the gardens were exactly huge, they were all well-kept.

"That the mountain rescue guy?" Tyler asked, as a man in a Gortex jacket stepped out of a large Renault and gave them a wave.

"Fulton. Aye. That's him," Logan said, unfastening his belt. Tyler moved to do the same, but the DCI stopped him. "You wait here. No point us both piling in. The lassie's going to have enough on her plate without you chucking your guts up all over her carpet."

"I'm feeling much better, boss," Tyler said, although this wasn't entirely true, and so he didn't lean too heavily into the protest.

Instead, he suggested that he take a walk around the village. Not that he expected to come across anything relevant to the case, but he needed a blast of fresh air before he could even contemplate the return journey.

"Don't go far," Logan instructed, as they both got out of the SUV. "Scene of Crime's expecting us shortly, and I don't want to have to listen to them whinging at me if we're late."

"No worries, boss. I'll just take a wander round the block," the DC said. He said it to Logan's back, though, as the DCI had already set off to meet Fulton beside the front gate of Hannah's house.

Fulton didn't bother with pleasantries. He looked too drained to even attempt them. His hand shook as he placed it on the top bar of the wooden gate, and while he may have been looking in the direction of the house, Logan couldn't help but notice how he studiously avoided glancing at the windows, like he was afraid he might make eye contact with someone inside.

"Are you sure you're up to this, Mr Randall?" Logan asked him. "If it's easier, I can do it."

Fulton swallowed. "Aye. Aye. That would be easier," he admitted. "Thank you." He took a breath, held it for a while, then let it out in one big blow. "But, no. No. I have to be the one to tell her. She should hear it from me."

He seemed to commit himself to the decision then. Pushing open the gate, he marched up the path, took a second to compose himself at the door, and was just about to enter when it was opened for him from the other side.

A woman—a girl, practically—stood in the narrow hallway, her face acutely conveying how sleepless a night she'd had. She was tall and skinny, with copper-coloured hair tied back in a loose ponytail.

Her face was an irregular pattern of pale brown freckles, like someone had flicked a loaded paintbrush at her from close range. They made her look younger still, and if Fulton hadn't already told him her age, Logan would've sworn the girl was in her mid-teens.

"Dad? Where's Carrie?" she asked. Her wide, worried eyes went from Fulton to Logan, then out to the street beyond before returning to her father again. "What is it? What's happened? Have you heard something?"

"Come on away inside, Hannah," Fulton said, stepping over the threshold and placing a guiding hand on her arm. "Come on away inside and we can have a chat."

Hannah started to let herself be led, then stopped. She twisted free of her dad's grip and turned to Logan. "Are you the police?"

"Hannah, let's go have a sit-down and—"

"Are you?" Hannah demanded. "Are you the police?"

"I am. DCI Jack Logan, miss. Like your father says, I think we should maybe—"

"He's dead. Isn't he?" Hannah asked. "Brodie, he's dead."

"Hannah, sweetheart—"

Fulton tried the hand on the arm again. The calming voice. The suggestion of a sad smile. None of it worked. Fury flashed behind Hannah's eyes, instantly changing her from a girl to a woman.

"Just fucking tell me!"

Fulton's intentions had been noble enough. Completely understandable. He'd wanted to tell her, to be the one to break the news. In the thick of it all, though, when it came right down to the moment, the words wouldn't come. His voice deserted him, and he could only gaze imploringly at Logan. Desperate. Pleading for him to end it. To do what needed to be done.

"Miss Randall, I'm sorry to have to inform you that Brodie was found dead this morning," he said.

And, like that, the woman was gone, replaced once more by the scared, uncertain girl. She fell against her dad, while simultaneously trying to pull away from him. She shook her head as tears weaved between the freckles on her cheeks.

"No. N-no, no, no. He's not. He's not. No. Brodie. *Brodie!*"

Her breathing became louder, more frantic and wheezing. She didn't resist when Fulton put an arm around her. It was possible that she didn't even notice.

"Come on, sweetheart. Come away inside," Fulton suggested.

"Carrie. What am I going to tell Carrie?" she whispered. "How am I going to tell her that her daddy's not coming back?"

Fulton swallowed. Tears blurred his eyes, and Logan had the good grace to glance away.

"We'll think of something," Hannah's father told her. He opened a door behind her and gave her shoulder another squeeze. "Now, come on. Let's go and get a seat and we can talk about it."

Logan hesitated outside the threshold for a moment, and took a quick look at the neighbouring houses. A net curtain twitched across the street, but he could still see the outline of a woman on the other side. Short and frail-looking. Pensioner, probably. Worth having a word with later, maybe. Often, a copper's best friend was the nosy old bugger across the road.

There was nobody at the other windows. Nobody he could see, at least. That was something to be grateful for. Fulton had managed to get his daughter inside just in time. Any more raised voices and one of the worst moments of her life could well have been turned into a spectator sport.

Logan was about to turn and head inside when he spotted a man in a tan coloured military-style jacket and baseball cap. He was standing at the corner of a house a little way back down the road, leaning a shoulder against the wall and making no bones about the fact that he was watching the events unfolding at the house.

He was too far away for Logan to shout to him without having to really belt it out, but close enough that the DCI could get a decent enough impression of him. Average height, but heavily built. From that distance, he couldn't say if it was fat or muscle, but he guessed the latter.

They regarded each other for a while, then Logan stepped inside the house, took out his phone, and rang Tyler's number.

"Boss?" came the reply after half a dozen rings.

"Where are you?" Logan asked.

"I'm just..." Tyler began. "God knows, actually. It's a confusing place, this. I think I'm just down from the school, though. Why, you ready to hit the road?"

"No. But get back up here. There's someone lurking about. Halfway back along the road, right-hand side as you're heading towards the house. Tan jacket. Red baseball cap. I don't like him. See what you can find out."

"No bother, boss. On my way," Tyler said.

"Be quick," Logan instructed, then he tapped the icon to hang up the phone, slipped it into his pocket, and headed through to face the grief of Hannah Randall.

CHAPTER SEVEN

There was an old-fashioned cuckoo clock on one wall of Hannah Randall's living room. That was the first thing Logan noticed. It was so out of place amongst the Ikea furniture and pastel-blue walls that his eyes were drawn to it immediately.

The fact that it was a noisy bastard of a thing with a tick like a metronome also helped it stand out.

Hannah was already sitting right at the middle junction of a leather corner couch when Logan entered, her dad sitting right in close to her, one of her hands clutched in his. The other hand was kneading a wrinkle in the leather, pulling and twisting on it, like she was trying to determine if it was real.

The room was small, but well-cared for. The only mess was over in one corner, which had clearly been designated 'the play area'. Some attempt had been made to arrange the dolls, cars, and teddies into a neat stack, but the toys were having none of it and had toppled over onto the floor.

There were thirty or more framed photographs on the wall. Mostly, they charted the growth of a baby into a toddler, but there were a good number of family snaps in there, too. Logan recognised Brodie Welsh in several of them. He and Hannah were together in a few of them. They looked like a nice couple. Happy.

A far cry from how Hannah looked now. Fulton was still holding one of her hands. The other was now thrust into the gap between the sofa cushions, and hooked under the one she was sitting on, like it was the only thing anchoring her in place.

She looked up and blinked when Logan closed the door, regarding him with a detached curiosity he'd seen on too many faces, too many times.

"Miss Randall, I'm Detective Chief Inspector Logan. Jack," he said. He'd told her already, but reckoned a reminder probably wouldn't go amiss. "I'm very sorry to have to be the bearer of such bad news."

"What happened?" Hannah asked, the words almost choking her. "To Brodie. What happened?"

"They don't know yet," Fulton said. He flashed Logan an apologetic smile, which the DCI dismissed with a subtle shake of his head.

"We're still working on it," Logan said, taking over. "We have a team at the site now trying to determine exactly what happened."

"'The site,'" Hannah repeated. Her voice was flat and hollow, but he could almost hear the quote marks around the words. Logan couldn't tell if she'd said it for his benefit or her own.

He waited to see if she was going to say more before he continued. The clock on the wall ticked loudly in the temporary silence.

"I won't pretend to understand what you're going through, Miss Randall. I can't. What I will say is that we will do everything we can to find out what happened to Mr Welsh."

"Brodie. He didn't like being called Mr Welsh."

"Brodie. Right," Logan said.

"Do you know who did it?" Hannah asked. She looked at him with hope in her eyes. It was tentative, but unmistakable. "Do you know who killed him?"

"We don't know for sure yet that Brodie was murdered," Logan told her. "We'll be able to determine that in the next day or two.

Hannah's movements became brisker, more agitated. "What do you mean? What else could've happened?"

She yanked her hand free from her dad's grip and stood up suddenly. Her eyes, which had been filled with hope, now blazed angrily. "Are you saying he killed himself? He wouldn't. No way. Not with... Not with..."

Her gaze crept over to the toys in the corner. Her legs seemed to buckle, and she found herself back on the couch. "He wouldn't do that," she whispered. "He wouldn't leave Carrie. He loves her too much. He wouldn't do that."

"I'm not suggesting he did," Logan assured her. "But until we have more information, it's important we don't speculate."

He gestured to a chair across from the couch. It was another Ikea contraption, with a bendy wooden frame and a folded padded cushion making up the seat and back. "May I?"

Hannah nodded absently, and Logan carefully lowered himself onto the seat. It started to tip forward as soon as his weight was on it, and he was forced to slide back to counteract the imbalance.

On reflection, he thought, he probably should've stayed on his feet. Still, too late now.

"Like I was saying, it's important we don't get ahead of ourselves. It's possible Brodie's death was entirely accidental. Did he go out walking often?"

"No. Never. He had no interest in any of that stuff," Hannah said.

"Not for want of me trying, eh, sweetheart?" Fulton offered, trying to lighten the mood a little, but failing miserably.

"He was supposed to be away at work. Offshore. Just for a few days this time," Hannah said. Her bottom lip wobbled, making her look even younger than she already did. "He was supposed to get back last night. We were going to have a chippy."

"Had you heard anything from his employers about him failing to turn up?" Logan asked.

Hannah sniffed and shook her head. "No."

"No phone calls?"

"No. Nothing."

Logan reached into his coat pocket and took out his notebook. He then spent several seconds fishing around in the other pockets trying to find a pen, until eventually Fulton took one from inside his jacket and handed it over.

"Here."

"Thank you. Always losing them," Logan said. The pen was cheap plastic, and had the name of some climbing guide company emblazoned across the side. Clicking the button on the end, the DCI held it above the pad, ready to write. "Do you have the details of Brodie's employer? We can inform them."

Hannah shook her head. "It's fine. I'll do it."

"Of course," said Logan. "I understand. But, we'd also like to talk to them. They may be able to provide some information."

Hannah squeezed the bridge of her nose between finger and thumb. "It's... I can't remember. It's on the bank statements. 'Orwatt,' or something. I can get it for you. They're Dutch. They gave us that thing."

She nodded in the direction of the cuckoo clock. A Swiss clock seemed like an odd gift from a Dutch company, but he decided not to question it.

"That would be very useful if you could get us their name, thank you," Logan said.

Fulton patted his daughter's hand and looked over at Logan. "I'll dig it out for you later. I can drop it off."

Logan fished in another couple of pockets until he found a business card, which he set on the coffee table between them. "Here. Keep this. You can call me any time. Either of you. Night or day. We'll also have a liaison officer appointed. These are specially trained officers who can—"

"It's fine. No," Hannah said.

Logan glossed over the interruption. "They're very experienced in helping families who—"

"I said no," Hannah barked at him, her eyes blazing with that same anger as before. "I'm not having someone in here scaring Carrie. It'll freak her out. She's used to her dad being away. She'll be fine for a while, but if someone's in here with..."

The words stuttered to a stop and the tears came. Big, gulping, silent sobs that formed balloons in her throat, cutting off her air. Fulton slid over on the couch, put an arm around her shoulder and pulled her in closer. She buried her head against him, her tears sliding off his waterproof jacket and down onto the couch between them.

"God, what about Margaret?" she managed, the effort of speaking further crumpling the lines of her face.

"Brodie's mum. She lives in Fife," Fulton explained. "Does she know?"

"I don't believe so, no," Logan said. "If you have a number or an address, we can get someone round to her."

Hannah shook her head and loudly cleared her throat. It took a few attempts. "I'll do it," she said. "It should be me."

"I'm not sure that's such—"

"I'll do it," Hannah insisted. "I know her. She should hear it from me."

Against his better instincts, Logan relented. "Right. OK, then. But, we'll still need to send someone round to talk to her, so if you can give us the address, that would be useful."

"Oh God. Margaret," Hannah said, her voice descending into sobs again. "What am I going to say?"

Logan leaned forward in the chair, being careful not to tip it off balance. "Like I say, Miss Randall. We can do it. We have trained officers who specialise in just this sort of thing."

If anything, this made the second shake of Hannah's head even more emphatic. "No. It shouldn't be a 'specialist' she hears it from, it should be family. I just... I mean..."

Her face crumpled, her eyes screwing tightly shut as she sunk her weight in against her dad. Fulton kissed her on the top of the head and gave her back a rub, then turned to Logan and spoke in a soft whisper.

"Can we continue this later? I can get you all the information."

Logan closed over his notebook. "Aye. Of course," he said, offering the pen back.

"Keep it. It's promotional. I've got hundreds," Fulton said.

Logan glanced at the text printed on the side of the pen again—*Nevis Walking and Climbing: Guided Walk's and Climb's Across Lochaber*—and tried not to wince at the apostrophe usage.

"Thanks," he said, tucking it into the same pocket as the notebook. "Much appreciated."

He stood up, a process that involved rocking himself forward in the chair, pressing both hands on the armrests, and launching himself to his feet, while simultaneously ruing the day that Ikea ever opened its doors in Scotland.

"Once again, Miss Randall, I'm sorry for your loss," he said. "I'll be in touch as soon as I have more information, and if you change your mind about the liaison—"

"I won't," Hannah said. She pulled her sleeve up over her wrist and wiped her nose on it. "But thanks."

"She's going to come stay with us for a few days," Fulton said, although the slight downward turn of Hannah's mouth suggested it was the first she'd heard about it. "Best for everyone. So Mum tells me, anyway. You've got my number."

"I'm not sure. Did someone take a note of it?"

"It's on the pen," Fulton said. "Mobile and landline."

Logan patted his pocket. "Right. Very good. We'll be in touch."

He was at the living room door when Hannah spoke.

"Do you think he was murdered?"

Logan stopped and turned.

"Like I said, Miss Randall, we really don't know at this stage."

"I'm not asking what you know. I'm asking what you think," Hannah said. She seemed to have shrunk, so her freckles took up more of her face than before. "Do you think someone killed Brodie?"

Logan stood with one hand on the door handle. On the wall beside him, the clock continued its steady *tick-tick-tick*.

"I think we need to prepare ourselves for that possibility," he told her.

And with that, he left her to her sorrow.

CHAPTER EIGHT

"Excuse me, mate. You local?"

The man in the crumpled tan jacket turned slowly, in no apparent rush to find out who had spoken to him. Down at his side, a small but mean-looking dog growled and strained on the end of a chain-link lead. DC Neish eyed it warily, then relaxed when he saw the muzzle fastened across its snout.

"Who's asking?" the man grunted. The accent was definitely local. If not specific to this area, then somewhere not too far away.

He was taller than Tyler, but not by much. There was a scar across one cheek, and he had the sort of crooked, wandering nose that suggested very few of his years on this Earth had been easy. His baseball cap was a faded red, almost a dark pink, and cast a shadow across his eyes that made them hard to see in much detail.

Fully dressed, it was hard to tell if his bulk had been caused by too much working out, or not nearly enough, but his angular chin and telegraph pole neck suggested he was a regular gym-goer, steroid abuser, or both.

Tyler produced his warrant card, deciding he was marginally less likely to be beaten to death by the guy if he knew he was polis. "Detective Constable Tyler Neish. We've had reports of someone acting suspiciously in this area who matches your description."

"From who?"

Tyler blinked. "What?"

"Who's reported someone acting suspiciously in the area who matches my description?"

"Just... It's..." Tyler waved a hand vaguely. "I can't give you that information. What's your name?"

"That's none of your business, Detective Constable Tyler Neish," the man told him. Down at his heel, his dog snarled its agreement. "I don't have to give you my name."

"Well, yes, you do."

"I don't. Not without good reason," he countered. "What grounds have you got for asking for my details?"

"Like I say, we've had reports of someone acting suspiciously who—"

"You haven't, though, have you? If someone had reported that, they wouldn't go sending out CID, or whatever you are. And anyway, I'm not acting suspiciously, am I? I'm walking my dog."

"Didn't look like you were walking," Tyler argued.

"He was having a piss," the man said. "No crime in that, is there? A dog having a piss?"

Tyler could feel himself losing control of the conversation. If he'd even been in control of it in the first place. The guy was right, he had no real grounds to do a stop and search. Nothing that would stand up to any scrutiny, anyway, and the man in the baseball cap seemed well-versed in what his rights were.

"Right, well, fun as this has been, I'm going to shoot off," the man said. He gave the dog's lead a jerk, and the dog stopped growling at Tyler long enough to let out a little yelp of surprise. "Nice to meet you, Detective Constable Tyler Neish."

"I'm sure I'll see you around," Tyler told him.

The man snorted out a half-laugh, looked the DC up and down, then shrugged. "Aye. Maybe you will at that," he said, and then with another jerk on the lead, he set off down the road in the direction of the school, whistling loudly and tunelessly as he went.

Logan and Tyler reached the Volvo at almost exactly the same time. Tyler opened his mouth to speak, but Logan gestured inside the car, then clambered in without saying a word.

When they were both inside with the doors closed, it was Logan who spoke first. "Well? You find the guy I told you about?"

"Eh, aye. Aye, boss. Found him. Think it was him, anyway. Dressed in black. Built like a brick shithouse. Horrible angry wee dog with him."

"I didn't see a dog," Logan said. "But sounds like him. Who is he?"

Tyler filled a moment by fastening his seatbelt. "I, uh, I didn't get a name, boss."

Logan turned slowly in his seat. "Eh?"

"He didn't want to give me his name," Tyler said. "Said I had no grounds to ask for his details. Seemed pretty clued up."

Logan swore below his breath. There were few things more annoying than a suspect who knew their rights. He sighed. "I mind the days when 'looking like a right shifty bastard' was justification enough," he bemoaned. "What was your impression of him?"

"A right shifty bastard," Tyler said. "He said he was just walking his dog, but it was definitely more of a lurk than a walk from where I was standing. Looked like he was watching the house."

Logan stole a glance in the Volvo's mirrors, but saw no sign of the mystery man in the hat. "We can ask around later. See if anyone knows him."

"How did you get on with the girlfriend?" Tyler asked, nodding in the direction of Hannah Randall's front door. "Anything interesting come up?"

"Not really. He worked offshore. Was away a lot. She thought he was working this week, and was due home last night."

"Explains why she didn't report him missing," Tyler said.

Logan drummed his fingers on the steering wheel. "Aye. Suppose."

DC Neish looked from Logan to the house and back again. "Something you're not telling me, boss?"

"Hmm?" Logan blinked as if coming out of a trance. "No. Probably not. It's just his work. They didn't phone."

"Phone who?"

"The house. They didn't phone when he didn't show up. I saw the body. It's been there a week, easy. He didn't make it to work, but nobody phoned to check up."

"Maybe they called his mobile?" Tyler suggested.

That was certainly a possibility, Logan admitted. Or, maybe Brodie had called them to tell them he wasn't coming in. There were a variety of very good reasons why the company wouldn't call the house.

And yet, it niggled at him, and he could never resist a niggle.

"The girl's father is going to get us the employer's details. I want you to follow up on it when we get them," Logan said. "Find out if he made it in or, if not, whether he gave them warning that he wasn't coming."

"Right, boss," Tyler said.

He tapped the button that kicked the engine into life and glanced at the time on the display. "Shite. I told the crime scene lot we'd be there ten minutes ago."

Logan's belt gave a definitive *click* as he slotted it into place. He shot DC Neish a smile that was perfectly balanced between 'apologetic' and 'amused.'

"Looks like I'll have to put the foot down."

Tyler swallowed, his mouth already filling with saliva in anticipation of the long and winding road ahead.

"Aw," he groaned. "Great."

CHAPTER NINE

Geoff Palmer, the head of the Scene of Crime team, stood with Logan by the narrow footbridge, listening to the distant retching of DC Neish.

Tyler had exited the Volvo before it had fully stopped, then gone tearing across the car park, one hand clamped over his mouth, his eyes practically bulging out of his head.

He had made it as far from the investigation site as he possibly could before erupting in quite spectacular fashion near the side of the road.

For the past few minutes, he had been alternately standing, crouching, and squatting there, emptying his guts over the bracken and heather, and receiving the occasional derisory horn-blast from passing articulated lorries.

"Christ. How much has he eaten?" Palmer wondered, as another *hurrrp* went echoing off the hillsides.

"Long as he gets it all up here and not in my car, I don't care," Logan grunted.

He wasn't Geoff Palmer's biggest fan. In fact, he wasn't even ambivalent about the man. He actively disliked pretty much everything about him, from his sneering, bulbous face, to the condescending way he spoke to everyone around him. He was good enough at his job, but seemed almost begrudging of that fact, like he'd had dreams of being something glamorous, and was now stuck dealing with crime scenes and corpses instead.

Every call out seemed like a personal affront to him. Every time he arrived on a scene, he acted like he was doing the world a favour, rather than simply doing the job he was being paid for.

Granted, he probably wasn't being paid enough—none of them were, when you got down to it—but that was the job, take it or leave it.

"Dramamine," Palmer said.

Logan raised an eyebrow. "What?"

"Dramamine. Travel sickness tablets. That's what he needs."

Across the car park, Tyler loudly threw up again.

"Drama *queen*, more like," Logan remarked, then he turned and gestured to the tent on the other side of the bridge. "So, you done?"

Palmer pushed back the hood of the paper suit he wore, revealing a hairline that seemed desperate to put as much distance between itself and the face below it as possible. "We're done," he confirmed. "We were done half an hour ago, but had to hang around for you to finally show up. The body's already halfway to Inverness, just like I should be."

"I told you to hang on to it until we arrived," Logan said.

"Aye, well, I didn't know when you were going to bother to show up, so I made an executive decision," Palmer replied. "Would you rather I'd let the body deteriorate further and risk compromising the evidence?"

Logan didn't rise to it. Now wasn't the time or place.

"No. Obviously," he said. "Fine. So, what have we got?"

"Shoes, mostly," Palmer said. "Come and see for yourself."

The bridge was solid, but he picked his way tentatively across it like he was terrified it would collapse at any moment. Logan took great pleasure in stomping onto it behind him and crossing it with a series of bouncing steps that made the whole thing shake.

"Can you not do that?" Palmer asked, shooting a look back over his shoulder.

"Do what?" asked Logan, feigning innocence.

Palmer tutted, then scurried the last few steps onto solid ground. Logan smiled at him as he reached the end of the bridge. It was petty, aye, but it was probably the highlight of his day so far. The way things had been going lately, it might well turn out to be the highlight of his week, so he was going to savour it while he could.

"Very funny. We'd see who was laughing if it had collapsed," Palmer whined.

"I don't know what you're talking about," Logan insisted, but he was already addressing the back of the other man's head.

"Let's just get through this quick," Palmer said. "Some of us have homes to go to."

As the SOC investigator had suggested, 'shoes,' was definitely the headline. One pair, size eight, had been active around the burial site in the past few days. Rain had washed most of the prints away, but a few had survived well enough for them to take casts.

"And they were definitely shoes?" Logan asked. "Not boots?"

"Not hiking boots, certainly," Palmer said. "Nothing that would really be suitable for taking to the hills with. Very little tread."

He gestured to the mountain rising up behind them. "You wouldn't get very far up that thing, put it that way."

"Right. And what do they tell you?"

"We don't know the make yet, and the weather means this isn't an exact science, but I'd say the wearer was pretty heavy, judging by the depth. Quite how heavy, I can't tell you, but no lightweight. From the size of feet, I'd say male," Palmer explained. "We found a couple of partial prints that were deeper, suggesting whoever it was, they were carrying something heavy."

"The body," said Logan.

Palmer shot the DCI a patronising look, but stopped just short of going, "Duh!"

"Speaking of which. You know the teeth were smashed in?" Palmer said. "There's something else, too."

"Fingers?" Logan guessed.

A flash of irritation crossed Palmer's face, his big moment spoiled. "Yes. Fingers. All removed. We didn't find them, but then leaving them nearby would sort of defeat the killer's point."

"Anything on the body?" Logan asked.

"No identification, if that's what you're hoping for."

Logan shook his head. "We know who he is. A family member was with the search team that found him."

Palmer looked into the tent at the hole in the ground. "They were looking for him?"

"No, they were looking for someone else. They found him by accident."

"Oh. Right. Well, that's lucky. Looks like the killers wasted their time trying to conceal his identity."

"What else have you got for me?"

Palmer glanced pointedly at his watch, then tutted, before continuing. "It'll all be in the report. He wasn't dressed for the outdoors. Jeans, t-shirt. Trainers. Size seven, before you ask, we've discounted them from the prints. There was no sign of his footprints anywhere in the area, in fact, although that's hardly surprising, given the time that's passed. We were lucky to get any casts at all."

"You discounted the prints the mountain rescue lads would've left? There were two of them," Logan began, but the chastising scowl on Palmer's face stopped him going any further.

"Of course we discounted them. Jesus." He motioned across to the car park, where the rest of the team were loading up a van. "We *have* been doing this a while, you know? We *do* know what we're doing. We also discounted the two idiots who set up the tent and trampled all over the place, and a certain Detective Chief Inspector who should've bloody well known better. I mean, seriously, what were you thinking?"

"I was trying to stop the scene becoming compromised," Logan protested.

Palmer gave a snort. "Next time, maybe just go the whole hog and invite the Orange Walk to march through. It couldn't make things much worse. You lot are all members, aren't you? Funny handshakes, and all that?"

"Only thing I'm a member of is the AA," Logan said, although he stopped short of specifying which one he was referring to.

"He wasn't killed at the scene," Palmer said. "Not enough blood in the surrounding soil. Killed elsewhere, carried here, then buried. I'd say, two, maybe three days ago."

Logan frowned. "Two or three days? Body looked older."

"Aye, well, the elements, maybe. Who knows? That's my estimate of when he was buried, anyway," Palmer said, visibly annoyed by the question. "If you can call it buried. They barely broke the surface. Going by the size, shape, and angle of some of the cuts in the soil, I'd say a large trowel or a small folding spade was used."

"No wonder they didn't go deep, if that was all they were using," Logan remarked. "Seems like poor planning, though. If you're taking someone out into the wilderness to bury them, you'd bring a shovel. Wouldn't you?"

"I'll just stick to giving you the facts, if it's all the same with you," Palmer said, practically lifting his nose in the air, "and leave the wild speculation to your lot."

Logan bit his tongue to stop himself saying anything he'd enjoy in the moment, but might later regret. He waited for the urge to pass, then got back to business. "Any thoughts on cause of death?"

"Again, not my department, so not really for me to say," Palmer sniffed. "But I'd say the big slit in his stomach probably did him no favours. Dr Maguire will be able to tell you more, I'm sure. She's waiting to receive the corpse."

He turned away from Logan and regarded the inside of the tent again. "She's very good, isn't she? Very thorough. Really knows her way around a body."

Something about the way he said it made the fine hairs on the back of Logan's neck stand up and the blood go *swooshing* through his veins. "Aye. She's an excellent pathologist," he said, choosing his words carefully.

"Oh. Yes," said Palmer. He glanced back at Logan, and there was a smile on his face that made the DCI's fingers twitch briefly into fists. "She's that, too."

"Is there something you're trying to imply, Geoff?"

Palmer shook his head. It was his turn to feign innocence. "Me? Imply something? What makes you say that?"

Logan stepped in closer so he loomed over the much smaller man. Whatever bravado had been puffing Palmer up escaped as a low squeak of fear.

"See me, Geoff? I don't imply. I'm not one for beating around the bush. Call a spade a spade, and a jumped-up wee bawbag a jumped-up wee... Well, you get my point," Logan told him. "So, I'll say this as plainly as I possibly can. Back in the lab, you might act the big man. Maybe you throw your weight around, trying to impress the new folk who haven't yet figured out quite what a wholly unappealing wee prick you are. But here?"

Logan pointed to the ground at their feet. "Out here, on one of *my* crime scenes, you do what I tell you. Alright? And you do not *imply* things about our mutual colleagues. In fact, you don't imply things about anyone. Like you said, you give us the data. That's it. We'll take care of the thinking bit. Is that clear?"

Palmer had a stab at standing his ground, but he crumbled immediately when Logan leaned forward a little, bringing his scowl closer.

"Fine. Yes. I was just... It was a joke, that's all," Palmer protested.

"Next time you try a joke, maybe have a bash at making it funny, eh? Or, better yet, don't bother. Stick to the day job, Geoff," Logan told him. He indicated the van with a jab of his thumb. "Now, fuck off and get me that report."

Palmer didn't say a word as he gathered up a couple of bags from outside the tent and went trudging off over the bridge. He shot Tyler the briefest of sideways glances as they passed on the other side, and then looked back once more just before he reached the van and the rest of his team. From the way their body language changed as he approached, Logan was satisfied that they'd all formed the correct impression of him a long time ago.

"I can't stand that man," Logan remarked.

"Who? Sex Pest Palmer?" Tyler asked. "Can't think why that might be, boss."

Logan raised a quizzical eyebrow.

"Nothing we could actually charge him for, even if we wanted to. Just stories. Cracking on to women half his age. That sort of thing," Tyler said. "He wrote a big rant on Facebook recently about some twenty-year-olds calling him out for being a creepy bastard after he tried chatting them up in a restaurant. Went a bit viral until he took it down."

"What do you mean it went viral? In what way?" Logan asked.

"Oh. People ripping the pish, mostly. Calling him out. Brutal they were," Tyler said. "He had to shut his account down in the end."

Logan gave a little grunt of satisfaction. Sometimes, justice came swiftly of its own accord.

While the Scene of Crime lot finished loading up their van, Tyler turned and stood, hands on hips, looking up at the mountains. "So. This is Glen Coe." He wrinkled his nose. "Just a big hill really, isn't it?"

"Mountain," Logan corrected. "And no. I mean, aye, that bit is, but it goes on for miles. It's actually pretty impressive. And I'm not an easy man to impress."

"Aren't you? You hide that well, boss," Tyler said. He looked around them again, taking in what he could see of their surroundings. The low clouds didn't help make the place seem all that remarkable, cutting off the mountaintops the way they did. "Didn't Jimmy Savile have a house up this way?" Tyler asked.

"Aye. It's back there," Logan said, indicating the road to the south. "You'll know it as soon as you see it. It's got 'Paedo' written all over it."

"Really? What, you mean like a vibe it gives off?"

"No, I mean it literally has the word 'Paedo' written all over it. In spray paint. Every time it gets cleaned off, someone writes it on again. And worse, too," Logan remarked. "Some of the spelling they use is really quite creative."

A chill wind swirled along the glen, rustling the tent and cutting both men to the bone. Shoving his hands in his coat pockets, Logan took one last look inside the tent, then back up at the mountain.

Finally, he set off for the bridge, beckoning the detective constable with a tilt of his head. "Right, then. Let's get back and get the kettle on," he said. "And if you could avoid heaving your guts up in my car, I'd very much appreciate it."

CHAPTER TEN

"Jack? Pop in here a sec, would you?"

Logan and Tyler had barely set foot in the station when the door to Chief Inspector Pickering's office opened and Hugh Pickering himself leaned out. The startling resemblance he'd once had to Velma from *Scooby Doo* that had earned him the nickname 'Jinkies' had faded over the years, and now it was a passing one, at best. Still, once a nickname was established in the polis, there was no shifting it, so Jinkies he forever would be.

Logan gave Tyler a nudge on the arm with his elbow. "Go fill the rest of them in. Get a door to door organised. I want to know who the guy with the dog is."

"On it, boss," Tyler said, continuing ahead towards the Incident Room.

"And stick the kettle on," Logan added. He looked very deliberately at the man in the office doorway. "This'll only take a minute."

Jinkies flashed an insincere smile, then stepped aside to allow Logan into the office. He was about to close it, when he had second thoughts, and leaned back out into the corridor, instead.

"Moira, no interruptions for the next twenty minutes," he said.

Logan let out a quiet snort. Twenty minutes. Aye, like that would be happening.

There was silence from out in the corridor. Jinkies ran his tongue across his lips, gave it a few more seconds, then shouted again. "Moi—"

"What?" Moira snapped, appearing around the corner at the end of the corridor.

"Ah. There you are. Did you hear me?"

"What, shouting my name?"

"No, the other bit. About not wanting any interruptions for the next twenty minutes?"

"No," came the reply. "I didn't hear that bit."

There was the slightest hint of desperation in Jinkies' voice when he spoke again. What was meant to be a demonstration of his authority was rapidly turning into a demonstration of something altogether less impressive.

"Well... No interruptions for the next twenty minutes," he said.

Silence.

"Moira."

"Yes! I heard. No interruptions."

"Right. Yes." Jinkies began to close the door.

"What if it's important?" Moira asked from along the corridor.

Jinkies opened the door again. "Well, obviously, if it's important, then that's... Right."

He closed the door, waited for a moment in case the receptionist was going to add anything else, then turned to find Logan sitting behind his desk. Jinkies opened his mouth to protest, before he ultimately decided that it wasn't worth the effort.

"Good to see you, Jack," he said, and he was almost convincing. "Although, I admit, I didn't think you'd be on my patch again quite so soon."

"Aye, well. Needs must," Logan said.

"The Highlands treating you well?"

"Certainly keeping me busy. Starting to think there's something in the water up here. The rate you're all killing each other off, there'll soon be no bugger left."

"Ha," said Jinkies, mirthlessly. "Quite. Terrible business up in Inverness recently. Good work on that."

Logan was fast approaching his maximum small talk threshold and steered the conversation on to more pressing matters.

"What was it you wanted?"

"Oh, just a catch-up, really. To let you know that our resources are at your disposal," Jinkies said, adding, "Within reason," after a suitable pause. "CID is close to a breakthrough in a local drugs case. Big business. They're pretty much flat out on that, so their assistance will be limited."

"Flat out? Aren't they off on some training course?"

"*Pretty much* flat out," Jinkies reiterated. "Important to keep up to date with all the current best practice, too."

Logan had only ever given the occasional passing nod to 'best practice,' and reckoned his idea of what that meant was likely very different to the Chief Inspector's. There were laws, there were rules, and then there was best practice. As far as he was concerned, one of those things could be safely bent, one broken, and the other ignored in its entirety.

"I'd ask you to respect that investigation," Jinkies continued. "And to be aware that any resource I do allocate you may have to be withdrawn at short notice."

"We're dealing with a murder here, Hugh," Logan said.

"Are we? Has that been confirmed?"

"As good as."

Jinkies rocked back on his heels. "So, that's a no, then," he said. He held up a hand before Logan could reply. "Of course, it's important. I'm not disputing that. But he's dead, and he's unlikely to get any deader. We have the opportunity here to shut down a big player in the local drugs trade. A big link in the chain. Huge."

Logan grunted. "Sounds like the kind of collar that could really make someone's career," he remarked.

Jinkies tried to look nonchalant, but the thick lenses of his glasses magnified the flicker of excitement in his eyes. "Well, I wouldn't know about that. I just want these people off the streets, Jack. We're just trying to make a difference, as always."

Aye, a difference to your pay packet, Logan thought, but he kept it to himself.

He stood up, making the unilateral decision that the conversation was now over. "Aye, well, we'll do our best not to tread on any toes."

"Good man. And, of course, my door is always open," Jinkies said. "Drop by any time."

Logan loomed over him. "Thanks. If you want to speak to me again, though, do me a favour and make an appointment," he said. He let the sentence hang in the air between them. "I'm a very busy man."

LOGAN WAS HALFWAY along the corridor when his phone rang. He stopped, hunted his pockets, then glanced at the screen. *Unknown Caller.*

"Hello?" he said, and was not particularly surprised when no reply came. "Hello?"

From the other end of the line, there came a *squeaking* sound. It reminded Logan of two balloons being rubbed together over and over. It was possibly interference, but—he checked the signal, and saw a full triangle of bars—more likely someone playing silly buggers.

"Who is this?" he demanded. "Is that you, Petrie? If it is, then—"

There was a laugh, not quite a snigger, and not quite a giggle, but somewhere in between. Male, he thought, but he couldn't be sure, and it lasted only a second before the line went dead.

Logan checked the screen, then checked his watch. He had just started to move when the phone rang again. A Glencoe prefix this time. Local.

"Hello?"

Fulton Randall spoke in hushed tones at the other end of the line. He explained that he was still with his daughter, but had stepped away to call in with the information the DCI had asked for. Logan asked him to hold on and went marching into the Incident Room, miming for someone to give him something to write with.

Hamza gestured to the open notebook on his desk and handed Logan a pen. As Fulton spoke, Logan scribbled.

The company Brodie had worked for was called 'Oswatt,' according to his bank statement. Fulton apologised that they didn't have a contact number, but Logan assured him it wasn't a problem, and that they'd find it.

The address and phone number of Brodie's mother was recited and repeated back, and then, after a brief enquiry as to how Hannah was holding up—not great, but that was only to be expected—Logan ended the call.

"Who was that?" Ben asked, handing over a cup of tea.

"Fulton Randall. Victim's partner's father." He looked down at the pad, already struggling to decipher his own handwriting. "You heard of Oswatt? Offshore company, I think."

Ben shook his head and took a sip from his own mug. "No. Don't think so. Why?"

"Victim worked for them. He was meant to be there this week. They didn't follow up on his whereabouts."

"Want me to give them a ring, sir?" asked Caitlyn.

Her offering to take on responsibility was not new by any means. She was driven and ambitious, and a damn good copper. What did take Logan by surprise was the way she said it—bright and upbeat, with the unmistakable suggestion of a smile.

"Eh, aye. Please," Logan said, after a pause. "Find out what you can. Did he turn up? If so, when did he leave? If not, why no phone call? When did they last see him?" He remembered who he was speaking to. "You know what we need."

"Aye. I'm sure I can figure it out," Caitlyn confirmed, then she turned to her computer and her fingers danced cheerfully across the keys.

Logan watched her for a few seconds, then shook his head and pressed on.

"We've got the address of Brodie's mother. She's in Fife. Hamza, can you get on to the local boys and get someone round there to talk to her?" Logan turned to Ben. "Who do we know over that way?"

"Fife? Hmm." Ben took another gulp of tea. "Duncan Donuts. He's over there, isn't he? Superintendent, I think, unless he's got himself demoted."

"Perfect," said Logan. He turned back to Hamza. "Get on to him. Use my name. Ask him to send someone decent. CID, not Uniform. The mother will already have heard the news from Hannah, but we need to know if she can tell us anything. Did she speak to him in the last week? Did anything seem amiss?"

Hamza glanced between the two senior officers. "Right, sir. Aye. But... Duncan Donuts?"

"Duncan Mitchell," Ben clarified. "Superintendent Duncan Mitchell. We call him Donuts."

"Right. Does he eat a lot of them?"

"What?"

"Donuts."

Ben frowned and shook his head. "Oh. No. God, no."

Hamza hesitated. His eyes narrowed briefly and his lips parted like he was about to ask a question, but then he shook his head. "Right. Fair enough. Superintendent Duncan Mitchell. Got it."

Logan clicked his fingers a couple of times and pointed to the phone. "Get on to him. I want someone speaking to her within the hour. She might try to come over this way. Tell him to dissuade her, if he can. For a few days, at least. Don't need a grieving mother under our feet until we've made a bit of progress."

"Right, sir," Hamza said. He tore the top sheet off his notepad, studiously copied down the address details onto a new page in more legible handwriting, then reached for the phone.

"Tyler, what have you got on our man?" Logan asked, wheeling around to face the other detective constable. Tyler had a phone handset cradled between his cheek and his shoulder, and was tapping at the screen of his mobile.

"Nothing yet, boss. I tried calling the Kinlochleven station, but apparently it's been a Bed and Breakfast for years. Who knew? Closest station is in Glencoe. It's not manned all the time, so we'll have to get some of the guys from here to head down that way." He pointed to the phone handset. "Just getting it authorised."

"What man's this you're talking about?" Ben asked.

"Shifty bastard. Seemed to be snooping around near the victim's house. Wouldn't give his name." The rest of the sentence came out through gritted teeth. "Knew his rights, apparently."

"Christ. One of them," Ben remarked. "Not like the old days. Eh, Jack?"

"No. Not like the old days," Logan agreed.

"I actually think it's quite good, sir," Hamza volunteered. He had the phone in one hand and a finger poised over the buttons, and eyed both men warily. "That folk know their rights, I mean. Rights are important. You know, like... checks and balances, and all that?"

Ben opened his mouth to reply, but Logan held up a finger to stop him. "That's a really good attitude to have, Detective Constable," he said, to the surprise of pretty much everyone in the room. "And I agree that rights are important. Vital, even. I have no problem whatsoever with people *having* rights. I just don't like it when they know what those rights are. It makes our job a hell of a lot more difficult."

He pointed to the handset. "Now, have you made that phone call? If not, would you mind getting down from your high horse for five minutes and doing it?"

Hamza turned his attention back to the task at hand. "On it now, sir."

Across at her desk, Caitlyn made a sound that could best be described as 'quizzical'. Her forehead furrowed despite the best efforts of her tightly-scraped-back ponytail, and all eyes went to her as she turned in her chair.

"Problems?" asked Ben.

"Uh, yeah. Maybe," she said. She gave a click of her mouse, waited for the next page of search results to load, then shrugged. "I can't find it. Oswatt. The company the victim worked for. I can't find any reference of it. Not as a business, I mean."

She gestured to the screen. "It's a surname, and possibly the name of a Pokemon—although, I didn't go too far down that particular rabbit hole—but I'm not seeing it as a business. Definitely nothing in the offshore sector."

Logan lowered himself onto the edge of Hamza's desk and crossed his arms. "You sure?"

"Positive, sir," Caitlyn confirmed. "I've Googled it, checked Companies House, Facebook, LinkedIn, Twitter. Nothing."

DI Forde rolled the question around inside his mouth a few times, before spitting it out.

"So, if there's no Oswatt, who the hell has been paying Brodie Welsh's salary every month?"

"And, more importantly," Logan added. "Where has he been going?"

CHAPTER ELEVEN

Logan sat in the small office at the back of the Incident Room, tentatively jabbing buttons on his keyboard while the woman on the screen mouthed silently at him, equal parts amused and exasperated.

"Now? What about now? Hello? Can you hear me now?"

On the monitor, the pathologist, Dr Shona Maguire, gave a double thumbs-up, pointed to her camera, then pointed to her ears.

"You can hear...? No. Me? No. I still can't hear..." He muttered a selection of obscenities under his breath, then raised his voice in the direction of the door. "Hamza! This stupid thing's not working. I can't hear a thing."

There was a moment of hesitation, while Hamza had a stab at diagnosing the problem.

"Are you wearing the headphones, sir?"

"Headphones? What bloody—"

He spotted the headphones hanging over the edge of the monitor, made a general sort of grumbling noise, then pulled them on.

"Hello?" Shona Maguire's Irish lilt was suddenly right there in his ears, like she was standing just a few inches away. "Can you hear me?"

"Aye. Got you. Can you hear me?" Logan asked.

"I've been able to hear you the whole time," the pathologist replied. "I was quite impressed by some of the language you were using at one point. I learned, like, four new swear words in the space of about eight seconds. That must surely be some kind of record."

Logan shifted awkwardly in his seat. "Aye. Well. I'm not really a big one for technology. All too complicated, for my liking."

"I know what you mean. Luckily, I've got a PhD, or I'd never have figured out how to put these in." She pointed to the Bluetooth earphones tucked into her ears, and smirked down the camera lens.

"Good one," Logan told her.

"Thanks," Shona said, her smile widening. "So, you cracked the case yet?"

"Oh, aye. All figured out," Logan said. "Piece of cake. I'm just calling you so you don't feel left out."

"Very generous of you," Shona said. "I'm putting the report together, and I'll fire it over shortly, but you want the top stories?"

Logan picked up a pen, clicked the button on the end, then held it ready above his notepad. "Go for it."

"Hang on, I'll pick you up," Shona said, and the image on screen lurched as she reached forward. There was a loud *crack*, and a panicky, "Oh, shit," and then the pathologist's face appeared again, this time viewed from below. It wasn't the greatest angle, but it also wasn't the worst. "Hello? Still there?"

"I'm still here," Logan confirmed.

Shona let out a sigh of relief. "Dropped the phone," she explained.

"I guessed."

Shona must've caught sight of herself in the little inset picture, because she quickly moved the phone so it wasn't capturing her from quite such an unflattering angle. As she moved it, Logan caught a glimpse of the corpse on the table behind her, a sheet covering its modesty.

"Right. OK, here goes, then," she began, turning the phone so the body filled most of the screen. "Male victim, obviously. Mid-twenties, but you know that. Teeth removed, fingers cut off from around the first interphalangeal joint."

Logan raised a hand and pointed to the middle knuckle of his index finger.

"Precisely. Well done. That was a test, and you passed. You know your knuckles," Shona told him. She focused in on one of the victim's hands. Her shaky camera work didn't make it easy, but Logan was able to see the blackened stumps of his fingers. "As you might be able to see, it wasn't a neat job. The fingers weren't removed individually, but in a couple of strikes with something like an axe. Machete, maybe. Once across the fingers, then across the thumb. Same on both hands."

"Pre or post-mortem?" Logan asked.

"After. I'd expect to see a lot of blood staining on his hands if he'd been alive, and the clotting situation would be very different. He wasn't bleeding when his fingers were cut off. Same with the teeth. Done after he was dead. Blunt instrument. Bad aim, too. Nose took a few cracks. One of the cheeks, too. You ask me, either the face was covered, or whoever did the smashing didn't want to look too closely at what he was doing."

Without warning, Shona angled the phone's camera to give a clear view of

Brodie's face. Logan had only seen half of it when the body was face down on the ground, and the damage was substantially worse than he'd first thought.

"Want a look?" the pathologist asked. Somewhat late, Logan thought.

"I'm looking," the DCI told her. "Christ. He'll no' be winning any beauty contests, will he?"

"Depends on who he's up against, I suppose," Shona remarked from behind the camera. "Someone didn't want him identified."

"Well, luckily, we got a break there," Logan told her. "What about the stomach? Palmer said something about a slit?"

"Bit of an understatement," Shona said. The image on screen moved down past the victim's chest, to an open wound in his stomach that caught Logan off guard.

"Jesus."

"Sorry, should've warned you. Yeah, it's a bad one," Shona said. "Bad two, actually. The initial cut went through the muscle and sliced open the stomach wall. There was then a secondary cut into the bowel. Neither were done particularly delicately. From what I can tell, both were done while he was still alive. There's also a stab wound to the chest. Close to the heart, but missed."

Logan wasn't particularly enjoying the view of the victim's insides, but leaned in for a closer look, anyway. "But the knife wounds were the cause of death?"

"Actually, no," Shona said. "I found sand and grit in his lungs. Breathed in. It's a close-run thing, but I'd say he suffocated before he bled to death."

"Buried alive," Logan remarked. His eyes narrowed. "Wait. Sand?"

"Yeah. And grit. Like... fine gravel, I suppose. I've sent it off for testing."

"Not soil?"

"No. Plenty of soil on the outside and in the wounds, but nothing in his lungs. I take it that doesn't match the scene?"

"It doesn't, no."

Logan scribbled a few notes in his pad. "When did he die?"

"Based on deterioration, conditions..." Shona said mulling it over. "Six days. Ish. I should be able to be a bit more accurate once some results come back."

"Palmer reckons the burial site was only a couple of days old," Logan told her.

"Geoff would know more about that than me, I'm sure," Shona said. "He knows his stuff."

Logan couldn't argue, but it annoyed him immensely to hear the pathologist praising that creepy bastard, particularly after what he'd said about her back at the burial site.

The image on screen changed to show Shona's face. "Body's definitely older, though. No way he was killed in the last seventy-two hours. Not possible."

Logan nodded, the suspicion that had formed while speaking to Palmer at Glen Coe now confirmed. "He was moved, then. Killed somewhere, left a few days, then relocated and buried."

Shona glanced down at the body which was now, mercifully, off-screen. "Maybe they were worried he'd be found?"

Logan sat back in his chair. "I don't think it's that," he said, although he didn't elaborate further.

"One other thing worth mentioning, his rectum was partially distended, and there was some damage around the anus. Not major, but worthy of note. I don't think it's particularly recent, either. Historical."

"A sex thing?" Logan wondered.

"I couldn't rule that out," Shona said. "But not necessarily."

"Right. Thanks," Logan said. He was still thinking about the body being moved, trying to figure out why. He folded his notepad closed, and drummed his fingers on the cover, lost in theories and 'what ifs'.

"Like I say, I'll get the report to you shortly," Shona said, interrupting his train of thought.

Logan blinked, then nodded. "Good. Thanks. I'll keep an eye out."

"Right. OK, then," Shona replied. Her tone changed, becoming more conversational. "How did your trip go, by the way?"

The DCI frowned. "Trip?"

"Glasgow. The hospital. I mean... *Carstairs*," she said, dancing around the hospital's name like it might be booby-trapped. "Did you get what you needed?"

Logan puffed out his cheeks and looked away, as if contemplating this fully for the first time. "No," he said. "Not really."

"Oh. Right. Well, sorry to hear that," Shona said. She raised the phone a little, so it was looking at her from a slightly higher angle. "Maybe, when you're back... If you want, like. Maybe we could have a chat about it? Problem shared, and all that. I'm sure one of us still owes the other one lunch, or dinner, or breakfast, or whatever it is." She smiled. "I've lost track."

Logan had just started to return the smile when there was a knock at the door, and DC Neish's head appeared around the door frame.

"Sorry, boss. Thought you'd want to know. The guy in the baseball cap? I think we've got a hit."

"Anyone of interest?" Logan asked.

Tyler made a weighing motion. "Aye. Worth a look, anyway."

"I'll be right there," Logan told him. He turned back to the screen. "Listen, I—"

"I heard. Go. We'll talk later," Shona said, then her eyes widened and she quickly garbled out a, "Wait!"

There was no real need for the urgency. Logan had no idea how to hang up the video call, and had been relying on the pathologist doing it from her end.

"What's up?" he asked.

"Forgot to say, got some very early toxicology reports. Basic stuff, but it might be something," she said. "Looks like he was a cannabis user. Regular, and long-term. Not sure if that's worth noting."

"I'm sure it is," Logan told her. "Thank you. Keep in touch."

"Will do," Shona said.

There was a hollow silence as they both sat there for a few moments, saying nothing.

"You'll have to hang up," Logan told her.

On the screen, Shona looked amused. "Is that the game we're playing, is it? No, *you* hang up."

Logan quietly cleared his throat. "No, I mean it. I don't know the buttons."

Shona's smile quickly fell. Her cheeks blushed red. "Oh. Right. Gotcha. Sorry. Bye!" she said, and then the tip of one of her fingers filled the screen, and the call was terminated.

"Well," said Tyler, and Logan winced when he realised the DC was still standing in the doorway. "That was all a bit awkward, wasn't it?"

CHAPTER TWELVE

There was an ugly bastard on the Big Board when Logan emerged from the office.

Usually, he tried not to judge people on their appearance, but it was difficult in this case. That was because it wasn't his appearance that was the problem. Not really. The ugliness Logan could see was all there on the inside.

You got to know it, eventually. You could see it in the eyes and in the lines of the face. A coldness, but something more, too. Something deeper. Something worse.

Sure, with his crooked nose, caterpillar eyebrows, and sunken, piggy-little eyes, the guy was certainly no oil painting on the outside, either, but the real ugliness lurked within, and Logan could see it as clear as day.

"That our man?" he asked, taking a seat on the edge of a desk.

"Aye, that's him, boss," Tyler confirmed. "We got a hit pretty much straight away from one of the neighbours. Old boy. He was the only one who pointed the finger, although Uniform reckons there were others who knew, but didn't want to say."

"And this is the man you spoke to?" Logan asked.

"Reckon so, boss, yeah," Tyler confirmed. "He's bulked up a bit since the mugshot was taken, and sorted out them eyebrows, but that's him."

"Sandy Gillespie," DI Forde said, reading from a printout. "Part of a local family of toerags. Youngest of three siblings, all of them with a record. Fighting, in his case, on the High Street, mostly. One charge of B&E a few years back, but it was dropped. Nothing major, just a recurring pain in the arse."

"Any connection to Brodie Welsh or Hannah Randall?" Logan asked.

"Only a disappointing one," Ben said. "Neighbours. He lives just around the corner."

"Regularly walks his dog up that street," Tyler added. "According to the neighbour who ID'd him, anyway. The old boy had plenty to say about him. No love lost there. But, he did back-up the dog walking story."

Logan tutted. "Bollocks." He ran his tongue across the roof of his mouth, eyeballing the photograph. Ugly bastard. No doubt. "Worth bringing him in on something?"

"On a charge?" asked Ben. "Because I can't see him volunteering to pop in for a chat."

"Anything we can get him on?" Logan asked, looking around for suggestions.

Ben and the others exchanged blank looks.

"Come on. Get creative," Logan urged. He pointed to the mugshot pinned to the board. "My gut tells me that bastard was up to something, but he'll be only too aware that we can't bring him in on that. So, what can we bring him in on?"

The silence that followed was eventually broken by an, "Oh!" from DC Neish. All eyes went to him.

"Tyler?"

"Dog shit, boss!" the DC announced. Quite proudly, too.

Logan's face remained impassive. "Dog shit?"

"Aye. That's one of the things the neighbour said. Here..." Tyler picked up his notepad and rifled through the pages. "Got it. Apparently, the dog shites on the pavement and Gillespie never bothers to pick it up. The old boy confronted him about it a few times, but he just laughs it off. So, he took photos. The neighbour, I mean. He took photos on his phone. Showed the lassie from Uniform. Dozens of pictures of dog shit, and a couple of Gillespie's dog in the act. He went through them all with her."

"Bet she was delighted," Hamza remarked.

DS McQuarrie tapped a pen against her desk. "Fixed penalty though, isn't it?"

"Aye." Ben looked doubtful. "Can we bring him in on dog shit?"

"I've brought people in on less," Logan told him, and Ben could only concede that point with a shrug.

"But, how's that conversation going to go?" Hamza wondered. "'We know we brought you in about the dog shit, but while you're here, did you happen to murder anyone recently?'"

DS McQuarrie nodded her agreement. "If he's clued up, like Tyler says, he's going to see right through it."

Logan shrugged off her concern. "He might know his stop and search rights, but that doesn't mean he knows his rights under the dog shite... Whatever."

"Dog Fouling Scotland Act, 2003," Caitlyn recited.

"Aye. That. Thank you," Logan said.

"Suppose, sir. But, if he gets a solicitor and puts in a complaint..." the DS continued.

"We'll cross that bridge when we come to it," Logan said. He rubbed his chin, his fingers rasping across the stubble. "Aye. Let's do it," he decided, giving Tyler the nod. "Let's go with the dog shit."

Sandy Gillespie was hurling abuse at a ten-year-old when the knock at the door came. He ignored it at first, his thumbs tapping on the X-button of his PlayStation controller, as he slide-tackled the legs out from under his online opponent, and cackled at the squeals of complaint in his headset.

"Fucking grow up, you wee Yank prick," Sandy sneered. "Away and greet to *Mommy*. You lot don't even fucking play football, so I don't know what you're even—"

The knocking came again. Louder and more insistent. Sandy recognised it, then. Not the specific knock, but the specific type. Polis. Fucking polis.

He dropped out of the game with a couple of button taps, swore a handful of times at the random kid he'd been paired up against, then rolled off his beanbag and onto the dirty carpet.

Snatching up the joint he'd left sitting in the ashtray, he stuffed it, his lighter, and a thumb-sized block of hash into a tin. Then, he shoved the tin into the little flap he'd created in the base of the couch, fastened it shut with the Velcro, and cracked open a window.

He'd just turned in the direction of the hallway when the hammering came again, shaking the front door in its frame.

"Mr Gillespie? We know you're in there," said a male voice. One of the local plods. Sandy couldn't remember the name, but he could picture his face.

"Alright, alright, I'm coming," he said. It was only when he shuffled past the kitchen door that the barking started on the other side. Sandy thudded a fist against it on the way past. "Shut the fuck up," he ordered, but this only egged the animal on, and the barking became ever-more furious.

"What?" Sandy asked, spitting the word out before the door was open. Not that it opened far. He'd left the security chain across it, so there was only a six-inch gap through which anyone could see in or out.

Two uniformed officers stood in the garden. The first was the guy he'd been expecting. Two or three years older than Sandy himself. Moved to the area a couple of years back. Thought he was the Big I-Am.

He stood up front on the step, chest all puffed up beneath the high-vis jacket. His fist was raised like he had been getting ready to knock again. It lowered to his side when Sandy squinted out at them through the gap.

Behind the first officer was a woman. Short. Squat. Unsure of herself. New, probably.

"Mr Gillespie?" the male officer asked. "Mr Sandy Gillespie."

"Aye. You know fine fucking well," Sandy said. He looked the man on the step up and down. "What's your name again? Farmer, or something, wasn't it?"

The officer opened his mouth to reply, but Sandy clicked his fingers and pointed. "Farler. James Farler. Jamie-Boy. That's right, isn't it?"

"Police Constable James Farler, yes," he confirmed. "Now, Mr—"

"Your kids go to the school, don't they?" Sandy continued. "Boy and a girl, isn't it? I see them go past."

PC Farler quietly cleared his throat. His shoes *creaked* as he shifted his weight on them. "That's not any of your business."

Sandy snorted, draining his sinuses, then swallowed it down. "Everything round here's my business, Jambo," he said. He turned his head back in the direction of the kitchen, bellowed, "Fucking shut up!" at the barking dog, then faced front again, flashing a smile that showed off his yellowing teeth. "Now, what can I do for you, orifice? Sorry, *officer*."

He looked past Farler to the female officer standing behind him. "I'm always making that mistake."

"Well, Mr Gillespie," she said, holding his gaze with a calm composure that disappointed him no end. "It's about your dog..."

CHAPTER THIRTEEN

Ben and Logan stood in half-darkness, peering into the brightly-lit room on the other side of the glass, where Sandy Gillespie slouched in a chair that had been carefully hand-selected for its uncomfortable back and complete lack of padding.

He hadn't asked for a solicitor. He'd seemed amused by the charge, by all accounts. He'd been cracking jokes when Uniform had checked him in, then had sung to himself as he was led along the corridor and into the interview room.

He still looked amused now, although boredom was starting to creep in. Logan and Ben both watched as he picked his nose, studied the findings, then flicked it in the direction of the glass.

"Can we hurry this up?" he asked, his voice stabbing at them through the speakers. "I haven't got all fucking day."

"Charming lad," Ben remarked. "Be nice if he did it, and we could wrap it all up before home time."

"Aye," Logan agreed. "That'd be handy."

On the other side of the soundproof glass, Gillespie started to chant. "Why are we waiiitiiing? Why are we waiiitiiing?"

"God. What a horrible little bastard," Ben said, his already low opinion of the man worsening by the second. He shot Logan a warning look. "You watch yourself in there. Don't go letting him under your skin."

"What, this wee dick? Come on, Benjamin. You know me better than that," Logan said. "How many times have we dealt with arseholes like him before?"

Ben nodded, but it was hesitant. "True. But, there's something about this one, Jack. He's got my guts churning."

"Sure that's no' Alice's cooking?" Logan asked, and both men shared a grim smile. "I'll be fine," Logan said. "Besides, I'm letting Tyler take the lead."

"Why are we waiiitiiiing? Why-aye are we waiiitiii—"

Ben tutted and turned the dial that lowered the volume from the speakers. Silence filled the viewing room.

"Tyler?" he asked, almost spluttering the word out. "I mean, he's coming along, but... taking the lead? Are you sure that's a good idea?"

"He wants another crack at him," Logan said. "After what happened down the road."

"What, you mean when he failed to even get so much as a name from the bastard?"

Logan nodded. "I'll be in there with him. I can jump in, if needs be, but it'll be good to observe Gillespie's reactions. I want you and Caitlyn through here. Leave Hamza digging into the employer thing. Oswatt."

Reaching into his pocket, Logan took out the promotional pen and handed it over. "Tell him to check in with Fulton Randall. See if Hannah will give him a copy of the bank statement. We might get an account number for them off there, or be able to check with the bank where the transactions have been coming from."

Ben took the pen, shook his head disapprovingly at the apostrophe usage, then tucked it into his shirt pocket.

"Hamza might need to go down there and talk to her himself. See what she knows about the company, if anything. When did Brodie start there? Does she have payslips? Has she ever spoken to his boss or colleagues? That sort of thing."

"Right. I'll get him on it," Ben said. He glanced at his watch. It was just after eight, and darkness had come creeping in a few hours ago. "Getting late, though. Maybe best leaving the visit until tomorrow?"

Logan conceded the point with a sigh. "Aye. But have him phone Fulton tonight. We can make a start there, at least, then follow up in the morning."

Ben tapped the breast pocket, and the pen it contained. "I'll go get him on it, and bring Caitlyn in. You going to give Tyler a pep talk?"

"Aye," Logan said. He put a hand on the back of his neck, kneading the muscle. "Something like that."

"Do *NOT* FUCK THIS UP. Is that understood?"

Tyler briefly regarded the finger jabbing in his face and gave a quick shake of his head. "I won't, boss. I've got this."

The finger dropped. Logan ran the other hand down his face, mumbled quietly, then pulled together something that could almost, under the right lighting conditions, be passed off as a smile.

"Aye. You've got this," he agreed. "But if at any point you feel you haven't got it, you let me know, alright?"

"Will do, boss."

"And, if I think you're struggling, then I'll jump in, and that's your cue to shut your mouth. We're only going to get one crack at this bastard. We cannot blow it."

"Got it. No bother, boss," Tyler said. He grinned. "But relax. I've got this. Honest."

Logan approached the door to the interview room, checked the code on the slip of paper he'd been given, then keyed it into the pad. The door *buzzed.*

Tyler took a deep breath. "Well, here goes nothing," he said.

Logan grunted. "That doesn't exactly fill me with confidence," he muttered.

And with that, he pulled open the door.

FULTON RANDALL SAT in his armchair, his granddaughter, Carrie, snuggled in at his side, a picture book spread across their legs. Realistically, the armchair was too big for the room, and it made the place look cramped and untidy. But Fulton had settled on it for just this very purpose. For moments just like this one, with Carrie coorying in beside him, one leg hooked over his, her wee body tucked in against his arm.

She should've been in bed by now. Should've been tucked up, fast asleep, oblivious to the fact her life had been irrevocably changed. But, she'd wanted to read the book again. 'Again-*again*,' in fact. She'd insisted on that, and he didn't have the heart to say no.

Hannah had refused to come and stay over. Point blank. Even when Fulton's wife, Sandra, had insisted, Hannah had stood her ground. She wanted to be home. She wanted to be in their room, her and Brodie's, in the bed they'd shared for the past few years. She wanted to be close to him.

Fulton and Sandra had offered to stay over with her. She'd refused that, too, but had accepted their offer to watch Carrie for another night. Hannah didn't want the girl to see her crying, she'd said. It would come. It was bound to come. But not now. Not yet. Not tonight.

"Look at the tutu. Is that funny?" Fulton asked, pointing to one of the pictures in the book. A cow was strutting around in a ballerina dress, and it was always one of Carrie's favourite pictures.

"Yeah!" she said, the word coming out as a giggle.

"Have you ever seen a cow wearing a tutu?" Fulton asked her, looking down. She grinned up at him and nodded enthusiastically. "You have?"

"Yeah! Two times."

"*Two* times? Wow!" Fulton said. "Lucky you. I don't think I've ever—"

His phone buzzed on the table. Normally, he'd have let it go to voicemail, but given everything going on, he knew he had to answer it.

His initial reaction was that it might have been Hannah, but the number wasn't one he recognised. Local one, though. He turned the page, pointed at another cow in fancy dress, then tapped the 'answer' icon.

"Hello?"

The voice on the other end was broad Aberdonian. It took Fulton's ear a moment to adjust.

"Mr Randall? This is DC Hamza Khaled. You spoke to one of my colleagues earlier. DCI Logan."

"Yes." Fulton sat forward, leaving Carrie looking at the book. "Is everything alright? Have you got news?"

"Sorry, nothing to report yet, Mr Randall. But we're pursuing multiple lines of inquiry, and working on getting a result as soon as we possibly can," Hamza said. "We were just hoping you might be able to help us with something."

Carrie tugged on Fulton's arm. He smiled, held up an index finger to indicate he'd only be a second, then returned to the call. "Of course. Anything. What do you need?"

"It's Brodie's employer. Oswatt. We're having difficulty tracking them down."

Fulton frowned. "Really? I think he said they're a Dutch company. Based in the Netherlands. Oil. Or... I assume oil. He never really specified, but he works offshore a lot."

He glanced sadly back at Carrie, then quietly corrected himself. "Worked offshore."

"I'm sorry for your loss, sir," Hamza said.

"Not my loss. Not really," Fulton said, giving his granddaughter's leg a squeeze. She beamed at him, then tapped a fist on the book impatiently. He made the same 'one-second' gesture with a finger again, then turned it into a tickle that made her squeal with delight.

"We were hoping there might be something on the bank statement that would help us identify the company," Hamza continued. "Do you have a copy?"

"No. I mean, yes. Hannah wasn't in much of a mood for going through the paperwork stuff, so I just took a photo on my phone so I could give you the details. I can email it to you, if you like?"

"That would be perfect, Mr Randall," Hamza told him. "I'll text you through my email address now. Easier than spelling it out."

"Right. Yes. No problem," Fulton said, then they said their brief goodbyes. He sat back, the phone in one hand, Carrie snuggling in against him again on the other side.

The text came through almost immediately. Fulton tapped it, attached the photo of the bank statement to the email window that popped up, and sent it off.

Returning to the phone's home screen, he selected the search box, then read a few lines of the book's next page while tapping his thumb across the phone's on-screen keyboard.

O-S-W-A-T-T.

A page of search results was returned. None of them relevant.

Glancing down, Fulton read off the next few lines of the story, then added the words, 'oil,' and 'Dutch' to the phone search. The screen refreshed. He swiped up, scanning the results. They were mostly links to sites selling Danish Oil for treating wood. In fact, not *mostly*. Exclusively. No offshore companies. No Dutch energy firms.

No Oswatt.

"Grandpa."

Fulton tore his eyes from his phone. Carrie pointed to the words at the bottom of the page and stared expectantly up at him.

"Sorry, sweetheart," he said, then he set the phone down, shuffled lower in his seat, and got back to reading.

CHAPTER FOURTEEN

On Logan's nod, Tyler pressed the button between them on the table. It illuminated red. On the other side of the room's large mirror, the display on a digital recorder began to count upwards.

"Interview begins at..." Tyler checked his watch. "Nine-sixteen PM. Present in the room is, um, me. Detective Constable Tyler Neish."

"Detective Chief Inspector Jack Logan."

Tyler looked across the table at the third man and waited.

"State your name for the recording," he urged.

"Sandy Gillespie," the other man said, after a few moments of unflinching eye contact with the DC.

"Thank you. We should note for the recording that Mr Gillespie has declined his right to a solicitor. Can you confirm that for us?"

"Aye. Whatever. Can we just get a fucking move on?" Gillespie asked.

He was slouching back in his chair, his arms draping down almost all the way to the floor. There was an air of a petulant teenager about him, despite him being old enough to know better. One of his legs was bouncing, so that the knee bumped softly against the underside of the table, shaking it.

At first, Logan had thought the movement was unconscious, a sign of nervousness, but he had quickly come to suspect Gillespie was doing it on purpose just to be annoying.

He was succeeding, too.

"Mr Gillespie. Sandy. Can I call you Sandy?" Tyler asked.

"Call me what you like."

"Sandy. Do you know why you're here?"

"Aye, but I want you to tell me," Gillespie said. "I want to hear you say it."

Logan sat in silence, eyeballing the man across the table, a look of mild irritation fixed on his face. It was a look he had honed carefully over the years. The 'mild' part was important, as he didn't want to come across as too aggressive from the off, but it was vital that the look implied that his irritation levels could become substantially less mild at any given moment.

"You're here because we've had reports of multiple offences you've committed that contravene the Dog Fouling Scotland Act of 2003," Tyler explained, briefly glancing at Caitlyn's notes to ensure he got the wording right.

"Bullshit," Gillespie spat.

Tyler flipped open a folder on the desk in front of him. "Dog shit, actually. And lots of it. We had some printouts done of the photos. Do you want to see?"

Gillespie ignored the ten-by-twelve glossy pictures that were pushed to his side of the table. "I mean bullshit, that's not what I'm here for." He jabbed a finger down on one of the photos. It showed a particularly impressive evacuation. "This is fixed penalty stuff. Forty quid. This is fucking council work, not you lot."

He flicked his gaze across to Logan. It was only the second or third time he'd so much as glanced in the DCI's direction since the detectives had entered the room. There was a flash of uncertainty there, but it was quickly pushed down.

"What's up with your face? You fucking constipated or something?"

Logan said nothing. He didn't even ramp his irritation levels up a notch. He just sat there, silent and staring, and let Tyler do the talking.

"What else would we have brought you in for, Sandy? What other reason would we have had to drag you all the way up here at this time of night?"

"You tell me."

Tyler clasped his hands in front of himself. Logan didn't like it. It didn't seem natural, like something the DC had seen on a training course, or an episode of *Prime Suspect*.

"We brought you in here to discuss the dog fouling, as I think we've made clear," Tyler said. "But, we're particularly interested in earlier today. Where you and I had our little chat. See, I've had a couple of officers go and check that area, Sandy, and they found not one, not two, but three dog turds all around the same spot. Three. That's a lot of shit for a wee dug."

He side-eyed Logan. "You think, boss?"

Logan nodded, just once, never breaking eye contact with the scrote across the table.

"All looked much the same. Similar size, shape, consistency. I had them check. They weren't happy about it, but I can't really blame them. Not a nice job," Tyler said. He stuck out his tongue, pulled a disgusted face, then shook his head. "The point is, though. They reckon it was the same dog. They took samples, in case we wanted to test it, but I don't think that'll be necessary."

"What's he fucking on about?" Gillespie asked Logan. Predictably, he got no response.

"Is your dog fit and well, Sandy? No problems with the plumbing?"

"No."

"Good. That's great. Because going three times like that would either suggest he's got a dicky tummy, or that you and he were hanging around there for a good wee while. In that same spot. Why would that be, Sandy?"

"No crime in standing on the street," Gillespie said.

Tyler shrugged. "There is if you let your dog repeatedly shite on it," he pointed out. "Why that spot, in particular? There are fields not far away. Nice walks through the woods. Why stand at that particular spot, outside those particular houses, long enough for your dog to empty its guts three times? That's what we're struggling to understand, Sandy. That's what we're hoping you can help us with. Why were you standing *there*? What were you doing there for that length of time?"

Gillespie glanced at the empty chair beside him. It had been set out for the solicitor he had chosen not to bring in, and for a moment he looked like he might be regretting that decision.

But then, the petulant teenager returned and he sat back, plastering a sneer across his weaselly little face. "I just like that spot."

"Certainly seems like it," Tyler agreed. "We checked, and the school has CCTV. You know? The one at the end of the road? It's not all that clear, but if you squint, you can see you walking up the street earlier today. Want to hazard a guess what time?"

"Not really."

"Quarter past eleven. Thereabouts. Eleven seventeen. May as well be exact about it. Eleven seventeen this morning. That's a good, what, three or four hours before I bumped into you? Something like that. We can check the school CCTV to get the exact time. I'm on there, too, wandering about. Looking for anything that might be considered suspicious."

Tyler gave that a moment to bed in. "Like, for example, someone standing in the same spot for four hours, letting their dog shite the place up. Some would consider that suspicious, Sandy. Especially given what's happened."

"There go you! Here it comes," Gillespie said. "Wondered when you'd get around to it. This is about Brodie Welsh, isn't it? You're trying to pin that on me."

Tyler looked surprised. Even Logan couldn't tell if he was feigning it, or if it was genuine. "Pin what on you, Sandy?" he asked. "What is it you're referring to?"

Another voice spoke before Gillespie could respond. It was amplified by the speakers on the wall, the tone clipped and authoritative.

"DCI Logan."

Logan recognised the voice as Jinkies'. What the hell was he doing here at this time of night? Not like him to show face outwith normal office hours.

"I'd like a word, please," Jinkies told him. "Urgently."

Gillespie drew in a breath and grinned, showing his scum-coated teeth. "Oops. Someone's in trouble."

Logan continued to stare Gillespie down as DC Neish hovered a finger over the recording button.

"Interview suspended at nine-thirty-four PM. DCI Logan leaving the room," Tyler said, and then he pushed down on the button and the recording stopped with a *click*.

"Bring us a coffee when you come back, will you?" Gillespie asked. "Milk and two. And not that shit from the machine."

Logan stopped at the door but didn't look back. "Coffee. Right," he said. "I'll see what I can do."

And then, he left the interview room and let the door swing closed behind him.

CHAPTER FIFTEEN

JINKIES WAS INSTALLED BEHIND HIS DESK, STAKING HIS RIGHTFUL CLAIM to the seat, when Logan entered. The Chief Inspector was tapping a pen against a pile of paperwork, and his teeth were digging into his bottom lip hard enough to leave a temporary mark in the flesh.

"You wanted to see me, Hugh?" Logan said, delivering the question almost like an accusation. He indicated the corridor with a tilt of his head. "Not sure if you noticed, but I was kind of in the middle of something back there."

"I noticed. Oh, I noticed. Close the door," the Chief Inspector said. He waited until the door clicked into place before ejecting a furious, "What the hell do you think you're playing at?"

Logan's shoulders stiffened and went back. He felt his chest expanding, but while the body was able, the mind was not willing. It had been a long day. He was in no mood for a fight.

"Interviewing a suspect, Hugh," he said, keeping his tone level. "I know it's probably been a while, but I thought you'd still be able to recognise it if you saw it."

"And he's a suspect, is he? Sandy Gillespie? You've got evidence that ties him to your investigation, have you?"

"He was outside the victim's house for several hours the day his body was discovered," Logan said. It was wafer-thin, but he said it confidently, like it was beyond questioning.

Jinkies, unfortunately, saw it very differently.

"You were asking him about dog shit, Jack!" he said. "You brought him in on a jumped-up charge that should've been a spot fine. It's ridiculous. Unacceptable. Completely unacceptable."

Logan shrugged. "Well, that depends on your point of view," he said. His gaze gave the Chief Inspector a quick once over. Jinkies was dressed in his civvies. Scruffy ones, at that. He'd come in for this, specially. He'd rushed in to pull Logan out of that interview and to put a stop to it. "You seem very invested in Mr Gillespie's situation, Hugh. Friend of yours, is he?"

Jinkies sneered. "No, he is not. What he is, *Jack*, is a major suspect in an ongoing CID investigation. An investigation which your little dog shit stunt is at risk of jeopardising."

Logan groaned inwardly but remained impassive on the outside. "The drugs thing?"

"Yes, Jack. As you so rightly say, *the drugs thing*," Jinkies retorted. "We've got a net around the whole Gillespie family right now, and it has taken us a long time to manoeuvre it into position. That net is going to close on them in the very near future. Our dominoes are all in a row, but if they get a clue—a snifter—that we're after them, then those dominoes fall over, and we're down the snake all the way back to square one."

"Pretty sure that's no' how Dominoes works," Logan remarked. "I mean, it's been a long time since I've played, but—"

"You think this is funny, Jack?" Jinkies demanded, leaning forward in his chair. He prodded the desk with a fingertip. "Thousands of hours have gone into building this case. Resources brought in from all over the country. We're trying to bring down one of the key suppliers of illicit substances to the whole of the Highlands here. To the whole of the north of Scotland, in fact. One of the big boys. And you're going to blow it all over... over some *dog shit*?"

"You know as well as I do that he's not here about the shite, Hugh," Logan said, still managing to keep his voice steady. He didn't want to give the other man the satisfaction of seeing him annoyed. Especially when, Logan hated to admit, Jinkies was in the right. "He's here about the murder of a young man. A father."

"A murder you can't remotely connect him to!"

Logan puffed out his cheeks and gave a grunt of acknowledgement. "Look. I didn't know. About the investigation. We didn't see anything about it."

It wasn't an apology, but it was as close to one as he could muster.

"The Gillespies have a lot of influence locally. We're keeping it low key, for fear it gets out and gets back to them," Jinkies said. "Which is why I told you—"

"You've got a leak?" Logan asked. The Chief Inspector ignored him.

"Which is why I told you, way back when you first came here for the missing boy case, that you need to go through me. You can't just go running around like you own the place like... like..."

He waved a hand, trying to conjure up a name.

"Like *Magnum, P.I.* There are procedures, Jack. There's a pecking order, and I'm at the top."

Jinkies raised the same hand and indicated a range of different heights. "There's me, bit down, you, bit down, everyone else. Stick to that. Keep that in mind at all times, and it'll prevent this sort of situation from happening again, won't it?"

The Chief Inspector sat back and smiled. It was a smile so intensely patronising that Logan had to physically plant his feet to stop himself lunging for the bastard.

"Next time you're going to do something like this, think, 'What would Hugh do?' And, if you don't know the answer to that question, by all means, just go right ahead and ask. Like I say, my door is always open."

THE DOOR to the interview room buzzed, then was thrown open. Logan entered, carefully carrying two cups of coffee, each with a chocolate digestive balanced on the saucer.

Gillespie smacked his lips together and grinned. "About time," he said, then his smile fell away as Logan set the cups down, one in front of Tyler, the other in front of his own empty chair.

The chair legs scraped on the floor as he pulled it out and sat down. He went back to holding Gillespie's gaze as he took a wee bite of the digestive, then slurped a glug of coffee to wash it down.

"Cheers, boss," Tyler said, raising his own cup in toast.

"No bother, son. I got us the good stuff," Logan replied. "No' that shite from the machine."

Tyler's finger moved over to the button that would start the recording, but Logan blocked it. "We've decided to let you go, Mr Gillespie."

Across the table, Sandy snorted. "Oh. *Decided*, did you? Were fucking told to, more like. What's the matter, someone higher-up give you a smack on the end of your cock?"

Logan and Tyler's eyes met. The DC shrugged. "New one on me, boss."

"I mean, I've heard of a slap on the wrist," Logan remarked.

Gillespie scowled at them, then stabbed a finger in the direction of the door. "So, I can go, then, yeah?"

"You can," Logan confirmed. He waited until Gillespie had moved to stand before finishing the sentence. "Once we issue you with your fixed penalties."

Across the table, Gillespie's face darkened.

Tyler drew a breath in through his teeth. "That's going to mount up."

"We're not going to pursue all of the alleged instances, obviously," Logan said, and a look of relief flitted across Gillespie's face. He took immense pleasure in stamping on it. "Just the ones we have photograph evidence for."

Logan turned to Tyler. "How many is that, Detective Constable?"

"Oh, not sure, boss. I'll have to look through. Thirty-odd, maybe?"

The DCI winced. He wasn't subtle about it. "Wow. You're right," he said, shooting an almost apologetic look at the man on the other side of the table. "That *is* going to mount up, isn't it?"

CHAPTER SIXTEEN

Hannah Randall was sitting on the end of the bed, gazing down at a pair of Brodie's dirty socks on the floor, when she heard the *crack*. It was low and muted, like something falling off a high shelf onto a linoleum floor. An unremarkable enough sound, but in the otherwise silent house, it made her breath catch somewhere at the back of her throat.

She listened, unmoving, her blood whooshing through her veins, her heart beating a staccato rhythm inside her ribcage. *Ba-dum. Ba-dum. Ba-dum.*

Twenty seconds passed. A minute. The house remained silent, and her breath emerged as a shaky gasp of fear, relief, and everything else between.

Getting up from the bed, she crossed to the window and peered outside, where the glow of the street lights did their best to push back against the gathering darkness. Everything looked normal enough. No cars she didn't recognise. Nobody hanging around. The same old street in the same old town, in a world that was never going to be the same again.

She turned back to the socks and, for a moment, considered picking them up like she'd done a hundred times before. Hannah thought about gathering his dirty washing, and putting away the stack of clean clothes he'd left balanced precariously on the edge of the chest of drawers.

That spot was where his clothes generally lived until either he'd worked his way through the pile, picking out what he was wearing that day, or Hannah had given up and put it all into drawers for him. They'd laugh about it sometimes, argue at others. She knew not to push it too far, though. He loved her—God, he loved her, and he never stopped telling her that—but his temper wasn't always easy to control.

That didn't matter now, though. Today, she wanted those clothes to perch there forever.

If she put them away—or worse, got rid of them—then it was over. If she put them away, he was gone.

One of his t-shirts was draped over the end of the bed, all creases and food stains. She picked it up, slowly and cautiously, like it was some rare and ancient artifact, then brought it to her face and sniffed. Smelled him. Breathed him in.

Grief hit her again then, a sucker-punch that made her slide down off the bed and onto the floor, still gripping the dirty t-shirt. What was she going to do? What would she say to Carrie? How would she explain to her daughter that her daddy was gone, and was never coming back?

She sat there for a while, alternating between sobbing and pulling herself together, going round and around in circles. After each teary outburst, she'd chastise herself, tell herself she had to get up, be strong, for Carrie's sake, as much as her own.

And then, the thought of her daughter and the days, weeks, months, and years that lay ahead would bring the tears again. She'd bury her face in the t-shirt then, and let the sobs take hold.

Hannah was on the fourth or fifth cycle of crying and self-recrimination when she heard the creak. The first sound she'd thought she'd heard had been downstairs. A concern, but a distant one.

This sound, though, had been closer. Upstairs, on the landing.

Right outside the bedroom door.

She checked her pockets for her phone, then remembered she'd left it downstairs after talking to her mum and dad. She could picture it on the windowsill in the living room, fully charged, but completely useless.

Leaning on the bed, Hannah quietly got to her feet. She had almost made it when the door flew open, and the room erupted into movement and noise. She saw a black balaclava, dark eyes glaring out through the holes, then the glow of the streetlights reflected off a knife blade.

Hannah tried to scream, but her chest had constricted and her throat had gone tight, and the sound that escaped was barely a gargle. A gloved hand clamped over her mouth and the world lurched until she was on the bed, the weight of her attacker pressing down on her, pinning her.

From downstairs, there came a series of loud bangs and crashes. She barely heard them. Didn't care. The hand on her face forced her harder against the mattress. The weight of the man's knee on her leg sent shockwaves of pain through her until they eventually escaped through her nose as a whimper.

The eyes blazed down at her through the balaclava. The man's voice, when it came, was raw with anger.

"What did he do with it?" he screamed at her, flecks of saliva hitting her face through the knitted material. He shook her violently, driving her harder against the bed. "*What did he do with our stuff?*"

CHAPTER SEVENTEEN

"Right, there've been a few developments in the last..." Logan glanced at his watch, then gave it a shake. "...Christ knows. Wee while. It's important we're all up to speed with the latest."

He stood on one side of a desk, leaning forward, his big hands gripping the edges like it was a lectern. Ben and the rest of the team sat on the other side, at least one of them doing his best to stifle a yawn.

"And yes, I'm aware it's late, Detective Constable," he remarked. "I'll try not to keep us all too much longer."

"Sorry, boss," Tyler said, forcing his eyes wider and sitting up straight in his chair. "Go on."

Logan motioned to DS McQuarrie, who handed around a small stack of printouts. "Caitlyn's got a summary of the pathology report. The full report is in your email inbox. What we have of it at the moment. Toxicology is still to come, and we're waiting for DNA testing from the lab bods, too. I want you to read the full thing before tomorrow morning."

Once they'd been given a copy, Tyler and Hamza flicked the report open. Ben, who'd already been through it, didn't bother.

"So, headline news is that he was murdered," said Logan. "He sustained two deep puncture wounds in the stomach and bowel. They'd have killed him in a matter of minutes, but it seems the actual cause of death was from asphyxiation. He was buried alive, during which he inhaled the gritty substance found in his lungs."

"Page two," Caitlyn told the detective constables, and they both turned the page in near-perfect unison.

Tyler winced at the photograph of Brodie's injuries. Hamza said nothing but instinctively moved a hand down to his own stomach.

"And we're sure that didn't kill him?" Hamza asked. "Looks like a fatal injury to me."

"Aye, well, it would've been, had he not suffocated before the injuries or blood loss could do the job. Although, as you say, it would've only been a matter of time."

Ben cleared his throat. "You probably don't need me to tell you what the wounds make me think of, Jack."

Logan shook his head, his mouth becoming small and tight as his lips drew together. "No."

"The truck," Ben said.

"Aye. I know."

Tyler glanced around at the others. "What truck?" His gaze tick-tocked between the two older men. "Care to fill us in?"

"No' really," Ben confessed. "But aye. I suppose we should."

And so, they did. Ben launched hesitantly into the explanation, but when he started to struggle to recall the details—either due to his advancing years or, more likely, through a sense of self-preservation—Logan took over.

They'd hunted the truck in question for days. It had come from the continent, delivering some unspecified cargo to a company in Glasgow. A random check had flagged it up before it left France, and while an initial search had turned up empty, it had niggled the powers-that-be enough that they'd put out a call for it to be pulled over once it reached the UK.

Somehow, they lost track of it. Somehow, despite all the manpower and technology at their disposal, they lost track of it.

The driver, they found. Eventually. It took the big boys two days to track him down. When he was eventually found in a Costa Coffee in East Kilbride, the then Detective Inspector Logan and DS Forde had found themselves with the job of questioning him, to try to find out what had happened to the truck.

"Did you find it?" Tyler asked. "Did he talk?"

"Eventually," said Ben, taking up the story again. "We guilt-tripped him, basically. Got him to spill the location."

"There was a false wall," Logan said. "Up the back. When the truck was fully loaded, it would've been impossible to see. Someone had emptied it by the time we turned up. Or, mostly emptied it, anyway."

He chewed his bottom lip, thrust his hands into the pockets of his trousers, then looked down at the floor.

"There were people. In the hidden compartment. From Syria."

"How many?" asked Hamza.

"Eight or nine," Ben told him.

"Nine," said Logan. "Five men, three women, and one girl. Aged six. We think. We never found out for sure."

"Dehydration?" Caitlyn guessed.

"No. No, not dehydration. Usually a good bet, but no," Logan said. He was still looking down at the floor with his hands his pockets, and did a little shuffle on the spot like he was physically unable to stand still. "Someone cut them open. Toxicology reports showed one of the men had a lethally high dose of heroin in his system. Bag must've burst. He died a full day before any of the others."

"Jesus," Tyler muttered.

"The girl was the last to go," said Ben. "She watched what happened to the rest. They *made* her watch. Course, we didn't know that at the time." He raised his head a fraction. His eyes met Ben's, just fleetingly. "But we got it out of them. Eventually."

"So, they were illegally bringing in immigrants loaded up with heroin?" Hamza asked. There was a flatness to his voice—a resigned acceptance that suggested he was saddened but not in the least bit shocked by the story. "And then, once they had them in the country—"

"They cut it out of them. Aye," Logan confirmed. "Had the truck not been flagged, if the driver hadn't been questioned, the bastards behind it might've waited. Let nature take its course. But, with the heat on, they had to move fast. They had to get them out the quickest way possible."

There was a hush as they all considered this. Tyler's eyes reluctantly returned to the photograph of Brodie Welsh's exposed innards.

"And what? We reckon that's what happened here, boss?"

Logan took his hands from his pockets, flexed his fingers, then shrugged. "He travelled a lot. At present, we still don't know who his employer is, and his house was being watched earlier today by someone considered a prime suspect in an ongoing sizeable drugs investigation."

"Likely, then," Caitlyn remarked.

"We can't get a conviction on 'likely.' It's a solid line for us to look into," Logan replied, not yet fully committing to the theory.

"Trips were a cover. He brought something back, swallowed it..."

"Or shoved it up his arse," Tyler interjected.

"He's hardly going to shove it all the way up into his lower intestine, is he?" Hamza said. "What did he use, a broom handle?"

"Well, no, but he did have bruising around the rectum," Tyler pointed out. He grinned triumphantly. "Top of page three. I skipped ahead."

Hamza flicked the page, looked briefly irritated, then continued. "Right. Well. So, if we assume he's a courier, and fails to drop off with the next man in the chain—"

"Or woman," Tyler said. He glanced at Caitlyn and gave a disappointed shake of his head. "Sexism."

"You know what I mean," Hamza said. "The next link in the chain. Male, female, transgender, gender fluid. Whoever they are. He doesn't make the delivery, so they come looking for it."

Caitlyn nodded. "Take him out into the middle of nowhere, cut him open, but find nothing there, so they bury him." She looked across the desk to where Logan stood. "It's plausible, sir."

"Last part's no' quite right," said Logan. "He was moved after death, but otherwise it isn't bad. Plausible, like you say."

Tyler sat back, crossed his arms, and eyeballed the sneering mugshot pinned to the Big Board. "Gillespie, you think?"

"Too early to say for sure," Logan replied. "But, if what CID are saying is right and he's as big a player as they reckon, then he's got to be worth a flutter."

He flicked a look at the mugshot. "Didn't strike me as the brightest, though."

"He knew all the legal stuff, boss," Tyler reminded him.

"Aye, but so do you," Ben pointed out. "That's no' exactly saying much."

"Doesn't take a PhD to hack someone's guts open, sir," Caitlyn said.

"True," Logan conceded. He stole another glance at the mugshot, then shook his head and turned back to the rest of the team. "Either way, Jinkies has made it very clear that he's off-limits for now."

"Since when did you listen to Jinkies, boss?" Tyler asked.

Logan sighed. "Generally speaking, I don't. But this is one of those rare occasions when he's right. We should've checked if he was under investigation. It's a big case, with the potential to take some right bad bastards off the streets. We don't bring Gillespie back in without good reason. Something more solid than dog shite."

"No pun intended," Tyler said. He grinned until the deadpan look from Logan wiped it clean off his face. "Sorry, boss."

Ben took a look at the clock, then it was his turn to fight back a yawn.

"Aye. That'll do us for tonight," Logan said. "We're not wrapping this up any time soon, so no point us all wandering about like half-shut knives. Did we get a hotel sorted?"

"Premier Inn, sir," Hamza said, as he and the others got to their feet. "We're all booked in. They're not doing breakfast, though. Restaurant's being refitted, so we'll have to eat somewhere else."

"Fine. I think there's somewhere just up the road. By Farmfoods. Grab something there on the way in."

Ben paused with his jacket half on. "You're coming, Jack?"

Logan rasped a hand across the lower half of his face. "I'm going to hang on here a bit." He indicated the board with a look. "See if inspiration strikes."

Ben lifted the DCI's coat from the table it had been dropped onto earlier. "Like you say, no point us wandering around like half-shut knives." He held the coat out. "Go and rest. You look like shite. More than usual, I mean."

"Besides, the restaurant's shut, but the pub's open, boss," Tyler said.

The awkward silence that followed made him realise his mistake. His grin became a flash of shock, then a clumsy series of aimless mouth movements that somehow managed to form words. "I mean... I'm sure they do soft drinks... You know, if you don't..."

Logan took his coat from Ben. "Aye. I'm sure they do, son," he said, throwing the DC a lifeline. "And for that, you're getting the first round."

Tyler conceded that this was more than fair, and headed for the door with Hamza and Caitlyn.

"It's by the Morrison's," Hamza said. "There's a McDonald's next to it, too."

"Maccy Ds!" Tyler cheered, and then they left the Incident Room and set off along the corridor.

In the silence that followed, Logan didn't even have to look at Ben to know what he was thinking.

"No. I'm not going to stand you up. I'll be there."

Ben grunted. "I've heard that before," he said, pulling on his jacket and fixing the collar. "If you're not there in twenty minutes, I'm sending Uniform to find you."

"I'd be worried, if I thought that lot could find their arses with both hands," Logan said. He gave his friend a nod. "I'll be there. It'll be... You know..."

"Good?" Ben guessed.

A frown troubled Logan's brow. "I wouldn't go that far. What's between 'OK' and 'bearable'? Is there a word for that?"

"Aye. 'Marriage,'" Ben said. He stopped by the door, took a look around the Incident Room, then fixed Logan with a stern glare. "Twenty minutes. I mean it, Jack."

"I'll be right out. Honest," Logan said, making a show of putting an arm into a coat sleeve. "See? I'm already on route. I'll just grab my phone and be right there."

Ben nodded. "What are you having?"

Logan blew out his cheeks. "Morgans and Coke?"

"Right you are," said Ben, opening the door. "I'll get them to hold the Morgans."

He was gone before Logan could argue. Not that he would have. Not that there would have been much point, even if he'd wanted to. Ben was more a guardian of Logan's sobriety than Logan himself could ever be. Much as he hated to admit it, he'd never have made it off the stuff without the older man's help.

Then again, without his influence, he might never have started. Not to the extent he did, anyway. Ben knew it, too. Probably why he'd been trying to make up for it ever since.

Logan had his coat on and was just taking what he told himself was a final quick look at the Big Board when a phone rang at one of the desks.

It took him a few moments to figure out which of the five phones in the Incident Room was responsible for the ringing, and it—predictably—cut off just as he reached it.

He prodded at a couple of the buttons on either side of the display, hoping to bring up the number that had been calling. Just as he hit on a menu option that looked promising, another phone rang behind him and two desks over.

Logan reached it more quickly. His fingers had touched the handset when it rang off. He brought it to his ear, anyway, to be sure.

"Hello?"

He heard the eager purr of a dial tone, ready and waiting to serve. He clicked the phone back into the receiver.

Brr-brr.

This one came from Ben's desk. Before Logan could even start to turn, it stopped, and was replaced almost immediately by the sound of Tyler's phone.

"What the hell is this now?"

Logan didn't bother grabbing for the phone. He stared it down, instead. It lasted three rings, then cut out halfway through the fourth and was replaced by an expectant hush, like the whole station was holding its breath, waiting to see what would happen next.

Another phone rang, further away this time. Logan had almost been expecting this one. It was muted by the door of the private office up at the back of the room. The office that was usually the domain of the person leading whatever investigation had set up shop in the Incident Room that week.

Logan's office.

It kept ringing as he approached the smaller room, grew louder when he opened the door.

He had time to read the single word that filled the display. *Unknown.*

The ringing continued right up until he lifted the handset from its cradle. He was on full alert when he spoke into the electronic void.

"Who is this?"

He said nothing more and just listened for a reply, the phone cradled between his shoulder and his ear as his hands grabbed for a pen and a notepad.

At first, the only response was the faint hissing of the open line. It was intriguing. Intoxicating, almost, tempting him to speak again.

He resisted.

He waited.

And then, there it was, the faintest suggestion of someone on the other end. Not a word. Not even a sound, really. Barely a breath. Barely anything.

But something.

Someone.

He resisted.

He waited.

The voice that emerged seemed amiable enough. Friendly, even.

"How's Vanessa, Jack?" it asked.

Logan's stomach knotted, processing the question before his brain could catch up. He had only just begun to form the first syllable of what would've been an extremely expletive-filled sentence when the line went dead.

He was out of the office in three big strides and storming out of the Incident Room in half a dozen more.

Out in the corridor, a uniformed sergeant jumped in fright at the sight of him. Logan recognised him as the one from the car park at Glen Coe. The sheep-lifter.

Great.

"Sorry, sir. Wasn't expecting to see you there," he said, pulling the bottom of his jacket down and then smoothing the front. "Thought you'd all gone home. I heard the phones ringing, so I thought I'd better check everything was—"

"I need to know who was calling those lines, Sergeant..." Logan clicked his fingers.

"Jaffray."

"Jaffray. I need you to do a trace on that call."

Sergeant Jaffray's smile remained fixed, but his eyes crept uncertainly in the direction of the Incident Room door. "Er..."

"Not you personally, necessarily," Logan told him. "Call someone in, if you need to. Find out if it's possible to get a number."

It wasn't. He knew that. Not unless the caller was very sloppy, or Logan's usual luck had miraculously changed for the better.

Neither of those things would be the case. He'd put money on it. But, still. Worth a try.

"Get them out of their bed, if you have to," he instructed. "I want to know by the morning who was calling, and heads will roll if I don't. Heads will be trundling up and down this corridor like fucking bowling balls. You won't be able to move for the bastards. Is that clear, Sergeant...?"

"Jaffray."

"Is that clear, Sergeant Jaffray?"

"Yes, sir. No problem, sir. I'm sure..." The sergeant's eyes flicked from side to side as if searching for a name. "*Someone* will be able to figure it out."

Logan shot the uniformed officer something that looked like a smile but was, in reality, a rather stark warning.

"Aye. Let's hope so, son," he said. "Let's hope so."

And then, with a final glance in the direction of the Incident Room, he buried his hands in his coat pockets and headed out into the cold, dark Highland night.

CHAPTER EIGHTEEN

The hotel bar was almost empty when Logan turned up, the arrival of the detectives having more than doubled the number of punters in the place.

Even if it had been busy, Logan reckoned it would've remained a pretty soulless affair. It was one of those generic bar/restaurants attached to the Premier Inn, and looked like an identikit version of every other one he'd ever been in.

It was fine in one way, in that you always knew what you were going to get. The problem was that what you were going to get was going to be a largely forgettable experience where the drinks were expensive, the craic was shite, and the air smelled faintly of disappointment.

There was a sharp whistle, followed by an "Over here, boss!"

Logan muttered under his breath and proceeded across the bar to the only occupied table in the place, where Tyler was beckoning him over with a wave.

"Thanks for the heads-up there, Detective Constable," Logan said. "Almost didn't spot you in amongst all this..." He gestured around them. "...fuck all."

"No bother, boss," Tyler said, either missing the sarcasm or deliberately ignoring it. Logan wasn't sure which of these possibilities annoyed him more, so decided not to dwell on it.

A pint of a dark brown liquid was lifted from one side of the table and deposited in front of him with a clunk. "Pint of Coke," Ben told him. "Well, it's Pepsi, but next best thing. And they only do diet, because of the sugar tax."

Logan regarded the glass with something akin to contempt, then sat down at the empty chair that the drink had been placed in front of.

"Great. Thanks."

"Oh, and the ice machine's broken, so it might not be very cold."

"Jesus Christ," Logan muttered. "Anything else wrong with it? Did you all take turns gobbing in it, too?"

"No. But, missed opportunity there, right enough," Ben replied. "I'll bear it in mind for next time."

Hamza and Caitlyn shuffled their own chairs aside a few inches, making room for the DCI to shrug off his coat. Hamza was drinking something that might have been alcoholic, but might equally have been just orange juice.

DC Khaled had once told Logan that he was a practising Muslim, but had admitted that he wasn't practising very hard. He'd demonstrated a vague preference for halal food in the past, but had also jumped on the odd bacon roll without stopping to ask questions, so Logan wasn't sure which direction the wind was blowing when it came to alcohol, and didn't really like to ask.

He had no such doubts about Caitlyn. She was sitting on his right, already a third of the way through a large glass of red, and had a look in her eye that suggested it would be the first of many.

Coppers drinking to forget, or to numb some unspoken pain was not unusual. Logan didn't think that's what was happening with Caitlyn, though. She swirled the drink around in her glass, half-smiling as if the red-purple liquid amused her in some way.

She'd been acting oddly, lately. She was different. Not in a way that made her any less excellent an officer, she was just... more animated, maybe. Less severe. He wasn't yet sure if he approved or disapproved. The jury was still out.

He looked along the table. Tyler, predictably, was on a pint. Stella, Logan assumed. Tennent's, maybe. Nothing too inventive, anyway. He raised it in the DCI's direction when he caught him looking. "Cheers, boss."

"Hold your horses, son, that's no' your job," Ben said. He looked around at the assembly of polis. "This, by my reckoning, is the first night out we've ever had. All of us together, I mean."

"It's not exactly a night out," Logan said.

"You know what I mean," Ben said, dismissing the objection with a wave. He nodded down at Logan's glass. "So. Toast."

The others all took hold of their glasses. Tyler cupped one hand at the side of his mouth and bellowed, "Speeeeech!" until the guy behind the bar shot the table a dirty look.

"Alright, alright," Logan sighed. He wrapped a finger and thumb around the top of the glass until they met at the other side, thought for a moment, then raised the Coke over the centre of the table. "To the bad bastards and the mad bastards. Without whom, we'd all be out of work."

The team echoed the toast back at him, then took a gulp of their drinks. All but Caitlyn smacked their lips together and made identical appreciative *aaaah* noises, before setting the glasses down again.

"That was emotional stuff, sir," Caitlyn said. "Really touching."

"Heartfelt," Hamza agreed, grinning.

"You should be flattered," Ben chimed in. "Last toast I heard him give started with, 'You're a shower of useless bastards,' and ended with, 'Get back to bloody work,' so, compared to that, this one was practically a tearjerker."

Logan took a gulp of his Coke, then flicked his gaze in the direction of the front door. "You got a minute, Ben?"

Ben sipped at the amber liquid in his glass. His lips drew back over his gums as if recoiling from the stuff, then he nodded. "Aye," he said. Standing, he motioned towards the door. "After you."

"VANESSA?"

"Aye," Logan confirmed.

"*Your* Vanessa?"

"Well, I mean, I don't know. He didn't specify, but I'm assuming so. I don't know any other Vanessa. Not that I can remember, anyway. Think there might have been one in my class in Primary Five, but I have my doubts he'll have been referring to her."

"Have you phoned her?"

Logan looked out across the hotel car park, the road, train tracks, and buildings beyond, and up to where the dark outline of Ben Nevis was imprinted against the night sky. He couldn't see the mountain, exactly, but he could tell it was there by the way it subtly altered the texture of the darkness.

"No," he said, with a shake of his head. "Not yet."

"*No*?" Ben spluttered. He gawped at the DCI in disbelief. "You get a call like that, and you haven't rung her to let her know?"

The dog-end of an abandoned cigarette was smouldering on the path between them. Logan ground it out under a heel.

"I thought maybe—"

"I'm no' phoning her," Ben interjected. "You can get that idea right out of your head for a start."

"It'll be easier coming from you," Logan insisted.

"Aye, easier for you, not for me. Or her, for that matter," Ben said. He caught Logan's dubious look. "Aye, well. But still, no."

"Maybe it's fine," Logan sighed. "Maybe I shouldn't even be worrying her about it."

Ben glanced back into the pub and lowered his voice a fraction. "If someone's playing silly buggers, Jack, she needs to know about it."

"Not someone," Logan said. He was still gazing up at the black-on-black outline of Ben Nevis, his hands thrust deep down in his pockets. "Petrie."

"Aye. Well. Whoever," Ben said, quickly glossing over that particular detail. "She needs to know, and she needs to hear it from you. If you think it's a serious threat, she might even need Uniform round there, keeping an eye on her."

Logan snorted, picturing his ex-wife's reaction to being put under police protection. "There wasn't a threat. Not really," he said. "She was just... mentioned. That was all. In passing. It's probably not even worth bothering her with, to be—"

The expression on Ben's face stopped him short. Logan might be the superior officer, but he knew this particular point wasn't up for debate. He had to phone her. Of course, he did. He should've done it as soon as her name had been mentioned on the call.

But it had been three years. Three years since the last conversation. Three years since the last argument. Three years since she'd told him she never wanted to see him again, and he'd assured her he was only too happy to oblige.

Three blissful, torturous years without her in his life.

Three years, that would end the moment he dialled her number and heard her voice.

"Christ's sake," Logan muttered. He reached into his pocket and slapped Ben with a look so sour it could've curdled milk. "Has anyone ever told you what a smug-faced wee bastard you look when you're right?"

"Aye, you. Regularly. And the wife, of course," Ben replied. "Although, she assures me that I'm never right, so it's no' really an issue."

He gave Logan a pat on the back and pulled open the bar's front door. The sound of Tyler swearing at the quiz machine rolled out from within.

"What? No way it was C! It was definitely D!"

"The wee cartoon quizmaster would beg to differ," Hamza replied, then both voices were drowned out by a sad '*wah-wah-wah-waaaah*' from the machine.

"Good luck, Jack," Ben said. "And assuming she lets you get a word in edgeways, say hello from me."

With a final smile of encouragement, DI Forde headed inside, leaving Logan alone with his phone on the bar's front step.

CHAPTER NINETEEN

The phone reception was pretty poor when Logan finally summoned the courage to make the call. The reception he received from his ex-wife wasn't exactly stellar, either.

Her voice had been light and airy when she'd first answered, like she'd just heard the punchline to a joke right before the phone had rung. For a moment, Logan had been reminded of better days and better times, back before everything had gone wrong between them. Back before the arguments and the divorce.

Back before Owen Petrie.

The levity had lasted right up until the point he'd opened his mouth.

"Hello. Vanessa?"

The tone had changed in an instant. The laughter had died in her throat, and the voice that came back to him down the line may as well have been accompanied by a blast of cold air.

"Yes. What? What's wrong?"

No small talk, then. Thank Christ.

"Yes. No. It's Jack," Vanessa said, her voice muted as she turned away to speak to someone else in the room. "Yes, *that* Jack. No. I won't be long."

"Sorry, did I catch you at a bad time?"

"It was a great time, actually," Vanessa said. "And then you called."

Logan chuckled mirthlessly. "Right. Aye."

"What is it, Jack? What do you want?"

"It's... I mean, it's probably nothing," Logan said.

Down the line, Vanessa tutted. "Then why the hell are you—"

"*Probably* nothing. But I thought it was worth calling to give you a heads up. Just in case it turns out to be, well, something."

There was a silence. It wasn't lengthy, but it was full and heavy with expectation.

"Are you ill?" Vanessa asked. Her voice was still cold and unwelcoming, but there was a faint thawing around the edges of it that almost made Logan wish that he was.

"No. No, nothing like that," he said. "It's just... God. OK. Earlier tonight, I had a phone call. Your name was mentioned."

Vanessa sighed irritably. "And?"

"The call was..." Logan glanced back into the bar, then out into the darkness, searching for the right words. "Well, it was threatening in nature."

"Threatening? Threatening who? Threatening me?"

"Aye. No. I mean, not threatening, exactly. Not, you know, overtly. But it was implied."

"How was it implied? Implied by who? What are you talking about, Jack?"

The door to the bar opened. A member of the kitchen staff emerged, barely old enough to shave. He drew a cigarette from his pack and was patting himself down looking for a lighter when Logan caught his eye.

"I'm in the middle of a conversation here," the DCI said.

"That's fine. Doesn't bother me," the lad replied. "Do you have a light?"

"No, I don't. And it does bother me, so going to piss off somewhere else?"

He could hear murmuring down the line, as Vanessa spoke to whoever else was in the room. Whatever she was saying was too low for Logan to hear, and he resisted the urge to even try.

"I'm on my break," the lad protested.

"Good. I'm delighted for you. But can you maybe be on your break over there?" Logan asked, pointing to the main hotel entrance further along the side of the building.

The lad looked Logan up and down, as if sizing up his chances. The door squeaked as he came to the conclusion that the odds were very much not in his favour.

"Need a lighter, anyway," he said, in a valiant attempt to save face.

Logan waited until the door had closed, before returning his attention to the call. "Sorry about—"

"Threatening how?" Vanessa demanded. "What are you talking about, Jack? Fucking explain. Am I in danger?"

"No. No, you're fine. As far as I know."

He pulled the phone from his ear as Vanessa's voice screeched out of the speaker. "*As far as you know?*"

Logan pinched the bridge of his nose, exhaled slowly, then just launched into it. "I've been getting calls lately. Silence, mostly. Heavy breathing. Coming through on numbers that nobody should even have. Christ, numbers I don't even know. Tonight, he spoke. He mentioned you."

"Mentioned me how? What did he say?"

"He said, 'How's Vanessa?'"

There was a moment of expectant silence.

"What? That's it? 'How's Vanessa?' That's all?"

There was a beeping from the handset. For a moment, Logan thought she'd hung up on him, but a quick glance at the screen told him the station was calling. He swiped the icon that he hoped would send it to voicemail.

"Jack?"

"Sorry, aye. That's all."

"How is that threatening?" Vanessa asked.

Logan shifted uncomfortably. Here we go.

"It wasn't so much what was said as who said it," he told her.

He should've continued then, but the knowledge of what would follow stopped him, and she was forced to drag it out of him.

"OK, then. So, who said it?"

The phone beeped again. He ignored it.

"It was... I mean, we're still looking into it, but I'm pretty sure... I'm almost certain..."

"Jesus. Spit it out, Jack. Who was it?"

"Petrie," Logan said. "It was... It was Owen Petrie."

If her voice had been cold before, it became an Arctic Tundra now. She snorted, but there was no humour in it. It was a snort of derision. Of mockery. Of incredulous disbelief.

"Right. Yes. I mean, of course, it was," Vanessa said. "Who else could it have been?"

"I know what you're thinking," Logan said. She jumped on it immediately.

"Do you, Jack? Do you really? Do you honestly believe you have the first fucking clue what I'm thinking right now?" she spat.

The voice in the room with her said something soothing, but she brushed it off. "No, he needs to hear it," she said, her voice momentarily muted again as she turned away, before returning more forceful than before. "Maddie told me. Phoned me earlier. Told me you'd stood her up, then told me why. You want to know what she said?"

Logan didn't. She told him, anyway.

"She said, 'I'm such an idiot, Mum. When am I going to learn?' That's what she said, Jack. That's what our daughter said. About you. She gave you a chance. I warned her. I warned her time and time again, but she gave you another chance, and you go and throw it back in her face. You keep hurting her, over and over, and she lets you. She lets you cause her pain."

Logan shook his head. "No. It wasn't like that. I didn't mean for... The traffic was—"

"Why are you telling me? Why am I sitting here listening to you trying to explain yourself? Again. I'm long past that, Jack. I'm years past that."

The volume of her voice had been steadily rising for the last few seconds. She stopped, took a breath to compose herself, and then continued in a much more measured tone.

"If your mystery caller gets back to you and asks how I am again, tell him I'm fine, alright? Tell him I'm better than I've been in a long, long time."

Logan winced at that one, although he knew her well enough to have seen it coming.

"Aye. Well. Just be careful, alright? If you see anyone acting strangely, or you don't feel safe, call—"

"Goodbye, Jack," Vanessa said, cutting him short.

The line went dead. A moment later, the beeping of the 'call waiting' notification transitioned into a full-on ring. Logan's thumb stabbed down on the green button and brought the phone to his ear.

"DCI Logan. What is it?" he demanded.

He listened to the officer on the other end of the line, his eyes slowly widening.

"Right. Aye," he said, once the message had been conveyed. He pushed open the door to the bar, and the *ka-thunk-ka-thunk* of the quiz machine spewing out pound coins emerged into the cool night air. "Tell them I'm on my way."

CHAPTER TWENTY

THE LIGHTS OF THREE SQUAD CARS AND AN AMBULANCE LICKED ACROSS the front of Hannah Randall's house, illuminating the cracks in the upstairs curtains of all the neighbouring windows. Logan shot looks of condemnation up at a few of them, and watched them twitch in response.

Hamza, who it turned out had indeed been drinking orange juice, stepped out of the passenger side of the car, gave his stomach a reassuring pat as if to let it know the ordeal of the drive was finally over, then scurried after the DCI as he approached the front gate.

A Uniform was stationed just outside the garden. Logan didn't recognise him, but the constable nodded curtly and opened the gate as he and Hamza approached, then quickly closed it over again behind them.

Another officer opened the door before Logan could knock. He vaguely recalled seeing this one around at the Fort William Station at some point, although he couldn't even guess at her name.

"She's in the living room, sir," the constable said, her voice low and sombre.

"How is she?"

"Not great. Her mum's with her, keeping her calm. Paramedics are here, too, checking her over."

Logan leaned back and looked up at the house, then around at all the flashing lights. "Can we get these turned off? It's like a circus out here."

"I can sort that out," Hamza said, backtracking along the path. He gave the officer guarding the gate a tap on the shoulder, then they both chose a different car and headed for it.

Logan glanced past the uniformed officer into the house beyond. "She ready to talk, do you think?"

The female officer made a non-committal sort of noise. "She's been talking to us. Not getting much useful out of her, mind you, though the mother's been a help. Maybe you'll have more luck, sir."

"Aye," said Logan, stepping past her. "Maybe."

Hannah looked up just briefly when Logan entered the living room. She was sitting in the middle of the couch, a woman in her fifties—her mother, presumably—pressed right up against her on the left-hand side, their hands clasped together on Hannah's leg.

Mrs Randall had the look of a crofter about her, with a reddish complexion and hair that looked like it had been ignored for some time. Her eyes were crinkled with a lifetime of laughter lines, and her teeth were so artificially white they could only have been a recently fitted set of NHS falsers.

"Who are you?" she demanded, glaring at Logan. She seemed to almost puff herself up until he produced his warrant card, at which point she returned to the job of squeezing her daughter's hand, and gently rubbing her back.

Across the room, the paramedics were in the process of packing up their kit. A bandage had been applied to one of Hannah's hands, and there were a couple of plasters on the side of her face, presumably to cover up smaller cuts.

What hadn't been covered was the purple-blue patch around her right eye that signalled the beginnings of what would soon be some not-insignificant bruising.

"Miss Randall. I came as soon as I heard," Logan told her. He gestured to the armchair across from the couch, being sure to avoid the Ikea monstrosity beside it, this time. "Do you mind?"

Hannah gave the briefest shake of her head, and Logan lowered himself onto the chair just as Hamza entered the room.

"It's fine. He's with me. That's Detective Constable Hamza Khaled. I'm Detective Chief Inspector Logan. Jack," he told the older woman. "You must be Hannah's mother."

"Sandra. Yes," she confirmed. "Hello."

"Hi, Sandra," Logan began, then the paramedics jumped in before the conversation could get fully underway.

"Sorry. We're just heading off," said the older of the two. He was almost Logan's height, but barely half as broad, with hair that was just clinging on and no more. He smiled down at Hannah. "You sure we can't take you in and get you checked over?"

Hannah shook her head firmly. "No. Thank you. I'm fine," she said, although there was a shake in her voice that told Logan she was nothing of the kind.

The older paramedic gave her a thumbs-up. "Right, well, if anything starts to feel worse, or you change your mind, just call the number on the card we gave you, alright? They'll get you straight in."

Hannah glanced around, as if trying to remember what she'd done with the card, then nodded. "Right. Thank you."

"I'll see you out," said Sandra, starting to rise. The paramedic waved her back before she could wrestle her way out of the couch's cushions.

"You're fine. We'll figure it out." He smiled at mother and daughter, gave Logan a look that may have been a warning, then led his younger companion out into the hall.

Logan waited until he'd heard the front door close before saying a word. "You've been in the wars," he observed.

"Aye, you can say that again," Sandra said. "Bastards."

"Who?" Logan asked. "Who did this? What happened?"

Out of the corner of his eye, he saw Hamza flicking open a notebook, and heard the click of a ballpoint pen being extended with the push of a button.

Hannah huffed out a shaky breath and ran a hand through her hair. Beside her, her mother gave her a nudge.

"Well, go on, then," Sandra urged. "Tell them."

"I've already told the woman. In the uniform. I don't know who he was," Hannah said.

"He?" Hamza asked.

Hannah raised her eyes to meet his. "Yes."

"It's just... 'Bastards,' you said," Hamza replied, directing that part at Sandra. "Plural."

"I only saw one of them," Hannah explained. "But I heard someone down here."

"You should see the mess they've made of the kitchen," Sandra interjected. "Trashed it, they have. And now we're not allowed to go in it because your lot have got it taped off. Can't even get a cup of tea."

Logan's gaze went to the two half-empty mugs on the coffee table between him and the women. Sandra bristled like she was being accused of something.

"The policewoman had one of the neighbours make us some," she explained. "But, still."

Hannah groaned, frustration furrowing her forehead. "Forget the tea, Mum. They need to block off the kitchen so they can look for, I don't know. Evidence, or whatever."

She looked across the table at Logan. "Right?"

"Aye. Aye, that's right," he confirmed. "Hopefully, it won't take too long."

He sat back in the chair, relaxing a little in the hope it rubbed off on both women.

"Can you talk me through what happened, Miss Randall? I know you've gone over it, but it'd be useful for me to hear it from you in your own words."

It was Sandra who jumped in to fill the momentary silence that followed. "She was upstairs—"

"In her own words," Logan reiterated. He smiled unconvincingly at the older woman. "Please."

Sandra's lips drew into a tight pucker. She clicked her tongue against the roof of her mouth once, but said nothing. Logan could see the strain on her face from the effort this was taking and almost felt bad about it.

Almost.

"Miss Randall?" he urged, his voice as soft and coaxing as it was ever likely to get. "Tell me what happened."

Hannah adjusted herself on the couch, shrugged, then adjusted herself again. She opened and closed her mouth half a dozen times during this process, as if about to start speaking, but then deciding against it at the last possible moment.

Finally, she found the words she'd been looking for.

"I was upstairs. In me and Brodie's... In the bedroom. I was just sitting there. Thinking, you know? About, well, everything. I heard a noise."

"What kind of noise?" Logan asked.

"I don't know. A noise. Like a thump. Movement. Down here," Hannah told him. "I didn't think it was anything at first. Just sort of ignored it. But then I heard it again, and then he was... I just turned around and saw him there, and..."

She drew in air in a big, shaky breath. Her hands shook as they squeezed her mother's. Tears trailed down both cheeks as if racing one another.

"He was just there. Out of nowhere. Shouting at me. He... he had a knife. I thought, God, I thought he was going to kill me."

Her voice grew fainter as her throat constricted. Sandra squeezed in closer and reached an arm across her daughter's shoulders, then pulled her in tight.

"It's OK. You're OK," she soothed. "You're fine now."

"Did you get a look at him?" Logan asked.

Hannah shook her head. "He had a mask on."

"What sort of mask?" asked Hamza, his pen scratching notes onto the pad.

"Like a ski mask. Or like, you know the SAS? A black mask with eyeholes and a mouth."

"A balaclava?"

Hannah gave the DC a nod. "Yeah. That's it. A balaclava. I couldn't see much, and it all happened so quickly."

"Anything else you can tell us about him?" Logan asked. "Tall? Short? Fat? Thin? Anything at all."

Hannah glanced up at the ceiling like she might find the answers written there somewhere. "No. Just, I don't know, normal. He felt..." She gulped in a few steadying breaths. "He felt heavy, though. When he was on top of me."

Beside her, Sandra's eyes widened while the rest of her face appeared to crumple. "On top of you? He didn't...? You weren't...?"

Hannah quickly dismissed the concern with a shake of her head. "No. Nothing like that. He just... He pinned me down. Put his knee on my leg and slapped me a couple of times."

"Oh, thank God," Sandra exhaled. "I mean, obviously that's bad enough, but it's not... At least he didn't..."

She left it there. There was no need to clarify.

"It must've been a very traumatic experience for you," Logan said. "And I appreciate how hard it must be to talk about it so soon after. Especially with everything else you're dealing with."

Hannah made a non-committal sort of noise and didn't meet his eye.

"You said he was shouting at you. What was it he said?"

A frown. A pause that went on just a fraction of a second too long for Logan's liking.

"He wanted money. Jewellery. Stuff like that. He asked if I had a safe."

"She doesn't," Sandra said. "Do you, love?"

Hannah shook her head. "No. Nothing like that. I told him I didn't have any money, and he..." She gestured to the bruise forming around her eye socket. "Well."

"It must've been terrifying. You're doing great," Logan told her. "Did he say anything else? Anything that might connect him to Brodie?"

Hannah looked straight at him and shook her head. "No. Nothing. Nothing like that. Just... He just wanted money."

"Right. Yes. I understand. Just thought it was worth asking, considering the timing," Logan said. He regarded the room around them. "Did they get anything?"

Hannah's eyes retraced the route Logan's had taken around the living room. "I don't... I'm not sure. Not that I've noticed."

"No cash? Cards? Your purse or wallet?" Logan gestured to the thin gold chain around the young woman's neck. "Jewellery?"

Hannah's hand went to the necklace as if trying too late to hide it. "They ran when my mum appeared."

"I couldn't stand the thought of her here on her own. Fulton stayed home with the wee one, and I came over. Thank God I did."

Logan shifted his attention to Sandra. "Did you see them? The intruders?"

"No, but I certainly heard them," she said. "They went out the back as I came in the front. Through the kitchen. Right racket they made."

"Any idea how many of them there were?"

Sandra shook her head. "Two. Three, maybe. Could be four. I don't know. Too much clattering for one."

Hamza chimed in with a question of his own. He pointed to Hannah with the end of his pen. "And you were still upstairs at that point?"

"Yes. In the bedroom."

"But the man who attacked you had left?"

Hannah picked at a ragged piece of skin next to her thumbnail for a few seconds, before confirming. "Yeah. He ran out when he heard the front gate. He panicked."

Logan picked up the DC's baton and ran with it.

"Fast, then," he said. When he saw the blank looks on the faces of both mother and daughter, he clarified. "To get out of the room, down the stairs, and out through the kitchen before you got the door open, Mrs Randall. He'd need to be nippy."

"Like I said, he was panicking," Hannah replied.

"Aye. Fear can certainly spur people on, right enough," Logan said. He jabbed a thumb back over his shoulder. "I think you've given us enough for now. You should get some rest. We'll no doubt need to talk to you again tomorrow."

"She'll be staying with us," Sandra said. "No way she's staying here."

"Aye. I was going to suggest that. We'll need to search the place." He offered Hannah a thin-lipped smile. "Evidence. Like you say."

THE DOORS of the Volvo clunked closed. Hamza had barely settled into his seat when Logan spoke.

"Thoughts?"

Hamza looked back in the direction of the house as he reached for his belt. "Well—"

"I don't buy it," Logan said, before Hamza could finish replying. "She's lying."

"About the attack?"

"No. About the reason for it. When I asked her if it was about Brodie, she looked me right in the eye when she said no. That's the one and only time she's done that since I met her earlier. And for it to happen on the same day her partner's body turns up? Hell of a coincidence."

"Suppose so, aye."

"And, for a gang of burglars, they didn't take very much, did they? By which I mean they took hee-haw."

Hamza shrugged. "The mother arriving could've scared them off."

"Maybe, but who turns over a kitchen looking for stuff to rob? Big telly in the living room. MacBook on the shelf under the coffee table. Handbag down the side of the chair I was sitting in. But what, they decide to make a grab for the Rice Krispies?"

He jabbed the button that started the engine. The Volvo spluttered into life as if caught off-guard, then settled into its usual throaty purr.

"She was literally wearing a gold necklace. She says the guy was on top of her. Even if he did panic—which I don't believe—he's come that far, he'd have at least grabbed that."

"You don't think they ran?" Hamza asked. "The mother said she heard them."

Logan adjusted his rearview mirror. "I'm not saying she didn't hear them. I'm saying it didn't happen like Hannah Randall says it did. How could it? He's upstairs, pinning her down, waving his knife about, making demands. He hears the gate opening, and then what? He turns into Billy Whizz?"

Hamza's brow creased. "Who's Billy Whizz?"

"What do you mean, *who's Billy Whizz?*" Logan demanded, turning fully in his seat so he was facing the younger officer. "Billy Whizz. The Beano."

"Oh. Right. Aye. I never read The Beano," Hamza said.

From the expression that settled on his face, Logan seemed to be even more incredulous about this than he was about Hannah Randall's story.

"What do you mean you never read The Beano? Who the hell didn't read The Beano?"

Hamza raised his eyebrows and puffed out his cheeks. "It's a cultural thing, sir. Religious reasons."

Logan winced like he'd just taken a low blow. "Oh. Right," he said, clearing his throat. "I see."

Hamza grinned. "Nah, not really, sir. I just thought it was shite."

Logan tutted.

"Aye. Hilarious. But, my point stands. There's no way some big knife-wielding mad bastard is going to be so freaked out by the sound of a gate opening that he'll sprint down the stairs, through the hall, into the kitchen, and out the back before the mother makes it up the path. What, was she crawling?"

He pointed through the windscreen at the entrance to the garden. "Also, did you notice on the way out?"

"Notice what, sir?"

"That gate doesn't make a sound. Latch is knackered. It doesn't even shut properly."

"So..." Hamza glanced down at his notebook. "What happened?"

"That, I don't know," Logan said. He jammed the gearstick into reverse, and the road behind him was illuminated in a pale white glow. "But I'm going to find out."

"Give us something to do, I suppose," Hamza said. His eyebrows raised.

"Oh! I got the bank statement from Fulton Randall. Showing the wages going in."

"And?"

"Doesn't give us much more detail. I'm going to chase up the bank tomorrow," Hamza said. "But I will say that whoever the employer is, they're not skint. Nine grand a month he was on."

Logan whistled through his teeth. "That's no' buttons. What was he doing, running the place?"

"Beats me, sir. I just know that I'm in the wrong line of work."

"Aye. You and me both," Logan agreed. "Get on the bank first thing. Find the company and let's speak to them."

"Will do, sir. First thing."

Logan eased the Volvo back from the squad car in front, then indicated to pull away from the kerb. Just before he did, he took a moment to fire a disparaging look in Hamza's direction.

"*Who's Billy Whizz?*" He tutted. "I mean, *honestly*."

CHAPTER TWENTY-ONE

Logan stood in the queue at the counter of J.J.'s Cafe, idly eyeing up a slab of Oreo brownie while he waited for the woman in front to finish placing her order.

Ben had volunteered to do the breakfast run on the way into the office, but Logan felt it was probably his shout after trying to coerce the DI into making the call to Vanessa the night before.

He opened the notes app on his phone as the woman in front moved off to take a seat, then he shuffled up until he was standing by the till.

"What can I get for you?" asked a man in a black apron. It had the word 'BOSS' emblazoned across the front in bold white letters, with: 'My Wife is the' written above it in a much smaller font.

Logan read off the list that Ben had dictated to him, briefly considered adding on one of the brownies, then decided against it for the sake of his waistline. "And no butter on one of the bacon," he added, as the man behind the counter jotted down the order. "One of them's a fussy bastard."

Once he'd handed over the cash and been assured the order would be ready in a few minutes, Logan stepped aside to let the next customer in line through.

The place wasn't particularly big, but it was busy. Of the eight or nine tables, six of them were occupied, and there were a couple of others waiting for takeaway orders like himself.

A dark-haired woman was struggling to reach a high shelf on the wall along from the serving counter. A couple of angular wooden clocks were perched there, price tags hanging from the hands.

"You need a hand?" he asked, reaching up for one of the clocks. The woman smiled gratefully as he passed it to her.

"Thank you," she said. She turned it over in her hands, examining its triangular frame.

"Ugly bugger of a thing, if you ask me," Logan said. "I wouldn't waste my money if I were you."

The woman's smile became significantly less convincing. "I made them," she said.

The ground, to Logan's dismay, failed to open beneath him and swallow him up.

"Did you?" he asked. "Well done."

The woman took it in good grace, and her smile returned. "Thanks. That's very kind of you. You want one?"

"I've nowhere to put it," Logan said, although he could definitely think of a few places the things probably belonged. "Otherwise, I'd be all over it."

The woman laughed drily, then gestured to the top shelf. "Get us that one down, will you? People aren't seeing them up there. I need to move them somewhere more visible."

Logan almost suggested that perhaps people *were* seeing them and that therein lay the problem, but elected not to.

He handed her the second clock, and she set both down on a lower shelf that was just below Logan's head height, and just above her own.

"There. They can be found now."

Logan regarded the newly positioned clocks, but he was distracted. Something the woman had said nagged at him. Niggled away. What was it?

"That's you," said the man in the apron, presenting Logan with a white carrier bag that bulged with the boxes it contained.

"Right. Thanks. Aye," Logan said, taking the bag. He looked back at the woman and her clocks, and something clicked into place.

"Good call on moving them," he remarked.

She stepped back, hands on her hips, considering the clocks' new placement. "Think they look better there?" she asked.

Logan answered honestly. "No' really," he said. "But then, what do I know?"

And with that, he was out the door.

Once the rolls were divvied up and the tea was in hand, Logan perched on the edge of a desk by the Big Board and let them in on his theory.

"We know the body was moved. Buried somewhere, then shifted," he said.

"I assumed that was because whoever killed Brodie was worried he'd be discovered, but given how and where he was reburied, that doesn't make sense."

He looked across the faces of the others, their mouths all moving as they chomped through breakfast.

"I don't think the killer was worried the body would be found. I think he was worried it wouldn't be."

Ben stopped chewing. "What?" he said through the side of his mouth. "You think they wanted it to be discovered?"

"I do," Logan confirmed. "I think he was moved there deliberately so someone would find him. Shallow grave, close to a well-used walking path. It's the only thing that makes sense."

He took a bite of his own roll. Square sausage. Tattie scone. Wee daud of brown sauce. He wasn't a believer in Heaven, but if he had been, that roll would've been close to the perfect definition of it.

He thought some more as he chewed, then swallowed.

"The rescue. What became of that in the end?" he wondered. "Did they find who they were looking for?"

Caitlyn washed down a mouthful of bacon with a gulp of tea. "No, sir. Called off. They think it might've been a hoax. I checked up last night."

"A hoax? Bastards," Ben remarked, and all but Logan nodded their agreement.

"I'm not convinced."

Ben raised his bushy eyebrows in surprise. "You're joking. Wasting time and money, putting people's lives at risk. They're definitely bastards, Jack."

"No, I mean I'm not so sure it was a hoax," the DCI said.

Caitlyn appeared confused. "Mountain Rescue team seem pretty confident, sir," she said. "You think there's someone out there?"

"No. What I'm saying is, I don't think it was just someone on the wind-up. I think it was deliberate. I think whoever made the call was trying to draw attention to the body."

Hamza rubbed his tongue across his teeth, sweeping up the debris of his breakfast butty. "Had to be the killer, then. Or someone who knew about it, anyway."

"See if you can find out any details of the call. If they rang nine-nine-nine there should be a recording. Get me a copy."

"Can I give that to Tyler, sir?" Hamza asked. "I've got the bank thing to follow-up, and he's doing bugger all."

DC Neish tried to protest, but his mouth was too full, and all he could do was extend a middle finger in the other DC's direction.

"I don't care who does it, just get it done," Logan said.

"Oh, speaking of calls," Ben said, perking up in his seat. "A uniform sergeant was in here looking for you when you were getting the rolls in. Said he got someone to look into the phones last night, like you asked."

Logan's legs stiffened, lifting him off the desk and into a standing position. "And?"

Ben picked up a notebook, squinted, then held it at arm's length as he tried to read what it said.

"Did they find anything?" Logan demanded.

"Hang on. They found..." Ben shook his head. "No. Nothing at all. No caller details."

Logan sighed. He hadn't been expecting a result, but he'd been quietly hoping for one, all the same. He should've known better, though. Whoever was calling him was clever. Or, at the very least, not a complete idiot.

To be able to find out the direct-line numbers of all the phones in the office meant they were well-connected, too. Someone in the station, most likely.

Someone sitting in this very room?

No. He dismissed that last thought.

For now.

But Jinkies clearly had concerns about security, or he wouldn't have been taking all the precautions with the drug investigation. Probably worth having a word with him about it at some point. See if he had any suspects.

Something to look forward to.

"Why would the killer want the body found?" DS McQuarrie asked, jolting Logan back to the matter at hand. "What would they stand to gain from that?"

"Glory, maybe?" Tyler suggested, finally managing to swallow down his food. "Notoriety."

"That can happen," Ben said. "Murderer kills someone, knows he should keep it secret, but also wants people to know what he's done, if not necessarily that he was the one who did it."

Logan couldn't argue. He'd seen that often enough, read about it in old case files even more often. It was fairly standard for certain types of killer.

And yet, this felt different.

"I'm not sure it's that," he said, pacing back and forth in front of the board. "It doesn't feel like that sort of murder. I don't think anyone's in it for the glory."

"What then? A warning to someone?" Hamza guessed.

"Guilty conscience?" Tyler suggested.

"Could be," Logan conceded. "Could be something else, too. We'll keep on it. Everyone had a chance to take a proper look over the full pathology report I emailed out?"

Most of them confirmed that they had. Tyler surreptitiously clicked to open his email inbox, and then side-eyed the screen.

"For those of you who haven't," Logan said, spotting the DC's woeful attempt at subtlety. "It confirms much of what we went over yesterday. Cause of death was not the dirty great knife wounds to the victim's torso, but the inhalation of a gritty, sand-like substance that we're working to identify. Teeth were smashed in and fingertips were removed in order, I think we can safely assume, to hinder identification."

"We caught a break there," Ben remarked.

"Not that big a deal, though, is it?" Tyler ventured, drawing his eyes away from the report on his screen. "Town this size, local guy, he'd have been matched up in no time."

DS McQuarrie nodded her agreement. "That's another thing about the body disposal I don't get. Why keep him local? If you're trying to hide his identity, why dump him so close to home?"

"Feels pretty half-arsed," said Tyler.

"Maybe it's whole-arse," Hamza suggested, which drew a confused look from the others for a number of reasons. "I mean, maybe it was all planned. If they moved him so he'd be found, maybe they wanted him identified, too."

"So, what's with the teeth and the fingers, then?" Tyler asked.

Ben looked up from his notes. "We're assuming it was the killer who moved him. What if it wasn't? We know he was originally buried elsewhere, then moved. Maybe the original site was miles away. Maybe someone found out about the murder and wanted to, I don't know, bring it to our attention."

"Could've picked up the phone," said Hamza. "Bit extreme to dig up a body and move it."

"True," Ben agreed. He looked down at his notes again. "But it makes as much sense as anything else we've come up with."

"We'll know more once we figure out where the first burial site was. Hopefully, we'll get a match on the sand in his lungs," Logan said. "I'll also draw your attention to the abdominal wounds. Any more thoughts on those?"

Tyler scrolled his mouse wheel, then grimaced at the sight of the pictures. "Looks painful," he remarked.

"Any thoughts other than the blindingly obvious?" Logan asked. "And yes, it would've been painful. Done while he was alive. Although, from the report, it looks like he was lying on his back at the time, so it's possible he was unconscious."

"Let's hope so, for his sake," said Ben.

"Got to be the drugs thing, hasn't it, sir?" Caitlyn said. "Too precise to be anything else."

Logan agreed. "They're surprisingly precise, actually. Whoever did this has likely done it before. Knows their way around the human body, anyway."

Ben's chair creaked as he sat back. "So, just so's we're all on the same page—we've got a young man, a recreational drug user himself, who travels extensively overseas for an employer we haven't been able to identify. He takes home... How much did you say, Hamza?"

"Nine grand a month."

"Fucking hell!" Tyler spluttered. "What was he, the Queen?"

"He takes home nine grand a month, and shortly after returning from one of these trips, he was murdered and had his insides cut open," Ben concluded.

"And there's the rectal damage mentioned on the post-mortem," Tyler announced, launching into his theory from the previous night. "Could've been shoving stuff up his arse, too."

"However he was doing it, presumably whoever killed him knew about it and took whatever he was carrying," said Caitlyn.

"Maybe," said Logan. "Or maybe they didn't find it, and so they went to his house last night to look for it. I don't believe they were there to rob the place, regardless of what Hannah Randall might be trying to claim."

"That all fits," Caitlyn said.

"Should we bring her in?" Ben asked.

"Bagsy no' being the one to drive down and pick her up, boss," Tyler said, visibly paling at the very thought of it.

Logan remembered his tea, which was sitting on the desk beside him, going cold. He picked it up and forced down an unpleasant gulp that made his lips draw back over his teeth. It was vile stuff, cold. Still, you didn't waste a cup of tea. It just wasn't done.

"Aye. Let's bring her in," Logan said. "But quietly. She's not a suspect, but she's also not telling us the truth. I want to know why, and I want her to tell us everything she knows about what Brodie was up to. Hamza, get on to the bank, see what you can find before she gets here."

"On it, sir," DC Khaled said, rolling his chair closer to his workstation.

"Tyler, get me that recording of the nine-nine-nine call."

DC Neish blinked a couple of times.

"The mountain rescue callout. Keep up."

"Oh. Right. Aye. Sorry, boss. Will do. You want me to finish reading the pathology report first?"

Logan tutted. "No, I want you to get me the recording now, and I want you to finish reading the pathology report last night, when I sent you the bloody thing. Can you do that for me?"

Tyler regarded his screen, then arranged his features into a nonplussed sort of smile. "Probably not that last part, boss," he admitted. He reached for his phone. "But, I'll see what I can do."

CHAPTER TWENTY-TWO

Jinkies appeared momentarily surprised to see Logan in his doorway, but it quickly gave way to a look of smug satisfaction.

"Ah. Jack. Two tics," he said, turning his attention back to the printed document he had been reading. He made a show of absorbing the contents, complete with nods, tongue-clicks, and the occasional utterances of, "Uh-uh," and, "Mm-hm," plus the occasional, "Well, well."

Logan endured it for as long as he could, which was almost a full twenty seconds, and a personal best.

"Sorry to interrupt, Hugh," he said, stepping fully into the room.

The apology was partly sincere. He deeply regretted that he had to come and speak to Chief Inspector Pickering, but the fact he was interrupting the other man's working day offered at least some small consolation.

Jinkies made a show of sighing and setting down the paperwork he'd been reading, before clasping his hands on the desk and smiling benevolently.

"What is it I can do for you, Jack?" he asked.

"I'm going to need to look at the drug case CID's building. Against the Gillespies."

Jinkies drew breath in sharply through his teeth. "Hm. Well. As I explained, Jack, we're playing that one close to our chest."

"Because you can't trust your own guys. Aye, you said. But, here's the thing, Hugh," Logan said. He stepped in closer and leaned down with both hands on the desk. "I don't care. I think that investigation may have a bearing on mine, so I'm going to need to see what you've gathered."

"Let me think about it."

"Fine." Logan shrugged, checked his watch, then crossed his arms and waited. "Take your time."

Jinkies ejected a single mirthless, "Ha," then rolled his tongue around inside his mouth as he considered the request.

Finally, he leaned forward so he was hunched over his own clasped hands. "Look, Jack. Between you and me? Fine. If it was just you, fine. Ben, even. I know you're both solid. I know I can count on you."

He motioned to the door and lowered his voice. "But the others? I don't know them. I don't know how... reliable they are."

"If they weren't reliable they wouldn't be on my team."

Jinkies raised an eyebrow. "So, you trust them?"

"With my life."

A smile tugged at the corner of the Chief Inspector's mouth. "Did I detect a wee hesitation there, Jack?"

Logan uncrossed his arms. "We're going to need to see the case you're building, Hugh," he reiterated, his voice dropping into a warning growl. "So, you can send it through to Ben, or—"

"Or what, Jack? You'll beat it out of me?" asked Jinkies, smirking.

"Or I'll ask Superintendent Hoon to put in a personal request for it," Logan continued. "And we both know that he won't just beat it out of you, he'll tear it out through your arse."

Jinkies unclasped his hands and drummed them lightly on the desktop. "Fine. Fine. I'll give you the summary. If you need to drill into the specific detail, we can discuss that at a later stage."

It wasn't a complete surrender, but it was the best Logan was likely to get without expending a lot more energy than he was willing to. The summary would be enough to be going on with. For now.

"Fine. See that Ben gets it," he said, turning for the door.

"Oh, Jack. Before you shoot off..."

Logan stopped and half-turned back. "What?"

"If you're planning to bring in any of the Gillespies, run it by me first. I'd like to observe."

Logan sucked in his bottom lip, then spat it out. "Tell you what, Hugh," he said. "Let me think about it."

"Got some information from the bank, sir. They won't give us much without a court order, but I was able to sweet-talk them a bit," Hamza reported, catching up with the DCI outside Jinkies' office. "I think the lassie liked the accent."

"What, *your* accent?" Logan asked, struggling to hide his surprise. Hamza spoke with a thick Aberdonian twang. As accents went, it was not one that was renowned for its charm or sex appeal.

"Aye. Fit's wrang wi' my accent, like?" Hamza asked, really playing it up. "It's a richt bonnie een this een, ken?"

Logan couldn't help but chuckle. "Aye. Music to the ears. What did you get?"

"She told me it was a virtual bank account. Like, with some online service."

"Like Paypal or something?"

"Similar, aye. Kind of. Actually, it's more like the Anti-Paypal. Sendfunds. Based in Central America and backed with Russian money. Or vice versa. No-one really seems to know which, but it doesn't really matter, because anyone can set it up from anywhere."

"Any connection to Oswatt?" Logan asked. "Beyond the name being on the transfer?"

"No, sir. And the name—Oswatt, I mean—is only in the reference field of the transfer. It was the bank woman who pointed it out. The sender's name is just a string of letters and numbers."

Logan tutted. "How did we not notice that before?"

"Dunno, sir. Just saw the name we were looking for and didn't think too much more about it. Sorry."

Logan shook his head. "Wasn't just you. We all did it. So, the account might not even be in the name 'Oswatt,' then?"

Hamza shook his head. "Almost certainly not, sir. The thing about Sendfunds is it's not meant for businesses. It's for individuals. Their big gimmick is that they allow anonymous account opening, and encrypt all transactions. Think it started on the Dark Web before moving mainstream. CIA and FBI in the States are both—" He made quote marks in the air with his fingers. "—'Warning of the dangers' of it."

"Untraceable global financial transactions. Aye, I can see why they'd be shiteing their kecks," Logan said. "Terrorist's dream come true."

"And the rest," Hamza agreed. "It's pretty clever, though, sir, I have to say. You pay in via Western Union to account details that change every twenty-four hours, and the money appears in your own account a day or two later. From there it's all completely untraceable. Scammers' Paradise."

Logan was beginning to get a picture of the service. It wasn't one that fit with a legitimate offshore energy company. "So, the payments were coming from a personal account?"

"I think so, sir, aye. Not a hundred percent, but that's what it sounded like. She did say, though, that getting more information from Sendfunds is likely to be impossible. Like I say, secrecy is their big thing, and what with them being based abroad... Well, I don't fancy our chances."

Logan agreed. A Central American online banking service was likely to be a brick wall too thick to even bother beating their heads against.

"Focus on the bank here. Get a request in and get Ben to escalate it. See if they can decipher that string of letters and numbers you mentioned. I want the name on the account that's been sending him the money," Logan instructed. "And chance your arm with the helpdesk again. Did you ask for a supervisor last time?"

Hamza confirmed that he had.

"Don't. Easier to put the wind up the front line staff. All we need is the name. Charm them, intimidate them, do whatever you can to get it. Alright?"

"I'll see what I can do, sir."

Logan clapped Hamza on the back. "Good lad. Tyler got me that call recording yet?"

"Just waiting on it coming through, I think. He's got the transcript, but not the audio."

He answered Logan's question before the DCI could even start to ask.

"Nothing really jumping out from the transcript. We got the call header, but the number was withheld. Audio should be through in the next few minutes, though."

"They give a name?"

"Aye, but didn't ring any bells. Tyler's following up on it."

"Right, good."

The door from reception opened along the corridor. Logan turned to see Hannah Randall being escorted in by two uniformed officers. Her father, Fulton, walked beside her, an arm offered out for support that she was making no move to accept.

Her face was difficult to read. She was worried, yes, but angry, too, Logan thought. Maybe more of the latter than the former. Her eyes were red with shadowy bags hanging beneath the lower lids. She looked like she hadn't slept a wink all night.

They had that in common, at least.

"Mr Logan. Jack. What's all this about?" asked Fulton, his voice racing along the corridor ahead of the group. "Hannah is... We're *all* very stressed and very tired. Couldn't this wait?"

Hannah looked irritated by Fulton's interjection. "Dad. I told you. It's fine. You don't need to be here."

"Well, I am here, Hannah. And I'm not going anywhere."

Her eyes flicked upwards and she sighed, but voiced no further objections.

"Sorry for the inconvenience, folks," Logan told them. "I've just got a few questions. I'm hoping you can help clear some things up. I won't keep you any longer than absolutely necessary."

He nudged open the door to one of the interview rooms, had a quick check inside, then motioned for them to enter. "We'll grab a seat in here. Can I get you a drink? Tea? Coffee? I think there's some orange juice in the fridge, although I can't vouch for how long it's been knocking about in there."

"Coffee wouldn't go amiss," Fulton said. "Hannah?"

Hannah shook her head.

"You sure?" Fulton pressed. "Tea?"

"I'm fine, Dad! I just want to get this done and go."

"Yes. Yes, of course, makes sense," Fulton said. He smiled up at Logan. "I'll still have a coffee, though, if it's going? Milk and one. Cream, if you have it, but milk's fine."

Logan glanced at one of the Uniforms, who nodded and set off for the kitchen. Almost as soon as he'd turned the corner, another uniformed officer came around it. This one, Logan recognised.

"Detective Chief Inspector. Can I have a quick word?" Sergeant Jaffray asked as he arrived at the group.

He met Fulton's eye and they exchanged nods of acknowledgement, then he shot a smile at Hannah that went completely ignored.

"Of course, Sergeant," Logan said, with just the vaguest suggestion of impatience. He asked the escorting constable to take the Randalls into the interview room and get them settled, then led Jaffray half a dozen big paces along the corridor away from the door.

"What can I do for you, Sergeant?"

"I just wanted to apologise about the phone thing, sir. I left a message for you about it. We couldn't get any information on who was calling last night."

"Right. Aye," Logan said. He glanced impatiently at the interview room. "Not to worry. I was a bit stressed out last night. Thanks for trying."

Jaffray relaxed a bit at that. "No bother, sir. Always happy to help. If there's anything else I can do for you?"

"That's fine. Thanks," Logan said. He started to set off along the corridor, then stopped a step or two in. "Actually... The Randalls. You know them?"

The sergeant's smile remained fixed, but he leaned from left to right a little as he shifted his weight from one foot to the other. "Everyone here knows Fulton," he said. "Through the rescue team. You soon get to know all the rescue boys, Lochaber and Glencoe."

"And Hannah?"

That one was the sore spot, Logan thought. Jaffray's eyes went to the door, and his rocking increased for a few seconds before he fixed his feet more firmly to the floor. He cleared his throat before he spoke.

"Couple of years below me in school, sir. We're not friends or anything. She used to go out with a mate of mine, yonks back."

Logan fixed him with a stare that bored into the sergeant like a drill. "That it?"

Jaffray swallowed. He tried to smile, but it came out more like a grimace. "Aye. Aye, that's it."

Logan wasn't convinced by the other man's response and made a mental note to come back to it later.

"Right. Fair enough, then. Anything about them you think I should know?"

Jaffray put his hands on his hips and glanced at the ceiling, possibly seeking inspiration. He mulled the question over like that for a few seconds, then shook his head. "No. Nothing I can think of. Hannah's got a kiddie. You know that?"

"Aye," Logan confirmed. "That relevant?"

The sergeant puffed out his cheeks. "Um, probably not, no."

He shot the corridor behind him a longing look. "I suppose I'll just... If there's nothing else, sir, I'll just be..."

Logan dismissed him with a wave. "Aye. I'm sure you've plenty to be getting on with."

"You can say that again. Work, work, work," Jaffray replied. "Sometimes, I think it's never—"

"That'll be all, Sergeant," said Logan.

Jaffray, to his credit, caught the cue to shut up, and hurriedly backed away along the corridor. He practically bowed as he retreated around the corner, and his disappearance was followed by a shout of, "Watch it," and a sudden yelp.

A moment later, the constable Logan had sent for coffee appeared, carrying a battered old tray with two mismatched mugs on top and what looked to be quite a disappointing plate of biscuits.

"Thanks," Logan said. He prodded around at the biscuits—two soggy looking fig rolls and a single digestive—flared his nostrils, then took a mug in each hand. "You're fine," he added, dismissing the plate with a look that didn't just border on contempt, but full-on invaded it.

And then, with mugs in hand, he nudged the door to the interview room open with a knee and headed inside.

CHAPTER TWENTY-THREE

"Should I have a lawyer?" Hannah asked. She was sitting beside her dad, directly across the table from Logan, leaning back in her chair with her arms folded.

Fulton snorted out a laugh. "A lawyer. Of course you don't need a lawyer." He shot Logan a worried look. "She doesn't, does she?"

"We can get you one if you like, but I'm sure it won't be necessary," Logan said. "You're not a suspect here, Miss Randall. Can I call you Hannah?"

She shrugged. Logan took it as her granting permission.

"You're not a suspect, Hannah. Not at the moment, anyway."

Fulton sat up straighter in his chair. "Not at the moment? What's that supposed to mean, 'not at the moment'?" he asked. "What are you trying to say?"

Logan took a sip of his coffee. It was the cheap stuff, and bitter. He briefly lamented dismissing the biscuits.

"We have no reason to suspect you were involved in Brodie's death, Hannah. Please, rest assured, I don't think that for a minute," Logan told her.

This wasn't entirely true, in that he suspected everyone pretty much equally until he could prove they weren't involved, but there was nothing that set Hannah apart from anyone else at this stage.

From none of the frontrunners, anyway.

"I just want to go over what happened yesterday, and maybe clear up a couple of things that have come up. Inconsistencies, really."

He set his mug down and indicated a button on the desk. "I do have to record the interview, though. Standard procedure. There are also a couple of cameras in here," he said, indicating them both with a point. "And that's a one-way mirror. During interrogations, we usually have people sitting on the other side of the glass. This isn't an interrogation, so we don't."

He smiled at them both in turn, his finger hovering over the button. "Everyone OK with all that?"

Fulton looked at his daughter like he was asking her permission. She nodded, and he granted his own approval with a, "Fine. Of course. Whatever you have to do."

Logan clicked the button, recited the usual spiel for the benefit of the tape, then forced back another sip of coffee. Fulton had taken a single gulp from his own mug, then set it down. Logan would be prepared to bet he had no intention whatsoever of going back to it.

It really was awful stuff.

"How you feeling this morning, Hannah? You get any sleep?"

"Not much," she said. Her mouth was tight and puckered, like she was grudging every syllable it was being forced to speak.

"Me neither," Logan told her. "Hotel beds. I hate them. I mean, it was comfy enough, but I can never nod off. See, when I'm in a hotel, it means I'm away from home, and when I'm away from home it's usually for a case and, well, the mind ticks over. Replaying stuff. Things people said."

He set the mug down on the table with the softest of *clunks*.

"Things they didn't. Tick-tick-tick. Round and round, all night long."

"Aye? Well, my fiancé was murdered, and my house was invaded by masked men with knives," Hannah spat. "So, sorry if I'm short on sympathy."

"Hannah," Fulton soothed. He smiled apologetically at the detective across the table. "Sorry. She's just... she's upset."

"Entirely understandable. I mean, who wouldn't be, after all you've been through? You're holding up better than most," Logan said.

Another pause. Another sip. He regarded the young woman over the rim of the mug.

"How's the wee one? What was her name?"

"Carrie," both Randalls said at the same time.

"Carrie. That's right. You mentioned. Have you said anything to her yet? About her dad?"

Some of the anger that had been shaping the lines of Hannah's body crumbled, becoming something more like grief. Her shoulders, which had been forced straight back, took on a forward stoop. She unfolded her arms and leaned her elbows on the table, supporting herself.

"No. Not yet."

"There's no real rush," Fulton said, placing a hand on his daughter's arm. "She's used to him being away for a few weeks at a time."

"Aye. Funny you should say that. That's one of the things I was hoping

Hannah might be able to clear up for us. Brodie's trips. Specifically, where he goes, and why," Logan said. "The *where's* not too big a deal. We can get a list of the places he's been from his passport records. It's the *why* that really interests me, though. What's he been going abroad for?"

"Well, work, isn't it?" Fulton said. He looked from Logan to his daughter. Neither of them were looking back at him.

"Yeah. He travels for work," Hannah said.

"Right. His work being...?"

"Offshore."

"For Oswatt, right. French company, wasn't it?"

"Dutch," Hannah corrected.

Logan clicked his fingers. "Dutch. Right. Of course. Sorry."

He clasped his hands loosely in front of him and leaned closer, confident and relaxed. "See, the thing is, we haven't been able to get hold of anyone at Oswatt. In fact, we haven't been able to find any reference to Oswatt anywhere. And we've looked. Believe me, we've looked. But nothing. Not here, not in the Netherlands. Nowhere. Bit odd that, isn't it?"

"It's on the bank statements. Oswatt. I've seen it myself. I sent it to your man," Fulton said.

"You're right. It's on the statement you sent. And thanks for that, by the way," Logan said. "But we talked to the bank. It's a virtual account from some Central American company. Not necessarily shady, but unusual for an alleged multinational energy company—who, again, we can find no record of—to be using it for their banking needs."

He looked from one Randall to the other, before settling on the younger of the two. "So, Hannah. Anything you'd like to tell me about Brodie's employer? Any additional information you can provide that will clear all this up?"

Hannah exploded into movement, leaning forward and throwing her hands up in the air. "What does it matter? Who cares? He's dead. Brodie's dead. My daughter's father is *dead*! Who gives a shit who he worked for? It wasn't them that killed him, was it?"

Logan maintained his composure. "How can you be so sure?"

Fulton ejected his second snort in as many minutes. "Come on, what are you saying? He was murdered by an energy company?"

Logan shifted his gaze in the man's direction. "You don't seem to get what I'm saying. As far as we can tell, there *is* no Oswatt. Brodie Welsh didn't work for an energy company, despite what appears to be a very elaborate attempt to make people believe that he did."

His chair creaked as he shifted his weight a fraction. "Now, if that's the case —if Brodie's job with Oswatt was some kind of cover—then that throws up a lot of important questions. Who did he work for? What was he doing?"

He fixed Hannah with one of his most probing looks. "And who knew about it?"

There was silence in the room for a few moments, as Logan kept the pressure on. Hannah tried holding his gaze, but buckled quickly and looked down at the table. So, she did know. Maybe not everything, but some of it.

"Brodie's beyond being in any trouble now, Hannah," he told her. "We're not trying to point fingers, we're trying to figure out who killed him. That's the focus. That's all we want."

"That's what we all want, Jack," Fulton interjected. He put a hand on his daughter's back and rubbed it. "Isn't it, Hannah? If you know something, you have to tell them. For Carrie's sake. Tell him. Tell us."

A tear fell on the table, leaving a tiny round puddle on the smooth wood. Hannah started to speak, but it came out as a croak. She coughed, clearing her throat, and then continued without looking up.

"He never said anything. Not really. When we got together, he just said he worked offshore. That he was away a lot. Lot of people round here work on the rigs, so I didn't think too much about it. Not to start with."

She sniffed and wiped a sleeve across her face.

"But then, when we got engaged, I said we should set up a joint bank account. Put both our wages in. I was working at the school at the time. He wasn't keen, though. At first, anyway. Kept putting it off and putting it off. I thought he was just worried I'd run away with it all or something.

"When I got pregnant, though, I talked him into it. He agreed it was best. For the baby. So, we set it up. I got my wages paid in, but he didn't."

Fulton frowned. "But I saw them. On the statement."

Hannah shot him a sideways glance. "Not at first. I asked him about it, and he said he got paid in cash."

"Cash?" said Logan. "Nobody pays that amount in cash every month."

"That's what I said," Hannah replied. She pulled the end of her sleeve over her wrist and used it to wipe her nose. "He got annoyed. Said I was accusing him of something. But then, after it had all calmed down—after *he'd* calmed down—he said he'd talk to the company and try to get it paid into the account."

She shrugged. Her face was slack, her eyes dull, like she wasn't quite present in the room. "And he did. It came in the next month, and every month since."

"Always the same amount?" Logan asked.

Hannah nodded. "Yeah. Why?"

"No overtime? Bonuses?"

She frowned, like this thought had never occurred to her. "I mean, he did work overtime. He'd sometimes get called away at the last minute."

"But no bump to the pay packet?"

"No. Not... No. Never."

"Maybe it was..." Fulton began. His eyes searched the space in front of him, hunting for an explanation. "He could've been on a fixed salary. Maybe the overtime wasn't paid, but covered in the normal wage. I mean, Christ, it was high enough."

Logan agreed that this was a possibility. As someone who had put in hundreds of overtime hours without ever seeing a penny extra in his wages, he knew it wasn't uncommon.

"Can I see him?"

Hannah's question took the DCI by surprise. He should've been expecting it, of course. Been ready with an explanation as to why it wouldn't be a good idea. But, the sincerity with which she asked, the big, wide, hopeful eyes, caught him on the back foot.

"Uh, aye. I mean, not right now, but maybe once all the tests have been..."

He saw her eyes well up again and her face go pale, like the reality of it all had just been brought home for her once more. There, in that moment, she looked fifteen. A wee scared lassie who didn't know what to do.

"I can only imagine how hard this must be for you, Hannah," Logan said. "Truth be told, it might be a few days before you can see Brodie's body. Even then, I'm not sure I'd recommend it. It's your decision, of course, I can only advise, but I advise against it."

Fulton took his daughter's hand in his. Judging by the look they shared, they'd already had this same conversation.

Hannah tried to speak, but all that emerged was a throaty wheeze. She looked to the ceiling, gulped down a few steadying breaths, then tried again.

"How did he die? Nobody's told me," she said. "How did he die?"

"Hannah. Sweetheart..." Fulton soothed, but she ignored him and fixed those big wide eyes on the detective across the table.

"Please. I have to know. I have a right to know. How did he die?"

Logan considered all the possible answers he could give to that question, including all the ways he might deflect it. In the end, he settled for the most direct.

"He suffocated."

Hannah's lips thinned. Her eyes blurred. Beside her, Fulton sat up a little straighter, his eyebrows meeting in the middle.

"What? I thought they said he'd been stabbed?"

Logan glanced at Fulton just long enough to reply. "He had. Yes. However, that wasn't the cause of death. He suffocated. Are you sure you want to hear this, Hannah?"

At the mention of her name, Hannah nodded. From the expression currently twisting the lines of her face, though, Logan doubted she was fully taking any of it in.

"Suffocated how?" Fulton asked. His hand squeezed his daughter's, the rest of him trembling at the very thought of it. "With what?"

Logan looked between them both and shifted his weight in his chair. "I'm not sure it's the right time to—"

"Tell us," Hannah said. A command now, not a request. "What happened?"

Logan let out a long sigh to signal that he thought this was a bad idea, before continuing.

"We believe Brodie may have been buried alive."

Hannah didn't react quite the way Logan had been expecting. There were no sobs, or gasps, or cries of anguish. Instead, she went very still and very quiet, like her brain had shut down all non-essential functions so it could process this new information.

Fulton, on the other hand, physically recoiled. A noise emerged from somewhere within him, raw and primal. His bottom lip shook like a toddler with a burst balloon, and then he sat back suddenly and forcefully in his chair and clamped a hand over his mouth.

"Oh, God," he whispered, choking back tears of his own. "Oh, Brodie, no."

CHAPTER TWENTY-FOUR

Tyler was scrolling through a third page of search results when something icy cold was pressed against the back of his neck. He twisted in his chair, ejecting a surprisingly high-pitched, "Fuck off!" and throwing an arm out for protection.

He had expected to find Hamza standing behind him, probably pissing himself laughing. The sight that did meet him was far better.

Tyler jumped up, the cold spot on the back of his neck instantly forgotten.

"Sorry, couldn't resist," said a young woman, holding a can of Irn Bru in one hand. From the way she said it, and the smirk on her face, she very clearly wasn't sorry in the slightest, but Tyler wasn't going to hold that against her.

"Sinead. What are you doing here?" he asked. He hesitated for a moment, overthinking it, then stepped in closer and gave her a slightly awkward hug.

She pressed the can against the back of his shirt, freezing him through the thin material.

"Argh! Quit that!" he said, although with far less venom in his voice this time.

"Sorry," Sinead said again, arguably even less truthfully than before. "Couldn't resist again."

She pointed to an empty chair at the next desk over. "Anyone sitting there?"

Tyler regarded the seat. "Aye. The Invisible Man. We use him for undercover work."

"His banter's still shite, you'll notice," remarked Hamza. He was on the phone at his own desk, one hand over the mouthpiece. "Hello, by the way."

Sinead smiled back at the DC as she wheeled the empty chair over to Tyler's desk. "Hi."

Hamza took his hand off the mouthpiece, but didn't speak. From the way he bobbed his head and tapped a finger on his notepad, Sinead assumed he was listening to some catchier-than-usual hold music.

"Where's everyone else?" she asked Tyler as she sat down beside him.

"The boss is doing an interview. The others are..."

He regarded the Incident Room.

"Not here. Dunno where they've gone, actually," he admitted, gesturing to his computer screen. "I've been tied up with this. Trying to find someone who called in a missing climber report."

"No joy?"

Tyler shrugged. "Not really, no. He gives his name as Robert Smith, so searching mostly just brings up the guy from The Cure. You know? 'Friday, I'm in—'"

He stopped himself from finishing the song title, smiled uncomfortably, then drew Sinead's attention to the screen again. "He's the most famous one, obviously, but there are loads of them. I've found at least four living here in town. I've managed to speak to three of them, but can't find a phone number for the fourth."

He gave his head a shake, then turned away from the computer. "Anyway. What are you doing here? You're meant to be at home resting."

"Yeah, but the thing is, it's really boring," Sinead said. "I've got nothing against 'Loose Women,' but there's only so many times you can watch it before you want to kill yourself."

She considered this point. "OK, maybe I do have something against 'Loose Women,'" she decided. "So, yeah. I got bored, and Harris is away on his school trip for the next couple of days, so I thought I'd come down and say hello. See if you were free for lunch."

Tyler groaned. "I'd love to be, but..."

He indicated the screen, and then the room around them. "Murder case, innit? All hands on deck."

"Right. Aye. Of course," Sinead said. "Sorry, should've phoned ahead. Stupid."

Brushing her hair back over an ear, she stood up, a plastic smile fixed on her face. "I'll leave you to get on."

"Or..." Tyler began. He took a Post-It from his desk and hastily scribbled down an address from the screen, then held it up for her to see. "You could come with me and talk to this guy."

Sinead sucked in her bottom lip. "I'm not on duty. Is that allowed?"

"Fuck knows," Tyler admitted. "Probably not." He tucked the address into the top pocket of his shirt and smiled at her. "But I won't tell anyone, if you don't."

Sinead gave a nod, then stepped aside. "Fair enough, then. I'm in. Lead the way."

Clicking off his screen, Tyler moved past Sinead and made for the door. Two seconds later, he yelped as an ice-cold can was pressed against the back of his neck.

"Sorry," Sinead giggled. "You just make it so tempting."

DI Forde sat in the shadows on one side of the glass, half-reading Jinkies' report on the drugs investigation, and half-observing the conversation taking part in the room beyond the mirror.

It was nosiness that had brought him into the observation room, if he was being completely honest. But then, it was nosiness that had driven most of his polis career, including several of his biggest busts, so he didn't see any shame in that.

Ben flipped through a page of the report, scanned a couple of random paragraphs, then went back to earwigging on the events in the room next door.

Logan had insisted Hannah Randall wasn't a suspect, but Ben had wanted to take a look for himself. Watching her now, he reckoned Jack was probably right. If she'd killed him, she deserved an Academy Award for the performance she was putting on.

You got to know the guilty ones. You learned to pick up on all the little ticks and habits that gave them away. There were dozens of them, hundreds, maybe, from the casting of an eye to the flaring of the nostrils. Usually subtle, and very easy to miss if you didn't know what you were looking for.

Hannah Randall hadn't displayed any of them.

That's not to say she wasn't hiding something—she was definitely hiding something—but had she murdered Brodie Welsh? No. Almost certainly not.

Ben turned to the next page in the report. It was dense with text, and the dim light of the room meant he'd have to squint to read it properly, even with his reading glasses on.

He'd come back to it.

Licking a finger, he turned a couple more pages until he found something marginally less trying on his eyes. It was still mostly text, but there were spaces between some of the paragraphs, at least. That sort of thing could go a long way.

Something buried in the writing on the page immediately nagged at him, but Logan had just delivered the bombshell about Brodie being buried alive, and Ben wanted to see how the Randalls reacted.

As was to be expected, both of them took it hard, albeit in their own individual ways.

Fulton was the most obviously cut up. Outwardly, at least. But Ben had seen that look on Hannah Randall's face on other people before, and was only too aware of the emotional turmoil that would be bubbling away below the surface.

His eyes returned to the page in front of him, practically of their own free will. At that first glance, something had jumped out at him. His subconscious had picked up on it, but the dominant part of his brain was struggling to find it.

He closed the report, holding the page between both thumbs, then opened it again in the hope that whatever he'd seen would appear again like magic.

It didn't. He angled the page towards the light from next door, and had just settled in to read the whole thing when he heard the door open behind him, and saw DS McQuarrie dimly reflected in the glass.

"Everything alright, Caitlyn?" he asked, turning away from the brightly-lit interview room. His eyes took a moment to adjust to the gloomier observation area, then settled on the DS.

"Fine, sir. It's just I found something that might be relevant to DCI Logan's interview. I was going to bring it to his attention, but thought I should run it by you first."

"Sounds wise. He generally doesn't like to be interrupted unless it's..." Ben thought about where that sentence was headed, then clarified. "Actually, he just doesn't like to be interrupted. What have you got?"

"It might be nothing, sir," Caitlyn said. She held up a printout. "Then again, it might be a pretty significant find."

Ben peered at the sheet of paper over the top of his reading glasses. "I'll swap you," he said, offering up the report. "See if there's anything on that page that, I don't know, jumps out."

"That you back on the pop-up books again, sir?" Caitlyn asked, swapping documents with the DI. It wasn't great, as jokes went, but it was so rare for DS McQuarrie to make them that Ben laughed, more for encouragement than anything else.

"Make for more entertaining reading, I'm sure," he said, smiling at her as he adjusted his glasses and considered the printout she'd given him.

The smile didn't hang around for long.

"Jesus," he muttered. He looked back over his shoulder into the interview room, then back at the page before finishing with another, "Jee-*sus*," for good measure. "How did we not know about this before?"

"Never followed up on, sir," Caitlyn said, speed-reading the page of the report Ben had given her. "No charges pressed. Everything denied."

"I mean, aye. Fair enough. But, still an' all."

Caitlyn nodded curtly. "Aye, sir. Bit of an oversight somewhere."

She turned the report back to him and jabbed a finger onto the page somewhere just below the middle. "That what you're referring to, sir?" she asked.

Ben pulled back from the page a little and peered through his glasses and along his nose. The writing swam in the half-light, but a bit of squinting eventually brought it into focus and he blasphemed for a third time. This one was louder than the two before.

"Aye. That's it," he said. Turning, he jabbed a finger against a button and bent in close to a microphone fixed in front of the window. "DCI Logan," he began, all his concerns about interrupting forgotten.

On the other side of the glass, the Randalls raised their eyes to the overhead speaker, where the voice had come from. Logan ignored it and looked straight at the mirror.

The voice hissed faintly through the intercom system.

"There's something I think you should see."

CHAPTER TWENTY-FIVE

"How do you say it? *Cor-patch*?"

Sinead tutted reproachfully and shook her head. "Corpach," she said, pronouncing the 'ch' as a soft sound at the back of her throat.

"Corpach," Tyler said. "Got it. Is that Gaelic?"

"Dunno."

"What does it mean?"

Sinead shrugged. "I don't know that, either."

"'Ridiculously steep hill,' maybe?" Tyler suggested, indicating the steep slope ahead of them with a nod.

He was behind the wheel of a marked police car, pulled in behind a row of parked cars while he waited for half a dozen other vehicles to pass in the opposite direction, and was quietly dreading the hill start that awaited him once the oncoming traffic had cleared.

Once the final car had passed, he raised the clutch, depressed the accelerator, and—to Sinead's delight—stalled immediately.

"Don't," Tyler said, seeing the glee on her face from the corner of his eye. He checked the handbrake, took the car out of gear, then started the engine again. "Just don't."

"I wasn't going to say a word."

"Good. Let's keep it that way."

With a not-inconsiderable amount of revving, Tyler drove on up the hill, muttering about not being used to the car as he growled it up the sweeping curve of the road.

"The address is up here on the right," Sinead said, indicating a semi-detached house just ahead of them.

"There's nowhere to stop," Tyler said, scanning for a space in the row of cars parked along the kerb.

"There's a car park further up. At the top," Sinead said. Her voice was suddenly hesitant, like this was not necessarily the good news it might appear to be.

"OK, cool," Tyler replied. He shot her a brief sideways glance. "You alright?"

Sinead tugged on her seatbelt, which suddenly seemed to be too tight. "Yeah. I just... I should've thought. When I knew we were coming up here, I should've thought."

"Thought about what?" Tyler asked, as he pulled into an almost empty car park and nabbed himself the first available space.

Sinead raised a finger and pointed out of the DC's side window. A sign stood by an open gate, with the words:

Kilmallie Cemetery.

"About that."

It took Tyler a second or two to catch on.

"Shite. Your mum and dad?"

Sinead nodded, her eyes fixed on the sign. An archway of trees blocked her view of all but the first row of the graveyard's collection of headstones.

"I haven't been back since we moved to Inverness," she said. "I should've brought flowers."

She let her gaze linger for a little while longer, then gave herself a shake and unclipped her belt. "Anyway."

By the time Tyler got out of the car, she was facing down the hill in the direction of the house they'd passed, her back turned on the cemetery. "It's just down here," she announced, not looking at him.

"Don't you want to...?"

"Murder investigation," Sinead reminded him. "All hands on deck. I can come back another time."

"Right. Aye. Fair enough," Tyler said. He put a hand on her arm. "Or, you could take five minutes now."

Sinead glanced at him, then over to the graveyard entrance. "I didn't bring flowers or anything."

"I'm sure they won't mind," Tyler replied. He flinched. "On account of them presumably being nice people, I mean, not because they're... I don't mean..."

Sinead took his hand and gave it a squeeze. Her expression lightened. "I know what you mean," she said. "And thank you."

She squeezed his hand again, then interlinked their fingers. "You sure it's OK?"

Tyler puffed out his cheeks. "Have to meet the parents at some point, I suppose. Might as well get it out of the way."

Despite everything, Sinead laughed as they started, hand-in-hand, up the hill. "Aye, I suppose you're right," she said. She bumped her shoulder against his. "But, just so you're forewarned, my dad is going to hate you."

BEN AND CAITLYN stood in the corridor along from the interview room, watching in silence as Logan read over the notes they'd drawn his attention to. He'd already echoed Ben's, "Jesus," a couple of times, and then elaborated on it with some quite creative swearing.

"And we're just finding out about this now? I'll murder Jinkies when I see him."

"They didn't make any concrete link between them, sir. He's only mentioned in passing," Caitlyn replied. "But aye, surprising the Chief Inspector didn't bring it up."

"Always said he was a useless bastard," Logan remarked. "Aye, to his face, like. No' behind his back."

"Let's hope being a useless bastard is all it is," Ben said. The way he checked the corridor around them and dropped his voice to a murmur made his meaning only too clear.

"You think he's on the fiddle?" Logan asked.

Ben frowned and double-checked that no one was listening in. "I'm not saying that, Jack, no." He tapped the report in the DCI's hands. "But this is one hell of an oversight. I'm happy to accept that he's just inept. Or maybe he was going to tell us, but wanted to piss up around a bit first. But, I think it'd be wise not to say too much in front of him until we know a bit more. That's all."

"I'm still leaning towards 'useless bastard,' myself, but no harm in playing things close to our chest," Logan agreed. "No' like he's not doing the same with us."

Caitlyn indicated the report with a look. "You're going to mention them both to the suspect though, right, sir?"

"Hannah Randall isn't a suspect," Logan replied. He tucked the paperwork under his arm, then exhaled through his nose. "At least, not yet."

"HERE YOU GO."

Sinead turned to find DC Neish standing behind her with a bunch of flowers. It was an odd assortment—a real mish-mash of varieties, assembled with care, but very little skill. Around half of them looked fresh and new, a quarter had started to wilt, and the rest were at the stage of requiring hospice care.

"Where did you get that?" she asked him.

"I nicked them from a few different bunches," Tyler explained. He saw the look of horror that flitted across her face. "I just took the odd one here and there from a few of the bigger bunches, like. Nobody will notice."

Sinead's eyes were still wide with shock, but she bit her bottom lip to stop herself smiling. "Well, thanks. I suppose," she said, accepting the bunch. "And I take it back. My dad would absolutely love you."

Crouching, she placed the flowers into the *Beloved Mum & Dad* holder that was pegged into the grass in front of the black marble headstone. "There you go," she whispered, adjusting the blooms in a futile attempt to make them look better. "It's the thought that counts, right?"

She plucked a few blades of grass from the headstone, wiped a spot with her sleeve, then stood up and stepped back so she was beside Tyler.

"It must've been... I mean, I can't imagine," the DC said.

Sinead swallowed and gave an almost imperceptible nod. For a moment, it looked like that would be her only response, but then she spoke, her words coming out slowly and hesitantly like she was having to slot them carefully into place.

"I was on duty when I got the call. I'd not long started. Back shift. I was on the speed gun on one of the straights through Glen Coe, when I got the shout."

She ground her teeth together, then clicked her tongue against the roof of her mouth.

"RTA. Two car collision. It was just up the road from where I was, so I was closest. I got there first."

Tyler slipped his hand into hers. It felt limp and lifeless, and she showed no signs that she'd even noticed his touch.

"As soon as I saw the car, I knew. It wasn't an unusual car, either. Loads of them on the road. It could've been anyone. I told myself it wasn't them, in fact. Really tried to convince myself," Her voice thinned, becoming softer, like a radio broadcast about to lose signal. "But I knew it was. And then, I saw this car sticker in the back window, and I had to stop telling myself that it wasn't. I knew it was them, and I knew there was no way anyone was walking away from that smash."

"I'm so sorry."

Sinead opened her mouth to say more, held it that way for several seconds, then closed it and wiped her eyes on her sleeve. "Jesus, look at me," she said, backing it up with a sound that approximated a laugh. "What a state. I'm a greetin' mess."

"Stop," Tyler told her. "It's no wonder. It's amazing how you've dealt with it all." He tightened his grip on her hand. "You're amazing."

"Ah, shaddup," Sinead said, hurriedly rebuilding the walls that had begun to crumble. She turned away from the grave and all the memories it held, and drew in a breath as she took in the scenery.

She and Harris had picked it specially. From there, you could look over the rooftops of Corpach, across Loch... what? Eil? Linnhe? She never knew where one ended and the other began. And from there up to Ben Nevis, with its snow-dusted peak.

It would've been quite breathtaking for the residents of the graveyard, had their breath not already been taken in a much more literal sense.

"Must be about the best view in town," Tyler remarked, following her gaze.

Sinead couldn't argue. "We wanted them to be somewhere nice. Somewhere they'd have something to look at. Stupid, I know."

"It's not stupid," Tyler assured her.

"Aye, it is. They're dead." She pulled on a smile. "Sorry. Being a bit morbid."

Tyler made a show of scoping out the graveyard around them. "Wonder what brought that on?" he said. "And it's not stupid. Just because someone dies, doesn't mean you stop caring about them. Doesn't mean you don't want them somewhere nice to..."

The words stopped coming. Sinead turned to see an expression of intense concentration furrow the lines of Tyler's face.

"What?" she asked. "What's the matter?"

It took a moment for Tyler to come out of his daze. "Hm? Oh. No. Nothing. It's nothing. Just a thought about the case. Not fully formed yet."

"Are any of your thoughts ever fully formed?" Sinead teased.

"Yes!" Tyler protested. "Usually. Occasionally."

Sinead raised an eyebrow, and Tyler sighed dramatically. "Well, OK, there was this one time..."

"I think even once is exaggerating," Sinead said, then laughed at the look of mock outrage on his face. "So, Robert Smith, then."

"What about him?" Tyler asked, before the penny dropped. "Oh! Our Robert Smith. I thought you meant the other one. Aye. Suppose we'd better. You ready?"

With a final look back at the headstone and its mismatched flower display, Sinead motioned down the hill in the direction of the gate.

"Aye," she said. "Lead the way, Detective Constable."

CHAPTER TWENTY-SIX

It took three rounds of knocking before Robert Smith appeared at the door, and three full seconds for the expression on his face to switch from 'furious' to 'terrified'.

He was in his mid-to-late fifties, with a head that had grown up through his hair, relegating what was left of it to an unkempt ginger horseshoe that ran around the back of his head from one ear to the other. He'd managed to drag a few long strands across the top of his head and had plastered them in place with something greasy. Presumably, he thought this was better than just giving in and embracing his baldness.

It wasn't.

His outfit was unusual, given the time of year, and where they were in the world. He had on a tight-fitting Hawaiian shirt unbuttoned all the way down to where his beer belly started to curve outwards from the rest of him, and a pair of white shorts so small and tight Tyler wondered if they might constitute a criminal offence in and of themselves.

He'd answered the door all bluff and bluster, demanding to know what the bloody hell Tyler thought he was bloody well playing at, hammering on his bloody door in the middle of the bloody day.

It was only when he saw the DC's suit and the police car parked at the top of the street that the anger—and the bloodies—fell away.

It wasn't until Tyler produced his warrant card that the beads of perspiration began to form on Robert's sizeable forehead.

"I don't... I'm sorry, I didn't mean to shout. I was just, I was in the middle of..." he stammered, before clamping his mouth closed, smiling weakly, and trying again. "How can I help you?"

The door was open only a foot or so. Robert wasn't tall, but what he lacked in height he made up for in girth, and his bulk was firmly plugging the gap in the doorway, his body language making Tyler feel decidedly unwelcome.

"Do you mind if I come in, Mr Smith?" he asked. "I've just got a couple of quick questions."

Robert's eyes crept sideways until he was looking into the house. "Uh. No. Sorry. I'm in the middle of something."

"It won't take long," Tyler insisted. "I tried to phone, but I couldn't find a number."

"We haven't got a house phone," Robert explained. He seemed to notice his open shirt for the first time, and quickly clenched the patterned fabric together with one sweaty hand. "I'm sorry, normally I'd invite you in, but it's just... I'm in the middle of something, like I said. Can you ask me here?"

Tyler peeked into the hallway over the top of the man's head. "Is everything alright, Mr Smith?"

"What? Yes!"

"It's just, you seem a bit on edge, sir. If you don't mind me saying? You sure everything's OK?"

"Fine! Yes. Fine. God. Yes. Fine, fine. Just... Just fine," he replied, punctuating the words with bursts of forced, incredulous laughter. "Dandy. Fine and dandy. All good."

Tyler blinked slowly. Once. Twice.

"Right," he said, dragging the word out. He looked into the hall again, trying to see further into the house, but Robert pulled the living room door shut.

"So, um, officer," he said. Swallow. Deep breath. Mop of the brow. "What was it you wanted to ask?"

Sinead stood just around the side of the semi-detached, listening to the conversation on the step. It had been her suggestion to hang back out of sight. She wasn't in uniform, or even on duty, and if Robert Smith turned into a person of interest, she didn't want technicalities to put the investigation at risk.

Of course, lurking around the corner listening in wasn't exactly a great look, either, but the man's point-blank refusal to let Tyler inside the house had piqued her curiosity.

The front garden, where Tyler was standing, was surrounded by a low hedge that was more brown than green, with patches of thinning almost as severe as the one on Robert Smith's head.

Sinead daren't get much closer to the front, or there was a very good chance Smith would see her, or at least hear her footsteps. Bad enough her being involved in his questioning while off duty, but it'd be so much worse if he spotted her skulking around at the side of his house.

Moving quietly, she sidestepped towards the back of the house, where a tall wooden fence surrounded the garden. There was nothing behind the garden but hillside. If you ignored the neighbours living in the other half of the semi-detached, it meant the garden was a quiet and secluded little spot. She could wait back there for Tyler to be done, then head back to the car with him. Nobody would see her. Nobody would know she was there.

Or, so she thought.

From beyond the fence, she heard a noise. A grunt. A groan, maybe.

She shifted position until she could see through one of the narrow gaps between the vertical planks of wood, and she felt her insides twist in panic. A man stared back at her from inside the garden. His eyes were dark, the rest of his face obscured by a tight-fitting black leather mask.

Around the corner, on the front step, Tyler had given up on his attempts to get inside, deciding it was best to just ask his questions and leave.

"It's about a phone call made to the emergency services in the early hours of yesterday morning, Mr Smith," he explained, taking his notebook from his pocket.

Robert practically sobbed with relief. "What, nine-nine-nine? Wasn't me."

"They asked for the Mountain Rescue," Tyler continued. "And they gave your name."

"Wasn't me. I don't know what else to tell you, mate. Wasn't me. I didn't phone—"

"Tyler!"

Sinead's voice was sharp and sudden and urgent. Tyler saw the look of relief on Robert's face be swept aside by one of raw panic.

"Shit, shit, shit, no!" Robert yelped. He shoved hard on the door, slamming it closed before Tyler could stop him.

The *clack* of a lock sliding home came a moment later, followed by a wail of anguish from the other side of the door.

Tyler gracelessly sprackled his way through the hedge and stumbled around the side of the house, but saw no sign of Sinead.

"Shite. Sinead!" he hollered, racing around the back, his head rapidly filling with a hundred different scenarios, none of them good.

He found her standing outside the back gate, one hand clamped over her mouth. At first, he thought this was because she was in a state of shock, but then he saw the lines creasing the skin around her eyes, and realised she was trying very hard not to laugh.

"What? What is it?" he asked. "What's wrong?"

Sinead indicated the gate with a tilt of her head. "See for yourself," she urged.

Tyler looked the fence up and down, then leaned in closer, putting one eye to a gap.

It took him a second or two to figure out what he was looking at, but then he jumped back so suddenly anyone watching would've thought the fence had been electrified.

He bit his lip. His nostrils flared. He couldn't look at Sinead. He daren't, in case it set them both off.

"Oh God," he whispered. "You have got to be kidding me."

CHAPTER TWENTY-SEVEN

Logan sat back at the desk with a bundle of paperwork and a half-arsed apology.

"Sorry about that. Something came up," he said, setting the cardboard folder down beside his empty mug. He looked across the table at the Randalls, his finger hovering over the button that would start the tape. "All set?"

"Will this take much longer?" Fulton asked. "She'd... we'd both like to get back."

"Hopefully you'll be on your way sooner rather than later," Logan replied. "I just have a couple of things left to go over, then we're done. Alright?"

He shifted his gaze from one to the other, giving them time to object. Then, he pressed the button, rattled off the required legal spiel, and jumped right into it.

"Was Brodie ever violent towards you, Hannah?" he asked.

He saw Fulton stiffen in his chair, but ignored the movement and kept his sights on Hannah.

"What do you mean? Of course not," Fulton said. He looked at his daughter. "He wasn't, was he? You'd have said, wouldn't you? You'd have said."

"No," Hannah replied.

"Whose question were you answering there, Hannah?" Logan asked her. "Just so we're clear."

"Yours," she said, her arms folded and defences fully deployed. "No. He was never violent."

The rigidity that had stiffened Fulton in his chair eased a little, but he was still sitting fully upright and alert.

"Right. I'm glad to hear that," Logan said. He opened the folder and plucked out the top page of the paperwork within. "It's just, we had reports from neighbours. Three separate incidents, in fact, over the past six months. They claimed they heard raised voices. Banging. Stuff being smashed. That sort of thing."

"Well, they're lying," Hannah insisted.

"Oh, no. They're not lying. Uniformed officers attended on all three occasions. You gave a statement each time saying it had been an argument. 'Just an argument,' you said. 'No harm done.'"

"Right. Well, it was that, then," Hannah said. "An argument. We argued. People argue."

"They do. I've got an ex-wife. Believe me, I know," Logan said. He consulted the sheet again. "But, on one of these occasions, four months ago, give or take, the constable who attended—Constable Jaffray. I believe you know him. He's made sergeant now, as it happens. Don't ask me how. Constable Jaffray wrote in his report that there was blood on your face, and visible signs of a struggle having taken place inside the house."

Hannah looked away, caught her reflection in the mirror, and looked back again. "I can't remember."

"That's alright, you don't have to. It's all written down," Logan said, indicating the report. He leaned forward and paraphrased some of what he read. "Neighbours say they saw you with a black eye in the days that followed. They also claim that during the argument, a female voice shouted—and I quote, 'Fucking touch me again and I'll kill you.'"

Logan set down the page. "Any idea who that might have been, Hannah?"

Fulton had contained himself enough to sit silently while Logan read from the notes, his face gradually becoming paler. He craned his neck, trying to read the writing on the page, but Logan flipped it over while maintaining his unwavering eye contact with the woman directly across the table.

"Hannah?" Fulton began. She dismissed it with a scowl.

"It was nothing, Dad. We argued. I stormed off. I fell, alright? That's all."

Logan clasped his hands together and leaned closer, as if about to share some big secret. "I want to help you here, Hannah. I want to protect you."

"Protect me? From what? From Brodie? I don't need protection from him. He's dead!" She wriggled uncomfortably in her chair. "And, even if he wasn't, I wouldn't. He wasn't like that. We just... We argued sometimes. Like everyone."

"Why didn't you say something?" Fulton asked, although it was whispered so quietly it might well have been rhetorical.

"I wasn't talking about Brodie, Hannah. I know you don't need protection from him. I was talking about his friends. Or colleagues, maybe."

He saw it in her face, that tightening at the corners of the mouth, that subtle change around the lines of the eyes.

"How long had he been dealing?" the DCI pressed.

"Dealing?!" Fulton spluttered. "What, drugs? Brodie? Brodie wasn't dealing drugs. Was he, Hannah? Not Brodie. Tell him."

Hannah had gone back to picking at the loose skin around her thumbnail. A spot of blood welled up where she'd scraped too deep.

"I don't know. A while," she said, her gaze cast down at the desk.

Fulton let his head roll back, buried his face in his hands, and made a succession of pained noises before sitting upright again.

"Right. No. This is... I think she should have a lawyer. This is, I don't know what it is. This is entrapment."

Hannah tutted. "Shut up, Dad. It's not entrapment, is it? He asked me a question, and I answered. Alright? That's all. That's his job."

Logan waited until the girl had finished drawing her father one of the dirtiest looks he'd ever seen, then pressed the advantage.

"How long a while. Roughly? Six months? A year?"

"I don't know. Since before I met him. Years," Hannah said. "I didn't know. Not at first. He never actually admitted it to me. Just deny, deny, deny. But I guessed. I figured it out."

She sucked the blood from her thumb, regarded the wound, then went back to picking. "Well, I thought he was shagging someone else to start with. I was actually relieved when I found out he wasn't." She shrugged. "I mean, not that I know of, anyway."

"How did you find out?" Logan asked.

"I can't remember."

Logan flexed his fingers, then clasped them again. "Try."

Hannah sighed and made a vaguely dismissive sort of gesture. "Just things he said. I don't know. I heard him on the phone a couple of times."

"Who to?"

"I don't know. And don't ask me what he said, either. I can't remember. It wasn't what he was saying, anyway, it was the way he said it. Cagey. But scared, too. Like he didn't want to say the wrong thing. When he realised I was listening, he hung up. Didn't say goodbye, didn't end the call, just hung up."

"What did he say to you after the call?" Logan asked.

"Nothing."

"Nothing?"

Hannah tutted. "I don't know. He was angry. He shouted. We argued. He told me I was paranoid. Called me a psycho. That was it. We didn't talk about it again, but I knew after that. I figured it out."

Fulton looked at his daughter as if seeing her for the first time. "You knew? You knew he was dealing drugs with Carrie in the house, and you didn't say anything?"

"He wasn't dealing from the house, Dad, was he?"

"I don't know, was he?" Fulton bit back. "You tell me! Was he?"

"No! Never. I never saw anything like that." She turned back to Logan. "Honestly. I knew. I mean, I suspected, but I couldn't prove anything. I never saw anything."

She was putting a brave face on it, but Logan could tell she was ready to crumble. There was a scowl fixed on her face, but it was a mask that was slipping away, revealing the scared wee girl hiding behind it.

"Tell me about Sandy Gillespie," he said.

The mask fell a fraction, giving a glimpse of the fear that flashed in Hannah's eyes at the mention of the name.

"What do you mean?"

"We believe Brodie met Sandy on a number of occasions over the past six months. We believe they may have been working together."

"I don't know," Hannah said. "I don't know anything about him. I mean, you hear things, but I've never really had any dealings with him."

"Really?" Logan asked. "I want you to think very hard about that, Hannah. It's important. You've never spoken to Sandy Gillespie?"

The hesitation was tiny, but Logan had been watching for it.

"No. Not really. Maybe a hello in the shops. In passing."

"And that's it?" Logan asked. He slid a sheet from the folder and watched Hannah's eyes get drawn to it.

"Wait. No," she said. Her brow creased like she was struggling to recall something. "Actually, I think he might've come to the house a couple of times. To see Brodie. I was in bed, though."

Logan nodded and slid the sheet back into the folder. He wasn't sure what that particular piece of paper actually said, but it had served its purpose.

"Do you know why he came round? What they spoke about?"

Hannah shook her head firmly. "No. Like I said, I was upstairs. With Carrie. I didn't see anything, I didn't hear anything, I don't know anything."

"Are you quite sure about that, Hannah?" Logan asked.

"Yes. I'm sure."

"Those people who came to your house last night. Could one of them have been Sandy Gillespie?"

There was no obvious physical reaction to the question. No widening of the eyes, no change to the colour of the cheeks, or to the shape of the mouth. Nothing to suggest shock or surprise.

"I only saw one. And I don't know. He had a mask on."

"What about his voice? Did you recognise that?"

She shook her head, although with less conviction than the last time. "No. Scottish, though. Pretty local, I'd say."

Fulton interjected, leaning forward in his chair until he was practically inserting himself between his daughter and the detective. "Wait, you think they killed Brodie, don't you? These drugs people. You think they killed him, and then came to the house."

"It's one line of inquiry," Logan confirmed. "It's possible they may have been looking for drugs Brodie brought back from his last trip abroad. It would explain some of Brodie's injuries."

He diverted his attention to Hannah. "We know they weren't there to rob the place, Hannah. It's time for the truth now. Did they ask about Brodie? Did they ask about the drugs?"

Fulton wasn't done with his interjection yet and jumped in before Hannah could reply. "Look, sorry. Is she under arrest? Is that what this is?"

Logan had a good idea about what was coming next. The look in Fulton Randall's eyes was one he'd seen countless times before.

"No," he said, smiling patiently. "She's not under arrest. She's just—"

Fulton's chair legs scraped on the floor as he got to his feet. "Right, then. Come on," he urged, motioning for Hannah to stand. "We're going."

Hannah looked from her dad to the DCI, then hurriedly complied. Logan sat back in his chair and folded his arms, demonstrating his disappointment without a word.

"If you want to talk to her again, then we'll have a solicitor present," Fulton said. "I'm not having you incriminating her, or pinning something on her she didn't do. I'm sorry, but I'm just not having it. Sorry."

Logan said nothing as the Randalls bustled past him. He heard Fulton pulling on the door handle, and the little gasp of exasperation when he discovered it wouldn't open.

"Sorry, can you...? Can you let us out?"

Logan uncrossed his arms and sat forward.

"Hannah Randall and Fulton Randall are now leaving the room," he said, then he terminated the recording with a jab of his finger, and reluctantly got to his feet.

After unlocking the door, Logan stood with a hand on the handle, blocking the way. Hannah wilted beneath his gaze as he looked down at her.

"Be careful out there, Hannah," he said. "If you feel like you're in danger at any point, contact us." He pulled the door open, but didn't yet step aside. "These people, whoever they are, are capable of some very nasty things."

CHAPTER TWENTY-EIGHT

AFTER SEEING THE RANDALLS OUT, LOGAN RETURNED TO THE INCIDENT Room to find DC Neish holding court in front of the Big Board.

Ben sat shaking his head in disbelief, while DS McQuarrie tried very hard to remain straight-faced. Hamza was taking a different approach, and was creasing up in his chair, literally holding his sides as if they might split at any moment.

It was the other occupant of the room who Logan acknowledged first. Sinead smiled at him as he entered, and he pulled an expression of mock outrage.

"Christ, are we letting anyone in here these days?"

"Looks like it, sir," Sinead confirmed. "How's it going?"

"Shite."

"Usual, then?"

"Pretty much," Logan said. He stopped between Ben and Caitlyn, and waited for Hamza to pull himself together. "Obviously, I've missed something good," he remarked, once DC Khaled had stopped giggling.

"You can say that again, boss," Tyler said, grinning like the cat who'd got the cream. "So, we were checking up on all the Robert Smiths in the area."

Logan frowned. "What, the singer? With the mad hair and the eyeshadow?"

"No. The nine-nine-nine call," Tyler said. "To the mountain rescue. The name the caller gave was Robert Smith. Fake number, from what we can tell. But, there are a few Robert Smiths locally, so I checked them out to see if any of them had made the call."

"Right. And?"

"They hadn't. None of them knew anything about it."

Logan glanced down at Hamza. His eyes were wet with tears of laughter, and he was still trying to get his breathing under control. A quick look at Caitlyn revealed she was having to hold it together, too.

"Am I missing the punchline somewhere?" Logan asked. "I mean, I enjoy a good joke as much as the next man, but I'm struggling to get this one. What's so funny?"

Tyler's face lit up like all his Christmases had come at once. He immediately launched into a lengthy and detailed explanation of the day's events, that quickly set Hamza off again, and earned more disapproving looks from Ben.

Once Tyler had finished, Logan could actually feel his mouth hanging open. He quickly snapped it shut.

"You're joking!"

"Nope. Straight up, boss. Pardon the expression." Tyler grinned. "He had all these cameras set up, and these two lads were both going at her. One at one end, one at the other. They were all in their fifties, except one of the lads, who must've been mid-twenties at a push."

"Jesus. And he was filming this?" Logan asked.

"Oh, aye. And none of your rubbish. Multi-camera set-up, boss. High end. I mean, I haven't seen the final edit, obviously, but I'd be disappointed if it wasn't some top production quality stuff. He's like a Sex-Tape Spielberg."

"His own *wife*, though," Ben muttered. He had been shaking his head when Logan entered, and was still shaking it now. "That can't be a healthy relationship."

"She certainly seemed to be getting plenty out of it," Tyler replied.

Ben scowled, like this only made it all that much worse. "In the back garden, too. And on stone slabs, you say? Christ. Be murder on the bloody knees, that."

This set Hamza off again. Laughter erupted out of him and almost caused him to roll sideways out of his chair as he tried in vain to contain it.

"What did you do? Did you arrest them?" Logan asked, raising his voice to be heard above Hamza's outburst.

"Not yet, boss," Tyler said. "Confiscated the footage and gave them a warning about indecency and ending up on the register. They tried to say the fence blocked the view from outside, so it wasn't indecent. I pointed out that the next-door-neighbour's house overlooked the garden and had a clear view of what was going on."

"And? What did they have to say to that?"

Tyler smirked. "One of the lads seeing to the wife *was* the next-door-neighbour. He said he didn't have any objections to it."

"Jesus," Logan said. He shook his head and cast disparaging looks at the others, like they were all somehow responsible. "That's the Highlands for you, I suppose. I should probably just be thankful they were husband and wife and no' brother and sister."

He waved a hand. "Give the footage to Uniform. Tell them to follow up on it. Thankfully, it's not our problem. We've enough on our plate without some amateur Hugh Hefner to deal with, too."

"Already passed it on, boss," Tyler replied.

"Good," Logan grunted.

"I hope you washed your hands, afterwards," Caitlyn added, eliciting one final outburst of laughter from Hamza.

The others watched him in silence as he struggled to compose himself, tears streaming down his cheeks. His voice, when he finally spoke, was a high-pitched squeak of delight.

"*Murder on the bloody knees.*"

Logan's phone buzzed in his pocket. To his annoyance, he felt himself tense, dreading finding another *Unknown Caller* message plastered across the screen.

To his relief, there was a name there. To his delight, it was that rarest of things—the name of someone he actually liked.

"I'm just going to take this in the office," he said, navigating between the desks and making for the door at the back of the room.

"Tenner it's the pathologist," Tyler remarked.

Logan shot a look back over his shoulder. "Tenner you'll be back in uniform this time next week if you don't get your finger out and get back to work," he barked, and then he swiped the button that answered the phone and said, "Hello. Superintendent Hoon? Always a pleasure to hear from you."

After flashing a smirk at DC Neish, he entered the office and closed the door. The voice on the other end of the phone sounded confused. It also very much did not sound like Superintendent Hoon.

"Eh, no. It's me," said Shona Maguire, her Irish twang unmistakeable.

"Aye. Yes, sorry. Long story," Logan told her. He walked around to the other side of the desk and took a seat. "How's it going?"

"Yeah. Alright. Got a result in that might be interesting," Shona said. "I was going to email it but thought I'd better phone it through. And besides, nobody else has died under suspicious circumstances, so it was this or play *Angry Birds* again."

"I'm honoured," Logan said. "So, what have you got?"

"Salt."

"Salt?"

"Aye. Lots of salt. On his skin, in his hair, in the wounds. All over him," the pathologist said. "I tried to think of a joke about him being *a-salt-ed,* but I couldn't come up with anything decent. Also, you know, him being murdered and everything..."

"Not really appropriate."

"Exactly. Not really appropriate. But, yes. Salt. Top to toe."

Logan scribbled the word 'SALT' on the notepad on his desk, added a question mark, then drew a couple of circles around it.

"What's that about, then?" he wondered. "You think he was buried in it?"

"I do," Shona confirmed. "I had Geoff Palmer help me look into it, and we reckon it's the type used to grit roads in cold weather. Which would fit with the sand and pieces of grit I found in his lungs."

"I bet Palmer loved that," Logan said.

"What's the matter? Jealous?" Shona teased.

"Jealous? Of that scrotum-faced bawbag? No' likely," Logan countered.

"Right. Well, that's good, because he offered to take me out to dinner."

Logan switched the phone from one hand to the other, buying himself time to formulate a suitably withering reply. At least, that was the theory. In reality, he couldn't come up with anything beyond, "Oh. Right. Well... fair enough. That'll be... Something."

"I said 'no,' obviously," Shona told him. "I might be desperate, but I'm not Sex Pest Palmer desperate. I have some standards. Not many, and they aren't very high, but they're higher than that."

Muscles relaxed that Logan hadn't felt tighten. "Aye. Good. Standards are important," he said.

"They are," Shona said. She fell silent, then, like she was waiting for him to say something. Logan had plenty he wanted to say, he just couldn't work out which order to put it in, or how to begin.

"Right, well," he said, just wanting to fill the silence. "Thanks for the update. I'd best get back."

"Right. Yeah," Shona said, brightly. Too brightly, it could be argued. "No problem. Any time. Happy to... you know. So, uh, bye, then."

"Aye. Bye. And thanks again."

"No bother. Like I say. Any time," Shona replied. "See you."

"Right, then. See you."

There was a knock at the door behind him.

"Boss?"

Logan hurriedly jabbed the 'hang up' button, then thrust the phone into his pocket, wheeling around on his heels in the same breath.

"Tyler. Yes. What is it?" he asked, making no attempt whatsoever to hide his annoyance.

"Sorry, were you in the middle of something?" DC Neish asked. His eyes went to the pocket with the phone in it, and one corner of his mouth curved into a smirk.

"I'm always in the middle of something, son. Now, unless you want my foot to be in the middle of your arse, what is it you want?"

"It's probably nothing, boss," Tyler said, sidling the rest of the way into the office. "It's just, I had a thought about how Brodie Welsh was buried."

Logan made a 'hurry up' gesture with one hand. "And?"

"Well, I was thinking, what if someone moved him because they cared for him? Like, even after they die, we want to know the people we care about are alright, don't we? I mean, not alright, obviously, but... alright. Like, we bring flowers. We spend a fortune on nice coffins, headstones, whatever. We want what's best for them."

"I don't follow," Logan said.

"I just mean, maybe whoever moved him was someone close to him. Someone who loved him, even. Maybe they wanted him found so he could be buried somewhere properly. Not guilt, exactly, just... I don't know. Respect, or whatever."

"That suggests who? Hannah Randall?"

Tyler shrugged. "Maybe. I don't know. Just an idea."

It was an idea, alright. He'd give the boy that much. Logan tried slotting it into the bigger picture, but couldn't find a way to make it fit. Hannah Randall might arguably have had motive, but she didn't have the means to kill him. Not on her own, at least.

Whoever had killed Brodie knew about the drug dealing and how he brought the stuff into the country. They were looking for it inside him, which meant it was almost certainly the same people who'd come looking for it at the house later.

Which meant there was really only one viable suspect.

Or, to be more precise, one family of them.

CHAPTER TWENTY-NINE

The other two members of the Gillespie clan were no more attractive than their younger brother. Like Sandy, they were ugly inside as well as out, and the family resemblance was evident in their matching sneers.

DS McQuarrie motioned to them both in turn, their grainy, blown-up photos pinned to the Big Board for the rest of the team to see.

"Maureen Gillespie. Age forty-seven. De facto matriarch of the Gillespie family, on account of their actual mother refusing to have anything to do with any of them," Caitlyn said, referring to her notes for the key points. "Been in and out of prison over the years, mostly minor offences. She once bit the ear off a constable who was two weeks into the job, and then swallowed it in front of him."

"Christ. And she looks like such an angel, too," Ben remarked.

"Hell's Angel, maybe," Hamza said.

"She did three years for that," Caitlyn continued. "Kept out of trouble ever since."

"Or no' been caught, anyway," Logan suggested.

"Aye. Not for want of trying, I'm sure," Caitlyn said. She indicated the other mugshot. It showed a man whose age was almost impossible to determine, thanks to the mess of homemade tattoos etched all over his face. "This is her brother, Thomas. Known locally as 'Tam the Bam,' which should give you a rough idea of the type of guy we're dealing with."

"A poet?" Tyler guessed.

"Aye, we wish," Caitlyn said.

"Jesus, look at the state of that coupon. He looks like my old desk from school," Logan said. "Scribble, 'Mr Fife is a prick,' on his cheek, and he'd be a dead ringer. I bet if you turn him over, the back of his head is all dried chewing gum and bogies."

"I'd say you shouldn't judge a book by its cover, but in this case, you can go right ahead," Caitlyn told the team. "Worst of a bad bunch by quite some margin. Convictions for robbery, GBH, sexual assault, and a dozen other crimes and misdemeanours. You name it, he's done it. The upshot of which is, he's currently doing a nine-stretch in Peterhead."

"Almost restores your faith in the justice system, doesn't it?" said Ben.

"My gran lives in Peterheid," Hamza announced. He glanced around at the largely disinterested looks this drew from the others. "Aye, no' the prison, like. Just the town."

"Great anecdote there, mate," Tyler remarked, slow-clapping. "Gripping stuff."

Hamza scowled at his fellow DC, then cleared his throat and smiled apologetically at DS McQuarrie. "Sorry, Sarge. Go on."

"Looking at the case CID is building, Maureen and Sandy Gillespie have been bringing cannabis, cocaine, and heroin into the country from a variety of suppliers, via a range of different routes. They've then been offloading it to contacts across the UK. Very hands-off, they don't seem to be involved in anything close to street level."

"They should be street level, though," Ben observed. "They *belong* at street level. How've they managed to get so high up the chain? Who's funded that?"

"Nobody seems to know, sir," Caitlyn replied. "They've got the cash to play with the big boys from somewhere, though, and now they're up there with the worst of them, if CID's investigation is right."

"Any reason to think it isn't?" Logan asked.

Caitlyn shook her head. "Solid enough police work, from what I can tell, sir."

"Anything in there about Brodie Welsh?" Tyler asked.

"A couple of references," Logan said, answering on the detective sergeant's behalf. "Nothing major. The Gillespies were the focus. He's included in the report as a potential accomplice, but he makes a couple of cameo appearances. Nothing else."

"There's a suggestion CID was going to try putting some pressure on him, sir," Caitlyn said. "Maybe bring him in and see if he would give them anything."

Logan's eyes narrowed. "Aye?"

It made sense, of course. It's what he would've done in the same situation. If the Gillespies had got wind of that, all the more reason to kill him. But how would they have gotten wind of it, if Jinkies was keeping the lid shut tight?

Clapping his hands on his thighs, Logan stood. "Right, my turn," he said, replacing Caitlyn at the board. "As you know, I was interviewing Hannah Randall earlier, and she told me she believes Brodie was dealing, or involved in the drugs trade in some way, at least.

"From what we can figure out, he was trying to cover his arse by funnelling cash through a Central American online payment website, which allowed him to make transfers into his and Hannah's joint account, posing as an offshore company, Oswatt."

"Which doesn't exist," DS McQuarrie added.

"Stupid move, that," Hamza said. "Why not just use the name of an actual company? Why make one up?"

"Christ knows," Logan replied. "Less hassle, maybe? No danger of her phoning them up, or meeting someone else who worked for the company and asking questions. I don't know. I'm sure he had his reasons. The point is, he was taking cash payments—presumably from the Gillespies—sending it via Western Union to this payment provider, and then returning it to himself as a wire transfer."

"It's almost clever," said Ben. "Were it not so bloody stupid."

"Aye. We're not getting much back from the payment provider or his own bank, but he left enough of a trail that we can pretty much figure it out."

"What about the home invasion, boss?" Tyler asked. "Did she give you any more on that?"

"Yes and no," Logan said. "She couldn't say that the guy who attacked her was Sandy Gillespie."

"Couldn't, or wouldn't?" Ben asked.

"That's the big question. There was definitely a reaction to his name—she's scared of him—but all she could give us on the attacker was that he sounded local. I asked her what they were really there for, told her we knew they weren't out to rob the place."

"And?" asked Ben.

"And that's when her dad jumped in and said she'd had enough. We want to interview her again, she's going to have a brief with her," Logan said. He shrugged in begrudged acceptance. "Can't blame them, I suppose. I'd do the same in their shoes."

After that, Logan told them about the salt on Brodie's body, and the possibility that it had been buried in a pile of road grit somewhere. Hamza made a note to find out where the council stored its winter supplies of the stuff.

Tyler's investigation into the various Robert Smiths had drawn a blank. If any of them had called in to report someone missing out on the hills, they were all denying it now. No alarm bells had rung while speaking to any of them—or none that didn't involve homemade pornography, at least—and the only conclusion he could come to was that the name had been as fake as the number.

"Which either makes it one hell of a coincidence, or whoever made the call wanted the body found," Logan said. "And I don't believe in coincidences."

"Assuming that's the case, and assuming it was the Gillespies that killed him," said Hamza. "Why would they want him found?"

"If we can figure that bit out, we've got the bastards," Logan said. "Gillespies or otherwise. We still don't know if it was the killer who moved the body, or someone else with their own motive. Either way, it's the key to putting this thing to bed, so I want everyone working on it."

He clicked his fingers and pointed to DC Neish.

"Have you listened to the nine-nine-nine recording yet?"

Tyler nodded. "Aye, sir. English accent, but put on, I think. Not a voice I recognise."

"Email it over and I'll have a listen later," Logan instructed. "In fact, email it round to everyone. CID, too. See if they recognise it. Maybe we can get a name."

"Maybe, sir, aye," said Tyler, although he sounded doubtful. "I'll get it sent out. Jinkies, too?"

"Aye, Jinkies, too," said Logan, then: "Wait." His eyes darted from side to side. His lips moved silently as if working on some difficult mental maths. "Aye. Bugger it. Send it to him, too. Mark it urgent. I'll have a listen, then go talk to him about it myself."

"I'm assuming you'll be wanting to talk to the Gillespies?" said Ben. "You running that by Jinkies first?"

"Away and shite," Logan said. "He might think he's the big I-Am, but we know different. But yes, in answer to your question, I think it's high time we had a more in-depth chat with the Gillespie clan."

"What about the CID investigation, boss?" Tyler asked.

"We'll just have to take our chances. This takes priority," Logan said. He jabbed a thumb at the mugshots. "Anyone got a preference?"

"Bagsy no' the ear biter," said Hamza.

"Fine. Caitlyn, you and Hamza go bring Sandy back in. Tyler, you're with me."

"Hold on, we're not going for the biter, are we, boss?"

"Afraid so," Logan told him. "If it's any consolation, I've always hated your ears, anyway. More than the rest of you, I mean."

He picked up his coat from where it had been abandoned across a desk, and gave Ben a nod that the older man understood only too well.

"I suppose I'll smooth this all over with CID, then, will I?" DI Forde asked.

"Aye, that's an idea," said Logan, in a way that suggested the thought had not even occurred to him. "You do that, then. Thanks."

Ben rolled his eyes. "Any time," he said, then he stood with a *creak* and watched as the rest of the team piled on out through the door.

CID was not going to like this. They weren't going to like it one little bit.

CHAPTER THIRTY

FULTON RANDALL INDICATED LEFT AT THE ROUNDABOUT BY THE POLICE station, waited for a couple of cars to pass, then pulled away with a heavy foot that loudly revved the engine and kangarooed the car into a series of brief lurching jumps.

"Shit. Sorry," he said.

It was all he said, in fact, until they were passing the leisure centre a mile or so up the road, and had left the station and its interview room far behind.

"So."

It wasn't a question, exactly. It wasn't much of anything. It was an invitation, he supposed, to a conversation he wasn't sure how to have.

In the passenger seat beside him, Hannah continued to stare ahead through the front windscreen. A smir of rain was falling, and the car's automatic wipers flicked lazily across the glass, eliciting a screech from the too-dry rubber.

"Anything you'd like to tell me, Hannah?" Fulton asked. Probing, but gentle. Like a tongue carefully testing a hole in a tooth, braced for the very real possibility of pain.

"No. Nothing."

Fulton tore his eyes off the road ahead and shot her a sideways look. "What? After everything in there? There's nothing you want to—"

"Dad!"

He faced front again and jammed a foot down on the brake, bringing the car to a stop just a few inches from the one in front. A couple of vehicles ahead, an elderly couple crossed at the traffic lights outside the hospital.

"After all that. Brodie. *Drugs*. There's nothing you want to say?"

"I've said everything, haven't I?" Hannah snapped. She crossed her arms and squeezed herself in against the passenger door, as if trying to put as much distance between herself and the conversation as possible. "You heard me say everything."

"Oh, I heard. I heard," Fulton said. He crunched down into first gear as the lights changed, then pulled away when the traffic started moving. "I just can't believe I'm only hearing now. I mean, what were you thinking? He was dealing drugs, and *you knew*? Carrie in the house, he's dealing drugs, and you knew? I mean, Jesus Christ. What were you thinking?"

She glanced at him for the first time since getting in the car. "Just leave it, Dad, alright?"

"No! Not alright. You were living with a drug dealer!" His hands tightened on the wheel. His jaw clenched as his back teeth ground together. "And he hit you."

There was no reply from the passenger seat. Fulton took the bypass turnoff, heading south out of Fort William.

This wasn't how he'd envisioned this conversation. He wanted to stop the car, to look at her, to put his arms around her, if she'd let him. Instead, he slowed as he approached yet another roundabout, and then accelerated smoothly across it.

"Talk to me, Hannah," he pleaded. "He hit you, didn't he?"

"Jesus, Dad."

"Just say it, sweetheart. You can tell me."

Hannah turned her head sharply and stared out of the side window, watching all the big B&Bs and hotels of the Golden Mile go blurring by. She flinched in surprise when her dad's hand patted her on the leg.

"It's fine. You don't have to tell me if you don't want to. Sorry, I shouldn't have pressed you," Fulton told her. He gave the leg a squeeze, then returned both hands to the wheel. "It's just... You're my wee girl, you know? I know you think you're all grown up—and you are—but you're still my wee girl. I worry. We both do. Me and your mum."

Hannah said nothing until the last of the guesthouses had been replaced by trees and hillside.

"It only happened twice," she said, not turning.

The leather of Fulton's steering wheel creaked beneath his grip.

"It was my fault."

"Don't you say that. Don't you ever say that!" Fulton managed to grunt. She still hadn't looked round, and so didn't see him drawing a sleeve across his eyes to wipe away the tears that had sprung out of nowhere.

He cleared his throat. Once. Twice. Bringing his voice under control.

"What happened?"

Hannah watched the world whizz by, her breath fogging the rain-flecked glass. "Doesn't matter now," she said. "He's gone."

"I just wish you'd told me. I wish you'd said something sooner." Fulton exhaled, a deliberate attempt to ease some of the tension he could feel building across his chest and shoulders. "At least it's out in the open now. No more secrets, eh?"

There was a squeak as Hannah wiped her breath-cloud off the window. "Yeah," she said. Her eyes met those of her reflection. "No more secrets."

CHAPTER THIRTY-ONE

Caitlyn's fingertips tapped on the steering wheel as she waited for the stream of oncoming traffic to pass so she could make the turn.

The tapping was not particularly unusual. Hamza had seen it often enough. It was a recurring tic of hers, usually appearing when she was growing impatient. Which was often.

Today, though, it was different. It wasn't the usual tap-tap-tap of irritation. There was a beat to it. A tune, almost.

He almost said something when the voice in his ear spoke again. Leaning forward in the passenger seat, he pressed his notebook against the dash and started writing, just as Caitlyn took the turn.

"Shit," he muttered, as the pen drew a line straight across the page.

"Sorry!" Caitlyn said. He glanced at her and caught her smiling in a way that made him think she'd done it on purpose.

"No, not you. Sorry," Hamza said into the phone. "Go on."

He listened, heart slowly sinking, as the Highland Council employee on the other end reeled off the answer to the question Hamza had posed earlier.

"Right. And there's no way that...? No. No, gotcha. Thanks for getting back to me. You, too. Thanks."

He stabbed a finger against the screen and muttered a couple of the milder curses below his breath.

"Good news, then?"

Hamza shot the DS a suspicious look.

"What?" she asked, raising an eyebrow.

"What's wrong with you?" Hamza asked.

Caitlyn took her eyes off the winding road ahead for a moment. "Eh? Nothing." She nodded at the phone in his hand. "What did they say?"

Hamza threw the phone a dirty look like it was somehow responsible for the information he'd been given.

"Council grit storage is covered by CCTV. People kept nicking it, so they beefed up security a few years back. Every depot has full camera coverage, highly visible, signs everywhere. They're going to go through the footage, but—"

"Nobody's going to be stupid enough to stuff a body there," Caitlyn concluded.

"Exactly," Hamza said. He sighed. "I suppose I should phone the boss and let him know."

"Yeah. You'd better."

Hamza regarded the phone for a while, then tapped an icon. "I'll text him."

The sound of a clucking chicken came from the seat beside him. The bottom half of his face broke into a smile, while the top half frowned deeply.

"What is up with you lately?" he asked.

"What? Nothing," Caitlyn said.

"You're acting weird. You're not dying, are you? Because, I can't deal with that."

"Aw, thanks," Caitlyn said.

"The conversation, I mean." He gestured to the door handle. "I mean it, if you tell me you've got six months to live or something, I'll jump out."

Caitlyn laughed. Even this was out of the ordinary.

It wasn't that she was usually miserable, exactly, she was just a little... stiff. Less inclined to join in with joking as the rest of them, maybe. Hamza had always put it down to her being fiercely ambitious. Tyler reckoned she had a poker up her arse. All things considered, Hamza thought his instinct was probably more accurate.

Recently, though, she'd seemed different. Not less driven, exactly, but less fierce in the way she went about it, maybe. Lighter.

Happier, dare he say?

"I'm not dying. I promise," she told him. "It's nothing. Honest."

She shuffled more upright in her seat, adjusted her rearview mirror, then indicated the car's satnav. "Now, stick in Gillespie's address, will you? We'll be arriving in Kinloch shortly."

"Christ. Aye. This is more like it."

Tyler sat forward in the passenger seat of the Volvo, eyes wide as he watched the scenery go rolling by.

Half of the sky had been smeared with blobs of wispy, grey cloud that clung to the tops of the hills and mountains rising steeply on the left. On the right, a bright, clear blue was fighting back, driving the gloom away and revealing a landscape that looked straight out of *Braveheart*.

During the drive south, they'd passed a couple of waterfalls, an impressive gorge, and the former home of disgraced TV and radio personality, Jimmy Savile. Sure enough, it had 'paedo' scrawled all over its whitewashed stone exterior, in a variety of creative spellings.

'Peedo' had been Tyler's favourite, and had started him on a monologue in which he imagined a world where the principal ingredient of the modelling putty, 'Playdo,' was urine. This particular flight of fancy went on for almost a full minute before Logan had politely instructed him to, "Shut the fuck up."

"Aye, no' bad, is it?" the DCI said, lifting his eyes from the road for a moment and briefly taking in their surroundings.

"I always wondered why people came up here on holiday," Tyler said. "I mean, no offence to the place, but it's not exactly jumping, is it?"

"People don't come here for 'jumping,'" Logan pointed out. "They don't want 'jumping,' they want..." He motioned to the sprawling landscape that stretched out ahead of them. "...that."

"Aye. That's what I'm saying, boss. I get it now," the DC said. "I understand. I've learned something today."

"First time for everything," Logan said. It was such an open goal that he almost felt guilty for taking the shot, but he knew Ben would never have forgiven him if he'd passed it up.

The car crested a little peak in the road, then dipped down suddenly on the other side. Tyler wriggled uncomfortably and took a steadying breath.

"Need to do something with the roads, though." He looked ahead, then turned in his seat and glanced back at the road already travelled. "I think Sinead's parents were killed round here somewhere."

"Bit further up, I think," Logan said. "Rannoch Moor sort of area."

Tyler blinked, gazed blankly at the landscape, then nodded as if he knew where that was. "Right. Yeah. Down this way, I meant." He blew out his cheeks. "Can't imagine it. Can you?"

Logan gave a single shake of his head. No. He could not.

"How is she? After everything."

"She's... aye. Doing alright. Itching to get back on the job, though."

"That's a good sign," Logan said. He'd seen too many good officers scared off by one bad experience. Not that he blamed any of them. He envied the buggers, if anything.

Logan side-eyed Tyler, who was being uncharacteristically reserved.

"You don't think so?"

"No. I mean, yeah. I do. I think it's great," the DC said. "It's just, is it not a bit soon? After what happened."

"She's obviously made of stern stuff," Logan said. They caught up with a Corsa pootling along the road, and he eased the Volvo past it without slowing. "If she thinks she's ready, then she's ready."

"Maybe. You're probably right," Tyler said. "I'm just worried, I suppose, boss. Can't help but think it's a bit soon for her to be getting back into uniform."

"Maybe she shouldn't, then," Logan said.

Tyler blinked in surprise. "Oh. What? You agree with me? Magic. Maybe you can help convince her?"

"No, I can't. That's not what I'm saying," Logan replied. "If the lassie thinks she's ready, who the hell are we to say otherwise? I'm just saying, maybe she shouldn't be back in uniform."

"I don't..." Tyler began, and then the penny dropped. "Oh. Right. Gotcha."

He went back to looking out at the scenery, giving the idea some thought.

After a while, his eyes went to the satnav, and the little triangle that ploughed smoothly through a flat, unremarkable patch of green that didn't even bother trying to do the place justice.

"Not long now," Logan said.

"She's proper arse end of nowhere, isn't she?" Tyler observed. "Be annoying if she's not in, after all this."

He looked out at the scenery again. "Still, nice to get out of the office, eh?"

Logan checked his mirrors, then turned off the main road. A long, narrow dirt track stretched out ahead of them, all potholes and puddles. The Volvo lurched violently on its suspension as Logan guided it up the winding incline.

"Actually," Tyler swallowed, one hand slipping onto his stomach, the other gripping the handle of the door. "Is it too late to take that back?"

"Mummy!"

Hannah bent and scooped up Carrie as she came running across the living room, her bare feet pit-patting on the laminate flooring.

"Oh, look! Dinner!" Hannah cried, dipping the girl backwards until her head was pointing to the floor and giggles came tumbling out of her.

"No! I'm not dinner!"

"No? You *smell* like dinner!" Hannah said, adopting a gruff voice. She snuffled furiously around Carrie's neck, ratcheting her laughter up until it was a series of high-pitched squeals of delight. Hannah licked her lips and smacked them together. "Do you *taste* like dinner, I wonder?"

"Nooooo!"

"For God's sake, don't keep me in suspense!"

Hannah stopped trying to eat her daughter, and instead looked over to her mother. Sandra stood in the kitchen doorway, a dish towel twisting over and over in her grip. "What did they say?"

Fulton looked very deliberately at Carrie, then back at his wife. "Probably not the time."

Sandra tutted. "Right, well, you come through here and tell me, then," she ordered, retreating into the kitchen.

Fulton locked eyes with his daughter and they shared something that was in spitting distance of being a smile.

"Alright, spud?" he said, giving Carrie a tickle on the way past. His touch caught her by surprise and she jumped in her mum's arms, then exploded into laughter.

After following his wife into the kitchen, Fulton closed the door, muting the sounds of merriment from the living room.

Sandra stood with her back to the draining board, vigorously drying a plate. Behind her, the window looked out onto the steep slope that led from the house down to the main road.

The snow would start making its way down from the higher peaks soon, turning the track into the usual winter ordeal.

Still, it was worth it for the view.

"Well?" Sandra demanded. "What did they say? What was it about? Do they know who killed Brodie?"

Fulton exhaled. "No. I mean... I don't know. Maybe," he said. Crossing to her, he gently removed the plate from her hands and set it down on the worktop. "There's a few things we need to talk about. Things that came up."

Sandra said nothing. Not vocally, anyway. Her eyes asked a hundred questions she wasn't sure she wanted to know the answer to.

"Brodie wasn't who we thought he was," Fulton told her. "He was involved in drugs."

"Drugs? What do you mean *drugs*?"

"I don't know. He was dealing. Or importing them, maybe. Bringing them into the country. That's what the trips abroad were about."

"He was working abroad. He was at work. For the oil people."

Fulton gave a little shake of his head. "It was a cover story. There was no oil company."

Sandra's back bumped against the edge of the worktop as she took a stumbled step backwards.

"Did she know? Did Hannah know?"

Fulton winced. "Aye. No. I mean... She suspected, aye," he said. He took a breath, bracing himself for his own reaction as much as his wife's. "He got... Brodie. He got violent. With Hannah."

The change to Sandra's face brought tears whooshing to Fulton's own eyes.

She shrank before him, one hand fumbling blindly for the edge of the worktop like it was the only thing in the world that could keep her on her feet.

He lunged for her, arms surrounding her, pulling her in close. She pressed her hands against his chest, like she might be about to push him away, but then let them both fall to her sides and just leaned there against him, her legs grateful for the support.

"When?" she whispered.

"It doesn't matter," Fulton told her. He sniffed and blinked back his tears, staring out of the window at the neat garden, and the wilderness beyond its boundaries. "She's OK now. That's the main thing."

Sandra tried not to ask the question. She didn't want to ask it, didn't want to know the answer, didn't want to think about what that answer might mean.

She asked it, anyway.

"Did she kill him?"

Fulton stepped back and stared down at his wife in shock. She looked older than she'd looked just a moment before, as if just saying those words out loud had taken years off her life.

"What? No. No, of course she didn't," he whispered. "Don't be so ridiculous!"

This time, she threw herself at him, her arms tightening around him as she sobbed against his chest.

He smoothed her hair and held her close, as his eyes travelled to the kitchen door. The giggling was louder than ever now. Happy and carefree.

"Of course, she didn't," he muttered.

Don't be so ridiculous.

CHAPTER THIRTY-TWO

The track up to Maureen Gillespie's house was the longest mile of Tyler's life.

By the time they reached the end of it, his guts were churning, his arse was aching, and he had half a mind to arrest the woman just for the state of her driveway. *Nauseating a Police Officer. Five years, minimum term.*

It wasn't even like the place was worth the effort. From a distance, it had looked like a quaint cottage set on the hillside. Up close, it could more accurately be described as a shack. Tyler himself had less generously proclaimed it, 'a heap of shit,' on the final stretch of the ascent. Now that they had arrived at it, he'd seen nothing that might change his mind.

He flexed his fingers, chasing away the numbness that had been brought on by his vice-like grip on the door handle during the drive up, then stepped out into a pool of dirty water that covered his foot all the way up to the ankle.

"Great," he muttered. "We're in a puddle, boss."

"Fine my side," said Logan, stepping down from the car onto the pock-marked dirt track.

The house was through a narrow gate and up a short path. It was made of wood that had once been painted white, but which had been stripped almost naked by years of wind and rain. The same weather conditions were likely responsible for the building's distinctive slouch, and the way its roof sagged in the middle.

A brick chimney rose up from the aged slate roof. It looked old and tired, like it had been standing for decades before the rest of the house was built around it. There was no smoke rising from it, although given the condition of the brickwork, that was probably for the best.

Tyler sploshed through the puddle, catching up with Logan as he strode through the open gate and onto a path that was little more than a track worn through overgrown grass.

"I thought it looked rough from down the hill," he said. "But it's worse up close and personal, isn't it?"

There was no need for a response. The question was obviously rhetorical, as there was no way that anyone in their right mind could argue against Tyler's point. It wasn't just that the house was a state, it was the area around it, too.

Bits of old scaffolding and broken guttering lay abandoned in the long grass. A couple of fence panels were rotting on the ground, bugs swarming through the damp and decay.

Twin wheelie bins—one blue, one green—were the most modern thing in the house's vicinity. Both had overflowed with beer cans and black bags, vomiting the contents into the tangle of weeds and bracken that surrounded them.

"Handy she's all the way out here," Tyler remarked. "Imagine some poor bugger having to live next to all this."

"Aye, I doubt she'd win herself any neighbour of the year awards," Logan agreed. He pointed around the side of the house. "Go keep an eye on the back door, will you? I can't imagine she'll leg it, but just in case."

"You be alright on your own, boss?" Tyler asked, which earned him a withering look from the DCI. "Right. Aye. Fair enough. I'll go watch the back."

Logan waited until Tyler had disappeared around the side of the house before he made his approach. The house looked empty, felt cold and unwelcoming, and he got the feeling that this would turn out to be the wasted journey DC Neish had joked about.

His phone chirped in his pocket as a message was received. That made sense. If Maureen was running a drug empire from out here, she'd need network access. The house must be in one of the rare phone signal oases that popped up along the route through the glen.

Logan checked the message as he walked the last few feet to the house. Hamza. Dead end with the council. Disappointing, but it had been a stretch, so not exactly a shocker of a result.

As he started to tap out a reply, he saw the signal bars drop away to zero again.

"Some bloody oasis," he muttered, then he returned the phone to his pocket as he arrived at the front door and rapped his knuckles on the peeling wood. It wasn't the full-on Polis knock. Not yet. No point spooking her, if he could avoid it.

He waited. A mile down the track, he heard the distant rumble of a truck heading south along the A82. From somewhere closer, he heard the calling of birds and the soft swish of the bracken blowing in the breeze.

From within the house, he heard nothing.

He tried again, louder this time. The side of the fist, as opposed to the knuckles. "Maureen? We know you're in there. We'd like a word."

No movement. No answer.

No great surprise.

"DC Neish. Any sign?" he called. His voice sounded too loud in the comparative silence of his surroundings.

"Nothing here, boss," came the reply.

Hunkering down, Logan opened the letterbox and peered through into the bare bones of a hallway. Flies looped in the air down by the door at the far end. Late in the year for them, unless conditions in the house were especially ripe.

The curtains were drawn across the windows, blocking Logan's view of inside. There was a slight gap where one set met in what he guessed was the living room, but it was too narrow, the room beyond it too dark, for him to be able to see anything.

"Reckon she's not home," announced Tyler, appearing around the corner. "Back door's locked. I was able to see into the kitchen—I wish I wasn't, but I was. No sign of anyone in there, just a big pile of dirty dishes. I tell you, boss, I don't know if she's a murderer, but she's definitely a clarty bastard."

Logan stepped back and gave the house another once-over. There was no denying that it felt empty. Abandoned, even. If it hadn't been for the build-up of rubbish in the bins, he'd have sworn nobody had lived here in months.

And yet, something about the place was nagging at him. Some detail he'd subconsciously picked up on was telling him not to leave. Not yet.

It was Tyler who spotted it.

"There's a hole in the window, boss."

Logan followed the DC's outstretched finger until he saw it. A round hole in the bottom corner of the glass, fracture lines splintering off from it like the legs of a squashed spider.

There were fragments of glass on the sill below the hole, outside the window.

"Shot came from inside," Logan muttered.

"Shot?" Tyler's head tick-tocked between the DCI and the hole. "What, like with a gun?"

"Aye. That's a bullet hole," Logan told him.

Tyler practically ducked. "Shite!" he ejected in a worried whisper. "So, someone might be in there? Armed?"

"Have to be helluva timing on our part," Logan said. He pushed down the front door handle. It was unlocked and opened inwards with a nudge.

The smell that rolled out went some way to confirming Logan's suspicions, but he had to see it. He had to know.

"Christ, it stinks," Tyler wheezed, covering his mouth.

"Stay out there," Logan instructed. "Keep your eyes open."

Tyler retreated gratefully, blew the last of his breath out through his nose to clear the stench away, then gulped down some fresh air.

Inside, Logan wrestled a hand into a rubber glove as he *clumped* along the bare wooden floor of the hallway. He heard the hum of the flies from inside the room, felt the stink of what was to come forcing its way through his airways and down his throat.

He creaked the living room door open, and there she was, spread out across the couch.

Maureen Gillespie.

Or, what was left of her.

CHAPTER THIRTY-THREE

Hamza tapped his phone screen to wake it, then swiped to the messages.

"Anything back from the Chief?" Caitlyn asked him, flicking the handbrake switch and turning off the car's engine.

"Nothing, no," Hamza said. "Signal's pretty weak, though. He might not have got it. Not a big deal, though. Not exactly breaking news."

"No," Caitlyn agreed. She peered ahead at a house just along from where she'd parked the car. "That one, is it?"

Hamza consulted his notebook, glanced at the numbers on the two closer houses, then nodded. "Aye. That's it."

He unclipped his seatbelt. "Fingers crossed he's in."

"Hopefully," Caitlyn said, unfastening her own belt.

Hamza had just started to open his door when she spoke again.

"I've met someone," she said. The words came out of her in a sudden rush, like she could no longer hold them back. She blushed when Hamza turned to face her, and tried with mixed results to wipe the smile off her face. "Sorry. That's not appropriate. Forget I said—"

"Like *met someone* met someone?" Hamza said.

Caitlyn's smile rallied. She nodded. The movement was quick and mouselike, and not like her at all. Hamza wholeheartedly approved.

He closed the passenger door. "That's great news, Sarge! Congratulations. I knew there was something different."

"You'll make a fine detective one day," Caitlyn told him. She tilted a hand from side to side and scrunched up her nose. "Or, well, average."

"I can but dream," Hamza said. "Who is he? Is he on the job?"

Caitlyn's smile took a bit of a dunt. "No. They're... I mean... *She*. Not he."

"Oh," said Hamza. He felt his eyes start to widen and fought to keep them regular sized. "Oh! Right. I... Gotcha. I didn't think you were... I mean, I didn't think you weren't, either, I just... Wow."

He punched her playfully on the arm, and both of them immediately hoped the other would never mention those last few seconds ever again.

"Good for you, Sarge," Hamza said. "I'm really... That's great."

"Thanks. And sorry. Shouldn't have said anything. Not very professional."

"Come on, seriously? I told you about my fungal nail infection," Hamza reminded her.

"In some detail, yes, fair point," Caitlyn said. "Well, thanks. I just wanted to tell someone. It's early days, but... Yeah."

"So, is she on the force?"

"No. God, no."

Hamza nodded his understanding. Being polis was one thing. Being in a relationship with one? He couldn't imagine much worse.

"And she's alright with you doing it?" he asked.

Caitlyn nodded. "Aye. She's fine with it."

"Well, give it time," Hamza said, which drew a staccato laugh from the DS.

"Aye, that's true."

She opened her door and stepped out onto the pavement.

"Well, come on then," she urged. "Let's get a shifty on. He's not going to arrest himself!"

Hamza got out of the car and joined her beside it. "Happy you is weird, Sarge," he said. "Good weird, though," he hastily added. "Just... it's going to take some getting used to."

Caitlyn screwed up her face. "New relationship. The novelty will wear off soon enough. I wouldn't bother getting too used to it."

Sandy Gillespie's house was in darkness when they opened the gate and headed up the path. It was barely after three, but the nights were drawing in, and several of the surrounding houses had some lights on.

"Reckon he's home?" Hamza asked.

"Fingers crossed," said Caitlyn, taking the lead. She hammered out a rhythmic knock on the door, then listened.

"I can't hear anything," Hamza remarked, then the barking of a dog from somewhere inside the house almost made him jump out of his skin.

"Well, we know the dog's home, at least," Caitlyn said. "Think we can convince it to open the door?"

She glanced at the upstairs windows. The curtains were open, but the rooms beyond the glass were in darkness.

Knocking again, she gestured to one of the downstairs windows. "Take a look."

Hamza picked his way across the gravel surface of the garden, carefully avoiding the half dozen dauds of dog shit scattered like landmines across it.

Cupping his hands, he peered into what turned out to be the living room. It was messy, but otherwise pretty unremarkable. An Xbox lay on the floor, wires trailing across the stained carpet to a large flatscreen TV. 4K, Hamza reckoned. Nice bit of kit.

He was about to report the place empty when he caught a glimpse of movement over by the door, there one moment, gone the next. A shadow, cast by someone out in the hall. Too big to be a dog.

"He's in there," Hamza whispered.

Caitlyn stepped closer to the door, raised a fist and hammered against the wood. *Thud-thud-thud.*

"Mr Gillespie? Mr Gillespie, open the door, it's the—"

Bang.

Around halfway down the door, a foot-wide section of the wood exploded outwards. The air behind Caitlyn became a fine mist of red. She made a sound —a gulp, a gasp—as she was propelled backwards off her feet.

A switch flicked somewhere, grinding the world into agonising slow motion.

Hamza watched helplessly as Caitlyn sprawled through the air. He followed her flight, his own feet rooted to the ground, as she tumbled back and hit the path with a damp *thack.*

He stared at the mess of raw flesh that was her stomach. Gawped as she coughed and choked, blood hiccupping up over her chin and running in rivulets from both sides of her mouth.

Her eyes met his. Wide. Desperate. Pleading. The world returned to full speed—faster, even—and he moved, dropping to his haunches and hauling her away from the door.

Blood poured from her, *fountained* from her. Hamza felt it, wet and warm, as it cascaded over his hands.

"Shit, shit, shit. Sarge. Caitlyn. Fuck!"

She gagged. Spluttered. Convulsed there in his arms.

"No, no, no, no!"

He heard movement—the creak of a door slowly opening—and threw himself over her, shielding her body with his, bracing himself for whatever came next.

"What happened? What's going on?"

The voice had come from elsewhere. Not Gillespie's house. Somewhere behind him.

A man in a dirty vest stood framed in the doorway of a neighbouring house, his dinner balanced on a plate in one hand. He was mid-chew when he saw the woman on the ground, and almost choked as he swallowed it down.

"Fucking hell."

"Ambulance! Call an ambulance!" Hamza bellowed. Caitlyn trembled beneath him, her teeth chattering together, her blood pooling between the gaps in the gravel. "Officer down!"

CHAPTER THIRTY-FOUR

"Anything, boss?"

Logan angled his phone down so he could see the screen. The signal he'd picked up earlier hadn't shown face again since, and he didn't want to go traipsing through Maureen Gillespie's house to look for a landline.

She'd been dead for a few hours, by Logan's reckoning. Five or six, maybe. No more. Her death had been swift, judging by the way in which her brains had exploded from the back of her head.

What had come after death would have been far more time-consuming.

Logan squinted as his screen. "Bugger all. You?"

Tyler took another look at his own phone, rotated a full one-eighty on the spot, then shook his head. "Nah, nothing."

With a tut, Logan angrily stuffed the phone in his coat pocket, as if this would somehow teach the thing a lesson.

"I'll take a drive down the hill and phone it in from there," he said, setting off for the car. "You wait here and guard the scene."

Tyler couldn't hide his disappointment. "Seriously, boss? It's freezing. And, it's not like there's another way up. Nobody's going to get past us without us seeing. As scenes go, it's already pretty guarded."

He had a point, much as Logan hated to admit it.

"Fine. Get in."

"Nice one," Tyler beamed, hurrying after him.

It was only when they were both back in the car and Logan was wrestling it through a tight five-point-turn that Tyler remembered the condition of the track. A track which he'd now have to endure twice more.

"Shite. Actually, maybe I should stay. Just in case," he suggested.

Logan had just ejected a particularly world-weary sigh when the Volvo's speakers announced a call coming through on his mobile. The dash display flashed up the caller's name.

Ben Forde.

"Must've picked up the signal," Tyler remarked, just in case the DCI had been unable to figure that out on his own.

Stopping the car, for fear of losing the signal again, Logan tapped a button on the steering wheel, and the ringing was replaced by a crackle of static.

"Ben?"

Ben Forde's voice was a broken hiss of interference.

"Ben? You're breaking up. Say again."

Tyler's phone *bleeped* in his pocket. He fished it out while Logan tried to decipher another string of garbled pops and hisses from the speakers.

"I'm not getting you, Ben. I'm going to try to..."

"—ello? Ja—"

Tyler's incoming message notification chimed again.

Again.

Again.

"Christ, I'm more popular than I thought," he mumbled, tapping the notification.

The sound from the speakers crackled again, then fell silent. Ben's name disappeared from the screen.

"Bloody thing," Logan muttered, sliding the car into first gear.

"Boss."

Logan turned and saw it on the DC's face. Something had happened. Something terrible.

"What is it?" he asked. "What's happened?"

"It's DS McQuarrie, boss. It's Caitlyn," Tyler croaked. He started to say more, but his breath got stuck somewhere between his lungs and his voice box. He turned the phone instead, letting Logan read the words on the screen.

"Oh, Jesus," the DCI whispered. He jammed his foot down on the accelerator and the Volvo lurched off from a standing start, churning the ground with its back wheels. "Oh, God, no."

By the time they arrived, the circus had descended on the street. Neighbouring houses had been evacuated, and cordon tapes had been set up at either end of the road, half a dozen Uniforms standing guard at each end.

Logan screeched the Volvo to a halt behind a row of police cars and vans, their lights painting the darkening street in overlapping shades of blue.

"Where is she?" he barked, jumping out of the car without bothering to shut off the engine, and startling a uniformed constable.

"Sir?"

"Fuck's sake! DS McQuarrie. Where is she?"

Ben Forde stepped out from the back of one of the vans.

"It's alright, son. I've got it," he said, dismissing the constable with a wave. "I think I saw one of the local journalists poking his nose around. Away and tell him to piss off, will you?"

The Uniform nodded. That, he could handle.

"Yes, sir. On it, sir."

Ben watched the constable go scuttling off in search of anyone with a camera, then turned back to Logan.

"Where is she?" the DCI demanded. "What's the story?"

"Ambulance took her about fifteen minutes ago. I've sent Hamza into the hospital with her. He didn't want to leave her. He's pretty shaken up."

"What the hell happened?"

Ben threw a scowl in the direction of Sandy Gillespie's house, and the gaping hole in its front door.

"Shotgun, we think. Close up from the other side of the door. He must've been standing just inside. Shot her clean through the wood."

Logan sucked air in through his teeth. "Bad?"

Ben nodded. "Bad. Aye."

"But not *bad* bad, though, right?" Tyler asked. "She's going to be alright, isn't she?"

Ben opened his mouth, then shrugged. It wasn't much of a movement, but it seemed to drain him of almost all his strength.

"Jesus Christ," Tyler whispered, running both hands through his hair. "Jesus Christ."

"Is it Gillespie?" Logan asked. "Is he still in there?"

"As far as we know, aye," Ben confirmed. "But he's not talking to anyone, and we daren't send anyone in. Armed Response are on their way. Be here within ninety minutes."

"Ninety fucking minutes," Logan said, spitting the words out as if the ETA was some sort of personal insult. He stared over at the house, fingers flexing in and out, making fists.

"His sister's dead," Tyler told Ben. "Maureen. Up at the house. Someone shot her, then cut her open."

Ben looked unsurprised. Or unbothered, maybe, like it was way down his list of concerns.

"Right. So, whoever was higher up the chain came looking for their missing gear," he deduced. "And she didn't have it."

"Aye. And my bet is that wee bastard in there knows what happened,"

Logan said, stabbing a finger in the direction of the house. "And he thinks that whoever came for Maureen is going to be coming for him, so he holed himself up with a gun and waited for them."

"And Caitlyn went and got caught in the middle of it," Ben said. He squeezed the bridge of his nose between finger and thumb. "Christ Almighty, what a mess."

A movement at the corner of Logan's eye caught his attention. Sergeant Jaffray stood a few feet away, raising his hand like a nervous schoolboy.

"What?" Logan demanded, making him jump. "What is it?"

Jaffray lowered his hand. "Um, just to let you know, he's still not answering," the uniformed sergeant said. "We've got his mobile number, too, but it's switched off."

Logan's glare became too much for him to cope with, and he shifted his attention to DI Forde, instead. "I didn't know if you wanted us to have a go with the megaphone again, sir?"

Ben deferred to Logan with a raising of his eyebrows. "Jack?"

Logan paced back and forth on the pavement, a few steps one direction, then a few steps back.

No. Not paced, exactly. He *prowled*, his gaze fixed on Gillespie's house like a predator on its luckless prey.

"We're sure he's in there?"

"Hamza reckons so," Ben replied. "Nobody saw him come out."

"And ninety minutes for AR?"

Ben nodded. "Aye. Bit less now, but near enough."

"Right. Fuck it," Logan said. He shrugged off his coat and let it fall to the ground at his feet, his eyes never leaving Sandy Gillespie's front door. "Megaphone."

Sergeant Jaffray looked down at the DCI's open hand.

"You deaf, son? What are you waiting for? Get me the damn megaphone!"

"Right, yes. Right," Jaffray blurted, practically jumping out of his skin.

He scurried into the back of the nearest van and returned a few seconds later with a battery-operated loudhailer. Logan took it, hefted it from hand to hand, checked the wrist strap was firmly attached, then nodded his approval.

"Right. Good. This'll do," he said, turning away from the sergeant like he'd suddenly ceased to exist.

"What are you going to say, boss?" Tyler asked.

Logan rolled up one of his shirt sleeves. "Say?" He switched the megaphone to the opposite hand and rolled up the other sleeve. "Who said I'm going to say anything?"

He set off in the direction of the house, then stopped when Ben caught him by the arm. "You should have a vest on, Jack."

Logan looked down at himself, then back at his friend. "Aye. I probably should," he agreed.

Ben puffed out his cheeks, shook his head, then released his grip on the DCI's arm. He, Tyler, and half the Lochaber area force watched as Logan marched across the street, threw open Gillespie's gate and set off up the path.

"What the hell's he doing?" Tyler asked.

Halfway up the path, Logan swung the megaphone by its strap and launched it at the living room window like the hammer of Thor. The street was filled with the sound of breaking glass, which was swiftly followed by a shout of panic from inside the house.

Logan was at the door a second later, inside a half-second after that.

Ben exhaled as he watched the DCI break into a run and go storming up the hallway.

"What he does best, son," he said. He folded his arms and waited for the fireworks. "He's doing what he does best."

CHAPTER THIRTY-FIVE

Sandy Gillespie was sweeping the shotgun across the living room, the weapon shaking in his hands, when the dog started going bananas in the kitchen, and he realised that he'd been played.

He spun, yelping in fright, finger just starting to tighten on the trigger of the shotgun when a man—no, not a man, a *beast*—came barrelling into the room like a force of nature: raw, and violent, and unstoppable.

Gillespie didn't recognise him. His anger disguised him, twisting his features into something monstrous. Rage radiated off him in rolling waves, stumbling Sandy back a pace as he desperately tried to bring the barrel of the gun into the gap between them.

The intruder was big. Bigger, in that moment, than anyone Gillespie had ever seen. Bigger than anyone who'd ever lived, he thought. Not a man. Not even a beast. A giant. A *god*. Fire and fury made flesh.

A bear-sized fist cracked against the side of his head. A wrecking ball. A juggernaut. An express train.

Pain exploded through his skull, filling it up, blinding him. The floor lurched beneath his feet like the deck of a storm-ravaged ship. He grabbed for the gun that was no longer in his hands, grasped for the air that was suddenly swooshing around him. And then he howled as his nose burst open on the carpet, and a broken tooth caught at the back of his throat.

He heard the breathing of the beast, raw air rasping in and out through its snarling maw. He saw the gun lying on the floor, just beyond his reach. One good lunge would do it. One kick of the legs, one swift grab, one single shot, and it would all be over.

The beast spoke then, each word booming out of him like the tolling of some terrible funeral bell.

"I dare you, son. I fucking dare you."

The floorboards whimpered as the beast took a step back, giving Gillespie room to manoeuvre. Giving him a chance.

"Do it," the voice urged. "Go for it. Pick it up."

Gillespie stared at the weapon. So close. Right there.

"*Pick it up*!" The voice was a roar, all rage and spit, and hot, fiery dragon breath.

When Gillespie didn't move, a clawed hand caught him by the back of the neck and dragged him closer to the gun. He hissed and whimpered as his broken nose and chin were burned across the rough carpet.

"There you go. Go on, what are you waiting for? It's right there," the beast told him. Sandy felt himself rise up an inch or two, before he was slammed down again onto his face. The floorboards gave another creak as the beast retreated a couple of paces. "Pick it up. Do it. This is your one and only chance. Now or never, Sandy. Do it!"

Gillespie wheezed, coughed, and spat out the broken tooth. For a moment, he just stared at it as it lay there in a puddle of blood and spit, not quite comprehending what it was, or how it had got there.

The beast growled.

The dog barked.

Sandy Gillespie's legs twitched.

And then, with a banshee yell, he grabbed for the gun.

THE SHOTGUN'S roar reverberated out from inside the house, shaking the remaining windows in their frames. Everyone but Ben Forde ducked for cover, and then they all listened to the sound of furniture breaking, something heavy hitting something hard, and then a desperate, terror-stricken scream that gargled into silence.

"Shit, shit. What do we do?" Tyler hissed, raising his head just enough to peer over the bonnet of Logan's Volvo. Despite the racket, there was no sign of movement from the house. "Do we go in? What do we do?"

Ben shook his head. "We don't go in, no. Relax, son. It's all under control."

DC Neish chewed on a thumbnail, his gaze going from Ben to the house and back again.

"But... the gunshot, boss. He might be in trouble. He could be hurt."

"Aye, well, that'll be his own stupid fault, won't it?" Ben said.

His phone rang, sharp and shrill, making half the officers in earshot jump with fright. He hurriedly checked the screen, and the name on it made his stomach flip itself all the way over.

DC Khaled.

Hamza.

"Like I said, son. Nothing to worry about. It's all under control," Ben reiterated, then he tapped the answer button, pressed the phone to his ear, and braced himself.

It was almost six minutes later when Logan finally emerged, shoving a bloodied and babbling Sandy Gillespie in front of him. Gillespie's legs were barely holding him up, but the threat of the detective at his back forced them to carry him down the path, through the gate, and out onto the street beyond.

He shuffled, zombie-like, off the pavement and onto the road, the spiralling lights of the polis vehicles dazzling him.

All around them, Uniforms watched in silence as Logan steered the bastard towards Ben and Tyler with a well-placed shove to the back.

"Keep walking," the DCI barked, drawing a little whimper and a burst of speed from the man in front. A bubble of blood burst on his lips. He spluttered, choking on the taste of his own broken nose.

A slab of a hand on Gillespie's shoulder jerked him to a stop at the kerb. His eyes went from Ben to Tyler and back again, half-panicked, half-pleading with them for protection. Neither of them made any move to help him. Judging by the look on DC Neish's face, in fact, Gillespie would be safer staying in the hands of the senior officer.

"Arrest this gentleman, will you?" Logan said. He gave Gillespie another shove that sent him tumbling to the pavement at Ben's feet. "And get him out of my sight."

Ben drew in a long, steadying breath. He shot Tyler the briefest of looks, and the DC took a half step forward, putting himself between Logan and Gillespie, blocking the way.

Logan looked between them, studied them, read their bodies and their faces, and understood. He knew, in that moment, what had happened. He knew what the charge was going to be, and wished he could somehow stop the words before they came tumbling out of Ben's mouth.

He couldn't, though. It was too late. The damage was already done.

"Sandy Gillespie," DI Forde intoned, not even looking at the snivelling bastard at his feet. "I am arresting you for the murder of Detective Sergeant Caitlyn McQuarrie."

CHAPTER THIRTY-SIX

A hush hung over Fort William Police Station. Smothering it. Stifling it. It invaded every corner, from the reception where Moira silently sat, to the empty interview rooms.

It pushed down hardest on the Incident Room, focused mostly on the Big Board, where Caitlyn had most recently worked her own particular brand of organisational magic.

Ben and Tyler sat at their desks, staring blankly at nothing in particular, lost in thoughts they were still too numb to think. Logan sat through the back, in his private office, the blinds drawn and door shut tight. He'd been in there since they'd got back.

"Give me a minute," he'd said.

That had been three hours ago.

Somewhere, far off in the building, a phone rang. It echoed along the silent corridors long enough to make Ben tut in irritation, then was silenced. Somebody answered, or someone rang off. Ben didn't care which. It had stopped, and that was the main thing.

"Still can't believe it." Tyler's voice was low and lifeless. Not shocked, or angry, but flat and matter-of-fact. "Still can't believe she's gone."

Ben nodded. He wished he had some words of wisdom to offer. Some comfort for the lad, but he didn't. The reality of it was, it happened. He'd lost other colleagues over the years. Friends. Family, almost. Tyler would, too. That was just the way of it.

You grieved. You processed. You moved on.

Somehow, you moved on.

"That prick been brought in yet?" Tyler asked. This time, his voice wasn't flat, or level, or matter-of-fact. There was anger there, raw and fierce.

"Still at the hospital," Ben replied.

Sandy Gillespie had sustained some injuries during his arrest by Logan. Nothing major. Nothing that couldn't be explained away by a violent tussle over a firearm. A couple of broken fingers, a shattered nose, a cracked rib. He'd heal. He'd recover. Physically, at least.

"Under guard, though?"

"Oh, aye. Uniform were queuing up. He's no' going anywhere. Be tomorrow before we can question him, though." Ben shot a look at the shuttered office. "Maybe for the best."

Tyler followed the DI's gaze. "The boss going to be OK?"

Ben's reply took a moment to come. "Aye. Jack? Aye. He'll be fine," he said, although there wasn't a lot of conviction in it. "He'll just be taking some time to process. It's been a long day."

Tyler couldn't argue with that. He checked his watch. After eleven. He stifled a yawn for as long as he could, then relented to it.

"Sorry," he muttered, once it had passed.

Ben caught the contagion and covered his mouth with both hands as he yawned, too. "You've got me started now." He got to his feet and took his jacket from the back of his chair. "Come on. Home time. Nothing else we can do here tonight. Tomorrow's going to be a big one."

Tyler didn't need to be told twice. He jabbed the button that turned off his computer monitor, then got to his feet.

"You heading to the hotel, or up the road, boss?" he asked.

Ben had been wondering that very same thing. The hotel was close, and the thought of climbing into bed was tempting. But after everything that had happened, he had a longing to be at home, to be with Alice. Just to see her, say hello, argue about something insignificant. Pretend everything was normal, just for a while.

But everything wasn't normal. Not by a long shot.

And there was still work to be done.

"Hotel," Ben decided. "You?"

Tyler, it turned out, had been having a similar debate with himself, and had come to the same conclusion as the DI.

"Much as I'd like to go home, hotel for me, too," he said. "Going to see this through, boss. For Caitlyn's sake."

Ben nodded his approval. "Aye. For Caitlyn's sake," he agreed.

Because, that's what you did. That's what you had to do. You grieved. You processed.

Somehow, you moved on.

"Any word from Ham?" Tyler asked.

"I sent him home. Aye, *home* home," Ben replied. "Told him to take a few days, and that we'd call him with any questions."

"Sounds sensible."

"Aye, well. Some of us have to be," Ben said, stealing the briefest of glances at Logan's office door.

Fishing in his pocket, Ben dug out his car keys and tossed them to DC Neish. "Here. Go wait in the car. I'll check on himself, then be out."

"No bother, boss," Tyler said. He looked the closed door up and down, then mouthed an almost silent, "Good luck," before leaving.

Ben didn't approach the office. Not yet. He eyed it warily, instead, like it was the lair of some great and terrible dragon. He wasn't scared of Logan. Not by a long shot. He could give as good as he got, and the DCI knew better than to try any of his shite.

He was afraid, though, of what else he might find lurking in the corners of the office. The grief. The misery. The guilt and self-blame.

It was fair to say that Logan disliked most people. Actively despised many of them, in fact. When something happened to those handful that he *did* like—especially those he considered his responsibility—the fallout could be painful to witness.

He knocked on the door, softly at first.

"Jack? Jack, it's me."

There was silence for a while, then:

"I'll just be a minute."

"Aye, well, you said that three hours ago," Ben told him. "I think your watch might be knackered."

There was a sigh, heavy and sullen.

"It's open."

Light spilled into the darkened office when Ben opened the door, making Logan hiss and blink. It pushed away the shadows and reflected in the bottle of amber liquid standing open on the DCI's desk.

A single measure was missing from the bottle, presumably having found its way into the *Cadbury's Creme Egg* mug that sat in the dead centre of the desk, an inch or two from Logan's hand.

"Jesus, Jack. Where the hell did you get that?" Ben asked.

Logan didn't look up, his gaze fixed like a tractor beam on the mug. "Does it matter?"

"Yes, it matters! Of course, it matters! What are you thinking?"

"What am I thinking? What am I *thinking*? I'll tell you what I'm thinking. I'm thinking I sent Caitlyn to that bastard's house," Logan said, tearing his eyes from the mug. "I'm thinking that one of my decisions has once again led to the death of a... of a *fucking excellent* police officer. That's what I'm thinking, Detective Inspector. If you must know."

His fingers crept around the mug. He lifted them off one at a time, then put them back, like the surface was too hot to hold onto for long.

"Why? What are you thinking?" he muttered.

"Oh, you know full well what I'm thinking, Jack," Ben said, shooting the bottle a look of distaste.

"I don't. I don't have a clue. Enlighten me."

"I'm thinking, 'Look at the state of this selfish bastard,'" Ben said.

Logan snorted a derisory laugh. "Oh, is that—?"

"I wasn't finished," Ben snapped. "I'm thinking we lost a very good officer today. One of the best I've ever worked with. I'm thinking we've lost a real asset and a good friend, and I refuse to just stand here and watch as we lose another. I won't."

Logan's shoulders straightened. His chest inflated like he was preparing for a fight.

But then, with a sigh, it all collapsed, and he sat there behind his desk looking smaller than Ben had ever seen him before.

"You're right. No. You're absolutely right," Logan said. "I wouldn't ask you to do that."

His fingers stopped their dancing and tightened around the mug.

"So, shut the door and turn the lights off on your way out," Logan instructed. "And I'll see you on the other side."

Sandy Gillespie surfaced groggily from the latest in a series of short, restless sleeps. For a moment, he couldn't remember where he was, but then a selection of aches and pains cut through the brain fog, and the metal bracelet around his wrist rattled where it was fastened to the hospital bed.

What time was it? There was a clock on the wall, but the room was in near-total darkness, making it difficult to see. Before he'd fallen asleep, light had been flooding in through the little window in the door, but someone must have pulled the curtain and covered it while he slept.

He squinted at the clock for a while, trying to force his night vision to kick in. Just after three, he thought. Or possibly a quarter past one.

They'd taken his watch. His clothes, too. Swabbed him down and taken his prints, and only then allowed him to receive treatment. He should sue. He should fucking sue. Take the bastards for all they were worth. Police brutality, that's what it had been. No question.

Pain burned through his ribcage, and he grimaced. That big bastard had done a number on him. He'd caught him off-guard. Caught him panicked. If he ever saw him again, the shoe would be on the other foot. Yes, next time, things would be very—

"Hello, Sandy."

Gillespie made a sound. It was not a sound he had intended to make, and not one he was particularly proud of. It was somewhere between a yelp and a squeal, like a puppy whose tail had just been trodden on.

The voice had come from the darkest corner of the room. There was a shadow there, big and bulky, imposing itself against the background of black.

Shit. Oh, shit.

"How the fuck did you get in here?" Gillespie demanded. His voice was an unsteady tremble, fraying around the edges. "You shouldn't be in here."

"Doesn't matter how I'm here, Sandy."

Gillespie's eyes were adjusting to the gloom, and saw Logan come stepping from the shadows. He had his coat on, his hands shoved deep down in the pockets. The coat and the stance made him look even larger and more intimidating than before.

"What matters—what you should be concerning yourself with—is *why* I'm here."

Gillespie swallowed. He pulled on the handcuff, but his hand remained trapped.

"Why *are* you here?"

Logan didn't answer. Not right away. Instead, he crossed to the end of the bed and leaned on it, his big hands wrapping around the metal frame.

"Honestly? Your guess is as good as mine," the DCI admitted. "I was wide awake and at a loose end. Thought I'd swing by and see how you were doing."

Gillespie shot a look to the door. The corridor light seeped in at the edges of the curtain. From there, strapped to that bed, it may as well have been another world.

"You can try shouting, if you like," Logan said. "See how you get on. I dare you."

Gillespie dismissed it with a shake of his head. He remembered very clearly what had happened last time the detective had dared him to do something. The multitude of aches currently ravaging his body were making damn sure of that.

"Don't hurt me."

Logan chuckled drily. "I'm not here to hurt you, Sandy. I wouldn't dream of hurting a man like you, who knows all his rights. And risk you getting away with everything on some technicality? No."

Sandy said nothing, just watched in nervous silence as Logan turned to look at the monitoring equipment by the bed. As the detective turned, something in his coat pocket *chinked* against the bed's frame. Glass. A bottle.

Christ, was he drunk? Sandy tried to wriggle out of his cuff, again, but he knew he was wasting his time.

"Your sister's dead," Logan said, almost absent-mindedly. He turned his attention away from the hospital machines, and back to the bed. "Maureen. We found her."

Sandy nodded. As suspected, this was not news to him.

"How?"

"Have a guess."

"I don't know."

"I didn't ask if you knew. I told you to guess," Logan said. His tone was dangerous, like another wrong response might ignite him and blow the whole room to kingdom come. "So, please. Humour me. Guess."

"Shot," Gillespie said.

Logan feigned surprise. "Well done. Spot on. Some guess there, Sandy. Shot. Through the head."

He formed a gun shape with two fingers and took aim at the man in the bed. "BANG!" he barked, and Gillespie's heart monitor spiked as he jumped. "Shot dead. Right through the forehead. Close up, they reckon. Downward angle, suggesting she was on her knees. Pleading."

Gillespie chewed on his bottom lip, biting back whatever response was trying to come out.

"Nasty business," Logan continued with a sad shake of his head. "And then, after she was shot, she was cut open. Like Brodie Welsh, only with less care and attention. Brutal, it was. Very messy."

Gillespie squirmed in the bed. He looked away from the detective, hiding the tears welling up in his eyes.

"Fuck you," he whispered.

Logan straightened. "Aye. Probably best not to dwell on it, right enough. Nasty business. Because, think about it, Sandy, if someone did that to her and didn't get what they were after, just imagine what they'll do to you." He flashed the wee scrote a smile that was all teeth. "And just think how easy it was for a clumsy big bastard like *me* to get to you in here."

He gave that a few moments to sink in, then headed for the door. "So, we'll maybe see you at the station tomorrow. If you're feeling up to it. With a bit of luck, we'll be able to put all this unpleasantness to bed, once and for all."

He opened the door, letting the light in. Gillespie blinked and shielded his eyes with his free hand.

"Wait!" he called, before Logan could leave. "The, eh, the cop. That woman. I didn't know she... She wasn't meant to..." He shrank beneath Logan's gaze, his voice becoming a squeak, like air escaping the neck of a balloon. "I'm sorry."

Logan clicked his tongue against the roof of his mouth, then nodded. "Aye. You will be, son," he said. "You will be."

He swallowed, his grip tight on the door handle like he was wrestling with himself over whether to stay or go. Was he finished here, or was he just getting started?

The weight of the bottle in his pocket pulled his coat down at one side.

And Logan knew what he had to do.

CHAPTER THIRTY-SEVEN

Ben Forde was the first one into the Incident Room the next morning. He'd promised Tyler a lift in at eight, but he'd been awake half the night, and by the time the clock showed seven, he was already halfway to the station.

"Jack?" he called, as he stepped into the room. The main bulk of the place was empty. The desks were untouched, their stacks of paperwork and evidence bags all exactly as they'd been left the night before.

The office blinds were still shut, the door still closed. Ben muttered a few of the more minor expletives below his breath, ran a hand through his thinning hair, then began his approach.

"Jack? It's me. You awake?"

There was no reply from within the office. Ben stopped by a window and tried to peek through the gaps at the edges of the blind, but the room beyond was too dark for him to see much of anything.

He swore again, with a little more venom this time, then knocked on the door.

"Jack? You in there?" he asked. He knocked again, louder this time. "Wakey wakey. Come on."

He gave it a few seconds, then tried the door handle. Locked.

Shite.

Ben's heart skipped into a higher gear. He gave the door the classic polis knock this time. *Thump-thump-thump.*

"Jack! Stop arseing about and open the door!"

He rapped his knuckles on the window, hard and fast and sharp. He called out again, close enough to fog the glass and loud enough to shake it.

"Jack! Open the bloody door!"

Ben listened, straining to hear over the sound of his blood whooshing through his veins. He gave it to the count of ten, before concluding that radical action was needed.

"Right. Fine. Don't say I didn't warn you," he called, then he stepped back, angled his shoulder towards the door, and lunged.

It had been a number of years since Ben Forde had last put in a door. They had been lighter back then, he thought, as pain went radiating down his arm and across his back. Flimsier.

He tried again, putting all his weight behind the second attempt. The impact was harder, the pain more severe. The bastarding door remained firmly shut.

Back in the day, he'd have put it in with a couple of well-aimed kicks, but the lock was at waist height, and there was no way he was getting his leg that high without risking permanent injury.

"You'd better be lying dead in there," Ben hollered at the office, then he took three big paces back, sucked in a couple of deep breaths, and charged.

His first instinct, when he heard the *crack*, was that he'd broken a bone. Certainly, that was what the agony that exploded across his shoulder suggested.

But then, he was stumbling into the office, the door swinging open and pouring light into the darkness.

Ben crashed awkwardly into Logan's desk and had to grip the edge to stop himself sliding right over the top of it.

The office was empty. No Logan.

Straightening, Ben gingerly moved his arm around, testing for damage. It throbbed, but there were no sudden sharp stabbing sensations that would suggest anything serious. That was something.

The *Creme Egg* mug was still on the desk. Ben stole a look inside. Just like the office, it too was empty.

He groaned. "Ah, bollocks."

This was bad. This was very bad.

He turned to leave, and then stopped and walked around to the other side of the desk. There was a bin there, tucked away under the desk, a round metal pail lined with a plastic bag.

The gold-coloured top of the whisky bottle jutted up above the rim, and Ben's heart fell all the way down to his feet.

"Christ. The whole thing?"

There was no saying where the DCI would be now. No saying what he'd be doing, or who he'd be doing it to. No saying what damage he might inflict on the ongoing investigations, or—

"You alright in there, Benjamin?"

Ben turned to find Logan looming in the doorway, a paper cup in each hand, a white paper bag poking out from a coat pocket.

"Jack! Where the hell have you been?"

"Cafe along the road. Got us rolls." He regarded the broken door frame. "Problems?"

"Problems? Aye. What? Aye, problems. I was shouting, but you didn't answer me."

Logan frowned. "I wasn't in."

"Well, no. I mean, aye. I know that now, obviously," Ben replied, throwing his arms up in exasperation. "I nearly broke my shoulder getting that open."

"I'm pretty sure there's a spare key somewhere," Logan said. He held out one of the cups. "Here. Coffee. I'm assuming you didn't get much sleep."

Ben resisted for all of three seconds, before tutting and accepting the cup. "Aye, and whose fault is that?"

He sat in Logan's chair and took a sip of the coffee. It was blisteringly hot, and he set the cup down on the desk to let it cool. A white paper bag landed next to it.

"Square sausage and a tattie scone."

"Making amends for something, Jack?" Ben asked, opening the bag. His stomach gurgled as the smell wafted out, and he realised he couldn't remember the last time he'd eaten.

"Aye. Something like that," Logan admitted. He sat in the chair across from the DI and opened up his own paper bag.

"How'd you know I'd be in here early?"

Logan tapped the side of his head. "Mind like a steel trap, Benjamin," he said. "Also, you've become a right predictable bastard in your old age."

He looked, Ben had to admit, remarkably fresh. Much fresher than the DI himself felt, that was for sure. There was none of the bleariness Ben had been bracing himself for, no bloodshot eyes, or gravelly voice. No shouting, or staggering, or out-of-character declarations of love.

He was, as far as the DI could tell, stone-cold sober.

"I went to the hospital. To see Gillespie," Logan announced, and Ben almost choked on his square sausage.

"Jesus Christ. You did what?"

"I know. I know," Logan said. "I wanted to..." He gestured vaguely with his roll. "I don't know. I thought it'd help."

"Help who, exactly? Not the case, that's for sure. Not us. Not Caitlyn."

Logan stuffed his mouth with bacon butty and chewed.

"And did it?" Ben asked. "Help, I mean?"

Logan made a weighing motion, then forced down a swallow. "Helped me realise I was being an arsehole," Logan said.

Ben grunted. "Huh. Well, that's something, I suppose."

There was a sound from out in the Incident Room. The squeak of a door opening.

Both men turned just as Hamza peeked tentatively into the inner office.

"Did I no' tell you to take a few days off?" said Ben.

Hamza shifted his weight from one foot to the other. "Aye, sir. You did. But... Well. You know."

Ben nodded. He knew. Of course, he knew.

"Coffee's on your desk," Logan said. "Bacon roll. Crispy, no butter. Right?"

Hamza smiled, albeit faintly. "Cheers, sir."

The door squeaked again out in the Incident Room. "Morning, Detective Constable," Logan announced.

Tyler appeared beside Hamza, thumbing sleep from his eyes. "Morning." He shot Ben a slightly accusatory look. "And cheers for the lift, boss."

"I thought you'd be sleeping."

Tyler yawned so wide he almost swallowed his face, then gave a shake of his head. "Couldn't. Not really. I got a taxi in."

"Go get some caffeine and grub in you, son," Logan said. "I left it on your desk."

Tyler rubbed his head, smoothing down a clump of hair that had been sticking up. "Right. Nice one. Cheers, boss."

"How'd you know?" Hamza asked. "That we'd be here?"

Logan tapped the side of his head again, but this time said nothing.

"Go get stuck in, lads," Ben told them. He picked up his own cup and took a sip. "Then let's get to work."

He and Logan waited for the DCs to leave the office, then Logan stood up and dusted the breadcrumbs off his crumpled shirt. "I'm going to go get cleaned up," he announced. "Then, we'll crack on. Alright?"

Ben raised his paper cup. "See if you can find some deodorant, while you're at it. No' putting up with you smelling like that all day."

Logan raised an arm, sniffed, and then pulled a face. "Aye. I take your point," he said, then he pointed to Ben, installed behind the office's desk. "Don't get too comfortable in that seat, by the way."

And with that, he was gone.

Ben waited until he heard the Incident Room door squeaking for a third time, then he set down his cup.

It took him a moment to prepare himself mentally, but then he rolled the chair back, leaned down, and took the whisky bottle from the bin.

Full. All the way to the top.

He sat back, exhaling, and shot a grateful look at the ceiling. He hadn't touched it. He hadn't given in. Aye, he must've been tempted, but he'd handled it. He'd resisted. He'd coped.

You grieved. You processed. And then, you moved on.

Ben gathered up the paper bags, drained the last of his coffee from his cup, and tossed them into the bin beside the bottle. That done, he took out the plastic bag and tied the whole thing tightly at the top. Double knot. Better safe than sorry.

"Just dealing with this," he told Tyler and Hamza as he crossed the Incident Room with the bag in hand. "And then, we'll get started."

Tyler swallowed a bite of breakfast and indicated the bag with a nod. "What is it, boss?"

Ben glanced down at the bag, its weight swinging it back and forth in his grip. "Nothing to worry about," he said. "Nothing to worry about at all."

CHAPTER THIRTY-EIGHT

Hamza couldn't bring himself to look at the others. Not yet. Not now. He had picked a spot in the gap between Logan and Ben, and was committing to it fully with a thousand-yard-stare.

"It just came out of nowhere. I thought... I mean, I saw a shadow moving in the house. I told Caitlyn. DS McQuarrie, I mean. I told her, and she knocked, and then... It just happened. Out of nowhere."

He frowned, like he still couldn't quite understand exactly what it was that *had* happened.

"Bang. Or boom. Aye. More a boom. Not a gunshot, an explosion. And there was... behind her, there was this mist. Red. Just so... Just so red. It was like it was swirling in the air there, like a firework, or something. And then, she was on the ground, and I just grabbed her and pulled her out of the way of the door."

He sniffed, his stare still fixed on a spot only he could see. "I didn't know what to do. I panicked. Totally bottled it. Just started shouting for help. For someone to help her. For someone to do something, because I... I didn't know. I didn't know how to. I didn't know what to do."

DC Neish put a hand on Hamza's shoulder. "You're alright, mate."

"Tyler's right, son," Ben added. "You got her help. You kept her safe until the ambulance came. There's nothing else anyone could've done. Nobody could ask any more of you, not me, not Jack, not Caitlyn. You did her proud."

Hamza sniffed again and drew one of his shirt sleeves across his eyes. "She, eh, she'd met someone. Recently."

"What, like, a guy?" Tyler asked.

"A girl. A woman, I mean."

"Aye? Wow! She was a dark horse, wasn't she?" Tyler remarked.

"Do we know who she is?" Ben asked.

Hamza shook his head. "No. She didn't say. It was quite new, I think. It's why she'd been acting differently." He shrugged. "Why she'd been happy."

"I get it, Hamza," Logan said. It was the first time he'd spoken in several minutes, and it snapped the DC out of his stupor. "I understand why you feel guilty. And you're right to."

Hamza's eyes grew a fraction larger. "Sir?"

"Not because it's your fault, or because you did anything wrong. It isn't, and you didn't. You're right to feel guilty because you're a good copper, son. You're a good man. And good men, in these circumstances, feel guilty. They feel like they should've done more, or should've acted sooner, or should've worked some miracle that would've somehow saved the day."

He glanced over at Ben, who gave him the briefest of nods in response.

"You're right to feel all that, because you're a good man, Hamza. But it wasn't your fault. You did all you could, and nobody thinks otherwise."

Hamza didn't look entirely convinced, but he gently cleared his throat. "Thanks, sir. Appreciate it."

"Has Hoon spoken to her family yet?" Logan asked, turning to DI Forde.

"Her parents, aye," said Ben. "They're on Orkney. He's got a liaison working with them and making arrangements. Funeral will be up there, he thinks."

"I'd like to speak to them, too," Logan said. "But I want to have some news for them first. What time are we getting Gillespie in here?"

Ben glanced up at the clock on the wall. "Doctor said he's all ours from around one. His solicitor is on standby."

"Right. So, we've got plenty of time, then," Logan said, standing. He fished in his pocket until he found his car keys. "Who's up for a wee road trip?"

Forty minutes later, Logan, Ben, Tyler, and Hamza stood in the shadow of Buachaille Etive Mor, listening to the distant rumble of passing traffic, and the irregular flapping of the plastic cordon tape.

The area had been meticulously searched by the Scene of Crime team, and all forensic materials taken away to be tested and catalogued. There was no reason the bridge and the path past the SMC hut couldn't be opened now—at least one climbing organisation was already demanding it, in fact—but Logan had insisted the place be kept cordoned off for another day or two, while he and the team continued to work on the case.

Of course, Brodie Welsh's murder wasn't the all-consuming urgent matter it had been just a day ago. There were two other murders to throw into the mix now, although from where Logan was standing, they were both pretty clear cut.

Sandy Gillespie had killed DS Caitlyn McQuarrie. Maureen Gillespie had been killed by someone she was involved with in the drugs trade. They'd get a name from her brother, sooner or later, and from there it should be straightforward enough. There was no great mystery to either.

Unlike Brodie Welsh.

Sure, Maureen and Sandy were probably responsible for his death. That made sense. It was clean. Easy.

Too easy, though?

Why move the body? Why stage the call-out? Why want him found? The main thrust of it—the actual murder part—that made sense, aye. But the rest? Sandy Gillespie was going to have to go some to make all the pieces fit the jigsaw.

Still, the evidence was there. The way Brodie had been cut open suggested someone who knew about his drug trafficking, and Logan was prepared to bet the footprints found around the grave would be the same size as one of the Gillespies'.

They had the motive, too, if they thought he was trying to cross them, or otherwise becoming a liability. Maybe they'd gotten wind that Hannah had seen through Brodie's cover story. Or maybe he'd been taking more of a cut than he was meant to. In that line of work, reasons to get yourself murdered were usually in abundance.

It made sense. The Gillespies, or someone working with them, must've done. It made sense.

And yet...

The sound of DI Forde's voice pulled the brake on Logan's train of thought and dragged him back to the here and now.

"Much as I enjoy getting out of the office, Jack, I can't help but wonder what we're doing out here in the freezing cold?" He gestured over the bridge at where Brodie's body had been discovered. "Something new come up?"

Logan shook his head. "No. I just wanted us to go over it one more time before we talk to Gillespie. See if we can make some sense of it. Also, aye." He inhaled deeply through his nose. "I thought we could do with getting out in the fresh air. Clears the head."

"Here! Boss!" Tyler gasped. He pointed up beyond the mountaineering club hut to where an animal stood watching them, its antlers raised to the sky. "Is that a moose?"

Ben snorted. "A moose? No, it's not a moose. It's a stag."

"Shite, aye. That's what I meant," Tyler said. "Stag."

"Jesus. Is that where he's up to now?" Logan asked. "Basic animal identification? They grow up so fast."

Ben chuckled, then went back to addressing the DC. "Aye, son, that's a stag. You get plenty of them out here."

He put a foot up on a rock and gestured south along the A82.

"I mind one incident a while back. Christ. Eighties, maybe? I was in uniform. Couple of lads were tearing up the road from Glasgow, and a stag jumps out in front of the car. Just throws itself out in front of them, too close for them to stop. They plough right into it. Heavy bugger of a thing. Smashes the front of the car in. Headlights gone, windscreen cracked. The works. Lot of damage."

"What about the stag?" Tyler asked.

"Killed. Big beast, it was, too. It's dead, but it's no' in bad nick. So, these lads, they reckon it'll fetch a few quid. At the butcher in town, like. Maybe pay for the car repairs, even. So, they fold down the back seats."

"Haha! No way!" Tyler laughed.

"They fold down the back seats," Ben continued. "And they manhandle it in. It's an estate, so there's a bit of room, but it's a tight fit. Like I say, it's a big bugger. Takes them a good twenty minutes of shoving it back and forth, but they eventually get it in the car, get the boot shut, and set off."

"And did they manage to sell it?"

Ben shook his head. "No. Halfway up the road, it woke up."

"What?!" Tyler spluttered. "Seriously?"

"Seriously. Wasn't dead, just stunned. It went from fully spangled to wide awake, like that," Ben said, clicking his fingers. "They stopped the car and jumped out, then stood at the side of the road and watched as it kicked its way out of the back. Took it three minutes. Wrote the whole car off, then it just gave them a dirty look and wandered off."

"That's mental," Tyler remarked.

"Aye, well, you don't mess with nature," Ben said. "That's the lesson I took away from it, anyway. That and never buy a Lada Riva Estate."

They all stood watching the stag on the hillside for a few minutes, none of them saying a word. The animal padded back and forth through the heather, paying them very little heed.

Occasionally, it would glance their way, but it seemed more curious than concerned. It would watch them for a while, mouth moving up and down as it chewed, then turn its attention to something else.

"He's a big lad, isn't he?" Ben observed.

"Aye. He's a beauty," Hamza agreed. He smiled faintly as he watched the animal go about its business. "Caitlyn would've loved seeing that."

None of the others corrected him. They didn't have to.

"She wouldn't, would she?" he said. "She'd just tut and roll her eyes, and ask us if we planned taking our fingers out of our arses and getting back to work anytime soon."

Logan laughed drily. "Aye. That sounds more like her style, right enough." He gestured back across the car park, to where the Volvo stood. "We should get up to Maureen's. Forensics have been and gone, and I'd like to do a walk-through. See if anything jumps out before we talk to Sandy. We're assuming someone else killed her, but there's no saying that wee bastard didn't do her in himself. He might've been trying to frame her for..."

His voice trailed away into a thoughtful silence. He looked across the bridge to the site where Brodie Welsh's body had been found.

"Everything alright, Jack?" Ben asked him.

Logan blinked, frowned, then nodded. "Aye. Grand," he said. He tore his eyes from the cordoned-off square of dirt. "Everything's just grand."

Maureen Gillespie's house held no real surprises. Logan had already seen the SOC report, although he'd figured out most of it himself on his initial look at the scene.

There were no signs of damage to the doors, which suggested either Maureen had left her doors unlocked—possibly, with the remote location, but unlikely given the company she would've been keeping—or had let her killer inside.

The bullet hole in the window had been caused by a stray shot, most likely. The room where Maureen's body had been found was in a real mess, and some minor injuries to her hands, arms, and neck suggested there had been a fight before the fatal shot had been fired.

The house had been turned upside-down, much like Maureen's own insides had been. There were no prints other than those of Maureen herself, and a few from Sandy, mostly on dirty glasses piled up by the sink.

Whoever had turned the place over had been prepared. They'd planned it enough to come equipped with gloves, at least, and there was a distinct lack of any physical evidence as to the killer's identity.

It would all come down to Sandy Gillespie, then, and whether he was feeling brave enough—or lucky enough—to speak out. The thought of offering that bastard protection stuck in Logan's throat, but he had a nasty feeling that's what the future would hold.

Aye, they'd get him for Caitlyn's murder, but he'd end up somewhere nice and cushy in return for selling out the bigger fish. He'd be detained, aye. Incarcerated. But he wouldn't be punished. He'd never be truly punished.

Not in the way Logan would like.

While DCs Neish and Khaled took a look around outside the house, Ben entered the living room at Logan's back.

"Alright, Jack? Find anything?"

"No."

Ben cast his eye across the room, sucked air in through his teeth, and shook his head disapprovingly. "Not a bad wee house, too. Untidy, aye, and it could do with some work. Bit out of the way, too, but no' bad."

"Aye, the bloodstains on the floor give it a certain ambiance, right enough," Logan said. He dropped onto his haunches by the window and studied the hole for a moment, then turned and followed some invisible line in the air. "There," he said, pointing to an upturned armchair.

The bottom had been split open, and judging by the amount of stuffing on the floor, the cushions had, too.

"There what?" Ben asked.

"That's where the bullet came from. Shooter was sitting down."

Ben frowned. "Thought you reckoned they were fighting."

"Aye. But the angle points to that chair. So, maybe they'd been fighting, Maureen knocked them onto the chair, then they pulled the gun and shot at her. They missed, but it bought them time to get back up and set about her."

Ben considered this. "That works, I suppose," he said. "Although, do we know Maureen didn't fire the gun? Aye, no' through her own face, but the window. She could've fired first, whoever was in here got the gun off her, and—"

"No. They checked her hands. No residue," Logan said. "Whoever killed her brought the gun with them and took it away afterwards. Same with the knife used to cut her open. Wounds don't match anything found in the house. It was all premeditated. Someone came here expecting to kill Maureen Gillespie, and then to gut her like a fish."

"And she let them in," Ben said. "She just opened the door and let them walk right in. Someone she knew, then."

"Aye," Logan said. He took another look around the room, then shoved his hands in his pockets and headed for the door. "And someone she trusted."

CHAPTER THIRTY-NINE

Logan regarded the solicitor like she was something he'd discovered sticking to the sole of his shoe.

"I'm sorry?" he said, in a tone that practically dared her to repeat the words she'd just said.

She gladly accepted.

"My client will not be taking part in any interview in which you are a participant," she said, meeting Logan's angry glare with one of practised indifference. "You can try to stare me down all you like, Detective Chief Inspector, but you physically assaulted my client not twenty-four hours ago, and then proceeded to pay him a midnight visit in hospital while he was recuperating."

She snapped her gaze in Ben's direction. "Were you aware of that? That DCI Logan snuck into Mr Gillespie's room last night? Threw his weight around a little."

"Bollocks, I didn't throw anything around," Logan protested.

"But you admit you entered his room without any sort of permission or clearance?"

Logan threw Gillespie a dark and dirty look. The bastard had been watching him, but quickly looked away when Logan caught his eye.

"I paid him a visit, yes. I wanted to inform him of what had happened to his sister."

The solicitor clasped her hands on the desk between them. "Yes. Well. You should consider yourself fortunate that we're granting you any sort of interview at all. We have not yet ruled out the possibility of pressing assault charges."

"Charges?" Logan said. He felt Ben's hand on his arm but ignored it. "Your client—" He jabbed a finger in Gillespie's direction, making him shrink in his seat. "That jumped-up wee arsehole right there, went for a gun. A gun, might I remind you, Miss..."

"Grey."

"...that he'd already used to shoot and kill one of my officers."

"Allegedly," the solicitor added.

Miss Grey was irritatingly composed for someone so young. She was early thirties at most, and had put herself together with well-rehearsed care and attention.

She wore an old-fashioned pinstripe suit—shirt, tie, jacket, and trousers—that was maybe a half size too big for her, but it all felt like a deliberate style choice, like she'd had it tailored too big on purpose. The outfit was perfectly matched by her short, meticulously sculpted quiff.

When he'd first seen her, Hamza had suggested the look may be some sort of feminist statement about being a powerful woman in a man's world. Tyler, on the other hand, reckoned she was a part-time Elvis impersonator.

Logan couldn't care less who or what she was. He was just annoyed by the fact that she clearly knew what she was doing. She had him over a barrel.

She knew that, too.

"I was defending myself from your armed client," Logan said. "I'd consider that justified use of force."

"You broke his nose, and two of his fingers, knocked out three of his teeth, and cracked a rib. He also sustained extensive bruising to the arms, back, throat, and neck, plus psychological damage still to be assessed."

"Psychological damage my arse!" Logan spat. "He killed one of my officers."

"Allegedly," the brief reiterated.

"He went for the shotgun. He was going to shoot me!"

"After you goaded him into it, Detective Chief Inspector. Yes? That is what happened, isn't it? You told him to pick it up. Dared him to."

"If I dared him to jump off the Erskine Bridge, would he do that, too?" Logan asked. He eyeballed Gillespie across the desk. "Because I'm game to put it to the test, if you are."

Miss Grey smiled and ejected a dry little laugh from the back of her throat. *Ha.*

"I'm the Senior Investigating Officer on this case, sweetheart. You don't come in here and lay down the law. That's my job."

"Right. I see. Well, I think in that case, we're done here," the solicitor said, reaching for the briefcase she had tucked beside her seat. "We came here in good faith, but I refuse to allow my client to be questioned by the man who physically assaulted him, then turned up drunk at his hospital bed in the middle of the night attempting to intimidate him."

Logan felt Ben's eyes on him.

"I wasn't drunk. I hadn't been drinking," he protested, as much for DI Forde's benefit as for the woman across the table.

"I'm afraid that my client disagrees."

"Aye, well your client's a nasty wee murdering bastard, and I don't care what he thinks, quite frankly."

The solicitor set her bag on her knees and gave a single shake of her carefully coiffured head. "I could almost forgive it, had you been drunk. Alcohol and grief. Never a winning combination. A lapse in judgement could perhaps be overlooked in those circumstances. But if you say you were sober... No. That's unacceptable. Sandy."

Gillespie looked around at the sound of his name, caught off guard.

"Huh?"

"We're going. Come on."

Logan's stare practically pinned Gillespie to the chair, but a sharp, "Sandy!" from Miss Grey dragged him out of it and up onto his feet.

"We'll be in touch," she said

They were almost to the door when Logan relented.

"Fine."

Miss Grey stopped. She stood motionless for a moment, controlling the smile that threatened to take over her face, then turned. Logan hadn't moved, and the solicitor found herself watching the back of his head as he spoke.

"I won't participate in the interview," he told her, his voice flat and measured. "DI Forde and another member of the team will question Mr Gillespie without me present in the room. I trust that will be acceptable?"

The solicitor nodded without bothering to consult her client first. "It's a start."

"Right, then," Logan said. He got to his feet. The movement was slow and filled with a calculated sort of menace, like a monster rising from the deep. "The pair of you, sit your arses down, and let's get on with it."

CHAPTER FORTY

Logan stood as close as humanly possible to the observation room window, as if trying to convince himself he was right there in the room next door where the action was, rather than just standing here, helplessly watching on.

"You make a better door than a window, Jack."

Logan didn't give Jinkies the satisfaction of a response. The one-way mirror was plenty big enough for the Chief Inspector to see through, even with Logan standing slap bang in the middle of it, so close his breath was blurring the glass.

"You sure about sending your man in there?" Jinkies continued. "Bit wet around the lugs, isn't he? For a case like this, I mean."

"He'll be fine," Logan grunted.

"I'm happy to partner up with Ben in there. Take the lead on this one. I do know a thing or two about Mr Gillespie's activities, after all, and I've crossed swords with the brief before, too. She's tough. Needs a firm hand."

"It's fine, Hugh," Logan said, trying not to physically recoil at the thought of Jinkies' 'firm hand'. "It's all under control. The lads know what they're doing."

He waited, poised on the balls of his feet, for Hugh to put himself forward again. The one-way mirror was largely soundproof, but it wasn't perfect. Logan wondered how loud a bollocking he could give Jinkies without everyone next door getting an earful of it, too.

Fortunately, they didn't have to find out, as the Chief Inspector wisely decided not to push the suggestion any further.

"Well, if you change your mind, you just have to ask," he said. "We're all invested in this one, Jack. We all want justice for DS McQuarrie. And, if we can get him to confess to Brodie Welsh, too, so much the better. If we get something there, I'll talk to Fulton and Hannah. God knows, they could do with a result."

"Bit premature to be running to them, isn't it?" Logan suggested.

"Fulton is a good friend of the station, Jack. He deserves to be kept in the loop."

Logan didn't bother to reply. Any breath spent on a conversation with Jinkies was a breath wasted, in his opinion. It was bad enough that he'd invited himself in to observe the interview, Logan didn't feel any obligation to humour the bastard with conversation, too.

Hamza sidled up to the glass beside Logan, drawing a tut and a sigh from Jinkies, followed by the sound of a chair being dragged across the floor.

"You think Tyler's up to it, sir?" Hamza asked. He kept his voice low, less concerned about the people on the other side of the glass hearing him as he was the man behind him. "Gillespie gave him the run-around before."

They both watched DC Neish set his notebook and pen down on the desk in front of him, as Ben Forde recited all the usual stuff about recordings and tapes.

To the casual onlooker, Tyler looked relaxed and confident. Logan and Hamza both knew him well enough to see through it, though. It was there in his movements and the lines of his face. He was nervous.

"He's going to be fine," Logan said, although it wasn't clear whose concerns he was trying to put to rest. "Ben's taking the lead, he's just there to make up the numbers."

He raised his voice a little, making sure Jinkies could hear. "Besides, he's a better copper than we give him credit for. They'll nail this bastard to the wall."

"I hope you're right, Jack," Jinkies said. "Now, scootch over a bit, will you? You're blocking the show."

A FEW FEET AWAY, beyond the glass, Tyler shot a surreptitious glance at his reflection, placed a second pen on the table beside the first, then clasped his hands in a manner that mirrored the body language of DI Forde.

Across the table, the solicitor, Miss Grey, sat with her own pen poised above a leather-bound notepad, a slightly impatient expression on her face. She looked like she was already waiting for a chance to jump in, before either of the detectives had even started their line of questioning.

She was going to be hard work, Tyler thought. His eyes briefly went to her slicked-up quiff and her stylishly oversized suit and tie.

Yes, definitely hard work.

"Mr Gillespie. Can I call you Sandy?" Ben asked. He was smiling and relaxed, as if chatting to a friend of a friend. "I'm Ben Forde. I'm one of the detectives brought in to work on the Brodie Welsh case. I'm sure you're familiar with it."

"My client isn't here to talk about that case," Miss Grey interjected. "He's here to answer questions relating to the death of Detective Sergeant..." She checked her notes with a glance. "...Caitlyn McQuarrie."

She didn't even know her name. At least four men in the immediate vicinity shared that thought at exactly the same time. *She didn't even know her name.*

"Aye. I know. But, to be honest, we don't have a whole lot of questions about that," Ben said. "Not directly, anyway. You see, we know he did that one. We've got witnesses. He was the only person at the scene. Forensics have his fingerprints on the gun, and gunpowder residue on his skin and clothing. No, that one's pretty open and shut. We're confident of getting a conviction there, aren't we, Detective Constable?"

Tyler nodded, his eyes fixed on Gillespie. "Yes, boss."

"Would you say we're confident, or very confident?" Ben asked.

"I'd say we're supremely confident, boss."

Ben's eyes widened in surprise and delight, then he turned his attention back to Gillespie and his solicitor.

"*Supremely* confident of a conviction. You hear that, Sandy? Supremely confident that you'll be found guilty of murdering a police officer. Plus all the usual stuff about owning an unlicensed firearm, assault with intent, and so on, and so on."

Ben frowned as if struggling to recall some detail. "What's the maximum sentence for murder these days? Miss Grey, can you remember?"

The solicitor sighed, clearly unimpressed by the DI's theatrics.

"Mandatory life sentence, isn't it, boss?" Tyler interjected.

Ben slapped the edge of the table. "That's the one! Of course, life doesn't mean *life*," he said, smiling benevolently at Gillespie. "I'm sure you know that. You'll get out eventually, after whatever minimum term the judge decides to set."

He leaned back, the confused expression returning. "What was that one that was just set recently?" he asked. "Set a new record."

"Thirty-seven years, boss," Tyler told him.

"Thirty-seven years," Ben repeated. He whistled quietly. "Thirty-seven years."

"Minimum," Tyler added.

"Good point, son. Good point. No saying he'll get out after that. No saying he won't do forty."

"I'm sorry," the solicitor interjected. "I was under the impression my client was here to answer questions, not to sit in on a personal and, if I might add, highly speculative conversation between two officers who really ought to know better."

She looked at them both reproachfully, like a disappointed teacher. "Now, my client will require pain medication within the next forty-five minutes, as a direct consequence of the beating inflicted upon him during his arrest. I suggest, if you have questions, you ask them soon."

Ben held both hands up, conceding the point. "You're right, you're right. No more messing around. Down to business."

On the other side of the mirror, Logan held his breath.

"Did you murder your sister, Sandy?"

Gillespie clearly hadn't been expecting that one. He opened his mouth, shot his brief a blank look, then spluttered out a series of incredulous sounds that he eventually followed up with a, "What?"

"Your sister. Maureen," Ben said. "Did you kill her? It's not a difficult question, son. It's a yes or no answer."

"No! No, I didn't kill her."

Ben tapped on Tyler's notepad. "Jot that down, will you, DC Neish? 'No.' Make a note of that."

He waited until Tyler had followed his instructions, then continued.

"Right, well, who did?"

"I don't... I don't know!"

"You don't? But you knew someone had killed her, right?" Ben pressed. "That's why you were holed up in your house with a shotgun, isn't it? That's what you told DCI Logan yesterday. You were, quote, 'protecting yourself,' unquote. You mistook DS McQuarrie for an invader. You thought she was someone coming to kill you, like they'd killed your sister."

Gillespie adjusted himself in his chair. "Right..."

"So, you knew about Maureen. About her being dead. How?"

"What do you mean?"

"How did you know Maureen was dead? You got a psychic connection? Did her ghost tell you?" Ben asked.

"What? No."

"Then how did you know? Either you killed her, or you know who did. That's the only way you could've known to prepare for them coming after you, too, Sandy. That's literally the only two options."

"No. I mean, that's not..." Gillespie caught the look from his solicitor, and then cleared his throat. "No comment."

"Did you kill Maureen?"

"No comment."

"Did you go to her house, get in a fight, and kill her?"

"No comment."

"Did you shoot your sister in the head, and then mutilate her dead body?"

Gillespie bit his bottom lip so hard all the colour drained out of it.

"No comment."

"You gutted her like a fish, Sandy. You carved her up. Your own sister."

"No! I didn't!" Gillespie spat, slamming his hands on the table. "It wasn't me! Alright? It wasn't me, it was..."

He crammed a hand in his mouth and bit down on the knuckle, stopping himself.

"It was who, Sandy? Who killed her? Who did all that stuff to her?" Ben asked, his voice becoming coaxing and gentle. "We're all ears. Aren't we, son?"

"We're one big ear, boss," Tyler said, picking up on the cue.

"Who was it? You can tell us. We're all friends here."

Gillespie's chair creaked as he leaned his weight back. "No comment," he whispered.

It was Ben's turn to take on the look of a disappointed school teacher. "Fine. OK." He nodded slowly. "Fine. We'll park that for now. We'll come back to it. I can see it's a sensitive subject," he said. "How about you tell me about Brodie Welsh, instead?"

"I didn't kill him, either, if that's what you're getting at," Gillespie said. "Don't try to pin that one on me, an' all. I had nothing to do with it."

"I never said you did," Ben replied, adopting a shocked expression that suggested the thought had never crossed his mind. "He was a friend of yours, wasn't he? I'd imagine you must've been pretty cut up about it all."

Ben shot a sideways look in Tyler's direction. "No' as cut up as he was, mind you. Same thing again as Maureen. Cut right open. Guts split wide."

"Nasty business, boss."

"Aye, you can say that again," Ben said, shuddering as he turned back to Gillespie. "Of course, Brodie was neater than Maureen. The killer, they took more care with him. It was less... God. What's the word?"

"Aggressive?" Tyler suggested.

"Demented, I was going to say. Less frenzied. Less... *visceral*. Brodie? Now, Brodie's wounds were nasty, but they were business-like. Professional, almost. Maureen, though? Yikes. There was emotion put into that. Passion, you might even say."

Gillespie flinched like he was imagining the scene. Or perhaps remembering it.

"Is there a question coming, Detective Inspector?" asked the solicitor. "Or are you going to continue to taunt my client about the death of his sister? Because, if it's the latter, I can't see that being looked favourably upon in court, can you?"

"Had you met Detective Sergeant McQuarrie before, Sandy?" Ben asked. "Before you shot and killed her, I mean."

The change of direction caught Gillespie off-guard, and he responded with a slightly bemused shake of his head.

"Shame," Ben said. "Although, to be quite honest, you'd have hated her. Exceptional police officer. Liked to do things by the book, and didn't mince her words. She'd have had you down as a lanky streak o' pish at first glance. She did, in fact. She pulled your mugshot and put it up on the board we've got. You know, like in the films? Where we track the investigation?"

Ben smiled at the thought of it. "I never tended to bother with them myself, but DS McQuarrie, she loved a Big Board. Always kept it perfect. Everything on there. Photographs, maps, statements, the works. She put you up there for us. You and Maureen. She had the measure of you right away, Sandy. Before she'd ever clapped eyes on you in person, she could see you for what you are."

"Could she?" Gillespie said, his nostrils flaring. "And what good did that do her?"

Through the glass, Logan saw Ben's smile solidify and hold in place. He wasn't going to give the bastard the satisfaction.

"Did Maureen see you for what you are, too, Sandy? In the end, I mean? Is that why you killed her?"

Gillespie snorted and folded his arms across his chest.

"I told you, I didn't kill her."

"You want to know what I think happened?" Ben asked. He gestured to the solicitor. "You might want to make a note of this. You too, son."

Tyler picked up his pen and placed the nib against the paper. "Ready when you are, boss."

Ben leaned forward and lowered his voice as if letting the others in on a secret. "I can't take all the credit. DCI Logan, he came up with it. I was dubious at first, I'll be honest with you, but it does kind of make sense." He smiled at Sandy. "Ready? Right, then, pay attention, and then you can tell me if we're getting close."

CHAPTER FORTY-ONE

Logan and Hamza had been joined at the glass by Jinkies, and a DS from CID who'd been investigating the Gillespies for drugs trafficking, and who was not overly impressed that his thunder had been stolen.

As they'd stood listening to the questioning, Jinkies had been emitting little mutters, groans, *mm-hms* and other verbal diarrhoea that did nothing but get on Logan's tits.

The CID man, DS Lowrey, had remained stoic and silent throughout. It was the only reason Logan continued to tolerate his presence in the room.

"Here's what we think happened, son." Ben's voice sounded a little tinny over the observation room's speaker system. "It's a bit complicated, so just ask if you lose the thread, alright?"

He gave Gillespie a few seconds to respond, then pressed on.

"Right, then. Here goes. We believe that Brodie Welsh recently returned from a trip abroad, and had been carrying drugs inside his body on behalf of you and Maureen, just as he'd been doing on a regular basis for the past few years."

"No comment."

"We believe you and Maureen were acting as middle-men, buying what Brodie—and no doubt others—brought you, and selling it up the chain to someone else outwith the area. Alternatively, rather than being freelancers, as it were, you were under the direct employ of this mystery person or persons. They provided the funds, you arranged the supply, and you were handsomely rewarded for your efforts."

Ben raised his eyebrows. "How am I doing so far?"

Gillespie shot his brief a sideways glance, then looked back at the DI. "No comment."

"Now, it strikes me—and please, don't take offence here—but it strikes me that Maureen was the brains of the outfit," Ben continued. He looked to Tyler for his input. "Would you agree with that assessment, DC Neish?"

"Aye, boss. Aye, I'd agree."

"I mean, I never got the chance to meet her, personally, but from what I've read and heard about her, I'd say she was the boss. Out of the two of you, I mean. Would that be a fair assumption?"

Gillespie ignored the question, and Ben didn't bother to waste any time forcing the issue.

"What size of feet are you?" he asked, instead.

"What?"

"Feet. Shoes. What size?"

Gillespie looked down, like the answer might be written at the bottom of his trousers. "Eight. Why?"

"And Maureen?"

Sandy shook his head. "I don't know. The same?"

"Big feet for a woman," Ben remarked. He turned to Tyler. "That's not sexist, is it?"

"No, you're fine, boss," the DC replied.

"Thanks." Ben rolled his eyes in Gillespie's direction. "Can't be too careful, these days. Too easy to accidentally offend someone, and then all hell breaks loose."

"What do Maureen's feet have to do with anything?" Gillespie asked.

"Doesn't matter. Forget it," Ben said. "So, here's what I think. What *we* think, I mean. Me and the rest of the team."

He tipped Miss Grey the wink and indicated her notebook. She stared back at him with professional disdain.

"We think that you and Maureen discovered Brodie had been scamming you. Pinching a bit off the top. Keeping a wee bit for himself and punting it locally," Ben said. "We think you waited until he'd come back with a shipment, you both confronted him about what he'd been up to, then you killed him and cut him open, hoping to retrieve what he had on him."

"That didn't happen," Gillespie said. "That's shite."

"But you didn't retrieve it, did you, Sandy?" Ben continued, glossing right over the objection. "You went through all that bother of cutting him open, and the stuff wasn't there. That's why you went round to the house. You and Maureen. That's why you broke in and trashed the place, terrorising Hannah Randall in the process. You were looking for your gear, weren't you?"

The answer came through gritted teeth. "No comment."

"Must've been pretty desperate to put yourselves at risk like that," Ben mused. "I mean, it's taking a big chance that she could recognise you." He turned to Tyler. "What do you reckon would motivate someone to put themselves at risk like that?"

"Fear, boss."

"Fear. Exactly. I couldn't have put it better myself, son," Ben said. "Fear. Fear that the folk up the chain were going to come looking for the shipment you were supposed to bring them. Had they already been asking about it? Had they been making noises about what would happen if you didn't find it?

"I mean, that's why you trashed Hannah Randall's house, isn't it? Fear of them up the chain. And that same fear's why you killed Brodie Welsh."

Gillespie's lips were desert-dry. He flicked his tongue across them, with little effect.

"No comment," he croaked.

"Do you think that's helping your case, son?" Ben asked, sitting forward. He waved vaguely at the solicitor without looking at her. "Is that what she advised you to do? 'No comment,' over and over? You're aware this is being recorded, yes? The cameras aren't just for show, you know. They work. They're recording everything, same as the tape."

Ben let that bed in for a moment, before continuing. "How do you think that's going to play to the jury? Local man murdered. Father. Aye, gone off the rails a bit, but whose fault was that? They'll see his girlfriend in the gallery. Wee daughter, maybe. And all they'll hear is you giving it, 'No comment.' How do you think that'll go down? Like a lead balloon, if you ask me."

He sat back and shrugged. "But hey. What do I know? I'm no' the one with all the fancy letters after my name. If she thinks it's worth the gamble, far be it from me to argue."

Inside the observation room, Jinkies let out a little snort. "It's quite the technique, isn't it?"

"Aye," Logan mumbled.

"I mean, I'm not sure how effective it's likely to be when it comes to—"

"Hugh?" Logan said, tearing his eyes away from the scene in front of them.

Chief Inspector Pickering turned, a half-smile playing across his face. "Yes?"

"Gonnae shut the fuck up?"

"I'm *sorry?*"

"Seriously. If you're not muttering to yourself, you're making clicking noises with your tongue, or tapping your teeth, or some other bloody thing. Even your breathing is annoying me. I'm trying to concentrate here, and all I'm getting is—" Logan inhaled and exhaled deeply like he was trying to stop himself hyperventilating. "It's like getting a dirty phone call from Darth Vader."

Logan eyeballed the Chief Inspector, whose face was still frozen in a mask of shock, daring him to respond. It was only when Ben Forde's voice came over the speaker again that Logan turned his attention back to the room on the other side of the glass.

"So, I'm going to ask you again, son. And I want you to think very carefully about the response. Did you murder Brodie Welsh?"

"You don't have to answer that," Miss Grey said.

Gillespie coughed quietly. "No. No, I didn't kill Brodie," he said. "But..."

"But what?" Ben asked.

"Maybe, I don't know, maybe Maureen did."

"Maureen?"

Gillespie nodded. "She didn't say anything, so I don't know. But maybe. She made us go to the house, anyway. She told me how much shit we'd be in if we didn't find the gear. Said what they'd do to us."

In the room next door, Jinkies and DS Lowrey both blinked in surprise.

"Did he just...?" Lowrey asked. "Was that a confession? To dealing, I mean? Did he just own up?"

Logan waved the man into silence as Ben continued the questioning.

"So, you think Maureen killed Brodie?" he asked. "That'd be handy, wouldn't it? For you, I mean."

Gillespie's eyes narrowed in confusion. "What?"

"Well, it conveniently gets you off the hook, doesn't it? She kills Brodie, then she goes and gets killed herself, meaning she's not here to answer for it. You get to walk free."

Tyler opened his mouth, but Ben beat him to it.

"Or you would, had you not shot and killed Detective Sergeant McQuarrie yesterday afternoon. I mean, we know that one. We can take that one as a given, can't we?"

On the other side of the glass, Logan and Hamza watched for it. Waited for it. Held their breath and prayed for it, even.

"Right, Sandy?" Ben urged.

And there it was. The nod. The acknowledgement. The acceptance.

They had an eye witness, forensic evidence, and now, in that nod, a confession.

Regardless of what else they got him for, regardless of what else he'd done, Sandy Gillespie was going to jail for the murder of DS Caitlyn McQuarrie.

And, if there was any justice in the world, he'd rot there for a very long time.

Ben shot a fleeting look at the mirror, then steered things back to Maureen and Brodie. He'd come back to Caitlyn later, of course, and cement the confession. But it was there on the video for all to see, and anything else was icing on the cake.

Logan wheeled around, turning from the glass.

"Did we get him, sir?" Hamza asked. "Did we get him on Caitlyn?"

"Aye," Logan said. "Aye, we got the bastard."

Hamza gave the DCI a quick look up and down. "You alright, sir?"

"Fine. Aye. Great," Logan said, hurrying past the younger officer. "Just going to get a cup of tea. Anyone else want one?"

"Aye, go on then, Jack. I wouldn't say no to a—" Jinkies began, but Logan was through the first of the observation room's two doors, and it was already clicking closed behind him.

CHAPTER FORTY-TWO

Logan stepped out into the corridor, ran his hands through his hair, and breathed out. It felt like he'd been holding that same breath since the phone call telling him Caitlyn had been shot. It was a relief to finally get rid of it.

Back in the interview room, Ben would be sticking to the plan. The discovery of Brodie's body pointed the finger of suspicion firmly at the Gillespies. They had to know that. Sandy was now putting it all on his sister, but what if that had been his intention from the start? What if the body was meant to be found so that the Gillespies—Maureen Gillespie, in particular—would be suspected?

Ben would be quizzing Sandy now. Had he done it? Had he killed Brodie and tried to pin it on Maureen? If so, why? And did that mean he'd killed Maureen, too?

Logan's eyes fell on the vending machine in the corridor. The tea from it was like dishwater, but he didn't want to be gone too long, and a traipse to the kitchen to boil the kettle felt like a step too far.

He begrudgingly jabbed the black coffee button, concluding that it was the most palatable thing on offer, and waited while the machine hissed and whirred into life.

"Come on, come on," he muttered, glancing back at the observation room door.

He felt bad about leaving Hamza in there with Jinkies, but he'd needed to step outside for a minute to compose himself, to take a moment's comfort from the knowledge that Caitlyn was going to get justice.

Now, though, he was itching to get back. He wanted to know what else Gillespie had to say, to get to the bottom of everything, and square it all away.

Had he tried to frame his sister for killing Brodie? It was the only explanation that fit, even if it had to be battered in a bit around the edges. Why else move the body? Why else put it somewhere it would deliberately be found, if not to stitch someone up?

And yet, there was no evidence to imply that the Gillespies had fallen out. Nothing to suggest why Sandy would deliberately try to frame his sister for Brodie's murder.

It could've been the next man up the chain, but that wasn't generally how it worked, in Logan's experience. Everyone dealt with the person below. You had a problem with the man two links down? You got the link between you both to handle it. You didn't skip over them. It was too risky, too easy to get yourself found out. Why put your face out there where it didn't need to be seen? Plausible deniability, that was the name of the game.

The Gillespies had to have killed Brodie. Then, when they'd failed to deliver the gear he'd been carrying, the people above had come after the Gillespies themselves. The chain had been maintained. It made sense. It all fit neatly together.

Or it would've done, had the body not been moved. Which brought him right back around to a stitch-up. Sandy had been quick to point the blame at Maureen in the interview. Was that a spur-of-the-moment survival instinct, or part of some bigger plan he'd had in place from the start?

If you ignored the bit about the body being moved, it was completely plausible that the Gillespies had murdered Brodie Welsh. And yet, it didn't feel right. Not in his gut. Not deep down, where it counted.

If Logan could get in there with Sandy Gillespie himself, he'd get the truth out of the bastard. One way or another, he'd make him spill everything.

The rattling of coffee into a plastic cup came to a stop. With a final hiss and a puff of steam, the vending machine released its grip on the cup, and Logan reached in to pick it up.

He had just got a hand around it and turned in the direction of the observation room door when a vaguely familiar voice called out to him.

"DCI Logan? Do you have a minute?"

Sergeant Jaffray bustled along the corridor, a couple of traffic cones clutched under one arm, a length of cordon tape trying its best to escape from beneath the other.

"What is it, son?" Logan barked. "Kind of busy here."

Jaffray regarded the coffee cup in his hand for a moment, then nodded so enthusiastically he almost dropped his traffic cones.

"Right, yes. Right. I just wanted to apologise, sir."

Logan rifled through his memory, trying to recall what the sergeant had to be sorry for. Beyond being a useless bugger, anyway. He drew a blank.

"For what?"

"For everything, you know, with Mr Randall."

Logan felt his eyebrows bump together above his nose. "What?"

Jaffray took a breath and straightened himself up. "I've been bracing myself for it since he was in. Kept waiting for you to come give me a bollocking. And, well, my nerves can't take it. I thought it best to get it out in the open. I'm sorry."

Logan took a step closer. "I'm not following, Sergeant. What are you talking about?"

"Oh. Right. I thought..." Jaffray's eyes darted shiftily along the corridor like he was looking for a way out. "It's nothing. Forget it."

Logan took another step, so he was now towering above the smaller officer. He leaned in, bringing his face close enough to Jaffray's that his breath made the sergeant's eyebrows twitch.

"What are you talking about?" Logan growled. "What were you going to say about Fulton Randall?"

Jaffray shifted on the balls of his feet. "I, uh, it was an accident. Slip of the tongue, really. I didn't mean to tell him. I thought he already knew."

"Knew about what?"

The sergeant was positively squirming now. His traffic cones slipped out from under his arm and hit the floor with a *thack* that echoed along the corridor.

"About Brodie and Hannah," he said. "About the domestic."

Logan blinked, stepped back, mind racing.

"What? You told Fulton that Brodie had attacked Hannah?"

"Like I say, it was an accident, I thought he—"

"When?"

Jaffray's mouth flapped open and closed. One of Logan's hands clamped around his upper arm, the fingers almost meeting around the other side.

"*When?*"

"At... at the time, sir. Couple of days after it happened."

At the time. Jesus Christ.

"What about the drugs stuff? Did you tell him that, too?" Logan asked.

Jaffray's eyes searched the DCI's face. "Drugs stuff, sir? I don't... What?"

"The dealing. The Gillespies!"

Nothing changed on the sergeant's face to suggest he had the faintest idea what Logan was talking about.

"What about the Gillespies?" he asked, but Logan didn't hear him. Didn't listen. There was another voice in his head, instead. An echo of one, at least.

Fulton is a good friend of the station, Jack. He deserves to be kept in the loop.

Logan's coffee cup hit the floor as he turned on his heels.

"Bastard!" he ejected, then he stormed across the corridor, threw open the door to the observation room, and charged inside.

CHAPTER FORTY-THREE

Ben Forde was drilling Sandy Gillespie about his relationship with his sister when the mirror shook in its frame. The corresponding *thud* from the other side caught the attention of everyone in the room, and all four of them turned in time to see the glass pane shaking for a second time.

"Problems, Detective Inspector?" asked Miss Grey.

Ben and Tyler exchanged glances.

"Eh, no. Just a... I'll just..." Ben hovered his finger over the button on the desk. "Interview suspended at two-seventeen PM. DI Ben Forde leaving the room."

He jabbed the button, shot Tyler another look, then hurried out, just as something heavy was slammed against the other side of the glass once again.

Gillespie and his solicitor both watched DC Neish expectantly. He smiled as casually as he could. "Probably just... the wind," he said. "Nothing to worry about."

Miss Grey sniffed. "Yes. Well. I think we'll have a break here. My client needs a break. We can reconvene tomorrow."

Tyler half-laughed, like he thought the woman was joking. As he watched her pack her notes into her briefcase, though, he realised she was being serious.

"Wait, what? You can't just go."

"I think you'll find we can," Miss Grey said, fastening the straps of her bag. She motioned for Sandy to stand. "We can continue tomorrow, at a mutually agreed time. For now, though, Mr Gillespie and I will be—"

"Sit down."

The firmness of Tyler's voice cut through the solicitor's bustling. She looked up from her briefcase straps, one sculpted eyebrow raising quizzically.

"I'm sorry?"

"You heard me. Sit down. We're not finished."

"I didn't say we're finished, I said we were taking a break."

Tyler sat forward in his chair, and fixed the solicitor with a look that Logan would have been proud of.

"We'll decide when we take a break. Not you. We've got your client for another..." He checked his watch. "Twenty-two-and-a-half hours."

The solicitor opened her mouth to correct this, but Tyler got in first. "I think we can safely say a senior officer will extend the usual twelve-hour period, don't you?" He said. "I can't imagine getting DCI Logan to agree to that will pose a problem."

He smiled, not unkindly. "So, I suggest you use this short interlude wisely, Miss Grey. Clear your calendar. Phone home. Let everyone know you're not going to be available, because you... we... have a very long night ahead of us."

He looked from the solicitor to her client and back again, then cast a meaningful look at their chairs.

They resisted. For a while, anyway. It was Miss Grey who caved first. She sat down heavily, like a sullen teenager after a telling off. Sandy muttered something below his breath, then plonked himself down, too.

Tyler nodded approvingly at them both, then rubbed his hands together. "That said," he began, beaming from ear to ear. "Who fancies a cuppa?"

Tyler entered the observation room to find Ben, Hamza, and one of the guys from CID trying to prise Logan's hands from Jinkies' throat. The Chief Inspector was pinned against the one-way mirror, the tips of his toes barely touching the ground.

"Jesus. What's going on, boss?"

"Get over and give us a hand here," Ben barked. "Jack! Jack, let him go! You're going to kill him."

"That's the general idea!" Logan hissed, but then he released his grip and stepped back, hands raised. Jinkies crumpled to the floor, coughing and spluttering, his eyes practically bulging out of his head.

"I'll have... your job... for this, Logan," the Chief Inspector wheezed.

"*My* job? Oh, you think so, Hugh? You think that *you'll* have *my* job? When I'm done with you, you won't even be left with your bloody pension, never mind your career!"

"What's happened?" asked Ben, setting himself up as a barrier between both men. "What the hell's this about, Jack?"

Logan stabbed a finger at the man on the floor. "You want to tell him, Hugh, or will I?"

Jinkies rubbed his throat. The skin was red and raw, but his breath was gradually returning. "I don't know what you're talking about."

"Fulton Randall. You told him. About the Gillespies. About Brodie's involvement with them," Logan spat. "You told him everything months ago. Didn't you?"

Down on the floor, Jinkies said nothing. Logan lunged at him, forcing Ben aside and grabbing the Chief Inspector by his tie. "*Didn't you?*"

"No! No!" Jinkies protested. "I mean, not like that." He shot Ben and the others a pleading look. "He makes it sound worse than it is. It wasn't like that. He's just, Fulton Randall, he's just..."

"A friend of the station. Deserves to be kept in the loop," Logan said, finishing the sentence for him. He released his grip, letting Jinkies sink back to the floor, then turned to DS Lowrey. "You were worried there was a leak? Well, good news. We found it. There it is right there. So, do us all a favour, will you?"

He sneered down at the snivelling shitebag on the floor. "Plug the bastard up."

While Logan had been dealing with Jinkies, Hamza had been processing the ramifications of the new information, and had quickly come to the same conclusion that Logan had.

"If Fulton Randall knew that Brodie and the Gillespies were dealing..."

"Oh, that's not the half of it," Logan said. "He also knew about the domestics. He knew all along that Brodie had been kicking the shite out of his wee girl. When he heard about it yesterday, he seemed surprised, but it was an act. It was all an act."

"You don't think..." Ben began.

"Aye, I think," Logan said. He pointed through the glass to where Sandy Gillespie and his solicitor were sitting in silence. "You two get back in there. See what you can get out of them. Hamza, give DS Whatever-His-Name-Is a hand with the soon-to-be-former Chief Inspector Pickering, will you?"

"Uh, aye, sir," Hamza said, briefly locking eyes with the CID man.

"What about you, Jack?" Ben asked. "What are you going to do?"

"I'm going to sort this mess out," Logan said. He flexed and tightened his fingers, imagining them back around Jinkies' throat. "One way or another."

CHAPTER FORTY-FOUR

The driveway leading up to Fulton Randall's house was steep and uneven. It zig-zagged as it climbed the hill, forcing Logan to creep the Volvo around the corners in low gear.

At the top, it opened onto a wide driveway. Fulton's four-by-four had been neatly reversed in so it was facing down the hill. The car was reasonably new, but the paintwork was currently faded by the veneer of dusty white that coated most local cars when the temperature dropped and the gritters came out.

Logan parked beside the big Range Rover, peeked in through one of the car's side windows, then went striding towards the house.

He was at the door when he spotted the big plastic chest stationed just along the wall. A hatch on top and another on the front gave easy access to the contents.

Salt and grit, for keeping the driveway clear. The driveway was long, which meant the container was large. Large enough to hide a body in, with room to spare.

He was about to knock when he heard the *thudding* of little feet go running past, followed by a shout.

"Come here, you wee monkey!"

A giggle followed, then a squeal of delight.

It all stopped when Logan rapped his knuckles on the glass panel of the front door.

Fulton Randall looked surprised to see him. He spent a few seconds staring at the detective through the glass, then hurriedly opened the door.

"DCI Logan. Hello. I wasn't expecting... Well, anyone," he said.

"Sorry to intrude like this," Logan said. "Mind if I have a word?"

Fulton glanced back into the house. "Uh, aye. Sure. No problem. Hannah's not here, though, if you're looking for her. She and her mother nipped out. I'm left babysitting again."

"Actually, Mr Randall, it's you I wanted to talk to." Logan gestured past the man at the hallway beyond. "Do you mind?"

Fulton's hand was still on the door, his arm blocking Logan's path. His expression didn't change, but the texture of it seemed to shift, like he was deliberately holding his features in place.

"Of course. Aye. In you come," he said, stepping aside. He waited until Logan had entered, then closed the door and squeezed past the detective into the hall. "Carrie! I'll just be a minute, alright?"

A couple of coats hanging from a rack on the wall rustled as they were pushed aside to reveal the girl hiding behind them. "OK," she said, then she let them fall back until only her legs were visible at the bottom.

"Tea? Coffee?" Fulton asked, leading Logan in the direction of the kitchen.

"No. Thank you."

"Sure? I'm having one."

"I'll be fine," Logan reiterated.

The kitchen was old-fashioned, but fresh-looking, like it had been done recently in a deliberate, if not entirely convincing, farmhouse style. Logan waited while Fulton filled the kettle from an ornate copper-coloured tap.

Only when the kettle had been plugged in and switched on did Fulton turn around. "I heard one of your officers was injured. By Sandy Gillespie. Is that right?" he asked, concern troubling his brow.

"She died," Logan said.

"Oh. God. I'm so sorry," Fulton said, covering his mouth with a hand. "I mean... God. You got Gillespie, though, right? You caught him?"

Logan nodded. "Questioning him now."

"Right. Right. Well, that's something, I suppose," Fulton said. The kettle rolled closer to the boil behind him. He turned to a cupboard and took out a mug. The words 'Grandpa's Tea' were printed on it, and he half-smiled as he read them. "Do you think he could've been responsible for Brodie? For his murder, I mean?"

"The thought did occur," Logan confirmed.

"Makes sense, I suppose," Fulton said. "It's what happens, isn't it? In that, I don't know, world, or what have you. You get involved in something like that, chances are there are going to be consequences."

"Aye. It happens," Logan said. "We see it all the time. And, you know, for a minute there, I almost believed it. Nearly convinced myself that it was Sandy Gillespie or his sister who had murdered Brodie."

Fulton set the mug down on the counter. The water rumbled inside the kettle.

"But it wasn't. Was it, Fulton?"

"Wasn't it?" Fulton asked. His voice was high, elevated by an artificial lightness. "Are you sure? If he was involved with them in some sort of drugs thing, then I'd have thought it was obvious, given his injuries, that they—"

"Aye. That's what we were all meant to think. It was staged, you see? All orchestrated to make it look like it was drug-related. Killing him. Cutting him open. Even removing his teeth and fingers. It was carefully planned to make us think it was connected to Brodie's drug trafficking."

Logan let that hang in the air between them for a moment, before continuing.

"But, it wasn't."

"Wasn't it?" Fulton asked. The tremble in his voice was unmissable.

"It's over, Fulton," Logan told him. "I know what happened. I know what you did."

Both men stood in silence, Fulton's hands splayed flat on the kitchen worktop, the mug filling the space between them.

There was a loud *click* as the kettle came to the boil. The sound was a starting pistol that drew Logan's gaze for a split-second and kicked Fulton into life.

He shifted, spun. The mug exploded against Logan's left temple, filling his skull with pain and noise and swirling lights.

The floor lurched. Logan staggered, grabbing at Fulton. He found only thin air, and then felt a *crack* as his forehead met the edge of the kitchen worktop. He saw blood, tasted it, too, and then the floor came up to meet him, and he was dragged down, down, down into a stifling, smothering darkness.

LOGAN AWOKE to a woman screaming at him. It was the sound he heard first, his eyes stuck fast with blobs of drying blood. She was somewhere close, right in his face, and he shoved her away before rolling onto his front and heaving himself up onto his feet.

"What the hell's going on? Where's Dad? Where's Carrie?"

Logan thumbed the crusts from his eyes, and opened them to see Hannah Randall practically squaring up to him, panic etched across the freckles of her face. From elsewhere in the house, he heard an older woman shouting Fulton's name, but receiving no answer.

"Shite," Logan spat. He staggered to the window, the world bobbing and weaving around him like it was trying to get out of his way. "His car's gone."

"We know! What happened? What are you doing here?" Hannah demanded.

"He's not here," said her mother, scurrying into the kitchen. Sandra rushed over to Logan and turned him with a yank on his arm. "Where is he? Where's my husband?"

"Where's Carrie?" Hannah demanded. "Who did this to you? Was someone here?"

Her face crumpled. Tears rushed in. Sandra caught the girl around the shoulders, sensing an imminent collapse. "Did someone take her?" Hannah whispered.

"What's the car reg?" Logan asked, fishing into his pocket for his phone. He opened the text messaging app, then barked out the question again. "His car reg. What is it?"

Sandra shut her eyes in concentration, then recited the plate.

Logan thumbed the characters into a message, rattled off a couple of instructions, then sent it to Ben, Tyler, and Hamza.

"What's going on?" Hannah pleaded. Her eyes flicked to the spot on his forehead that was currently throbbing like a bastard. From the way she flinched, he reckoned it was a bad one. "Who did this?"

"Fulton did. Your dad," Logan said.

Both women exchanged looks of disbelief.

"What? No. Fulton?" Sandra said. "What are you talking about? What do you mean?"

"There's no time to explain," Logan told them. "I need you to think where he might be. Where he might have gone."

"Gone?" Sandra said, her pitch rising. "What do you mean? Why would he have gone anywhere? What are you talking about?"

Logan had lost enough time. He wasn't about to throw away any more.

"I have reason to believe Fulton killed Brodie."

"*What*?" Sandra spat. "Have you lost your mind?"

"When I started to question him, he did this." Logan pointed to his head injuries. "Now, he's gone, and he's taken your daughter with him, Hannah. He's taken Carrie. I need you to think where he might have gone."

Hannah's hands fumbled for the worktop, searching for support. "Mum?" she said. "What's he talking about?"

"I don't know. I don't know. It's nonsense. It's all nonsense!"

Logan shook his head, trying to clear away the cobwebs. The effect was almost exactly the opposite, and the world went blurry around the edges. He ignored it, and focused on the parts in the middle.

"Hannah, listen to me," he urged. "Whether he's guilty or not, your dad did this to me. He panicked. He's out there now somewhere, scared. Not thinking straight. And he's got your little girl with him."

Hannah covered her mouth with a trembling hand. "He wouldn't hurt her. He won't."

"Not deliberately, maybe," Logan said. "But she's out there with him now, and she'll be scared, and confused, just like he will be. But, she won't understand what's going on. She won't understand what's happening."

He stepped in closer. "So, I need you to think, Hannah. I need you to think about where he might go. Where he might've taken her."

Hannah shook her head, like she didn't want to think about it, didn't want to face up to the reality of what Logan was telling her.

For a moment, she looked like she was going to burst into tears, but then she sucked it up and swallowed it down. Her voice, when it came, was stronger than Logan had been expecting.

"He'd have headed down the road. Glasgow way, probably. He knows a lot of people down there."

"We've got a holiday rental," Sandra added. "Near Largs."

Logan's phone buzzed in his hand. He glanced at the message from Hamza.

"Right, well, we're on the lookout for the car. If he does head down that way, he'll get picked up on the cameras, if not before."

"I'm sure it's all just a... a misunderstanding," Sandra said. "Why would he kill Brodie? It's ridiculous! It doesn't make sense!"

"Aye, well, what matters right now is finding him. Everything else we can sort out after that, OK?" Logan said. "We've got eyes on the roads in all directions. Whichever way he goes, we'll find him, and then we can get to the bottom of it all once Carrie's back home safe. Alright?"

"Unless..." Hannah began.

She fell silent again, only continuing when Logan prompted her with a raised eyebrow, and an, "Unless what?"

Hannah met his gaze. Her eyes were wet with tears, and heavy with worry. "Unless he doesn't take the road."

CHAPTER FORTY-FIVE

He could feel the girl shivering in his arms, her wee body trembling under the blanket he'd grabbed from the back of the car.

"It's cold, Grandpa," she said, her chin wobbling as her teeth chattered together. "It's *fleezing*."

"I know, sweetheart. I know it's *fleezing*," Fulton said. His breath came out as a cloud of white mist, illuminated in the glow of his head torch. He rubbed her back through the blanket as he picked his way across the scree that covered this stretch of the mountainside. "We'll get you inside soon, OK? We'll get all warmed up."

"When?"

"Soon, OK?"

"How soon?"

"Just *soon*, Carrie, alright?"

He regretted his tone immediately, tried to make up for it by jiggling her in his arms and plastering on a smile. "It's an adventure! Just you and me, off on an adventure together. It's going to be fun. Won't it?"

He heard her sob beneath the blanket. *No, no, no.*

"How about a song, eh? Will we sing a song? What's that one you like? The wheels on the bus go..."

The voice that emerged from under the blanket was small and strained. "Round an' round."

"That's it! Round and round, round and round. The wheels on the bus go—"

His boot slipped on the loose stone shards, and he yelped as a leg went skiting out from under him. Twisting, he managed to land on his back, instead of his front, but the jarring impact brought a gasp, then tears from the girl in his arms.

"I'm sorry, I'm sorry, you're alright, you're OK," he soothed, rocking her back and forth. "I've got you, Carrie. We're alright."

Her cries settled down into sniffles, as Fulton got back to his feet. His back and shoulder ached from carrying her, and she clung to him as he swapped her from one arm to the other.

How long had they been walking for now? Two hours? Three? He'd left his watch and his phone back at the house, so he couldn't say for sure. The sun had dipped below the horizon a few miles back, though. If he hadn't had the head torch in the car, they'd be wandering blind by now.

The bothy had to be nearby. Ten minutes of trudging. Less, if he hurried. They could get a fire started in there, get them warm. Once he was warm, he could plan. He could figure out what to do. Figure out how to fix this mess.

But the girl was so heavy, and the fall had hurt his back. And ten minutes might as well have been a lifetime.

"I want to go home, Grandpa."

"Well, we can't right now, darling. Alright? Not yet. But we're going to somewhere even better. Just me and you. We'll get warm, you can have some chocolate—"

"I want home."

Anger bubbled up inside him, sharply tightening his grip on the girl. "Well, you can't go home, Carrie! Not yet. So stop complaining, alright?"

More tears came then. More wailing. Fulton marched on, the circle of torchlight sweeping across the scree, Carrie wrestling against him like she wanted to break free.

"Stop it! Stop it, you'll fall. Is that what you want? Is it? To fall? Because it's a long way down from here, and you won't like what happens when you get to the bottom!"

The crying intensified. The struggling, too. His arms burned like they were on fire. She was so heavy, and he'd been carrying her for so long.

"Shh. Stop. Stop it!"

She twisted in his grip. An elbow was driven into his throat. He felt her slip beneath the blanket, realised too late that she was going to fall. He grabbed for her, but found only the rough, woollen material.

There was a *thack* from the stones at his feet.

The crying stopped, and silence rushed in to fill the space it had left behind. The circle of light from the head torch picked out the lifeless shape on the scree, one arm folded in beneath her, one leg bent atop the other.

Fulton snatched her up, shook her, hugged her against him. She felt tiny and limp against him. And cold. So very cold.

"Carrie? Sweetheart. Come on. Come on, wake up," he whimpered. "Wake up, come on, darling, come on. Please. Wake up for Grandpa, alright? Wake up for—"

She screamed. It was simultaneously the best and worst noise Fulton had ever heard. He kept her pinned against him as she howled and wailed and screeched in his ear. She was cold, she was terrified, and she was hurting.

But she was alive. Thank God, she was alive.

It took her a good few minutes to run out of energy. The adrenaline spike that had fuelled the screaming session was exhausted, and she sagged in Fulton's arms.

With the crying over, the silence returned. Only, it wasn't silence this time. Not quite. There was another sound in there, too. A *whum-whum-whum* that he was only too familiar with.

Hugging Carrie closer to him, Fulton clicked off his torch and began to run just as the helicopter crested the top of the mountain ahead of them, its spotlight slicing through the darkness. The roar of the rotors was deafening, their downdraft flattening the heather and bracken further up the mountainside.

Down there, on the scree, they were too low for the spotlight to reach them. If they could make it past, get to the next ridge without being seen, they could still make it to the bothy.

They couldn't stay there now, of course. Not for long. But he could take a few minutes to rest. He could find a way to get Carrie on his back, make her easier to carry. He could think. For a minute, he could just stop and think.

A bundle of stone fragments slipped out from beneath his feet. He was ready for it this time and kept his balance as they slid a few dozen feet down the hillside, further away from the beam of the helicopter's spotlight.

There were trees ahead. Not many, but enough to offer some cover. Slipping and skidding across the scree, he stumbled into the bracken, and went scurrying through the copse of trees.

The thundering of the rotor blades faded as Fulton emerged from the thicket and rounded the shoulder of the mountain. Clinging to his granddaughter with one arm, he kicked and pulled them up the steep incline, making hand-holds from whatever foliage he could reach.

They were both breathing heavily when he finally got them to the ridge. The helicopter was half a mile away and still going, and Fulton felt safe enough switching his head torch back on.

The circle of light immediately picked out the old stone wall of the bothy. It had been a hill crofter's house, once upon a time, but was now open to climbers and walkers passing through the area. A place for rest and respite from the unforgiving terrain.

There was no smoke from the chimney, and no signs of movement from inside. Fulton hurried to the front door and shouldered it open, then turned and closed it behind him, before wedging it shut with the back of one of the bothy's rickety wooden chairs.

"Here we are, here we go. What did I tell you?" Fulton whispered, rubbing the warmth back into Carrie's shivering body. She hadn't said anything since the fall. Barely made a sound since she'd stopped crying, in fact.

She was probably tired, that was all. Tired, and cold, and hungry. Half an hour here would see them both right. Half an hour with the fire on, and they'd both be ready to set off again.

He found a box of matches on the mantle. There was a candle, too, the wax mostly melted until it was little more than a stumpy little stub with a blackened wick. It wouldn't be bright enough to see from outside—not from the helicopter, certainly—but a bit of light might help set Carrie at ease.

He wasted a couple of matches before he was able to get the thing lit. The flame burned tall and bright for a few seconds, before settling down. In that moment, though, he saw the shadow dancing across the wall.

"Well, well, well. Fancy seeing you here, Mr Randall."

Fulton tightened his grip on the girl as Logan stepped forward into the shallow pool of the candlelight.

"I was starting to think you weren't going to show."

Fulton's mouth flapped open and closed. "I don't... It's not what it looks like. None of this. I don't know what you think happened, but it's, it's, it's not that."

Logan pointed to his face. One side of it was a mess of bruising, swelling, and blood that had dried almost black.

"You didn't wallop me with a mug?" he said. "You didn't put your granddaughter at risk by fleeing with her into the mountains?"

The floorboards creaked as Logan came to a stop. "You didn't murder Brodie Welsh?"

"No, I... It's not like that. You've got it all wrong!"

"Enlighten me then, Mr Randall," Logan said. "Tell me what happened. Explain it to me."

Carrie wriggled in Fulton's arms. He rubbed her back and rocked from foot to foot, trying to soothe her. "I don't... I can't..."

"How about I tell you what I think happened? Make it easier," Logan said. "I think you found out exactly who and what Brodie was. I think you were so angry with him, so disgusted by him, that you decided to get rid of him. For Hannah's sake. And Carrie's."

Fulton flinched at the sound of the girl's name and hugged her so tightly she whimpered beneath the blanket.

"I think you thought you could pin it on the Gillespies. Make it look like a drugs thing by cutting him open. Shift the blame to them, kill two birds with one stone," Logan continued. "But, for that to work, he had to be found, didn't he? You kept him in your grit bin until you could move him, and then, once you'd buried him and left a few Gillespie-sized footprints around the place, you made the call to the mountain rescue, knowing someone would find his body."

The windows of the bothy shook, and a trickle of dust fell from the rafters as the helicopter came circling back towards the building.

"That's about the size of it, isn't it, Mr Randall? That's pretty close."

Fulton's throat was tight and narrow, and barely able to get the words out.

"He was hitting her. He was hurting my daughter."

"Aye. I know," Logan said.

"What if he'd hurt Carrie, too? Hmm? What if he'd started hitting her? Or worse! What then?"

"I understand your concerns, Fulton. I do. I've a daughter myself. If I found out someone was hurting her. Causing her pain. Well..." Logan's eyes briefly glazed over, like some internal realisation was drawing power from the rest of him. "Well, I'd never forgive them. I'd hate them for it."

Fulton shook his head, sending tears plopping to the dusty wooden floor. "I didn't hate him. Not really. I didn't want him to suffer. I just... When I found out what he'd done. What he was doing. I couldn't just let it go on. I couldn't. I had to do something. For Carrie's sake. I didn't want to, but I had to. I had to!"

The *whumming* of the helicopter rotors grew louder overhead. Outside, the beam of the searchlight came sweeping across the heather.

"Aye, well, let's go get you both warmed up, Fulton," Logan said. "We can talk about this somewhere a bit less..." He gestured around at the bothy. "...grim."

Fulton rocked the child in his arms. She had stopped struggling now. He could hear her breathing, soft and slow, feel its warmth against his neck.

He'd never have this again. Never have this closeness. Never have another moment like this one, with her holding him, trusting him, loving him.

He'd killed her daddy. She'd never forgive him. He might not even see her again.

The thought of it kicked his weary legs into life and he raced for the door, Carrie clutched to him like a rugby ball as he went barrelling outside into the blinding bright storm of the helicopter.

"Fulton, wait!"

Logan's voice was right behind him. Close. Too close. Fulton slammed the door on him and broke into a run, tripping and stumbling through the spotlight's beam.

They were going to take her. Take Carrie. Take her away from him forever.

He couldn't let them. He couldn't lose her. Wouldn't. Not here. Not now. Not like this.

The edge of the ridge came up quickly, catching him by surprise. He skidded to a stop just inches from where the ground fell away, and heard the distant clatter of sliding rocks on the mountainside far below.

The chopper's downdraft was like a hand on his back, forcing him closer to the edge, and the long drop beyond it. He was a step away, that was all. One step. Just one, and he'd never have to see the look of betrayal on his granddaughter's face. He'd never have to hear Hannah tell him he'd never get to see either of them again.

He'd never have to face up to what he'd done.

One step.

Just one.

Fulton's foot trembled as he raised it off the ground.

"Don't you fucking dare!"

The tone and the wording of the shout took him by surprise. He wobbled for a moment, then his foot returned to join the other on the ground.

He shuffled around in a tight half-circle to find Logan silhouetted against the spotlight's beam, his coat billowing around him like a cape.

"What the hell do you think you're playing at, you daft bastard?" the detective demanded.

It was not the sort of negotiation strategy that Fulton had been expecting, and his brain struggled to formulate any sort of response.

"You're going to jump. Is that it?" Logan asked. "You're going to jump off there with your granddaughter in your arms?"

Fulton glanced back at the drop. Six inches behind his heels, the world fell away into darkness. It would be quick. She'd never even know.

"They won't let me see her again," he sobbed, raising his voice over the thunder of the rotor blades. "I'll go to jail, and they'll all hate me, and I won't get to see her again."

"Aye, well, can you blame them? You're threatening to kill her, Fulton," Logan said. "Does that sound like the sort of person that should be involved in her life? Honestly?"

Fulton tightened his grip on the girl. She groaned in her sleep, or her exhaustion, but otherwise didn't react.

"You say you care about her—"

"I do! Of course, I do! I did all this for her! I love her!"

"Not from where I'm standing, you don't," Logan said. "From where I'm standing, you're a selfish bastard who'd rather end her life here and now than have her find out what you did. If you can't have her, no one can. Is that it, Fulton?"

"No! No, it's not like that!"

Logan sighed. "Look, if you want to jump, be my guest."

Fulton blinked. "What?"

"I mean it. I'd rather you didn't, but honestly? I don't care. Jump. Don't. It's up to you," Logan said. He took a step forward and held out a hand. "But give me the girl, Fulton. Give me Carrie. She doesn't deserve this. She deserves to go to school, make friends, fall in love. She deserves to have a life."

He shuffled forward a step. Fulton didn't flinch or draw back.

"Are you really going to take that from her?" Logan pressed. "Or are you going to be her grandfather, and do what's right?"

Fulton rocked the girl, whispering to her, as tears cut tracks down his cheeks. She was cold. So cold. Her breathing so shallow.

What was he doing? What had he done?

He pulled the blanket aside, just a fraction, and kissed the top of her head. He inhaled her, breathing in the smell of her for what he knew would be the very last time.

She stirred, opened her eyes, and looked up into his. She smiled, just for a moment, then her eyelids grew heavy again, and her head fell against his chest.

Fulton nodded, just once, and held the precious bundle out. "Here. Take her," he said. "Hurry."

Logan approached quickly but cautiously, one hand outstretched, the other emerging from his coat pocket. He took the girl, blanket and all, and hugged her against him.

Fulton opened his mouth, and something primal emerged. Fear, and angst, and anger, and shame, all mixed up in one desperate, pitiful cry.

He turned away. Took a step. His foot found nothing but empty air.

And then, metal dug into his wrist, pain shot up his arm, and he was dragged back from the edge of the abyss.

Fulton stared in disbelief at the handcuff around his wrist. At the other end of it, DCI Logan drew himself up to his full, terrifying height.

"Fulton Randall," he began. "I am arresting you on suspicion of the murder of Brodie Welsh."

CHAPTER FORTY-SIX

Four days later, Logan muttered to himself as he readjusted his tie for the fifth time in as many minutes. He hated the bloody things, and this one seemed determined to be as difficult as possible. It was either too long or too short, or all twisted at the knot.

He'd tried everything—using the mirror, not using the mirror, tying it first then pulling it on over his head, calling it an arsehole and throwing it across the room. You name it, he'd done it, and still the thing wasn't sitting right.

"You no' ready yet?" asked Ben.

"It's this bastarding tie," Logan said. He grimaced as he tried to flatten down the twisted knot. "It's broken."

"It's a tie. How can it be broken?" Ben asked. He swatted Logan's hands away and stretched up, adjusting the tie for him. "Here. Let me have a look."

Logan tilted his head back, giving the DI free rein.

"Maybe if you didn't have such a fat neck," Ben muttered.

"It's no' a fat neck, it's a boxer's neck," Logan insisted.

"Aye, and I suppose they're boxer's chins, too, are they?"

Logan started to protest, but a sudden tightening of the tie choked him into silence.

"There," Ben said, stepping back. "How's that?"

Logan tucked a finger into his shirt collar and loosened the tie a fraction, then checked his reflection in the hotel mirror. "Aye. Fine."

His phone *dinged,* and he searched the pockets of his suit until he found it. Ben watched him as he checked the screen.

"Anything exciting?"

"Email from Hoon," Logan said, scrolling through the message. "Fulton Randall's court date has been set."

"That was quick."

"Aye, well, he's confessed to everything. Murdering Brodie, trying to frame the Gillespies. The works."

Back at the station, Fulton had been quick to sing, and slow to stop. He'd confirmed that Sergeant Jaffray had let slip about the domestic assault. Once he'd heard about that, he'd gone straight to Jinkies, who'd revealed Brodie's connection to the Gillespies. He'd done it 'one friend to another,' Fulton insisted, but that would make no difference to the internal investigation, Logan knew. Jaffray might get through it with a demotion, but Jinkies was done for.

Good riddance.

It hadn't all tied up neatly, though. Fulton insisted he had nothing to do with Maureen Gillespie's murder, and there was no evidence to connect him to it. He also hadn't found any drugs when he'd cut Brodie open, so there was very probably some sort of missing shipment out there somewhere. Whose hands it was in, if anyone's, remained a mystery.

Sandy Gillespie wasn't talking, either. He claimed that Maureen had been the mastermind behind their little drug empire, and that he'd never even heard the names of the people she was working with, never mind met them.

He was scared. That much was obvious. Someone had to have told him about Maureen's death, and unless they had some sort of psychic sibling link that extended beyond the grave, it was likely that the someone in question was directly involved in her murder.

Still, they would have plenty of time to work on him. They had him bang to rights on Caitlyn's murder. He wasn't going anywhere for a long, long time.

"You spoken to the family again?" Ben asked, as he unhooked his suit jacket from the hanger on the back of the door.

"Bit snug that, Benjamin," Logan remarked, as the DI squeezed himself into it. "And aye. Yesterday. Just briefly."

"How's the wee one?" Ben asked. He started fastening a button, then realised it was a bridge too far, and decided just to let the jacket hang open.

"Full of the cold. Confused. Wondering where her dad and her granddad are."

Ben sucked air in through his teeth. "They've not told her?"

"How do you explain it to someone her age?" Logan asked.

"Aye. Rather them than me, right enough," Ben said. "How are the wife and daughter?"

"About how you'd expect," Logan said. "It won't be easy for them."

He fiddled with his tie again, earning himself a slap on the arm from the older man.

"Leave that. It's fine."

Logan rubbed a hand across his chin. For once, it was completely smooth. Well, mostly. He'd found a tiny patch he'd missed between his chin and his neck, and it had been annoying him ever since. Not enough for him to go dig out his shaving gear again, but enough that he kept feeling it with his thumb and tutting.

There was a knock at the door. Ben checked his watch, adjusted his own tie, then gave Logan the look both of them had been quietly dreading.

"You ready, then?" he asked.

Logan wasn't ready. He never was for these things. Not really.

"Aye. Ready," he lied, then he pulled on his coat as Ben opened the door.

Hamza, Tyler, and Sinead stood out in the corridor, sombre and silent, all dressed up in shades of black.

Logan adjusted his collar, shoved his hands deep down in his pockets, and checked his reflection one more time. He nodded, accepting that his reflection was as good as it was likely to get.

"Right, then. We fit?" he asked.

"Ready, boss," Tyler said, and the others murmured their agreement.

Ben joined them in the corridor. Logan stepped out, letting the door close behind him.

"Nice day for it," Ben remarked, as they stepped out of the hotel and into the bracing Orkney air a couple of minutes later.

Logan looked up. The sky was lined with shades of grey. A blanket of thick cloud hung over everything, dark, and heavy, and oppressive.

"Aye. Pretty much perfect, I'd say," he observed.

His phone buzzed in his pocket. He checked the screen.

'Unknown Caller'.

He regarded it impassively for a few moments, letting it vibrate in his hand.

"Everything alright, Jack?" Ben asked.

Logan thumbed the button to reject the call and switched the handset off.

"Aye. Everything's fine," he said.

And with that, they joined the slow procession heading to the church, and set off to say their final farewells.

Together.

THE LAST BLOODY STRAW

DCI JACK LOGAN BOOK FIVE

CHAPTER ONE

The final evening of Iona Wallace's life started well enough. A couple of drinks in the house, the last of the oven chips—plenty of salt and vinegar—and a quick wash of the nether-regions over the bathroom sink, because you never knew your luck.

The weather had seen to it that the ferries were off more than they were on lately, but there might still be the odd tourist looking to have some fun. God knew, the island was in short supply of anything else that might pass for entertainment.

After a wee skoosh of perfume in all the wrong places, she wrestled herself into a dress. It was a figure-hugging burgundy number that matched her favourite shade of lipstick, which was about the only thing the dress had going for it these days.

She'd bought it a decade ago in Inverness. It hadn't been figure-hugging then. Nor, she suspected, was it ever designed to be.

Iona checked her cleavage, twisting and bending at the waist to survey it from every possible angle. Perfect. Sure, it was taking more and more scaffolding to keep it that way, but to the casual observer, she looked as young as she ever had.

Her reflection met her eye in the mirror.

Aye, right.

When she stepped outside, the cold grabbed her lungs and twisted, ejecting twin snorts of steam from her nostrils, and instantly cutting through her carefully cultivated alcohol fuzz.

"Jesus fuck!"

She pulled her coat tighter around her shoulders, hugging herself through it. The fur collar, once thick and luxurious, was now a sparse, paltry thing. She'd found it in a charity shop longer ago than she'd care to remember, and it had served as an important part of her armour ever since.

The identity of the animal that the fur had once belonged to had been a mystery back then, and was even more so now. Most people guessed mink. When they did, Iona would just wink and smile enigmatically, confirming nothing, and denying even less.

It was half a mile to the pub if you went by the track, a good bit less if you cut across the field. Her boots were reasonably sensible—between the island terrain and her back, heels were out of the question these days—but with the rain they'd been having of late, the field would be a marsh.

She shut the cottage's front door with a *clunk* that rattled the windows in their frames. There was no need to lock it. Not out here.

"You'll keep an eye on the place, won't you, Archie?" Iona cackled into the darkness. Fifty yards across the field, the pale moonlight picked out the eyeless hollows of a crudely-formed face.

Lighting the last cigarette from her crumpled pack, Iona took a draw, savoured the swirl of smoke as it warmed her lungs, then set off down the track under the empty-eyed gaze of the scarecrow.

"Christ. What's she doing here?"

Isaac Young found himself taking cover behind the double-doors of the pub, the sight of his mother stumbling from table to table freezing the blood in his veins more effectively than the cold wind blowing in off the water could ever hope to.

A hand slipped into his, fingers interlocking like they were a custom fit, built to be together. His fiancée, Louise, offered him the most convincingly authentic smile she could muster and gave his hand a squeeze.

"It'll be fine. It's a Tuesday night, and it's hardly party central in here. She probably won't stay long."

Isaac exhaled slowly. "Aye. She might get a lumber," he said. He returned the smile, but it was even less genuine than the one Louise had plastered on. The pain in his eyes almost made her recoil.

Through the glass of the door, Isaac watched his mum draping herself over the bar, cleavage aimed squarely at the Australian barman, eyelids fluttering.

"Jesus, he's younger than me," Isaac muttered.

"We can go somewhere else," Louise suggested. "There's always..." She ran through her mental list of available options. "...home."

Isaac was tempted. She could see it on his face, and in the way the tension in his shoulders eased off.

But then, he shook his head.

"We came out for a drink. We're having a drink," he said, then he pushed open the door, and they both stepped inside.

The warmth of the place reached out to welcome them, the fire blazing in the grate a Siren-call from the other side of the wood-panelled room.

There were half a dozen other people gathered near the fire. Most of them were local, and so made a point of not catching Isaac's eye, sparing all concerned from that moment of embarrassment.

A fella in his forties looked up from where he'd been studying a map at the corner table. He wasn't native to the island, and the big backpack propped up on the seat beside him suggested he had no intentions of becoming one.

Nevertheless, he gave the newcomers a nod and a smile, tentatively attempting to initiate a conversation that neither of them had any interest in being part of.

"What you having?" Isaac asked Louise, his gaze still fixed on his mother's back. She was wearing that ugly fur coat and the burgundy dress that was too young for a woman half her age and a third her size.

"Bottle of Fraoch," Louise said. "Sure you don't want me to—?"

"It's fine," Isaac said, already approaching the bar.

He took up a spot as far from his mother as it was possible to get. The bar was small and curved, though, so the distance between them was no distance at all.

The barman, Bruce, noticed him first, relief spreading across his face like a fast-acting rash as he extracted himself from the conversation with Iona and came striding over to Isaac, a slurred, "Ah, fuck off, then," following behind him.

"Evening, mate. What can I get for you?" asked Bruce, his Australian accent so thick as to almost be a parody of itself.

"Pint of cider and a bottle of Fraoch," Isaac said. He'd gone from glaring at his mother to studiously avoiding meeting her eye. It was coming, of course—there was no escaping that—but he was happy to delay it for as long as he could.

Bruce's big forehead furrowed behind the curtains of his blond hair. "Cider and...?"

"Fraoch," Isaac repeated. He pointed to the fridge at the back of the bar. "The heather ale."

"Right. Gotcha. Sorry. Still getting the hang of the lingo," Bruce beamed, reaching for a pint glass.

"Zac!"

Isaac took a slow breath through his nose. Here it came.

"Mum."

She shambled closer, one arm in constant contact with the bar, like it was playing a vital part in her remaining upright.

"Ditched the bitch for the night, have you?" Iona asked. She grinned, showing a smudge of lipstick on her teeth. Each of her eyes seemed to be blinking independently of the other, and the wafts of her breath had probably pushed Isaac over the drink-drive limit before he'd touched a drop.

"Louise's over there," Isaac replied, pointing to one of the tables by the fire.

Iona turned and spent a few seconds trying to focus, before she raised a hand and gave a little wave. Louise's reply was a curt nod, then a questioning look at Isaac that he dismissed with a shake of his head.

"Shite, aye, so she is," Iona said, turning back to her son. "You still...?"

"Yes. And we're happy."

Iona pulled a face that suggested she couldn't possibly comprehend how, then shrugged and showed the lipstick on her teeth again. "Buy your mum a drink."

"I think you've had enough."

She laughed at that. He didn't.

"Funny. Like your dad."

Isaac blocked his mother's hand before she could reach up to stroke his hair. He'd been ready for it. For the insincerity of it. Of her.

"Come on. One drink. For your old mum."

"Four-eighty, mate."

Mother and son both turned as the drinks were set down. Bruce looked between them, settling in the end on Isaac.

"Or... Sorry, did you want something else?"

Isaac fished in his pocket and pulled out a handful of coins. "No," he said, counting out the exact amount and handing it over. "No, that's everything."

The words were shouted at his back, each one louder and packed with more venom than the one before.

"Fucking selfish little *twat*!"

The pub was all but silent as Isaac took his seat, the only sound the crackling and popping of the logs on the fire, and the faint droning of the background music.

"You know what I gave up for you? What I fucking sacrificed?"

Louise answered on Isaac's behalf. "Yes, everyone's very aware of what you sacrificed, Iona. Nothing."

"The fuck's it got to do with you?" Iona snarled. She released her grip on the bar and stumbled, untethered, towards the group knotted around the fire. "You snooty fucking jumped-up fucking... fucking... cow."

Chair legs scraped on the rough wooden floor. One of the men who had been sitting staring into their drink straightened to his full, impressive height.

His voice was slow and methodical, like each word was having to be thought about in advance.

"I think you should go."

Iona almost collided with him, only stopping herself by placing a hand on his broad chest. It felt solid beneath his thick checked shirt.

"Dudley. You don't get it," she spat. "You don't know what the bitch is like."

"You want to say that to my face?" Louise snapped.

"Gladly. If this big fucking... retard gets out of my way."

Half a dozen heads turned her way.

"Hey, now!"

"That's enough of that."

Iona looked across the angry faces glaring up at her. Her neighbours. Her 'friends'. What was it to do with them? What was it to do with anyone?

She turned away from them, and the backpacker in the corner was too slow in looking down.

"Haw. You," she called over to him. "Want to buy me a drink?"

The tourist raised his head just long enough to give it a shake.

Iona shifted her weight, creaking her leather boots. She adjusted her cleavage before trying again.

"You want to come back to my place?"

"Jesus Christ," Isaac muttered, choking down a sip of his pint.

"Uh, no," said the tourist. "Thank you."

"What are you? A poof, or something?" Iona demanded, her face twisting into a scowl. She turned on the spot, arms out, presenting herself to the rest of the bar. "Anyone else up for a go? Hmm? Buy us a drink and I'm all yours."

Louise bounced to her feet, her knee clonking against the table and rocking the drinks in the glasses. She dodged past Dudley and slammed both hands against Iona's shoulders, sending her staggering clumsily towards the door.

"Oh, just fuck off, will you?" Louise spat. "Look at you! Look at the state of you! You're an embarrassment, Iona. You're a complete fucking horror show, and you need to go. Seriously. Go."

Iona stood by the door, her chest heaving, her face reddening with rage or shame or some rich blend of the two.

For several seconds, both women just stared at one another in the near-silence. Then, with a shifting of her gaze, Iona looked to Isaac. To her son.

"Are you going to let this bitch talk to me like that?"

Isaac looked up from his drink, just briefly. Just once.

"Go home, Mum," he said. "Just go home."

The world lurched sickeningly, the slick, sodden ground contorting beneath her bare feet as if it were alive. She stumbled on through the dark, pain radiating from the wound on her head, blood nipping at eyes already blinded by the darkness.

She could hear the footsteps behind her. A little slower than her own, but more controlled. Less frantic. Gaining. Always gaining.

"Leave me alone!" she screamed into the chasing void.

Only the wet *thacking* of those footsteps replied. Stable. Steady.

Inevitable.

Her fur coat trailed behind her through the mud, flapping from one arm. Her shoes were gone. Her dress was torn. The alcohol and the head wound were working together to spin the world in looping circles around her, and she had no idea where she was running to. No idea where she was going.

Anywhere but here. Anywhere but now. Anywhere. Somewhere. Please, God, let her get somewhere.

The ground rolled like the deck of a ship in a storm. Thrown sideways, she caught sight of a figure standing in the darkness and grabbed for its outstretched arms, eyes pleading, mouth already babbling a cry for help.

"P-please, help me! Help me!"

The crudely stitched mouth couldn't have replied, even if it had wanted to. The empty, eyeless gaze of a hessian sack peered down at her, like Christ gazing down from the cross.

A breeze swirled around them, fluttering the scarecrow's ragged clothes, and almost disguising the *slap-slap-slap* of wet footsteps approaching.

Almost.

"Please, don't," she whispered, still clinging to the scarecrow like it might yet leap to her defence.

The footsteps stopped. A weapon raised.

And Iona Wallace died screaming in the dark.

CHAPTER TWO

DCI Jack Logan regarded the man in the chair like one might regard a big daud of shite on a clean kitchen worktop. The big daud of shite in question smirked up at him from behind his expensive desk, his Italian leather seat creaking over and over as he rocked it incrementally back and forth.

"I would like to say I was expecting you, my friend. But this would be a lie, yes?"

Bosco Maximuke held his hands out in a welcoming gesture and ratcheted his smirk up a notch or two. "Still. Is nice surprise. To what am I owing this pleasure?"

Logan didn't return the smile. He had no interest in exchanging pleasantries with the podgy Russian bastard. This was anything but a social call.

Not that Bosco had any real intention of making nice, either. Logan could feel Valdis, the largest and most Neanderthal-like of Bosco's small army of henchmen, looming a pace or two behind him. He could hear the faint whistle of the man's breathing, hear the rustling of his gloved fingers as they curled into fists over and over and over again. Classic intimidation strategy.

Aye, good luck with that.

Logan shot a glance over to the corner of the room, where Bosco's daughter was tapping away on an iPad, a set of *Pokémon* headphones clamped over her ears.

"In-service day," Bosco said, reading the detective's mind. "I swear, I should've been teacher. So much time off."

"Teachers work in-service days," the girl said without turning.

"Oh. Well. Good," Bosco said, after a moment's thought. "This is what my taxes pay for. This and..." He gave a dismissive wave in Logan's direction. "... you people, of course."

Clasping his hands on the desk in front of him, the Russian leaned forward. "Please, my friend, speak freely," he told the DCI. "What brings you here to my workplace? Have you come to scratch my back, or are you hoping for me to scratch yours?"

"Neither, actually," Logan replied. "I met some friends of yours recently. Or... associates, maybe. Sandy and Maureen Gillespie. Down near Fort William."

Bosco puffed out his acne-scarred cheeks, his smile fixed in place. "Never heard of them."

"See, I think you have," Logan argued. "I think you knew them well. I think you and they had a business relationship going on, Bosco. A thriving business relationship."

"Oh! They were in building trade?" the Russian asked, with an air of innocence that didn't remotely suit him.

"The other business," Logan said. "And I think it turned sour after one of their guys went and got himself killed, when he was supposed to be bringing in a shipment of merchandise from abroad."

He took a hand from his coat pocket and jabbed a finger in the Russian's direction. "Your shipment. Your merchandise."

The floor of the Portakabin office creaked as Valdis shifted his weight. Bosco shot him a look, and Logan could swear he felt the henchman's internal struggle as he fought to contain himself.

"I, of course, have no idea what you mean, Detective Chief Inspector," Bosco said. "I resent any suggestion that I may be mixed up in any... how would you say? Criminal activity. If this is what you are suggesting."

"Do us both a favour and cut the shite, Bosco. I know you were funnelling your gear through the Gillespies," Logan said, his voice dropping into a guttural growl. He jabbed a thumb over his shoulder. "And I know that you—or, more likely, this big streak o' pish—killed Maureen."

"Oh, and how would you know such a thing?" Bosco asked.

"Sandy," said Logan, and the word seemed to hang there in the air between them. "Sandy told us everything."

Bosco stopped rocking in his chair. The creaking of Valdis's gloves fell silent, too, and the only sound in the office was the tapping and swiping of Olivia's fingers on the iPad screen, and the faint *tshk, tshk, tshk,* of music playing over her headphones.

Eventually, the Russian cleared his throat. His smile, which had all but died away, returned, bringing reinforcements with it. "Oh. Did he, now?"

Logan said nothing.

Damn it.

So much for that plan.

"No, I think he did not. I think if this 'Sandy' you speak of had told you the things you say he told you, then you would not be standing here in my office alone. You would not be—what is word? Fishing. You would have cars, and vans. Helicopters, maybe. You would have idiots in uniform scurrying around, poking their noses in. Poke, poke. Pry, pry."

Bosco rolled his chair back and stood up. The shirt he was wearing probably cost more than Logan made in a week, but the Russian's squat, bloated frame did it no favours at all.

Logan watched in silence as Bosco unfastened his gold cufflinks and began to roll up the shirt sleeves with slow, calculated precision.

"You know what I think, old friend? I think that nobody knows you are here. I think you are here on personal vendetta. I think you are looking for someone to blame for death of... police woman. What was her name again?"

Logan bristled. Deep in the pockets of his coat, his hands became fists.

"Caitlyn? This is right, yes? Caitlyn... Silly Scottish name..." Bosco clicked his fingers, like the name was dancing around on the tip of his tongue. "McQuarrel?"

"Detective Sergeant McQuarrie," Logan said. "And yes."

Bosco finished rolling up his sleeves and raised an eyebrow. "Yes?"

"You're right. Nobody knows I'm here. Honestly? I don't care if you were supplying the Gillespies. Not really. That'll all come out in the wash sooner or later. That's CID's job, no' mine."

He took a half-step forward so he was towering over the desk, and the man standing behind it.

"But yes, Bosco, I'd very much like to blame someone for the death of DS McQuarrie. Don't get me wrong, Sandy Gillespie pulled the trigger, and I'm going to make damn sure that he spends every waking moment of his miserable life deeply regretting that decision."

Taking his hands from his pockets, Logan leaned down. He placed his knuckles on the desk and rested his weight on them, like a silverback gorilla demonstrating its dominance.

"But I also hold the individual who drove him to pull that trigger equally responsible," he continued. His voice was flat and measured. No nonsense. Matter-of-fact. "I also blame the person who got him so scared, so wound up, that he shot one of my officers dead. You see, *that* person? That's the one I'm gunning for now, Bosco."

He gave that a moment to sink in, before standing up straight.

"And, let me be very clear when I say that I will stop at nothing to bring that bastard down. I'll dedicate my life to it, if I have to. Whatever protections he's built around himself, whatever wee empire he thinks he lords it over, I will burn it all to the ground with him inside it, and I will dance on the fucking ashes. Is that understood?"

For a moment, Bosco almost looked concerned, but then he nodded sympathetically. "I understand, my friend. I do. It was tragic loss. We were all very cut up when we heard about her having her guts blown out."

Bosco made the sound of a gunshot, then clutched at his stomach before beaming broadly over Logan's shoulder. "Weren't we, Valdis?"

"Heartbroken," agreed Valdis. His accent was thicker and less polished than Bosco's. The voice came from closer than Logan had expected. A pace. Half a pace, maybe. No distance at all.

"You know what else upsets me?" Bosco continued. He was peering down at his metal desk organiser, fingers dancing above an assortment of pens and pencils.

He finally selected a metal fountain pen, removed the lid, and tapped his finger gingerly against the pointed tip. He hissed as it drew blood, then gave the fingertip a quick suck before continuing.

"Your arrogance. Your stupidity. You are suggesting that I am big bad guy. That I am evil villain, but you come barging in here making accusations. Making your threats. In front of my employees. In front of my family."

He gestured to Olivia, who was still glued to her iPad, paying them no heed whatsoever.

"You have no evidence. No proof," Bosco said.

Logan heard the *clunk* of the door being locked behind him.

"No back-up. No support. No-one who knows where you are."

Bosco's smile broadened, showing his yellowing teeth.

"Death of the woman cop has made you forgetful. Careless, maybe," the Russian continued. "You forget that I know things, my friend. That I have scratched your back in past. Do your bosses know this? Your subordinates? I think not. What would they say? What would they think of you? What would they do to the great Detective Chief Inspector Jack Logan if they knew what you really are?"

Bosco rolled his chair in all the way under his desk, and untucked his shirt from his belt. Freed from this constraint, his stomach flopped out over the top of his belt. One of the bottom buttons had come undone, revealing a diamond of hairy flesh.

"I think maybe you need reminder of who is in charge here, yes?" Bosco said. "I think we must do you favour, and jog your memory."

Logan sensed the looming presence of Valdis behind him again. He felt the heat of the man's breath on the nape of his neck, breathed in the stink of it. He watched as Bosco turned the pen over and over in his hands, the pointed nib glinting in the office's artificial lighting.

He knew what was coming next. Of course he did. He'd known from the moment he'd set foot inside the office. From the moment he'd made his excuses to get out of the station that afternoon.

From before then, even. When he'd woken up that morning. When he'd stood at Caitlyn's graveside. When he'd sat at the back of the church watching her parents crying in the front row.

When he'd seen the hole in Sandy Gillespie's front door, and the spray of blood on the path.

Yes, that was it. Then. That was when he'd known this moment was coming. That was when he knew he'd be standing here. Now. In this room.

"You not going to send her out of the room first?" Logan asked, indicating Bosco's daughter with a nod. "She doesn't need to see this."

"Forgive me, old friend, but I do not think you are right man to give parenting advice. Anyway, I disagree. One day, this will all be hers," Bosco said, gesturing around at the world in general. "She must get used to the business of doing business sooner or later. Yes? Why not today?"

"You sure that's wise? I mean, how old is she?" Logan asked.

Bosco's smile was swept away by an indignant sneer. "None of your fucking business. That is how old," he snapped, then he gave a wave of his hand, and Logan felt a burst of movement behind him.

He was ready as the bastard made a grab for him. A half-step back, a sudden jerk of the head, and Valdis's nose exploded against the back of Logan's skull. The detective followed it up with an elbow to the henchman's solar plexus, then turned and capped it all off with a particularly satisfying knee to the balls.

Satisfying for him, at least. Less so for Valdis, judging by the way he buckled in the middle and dropped to the floor, choking on snot, tears, and a not inconsiderable amount of blood.

Bosco stared, open-mouthed, as Logan rounded on him. He tried to retreat, but there was nothing but wall behind him, leaving nowhere for him to go.

He yelped in fright as Logan lunged across the desk and grabbed him by the shirt, cried out in shock as the pen was ripped from his grasp and his hand was slammed onto the desktop.

Logan raised the pen, nib pointing downwards. Bosco's face came alive with panic.

"No, no, please, no! My daughter! My daughter is here!"

"Come on, Bosco. Got to get her used to the business of doing business, sooner or later, eh?" Logan spat, his grip tightening on the pen's metal casing. "Why not today?"

He brought the pen down hard. Bosco screamed—a high-pitched squeal like a pig going to slaughter—as the pointed nib tore through the web of flesh between forefinger and thumb, and was embedded into the desktop below.

"You... fuck! Crazy fuck!" the Russian sobbed.

Logan turned and looked over his shoulder at Olivia, who was gazing at them in rapt fascination.

"You. Outside," he told her. "Now."

The girl's brow furrowed in complaint. "Aw, but I want to—"

"Just do as you're told, alright?" Logan instructed.

She looked between the detective and her father for a few moments, then tutted and picked up her iPad.

"Fine," she muttered, stepping over Valdis on her way to the door.

She stopped there and shot a look back at her father. Her expression wasn't one of concern, more a sort of mild irritation.

"Should I, like, call the police or something?"

"Fuck, no!" Bosco hissed. He swallowed, steadying his voice. "I mean... No. We are... chatting. Is all. Having conversation. Yes?"

Olivia rolled her eyes. "Fine. If you die, it's your own stupid fault," she said, then she opened the door so wide it thumped the foetal Valdis on the back of the head, and left.

"Apple doesn't fall far from the tree with that one, eh, Bosco?" Logan said, once the door had slammed closed behind the girl. "I'll have to keep my eye on that one when she's older."

He twisted the pen, then yanked it free. Blood seeped from Bosco's wound, pooling over the paperwork that lay scattered across the desk.

"Now," Logan growled, leaning closer to the whimpering Russian. "What was that you were saying about being in charge?"

Logan's phone rang just as he shut the car door. He tapped the ignition button and let the Volvo's Bluetooth connect. The words, 'Yon Arsehole' flashed up on the radio screen. Logan sighed before tapping the green phone icon.

"Detective Constable Neish," he said. "What can I do for you?"

Tyler's voice sounded uncharacteristically rich and deep over the car's speaker system, yet somehow still retained the fingernails-down-a-blackboard effect it usually had on Logan.

"Alright, boss? Where are you?"

"Ach, just out and about," Logan said. "Nowhere exciting."

He glanced in his wing mirror as a flash of blue light caught his eye. Tyler started to reply, but the screaming of passing sirens made it impossible for Logan to hear him.

"What was that?" the DC asked, once the racket had thundered by.

"Fire engine," Logan said, reaching for his seatbelt.

He watched the big red vehicle take a corner, headed for the growing column of grey-black smoke rising a couple of streets away.

"There a fire, or something?" Tyler asked.

"Naw, they probably just fancied a wee day out," Logan replied. He rolled his eyes at the silence that followed. "Aye, son, there's a fire. Now, what do you want?"

"Oh. Aye," Tyler said, remembering his reason for calling. "We've had a shout. Body found on one of the islands."

"Which one?"

"Eh, a woman, I think. Forties. There's not a lot of info through yet."

Logan's brow furrowed. As with most conversations involving Tyler, he could feel a low-level headache developing behind his eyes.

"I hope that was a joke, son. Which island, I mean, no' which body."

"Oh. Haha. Aye. Just kidding, boss," Tyler said, but Logan had been in the job long enough to know bullshit when he heard it.

There was a rustling of papers down the line before Tyler spoke again.

"Canna, boss. Heard of it?"

"Of course I've bloody heard of it," Logan said.

"Right. Aye," Tyler said, in a tone that suggested he hadn't. "Ferries are off with the weather, so they're choppering us over."

Logan grunted and put the car into gear. "Christ, Ben'll be like a kid at Christmas," he remarked.

"No, boss. DI Forde and Hamza are both on their way back from Dundee. Won't arrive in the office for a couple of hours. They're not heading over yet."

Logan stiffened in his seat. "Right. Then who's all going?"

Even down the phone, he could hear the DC grin.

"Just me and you, boss."

Logan's response was mercifully drowned out by the wailing of another passing siren.

"Was that another one? Big fire, is it, boss?"

"Aye, pretty substantial," Logan said. He shot a glance at the column of smoke and allowed himself a grim smile. "If I do say so myself."

CHAPTER THREE

The only part of DC Neish that was currently whiter than his knuckles was his face. It had taken on a greyish hue soon after take-off in Inverness, and in the forty-five minutes that followed had paled to the point of near translucence.

His eyes were shut, and Logan could hear him groan over his headphones whenever the helicopter ascended, descended, turned, or otherwise made any sort of movement whatsoever.

A light sheen of sweat glistened on Tyler's forehead. Light danced across it whenever his head bobbed around. Which, given the current turbulence, was constantly.

"Mayday! Mayday!"

Tyler's eyes snapped open. Somehow, his face managed to turn a full shade whiter.

"What? Fuck! What's wrong?" he yelped, eyes fixed desperately on the DCI.

Logan looked up from his phone. Despite the headset comm-system, he still had to raise his voice to be heard over the thrumming of the rotor blades overhead.

"Hmm? Oh. Sorry. There's nothing. I'm just planning my holidays for next year. I'm thinking of taking the Mayday weekend."

"Aye. Funny. Good one, boss," Tyler croaked, closing his eyes and settling his head back against the seat.

He was sitting behind the pilot, a stern-looking older man who had barely spoken a word to them since the pick-up, and who looked entirely unimpressed by Logan's attempt at humour.

Not as unimpressed as DC Neish looked, granted—not by a long shot—but unimpressed all the same.

Logan sat up front, watching the water roll by below them. Rain lashed at the windscreen, and the pilot's lack of conversation was probably down to how hard he was concentrating on fighting against the wind and keeping them in the air.

"We nearly there yet?" Tyler asked, not for the first time.

The pilot gestured ahead. "That's it," he muttered. Which, for him, was positively chatty.

Tyler risked opening an eye and leaned over so he could see between the front seats. An island rose out of the storm a mile or so ahead. From this distance, it looked wild and unwelcoming, but Tyler had never been more grateful to see anywhere in his life.

"Is it your first time in a chopper, or something?" Logan asked.

Tyler shook his head. "No. First time in this weather, though."

Right on cue, a gust of wind buffeted the helicopter, forcing the pilot to wrestle with the stick.

It hadn't been too bad in Inverness. A few spots of rain. A bit of a breeze. Practically tropical for the area.

Ten minutes into the flight, though, everything had taken a turn for the worse. Since then, it had seemed like the gods themselves had been conspiring to turn the helicopter back. They'd gone through every possible type of precipitation, from rain to hail and back again, all hammered into them by gale-force winds.

"Aye, it's a bit of a rough one, right enough," Logan said. He shrugged. "Still, on the bright side, at least we're not in the same chopper as Geoff and his lot."

Geoff Palmer and the rest of the Scene of Crime team had set off for Canna almost as soon as the call had been received. Apparently, they were hoping to beat the weather front that was rapidly moving in.

"What are they flying in? A fucking time machine?" Logan had asked, after just the briefest of looks at the weather map.

There was no chance of them getting to the scene before the storm hit, but if it meant not having to spend the better part of an hour cooped up with Palmer, Logan was all in favour of them trying.

The helicopter began its descent without any warning. It was far less smooth than even Logan would've liked, and the contents of his stomach sloshed unpleasantly upwards as he heard a whimper from Tyler crackling in his ears.

"Soon be on the ground, son," he said.

Tyler swallowed. "Cheers, boss."

"Whether we'll be in one piece or not," the DCI continued. "That's another question..."

"They could've at least given it a clear-out first," Tyler grumbled. He had been inside the Land Rover for less than five seconds, and was already complaining.

It was, Logan feared, going to be a very long trip.

"I mean, look at this."

Tyler lifted a partially crumpled Red Bull can from the passenger footwell. A smattering of ash around the hole on top told them someone had been using it as an ashtray.

"There's loads of empty crisp bags on the floor, too," Tyler continued. "Did nobody tell them we were coming?"

Fewer than fifty people lived on the island—not enough for a full-time police presence—and the only available vehicle was an ancient National Trust for Scotland Land Rover that had probably seen more welders than the Clyde shipyards.

"You could always walk," Logan suggested. "It's only a couple of miles."

Tyler peered out through the blurry windscreen. The wipers were going at full-tilt, but it was very much a losing battle. When the wind wasn't angrily slamming itself against the Land Rover, it was whistling in through a thousand tiny gaps, filling the vehicle with the kind of air that fogged the inside of all the windows.

Tyler tossed the Red Bull can onto the back seat, where it joined half a dozen others.

"Nah, you're alright," he said, kicking aside the carpet of litter to make room for his feet. "I'm sure I'll cope."

"What a trooper," Logan remarked. He cranked the key until the engine coughed into life, then studied the controls on the dash. "Now, where the hell's the blower on this thing?"

Twenty minutes of partially-blinded directionless driving down dirt tracks later, Logan and Tyler finally arrived at the scene.

They parked the Land Rover at the edge of a field where several members of the SOC team were struggling to fasten down a tent under the direction of Geoff Palmer.

They were too far away to be able to hear what Palmer was saying, but from the way he was stomping and flailing his arms around, it was clear he wasn't having an enjoyable time.

Another helicopter, larger than the one they'd flown in, stood at the far end of the field. They could just make out the pilot sitting watching on from the cockpit and occasionally sipping from a Thermos flask.

Logan cursed himself. Tea. Why hadn't he thought of that?

"We should probably give them a hand," Tyler said, as the SOC team grappled with the writhing sheet of white canvas.

"We probably should, aye," Logan agreed.

Neither man moved.

Across the field, one corner of the tent was whipped up into the air, and Geoff Palmer literally jumped up and down on the spot in rage.

"God. He's having a hell of a time of it," Logan remarked.

"Terrible, boss."

They sat observing in silence. The Land Rover groaned in a sudden gust of wind.

Outside, Palmer raised his face to the sky and shouted loudly enough for them to hear it, if not make out any of the actual words.

"Aye. Just terrible," said Logan. He indicated the folder in Tyler's lap. "The victim. How long did the report say she's been missing for?"

Tyler consulted the printout through the transparent plastic. "Last seen five nights ago in the local pub. Nobody's heard from her since then."

Logan nodded. "They're going to get bugger all evidence from the scene anyway, then," he said. His seat squeaked as he settled himself back into it. "Might as well give it another few minutes."

CHAPTER FOUR

Palmer didn't hold back when Logan and Tyler joined them inside the tent.

"Oh, look who finally decides to show their faces," he spat. "Thanks for the assist, lads. Good of you to help out."

"Ach, come on now, Geoff. You lot know what you're doing. We'd only have got in the way," Logan said. "Besides, someone had to film it for YouTube."

The circle of Geoff's face that was visible within the folds of the white paper hood contorted in displeasure. Behind him, the rest of the team bustled around, already taking their photographs and measurements.

"New member of the team?" asked Logan, nodding past them to the far end of the tent.

A scarecrow slouched there, knocked onto an awkward angle, like something had crashed into it. Despite the angle, the top of its head almost touched the canvas roof of the tent. Down at its feet, a person-sized lump was covered by a sheet that was already going damp around the edges.

The ground was a quagmire of mud and wet grass. By all accounts, it had been raining pretty constantly for the past week, and if the victim had been here since she went missing—and the cloyingly sweet smell of decay that was starting to pollute the tent suggested she had—then the chances of getting anything useful from the scene were low.

Still, much as Logan hated to admit it, Palmer's lot had a better chance than most. Palmer himself was a horrible bastard, but he and his team knew their way around a murder scene.

"What have we got?" Logan asked.

"What have we got?" Palmer parroted. "A body, a scarecrow, and two massive pains in my arse, that's what we've got."

He looked both detectives up and down, making his point very clear.

"If you want more than that, you'll have to wait. Maybe if you'd given us a hand to get the tent set up, we'd be further along, but for now, that's all you're getting."

"Aye. Right. Very good," said Logan, who had tuned Palmer out midway through the man's first sentence, when it was obvious he wasn't going to prove himself useful.

Picking his way carefully over to the body in his paper boots, he took a pencil from his pocket and lifted the edge of the sheet.

"Do you mind?" Palmer snapped.

Logan glanced up at him. Palmer's angry red face was a swollen circle surrounded by the white hood of his suit.

"Jesus, Geoff. You look like the Japanese flag. Take a breath, man," the DCI said, then he turned his attention back to the lifeless shape beneath the sheet. "Head injury," he observed. "Looks like it would've bled a lot, but the rain's washed most of it off. Plenty on her coat, though. Still looks pretty superficial, though. Not deep."

He squatted down, taking a closer look. A deep red welt ran across the victim's throat, a line of bruising cushioning it on either side.

"Strangled, by the looks of it. Thin rope or wire." He shot Geoff a look. "Keep an eye out for it."

Palmer tutted, then raised his voice, addressing the rest of the team. "Hear that, everyone? Since we're all here, the Detective Chief Inspector would like us to look out for a murder weapon. Add that to your To-Do lists, will you?"

There was a murmur of half-laughter from the others, and Palmer drew Logan a filthy look. "Anything else you'd like us to look out for, Jack? Clues, maybe? Evidence of some description?"

"Aye, very good," Logan muttered.

"I tell you, it's a good thing you're here, or we'd be fumbling about in the dark with our thumbs up our arses, trying to figure out what to do next."

Logan gave Palmer a cool, protracted stare that suggested the point had been made, and it would be in everyone's best interests if he shut his mouth and got back to work.

Palmer shook his head, mumbled, "Keep a bloody eye out for it," but then turned away before Logan's stare bored a hole right through his skull.

After a brief check to make sure Tyler was writing down his observations, Logan turned back to the corpse.

She was in her mid-forties, by the looks of her. Roughly around Logan's age. Her eyes were open, the red fractures on the whites of her eyeballs supporting the strangulation theory.

There was a small mole, like a beauty spot, on her left cheek. She would've been a looker back in the day, but the years had taken their toll on her complexion.

Being murdered almost certainly hadn't helped, either.

Logan's brow furrowed. He craned his neck so he was looking at the victim's face straight-on.

"See something, boss?" asked Tyler, his pencil hovering over his notepad.

"What did you say her name was?" Logan asked, not looking up.

"I didn't. I don't think so, anyway," the DC replied. He wiped the rain off his plastic folder with a sleeve, and consulted his notes. "It's, eh... Wallace," he said, angling the printout towards one of the lights the SOC team had set-up. "First name..."

"Iona?"

Tyler looked up from his folder. "Eh, aye. Aye. How'd you know that?"

"Formerly Iona Kerr," Logan said. He let the sheet drop back into place, then stood up. He sighed. It was a heavy, weary thing that came from somewhere deep inside him. "That there's the lassie who took my virginity."

Logan sat in the Land Rover, watching Tyler trampling around in the rain as he tried to get a signal on his phone.

After leaving the SOC team to do their stuff, they'd driven to the most south-westerly point on the island, in the hope of picking up a network bar or two. Judging by the convoluted interpretative dance Tyler was in the process of performing, Logan reckoned their odds were not good.

He flicked on the wipers, clearing the screen. Across the water, the Isle of Rum rose darkly through a bank of grey mist. To most folk on the mainland, Rum was the very definition of 'the arse end of nowhere'.

Canna was a step further still. It was right at the arse end of the arse end of nowhere. In fact, if the arse end of nowhere sprouted a tail, Canna would be clinging for dear life to the tip.

It was probably nice enough, Logan thought. Given that his only experience of it to date was pishing rain, a Land Rover almost as old as he was, and the body of a former fling lying rotting in a field, it was unlikely to make his list of top places to visit.

Iona Kerr. Jesus. That was a name he hadn't thought of in a long time.

He'd first met her in Primary School, where her name had provided countless hours of mirth.

Iona Kerr.

Oh, really? What colour is it? How fast does it go? Can you gie us a lift hame in it?

That sort of thing.

They were in different classes and social groups in high school, and hadn't really spoken to each other until the night of the fourth year school disco, when they'd reconnected in the most literal of senses.

That would make them, what? Fifteen or sixteen when they'd done the deed. A clumsy, late-night fumble in an unfamiliar close in the east end of Glasgow, that had painted neither of them in a particularly good light, and which they never spoke of to each other again.

Her big brother had gotten wind of it a few weeks after it had happened. Him and a couple of his mates had leathered seven shades out of Logan. They'd given him his first broken nose of what was, over the decades since, to be many.

Still. Absolutely worth it, though.

The family had moved away a couple of months later. Iona's old man was a minister, or a priest, or something, Logan dimly recalled. Strict old bugger, always a bit too eager with the belt, by all accounts.

The mother wasn't on the scene, hadn't been for a few years. Logan had never known why. A lot of folk locally reckoned that was why Iona had ended up the way she was. Loud. Reckless.

Desperate.

He'd wondered about her occasionally in the weeks and months that had followed her leaving. Until, one day, he hadn't. One day, she was just no longer occupying any space in his head.

Until today.

"Getting wilder out there, boss," said Tyler, breathlessly ejecting the words as he pulled open the passenger door.

Seizing its chance, the wind swirled in around the footwell, whipping half a dozen crisp bags and an empty Jaffa Cakes box out of the car and into the air.

Tyler grabbed for them, frantically snatching and grasping like a contestant on *The Crystal Maze*. He came away empty-handed, and Logan could only tut his disapproval as the wind carried the litter towards the water that crashed against the rocks at the island's edge.

"Well, that's a turtle dead," Logan remarked, as the crisp bags alighted on the tide. "Good work, son."

"I tried to grab them," Tyler protested, sheepishly clambering into the car and pulling the door closed.

Logan nodded. "Aye. And breathtaking it was to watch, too. Like a gazelle having a seizure."

Tyler pulled on his seatbelt, hands shaking from the cold. Logan nudged up the heating a few degrees. Not too far, obviously. No point spoiling the lad.

"I'm guessing from your performance out front that you didn't get a signal."

"Not a thing, boss," Tyler said. "Didn't even flicker."

Logan nodded. No surprise. "Aye. That figures," he said, staring blankly out through the rain-blurred windscreen ahead.

"You alright?" Tyler asked.

Logan blinked and turned to the junior officer. "What? What do you mean? Aye. Why?"

"Just... You know. The victim. Iona," Tyler said, shifting uncomfortably in his already uncomfortable seat. "You and her. Your relationship, and all that."

Logan let out a derisory grunt. "We had a drunken teenage fumble. She wasn't exactly the love of my life."

"Aye. No. I know," Tyler said. "It's just... If you need to talk, or anything..."

"I'm pretty sure I'll cope, son," Logan said, cutting him off. "I don't need an agony aunt. What I need is a competent—no, a *vaguely* competent—police officer to assist in this investigation."

He turned the key in the ignition, and the Land Rover's engine reluctantly turned over on the third try.

"But since I don't have one of them available at the moment, you'll have to stand in," Logan concluded. He checked his watch. "Right, we've got a couple of hours before Palmer finishes up. What's say we go meet the locals?"

CHAPTER FIVE

CANNA'S MAIN, AND IN MANY REGARDS *ONLY* STREET RAN FROM THE ferry terminal, past a shop, a café, and a pub, then meandered off into the wilderness never to be seen again.

As much through old habits as any sort of strategy, it was outside the pub where Logan elected to pull up in the Land Rover, smoke farting in great grey guffs from the vehicle's rattling exhaust.

The pub was housed in a whitewashed old stone building. Its name, 'Canna Come Inn,' was painted on a wooden board above the door.

"Quality," Tyler remarked, when he saw the sign, although Logan couldn't tell if he was being sarcastic or not.

There were no other cars parked along the road, and a solitary older woman stood watering a basket of flowers that hung from an arm fixed to a street light a little further along from where they'd parked.

Were it anywhere else in the world, Logan would've said the place was deserted. For here, though, it was practically rush hour.

Still, at least the rain was off. For now.

Tyler's phone gave a *bleep*, and he quickly fumbled in his pocket for it. A text displayed on the screen, letting him know he had three voicemails. He flicked his gaze up to the notification bar at the top of the screen in time to see the single signal bar become an empty triangle once more.

"Bastard," he muttered. "Missed it."

Logan checked his own phone. No signal. No messages. No missed calls.

No point.

He switched it off to save the battery, then shoved it back in his inside coat pocket.

Truth be told, it was almost a relief to be out of signal. Given the barrage of anonymous phone calls he'd been receiving lately, he wasn't going to complain too much about being out of reach.

Besides, Detective Superintendent Hoon was bound to be gunning for him soon. The longer he could delay that particular conversation, the better.

"Right. Let's go see what we can find out," he said, jabbing the button that unfastened his seatbelt.

They had both barely opened the doors before the woman with the watering can came tearing up the pavement towards them.

"Hey. No, no! You can't park that there!"

Logan stepped out, very deliberately closed his door, and produced his warrant card as the woman rushed up, brandishing the watering can like an offensive weapon.

She wasn't as old as she'd looked at a distance. What he'd taken as wrinkles seemed to just be her default resting face—mouth puckered up, eyes narrowed in suspicion.

"Police," Logan said.

"I don't care if you're the Queen of bloody Sheba, you can't park there," the woman insisted. "It's an obstruction."

Logan and Tyler looked along the street in both directions. There didn't seem to be a whole lot of anything to obstruct.

The DCI's instinct was to point out that there were no yellow lines or 'No Parking' signs, and to tell the woman to ram her objection up her hoop, but it was a tight-knit community, and he suspected it wouldn't do to get on the wrong side of this one.

"Of course. We'll get it shifted," he said, in a display of diplomacy that drew a faint gasp of surprise from DC Neish.

"Right. Yes. I should think so," the woman replied, none of the fight going out of her.

"Where do you suggest we stick it?" Logan asked, even though he could think of a few places. One in particular.

"There's a parking spot further down," she said, a little waspishly. A quick jerk of a hand indicated a painted white box a dozen yards along the same road. If the car was an obstruction in its current spot, it would be no less of one over there.

It took all Logan's self-control to toss Tyler the keys. "Shift it, will you, DC Neish? Like Mrs...?"

"Bryden," the woman sniffed. "Joy Bryden."

Joy. Logan almost laughed. Her parents must've been sorely disappointed.

"Chair of the Community Council," she added. Logan wasn't in the least bit surprised by this information, but still felt a shudder of dread ripple through him from head to toe.

How many Community Council meetings had he spoken at over the years? How many times had he been forced to field questions so banal and inane that just a modicum of common sense and five-seconds thinking time would've negated their need to be asked?

Once you took murderers, rapists, and all that lot out of the equation, the only thing Logan despised more than the average Community Council chairperson was a member of the tabloid press. And, truth be told, it was quite a close-run thing.

"Of course you are," he said, smiling at the woman in a way that showed far too many of his teeth.

He joined her on the pavement while Tyler climbed into the driver's seat of the Land Rover. Logan watched him adjust the position of the seat and the angle of the mirrors before telling him to, "stop pissing about," in no uncertain terms.

"It's literally driving two car lengths down the hill. We could've just taken off the handbrake and let it roll down," he concluded, but Tyler was already over-revving the engine, and pointing at his ear to suggest he couldn't hear what the DCI was saying.

Logan and Joy both stepped into the pub doorway as a haze of blue-black smoke came hissing from the exhaust, and the Land Rover creaked off down the incline towards the designated parking space.

"You'll be here about the body," Joy said. Her nostrils flared, like she didn't approve of that sort of thing. *Bodies*. "It's Iona Wallace, I hear."

The way she said the name made a little light blink on inside Logan's head. He got the sense that Joy probably didn't like very many people, but from the tone she took and the way her mouth turned down at the corners, she'd disliked Iona more than most.

Logan could see it. The Iona he remembered would've been the complete antithesis to the sour-faced specimen standing before him now. The average Community Council wouldn't last five minutes in the same room as the Iona Kerr of old.

"Did you know her?" Logan asked. Stupid question on an island whose entire population could fit on one double-decker bus, but he wanted to gauge her reaction.

"Of course I knew her. Everyone knew her. Everyone knows everyone," Joy replied. "But her, especially."

"What do you mean by that?"

"Let's just say, her own business was rarely her own business. She'd enough dirty laundry to start her own laundrette, that one. If you find anyone with a good word to say about her, you'll be doing well. And they'll be lying," Joy said.

She sniffed and pulled her jacket tighter around herself. It was an expensive waterproof number. Probably a necessity of island life, if the wind was anything to go by.

"Not that I'm one to talk ill of the dead," she added, clearly as an afterthought. "And it's all poor Abraham needs at his age."

Logan raised an eyebrow, but didn't need to ask the question.

"Her father. The minister. Years of trouble she's given him. Years of it. He's been very tolerant, considering, and how does she thank him?"

"Well, Mrs Bryden, I highly doubt she got herself murdered on purpose..."

Joy's ears visibly pricked up. Logan bit down on his tongue, but far too late.

"So, it is murder, then? I'd heard a rumour, but I didn't want to say anything. I'm no' one for gossip."

That, Logan thought, was very hard to believe.

"We're still investigating. We'll know more when the forensics team has finished up, and a full post-mortem has been carried out."

He glanced around and lowered his voice. "But between you and me, Joy? Just between us? Aye. I think she was murdered. I think she was murdered, and I think there's a very good chance that whoever did it is still here on the island."

Joy stepped in closer, enjoying being part of the detective's inner circle. "I mean, that would make sense. The ferries haven't been running for days. I haven't seen any other boats coming and going, not with the gales."

She put a hand to her chest to steady herself, then squinted up and down the street, like she might spot the killer lurking there behind one of the windows.

"You'll keep your eyes open for us?" Logan asked.

"Of course. I'm Secretary of the Neighbourhood Watch," Joy told him. "I'll rally the troops, find out if anyone has seen or heard anything."

"Aye. You do that," Logan told her.

From experience, this could go one of two ways. Either it would keep her out of his hair until the case was all wrapped up, or he had just opened himself to a regular bombardment of irrelevant information and gossip.

Still, if it meant getting her on-side, it could only make his life easier in the long run. The smaller the community, the more power the Community Council tended to wield, and communities didn't come much smaller than this one.

"Hey! No!" Joy shouted, derailing Logan's train of thought. She glowered angrily at Tyler, who was walking back from where he'd parked the Land Rover.

He stopped walking and looked at Logan in alarm when Joy started marching towards him, gesturing down the hill to where he'd parked.

"Not *that* white box. That's the disabled space," she bellowed. "What are you? Blind, as well as stupid?"

Logan sighed through his gritted teeth. *On-side.*

Aye, right.

CHAPTER SIX

The pub's front doors were shut tight, and no amount of hammering was drawing the attention of anyone inside.

Joy Bryden had personally supervised Tyler as he'd moved the car forward six feet into the adjoining space to the one he'd parked in, guiding him with shouted commands, indecipherable hand gestures, and an assortment of disapproving looks.

That done, she'd nodded curtly at Logan, before crossing the road and vanishing into an alleyway between two whitewashed houses.

"She's a bit scary, eh?" Tyler observed, once he was confident she was well out of earshot.

"She's a slightly built Community Council leader in her late-fifties," Logan pointed out. He blew out his cheeks and shuddered. "So, aye. Bloody terrifying."

He thumped a fist on the pub's wooden doors again, then glanced up at the darkened upstairs windows.

"Notice anything strange about her?" he asked, shooting Tyler a brief look.

"Eh... Like what?"

Logan tutted. "That's what I'm asking you. Did you notice anything?"

"She's got issues with parking?" Tyler guessed.

"I'd imagine she's got issues, full stop," Logan replied. He watched the DC for a few more seconds, giving him time to offer something else. *Hoping* that he would.

"I don't know then, boss," Tyler was forced to admit.

Logan made no attempt to hide his disappointment. "Jesus. It's been raining solidly for several days, has it not?"

"Think so, aye."

Logan nodded past him, to where a hanging basket *creaked* back and forth on the breeze.

"So, what was she doing out watering the flowers?"

Before they could dwell too much on this, there was a loud *clack* from the other side of the doors, as a bolt was slid aside.

One of the doors opened a crack, offering a tall, narrow glimpse of a grey-haired man with a moustache and glasses. His eyes were sunken deep into a skull that looked a half-size too small—an effect not helped by the thickness of the lenses in his NHS style frames.

"We're not open yet," he said. There was a rasp to his voice that implied he was a heavy smoker. Or, could he be upset? "Opening at five tonight."

He started to close the door, but the judicious positioning of Logan's right foot stopped it shutting all the way. He held up his warrant card.

"Detective Chief Inspector Jack Logan, Major Investigations Team."

The man on the other side of the door blinked several times in quick succession. He looked from the ID to each of the detectives in turn, then back again.

It took him three full circuits of this before he said anything.

"The police?"

"Aye. That's right. The police," Logan said. He gave Tyler a nudge, and the DC presented his own identification.

"Mind if we come in, sir?" Tyler said. "Ask you a few questions?"

"Questions? Me?" the man asked through the gap. "What for?"

"We're investigating... an unexplained death," Logan told him. "We're just trying to get a feel for the place."

He returned his ID to his pocket, and arranged his features in a way that made it very clear they weren't going anywhere except inside.

"We won't take up too much of your time," he said. "I appreciate you're probably very busy."

The man gave a little groan below his breath, then let the door swing open. He was wrapped in a faded brown dressing-gown the letters, 'RM' embroidered inexpertly on the left breast. Below the dressing-gown was an old grey t-shirt patterned down the front with a multi-coloured assortment of food stains.

There was a smell of alcohol about him. Not the usual pub smell that Logan had subconsciously been bracing himself for, but some stale, stagnant variant that came seeping from the pores of the man standing in the narrow wood-panelled corridor beyond the front doors.

"Right. You'd best come in, then," he told them, shuffling around on his bare feet.

He motioned to a door marked 'Private' that led off from the corridor, and winced at the thought of what lay behind it.

"I'd take you up to the flat but, well, I need to give it a tidy," he said.

There was another set of double-doors behind him. Unlike those out front, these were mostly made of textured glass, with curved brass handles and matching kick plates down at the bottom.

"We can go through to the bar, though, if you like?" the man suggested, then he shook his head like he was admonishing himself, and lunged for Logan with a hand extended. "Sorry, sorry. I'm Roddy. MacKay. Roddy Mac, they call me. I'm the landlord. This... This is my place. My pub."

He looked down and reacted in surprise, like he'd suddenly realised what he was wearing.

"But then, you know that, don't you?" he said, self-consciously retying the belt of the dressing-gown around his narrow waist. "Of course, you know. Of course, you do. That's why you're here. Why you've come."

Logan felt Tyler's gaze slide in his direction, but ignored it.

"I don't follow, Mr MacKay," the DCI said.

"Well, this was it, wasn't it?" Roddy said. "Here. The pub. This was it."

"This was what?" Logan pressed.

"This was the place Iona was last seen alive."

Roddy shoved his hands in his dressing-gown pockets, but not before Logan saw how badly they were shaking.

"I didn't see her. The night she died, I mean. I was upstairs."

He flinched, realising his error almost as soon as the words had left his mouth.

He wasn't the only one.

"We don't know what night she died, Mr Mackay," Logan said.

Roddy's face reddened behind his silver-grey moustache. For a moment, his mouth just flapped open and closed like a fish out of water, before words began to babble out.

"No. I mean, yes. I mean, I know. But... The night she... The last night she was here, I mean. The night she disappeared. That's the one I was... I didn't see her. I was—"

"Upstairs. Aye. You mentioned," said Logan. He gave the door that led to the flat a very calculated once-over, before turning back to the landlord. "To be honest, we were really just hoping to grab a cup of tea and use your phone, Mr Mackay. But, since we're on the subject, why don't we step into the bar? And you can tell us everything you know about the night Iona Wallace went missing."

There was a knock at the front door, which still stood ajar. Roddy practically sagged with relief when the door was nudged open from outside, and a young Asian woman with her hair tied up in a bun smiled nervously at the towering detective in the hallway.

She couldn't have been older than twenty-two or twenty-three. There was something vaguely familiar about her, although Logan couldn't quite place where he'd seen her before.

"Uh, hi," she said, shuffling on the front step. "Hoped I might find you here."

"Alright?" asked Tyler. The way he was frowning suggested he was struggling to work out who she was, too.

It was only when she jabbed a thumb back over her shoulder and said, "Geoff wants to see you," that both men realised she was a member of the SOC team.

It was the first time either of them had seen her without a paper hood and a mask covering her head and half her face.

Her eyes were a dark walnut brown, and the smile she was plastering on her face had formed little dimples in her cheeks. There was a glow about her that suggested she'd run all the way here to find them.

Young, fit, and attractive, then. No doubt Geoff himself had taken a keen interest in her recruitment. They didn't call him 'Sex Pest Palmer' for nothing. The poor girl probably spent half her day fending him off with a shitty stick.

"Storm's coming in," she said. "Chopper wants to get going. We're done at the site, and going to take the body back to Inverness. I'm Samira, by the way. Hi."

"Hi. You're packing up already?" asked Tyler. "Bit quick that, isn't it?"

"Site's badly compromised," she replied. "We've got what we can."

"Which is...?" asked Logan.

The young woman gave an embarrassed sort of shrug. "Not much, I'm afraid."

"Great," said Logan, his chest heaving with a sigh. Half-turning, he pinned Roddy to the spot with a steely glare. "Don't go too far, Mr Mackay," he warned. "We'll be back to have that chat."

THE LAND ROVER bounced up the track leading to the field, Logan behind the wheel, the SOC lassie in the front passenger seat, and Tyler relegated to the back.

"It's a complete shithole back here," DC Neish had been quick to point out, and the soundtrack for most of the journey had been the rustling of crisp packets, the rattling of empty cans, and a low-level muttering about basic standards of hygiene.

"There they are. Looks like they're about loaded up," Samira said, indicating the helicopter that sat crouching in the field, its blades rotating lazily like it was stretching itself awake.

The tent had been folded down and packed away, and the body was presumably already on board the chopper, along with most of the team. Geoff stood by the side door, watching a younger guy cordon off a ten-feet by ten-feet square of field.

Right at the centre of it, the lop-sided scarecrow stood with its arms outstretched, its rough canvas face turned in the Land Rover's direction.

Logan steered them towards the layby near the edge of the field, where they'd watched the farce with the tent earlier. He had just pulled on the handbrake when Tyler let out a sudden yelp of panic.

"There's a fucking mouse in here!"

Logan's chair groaned as he turned and looked into the back. Tyler was already out of his seat belt, and grabbing for the door handle.

"What?"

"There's a mouse! An actual mouse! The cheeky wee bastard ran right over my hand!"

He shuddered in revulsion, then tugged on the handle, but the door refused to open.

"Fuck's sake! Who put the child lock on?" he cried, rattling the handle over and over again. "Come on, let us out, boss."

"Calm down. It's just a mouse, no' a rat," Logan said. He sucked in his bottom lip. "Unless... maybe it *is* a rat. Big hairy bugger of a thing. Full of disease."

He looked across at Samira in the passenger seat, his face a picture of concern. "God, would that not be terrible?"

"I'll climb through, boss," Tyler warned. "I mean it, I'll climb right over you, if that's what it comes to."

Logan shook his head. "Jesus. Pull yourself together, Detective Constable. All this fuss over a wee..."

He fixed his gaze on Tyler's shoulder, his eyes widening. "Christ. Aye. It's a big brute of a thing, right enough."

Tyler contorted, swiping at his shoulder, and was halfway towards a panic attack when he spotted the smirk on the DCI's face, and realised he'd been had.

"Sorry," Logan said, opening his door and squelching down onto the muddy grass. "Couldn't resist."

When Samira had said the SOC team didn't have much, she wasn't lying. She may actually have been exaggerating. 'Not much' was a step-up from what they did have, which was practically nothing at all.

"Given the conditions onsite, anything I can give you is pretty much just speculation," Palmer told Logan, while Samira helped load the final few boxes into the chopper.

A bank of truly murderous-looking cloud was moving in from the west, and the pilot was starting to get antsy. He was keen to get off—a sentiment Palmer himself shared, judging by how quickly he was talking.

"It's likely she was killed here, although given the condition of her clothing I can't rule out her being dragged through the mud. There has been a lot of animal activity around the site, both before and after she was here. Them, probably."

He pointed to a flock of sheep scattered across one of the low hills that rose up just beyond the crumbling wall that marked the far edge of the field.

"Whoever found her wasn't canny about keeping their distance, either. At least two people. Looks like they attended the body, then either paced around waiting for help to arrive, or maybe had themselves a wee ceilidh. Either way, their prints have obliterated whatever else was below. Although, I doubt we'd have got much even if they hadn't been around."

"Who found her?" Logan asked.

Palmer tutted and shrugged. "The bloody hell should I know?"

There was a knocking on the helicopter's windscreen, and the pilot made a show of tapping his watch.

"We need to get off," Palmer said.

Logan blocked his route to the chopper. "Wait. That's it? There's nothing else?"

"Oh! No! We found you an eyewitness," Palmer said.

Tyler looked up from where he'd been writing in his notepad. "Aye?"

Palmer indicated the partially toppled scarecrow with a nod. "He's the strong, silent type, but I'm sure you two can talk him into giving a statement!"

Logan's expression made it very clear that he did not appreciate Palmer's attempt at humour. It made it clear, in fact, that he did not appreciate Palmer's very existence.

"It's a puddle of mud and sheep shit. What did you expect us to find?" the SOC boss asked. "Dr Maguire might get something from the body, but... Come on, Jack. There are, what? Fifty adults on the island? Nobody's been or gone in days."

He backed towards the helicopter, his mouth wrenching into a sneering smile. "A couple of bright lads like you? With your experience, Jack, and his..." He gestured at Tyler, racked his brains for a moment, then shrugged. "Whatever it is he brings to the table. Just how hard can it be?"

CHAPTER SEVEN

Logan stood just beyond the cordon tape, eyeballing the ground as a fine drizzle dampened everything that wasn't already soaked through.

He was hoping he might spot something that Palmer's team had missed, although he knew that the likelihood of that happening was slim.

Palmer was right. It was a puddle of mud and sheep shit. Even the indent where the body had been lying had now been almost completely smoothed away by the rain. The site was so far beyond compromised that even if they'd found a written confession, it was unlikely to be admissible as evidence.

"What's the scarecrow for?" Tyler asked.

"Scaring crows. I'd have thought that was pretty self-explanatory," Logan replied without looking up.

There was a soft *squelch* as Tyler picked his way forward through the mud until he was standing at the DCI's side by the cordon tape. The scarecrow looked sturdy and well-made, its straw body and workman-like clothing holding together well, despite the ravages of the recent weather.

"No. I know what scarecrows are for, boss. I meant what's this one particular scarecrow for?"

Logan looked at the mud-pit around them. It was a field in name only. Beyond a few clumps of waist-high weeds, nothing grew here, and almost certainly hadn't for a number of years.

"What's it guarding?" Tyler pressed.

"Huh. Good question," Logan said, somewhat begrudgingly. "Why's it here? The mud's no' exactly worth protecting, and he doesn't look all that old."

He met the hollow gaze of the scarecrow, ran his hand through his hair, then tapped on Tyler's breast pocket, where he kept his notebook. "Write it down. Probably nothing, but... Good spot. Well done."

"Cheers, boss," Tyler chirped, pleased with himself. He whistled below his breath as he made a note in his book, then flipped it closed and returned it to his pocket.

A line of shadow was creeping closer across the field, mirroring the progress of the vast dark clouds above. Tyler regarded it with growing concern.

"Looks like it's going to get rough soon. Maybe we should go hole up somewhere until it passes?" he suggested. "We could go back to the pub, talk to your dressing-gown fella. Should probably phone the office, too, see if they've sorted us out somewhere to stay."

Logan gave a non-committal sort of grunt, then paced around the outside of the cordon tape, checking out the scarecrow from every available angle. It was, as far as he could tell, just a bog-standard scarecrow. Palmer's team would've gone over it when they were searching the site, so if it had any secrets to give up, it would've already handed them over.

And yet, Tyler had got his mind racing. Why was it here? What was the point? And how come Iona Wallace's body had been found right there in front of it?

"Aye. I'll get it out of you yet," Logan muttered.

"Sorry, boss?"

"Nothing. Doesn't matter," the DCI replied. He took the keys from his pocket and used them to point in the direction of an old thatched cottage that squatted on a low hill just beyond the field's edge. "That must be Iona's house. Let's go get inside and check it out before the storm hits."

Tyler didn't need telling twice. He trudged, splashed, and skidded back in the direction of the Land Rover, with Logan following behind.

And the scarecrow watched them, every step of the way.

DCI Logan and DC Neish entered the house wearing gloves and shoe protectors. Given the vicinity to the crime scene, SOC would usually have given the place a going over, but their rush to get the body back before the storm cut them off had meant it would have to wait for another day.

The door was unlocked. Not really a surprise way out here, where everyone knew everyone, and crime was a thing that happened to people on the mainland.

From outside, the cottage was quaint, if a bit run-down. The few single-glazed windows that weren't cracked were desperately in need of a power washing, and while Logan would never claim to be an expert on roof thatching, he was reasonably certain it was never meant to look quite like that.

The stone walls were solid, though, despite no-doubt having been there for generations. An attempt had been made to brighten up the garden at one point, with half-sized whisky barrels used as planters for flowers by the front door and along both sides of the narrow path.

Whatever had been planted in them was long-dead, though, the compost now crusted with moss and a selection of short, stubby weeds.

Inside, the situation was much the same. There was potential for it to be a lovely wee place, from the exposed beams of the ceiling, to the rustic-looking log burner set back in a stone fireplace, topped with a driftwood mantelpiece.

But it was all so grimy and grim. The windows were as filthy on the inside as they were on the outside, and rings of damp were congregating between the ceiling beams.

An area of several square feet around the log burner was caked in ash and soot, with footprints trampling various paths through it and across the threadbare carpet.

The kitchen sat at one end of the living area, a mishmash of different units, half of them with grubby curtains instead of doors. The sink was stacked high with dirty dishes. Judging by the smell, and the colour of the water they were half-submerged in, they'd been that way for some time.

But it was the general odour of the place that was most overwhelming. The twin aromas of tobacco and cannabis permeated every fibre of the cottage, right down to the stone that made up the walls.

Ashtrays sat in various spots around the room—on the arm of the chair; on the mantelpiece; two on the kitchen worktops—each one overflowing worse than the one before.

Clothes lay scattered on the floor, and across the tired old sofa that slouched indignantly in the far corner of the room, like a teenager who'd stormed off in the huff.

"I like what she did with the place," Tyler remarked, picking up a lacy black bra with the end of his pen and examining it like it was some alien specimen. "Really homely."

It was chaotic. A bloody shambles. It told him that Iona hadn't changed much in the years since he'd known her. If he'd been asked to describe how he pictured her living, it would've been almost exactly this.

"Any idea what we're looking for?" Tyler asked. He'd returned the bra to where he'd found it—draped across a cheap plastic kettle—and was now poking around in a cutlery drawer.

"No' really," Logan admitted. He hadn't moved from the middle of the room since they'd entered, and was slowly turning on the spot, taking the place in. "We want to build up a picture of her last few days. See if anything jumps out. Notebooks. Mobile phone and laptop, if she had them. Letters."

Tyler snorted. "No one sends letters these days, boss," he said, closing the cutlery drawer and crossing to the fridge.

"Aye, well, maybe they do out here. Keep your eyes peeled, anyway."

Outside, the storm was building. The wind had started to whistle in through gaps in the roof and the windows, and there was a steady drip-drip-drip from somewhere above the worst of the damp stains.

"You look in here, I'll check the bedroom and bathroom," Logan instructed.

"Right you are, boss. One thing I will say about her..." Tyler opened the fridge door all the way, revealing shelves filled with cans of cheap cider and lager. "She liked a drink."

"Aye. She did that, alright," Logan confirmed, recalling the girl he used to know. "Now, get going. I want us done and out of here sharpish. I don't know about you, but I'm bloody starving."

Leaving Tyler to search the living room and kitchen area, Logan headed through an open door that led to a hallway which would've been a squeeze for two full-sized adults. Three other doors ran off from the hall, two of them open, the other closed.

He could see a bathroom and bedroom behind the two open doors, and a quick check behind the third revealed a cupboard containing an old vacuum cleaner, an ironing board, and about three months' worth of ironing spilling out of a plastic basket.

Closing that door, Logan opted to check the bathroom first.

It was freezing. That was the first thing he noticed. It was right at the back corner of the house, and the wind was busy chilling both outside walls. There was no heater that he could see, although an ancient towel rail that was no longer wired into the wall had probably doubled as one at some point.

There wasn't much else to report. Another ashtray was balanced on the edge of the chipped and stained bath, half a hand-rolled cigarette propped up in one of the grooves.

Logan picked it up in his gloved fingers and sniffed the end. The smell of cannabis was unmistakable.

A check of the bathroom cabinet revealed mostly painkillers, some antihistamines, and a couple of near-empty containers of thrush cream. The tube of toothpaste, by comparison, was almost new, and the only toothbrush he could find was mostly hidden behind the half-used blister strips of paracetamol, ibuprofen, and...

Hello.

Reaching into the cabinet, Logan took out a small stack of blister strips that didn't fit in with the others. There were five strips, each containing four tablets —twenty in total.

Each tablet was diamond-shaped and pale blue. Distinctive enough that he recognised them at once. They were a common find during shakedowns back in Glasgow.

Viagra.

He angled one of the packs to the light, checking the dosage printed on the pills. A hundred milligrams. Max strength, he thought, but he'd have to double-check.

What was a single woman living alone doing with five packs of a male impotence drug? Selling them? Maybe. An insurance policy in case some late-night hook-up couldn't fulfil their end of the bargain? Very possibly.

Logan returned them to the cabinet and jotted down a note in his pad. Then, after a further check of all the likely hiding spots in the bathroom, he left the room and headed to the one across the hall.

Compared to Iona's bedroom, the rest of the house was positively presentable. It had seemed like half of her clothes had been strewn across the living room, but that was a fraction of what lay in piles around the bedroom, hung on hooks from the curtain rail, or sat teetering on the short, wooden poles at the end of the unmade double bed.

"Jesus."

"Alright, boss?" Tyler called through to him.

"Aye. Just marvelling at what a clarty bastard she was," Logan replied.

He tried to ignore the mess, and concentrate instead on anything that might help with the case. It was difficult to know where to start.

The arrangement of the covers and pillows on the bed suggested only one person had slept there recently. Looking closely at the exposed sheets revealed a rainbow of different stains, which he'd have to get forensics to look at.

Some of them he could dismiss as food stains. Others either suggested that Iona had enjoyed a highly active sex life in recent weeks, or that she hadn't washed the sheets in a very long time. Again, hopefully forensics could tell him more.

There was a phone charger plugged in by the bed, which suggested she must have a mobile somewhere. Logan checked in the bedside drawers, but found no phone. He did find several other *devices*, though, all battery-operated, and all different sizes—if broadly similar in shape.

Beneath the bed was a clutter of more clothes, several pairs of shoes, and a couple of cardboard boxes. With a bit of effort, Logan managed to reach both boxes, and pulled them out to check inside.

The first box was filled with old video cassette tapes. There were fifteen of them in all, at least six of which had variations on the theme of Tom Cruise staring smokily out from the cover.

The rest were a mix of various trashy horrors, a couple of 80s rom-coms, and *G.I. Jane*, starring Demi Moore. Logan opened a few of the boxes, checked the tapes corresponded with the covers, and then set the box aside.

The second box was older and more battered. It had a removable lid that was taped down on one side, so it moved as if on a hinge.

Flipping it open, Logan let out a little grunt of satisfaction. In it, there were a dozen or more diaries, the year hand-written on some of the earlier ones, and embossed in gold on the two most recent, which covered the years 2013 and 2016. Not current, then, and not continuous, but recent enough that they might reveal something about her relationships with the other people on the island.

A quick flick through confirmed that she'd written entries on at least a handful of the dates, which made the box an important find. If luck was on their side, the identity of the killer might be written somewhere on those pages.

"Aye," Logan muttered, folding the lid back into place. "We can but hope."

WHEN LOGAN RETURNED to the living area, cardboard box under one arm, he found Tyler on all-fours in front of the couch, using the torch on his phone to peer into the gap beneath it.

"What've you got?" the DCI asked, as Tyler carefully slid a hand into the narrow space.

"One sec..."

After a bit of squirming, Tyler removed his hand, the blade of a knife pinned beneath the tip of one finger.

The blade was long, curved at the end, with a serrated edge running down its back. The handle was a rubberised grip, with a black metal hilt to protect the hand of anyone wielding the weapon.

"Jesus. That's a serious blade," Tyler remarked.

"Hunting knife."

"Aye, but what the fuck's she hunting? Bigfoot?"

Logan considered the knife, its position beneath the couch, and the couch's relative position to the front door. "For self-defence, maybe?"

"Hardly handily placed for an emergency, boss," Tyler said. "I've been trying to fish the bastard out for the past five minutes."

Logan regarded him impassively. "Couldn't you have tilted the couch back?"

Tyler opened his mouth to reply to this, hesitated, then sighed and said, "Shite, aye."

"Bag it up," Logan instructed, indicating the knife. He patted the box under his arm. "Found some old diaries. Don't expect to get much, but good background."

"Maybe you'll be mentioned in them, boss," Tyler teased. He took an evidence bag from his pocket and carefully dropped the knife inside.

"Although, did they have pen and paper back then, or was it all chisels and slate?"

"Aye, good to see you're still as witty as ever, son," Logan said. "By which I mean, not at all."

He set the box on the floor beside the door, took the knife from Tyler, and placed it on top, then turned and surveyed the room again. The wind was howling through the gaps in the windows now, and the dripping above the ceiling was now a steady *pitter-patter* of trickling water.

"Right, let's give the place one more going over, then get the hell out of here before the bloody roof comes down."

CHAPTER EIGHT

Roddy Mackay was nowhere to be seen when Logan and Tyler returned, dripping wet and windswept, to the Canna Come Inn. The pub was open, though, and a tall, blond-haired man with a chiselled jaw smiled at them from behind the bar, showing the most perfectly aligned, impeccably white teeth either of the detectives had ever seen.

"G'day," he said, in an accent that was straight out of Ramsay Street.

He had a bungee-cord braid around his wrist, fastened with a clasp made from a polished shell, and wore a shark's tooth on a leather strap around his neck. If the man wasn't a surfer, Logan reckoned, then he had missed his life's calling.

"How can I help you gents?" he asked, reaching under the bar and producing a couple of laminated menus. "You after a bite to eat?"

"Aye. Maybe," Logan said, taking both menus. "We're looking for Mr Mackay. We were having a chat with him earlier, but got called away."

"Oh! Right! You must be the cops!" the barman said. "Roddy said you'd be in. I'm Bruce."

"Of course you are," said Logan. He glanced around at the empty pub. A back door stood open, an arrow on the wall informing anyone who might be interested that this was the way to the beer garden.

Given that the sky was in the process of falling, and the rain was rattling off the ground like bullets, it was unlikely anyone would be out there enjoying the fresh air now.

"Is Mr Mackay around?" asked Tyler, half looking at Bruce, and half eyeing up the menus that Logan was still keeping a firm hold of.

"Nah, he nipped out. Said he'd be back... Actually, I don't know when he'll be back. I mean, he did say, but I was only half-listening," Bruce told them. "He said to get you boys a bite to eat, though. On the house."

"Very kind of him. But we couldn't accept that," Logan said.

"He says it's no problem. Honestly."

"No, I mean we literally can't accept that," Logan told him. "Wouldn't want anyone to suggest that Mr Mackay was bribing us with a couple of juicy steaks."

Bruce blinked a few times, like he didn't quite understand. "We don't do steaks," he said, which was up there with the most disappointing things Logan had heard all day.

Tyler was practically salivating beside him, so Logan slid one of the menus onto the bar in front of him. "Mind if we use your phone, Bruce?"

"Ah, defo. Fire on," Bruce said, indicating the payphone sitting down at the far end of the bar, near the door leading to the beer garden. "You got on the Wi-Fi alright, though, yeah?"

Tyler looked up from the menu, a hand already slipping into his jacket pocket. "The pub's got Wi-Fi?"

Bruce grinned at both of them, his forehead furrowing a little like he wasn't sure if DC Neish was joking.

"Nah. Whole island, mate. Complete coverage, end to end. All free. It's a bloody marvel."

Logan turned his head towards the pub's windows, like he might be able to catch a glimpse of the wireless internet signal bouncing around out there.

"The whole island has free Wi-Fi?"

"Yeah, I reckon," Bruce said.

"You reckon? You mean you don't know?" Logan asked him.

Tyler shook his head. "That's just what they say, isn't it? It's the way they talk."

Logan scowled at the younger detective. "So, does it have Wi-Fi or not?"

Tyler thumbed his screen, then held it up for Logan to see. The words, 'Canna Community Network' filled a couple of lines on the screen. As Logan watched, a little tick appeared beside it, and Tyler's phone *ding-d-ding-dinged* as a couple of emails and a Facebook notification all arrived at the same time.

"Looks like it, boss," Tyler confirmed. "Fast, too."

"Community Council put it in, I think. They got a grant, or a loan, or whatever. From the Government, I think. Everyone was pretty stoked," Bruce explained. "The phone signal is pretty bad out here, but the internet's slick. I think it uses satellites. Or maybe tunnels? Undersea wires, or something, I mean."

"We can use the Wi-Fi for VOIP calls," Tyler suggested.

Logan took out his phone and regarded it as if it had suddenly morphed into a piece of tech from the distant future. "We can what?"

"Voice Over IP. If we download Skype—or, no, WhatsApp—then we can use that to send messages, make calls and—" Tyler began, but Logan handed him the phone and gave a dismissive wave designed to shut him up.

"Aye, well. I'll let you handle that, then," he said, finally taking a look at the menu he was holding. "While I order us up some grub."

Detective Inspector Ben Forde shot a sideways glance at the office door as he flopped into his chair and rolled it closer to his cluttered desk. He had a haunted look about him, like he'd just been confronted by the grim reality of his own mortality.

Which wasn't a million miles away from the truth.

"The DS didn't sound best pleased, sir," said a junior detective sitting at a neighbouring desk. His voice was little more than a whisper, like he was afraid the walls had ears.

"Aye. Well, you can say that again, Hamza," Ben muttered. He puffed out his cheeks, tore his eyes from the door, and offered a wafer-thin smile to Detective Constable Khaled. Hamza, for his part, bounced it right back with added sympathy.

After more years on the force than he had any inclination to count, it took a lot to rattle Ben's cage. The past ten minutes with Detective Superintendent Hoon, however, hadn't so much rattled his cage as hurled it against a brick wall and then furiously stamped it to bits.

"I mean, I always go in there expecting him to rip me a new arsehole, but it's like Swiss bloody cheese today. Something's got him wound up worse than usual," Ben said.

He checked the door again, then rolled his chair a little closer to Hamza's, so he could drop his voice even further.

"Usually, there are at least a couple of non-swear words scattered here and there amongst the barrage of abuse. The occasional oasis of clean language. But that? That was just relentless from the get-go. I mean, there were swear words in there I've never even heard of, and I like to think of myself as a fairly educated man when it comes to that sort of thing."

Reaching for his shirt pocket, he took out his notebook and flicked through a few pages. "I even wrote one down. Hang on..."

Hamza took a sip from his mug of tea while he waited for the DI to find the right page.

"Right. Here we are. At one point, he said I was a 'scumbering fuckstick,'" Ben announced. He looked up from his pad, his expression suggesting he was a little hurt, but mostly confused. "I mean, what's that when it's at home?"

"Well—"

"The 'scumbering' bit, I mean. I can figure out the 'fuckstick.'" He pointed down at his pad. "'Jeb end.' That's another one. I mean, I've heard of a knob end. I wouldn't have minded knob end. Bell end, even. But *jeb end*? What's a jeb?"

Hamza bit his lip, fighting hard to contain the urge to laugh. "Aye, sounds like he was off on one, sir," he said. "What's got him so riled up this time?"

"Oh, Christ, don't ask me. Would you believe, I stand there and take all that dog's abuse, and I'm still none the wiser as to what the problem is? Something to do with Logan, though. Hoon's gunning for him. Probably just as well he's tucked away on Canna. Short of the dark side of the bloody moon, a remote island's probably the safest place for him."

He rolled his chair back to his own desk, picked up his mug, and was unable to hide his disappointment when he found it was empty.

"Any word from him yet?" he asked, depositing the mug back down with a sullen *clunk*.

"SOC team landed forty minutes ago. Body's off to Raigmore for the PM," Hamza said. "But no, nothing yet from the boss."

Ben rummaged in his desk drawer until he found a packet of Polo mints. They were a poor substitute for a hot cup of tea, but making a fresh brew would mean leaving the safety of the office, and he didn't want to risk bumping into Hoon again.

Where the hell was DC Neish when you needed him?

"You ever been to Canna, Hamza?" Ben asked.

"Can't say I have, sir, no," said Hamza.

DC Khaled had been brought up in the east. The *far* east.

Aberdeen, to be precise. Anything west of Inverness and south of Dundee was generally something of a mystery to him.

Ben wrinkled his nose. "You're not missing much. I mean, it's nice enough, don't get me wrong. And if rocks or sheep are your thing, then you'll be like a pig in shit. But, it's not big. No' exactly well equipped. I'd be very surprised if they can even get a mobile signal all the way out—"

The phone on Ben's desk rang. He pounced on it quickly, grabbing for the receiver before Hoon could get wind of it.

"Detective Inspector Ben..." he began, then an echoey voice down the line cut him off.

"Benjamin."

Ben lowered both his head and his voice, cupping a hand around the phone's mouthpiece like he was sharing some big secret with it. "Jack. It's yourself. Your ears must've been burning. Hamza and I were just talking about you."

"Aye? All nice things, I hope," came the voice down the line.

"Nicer than the stuff Hoon was saying, that's for sure. It's fair to say he was being less complimentary about you than we were. He's gunning for you. Wants you to get in touch, pronto. What have you done to piss him off this time?"

"No idea," Logan said, but Ben knew him well enough to know a lie when he heard it.

"Right. Good. Fair enough, then," Ben replied. "On an entirely unrelated note, I hear Bosco Construction had a fire on the premises earlier this morning. One of the Portakabins went up like a match."

"Did it, indeed? I hadn't heard a thing," Logan replied. "One of the downsides of being stuck in a storm in the arse end of nowhere, I suppose."

"Suppose so," Ben said. "Well, if I see Bosco, I'll pass on your condolences."

"Aye. Do that," said Logan. "That'd be lovely. Now, has Hamza sorted us out somewhere to kip yet?"

"Hang on, I'll put you on speaker," said Ben, setting the phone on the desk between himself and DC Khaled. "But keep your voice down. Hoon's bastard-sense is no doubt already tingling."

"Alright, sir?" said Hamza, once Ben had tapped the loudspeaker icon on the phone's screen. "Enjoying your quality time with Tyler?"

"God, aye. It's like all my Christmases have come at once," Logan replied. "You get us somewhere to stay?"

"Uh, yeah. I did."

There was a slight change to the tone of Logan's voice. A subtle sort of wariness creeping in around the edges.

"What's wrong with it?" he asked.

"Nothing, sir. It's a nice wee B&B. It's the only B&B on the island, actually. It's not big. They've only got two rooms."

"We only need two rooms."

Hamza's chair gave a soft groan as he shifted his weight back a little, putting more distance between himself and the phone, like he was worried it might suddenly make a grab for him.

"That's the thing, sir. One's already taken."

There was silence from the handset. Hamza stole a look at DI Forde. It was Ben's turn to be struggling to contain his laughter.

"What?" Logan finally asked.

"The other room's taken, sir. There's only one available. It's a twin, though, so... there's that."

Despite his many years of investigation experience, it seemed to be taking a long time for Logan to process what Hamza was telling him. Either that, or he was simply refusing to believe it.

"What are you saying here, DC Khaled? *Exactly*?" the DCI asked. "You're telling me that... What?"

Ben cleared his throat. "Hello, Jack? It's me. Ben."

"You've both got different voices, Ben, I know it's you," Logan snapped.

"Right. Aye. Well, I think what Hamza's saying is that, despite his best efforts—and he worked hard on this, I saw it myself. Despite those best efforts, he has only been able to secure you a twin room for tonight."

Another burst of silence from the other end of the line. Hamza and Ben exchanged looks, and both men found themselves struggling to hold it together.

"Well, where's Tyler going to...?" Logan began.

And then, it happened. Then, the penny dropped.

"Wait a minute! Wait just a fucking minute. Are you saying...? I'm no' sharing a room with this bawbag."

Tyler's voice echoed tinnily in the background.

"Are we sharing a room, boss?"

"No, we bloody well are not!" Logan barked at him. His voice became clearer as he turned back to the phone. "There must be something else."

"There's..." Hamza coughed, concealing a chuckle that he hadn't managed to contain in time. "Sorry. There's not, sir. There's the caravan park, but it's shut until summer. The other guest at the B&B is due to move on as soon as the weather lifts, so I've pre-booked that room for when he does, but until then..."

He wasn't sure how to finish that sentence without getting shouted at, so just let it trail away into silence.

Ben was quick to take up the mantle. "Think of it as a chance to get to know each other better, Jack," he said. "Think of it as bonding time."

"I'll bond the toe of my boot to his arse if I've to put up with him all night," Logan replied. "And why would I want to get to know him better? Have you met him? I'd like to get to know him *less*, if anything."

"You know I'm standing right here, boss, aye?" Tyler asked.

"Yes, Detective Constable. I know. I can sense you looming behind me like the spectre of fucking Death," Logan snarled. "Away and sit down, for Christ's sake. You're making the place look untidy."

Ben bit hard on one of his knuckles. Hamza buried his face in the crook of his elbow, his shoulders heaving.

"Are you pair laughing?" demanded the voice from the phone.

"Us? No," Ben said, the words squeaking out of him like air escaping from a balloon.

"You'd bloody better not be," Logan warned them.

And then, it all became too much, and Ben and Hamza both exploded with laughter so loud and uncontrolled, that they missed the entirety of the expletive-filled rant that came spitting at them through the speaker.

CHAPTER NINE

Logan and Tyler stood in a small, fussily-decorated bedroom, staring in mute horror at a double bed.

The owners seemed nice enough. Patricia and Norman Dawson, originally from Beith in Ayrshire. They were a couple at opposite ends of their thirties, Patricia not much out of her twenties, Norman approaching forty. They'd seemed genuinely apologetic when explaining the shortage of rooms.

"It's Kevin, the other guest. He was meant to leave, but, well, the ferries," Pat had explained, before launching into another round of apologies.

After a quick tour of the house—the shared bathroom, the dining area, and the lounge with its big bay windows currently looking out onto a wall of grey fog—they were given the key to the room and left to their own devices.

And here they were now. Standing there.

Right at the foot of the double bed.

"This can't be right, can it, boss?" Tyler asked. He'd seemed pretty amused about the sleeping situation until that point. Now, he looked almost as concerned as Logan felt. "We can't be sharing a bed, can we?"

"I'll chainsaw the bastard down the middle, if I have to," Logan said.

He dropped his bag by the door and had just turned to head back down the stairs when he heard the hurried *thudding* of racing footsteps.

Pat's head popped up above the gloss-painted bannister, her face red, her bob of brown hair practically standing on end.

"Sorry! Sorry! I thought Norman had split the bed into singles. He just told me he thought I'd done it!"

"Oh, thank God," Tyler muttered, physically sagging with relief.

"Give me fifteen minutes, and I'll get it all sorted," Pat said, squeezing past them. She had a small stack of sheets and single quilt-covers draped over her arms, and a screwdriver sticking out of her back pocket.

"You need a hand?" Logan asked, as she set the linen on an ancient-looking bureau, and reached for the screwdriver.

"No, I'm a dab hand these days," Pat said, shooing them both towards the door. "Away you go downstairs. Norman's got the kettle on, and I just made a carrot cake."

Logan nodded graciously. "Aye. Well," he said. "Now, you're talking my language."

AFTER DISHING out the tea and a couple of generous slices of carrot cake, Norman left the detectives alone in the lounge.

Like the rest of the house, it could generously be described as 'quaint' and less generously as 'horribly dated.'

The walls, with their swirling brown and cream floral print, felt like they were closing in on the mismatched leather couches and wingback chairs.

A small television was balanced on a bookcase in one corner, positioned so impractically that it would be almost impossible to see from all but one of the available seats, and even from that one, you'd have to hope nothing important was happening in the bottom left corner.

There were two big display units, all smooth, curved wood and scuffed glass. Inside one was a veritable safari-park of animal-themed ornaments, arranged in groups according to species.

The other case held stacks of old crockery. Teacups and saucers, mostly, and the occasional big plate. Logan couldn't say if they were valuable, but he could say, with some conviction, that they were a bloody eyesore.

Somewhere in the house, a cuckoo clock called out nine times. Logan wanted to throttle it by the fourth.

He didn't know enough about Pat and Norman to make the call yet, but he had a feeling they didn't really fit with the style of the house. The cups and plates the detectives had been given with their tea and cake were plain, unfussy things. A world away from the dated clutter of the rest of the place.

"Jesus, that's hard," Tyler remarked, attempting to settle himself down in one of the wingback chairs. "I thought what it lacked in looks it might make up for in comfort, but nope. Does it fuck."

He got back up again and joined Logan by the big bay window, face to face with the storm. It screeched and battered against the other side of the glass, like a monster trying to force its way inside.

Logan sipped his tea, unblinking and uncowed by it, and enjoyed a bite from his slab of cake. They'd grabbed dinner in the pub—a couple of toasties, and some underwhelming chips—but the cake was undoubtedly the culinary highlight of the day.

"Forecast says it's supposed to ease off overnight," Tyler said, indicating the weather with a tilt of his cup. "Still going to be grim, but not as bad as this."

Grim. It was how Logan always imagined life out on the islands. A relentless parade of drudgery beneath an overcast sky. Backbreaking labour on too-salty soil. A life spent squinting in the wind.

The rain raged against the window, doing nothing to change his mind.

"Right, where are we?" Logan asked, turning his back on the storm. "What have we got?"

He took a seat on one of the couches, and Tyler returned unenthusiastically to the wingback. The DC had spent most of the evening emailing and messaging back and forth with Hamza, who was co-ordinating with SOC and Pathology.

The hope was that, between them, they could build up an early picture. What they'd actually pulled together wasn't so much a picture as a child-like scribble, and Tyler had been dreading the moment he had to deliver his report.

He took a bite of his cake, washed it down with a gulp of tea, then swiped at his phone until he found his notes.

"Right, boss. Iona Wallace, aged forty-six. Formerly Iona Kerr."

"Aye, I know that bit," Logan said.

"Moved to the island with her father and older brother back in—"

Logan raised a hand, silencing him. "And that bit. What else?"

Tyler glanced up from his phone, then swiped the screen with a thumb a few times, scrolling through a lot of text he'd typed out that, now he came to look at it, didn't actually say very much.

"Uh, her dad's the minister. Abraham Kerr. He's with the Wee Free church."

"Jesus. Don't beat around the bush. Give me the headlines, son. Has cause of death been confirmed?"

"Not yet, boss. Dr Maguire's still on the post-mortem, last I heard. You reckoned strangulation though, didn't you?"

"Aye, but hard as this may be for you to believe, I've been wrong in the past," Logan said. "Very occasionally. So, I'd like an expert opinion to confirm."

His eyes went to Tyler's phone. "Can we Skype on this connection?"

Tyler's brow furrowed. "What, each other?"

"No! Why the f--?" Logan pinched the bridge of his nose, muttered quietly, then shook his head. "Why would you and I Skype each other? We're sitting in the same room. Off the island, I mean. Can I Skype, I don't know, Dr Maguire, for example?"

A smirk tugged at the corners of Tyler's mouth. "Ah. Gotcha. Aye. No bother, boss. Connection's good. You'll be grand. I installed WhatsApp for you, too, if that's easier."

"Skype will be fine," Logan said. He knew how to use Skype. Vaguely. He had enough on his mind without worrying about some new bloody technology.

He shifted his weight on the couch, making the leather creak beneath him. "I'll do that later, then, when you're not lugging in. Where are we at with getting back-up? Not that there's anywhere for them to stay, mind you."

"Can't do much until the weather clears a bit," Tyler said. "DI Forde said he'll get a team of Uniforms across on the ferry as soon as it's back up and running, but no saying when that'll be."

"That's fine, but I don't want any other ferries running until we give the say-so. We don't want anyone leaving before we've had a chance to speak to them," Logan said.

"Shouldn't take us that long, boss. Population's only forty-seven, Hamza tells me."

"Is that before or after someone murdered Iona?"

Tyler hesitated. "Forty-six," he corrected. "And are we sure it's definitely murder, aye?"

"Well, unless she clonked herself on the coupon and then throttled herself to death, I'd say so," Logan replied.

"She couldn't have hanged herself? The way the body was lying at the foot of that scarecrow, I just wondered..."

Logan shook his head. "Briefly contemplated it myself, but it doesn't fit. If she did away with herself, where's the rope? Not enough height on the scarecrow, either. To get enough weight on her neck, she'd have to have lifted her feet off the ground and kept them there until she choked to death."

"Suppose. She'd have had to have been determined."

"She'd have had to have been a bloody miracle worker," Logan retorted. "Before she died, she'd have passed out. I'd have liked to see her keeping her legs up then."

He took another mouthful of tea, rolled it around, then swallowed it. "No. She was murdered. And right now, we're in the fortunate position of having a finite number of possible suspects. Forty-six people, take away... what? Ten or so kids, probably. She was found in a pretty remote location, and it'd have taken some strength to throttle her, so rule out the older folk, and we've probably got twenty or so possibilities."

"Assuming whoever killed her didn't get off the island before she was found, boss."

"Ferries haven't been running. Private boats are a possibility, but someone will have seen something, so at least we'll know," Logan said. "Right now, though, let's work on the basis that the killer's still on the island, and concentrate on catching the bastard before they can get their arse off it."

Tyler stifled a yawn that prompted Logan to check his watch. Twenty to ten. No point getting stuck into anything more tonight.

"Tomorrow, we'll start the house calls. I want to speak to Iona's father, find out who her friends are, and build up a picture of the last night she was seen alive. We'll have to find somewhere to set up an Incident Room, or at least to do more formal interviews, if it comes to that. Ask Pat and Norman, or get on Google Maps. See if there's anywhere that might fit. A school, maybe."

He clicked his fingers, a thought occurring to him. "I bet the Community Council has got an office somewhere. If so, we can use that."

"I'll get on it, boss," Tyler said. He yawned again, and there was no holding this one back. "Sorry, long day," he said, once it had passed. "I was pitching in with CID on some of the donkey work for the Gillespie case from early this morning."

Logan regarded the DC with surprise. "Were you?"

Tyler fiddled with the handle of his mug, then poked a couple of crumbs around on his plate, not quite looking up. "Caitlyn's case, isn't it? Just want to help make sure the bastard goes down."

"Aye. Well," Logan said. It was the only words that were really needed. "Go and get your head down. We can carry on in the morning. With a bit of luck, we'll have it all wrapped up by lunchtime."

"Cheers, boss," Tyler said. "I'll maybe just give Sinead a ring first. See how she's doing."

"Tell her I said hello," Logan said. "And remind her that she could do much better for herself."

"Will do," Tyler said. He set his cup on his plate, looked around for somewhere to put them that wasn't cluttered with bowls, vases, and assorted other nonsense, then just placed them on the floor next to his chair.

He was almost at the door when Logan called to him.

"Oh, and Tyler?"

"Yes, boss?"

"If you snore, I swear to God, I will smother you with a pillow."

Tyler grinned. "No promises, but I'll see what I can do."

When he was gone, Logan swallowed the now nearly cold remnants of his tea, winced at the taste of it, and crossed to the window. It was dark now, but the way the window shook in its frame made it clear that the storm was still raging away.

Logan saw himself reflected in the window. His face heaved and moved, like his flesh was alive and squirming beneath his skin. An optical illusion caused by the rainwater running down the outside of the pane. But still, it did nothing to boost his confidence as he smoothed down his hair, adjusted his shirt collar, then took out his phone and tapped on the big blue icon that opened the Skype app.

CHAPTER TEN

Shona Maguire was not midway through the process of cutting up a corpse when she answered. This was always a pleasant surprise.

She wasn't even in the hospital, unless the staff areas had been given a complete redesign since he'd last been in.

Shona was half-sitting, half-reclining on a couch, the colour of which could only be described as 'organ purple'. She had on an oversized checked shirt, her hair was hanging loosely around her shoulders, and she was a good two-thirds of the way through a generously-sized glass of red wine.

On the wall behind her were three framed movie posters: *Ghostbusters 2*, *Gremlins 2*, and *The Empire Strikes Back*. A satin gold scarf was pinned to the wall beneath them with the words, "Rock On, Tommy!" emblazoned across it in faded black print.

There was another framed picture to the right of the posters, only half in shot. It was a photograph, and showed a grinning Shona with an arm around what looked like one of the *Doctor Whos*. One of the originals, Logan thought, not the new lot.

At the bottom of Logan's screen, right at the very edge of the camera's frame, the top of a Chow Mein flavoured *Pot Noodle* rose into view like an obelisk. The thin metal handle of a fork stuck out of the top like a tiny lightning rod.

"I wondered when you were going to call," Shona said, her Irish lilt drifting from the phone's speaker like music. "You're cutting it fine. I was getting ready to head to bed."

Logan swallowed, coughed, and cleared his throat, all in one movement.

"Jesus, are you choking?" Shona asked, leaning forward in concern.

"What? No. No. I'm fine," Logan assured her. "Sorry to call so late. I thought you'd still be... you know."

"Elbow deep in a chest cavity? Nah, she's on ice until tomorrow. Had an OD and a car accident earlier. Worked too many hours, so they made me go home."

"Ah right," Logan said. He fumbled around for the right words. God, why wasn't he better at this? "Rough day, then?"

Shona shrugged. "Pretty standard, really. You? I hear you got a burl in a helicopter. That must've been exciting."

"No' quite the word I'd have used to describe it," Logan said. "And now I'm stuck sharing a room with DC Neish."

"Is he the good-looking one?" Shona asked, smirking behind her wine glass.

"No, *I'm* the good-looking one. He's the glaikit one with the stupid hair."

She laughed at that, and Logan was almost annoyed by how grateful he felt for it.

Shona leaned forward again, squinting at the camera. She was using her laptop, presumably, propped up on a table to give a wider angle of the room.

"Where even are you? The nineteen-hundreds?" she asked.

Logan looked over his shoulder at the dated furniture and yellowed wallpaper. "Aye, something like that," he said.

He wanted to say more to her. To just chat for a while. Enjoy this moment of connection with her, just the two of them there on their wee screens.

Unfortunately, he'd completely run out of things to say, and so he defaulted back to what he knew best.

"So, when do you think you'll get a look at the body?"

"Officially? About half-eight tomorrow morning," Shona said. "Unofficially?"

She reached out of shot and returned with an A4 notebook.

"I already had a quick peek and did some swabs. I'll start getting results from those tomorrow. This is all subject to change, and the body wasn't in great condition, but I'm putting cause of death most likely as asphyxiation caused by strangulation. Definitely murder. Someone standing behind her with a wire of some sort, I'd say. Either substantially taller than her, or she was kneeling. The wire wasn't sharp, but fairly thin and pulled tight, so it cut into the flesh. You know your phone charging cable? Something like that. Slightly thinner, maybe, but touch and go."

"There was a head wound," Logan said. A teasing smile started to form at the corners of Shona's mouth, and he jumped in before she could say anything. "You know, in case you hadn't noticed."

"Actually, now that you mention it, I think I did spot something along those lines," she said. "Not fatal, though. Not even all that serious. Bled a lot, but these things do. Would've been distressing, though. Probably blinded her temporarily. All in all, it wouldn't have been a very pleasant final few minutes."

"They very rarely are," Logan said. "Any ideas on when she died?"

"Few days ago. I'd have to check the weather and temperature records to get a better idea of decomposition rate, but she's obviously been somewhere wet. The skin on her fingers is what I'd expect to find on someone who drowned."

"She was in a big muddy puddle, and it's been pishing down," Logan told her.

"Sounds about right. I'd estimate tail end of Tuesday, first half of Wednesday, but call that an educated guess until I've had a chance to look at her properly."

"That fits. Tuesday was the last night anyone saw her alive. As far as we know at this stage, anyway."

"Close-knit community, and not a big place. Chances are, if she was still alive after that, someone would have seen her," Shona reasoned. "And decomposition would rule out her being alive even by Wednesday evening, so you've got a decently small window."

"Aye. It's looking like the Tuesday night, right enough."

Logan shuffled his feet on the lounge's awful carpet for a few moments, before continuing. "I knew her. The victim, I mean. Way back. We were in school together."

Shona stopped swirling her glass and sat it down on the table in front of her. "Oh. God. I'm sorry. I didn't know. Were you close?"

"Eh, no. Not really," Logan said, skirting around the edges of the truth. '*Not often,*' would've been more accurate. "She moved away when we were in high school. Hadn't really thought about her until I saw her under the sheet today."

"Still, though," Shona said. "Must've been a shock."

"Ach, yes and no. From what I remember of her, it was only a matter of time before she got on the wrong side of some bad bastard. But, aye, I've a bit of a personal stake in this one. I'd like to nail whoever did it, pronto. So, anything you can get me tomorrow..."

"Yeah well, sure, you can count on me, Jack," Shona told him.

"Aye," he said, with a nod and a smile. "Aye. I know."

He cleared his throat again. Christ, his mouth was dry. He wished he hadn't polished off the last of the tea before the call. He wasn't prepared. Not properly. Now probably wasn't the time.

Although, it was rare that they were having a conversation that wasn't taking place above the remains of a murder victim, so maybe now was as good a time as any.

Sod it. He was going in.

"So, listen, I was thinking. I know we've made plans before, and something's come up, so we've never really… You know? I mean, we spoke about maybe…. Before, I mean. We'd discussed the idea that…"

He forced himself to shut his mouth, cutting off that awful bloody babble before it could go any further. On-screen, Shona was watching him in silence, her expression giving nothing away.

"I suppose, what I mean is, will we just do it?" he said, then his eyes widened in horror as he heard the words out loud. "Have dinner, I mean! Dinner. Not, not… I wasn't saying… Just, we could have dinner. I'd like to take you to dinner. Somewhere nice."

Logan's mouth was racing ahead of his brain, which was currently fixating on what a weird word 'dinner' was. He'd said it so often in such a short space of time, it had lost all sense of meaning. Was it even a word?

Shona still hadn't replied, and Logan's instinct for self-preservation quickly kicked in.

"Somewhere nice-ish, I mean. Nowhere crazy. A kebab, or something. I'm no' made of money!" he said.

She was still saying nothing. Logan held his phone a little further away and squinted at the display.

"Hello?"

He tapped the screen. Shona's face remained completely frozen. The timer in the bottom corner that had been ticking up the minutes, ticked no longer.

"You are bloody kidding me," Logan muttered, then a movement from behind him made him turn.

Norman was leaning into the lounge from the hall, offering up an apologetic smile.

"Sorry, forgot to say, the internet goes down at ten," he explained. "Cost-saving. It's back on at eight."

"Sunday," called Pat from elsewhere in the house.

"Oh, aye. Tomorrow's Sunday, so it won't be back on until after twelve. Reverend Kerr insisted."

"Did he?" Logan sighed. He looked back at the screen in time to see Shona replaced by the Skype logo. "Well, who am I to argue with a man of the cloth?"

"Aye. Well. Sorry, again," Norman said. He started to leave, then leaned back in. "Would you like a glass of wine, or something?"

"No. Thank you," Logan said, the response coming on auto-pilot.

"Whisky? Gin? We've a nice Lochaber one we haven't tried yet."

Logan shook his head. "You're fine. Honest."

Through the ceiling above him, he heard the muffled rumble of a snore. He picked up his cup and plate.

"But I wouldn't say no to another cup of tea, if you're making one."

CHAPTER ELEVEN

When Norman returned with the tea—and, to Logan's delight, another slice of cake—the detective took the opportunity to gather some background on Iona, and her relationship with the others on the island.

The relationship could generously be described as, 'not great,' it transpired. Norman seemed reluctant to speak ill of the dead, but with a bit of reading between the lines, Logan got a picture of a woman who had turned almost everyone against her.

"It was the drink that was her downfall," Norman said. "I mean, so they tell me. She's been here a lot longer than we have. All we've ever seen her as is a bit... desperate. No offence to her, or anything," he added, shooting a glance skyward. "She was never far from drama, put it that way. And usually of her own making."

"Some things never change," Logan remarked.

Norman raised his eyebrows and tilted his head, like he hadn't quite heard. "Sorry?"

"Doesn't matter. Her dad's on the island. What about the brother?"

Norman shook his head. "Didn't know she had one. She's got a son, though. Grown-up now. Isaac. Isaac Young. Goes by his father's surname. He's got a house here with his girlfriend. Don't think his grandfather approves, unmarried couple living in sin, and all that, but then I don't think the Reverend approves of very much, really." He shivered. "Certainly not central heating, judging by the temperature in that bloody church of a morning."

"The boy. Isaac. What was his relationship like with his mother?"

"Oh, I'm not sure... I wouldn't really know," Norman said, but the uncomfortable look on his face told Logan enough.

"And Isaac's father? Is he around?"

"No. Lives in England somewhere, I think. Never known him to come out here. Probably doesn't like the idea of running into Iona." Norman smiled thinly. "I suppose there's no chance of that now, mind you."

He had been sitting forward in the same chair Tyler had sat in earlier, but now leaned back and gazed through his reflection in the window at the darkness outside. The wind and rain had abated a little, so it was now just low-level background noise, and not the attention-demanding racket it had previously been.

"Murdered. I still can't believe it," Norman remarked. "I mean, we came here to get away from that sort of thing. Drugs and crime. Wee neds chucking stones at your windows. That's why we bought this place. Get away from it all. Somewhere you can leave your doors open, and not have to worry about who might be watching you coming and going."

He blew out his cheeks and rubbed the arms of the chair with the flat of his hands. "So, *murder*? An actual murder? I still can't believe it."

"Any thoughts on who might've done it?" Logan asked, prompting a shocked look from Norman. "Off the record, I mean. Just between you and me. I promise, I'm not going to go arrest someone on your say-so. Just thought you might have some personal insight, being local."

"Oh, we're not local. Not by a long shot," Norman said, deflecting the question. "You've to be here at least three generations before you can call yourself local. We've barely been here a year and a half. If we said we were local, we'd be bloody crucified!"

He clocked the way Logan was looking at him, and hurriedly clarified. "Metaphorically. There's nobody I'd put down as violent. I mean, obviously it seems that there is, but... There's no-one I know who's capable of..."

He shook his head, visibly appalled by the very thought of it. "So, no, Mr Logan. Sorry. I don't have any thoughts on who might have killed Iona."

He stood up, collected Logan's empty cup and plate, then gave a nod. "But I really hope you find them."

CHAPTER TWELVE

Logan found himself on page ninety-seven.

He hadn't been ready to face a night lying awake listening to Tyler snoring, and so had settled down beside an ugly lamp in the otherwise darkened lounge with the box of diaries they'd taken from Iona's house.

Logically, he should've started with the most recent, but he told himself it was important to build up a more long-term picture of the victim's life, and had gone straight for the one most likely to contain reference to their not-so-secret liaison.

It wasn't a diary, exactly, just an old school jotter Iona must've nicked from a class supply cupboard. She'd written 'The Secret Diary of Iona Kerr' on the front in bubble writing and shaded it with coloured pencils. Under it, in brackets, was another name, *Desiree Shanelle*, which didn't ring any bells for the detective. A pen name, clearly. Some teenage escapist fantasy.

The rest of the cover was decorated with little cartoon animals, the personalities shining off the page. She was good. Or had been, at least.

He'd looked through many diaries, private letters, and personal effects over the years. It was all part of the job. And yet, he found himself glancing cagily around before he opened the cover of this particular journal, and began scanning the pages for his name.

And there he was. Page ninety-seven.

"Jack Logan is a total knob."

This wasn't the reference he'd been expecting, and he quickly read the rest of the entry, his frown deepening as he followed the whirling, twirling handwriting down the page.

They were in third-year at the time of the diary entry. Roughly six months before their post-disco get-together.

Logan had no recollection of it himself, but according to the diary, some sixth-year lads had been giving her grief after school, and she'd asked him if she could walk home with him.

He'd said no.

A weight formed low down in his stomach as he read the rest of the entry. Read the abuse she'd taken. Read how they'd pawed at her, ground themselves against her, before shoving her down the steps at the back of the Co-op and leaving here there in a dirty puddle.

Her old man had gone ballistic at the state of her uniform when she'd finally got home. Leathered seven bells out of her. Made her pray for forgiveness kneeling in her underwear on the cold kitchen floor.

And all because of him. All because he'd told her no. All because, for whatever stupid reason, he'd told her he wouldn't walk home with her.

"Aye," he grunted, turning the page in shame. "What a total knob."

He wasn't mentioned again until the night of the disco. Even then, it was barely a cameo appearance, and not worth writing home about.

'Shagged Jack Logan,' it read. 'What was I thinking?!?'

There was a wee drawing of a girl next to it, that Logan took to be Iona herself. She was holding her head in her hands.

It was, he thought, the single most damning review of his sexual performance he'd ever been privy to. He supposed he should be grateful that she hadn't used a star rating system.

Over in seconds. No stars. Wouldnae ride again.

Somewhere in the house, the cuckoo called midnight.

Skimming through the rest of the book, Logan got a clear impression of an unhappy home life, mostly caused by her father's temper and strict religious bent. Iona had it bad, but her older brother, Jacob, got it far worse.

Logan remembered the sight of Jacob coming marching along the road towards him that night, his face twisted by rage into something monstrous. He'd had a couple of mates with him, but he wouldn't have needed them. Not with anger like that driving him on.

Logan had assumed at the time that all that rage was because of him. Now, though, he could see where it had really come from. Aye, it had been directed Logan's way that night, but it had been fuelled by years of violence and abuse from a father who punished frequently and, from what Logan could gather, loved rarely, if ever.

After sealing the book in an evidence bag, Logan wrote the details on the plastic label, and placed it back in the box.

He was reaching for the most recent diary when he heard footsteps shuffling softly along the hall. Someone was creeping about downstairs.

He could rule out Tyler, who was still snoring his head off on the other side of the ceiling.

Easing himself up out of the chair, Logan made his way quietly towards the door of the lounge. The top lights were out in the hall, but a couple of particularly hideous wall lamps were casting a thin, watery sort of glow across the walls.

A floorboard creaked. A shadow moved. Logan stepped out into the hallway, and a man in an orange cagoule screamed in fright.

"Shh. Jesus!" Logan hissed. "People are sleeping."

"Wh-who are you?" the man asked in a shrill whisper. His accent was south of England. Refined by years of expensive private education, the detective guessed.

"I was about to ask you the same thing," Logan replied. "Detective Chief Inspector Jack Logan. Mind telling me what you're doing sneaking about this house?"

A light came on at the top of the stairs, and footsteps hurried down. Pat practically jumped the last few steps, a sturdy-looking shoe clutched in one hand like a weapon.

Her relief when she saw the men in the hallway was immediate and palpable.

"Oh. God. It's just you two."

"You know this gentleman?" Logan asked.

Pat smiled and nodded. "That's Mr Tillerson."

"Kevin," the man added.

"He's the other guest," Pat explained. "The one in the double."

"I've been stuck. With the weather," Kevin said. He held up a pack of cigarettes. "I was just nipping outside for a quick puff before I turn in."

"Everything alright down there?"

That was Norman calling. Safely from the top of the stairs, Logan noted, and not down here in the thick of it with his wife.

Pat looked quizzically at the shoe she was carrying, like she couldn't remember picking it up. "Aye. All fine," she replied, backing up to the stairs. She smiled apologetically at her guests. "Sorry. I'll leave you to it."

Both men listened to her footsteps as she made her way back up to bed. Kevin raised his eyebrows and pulled a 'well, then,' sort of face that suggested he'd really like to go and have his smoke now.

Logan had his own ideas about that.

"You didn't happen to see Iona Wallace on the night she died, did you?" he asked.

"Uh, I don't think so. I'm not sure I know who that is."

Logan nodded. "Right. I see. It's just, I was in the pub today, and the barman there—Australian boy—gave us a list of people who were in there the night Iona was murdered. You were on it."

"Oh! Yes! The woman in the pub! The loud one? Is that her?" Kevin asked. He was fiddling with a cigarette, rolling it between finger and thumb. "Yes. Sorry, yes. I did see her."

"Right, then," Logan said. He moved aside and motioned into the lounge. "Would you mind stepping into my office, Mr Tillerson? I think it'd be useful if you and I had a little chat."

CHAPTER THIRTEEN

Kevin Tillerson was a refreshing change from most of Logan's interview subjects. Despite the informality of the set-up—him on the couch, Logan sat higher on one of the wingbacks—Tillerson spent the entire conversation wide-eyed in terror, babbling out answers almost the moment that Logan had finished asking the questions.

They'd started easy. Background stuff. What had brought him to the island? Who was he travelling with? Where was he going, and where had he been. That sort of thing.

Logan hadn't written down most of the answers. He'd just scribbled a catch-all, 'post-divorce mid-life crisis,' and then steered the conversation onto more important matters.

Tillerson had become even more willing to talk at that point. With no loyalties to anyone on the island but himself, he was holding absolutely nothing back.

The daughter-in-law had really hated her, he thought. He hadn't caught her name, but there was definitely no love lost there.

The son? Well, he had seemed mostly embarrassed by her, but angry, too. A cold sort of anger. Deep-rooted. Enough to drive him to murder? Kevin wasn't sure, but he wasn't ruling it out.

She'd had a go at a big chap. Got quite cruel. Kevin couldn't say for sure if he'd had learning difficulties, but he wasn't ruling that out, either. *Worth having a word, anyway, I'd say. He certainly looked capable.*

"Between you and I, I got the impression she was about as welcome as a fart in a spacesuit," Kevin said. "To, uh, to quote one of your countrymen."

Logan regarded him blankly.

"Billy Connolly, wasn't it? Fart in a spacesuit?"

"I wouldn't know," Logan said. "So, she wasn't there with friends?"

"Goodness, no. I got the impression she didn't have any. Not among that lot, anyway. You could feel the hostility when she walked in—or staggered in, more accurately. And then, when the son and daughter-in-law arrived... Oof. I'd swear the temperature dropped half a dozen degrees. Which is impressive, given the place is constantly ruddy freezing."

"How long was she there?"

"Before they arrived? Maybe an hour. Afterwards? Oh, I don't know. Five, ten minutes?" Tillerson recalled. "She became quite abusive to, well, to everyone. The big lad, as I mentioned, but the rest of them, too. The daughter-in-law got right up in her face by the end, screaming at her to go. And, well, she did. I think she was out of money, personally. No one would buy her a drink, so off she went."

Logan scribbled in his pad. "And that was the last you saw her?"

Tillerson's eyes went to the pad, drawn there by the movement of the pencil.

"Hmm? Oh. Yes. Yes. That was the last I saw of her."

"And what was the atmosphere like once she'd left?"

"Fine."

"Fine? Can you elaborate?"

Tillerson shrugged. "Uh, well, I was sitting by myself, so I wasn't involved in anyone's conversations, exactly, but everyone seemed to relax after that. Well, almost. The son and daughter-in-law looked pretty shaken, still, but they left themselves soon after."

"They left? Together?"

"Yes. Yes, I think so. I didn't see them go, just looked up from my map at one point and they were gone."

"And how soon was this after Iona went?"

Tillerson made a weighing motion with his hands. "I'd be lying if I said I knew for certain, but... ten minutes? Thereabouts."

He gave a little jump as the cuckoo clock called once.

"Goodness. Is that the time?" he asked. It was diplomatic, if not exactly subtle.

"Aye," Logan said, flipping his notebook closed. "Thank you for your help, Mr Tillerson."

"Right. Yes. Of course. Happy to."

Tillerson sprang to his feet, already opening the top of his cigarette packet. "If there's anything else I can help with while I'm here, do let me know. It's a lovely island, and such a terrible thing to happen. The community must be..." He smiled grimly. "Well. It's very sad."

"It is," Logan agreed. "And thank you. If we need anything more, we'll be in touch."

"Well, you'll certainly know where to find me! I think we're right next door," Tillerson said. "Oh! That's a point. I don't suppose you know if they take cards at this place, do you? Been here longer than expected, and running a bit low on cash. Not sure if there's a machine anywhere."

"No idea," Logan told him, safe in the knowledge that he wouldn't be the one paying the bill at the end of his stay.

Tillerson looked a little disappointed, but then shrugged. "Ah well. It'll all work out, I'm sure. I can do a cheque, if it comes to it."

He nodded a farewell. "Goodnight, Mr Logan," he said, his waterproof jacket rustling as he headed for the door. "And good luck."

If Logan slept, it was brief and fitful, although he was fairly certain he didn't sleep at all. Partly, that was down to his mind whirring over the details of the case, but mostly it was because of Detective Constable Neish's incessant bloody snoring.

He wouldn't have minded so much, if it had been constant. If the snoring had taken just one form, and stuck to it. It was the variation that was the problem. One minute, he'd been roaring like a buzzsaw, the next he'd be whistling tunelessly through both nostrils, or making a clicking sound like a bubble bursting at the back of his throat, or one of a dozen other noisy ejections his airway decided to form while he slept.

Logan had woken him up six times, each time more irate than the last. Tyler had apologised every time, then immediately fallen back asleep before launching into some previously unheard nasal concerto.

After that, Logan had decided there was no point in waking him again, and had tried to learn to live with the racket.

This had not gone well. The couple of times he'd come close to dropping off, that bastard of a cuckoo clock had jolted him awake again.

And so, with time on his hands, and a ceiling to stare at, Logan had gone through what little he knew of the case so far, and made plans for the following day.

Talking to the family was going to be the priority, of course. Tomorrow—or today, technically—was Sunday, and Abraham Kerr was due to be running his church service as usual. The murder of a child might put lesser ministers off their stride, but not him. Not that bastard. Logan was very much looking forward to their chat.

Same with the son and daughter-in-law. They'd argued with Iona the night she'd died. Sounded serious, too. That conversation was another priority.

Roddy Mackay hadn't shown his face at the pub again, so he was on Logan's hitlist, too. The 'big chap' Kevin had referred to would be worth a word, and then it would be a case of asking around, talking to anyone else that might be able to shed some light on her final movements, to see if anything interesting emerged.

Shona should hopefully be able to provide him with some more information by early afternoon, and now that the weather was easing off a bit he'd like to get back out to where the body was found.

He lifted his head off the pillow, a thought striking him. Who'd found the body? He didn't recall seeing or hearing a name anywhere. He'd have to check.

A lot to do, then. And only him and the noisy snorting bastard in the next bed to do it.

He checked his watch. Almost five. Probably no point even trying to rest now. It was a complete waste of time. He might as well get up and get cracking. Get a head start on the rest of the world.

"Early bird catches the killer," he mumbled.

And then, with Tyler wheezing across the room, and the cuckoo clock *sproinging* into life downstairs, DCI Jack Logan finally surrendered to sleep.

CHAPTER FOURTEEN

Breakfast was the stuff that dreams are made of. Perfectly poached eggs, crispy bacon, three fat sausages, and some of the best tattie scones Logan had ever tasted, all accompanied by the usual beans, mushrooms, hash browns, and a nice wee slice of Stornoway black pudding.

Even the toast, which Logan could usually take or leave, was something a bit special. Homemade bread, apparently. You could taste the difference.

Tyler had been halfway through his breakfast by the time Logan came down. The DC grinned as he chewed a piece of bacon.

"Aye aye. Sleeping Beauty awakes," he'd remarked, pronging a bit of square sausage with a fork.

Logan had said nothing as he pulled out the chair opposite him and sat down. He had waited until Pat had come to take his order, in fact, before launching into a whispered-but-passionate tirade about 'some bastard snoring all bloody night!'

"Who? The boy next door?" Tyler had asked, prompting a substantially louder outburst from the DCI.

Over breakfast, Logan had filled the junior detective in on his discussion with Kevin Tillerson the night before, and recounted some of the details of the diary he'd read, being careful to leave out any mention of himself.

The focus was mostly on Iona's relationship with her father. While there was no reference to any sexual abuse, it was clear the old man was a violent bampot, and that both children had suffered regularly at his hands. Or, more regularly, his belt.

"Sounds like a piece of work," Tyler said. He pointed with a fork to Logan's plate. "You going to eat that tattie scone, boss?"

"Yes, I bloody am!" Logan said, fending the DC's fork off with his knife.

"Oh. Right, aye," said Tyler, crestfallen. He picked up one of his toast crusts and dragged it through what was left of his baked beans. "How'd you get on with Dr Maguire last night?"

Logan chose to ignore the smirk and the waggling of the eyebrows that accompanied the question. "She hasn't had a proper look at the body yet. Definitely strangled, though, and she reckons Tuesday night, early hours of Wednesday fits the time of death. She'll know more this morning."

Logan stopped when he became aware of movement by the door that led through to the kitchen. Pat hovered there, clearly unsure whether she should come in or not. She smiled with relief when Logan beckoned her through.

"How was it?" she asked, looking from one detective to the other. "Everything OK?"

"Bloody marvellous," Logan told her.

"Great! Would you like anything else? More toast? Tea?"

"I wouldn't mind another of those tattie scones, if it's—" Tyler began, but Logan picked up the DC's plate and held both it and his own out for Pat to take.

"He's fine. We're grand. Thank you."

"Sleep OK?" Pat asked, taking the plates.

"Out like a light," Tyler said.

"Oh, I'm sure the whole house is aware of how well you slept," Logan said, shooting him a sideways look.

"Cuckoo clock didn't keep you up, did it?" Pat asked.

"No. I mean, not really," Logan said. "It was mostly this bugger."

"Lucky you. Took me months to stop hearing the bloody thing," Pat said, rolling her eyes. "We wanted to get rid—wanted to strip the place right back and modernise it, in fact—but we weren't allowed."

Logan frowned. "No' allowed? How d'you mean?"

"Well, I mean, yes, I suppose we were allowed. It was just..." Pat shook her head and pulled an amused little smile, like she knew how ridiculous what she was saying sounded. "The Community Council, they suggested we leave it as it was. For posterity's sake, sort of thing. Joy—the council, I mean—made it quite clear that they wouldn't be impressed if we changed it. Even specified that bloody clock. Said the house was of 'local historical interest' and that the locals liked it as it was. We didn't want to make ourselves unwelcome, so we decided to hang off on the refurbishment. Just until we'd settled in a bit."

"Right. I see," said Logan. He glanced around at the faded wallpaper and garish curtains. "How long have you been in?"

"Year and a half," Pat said. "We've owned it a bit longer, but that's when we moved in. Joy stops by every so often to say hello. Although, she's really just checking to make sure we haven't started redecorating, I think."

"Aye, we ran into her yesterday," Logan said. "She seems like she could be..."

"An interfering old arsehole?" Pat suggested.

"Well, I was going to say 'stubborn' but aye. That, too," Logan said. He stood up and took another look around the place. "If it's any consolation, I quite like it."

"Do you?" asked Pat, her eyebrows rising in surprise.

Logan shook his head. "No." He smiled, apologetically. "No' really."

THE RAIN HAD DIED DOWN into a light drizzle, so they started the morning with a trip back to the site where the body had been found.

The scarecrow seemed to grin down at them as they sloshed carefully through the mud, the indentations in the hessian sack of its face carefully positioned to form rudimentary features.

"What is it we're looking for now, boss?" Tyler asked, pulling his jacket tightly around himself.

The coat he'd brought hadn't been particularly waterproof, and Pat had insisted both men take one of Norman's Gore-Tex jackets before heading out. Tyler had gladly accepted, but Logan had kept hold of his own overcoat. It was a large, heavy woollen thing, and was good for cultivating a nicely intimidating presence.

Also, he liked the big pockets.

Logan approached the scarecrow, snapping his rubber gloves into place. He hadn't yet heard any more from Shona—it was just after nine, and she'd barely be back at it yet—but something she'd said last night had made him think the site was worth another look.

With his hands protected, he reached up and began running his hands along the scarecrow's arms, patting down the padded sleeves from shoulder to wrist.

"Shouldn't you read him his rights first, boss?" Tyler asked. "Or is this some sort of personal interaction? Should I even be watching this?"

"Shut up and give me a bloody hand," Logan barked.

Pulling on his own gloves, Tyler joined him by the scarecrow. He didn't have the height advantage of the DCI, so felt around the legs and lower torso on the left side, while Logan focused on the right.

"What we actually looking for, boss?"

"Wire," Logan said. "Iona was throttled with a length of wire. I thought this thing might be held together or tied to its stand with the same stuff."

"Doesn't feel like it," Tyler said, after another half-minute of searching. He glanced back over his shoulder at the road. "I hope nobody drives past. We'll look like a right pair of weirdoes standing here touching up a scarecrow."

"It's the islands," Logan remarked, still prodding at the thing. "This probably qualifies as a good night out."

"Creepy bloody thing, isn't it?" Tyler said. "Or have I just watched too many horror movies?"

"*Wizard of Oz* doesn't count as a horror movie, son," Logan said. "Don't try to make yourself sound like the big man."

They searched until they were sure that they weren't going to find what they were looking for. The scarecrow was attached to its post with wire, but it was thick metal fence wire, that would've had to be bent into shape with tools. Not the sort of thing you could really strangle someone with, and it didn't match the description that Shona had provided.

So much for that idea.

Peeling off the gloves, they trudged back to the Land Rover, the wind nudging and shoving at them as it came whistling in off the water.

"Internet back on yet?" Logan asked, once they were safely installed back in the Land Rover. He turned over the engine and cranked up the heating. The vents emitted an acrid burning smell, but not a whole lot else.

"No. After twelve today, boss," Tyler said, although he took out his phone and checked, just to be sure. "I asked Pat when she was taking my brekkie order."

"Oh, aye. They said last night."

Logan checked the clock on the dash. The bottom row of the LED lines were permanently off, but there was enough left for him to piece the time together.

"Not too long, though. We'll see if Hamza's got anything for us when it's back up and running. Soon as you can, I want you to fire him over names of everyone we've spoken to. Have him run background. On the family, too, if he hasn't already. And pay attention to the daughter-in-law."

"Will do, boss," Tyler said. He rubbed his hands together, then held them in front of the heater, in the hope it might start spitting out hot air at some point in the not too distant future. "What's the plan now?"

"Now?" Logan began. He took a breath, readying himself to say words he hadn't spoken in a very long time. "Now, we're going to church."

CHAPTER FIFTEEN

"Anything back from them yet?" asked Ben, checking his watch for the fifth time since he'd entered the Incident Room.

He'd had a bash at putting together the Big Board, but without Logan and Tyler here, there didn't seem much point. Besides, that had been Caitlyn's area of expertise, and Ben's efforts looked positively amateurish by comparison.

Right now, it consisted of a few scribbled Post It notes, a Google Maps printout of Canna with a red X marking the location of the body, and not very much else.

"Not yet, sir, no," said Hamza, after clicking 'refresh' on his email for the umpteenth time that morning. "Tried getting Tyler on WhatsApp, but he's not showing as online."

Ben grunted. "Probably dead, then. Maybe Hoon caught up with them."

"Preliminary pathology report's in, though. I was going to forward it over, but we've all been CC'd in, so it'll be in your inbox. There's an update from Geoff Palmer in there, too."

"Anything exciting?"

"Potentially," was all Hamza would say on the matter. "Worth having a look."

Ben clicked his mouse a few times, then gave it a shake, waking the computer from its slumber. Judging by the series of whirring and grinding noises it made, it wasn't impressed.

"Any word on the ferries?"

"Not due to start running today, sir, but they're eyeballing tomorrow as a possibility. Weather's supposed to get worse this afternoon, then improve from there. We should be able to get a chopper over without too much bother, if you fancy a wee trip."

From the look on Ben's face, he very clearly did not fancy a trip, wee or otherwise. "Best if we head things up from here," he said. "No point in us all being stranded out there, is there?"

Hamza looked at his PC screen. The weather forecast for Canna for the rest of the week was laid out across it. There was a marked improvement by Sunday evening, but it was still due to be raining for most of the next seven days.

"Aye. That's true," he agreed, picking up his mug of tea. "It's a dirty, thankless job, but someone has to stay here and man the fort."

The two men raised their mugs in a toast. "We make a hell of a home team," Ben said, and then they both jumped in fright when the door to the Incident Room was thrown wide, framing the hulking silhouette of Detective Superintendent Robert Hoon in the doorway.

Yesterday, while giving Ben the third degree, Hoon had looked angry. Furious. Apoplectic, even.

Today, though, he looked *evil.* Today, he looked inhuman. Steam practically blasted in great, billowing clouds from his nostrils as he jammed his hands against the door frame and pushed. Hamza and Ben both found their eyes drawn to the wood as it creaked and groaned in complaint.

"Have you heard from that fucker yet?" he hissed.

Taking his life in his hands, Ben played dumb. "Which fucker are you referring to, sir?"

"You know full fucking well which fucker I'm fucking referring to! Logan!" Hoon jabbed a meaty finger in Hamza's direction. "You've fucking spoken to him, haven't you? Haven't you?!"

Ben opened his mouth to speak, but Hoon was on it in a heartbeat. "Keep your fucking mouth shut, Benjamin. Does it look like I was asking you, you Muppet-faced cockrash?"

Ben closed his mouth again, and made a mental note to write that one down later, assuming he survived the next few minutes.

Hamza's mouth flapped up and down like a ventriloquist's dummy with a faulty hinge. "I, uh..."

"Let me make it very fucking easy for you, son. Let me simplify it for you," Hoon growled, advancing into the office like a lion in search of prey. "I know you fucking spoke to him. I know everything that goes on in this fucking place. See me? In this place? I'm God. I'm the Lord fucking Almighty. I'm everywhere. I'm all around. You can't go for a shite without me being there.

"So, I know you fucking spoke to him. That's not a subject that's open to fucking debate. What I want to know is, did you tell him that I'm looking for him? Did you tell him to take his bastarding thumb out of his puckered fucking ring and call me?"

Hoon leaned over Hamza's desk, his eyes practically bulging out of his head, like all the anger swelling inside him was trying to force its way out through the sockets.

"Did you say that to him, son?" Hoon asked. "Did you tell him that from me?"

Hamza's chair squeaked. Or, it might have been Hamza himself. "I, uh, I mean, not in so many words, sir, but aye. I passed the message on."

"Oh, you did, did you?" asked Hoon, his mood lightening, his mouth forming something that was like a smile, but very much wasn't one. "You passed the message on, did you?"

Ben knew full well what was coming, and started to speak. Hoon held up a finger for silence before the DI had got halfway through the first syllable.

"Benjamin. Please," he said.

Then, when he was sure Ben wasn't going to continue, he placed both hands on Hamza's desk and leaned forward, forcing the DC to roll his chair back a few inches.

"So, tell me this, son," he began. His voice was quiet, but it had lost the levity of a few seconds before. "If you passed on the message—if you told him to call me—then why *the fuck* hasn't he?"

Hoon straightened, turning, threw his arms out to the side like a gladiator addressing a baying crowd. "Eh? Can anyone tell me that? Benjamin? You were so fucking keen to say something a minute ago. Can you explain to me why Detective Chief Inspector Logan has ignored a direct fucking order from on high?"

"The, uh, the signal's not great," Ben said.

"Do they have landlines?"

Ben squirmed under the heat of Hoon's glare.

"Um, aye. I think they—"

"Then what's the fucking problem?"

"Maybe... Maybe the storm—" Hamza ventured, but Hoon spun on the spot and silenced him with a look.

"Your shot's over, son. Let the adults fucking speak now, eh?"

Ben stood up. "Look, sir, it wasn't DC Khaled who spoke to Jack, it was me. I told him you wanted him to get in touch. Whether he did or not, that's not on us. He's a big boy, and can make his own decisions."

"Oh, he's—"

"I wasn't finished. Sir," Ben said. The firmness in his tone caught Hoon by surprise, shutting him up.

Across at the other desk, Hamza quietly rolled his chair back another few inches.

"With all due respect, Detective Superintendent, DC Khaled here is a good officer. He's a valuable member of my team. You want to give me a bollocking? You want to scream, and shout, and call me a... a... Hamza?"

"Jeb-end, sir."

"A jeb-end? Fine. Go for your life." Ben stepped closer to the DSup, craning his neck to look up at him. "But you do not come in here and take that approach with my officers. No' even if DC Neish is here. I won't have it. I'm pretty sure HR won't have it, and I know for a fact that the press would have a field day if they knew a senior officer was throwing around racist language like that."

Hoon's eyebrows, which had been knotted together with fury, tightened further in confusion. "What the fuck are you talking about? What racist...?"

The penny dropped.

"Oh. I see."

Hoon drew himself up to his full height. Ben stood his ground. Hamza quietly wondered what the current jobs market was like.

When Hoon spoke, there was a note of amusement in it. "I always did like you, Benjamin," he said, then he wheeled around in a crisp about-turn and marched out of the Incident Room, bellowing, "And get that fuckwit to phone me!" as he went.

Once the door had swung closed, Ben sunk back down into his chair like a punctured balloon.

"Cheers for that, sir," said Hamza. "I owe you one."

"One? You owe me about three years of my bloody life," Ben said, clutching at his heart. "Twelve years military service, getting shot at and dealing with bloody IEDs in the Gulf, and it still doesn't prepare you for that bugger when he's off on one."

"Didn't know you were in the army, sir," Hamza said.

"Aye. Long time ago," Ben replied. He reached a shaking hand for his mug, then motioned to the DC's PC with it. "Now," he said. "Any word?"

CHAPTER SIXTEEN

The internet signal returned halfway through the church service, sending Tyler's phone into a frenzy of pings and bleeps, and drawing him dirty looks from much of the congregation, and the old man standing at the head of it, in particular.

The Reverend Abraham Kerr was a minister very much in the fire-and-brimstone mould. He hadn't yet addressed the death of his daughter, choosing instead to devote the first part of his sermon to the importance of fearing God. Not loving God, which Logan dimly recalled being generally encouraged at other services he'd been dragged along to in the past, but *fearing* him.

Fear of God, according to Reverend Kerr, was key. Fear, not love. That was the main thing. Those who didn't fear the Lord would find themselves in hot water come the Day of Judgement—a day which, going by the way the old man spoke about it—he felt couldn't come soon enough.

"Turn that thing off!" the reverend roared, his narrow eyes blazing righteous fury all the way from the front of the church to the back, where DC Neish was fumbling with his handset.

This was not actually all that impressive, each end of the church being only half a dozen pews away from the other.

Once Tyler had finally managed to switch his phone into silent mode, he cleared his throat, smoothed his hair, and shot a sideways look at the man beside him, who sat shaking his head in disgust.

"You're a disgrace," Logan whispered, enjoying every moment of Tyler's embarrassment.

The sermon resumed. Fear this. Worship that. Do as you're told and, if you were very lucky, you might not end up having a hot poker rammed up the jacksy on the regular for the rest of eternity.

The usual.

Logan let it wash over him and indulged instead in one of his favourite pastimes: people watching.

Judging by the numbers, most of the island had turned out for the service. That might be unusual—they might've turned out to hear what the minister was going to say about the death of his daughter—but Logan suspected it was probably the norm.

He didn't know most of the congregation, but he recognised a few of its members. Pat and Norman from the B&B were there, sat in the second row from the back, like they weren't too sure of their place.

They'd smiled and waved at the detectives when they'd entered, before being frowned at by a stout woman with copper-coloured hair who sat a few feet along the same pew.

Joy, the Community Council chairwoman, had parked herself right down the front. She was really putting her back into the whole Sunday worship thing, and sang the dreary selection of hymns louder than anyone else.

Although not, it had to be said, particularly well.

Roddy Mackay from the pub was pretty much slap-bang in the middle—third row from the front, six from either end. He didn't seem to have come with anyone, and while Logan couldn't see his face, he shifted and fiddled like someone who was on edge, much to the chagrin of the well-dressed families on either side.

A couple down the front caught Logan's eye. They were sat off to the side, so he could make out at least part of their faces. He'd put them in their late twenties or early thirties, and while the woman was listening intently to the sermon, her partner had his head down, eyes fixed somewhere on the floor.

He hadn't seen the man before, but there was something instantly familiar about his profile. Logan had seen it before. Or seen one like it, at least.

Nudging Tyler, he pointed subtly in the direction of the couple. "Son and daughter-in-law," he whispered. "Sure of it."

Over on Logan's right, tucked in at the back corner, was a giant of a man. The DCI dwarfed most people, but this guy was bigger in every direction. It was as if someone had taken a man of Logan's build, and scaled him up by another fifteen percent.

He held a hymn book in his hands. The book was sizeable, but in the man's hands, it looked comically small. The man was listening intently to the minister, his lips moving as he silently repeated the words being spoken from the pulpit, like his mouth was helping his brain to process the information.

This had to be the 'big chap' Kevin Tillerson had mentioned. The one who'd received the tongue-bashing from Iona the night she'd died.

Logan was still sizing the guy up when, up front, Abraham ratcheted up his volume half a dozen notches.

"And speaking on sin..." he boomed, his beady eyes darting across the congregation.

They'd all been sitting silently until that point, but now they went a few steps further. They froze, held their breath, unmoving. This was it. This was what they'd all been waiting for.

"You will all now have heard the news of the death of Iona Wallace."

Logan felt that one on the victim's behalf.

Iona Wallace.

That was what he called her. Not 'my daughter.' Not even 'Iona.'

Iona Wallace.

"Some of you, no doubt, will feel I have something of a vested interested in this news. Some sort of..." His nostrils flared, like the words disgusted him. "*...personal connection.*"

His gaze swept across them again. Not a hair moved. Not a breath was taken. Even the children, who'd been kicking their feet and twiddling their thumbs now sat quietly, not quite understanding what was going on, but knowing it was significant, somehow.

"And you would be correct. Of course, I have a personal connection. I stand here as a servant of God, and you are all—even Iona Wallace—God's children. Still, as the Bible tells us: 'The body that is sown is perishable, it is raised imperishable; it is sown in dishonour, it is raised in glory; it is sown in weakness, it is raised in power; and it is sown a natural body, it is raised a spiritual body.'"

He glanced up to the apex of the church's roof, and for a moment Logan thought there might have been a flicker of emotion on the old man's face. If there was, though, it didn't last long.

"We are all sinners, Iona Wallace perhaps more than most. We can only hope that the Lord, in His wisdom, will see fit to forgive her many, many transgressions."

He reached for a hymn book and gave the nod to a stern-looking silver-haired woman who sat by an old cassette player. "And now, we shall sing Hymn ninety-two, 'Praise God, For He is Kind.'"

The button of the tape machine *clunked* as it was pressed. The speaker had just started to crackle when a voice piped up from the centre of the middle row.

"*Kind*? What do you know about kind?"

A collective gasp went up. The cassette player was hurriedly *clunked* off again.

The families on either side of Roddy Mackay all shuffled sideways on their pews, making a show of distancing themselves from him as he jumped to his feet.

"You treated her like dirt. Like something on your shoe!" Roddy said, his voice trembling. He shot accusing looks at the congregation around him. "You all did. Every last one of you. She didn't need your bloody... judgement. She needed your support. She needed compassion. She needed help. And where were you all? Her neighbours. Where were any of you?"

He turned his attention back to the minister, who was peering at him like a buzzard eyeing up a juicy rabbit. "And where were *you*? You were her father. You were supposed to watch out for her. To protect her. It's supposed to be your natural instinct. It's a... It's fucking *genetics*!"

"Hey now," said a man in his fifties from the row in front. "Settle down. There's kids present."

"Good! They should hear this!" Roddy cried. He stabbed a finger up at the pulpit. "They should know that *that*—him there—that's not what a parent should be like. A parent should love you. A parent should care. The only thing that bastard loves is the sound of his own voice. He's the reason Iona's dead. Him, and you, and you, and all of you!"

He leaned on the back of the bench in front, some of the fight going out of him. "All of us," he said, his voice cracking. "Iona had her problems, but she was funny, and she was sad, and she was kind. She was one of us. And we let her down. We all let her down."

The silence that followed was an uncomfortable one. It pressed down on the place, bending the necks of almost everyone in it, until their gazes pointed to the floor.

"Well, then, now that you've said your piece," said Abraham, his voice calm and measured. He indicated the door with a single sharp nod of his head. "Get out."

For a moment, Roddy looked like he was going to protest, but then he began sidestepping past the family on his right, who were forced to half-stand, or turn their knees in to let him pass.

Roddy caught Logan's eye, but said nothing as he scurried past, his mouth drawn tight, his eyes shimmering.

"And if you're lucky," bellowed the man of the cloth from up front, "we'll consider saying a prayer for your soul."

Logan leaned in closer to Tyler. "Stay here. I'm going to go talk to him."

"Aw, what? Can't I come?"

The DCI shook his head. "Stick it out. See if anything else happens. Meet me outside after."

He started to move, then turned back, "Oh, and try to at least look like you're enjoying yourself." He flicked his gaze upwards. "The big man's got his eye on you."

LOGAN CAUGHT up with Roddy halfway down the hill that led to the pub. Despite the detective calling after him, Roddy didn't stop until a hand like a twenty-ounce steak slapped down onto his shoulder.

"Mr Mackay?"

Roddy sighed below his breath, inhaled deeply through his nose, then turned, an attempt at a smile plastered in place. Logan was much taller than he was, and the angle of the hill didn't help matters. Roddy's smile wavered at the sight of the detective towering above him, but he did his best to hold it in place.

"Oh. Hello. Yes. Sorry. I wasn't... I was miles away."

"Understandable," Logan said. "That was quite a speech you gave back there. I get the impression Mr Kerr doesn't often have anyone talk back to him."

"Just Iona," Roddy replied. "And only if she'd been drinking."

"You knew her well?"

Roddy's eyes darted down to the detective's chest, purposefully avoiding eye contact. He shrugged.

"Aye. I mean... We weren't close, but, she'd... We'd..."

He squeezed the bridge of his nose, shook his head, then tried again.

"Yes. We were friends. There. Iona and I were friends. OK?"

"Why wouldn't it be?" Logan asked.

"She wasn't like they all say. All of *them*," Roddy said, his voice shaking like it had back in the church. "They sit there every week and they go on about turning the other cheek, and loving thy neighbour, but they don't. None of them do. They all hated her, and they bloody well went out of their way to make sure she knew it."

Logan followed Roddy's gaze back in the direction of the church, then motioned down the hill to the pub. "Mind if I ask you a few questions inside?"

Roddy shifted his weight from foot to foot. He wrung his hands together. Logan could practically hear his brain whirring as he searched for an excuse.

"It'll only take a few minutes," the detective said. He placed his hand on Roddy's shoulder again and guided him down the hill. "And who knows? It might even help the both of us."

CHAPTER SEVENTEEN

He wasn't saying she was an angel. Not by a long-shot. He wanted to make that clear.

Logan had asked just one question in the past ten minutes—"Can you describe your relationship with Iona?"—and Roddy had taken it from there.

She'd been a customer to begin with. That was all. A regular, from the day that Roddy came to the island and reopened the long-dormant pub, right up to the day she died.

Over the years, Roddy had developed 'a soft spot' for her. Nothing romantic, he wanted to make that very clear, but he'd seen the way she was treated by most of the other people on the island, and he'd taken pity on her.

He'd given her a few shifts. Cleaning at first, then a few goes behind the bar. She wasn't half-bad, but nobody was keen on having her serve them, and so sales steadily dropped until he'd had no choice but to let her go.

Somewhere along the way, they'd become friends. It was mostly one-way, Roddy was the first to admit. She took far more than she ever gave, borrowed money that he often didn't even have. But she was wild, and unpredictable, and fun to be around.

"No wonder the rest of the island hated her," he concluded, before downing a gulp of the thick, stodgy-looking pint of real ale he'd levered from one of the bar taps. "She was everything they're not."

Logan asked his second question. It was a belter.

"Were you in love with her?"

He'd expected a quicker reaction. An incredulous shake of the head, maybe. A gasp and a raising of the eyebrows.

Instead, Roddy considered the question carefully, sucking the foamy head of his pint off the bottom half of his moustache.

"No. Not really. I mean, not in the way you're meaning," he said, after a period of contemplation. "Did I love her? Yes. Yes, I think so. I think I was probably the only one who did."

"Were you ever involved in a sexual relationship?"

Roddy's flinch was there one moment, gone the next. Had Logan not been watching for a reaction, he'd have missed it.

"No. No, never. She wasn't interested in me in that way," he said, then hurriedly clarified. "And I wasn't interested in her in that way, either. That was mutual. We were friends, like I say. Just friends."

He hadn't seen her the night she went missing, he said. He'd spent most of the evening upstairs in his flat, cashing up the weekend's takings. He'd only heard about the argument at the end of the night, when Bruce had filled him in on all the gory details.

"Don't suppose you've got any CCTV in here, have you?" Logan asked, gaze flitting around all the likely locations.

"No, never needed it. There's rarely any trouble," Roddy replied. "I mean, there are arguments, of course. Plenty of those. But nothing we'd need CCTV for."

"Fair enough. Just thought I'd ask on the off-chance," Logan said.

"There is the webcam, though."

Logan blinked. His gaze gave the place another once-over. "Webcam?"

"No, not in here. Sorry. I mean outside. It looks down from the shop out across to Rum. Runs on the Wi-Fi. It won't show in here, but it might show people coming and going."

"Right. Got you," said Logan, unable to fully hide his disappointment. "But only up to ten o'clock?"

Roddy winced, then nodded. "Yes. Good point. Only up to ten o'clock," he confirmed. "Still, Iona left before then, I think. Maybe it'll show something."

"Maybe," Logan said, making a note. "I've come across a few of these sort of things before, though, and most of them don't record. They only... what's it called? Stream."

"Oh no, this one records," said Roddy. "I helped them set it up when it was first being installed. It all gets backed up onto a server."

Logan was more interested now. "And who's responsible for the server?"

"Community Council. Joy. She made me walk her through the set-up step-by-step, then changed the passwords, so I don't have access. But yes, she'll be able to pull up the footage from the night Iona died. It should all be there."

Logan wrote something else in his pad, then underlined it.

"That's useful to know, thank you. I have to go talk to her today, anyway. Do they have an office, do you know? The council?"

"Yes. Sort of. It's part of the school building," Roddy said. "It's not big—they hold any public meetings in the dinner hall—but yes. They have one."

"Also useful to know," said Logan, already relishing the thought of how Joy would react when he commandeered the place. It would be nice to have something to look forward to.

Logan checked the time, then pressed on with the interview. Roddy was fully forthcoming about Iona's relationship with her father, or what he knew of it, anyway.

He'd disowned her, apparently, in her thirties. Or, she'd disowned him. One of the two. Either way, they'd rarely spoken since, and when they had, the words they'd exchanged weren't kind.

"She owed him money. A lot of money, I think," Roddy said. "She'd talk about it when she'd had too much to drink. Cried about it, sometimes. She was paying it back for a while, but she stopped a few weeks ago. She told me she'd had enough, that he wasn't getting another penny out of her. She wished she'd never started paying him back in the first place."

"What did he give her the money for?" Logan asked.

Roddy shrugged. "I don't know. She didn't say. I asked, but she always seemed... I don't know. Ashamed."

"She never gave you any idea?"

"No. Although, she did once say she didn't owe him anything. That it 'wasn't normal' for him to be asking her for it."

Logan's pen paused above his pad. "Wasn't normal?"

"That's what she said. She'd been drinking a lot, though. She wasn't making a lot of sense. I had to put her to bed upstairs in the end."

Roddy's eyes widened, like he was suddenly worried he'd said too much. "I slept on the couch. Nothing went on."

"I understand," Logan said. He made another note, which prompted the man opposite to take another big swig of his pint.

Roddy wasn't as keen to talk about Iona's son, beyond to confirm some basic details. His name was Isaac, he'd lived off the island for a number of years, before returning with his then-girlfriend, now fiancée, Louise.

Isaac had studied Economics at Glasgow University, but he and Louise now ran a small business making soaps and candles for customers all over the world.

"Iona was proud of him. So proud," Roddy said. "But he was mortified by her. You could see it whenever they crossed paths, he desperately wanted to be somewhere else. Somewhere she wasn't."

"So, why come back?" Logan asked. "Big world out there, why settle back here?"

"I think his grandfather put up the money for the business," Roddy said.

"Maybe there were conditions on it. Or maybe being here was good for branding. I honestly don't know."

And that was about as far as Roddy would go into the relationship between mother and son. Best Logan asked Isaac about it himself, he suggested. It wasn't for him to say.

The impression Logan got was that Roddy was protecting Iona more than he was looking out for her son. It was like he didn't want to badmouth the lad, because he knew she wouldn't have approved.

Logan could've pressed, of course. Pressing was one of his strong points. Often, it involved the sole of his boot. But he elected not to, on this occasion. Roddy wasn't going anywhere. If he needed to come back and do some pressing, he wouldn't have far to go.

He stood up, flipped his notebook closed, and returned it to his pocket. "Thanks for your time, Mr Mackay. I won't keep you any longer. For now."

"Thanks. Aye. I should crack on and get set up. Think I'll be on my own today."

Logan looked over at the empty space behind the bar. "Not got your Ozzy on the night?"

Roddy blew out his cheeks. "Your guess is as good as mine. Bugger didn't come back after his break last night."

Something in Logan's gut stirred. "He didn't?"

"No. Said he'd be fifteen minutes, then never came back."

"And when was this, exactly?" Logan asked.

"Eight, maybe. Thereabouts," Roddy said. "He's staying in the wee flat out the back of the shop. I meant to go round there, but... Other things on my mind."

"I'll look into it," Logan said.

"If you see him, kick his arse."

"Will do. And, I must say, Mr Mackay, what you did back there? What you said at the church?"

Roddy looked up from his now almost empty pint glass. He appeared shrunken and cowed, like he was bracing himself for the worst.

"What about it?" he asked.

One corner of Logan's mouth turned up in a smirk. "I reckon Iona would've loved every bloody minute of it."

CHAPTER EIGHTEEN

The service was still dragging on when Logan returned to the church. Wee Free services tended to do that, if memory served. The prayers alone could go on for twenty minutes apiece—longer if the person leading them got sidetracked into slagging off Catholics, and denouncing the Pope as the Antichrist.

The rain was off—although, the colour and formation of the clouds suggested the respite was a temporary one—and so he took a wander a little further up the hill, and killed some time just looking out to sea.

He could see Skye rising from a bank of grey fog to the north, looking positively Jurassic from this angle.

To the east was Rum and, beyond that—though currently invisible—lay the mainland. Mallaig, Morar, and then a run down the A830 to Fort William, via Glenfinnan.

Out west, almost completely lost to the mist, lay... what? Another island, but which one? He tried to picture his placement on the map. Outer Hebrides. Barra, maybe, with its airport on the beach? South Uist? One or the other.

He breathed in. Deliberately. Growing up in Glasgow, this wasn't something he tended to do often, but this place practically insisted on it. There was a freshness to the air that made him cough, like the years' worth of gunk built up in his lungs was protesting against the sudden intrusion.

And God, the place was quiet. Other than the faint rustling of the grass on the breeze, and the distant call of a sheep, there wasn't a sound beyond those he made himself. It was a world away from Glasgow, and a stark contrast to even Fort William or Inverness.

Hell, it was a stark contrast to the room in the B&B last night, which had probably endangered his hearing at points.

He'd always had a faint dislike for the islands. Or for the idea of them, maybe. Growing up in the city, they'd seemed snobbish, somehow. Their remoteness making them seem standoffish and aloof. He imagined them to have some sort of superiority complex, some greater claim to Scottishness than he, in his tenement block, had any right to.

And maybe they did, he thought, standing there at the top of the hill, looking out at the world through a veil of mist and fog. And maybe that was OK.

Or, maybe the claim they had wasn't greater or more authentic than his own, but just different. And maybe that was OK, too.

He enjoyed another big breath, really sucking this one down and letting it expand his chest. The freshness of it was flavoured with salt and *just* the faintest hint of sheep shit.

Since arriving on the island—and barring those few hours in the middle of the night—he'd felt calmer. More relaxed. He'd put it down to being out of phone range, beyond the reach of whoever had been plaguing him with all those mystery calls.

But what if it was something more than that? What if, God forbid, he actually *liked* the place?

He was just starting to come to terms with that possibility when he spotted the scarecrow. From where Logan stood, the hill dropped down before rising up again, forming a little gully of bracken and heather. The scarecrow was fixed in place near the top of the other slope, half-hidden by the shade of a large Scots pine.

It wasn't the same scarecrow as the one near Iona Wallace's house. Not unless it could move about and change its clothes. This one was fatter and squatter, with an old bowler hat fixed to the knotted ball of straw and canvas that made up its head.

Like the one at Iona's, there was no need for it. It made no sense. The point of a scarecrow was to protect crops, surely? Unless that tree was going to miraculously start sprouting fruit, there was no purpose for the thing being there.

Or none that was currently clear, at least.

Its ragged outfit fluttered in the breeze as it held Logan's gaze, its long dark coat blowing around it like Dracula's cape. They stood there, eye to eye across the gully, and the world waited to see which would draw first.

The sound of the church's front door opening broke the spell. Thrusting his hands deep in his coat pockets, Logan turned his back on the scarecrow and trudged down the hill in time to meet DC Neish scurrying out of the church and onto the pavement, a conga-line of congregation members hot on his heels.

"Fuck's sake, boss. You got off lightly there," Tyler grumbled.

Both men stood out of the way of the door as most of the rest of the island's population came filing out, all pulling on their jackets and shooting wary glances up to the sky.

"Anything interesting happen after I left?" Logan asked.

"Not a thing. Literally, not a thing," Tyler said. He leaned in closer and dropped his voice to avoid anyone else hearing. "Although, I did come to the conclusion that God can be a bit of a prick when he wants to be. Or maybe that's just your man in there's interpretation of it."

Logan shook his head. "No. I hear he can be, right enough."

He spotted a familiar face in the crowd and stepped past Tyler. "Come here, this'll cheer you up," he told the DC, pushing into the crowd. "Mrs Bryden? Do you have a minute?"

Joy Bryden stopped, looked around for the source of the voice, then folded her arms across her chest when she spotted the detectives. Her face took on the look of someone who'd just sucked a whole lemon in through their teeth, and Logan felt a little surge of happiness that made it all the way to his face as a smile.

"Yes? Can I help you?" she asked, her expression making it abundantly clear that she'd much rather not.

"You can, actually," Logan said. "You've got an office, right? The Community Council, I mean?"

She eyed them both suspiciously. "We do. Of course. Why?"

"We need it," Logan said.

Joy's face didn't so much as twitch. "I beg your pardon?"

"Your office. We're going to have to take it over," Logan said.

"I'm sorry, no. You can't."

"Oh, we can, Mrs Bryden."

"*Ms*," she corrected.

"Apologies. *Ms* Bryden. We're investigating a murder. But then, you already know that. In order to facilitate that investigation, we're commandeering your premises as of now."

Truth be told, Logan had no idea what the legal position was on this. If DS McQuarrie had been here, she'd have known. She'd have been able to quote the exact law or regulation that gave him permission to take over the Community Council's premises.

But DS McQuarrie wasn't with him. She never would be. And DC Neish, despite his heart being more or less in the right place, was a poor substitute.

"You want to kick us out of our own office, so you can use it?" Joy said, her voice adopting a shriller tone.

"That's about the size of it, aye," Logan confirmed.

"Under what authority?" she asked.

Logan groaned inwardly. This would be the sticking point. He didn't think intimidation would work on the woman, but he drew himself up to his full height, fixed a suitably disgruntled look on his face, and prepared to give it his best shot.

"*Under what authority*?" he growled.

"The Joint Services Co-ordination of Municipal Buildings Act, two-thousand-and-eleven."

Logan and Joy both turned to Tyler. He beamed back at them. "That's right, isn't it, boss?"

The DCI blinked, frowned, raised his eyebrows, then repeated this entire process again. Finally, he nodded. "Oh. Aye. Exactly. Under that authority."

He faced Joy again. There was a look of resigned indignation on her face that told him, without her having to say anything, that they'd won.

"So, do you have the keys handy? Or would you rather show us around in person?"

Joy heaved out an exaggerated sigh, then turned on her heels and started marching down the hill. "Fine. I'll show you. But you had better not make a mess."

Logan fell into step beside Tyler as they set off after Joy.

"Looks like someone's done his homework," he remarked. "Where'd you pull that one out of?"

"My arse, boss," Tyler said.

Logan peered down at him. "Eh?"

Tyler winked. "Made it up. Sounded good though, eh?"

Logan nodded slowly, then gave just the tiniest and most begrudged of chuckles. "Aye. Maybe there's hope for you yet, son," he said, and then they hurried down the hill, closing the gap on the furious Joy Bryden.

The Canna Community Council office was small, sparse, and immaculately tidy. It was so tidy, in fact, that Logan had his doubts the place had ever been used for anything more than storing a couple of desks and a filing cabinet.

The only giveaway that anyone actually used the place on a regular basis was the A1-sized wall calendar, which displayed a number of past and upcoming events.

A printed sign above it read: 'COMMUNITY CALENDAR: IMPORTANT!!!!" and Logan was already making plans to Tipp-ex out those exclamation marks as a matter of priority.

A quick glance at the events on the calendar cast further doubt on their importance. There were six events listed—including two AGMs, for some reason—and none of them struck the DCI as particularly vital.

The other events ranged from a shore clean-up to 'duck tagging,' whatever that was.

Twice a month, there was a little red sticker stuck to the calendar—the first and third Wednesday of each month. The most recent was a few days ago, right after Iona Wallace had been murdered.

"What's all this?" Logan asked, pointing to the latest sticker.

DC Neish, who was standing in the corner scrolling through his phone, briefly looked up, before realising the question wasn't directed at him.

"Battery change. For the webcams," explained Joy, grudging every word. She set the keys on the faded green padding that topped the larger of the two desks. "Now, I'm going to leave you with these, but I want you to promise—"

"Webcams?" asked Logan, jumping on the remark.

Joy hesitated. "Sorry?"

"You said 'webcams'. Plural. Is that right?"

The woman's expression tightened. Solidified. Fixed in place. "Webcam. Singular. Slip of the tongue."

Logan sat in the largest chair—her chair, he thought—not taking his eyes off her. "Right. Easily done," he said, after a lengthy pause. "I meant to ask you about that, actually. I need the footage from Tuesday night. We believe it might show Iona Wallace leaving the pub."

Joy threw her arms up and gave a heavy, emphatic sigh. This wound Logan up no end, and the next few words were out of him before he could stop them.

"I'm no' asking you to travel back in fucking time and fetch it for me," he told her.

He took a moment to compose himself, lowered his voice a few decibels, then continued. "It'll be backed up on the server, right? The one Roddy helped you set up. You can either get us the footage or you can give us some way to log in and get it ourselves. Up to you."

"Fine. Fine, I'll get it looked out," Joy snapped. "Anything else you'd like me to get for you while I'm at it? Cup of tea? Home-made scone?"

"Only if you're making one," Logan said, which earned him a fierce look.

"Kettle's in the bottom drawer of the cabinet," she snapped. "If you use any teabags, you'll replace them. Fair's fair. And leave the biscuits, they're diabetic."

"Right. Well, they have my condolences," Logan said, sitting forward in the chair.

He motioned for Tyler to open the door. The office building was attached to the school, but it had its own entrance out onto a small rectangle of tarmac that made up the playground.

"And when you've got that footage," Logan began, as Tyler opened the door at Joy's back. "Just drop it in here. At our office."

Joy bristled at that, but said nothing. She caught the door handle on the way past Tyler, and pulled it hard behind her. The effect was lessened somewhat by the slow-close hinge that prevented any impressive farewell slam.

Tyler only glanced up from his phone once the door had eventually eased itself shut. "Bit harsh there, boss," he said, before going right back to reading.

Behind the desk, the DCI shrugged. "Good enough for the sour-faced cow," he said, then he stood up, retrieved the keys from the desktop, and tossed them to DC Neish. "Right, we're going to check out the shop. Bruce, the Australian fella from the pub? He didn't turn up for his shift last night. Seemingly, he rents the flat out back."

Tyler said nothing. His lips moved silently as he continued to read.

"Sorry, am I keeping you from something?" Logan asked, his shadow falling over the junior officer.

"Hmm? Oh, sorry, boss," Tyler said. "It's just, have you seen the pathology report?"

"Didn't know it was in. Why?"

"It's just preliminaries so far. But, it's Iona Wallace, boss..."

"Aye, well I should hope so. What about her?"

"The swabs. They found semen," Tyler said. He turned his phone to show Logan the gory details of the report. "Looks like she'd had intercourse the night she died."

CHAPTER NINETEEN

Logan had knocked three times now, but had heard nothing from the other side of the door. He knocked again, a proper policeman's knock that shook the dimpled glass panel that ran the height of the door on one side.

"Bruce?" he called, having realised after the first knock that he had no idea what the Australian's surname was. "You in there, son?"

He'd left Tyler talking to Hamza back at the newly commandeered office, and had taken a stroll across the street to check the flat at the back of the shop.

Part of him had thought he might find Bruce curled up under a blanket, loaded with the cold, but a much larger part had told him not to be so bloody stupid. The barman had upped and vanished shortly after the detectives had left the bar. Even if he believed in coincidences, Logan would have been highly sceptical of that one.

The door was flimsy. One good kick would do it. One good shove, maybe.

He contemplated it for a few moments, then decided to try the shop, on the off-chance they had a spare key.

The shop was essentially a *Spar* without the branding. It had the same limited selection of tinned and dry foods, a few racks of household products, and a fridge full of milk, cheese, yoghurts, and assorted soft drinks.

On the top shelf of the fridge sat a row of sad-looking sandwiches. They were all lined up like puppies at a dog pound, all sitting there side-by-side, hoping that today was the day they'd finally be chosen.

There was no one at the counter when Logan approached it. A door stood open behind it, and he could hear the rustling of someone moving about in there, and a tuneless mumble of whoever it was singing below their breath.

"Hello?" he called.

The singing came crashing to a halt. A small, wiry man in his late-seventies shuffled out, his coat hanging from one arm. His gaze went the length of Logan, top to bottom and back again. His expression was one of utter and total confusion, like he had no idea what he was looking at.

"We're not open," he eventually said.

His voice was stronger than it had any right to be, given how withered the rest of him was. He didn't sound annoyed, exactly, more sort of bemused, like he couldn't get his head around how anyone could've made such a fundamental error of judgement.

Logan very slowly and deliberately regarded the shop around him before replying.

"Aren't you?" he asked.

"Sunday. We're not open for another half hour."

"Right. But the door's open. You look open."

"Looks can be deceiving. You'll have to come back."

Logan almost let himself get drawn into a debate on the matter, then remembered what he was there for. He produced his warrant card, which went almost completely ignored.

"Do you own the flat out back?"

"Apartment."

"Sorry?"

"It's not a flat. It's a self-contained apartment," the shopkeeper said.

"Whatever it's called. Do you own it?"

The old man shook his head. Logan could've sworn he actually heard his neck creaking like dry wood. "No."

"Well, do you know who—"

"The business does," the shopkeeper continued. "And I own the business. I'm the shareholder. It's a limited company."

Impressively, given his past form, Logan held it together.

"OK, so you're responsible for the fla—" He stopped himself just in time. "For the apartment? And it's currently being rented to Bruce from the pub. That right?"

"That's correct."

"Do you have Bruce's surname?" Logan asked, taking out his notepad.

"I do."

Logan clicked the button on the end of his pen, flipped open his pad, and waited.

The old man said nothing.

"Can you tell me what it is?"

"Anderson."

Logan wrote the name in the pad. "When did you last see Mr Anderson?"

"How do you expect me to know that?"

By fucking remembering, Logan thought. He managed to avoid saying it out loud, and instead just gave the shopkeeper a hopeful, expectant sort of look.

"Wednesday, maybe? Thursday? He comes and goes. I come and go. We don't often come and go at the same time. He was in here doing his shopping one morning, though. I think it was Wednesday. I don't know. I can't be sure." He waved a hand as if trying to swat away a particularly irritating fly. "I think it was Wednesday."

"Notice anything unusual about him?"

"Not really," the shopkeeper said. "I mean, I barely understand a word he says at the best of times. He's foreign."

"Nothing strange about the transaction?"

"Strange? Like what? He wasn't standing on his head or, or wearing a dress, if that's what you mean."

Logan counted to five in his head before continuing. "Anything unusual about his purchases, I mean."

The old man grunted gruffly. "Right. I see. Well, yes, as it happens. There was."

Logan raised his eyebrows. "Oh?"

"Cleaning stuff."

Logan's grip tightened on his pen. "Cleaning stuff?"

"Whole basket of it. Bleach. Disinfectant. Cloths. That sort of thing. Shoe polish. Brown. Two wee things of it."

"I see..."

"And a Twix," the old man concluded. He placed his forefingers about eight inches apart. "One of the jumbo ones."

"And that was unusual?"

"Oh, no. Not unusual at all. He's partial to a Twix."

"The cleaning stuff, I mean," Logan said, who really should've seen that one coming a mile away. "Would he normally be buying stuff like that?"

"No. Not at all."

"You're sure?"

"Well, he's never bought it from me, and I'm the only bloody shop on the island, so you work it out."

Logan jotted down a note as the shopkeeper continued. "I remember I said to him, 'What's all this for? You'd better not have made a mess of the place,' I said. 'Or you'll be out on your arse,' I said."

"What did he say?" Logan asked.

The old man shrugged. "No idea. He's foreign. I can't for the life of me get to grips with the accent."

Cleaning products. Wednesday morning. Hours after Iona Wallace was killed. And now he'd vanished, right after chatting to the two investigating officers.

"The flat—"

"Apartment."

"The apartment," Logan said. "Don't suppose you've got a spare key?"

"Why do you ask?"

"It's just, we're having difficulty getting hold of Mr..." His eyes flicked to his pad. "...Anderson. He didn't show up for work last night, and now he's not answering the door."

The old man gave Logan another look up and down, sniffed noisily, then pressed a button on the till that sat on the counter between them. The bottom drawer shot out with the force of a battering ram, ejecting a small pile of loose change onto the floor.

Muttering to himself, the shopkeeper fished around in the drawers, rattling the coins and rustling the notes.

After a good thirty to forty seconds of this, he finally produced a large copper-coloured key and held it out for the detective to take.

"Don't make a mess," he instructed, as Logan took the offered key. "And if he's in there, tell him he still owes me this month's rent."

Logan entered the flat quietly, and stopped in a hallway no larger than a public toilet cubicle. Odours hung from the walls like paintings in a gallery. Cigarette smoke, cannabis, cheap beer, and sweat.

Whatever Bruce had bought the cleaning products for, it wasn't to tackle the hallway.

"Mr Anderson?" he called, projecting the greeting through the three closed doors that surrounded him. "It's Detective Chief Inspector Jack Logan. We met yesterday. At the pub."

Silence. Not a creak. Not a whisper. Nothing to suggest anyone was home.

Of course, Caitlyn probably thought the same thing back in Kinlochleven, right before Gillespie had shot her through the door.

One of the doors was half the width of the others. Storage cupboard. Had to be. He checked that first, tugging on the little brass doorknob with a rubber-gloved hand. It sprung open at the first pull, and he brought up an arm to deflect a flurry of movement from within.

The falling broom toppled as far as it could in the narrow hallway, then the handle *clonked* against the opposite wall. Logan retrieved it, had a quick squiz inside the narrow space behind the door, then returned the brush to its rightful place and pushed the cupboard closed.

That done, he turned to the door directly opposite, and gave the shoogly handle a downwards shove. The door opened into a small, messy bathroom. Toothpaste was flecked across a grimy mirror, and a bar of soap had all but dissolved in a basin of water.

The toilet was blocked, a gelatinous papier-mâché of bog roll and brown water filling it all the way up to the rim.

"Clarty bastard," Logan muttered, burying his nose in the crook of his elbow and dropping the lid back into place.

He had a quick check behind the grim-looking plastic shower curtain, then quickly backed out of the room and closed the door behind him.

The other door led to an all-in-one living room, kitchen, and bedroom set-up. A bed seemed to have partially exploded out of the sofa, its curved metal legs not quite hitting the floor. There was a thin mattress on top, with a knot of bedclothes slung over to one side, and a couple of pillows so lacking in stuffing they barely made one good one between them.

The rest of the room was clean. Spotlessly clean, in fact. Logan pressed the pedal on the kitchen bin with the toe of his boot, flipping the lid to reveal a nest of disinfectant wipes and crumpled paper towels.

There was a smell of bleach that became more choking the closer he got to the small stainless steel sink. Like the rest of the kitchen, the sink had been scrubbed to a dull shine. A selection of half-empty bottles of cleaning products suggested Bruce had thrown everything at the place. And in a hurry, too, going by the way the bottles had been abandoned on the kitchen floor.

A theory began slotting itself together as Logan poked around the rest of the flat.

Bruce Anderson had had sexual intercourse with Iona on Tuesday night. Raped her? Possibly, although it could've been consensual.

After that, he'd killed her and left her body out of the way. Someone would find it, of course, but it'd take a few days. Time enough for him to clean the place up and remove any evidence of her having been in the flat.

He bought the cleaning products on Wednesday morning and set about scrubbing the place. He'd only cleaned the living area, which told Logan that he'd either run out of time, or he knew there was nothing incriminating in the bathroom. Maybe Iona hadn't gone in there.

The only thing was that Bruce had seemed perfectly calm when Logan and Tyler had spoken to him. Nothing he'd said or done had rung any alarm bells, and Logan prided himself on his ability to spot when someone was being a shifty bastard.

Still, his senses had occasionally failed him before, and Bruce's decision to pull a vanishing act almost the moment the detectives had left the bar was not helping to paint him in a particularly good light.

There wasn't much else of interest in the living area of the flat. The fridge was stocked with everything a young, single, Australian man would require—

namely, several cans of cheap lager, a couple of microwave curries, and something that might once-upon-a-time have been a lettuce.

A quick finger-tip search of the bin produced nothing but the used cleaning products. Logan tied the bag off at the top and set it by the door to take away as evidence.

His hands were starting to sweat inside the rubber gloves he'd pulled on before entering the place. He'd never been able to bear the feel of the bloody things for long.

What else?

Standing in the doorway, he looked around the room, searching for anything out of place. Anything that shouldn't be there, or anything that should be, and wasn't.

Nothing jumped out at him. Nothing obvious.

Ducking, he took a look beneath the fold-out bed. At first, he thought there was nothing under there, but then he saw it, tucked away in the shadows at the back.

A box. A green plastic storage box.

Kneeling down, Logan reached into the gap until his fingers brushed against the smooth plastic. Catching the underside of the rim, he slid the box out, weaving it between the metal legs of the bed.

And then, he stared. For several long moments, he just knelt there, gazing blankly at the spaghetti of cables and wires that were spilling out of the box. Power cables. HDMI cables. Phone charging cables. All different lengths, all different thicknesses, all tangled together like some sort of diabolical Chinese puzzle.

"Well now," Logan whispered. He poked around in the mass of wires. "Isn't that interesting?"

CHAPTER TWENTY

Tyler watched in silence as Logan deposited the black bag and the box of cables in the corner of the office, his mobile tucked into the crook of his neck, his fingers poised on the keyboard of his laptop.

"Who's that?" Logan asked, indicating the phone with a nod.

"It's Hamza, boss."

"Get him to run a full search on Bruce Anderson."

"The Ozzy?"

"I want a full background. Who he is, where he's been. Has he got any priors or warrants? If he's had a parking ticket, I want to know about it, and I want to know within the next half hour."

Tyler spoke into the phone. "Get all that, Ham? Aye. Bruce Anderson. Australian."

He looked up at the DCI. "Any other info to go on?"

"He's got good teeth," Logan said. He scowled. "No, I don't have any other info to go on, so tell him to get his finger out and get on with it."

"Get your finger out and get on with it," Tyler said. He grinned at the response. "Want me to pass that on to the boss for you?" he asked. "No. No, thought not. Keep in touch."

He tapped the hang-up icon, then sat the phone on the desk.

"We got a suspect, boss?" Tyler asked.

"Aye. Maybe. Bruce Anderson bought a sizeable number of cleaning products on Wednesday morning. Bleach, Flash wipes, Dettol spray."

"Could just be a neat freak," Tyler suggested.

"You wouldn't be saying that if you'd seen the bastard's bathroom," Logan replied. He pointed at the green plastic tub in the corner. "Also found that little lot tucked under the bed."

Tyler meerkatted up and peered over the top of his screen. "Cables?" he said, initially confused, then quickly catching on. "Oh. Right, aye. You think one of them's the murder weapon?"

Logan shook his head. "I doubt he'd have strangled her with one of them, then put it back in the box. But we know he had access to the same sort of weapon used in the attack."

"To be fair, boss, so does everyone."

"I know. Neither one's much to go on on its own, but throw in the disappearing act and it gets a bit tastier."

Tyler nodded. "If there's something to find on him, Ham'll dig it up."

"What else did he have for us?" Logan asked.

DC Neish looked down at the notes he'd taken during the call with his colleague back in Inverness.

"Couple of things. Body showed no sign of there having been a struggle, beyond the blow to the head and the strangulation. A few bruises, but day-to-day stuff. A bump on the shin and some light scrapes on both knees. No defensive injuries that would suggest she'd tried to fend off an attacker."

"So, it's not impossible that the sex could've been consensual," said Logan.

"Nothing to suggest otherwise at the moment, boss," Tyler said. "I mean, other than her being murdered shortly afterwards, obviously."

"What else did they get?"

"From a pathology point of view, not much. Something about gastric alcohol concentration levels—she was drunk, basically, but we knew that. Marijuana user, too. Long term, judging by the build-up. No DNA news on the semen sample yet." Tyler scanned down the rest of the page. "That's about it. More broadly, they found forty quid on the body. Two twenties."

Logan stopped and straightened. "Huh."

Tyler raised an eyebrow. "Something the matter, boss?"

"Kevin Tillerson—the other fella at the B&B—he said she was mooching about for drinks on Tuesday night. Very much gave the impression she was skint."

"Maybe just tight," Tyler suggested. "Why spend your own money when you can get some other idiot to spend theirs?"

"Aye. Maybe," Logan said. "Or maybe she earned herself forty quid between the time she left the bar and the time she was murdered."

"Earned?" said Tyler. "How do...? Oh. You reckon she was on the game, boss?"

Logan let the thought percolate around for a few seconds, then gave a non-committal sort of shrug. "I'm not ruling it out," he said. "Have we got anything else?"

Tyler flipped forward and back a page in his notes. "That's about it, boss. Oh, although she had some scarring on her wrists. Old, though."

"Suicide attempt," Logan reasoned.

"That's the most likely explanation, aye," Tyler agreed. DI Forde and Hamza are going to run her medical records, see if there's anything on there about it.

"Right, good. But text him, and make sure he prioritises Bruce Anderson. He's our best lead."

Tyler had picked up his phone halfway through the sentence, and his thumbs were already tapping on the screen.

"Done," he announced, just a couple of seconds later. "Oh. There was something else, boss. Not from Hamza, just..."

He stood up and crossed to the filing cabinet. "It's probably nothing. Just a bit odd, is all. I was having a snoop around and found these."

Tyler opened the top drawer of the cabinet, rifled through the paperwork for a moment, then took out a suspension folder.

"Meeting minutes. For the Neighbourhood Watch," he said, handing Logan the folder.

The DCI opened it, revealing a neatly-typed set of minutes, dated a couple of weeks before. There was a stack beneath the top one, presumably from different meetings.

Logan scanned the page. It listed several incidents so mind-numbingly minor, he wasn't sure they should even be referred to as 'incidents' so much as just 'things that happened.'

A couple of teenagers had been observed milling around outside the pub one night. Part of a visiting family of wild campers. They'd tried to get a couple of people to buy them alcohol, but had been refused.

A woman—another visitor—had dropped her purse down near where the boat came in, but had found it again almost immediately.

A couple of locals had been seen smoking in the beer garden of the Canna Come Inn, despite the fact it was supposed to be a no-smoking zone.

That sort of thing.

"What's odd about this? Besides the fact anyone bothered their arse to write it down, I mean?" Logan asked.

"Look at the top, boss. 'Members present.'"

Logan's eyes flitted up the page. There was only one name listed. "Joy Bryden," he said. "Just her? Quiet night."

"Not just that night, boss," Tyler said. "Check the rest."

Logan skimmed through the next few pages of minutes.

Members Present: Joy Bryden.

Joy Bryden.

Joy Bryden.

"She's the only member ever mentioned," Tyler said. "Like, ever. I went right back."

"A one-woman Neighbourhood Watch," Logan said. He shook his head and closed the folder. "Still, if it was going to be anyone, it was going to be her. Struck me as a right bloody busybody."

He passed Tyler the folder back. "Odd, right enough," he said. "But each to their own. Now, we've got half an hour to kill before Hamza gets back to us. I think it's time you and I paid the Reverend Kerr a wee visit."

CHAPTER TWENTY-ONE

"Christ. He's no' short of a bob or two, is he?" Tyler whispered, as he and Logan waited in the hallway of the minister's house. It was attached to the back of the church, but overshadowed that building in every sense.

Logan's whole flat would've fit in that one room, and the oak and mahogany furniture was probably worth more than everything the DCI owned.

The floor was all exposed boards, carefully varnished and polished to a rich shine. Much of it was covered by a thick rug that would've carpeted several rooms of a normal-sized house, although the homeowners would have to be pretty desperate to put up with that pattern.

There were four large paintings, one on each wall. They each depicted famous moments from the Old Testament. There was Noah living it up on his boat while dozens of people flailed and thrashed in the water around him.

On the wall opposite, a pillar of salt looked back as Sodom burned. Flanking those on the other walls, choirs of angels slaughtered men, women, and children.

Aye, Tyler wasn't wrong, Logan thought. God could be a right prick, when he wanted to be.

"Does the church pay for all this? No' exactly cheery, is it?" Tyler said, following Logan's gaze to the paintings. "Quite impressive, mind you."

"I'm more of a *dugs playing snooker* man, myself. Maybe a nice watercolour landscape," Logan said. "Babies getting rammed onto spikes isnae really my cup of tea."

They'd been shown into the hall by a meek wee woman in her fifties, who might have been an employee, but might equally have been a particularly submissive spouse.

Iona's mother had never been on the scene from as far back as Logan could remember, but it was possible that Abraham had remarried. To a certain demographic of women—the God-fearing, self-hating, low self-esteem demographic—the vicious old bastard was probably quite the catch.

The wee woman appeared through a set of double doors at the far end of the hall, and practically curtsied as she addressed the detectives.

"The Reverend will see you now," she announced, her head down as she studiously avoided meeting either man's eye. "But he's asked me to inform you that he doesn't have long, so he's requested that you don't take up too much—"

"Aye, no' bother, pet," Logan said, striding past her and into the room beyond.

"Cheers," Tyler told her, smiling awkwardly as he followed Logan into a high-ceilinged study with wood panelling on the walls.

There was one desk, placed slap-bang in the middle of the room. This had the effect of making the person sitting behind the desk the focal point of anyone walking in. An effect, Logan thought, that was not accidental.

The Reverend Abraham Kerr sat forward in a luxuriously padded brown leather chair, his pointed elbows on the walnut desktop, his chicken-bone fingers interlocked as if in prayer.

His eyes blazed out from beneath eyebrows the colour of freshly driven snow. There were matching clumps of hair on his cheeks, too, like miniature mirror images of the eyebrows above. Given that the rest of him was clean-shaven, it was an odd choice on the facial hair front, Logan thought, but each to their own.

The minister said nothing, his hawk-like gaze inviting them to be the first to speak. *Daring* them, maybe.

Logan could never resist a dare.

"Mr Kerr?" he said, purposefully neglecting to address the man by his correct title.

"Reverend. But yes," the minister replied. His voice was crisp and clipped. It wasn't booming with the righteous wrath of his sermon, but gave the impression it could head in that direction any time he chose. "I am he. To whom am I speaking?"

Five seconds. That's how long it had taken. Five seconds, and Logan already felt rubbed up the wrong way by the bastard.

Granted, he hadn't been a fan of the man going in, but it had been a second-hand dislike of him, borrowed from the pages of Iona's diary. The near-instant contempt he'd felt when Kerr had opened his mouth was much more personal and authentic.

"Detective Chief Inspector Jack Logan, and Detective Constable Tyler

Neish. Police Scotland Major Investigations Unit. We're investigating the death of Iona Wallace," Logan explained, adding, "Your daughter," in case the minister was having difficulty placing the name.

Kerr's fingers flexed to form a tent-shape, then locked together again. He peered at Logan over the top of his knuckles, his tongue licking drily across his puckered lips.

"Jack Logan?" he said. "Not *the* Jack Logan? From Castlemilk?"

"The one and only," Logan said.

"You've a nerve coming here."

"I'm here to do my job, Mr Kerr," Logan said.

"Reverend. And how can you investigate the death of Iona Wallace?" Kerr sneered. He shot Tyler the briefest of looks. "They were in a relationship, you know? Back in the day." He focused his attention on Logan again. "How can you *possibly* be considered impartial?"

Logan wanted to say, *Because it wasn't a relationship, it was a twenty-second fumble up a darkened close,* but chose not to, more for Iona's sake than her father's.

"Aye, well, like it or not, I'm who they've sent," was what he settled on, then he helped himself to one of the two chairs on the other side of the desk, and gestured for Tyler to take the other.

"I didn't invite you to sit," Kerr said.

"Aye, we noticed," Logan replied, making a show of getting himself comfortable. "We'd like to ask you a few questions about Iona. Your daughter."

Kerr gave a dry, mirthless chuckle. "I'm sure you would," he said. "And how long will that take?"

Logan sucked in his bottom lip, then spat it out again. "Oh, I don't know. How long will that take, DC Neish?"

"Suppose that's up to Mr Kerr, boss," Tyler said. "Depends on how forthcoming he is."

"True," said Logan, nodding sagely. "Good point, well made, Detective Constable."

He interlocked his fingers and leaned his elbows on the desk, mirroring the man opposite. "Did you kill Iona?" he asked.

A little explosion of air escaped simultaneously through the minister's mouth and both nostrils. His expression was midway through a particularly impressive bit of contortion when Logan held up a hand to stop him.

"Sorry. Sorry," he said. He held Kerr's gaze while addressing Tyler. "Would you mind recording this interview, Detective Constable? Let's have an accurate record of what Mr Kerr here has to say."

"No bother, boss," Tyler said, producing his phone. He opened the voice recorder app, set the phone on the table, then spoke into it. "Interview with the Reverend Abraham Kerr."

Tyler checked his watch and recited the time and date, before continuing.

"Present are Detective Chief Inspector Jack Logan, and Detective Constable Tyler Neish."

Logan hadn't taken his eyes off Kerr the whole time. The minister's face was stuck somewhere between 'shock' and 'outrage' but he was returning Logan's stare with interest. Even his eyebrows were joining forces in the middle in an attempt to muscle in on the action.

"That us recording?" Logan asked.

"That's us recording, boss," Tyler confirmed.

The DCI lowered his clasped hands until they were resting on the desk in front of him. "Did you murder your daughter, Mr Kerr?" he asked again, drawing another outraged exhalation from the man opposite.

"No, I did not! How dare you even suggest such a thing?" he blustered. "How *dare* you? And it's *Reverend*. Reverend Kerr. I won't tell you again."

"Your relationship was... difficult, was it not?" Logan pressed.

"Our relationship was non-existent. But that was as much her choice as it was mine, and it certainly did not mean I had any part to play in her death, Mr Logan."

"It's *Detective Chief Inspector*," Logan took pleasure in correcting. "Iona owed you money."

"She did."

"How much?"

Kerr sniffed. "I fail to see how that's relevant."

"Well, how about you let us be the judge of that?" Logan suggested. "How much did she owe you?"

"I don't have the exact figure to hand," the minister said.

"Roughly, will be fine."

Kerr's tongue moved from side to side in his mouth, like he was rolling the number around in there. "Total, or still outstanding?"

"Let's go for outstanding," Logan said.

"Eighty thousand pounds."

"Bloody hell," Tyler remarked. When the outburst drew a fiery look from the minister, he offered an apology, cleared his throat, and stared at his phone screen like it was the most fascinating thing in the world.

"Raising a child single-handed is not an inexpensive endeavour," said Kerr. "The costs soon mount up."

Logan replayed the sentence in his head. Then, he replayed it again.

Surely not? Surely the man didn't mean what Logan thought he meant?

"What are you saying?" the DCI asked.

Across the desk, Reverend Kerr gave a curtly efficient little shrug. "She said she was 'disowning' me. Said she no longer considered us to be father and daughter—which, by the way, suited me just fine."

He was. He bloody was. He was actually saying what Logan thought he was saying.

"So, you're saying you *billed* her? You billed her for the cost of bringing her up?"

"Precisely that," Kerr confirmed. "Why should I be left out of pocket for the sake of an ungrateful wretch like her?"

Logan and Tyler both sat mute and dumbstruck by the very idea of it.

"Iona brought nothing but shame and embarrassment on me, from the day she was born until the day she died. Drinking. Drugs. *Whoring* it around to anyone who'd have her," the Reverend continued, his nostrils flaring and drawing further upwards with every word.

It was like even the mention of her name offended him. Like it had a stink to it that left a bad taste in his mouth and snagged at the back of his throat.

"I dedicated the best part of my life to that girl. Her brother, too. And did they appreciate any of it? Were either of them grateful? I gave them everything, and for what? How did they thank me?"

"Your son. Jacob. You hit him with a bill, too?" Logan asked.

Kerr barely skipped a beat. "Jacob is dead."

"Dead? Sorry, I didn't know. Since when?"

"Since he took his own life. Six years ago. Well, closer to seven now, I'd imagine. I don't keep count."

He doesn't keep count, Logan thought. *What sort of heartless bloody husk of a human being wouldn't keep count?*

"I'm sorry to hear that," Logan said.

Kerr's expression did nothing to suggest that he was. "Yes. Well, it was unfortunate, but these things happen."

These things happen. Jesus.

"The money Iona owed you," Logan said, steering the conversation back on track. "She'd stopped repaying it, hadn't she?"

The briefest suggestion of surprise went darting across the minister's face, then was gone. "Who told you that?"

"A little birdie. Is it true?" Logan asked. "And, not that I'd expect a man of your standing to lie to me, but we can check with the bank, so please answer honestly. Had she stopped her repayments?"

"She had. Yes."

"And how did you react to that?"

"Not by killing her, if that's what you're driving at. It was all in the hands of my solicitor in Inverness. It's all documented and above board. She agreed to the monthly payments, and then she stopped making them, placing her in breach of contract. My intention was to settle it through legal means. Not violence."

"But you've been violent before, haven't you?" asked Logan. "Quick to anger, quicker with the belt."

"Children need discipline. Mine more than most. Punishing a child for their transgressions is not the same as murdering one. I shouldn't even dignify your original question with a response, but I will reiterate. I did not kill Iona. I do not know who killed Iona. Her death, while hardly a surprise, is as much a mystery to me as it evidently is to you."

He looked at his watch, sighed, then tapped it twice with a long, bony finger.

"Now, could we possibly hurry this up? I have an evening service to prepare for."

"Evening service? We don't have to go twice, do we?" cried Tyler, practically spitting the words across the table in panic. "The, uh, the congregation I mean. Surely they don't sit through that twice?"

"Many of them choose to, yes. Particularly at difficult times such as these. So, if we could draw this to a close..."

"Does it no' make you angry?" Logan asked, his stare boring deep into the minister, like he was trying to see inside his skull.

"Doesn't what make me angry?"

"You down here, nose to the grindstone, doing the work of the big man upstairs, and yet he goes and takes your kids from you. First your son, now your daughter, both gone before their time."

Logan leaned forward, resting more of his weight on his forearms. "I know I'd be raging. Putting in all them hours singing his praises, and then he goes and does something like that to you. How'd you feel about that, Detective Constable Neish?"

"I'd be fuming, boss," Tyler replied.

"You and me both, son," Logan said. "And you, Mr Kerr? How does it make you feel knowing the God you've dedicated your life to could allow your children to end up the way they did? Doesn't that upset you?"

Kerr had only shown a single flicker of annoyance during Logan's latest line of questioning, when the detective had once again failed to address him by his correct title.

His reply, when it came, was calm and level, all but devoid of emotion.

"Why would it upset me? God gives life, and He takes life. Everyone who dies does so because God wills it."

Logan started to respond, but the minister raised his voice to speak over him.

"Everyone acts like God owes them something. God owes us nothing. He rules and He governs, and everything He does is just and right and good."

"Says who?" asked Logan.

"Says me. Says *Him*. If He does something, whatever that thing may be, then it's right. Then, it's just. The Will of the Lord is infallible. We are only breathing, all of us, through His kindness and grace. If He kills us all tomorrow, He'll have done us no wrong. Our lives do not belong to us, they belong to Him. We *all* belong to Him."

"And what about murder?" Logan asked. "Your daughter was murdered. That's frowned upon, isn't it? It's in the Ten Commandments, if I remember rightly. 'Thou shalt not kill.' It's not acceptable to commit murder, is it?"

"Of course not. But, we are all just cogs in the Lord's great machinery. Even if we knew His plan, we're not equipped to understand it."

He gave that a moment to bed in, then pushed his chair back from the desk and stood. "Add to the fact that we're all sinners, mired down here in our own arrogance and filth, and it's a miracle that He tolerates our existence at all. No, *Mr* Logan, I am not angry at God for taking my children. If I were to be angry at Him for anything, it would be for inflicting them upon me in the first place."

The minister checked his watch again, shook it, and briefly placed it to his ear before continuing in a tone that made it clear the interview was over.

"Now, unless I am under arrest, I'm afraid we'll have to reschedule the rest of this conversation for another time. At times like these, the community looks for guidance. And if I don't give it to them, then who will?"

He motioned with both hands for the men to rise. "Helen will see you out," he said, putting heavy emphasis on the name that Logan only realised wasn't for their benefit when the doors to the office were opened from the other side, revealing the woman who'd originally shown them in.

"Is Helen your wife?" Tyler asked.

"Good gracious, no," Kerr replied, visibly appalled by the very thought. "She's staff. If you wish to question her at any point, kindly arrange it for when she's off-duty. I don't pay her to sit around and chat."

"We'll see what we can do," said Logan, unconvincingly.

"A word of advice," Kerr called after the detectives, as they headed for the door.

Logan and Tyler both stopped. Turned. Waited.

"The man who stood up in church today. Roddy Mac."

"What about him?" asked Logan.

"I'd talk to him. He and Iona were... Well, they *made videos*. Of a sinful nature, I believe. Together. I'll let your imagination do the rest. But, if I were you—if getting to the bottom of this were my concern—then I'd be starting with Roddy Mac."

CHAPTER TWENTY-TWO

Neither detective said a word as they trudged through the drizzle in the direction of the Community Council office. But by the time they were halfway, well out of earshot of anyone from the church, Tyler couldn't hold his tongue any longer.

"Jesus Christ, boss," he remarked in an incredulous whisper. "How's that for mental? You think he genuinely didn't give a shit about Iona's murder, or was he putting it on?"

"I don't think he could care less," Logan said, as they opened the squeaky school gate and went striding along the side of the building, headed for the office door. "Going by Iona's old diaries, he was always like that. Cold-hearted. Think he resented her from day one. The brother, too."

"No wonder the poor bastard did away with himself," said Tyler. "Five more minutes in there and I'd have been giving it some serious consideration myself."

"Aye. Charming fella," Logan said, unlocking the office door and opening it. He ushered Tyler through, before following.

"We going to talk to that Roddy Mac guy from the pub again?" Tyler asked.

"That's him. And aye, we will," Logan said. "I'm in two minds about him. After speaking to him, I mean. I want to think he's being genuine. He says he and Iona weren't sexually involved, but it's very possible that he wanted to be, and she shut it down."

"By all accounts, she'd shag anything with a pulse," Tyler said.

"The fuck are you trying to say, Detective Constable?" Logan demanded.

Tyler's face fell. "Shit. I mean... I didn't mean you, boss. On the island, I mean."

Logan grunted. "Aye, well. All the more reason for Roddy to get jealous. If he's been shooting porn with her, and has to watch her getting it from all and sundry, then it might just have tipped him over the edge."

"We headed there now then, boss?"

Logan shook his head. "Soon. But I want to put a call in back to base first for a catch-up. See what Hamza's dredged up on Bruce Anderson. But, before that..."

Logan plucked a mug from a line of them hanging on hooks from the wall above a box of teabags. "Is it no' high time you stuck the kettle on?"

DI Ben Forde peered along the length of his nose at Hamza's phone screen, and his own mirror-image peered back at him. "That's no' Jack. I thought we were calling Jack?"

"We are, sir. Well, we're calling Tyler's phone, but they haven't picked up yet. Once they do, then they'll appear."

"On the screen?" said Ben.

Hamza hesitated. To his credit, he resisted the urge to say, 'Naw, in person, like genies,' or to use any of the other sarcastic responses that had immediately popped into his head. "Aye. On the screen."

They sat side-by-side at Hamza's desk, the phone propped up against the base of the monitor. Ben took the opportunity to check himself out.

"Christ, you're looking old, Benjamin," he muttered, running his hand down his face, then through his thinning hair. "The scrapheap beckons."

"Scrapheap's been beckoning you for years, ye old bugger," boomed a voice from the phone, as Logan and Tyler materialised on the main screen. "Hasn't stopped you so far."

"Hello, Jack," said Ben, projecting his voice. "Can you hear me?"

"Pretty sure I can hear you through the bloody window," Logan replied. "You don't have to shout. It's just like a phone."

He turned to look off camera. "That's right, isn't it? It's like a phone?"

"Pretty much, boss, aye. It's WhatsApp. Video calling."

"Alright, alright, I don't need the technical breakdown," Logan said, then he faced front again. "Hamza there?"

"Here, sir," DC Khaled said, leaning into shot.

"Oh, look. There's us up the top," said Ben, marvelling at the wee box in the top right corner of the screen that now held his and Hamza's image. He gave a little wave and chuckled as he waved back.

He was still waving when he realised that everyone else had fallen silent. He lowered his hand, quietly cleared his throat, then gave Logan a nod.

"Sorry. Got a bit over-excited," he said. "Hamza's been digging into Bruce Anderson, like you asked."

"Good. We've just had quite the interesting conversation with Abraham Kerr, the victim's father," Logan said.

Ben's eyebrows raised. "Interesting how?"

"Interesting in that he's a fucking bampot," the DCI replied. "Basically, he reckons it's fair enough that his kids are both dead, because that's the way God wants it."

"Sounds like a charmer," said Ben. His eyes were flitting around the screen, like he wasn't quite sure where to look. "Both kids?"

"Iona had a brother. Topped himself, apparently. Jacob, his name is. Can one of you look into it and make sure the story checks out?"

Hamza nodded, and jotted a note on his pad.

"He a suspect?" Ben asked. "The father I mean, no' the dead son."

"That's the big question," Logan replied. "I'm undecided. I think he's an arsehole. I think he made those kids' lives hell. Depending on what's in the rest of Iona's diaries, I think we might be able to build a case for abuse. But did he kill her? I doubt it. Honestly? I think he'd tell us if he had. I think he'd say he was doing God's work and bloody revel in it."

"Proper nutter, then?" Ben said.

"Bananas, boss," Tyler chipped in. "Proper heid the baw."

"What did you get on Bruce Anderson?" Logan asked.

Ben shuffled aside a little, letting Hamza take centre stage. "I haven't been able to look into him fully yet, but early signs are promising. Australian, as you know. Haven't been able to scare up any info from over there yet, but he's got an international arrest warrant out for him for a suspected sexual assault in Vietnam. Issued in July last year."

"How did he get into the country with that?" Logan asked.

"He didn't, sir. Not officially, anyway," Hamza explained. "Must be here illegally."

"Sounds like we might have our man, boss," Tyler said.

"Aye, if we can find the bastard," Logan said. "Ben, what's the latest on getting us some reinforcements over here? We could do with some Uniform for the search. The island's no' exactly huge, but too big for the two of us."

"We're hoping to get a chopper over to you later tonight. Ferries might start running tomorrow."

"Hold them back as long as you can. At most, I want inbound only," Logan instructed. "Nobody gets off this island without my say-so. Anderson is our main target, but the victim wasn't winning any popularity contests around here, so there's no saying it was definitely him who killed her. Until we know more, I want this place as locked down as possible."

"We'll get it sorted," Ben said. "Only slight problem is manpower. It's a big week."

Logan frowned. "How so?"

"Jesus, Jack. Royal visit this week, isn't it? Tomorrow, Her Majesty herself is gracing the good folk of Inverness with her presence."

Logan stared blankly back at him from the screen.

"The Queen. It's been briefed for weeks. Two-day visit while she's up at Balmoral. I think she's opening something somewhere."

"And?"

"And security's high. They're having to cancel all non-urgent leave as it is. We can get you some resource, but it'll be limited until she's been and gone."

"Christ Almighty. Fine. Just get us who you can when you can. Hopefully, Anderson isn't going anywhere."

Something caught the DCI's eye and he leaned closer to the camera. The tip of an enormous finger blocked half the screen as he pointed to something behind Ben and Hamza.

"What's that?"

The two men looked back over their shoulders. Ben's face had reddened slightly when he turned back to the phone.

"Oh, thought I'd have a go at doing a Big Board," he explained. "Haven't got Caitlyn's knack for it, though."

Logan ejected a short exhalation through his nose. It wasn't quite a laugh, but it was in that neck of the woods.

"Aye, you can say that again," he said. "She'd a gift for the old Big Board."

"Be better organised than that one, sir, that's for sure," Hamza chimed in.

"She'd be raging, wouldn't she?" Ben laughed, shooting a glance back at the board again. "She'd have taken one look at it, hauled everything down, and started again."

"Aye, you can say that again, boss!" said Tyler. "She'll be turning in her bloody grave."

Everyone fell silent at that. Tyler wilted under the glare Logan shot his way. "Bit fucking morbid."

"Aye, come on, son. There's a line," Ben said, shaking his head disapprovingly.

"Show some bloody respect," Hamza scowled.

Tyler looked between them all. "What? No! I wasn't being... I just meant..." he began, then he caught just the faintest smirk on Logan's face. "Bastards!" he said, wheezing the word out in relief. "You're all bastards."

"Are you only just realising this now?" Logan asked. He checked his watch, then tapped the table with both hands, making the image on Hamza's phone screen shake. "Right, places to go, people to harass. Get me them Uniforms, see what else you can find out about Mr Anderson, and let's talk again later tonight."

"Right you are," Ben said.

"Oh. And send us a picture of the Big Board."

Ben looked back again. "I was going to scrap it. You think we should keep it?"

Logan shrugged. "Aye. Why not? DS McQuarrie would've, and that's good enough for me."

Ben and Hamza both nodded their agreement. "Aye. Good enough for me, too," Ben said. On-screen, Tyler started reaching for the phone, but Ben jumped in quickly before the DC could end the call. "Wait. Did Hoon get you, Jack?"

"Thankfully not," Logan replied. "He still on the warpath?"

"Like I've never seen before," Ben said. "He's bloody fizzing."

"Aye, well, if I'm lucky, he might have a heart attack before he catches up with me. Tell him you passed the message on, and that I'm going to get back to him as a matter of urgency."

"And are you?" Ben asked.

"What do you think?" Logan asked.

And then, with a nod from the DCI, Tyler's finger filled the screen, and the call came to an end.

"What do I think?" asked Ben. He sucked in his top lip and shot a wary glance at the Incident Room door. "I think that daft big bugger's going to be the death of all of us."

Tyler shoved his phone back into his pocket and rolled his chair away from the desk that Logan had claimed as his own.

"How come the Superintendent's gunning for you, boss?" he asked, positioning himself behind the room's second, far smaller desk. The 'Lesser Desk' as Logan had named it when they were sorting out the seating arrangements. *Desk Minor.*

"Who knows?" Logan asked. "Probably nothing. Or maybe... You know Bosco, right?"

"Bosco Maximuke? The builder with the drug connections?" Tyler asked. "Sorry, 'alleged' drug connections," he corrected, making quote marks in the air with his fingers. "What about him?"

"I've got reason to believe he might have been supplying the Gillespies."

"What reason's that, boss?"

"Because I know the crooked bastard," Logan said. "The shot that killed

Caitlyn? I think it was meant for him. I think, if it wasn't for Bosco, DS McQuarrie would still be with us. Course, I've got no evidence to back that up. Nothing that would stand up in court, anyway."

"So... what?" asked Tyler. "Did you go round and accuse him?"

"In a manner of speaking, aye," Logan said. "In a way."

"What way would that be, boss?"

"In a 'leathered shite out of his henchman and burned his office to the ground' kind of a way."

Tyler's eyes became two miniature globes of surprise. "Fucking hell, boss! What were you thinking?"

"I was mostly thinking, 'I'm going to burn this bastard's office to the ground,' truth be told." Logan clicked his tongue against the back of his teeth and shrugged. "I didn't really think it through beyond that. Got a bit carried away in the heat of the moment."

"Jesus, you didn't kill him, did you?" Tyler asked.

"Of course, I didn't kill him! Jesus Christ, son, what do you take me for?" Logan barked. He shifted his weight on his feet and shrugged. "I mean, I can't say I wasn't tempted. But, no."

"That's something. But still, boss." Tyler's eyes darted left and right, like he was seeing all the potential consequences of Logan's actions being played out before him. "That could be career-ending. You could get your cards for that. You could get the bloody jail!"

Logan nodded slowly. Clearly, he'd come to the same conclusion some time ago. "Aye. But I'll worry about that later. For now, while I still have one, we've got a job to do. There's still a lot of people to talk to, and Bruce Anderson isn't going to find himself. We get this done, we find out who killed Iona, and then Detective Superintendent Hoon, the PCC, and whoever else wants to throw their oar in can do what they need to do."

He necked the last of his cold tea, pulled a face, then clonked the mug down on the desk. "Right, you fit? Let's go see if Roddy Mackay'll gie's a swatch of his mucky videos."

CHAPTER TWENTY-THREE

They were outside the pub when they heard the shout from inside.

"Hey! What are you doing? Stop!"

Through the glass, they saw Bruce Anderson stuff his pockets with money from the till, then shoulder his way past Roddy, sending the pub's owner spiralling to the floor.

Anderson was out through the back door before either detective could react, already vanishing up the metal steps that led to the beer garden.

"Shite. Get after him," Logan barked, practically throwing Tyler at the pub's front door.

The DC set off at a clip, powering through the pub, hurdling the fallen Roddy, and vanishing through the door, hot on Anderson's heels.

Logan offered up a hand as Roddy sprackled back to his feet, and pulled the man upright with a single jerk.

"You alright?" he asked, not waiting for an answer before adding, "What happened? Where did he come from?"

"Robbed me," Roddy wheezed, rubbing his chest with the heel of his hand. "Nipped upstairs, then came down and caught the bastard with his hand in the till."

He limped behind the bar and rummaged half-heartedly in the till drawer. "He's got most of the float. All the notes, anyway. There was fifty quid there."

Logan looked to the back door. The sound of footsteps had been lost to the soft rattle and clank of the rain falling on the metal staircase out back.

"Is there a way out past the beer garden?" he asked.

Roddy nodded breathlessly. "Aye. Backs onto wilderness. Trees, bushes. Hills. Your man'll have to get a shift on, if he wants to catch him. Is he quick?"

"Depends in which sense you mean," Logan sighed. "Let's just keep our fingers crossed, eh?"

He pulled a chair out at one of the tables. "Here. Take a seat. I'll get you a drink."

Roddy looked across the optics, like he'd just remembered they were there, then emerged from behind the bar. He and Logan crossed paths as Roddy headed for the seat and the detective sidled in through the bar's narrow hatch.

"I'll have a wee Grouse," Roddy said. "Glasses are down below."

Logan reached under the counter and found a suitable glass. He jammed the rim against the bottom of the optic and watched, transfixed, as a gurgle of golden liquid sloshed into the glass.

The smell of it was... something else. It transported him back to other places, other times. Better times.

And worse.

Something writhed and raged at the back of his brain, like a trapped animal hurling itself against the bars of its cage, demanding to be released, demanding to be set free.

"Everything alright?" Roddy asked, and Logan realised he'd been staring at the contents of the glass for several seconds.

"Fine. Aye," he said, quickly turning. He joined Roddy at the table and deposited the glass in front of him without looking at it, then went to the back door and stepped out into the rain.

The metal steps were slippery as he stormed up them. The beer garden spread out in a semi-circle from the top step, a poorly-maintained wire fence the only thing separating it from the expanse of sweet-fuck-all that stretched out beyond it.

Logan could see two figures out there. One was a few hundred yards beyond the fence. The other was much closer.

At first glance, he assumed it must be Tyler and Anderson, but quickly realised that this wasn't the case. One of them was Tyler, right enough. He was the one furthest away, thundering across the uneven terrain, presumably in dogged pursuit of Anderson, although Logan couldn't see him.

The other figure stood crucified a relatively short distance away on the right. Another bloody scarecrow. How many was that now? Three? Four? Too many to make sense.

Firing another glance in the now much smaller DC Neish's direction, Logan thrust his hands in his coat pockets, and clumped his way back down the stairs.

Tyler ran.

He ran, despite his lungs burning, his knees aching, and the pervasive aroma of sheep shit playing havoc with the contents of his stomach.

He ran, despite his tightening chest, his inappropriate footwear, and the lingering sense that it was all a complete waste of time.

Bruce Anderson had been over the back fence of the beer garden and halfway to bloody nowhere when the DC had crested the top of the stairs. The Australian was solidly built, but the bugger was fast, too, and wasn't hindered by his choice of footwear.

Even as Tyler threw himself over the fence, he knew the chances of catching him were slim. If he could keep him in sight, then there was a chance Anderson would tire out first, but the area out back of the pub was dotted all over with trees and bushes, and the ground undulated in rolling dips and hills that offered ample opportunity for cover.

A little nagging voice at the back of Tyler's head told him he should probably just give up now. Another, much louder voice—one that sounded a lot like DCI Logan's, Tyler thought—warned him he had better not come back empty-handed.

And so, despite everything, Tyler ran.

And he kept on running.

He buried his face into the crook of his arm, trying to muffle the rasping of his breath, as he tucked himself into the undergrowth.

Stupid. *Stupid, stupid, stupid.*

He should've stayed away. Should've waited it out. Should've hidden until the boats started, then snuck aboard and got the fuck off the island at the first possible opportunity.

But, he'd need money when he got to the mainland. He'd get nowhere without it. What choice did he have but to raid the till? Roddy had been upstairs. Why the fuck hadn't he stayed there?

The foliage around him was wet, the ground soaking him from below. A rock or a root—something bloody uncomfortable, anyway—was digging into his ribs, but the footsteps of that cop were coming closer, and he didn't dare move. Didn't dare give himself away. If he was caught, it was over.

If he was caught, he was fucked.

The footsteps slowed as they drew closer to the overgrown clump of heather and bracken that was hiding him.

No, no, no.

Shit, shit, shit.

He could hear the cop wheezing, sounding even more out of breath than himself. The footsteps swished through the grass, cautious now. Approaching steadily. Had he seen him? Was it already over? Was the game already up?

He slid his hand beneath him, cautiously feeling for the painful lump.

A rock. A sharp, pointed rock.

A weapon.

He wrestled it out from beneath him, keeping his movements slow and subtle. There had been no shout from the cop yet. No barked orders. No sudden weight on his back, or wrenching together of his wrists.

The cop hadn't seen him. Yet. But, it was only a matter of time. And that meant, it was only a matter of time before he was in a cell. Only a matter of time before he was standing before a jury, facing a life stretch.

No. Not going to happen. It couldn't. He wouldn't let it.

His hand tightened on the rock. The footsteps came closer, then stopped. The cop breathed deeply.

Down in the damp foliage, his heart thundered in his chest.

"Ah, bollocks to this," said the cop.

And then, to his relief, the footsteps turned and walked away.

"What's with all the scarecrows?"

It was the first question Logan had asked as he'd plonked himself down in the seat across from Roddy, and it had evidently caught the bar-owner off guard.

"What? Oh. Them. I don't know. It's a thing."

Logan waited until Roddy had drained the last of his whisky before pressing him on it further. "A thing?"

"Like a... Oh, I don't know. Gimmick. Dudley does them. For the kids and tourists mostly. The Tattiebogle Trail. Another of the Community Council's 'great ideas.'"

"Tattiebogle?"

"Another name for a scarecrow, seemingly," Roddy explained. "Old. Think it goes back a bit."

"Right. Who's Dudley?"

"Dudley Broon. Well, Dudley Brown, but... You'll have seen him at church. Can't miss him. Great big lad."

"Him. Aye. I clocked him, right enough," Logan said. "I'm told he and Iona had a bit of a set-to the night she died."

Roddy shook his head, already anticipating the suggestion before Logan could propose it. "Dudley wouldn't hurt a fly. He looks scary, sure, but he's a heart of gold in him. You'll find no one with a bad word to say about him."

"Except Iona, by the sounds of it."

Roddy picked up his glass, looked at it mournfully, then set it down again. "She had a temper when she'd had too many. She'd have said things she didn't mean. She did that, but she always felt bad about it afterwards. Once she'd..."

"Sobered up."

Roddy smiled, but it was a thin and unconvincing thing. "Sobered up. Yes. Exactly."

The more time Logan spent in Roddy's company, the more he found he liked the man. Despite everything currently going on, he had a down-to-earth air about him. Even now, he radiated a level of friendliness that made it abundantly clear why he'd ended up in the hospitality trade.

All that, however, just made what Logan had to do next all the more difficult.

"Tell me about the videos you made together," he said, then he shut his mouth and took note of the reaction.

There was shock at first, a little widening of the eyes, a slight dropping of the bottom jaw.

Something like shame or embarrassment came next. The reddening of the cheeks. The darting of the eyes. The heavy swallow.

And then, to Logan's surprise, came amusement. The embarrassment was still written there across his face, but he was smiling, too. Laughing, almost.

"God. You heard about them, did you?"

Logan nodded.

"Who from? Was it Joy?" Roddy asked. "Or, no. Wait. The minister. Reverend Kerr. It was him, wasn't it? What did he tell you they were?"

He stood up suddenly, still smiling but clearly annoyed. Not at Logan, the detective thought, but at whoever had told him about the footage.

"Fine. You want to see? You want to see the videos? I'll show you. They're upstairs. They're on my laptop."

"One sec," Logan said. He got up from the table, climbed the stairs out back, and saw Tyler trudging dejectedly back towards the beer garden.

Alone.

"Useless bastard," the DCI grumbled, then he turned and clanked down the steps, and headed off with Roddy to watch some home-made porn.

CHAPTER TWENTY-FOUR

LOGAN SAT AT RODDY'S KITCHEN TABLE, EYES FIXED ON THE LAPTOP screen, watching Iona giein' it laldy.

He'd recognised her at once, not as the corpse he'd seen the previous day, but as the girl he remembered from years back. Sure, the years had taken its toll, and the booze had lent a hand, but it was still her behind the eyes. Still her in all those surprisingly energetic movements.

On-screen, Iona strutted around in the bar area, a microphone in her hand, belting out Cyndi Lauper's *Time After Time* to a backing track. She was performing as if to a full-house, but from the lack of response, it was clear that the pub was empty.

The video had been edited well, cutting to a tight close-up on the more emotional moments, when Iona would stop striding around and perform over-sincerely right down the camera lens.

Closing that window, Logan double-clicked another of the video files. In this one, Iona was earnestly murdering Tina Turner's *Simply the Best* while shuffling around the bar like a cowboy who'd lost his horse.

"She wanted to put them on *YouTube*," Roddy explained. He was standing in the kitchen doorway, and Logan couldn't help but notice he wasn't watching the videos. The memory was too painful, maybe. Or too embarrassing.

"And did she?"

Roddy shook his head. "Wanted to build up a bunch of them before she launched. A *portfolio*, she said. I've no clue how many she was aiming for. We did dozens, and she used to borrow the camera herself sometimes, so no idea how many she made on her own. Whatever it was, it clearly wasn't enough. She never got around to putting them up."

"And that's it?" Logan asked. "Just singing?"

"Just singing," Roddy said.

"Never anything sexual?"

Roddy gestured to the laptop. "You'll be taking it away anyway, won't you? Go through it yourself and see," he said, his anger bubbling just below the surface. "I know what the gossip was, but we never did anything like that. I wouldn't. It was just singing, that's all."

Logan closed over the laptop lid and turned to the man in the doorway. "When you say you 'wouldn't'. Does that mean she asked you?"

"No."

"Never?"

"Never. No. Just singing. That's all she ever asked me to film, and that's all I ever did."

Logan held his gaze for several seconds, giving Roddy the chance to change his story. The bar-owner stood his ground, though, and Logan eventually relented with a single nod of his head.

"Good. Well, we'll go through it and get it back to you as soon as we can," he said, standing and drawing an evidence bag from his pocket.

Roddy watched, transfixed, as Logan placed the laptop in the bag and sealed it shut.

"Is that necessary?" he asked, his gaze flitting up to Logan's face and back again. "I'm not... You don't think I did it, do you?"

"We're still at an early stage in the investigation, Mr Mackay," Logan said, and the use of his title and surname made Roddy look even more worried. "We can't rule anyone out yet."

Logan tucked the bagged laptop under his arm. "But, if it helps any... No, I don't think you did it."

Roddy stepped aside as Logan headed for the front door of the flat. The detective stopped there and looked back, his features fixed in a grim smile. "For your sake, I really hope you don't prove me wrong."

"I... I won't. And thanks. For believing me."

"Call 101. Get the robbery logged. If we can get you your money back, we will," Logan said, and then he pulled open the door, and ducked down the narrow staircase that led to the pub corridor below.

"There you are, boss," said Tyler, when Logan appeared through the door at the bottom of the steps. "Bad news. I lost him."

"Don't worry about it, son. I knew you would," Logan said. "To be honest, I just wanted you out from under my feet for five minutes."

Tyler laughed, although he wasn't entirely convinced that the DCI was joking. His eyes went to the laptop tucked under Logan's arm.

"He show you the vids?"

"He did, aye," Logan said.

"And?"

"And they were... eye-opening," Logan said. He handed over the laptop, and Tyler's face practically lit-up. "You can comb through them when we get back to the office."

He checked his watch. After five. The day was slipping away from him, and while they had a solid suspect, they were no closer to catching Iona's killer.

"But before you get stuck into that, we're making a house-call," he announced.

"That'll be a nice surprise for someone," Tyler said. "Who we dropping in on?"

Logan set off for the pub's front door. "We've spoken to Iona's old man," he said. "Now, let's go see what her son has to say."

"What the fuck do you want? Have you found him?"

Ben had made it just a third of the way through knocking on the door when Detective Superintendent Hoon pulled it open, leaving the DI swiping his knuckles at thin air.

As usual, Hoon's face was all rage and thunder. He still had one hand on the handle, like he was ready to slam the door in Ben's face at any moment. Perhaps repeatedly.

"Well?" he barked, before Ben had a chance to reply. "I don't have the luxury of standing here all fucking day, Benjamin. Have you got him for me? Is he on the phone?"

"Uh, no, sir," Ben said.

He stepped back as the door was slammed shut, and stood in awkward silence for several seconds while the man in the office gnashed and roared.

Eventually, the door opened again. "What, then?"

"We, uh, we think the weather's going to improve. Looked like it'd be tonight, but forecast is now saying tomorrow morning. We want to fly Uniform in. To Canna, I mean. Back-up."

"Back-up? You know what's got my fucking back up, Benjamin? That useless great cocksplash of a DCI we both have the misfortune of knowing."

Ben wasn't quite sure how to react to that, so he gave a dry, slightly nervous chuckle.

This, it transpired, was a mistake.

"Something funny?" Hoon demanded. "Eh? Are my elevated fucking stress levels amusing you, Detective Inspector? Is my mounting blood pressure proving to be enter-fucking-taining?"

Ben shook his head, but Hoon was off on one now. He gestured to the floor. "Maybe I'll have a fucking heart attack, and give you a really good laugh, eh? Maybe I'll drop dead on the floor, and you can send it in to *You've Been* fucking *Framed*, so everyone can get in on the fucking joke."

He glowered at the DI, his eyeballs bulging in that way they did, his lips moving as he swore repeatedly below his breath.

"One," he said.

Ben blinked. "Sorry, sir?"

"One. You can have one. Uniform."

"One? But—"

"Take it or fucking leave it. We've got the bastard Queen coming. I can give you one officer, and you can fuck right off with the helicopter. Boat them in."

"Ferries aren't running, sir," Ben pointed out. "And I'm not sure one is—"

"Did I say the word 'ferry,' Benjamin? Did you hear me mention a fucking ferry? Find a speedboat, or a yacht, or whittle sticks to make a fucking raft, I don't care," Hoon snarled. "In fact, you know what? Fuck it, pick a good swimmer and give them some goggles. I'm no' spunking money on a helicopter for one fucking Uniform."

"Right. Aye. Fair enough," said Ben. He cleared his throat. "I just think, given the geographic area they have to cover, one is—"

"It's Canna, Benjamin. It's in the Small Isles. Key-fucking-word being 'small.' It's no' fucking... fucking..." He flailed a hand about, searching for a name. "*Botswana.* They can have one, and you're boating the bastard in. That clear?"

Ben stood up straight. There was no point in arguing. Not now. Not when he was like this.

Mind you, when was he ever not like this?

"Clear, sir," he said, and the door was closed in his face before he'd even reached the second word.

CHAPTER TWENTY-FIVE

Isaac Young and his fiancée, Louise Beaton, were at their dinner when Logan and Tyler came knocking. They'd done a big roast chicken, and the smell of it cranked Logan's saliva glands into overdrive and set his stomach rumbling.

The detectives had offered to wait in the living room while they'd finished, but Isaac had waved the suggestion away, albeit with a certain level of irritation. He led the detectives through to the front room, while Louise stuck everything back in the oven to stay warm.

Up close, there was no mistaking Isaac's parentage. He had Iona's eyes. Nothing much else of hers, but the eyes were enough. They immediately marked him as Iona's son, and when Isaac looked at him, Logan felt a twinge of something like nostalgia.

"We're sorry to trouble you, Mr Young. We appreciate that this is a difficult time," he said. "I'm DCI Jack Logan. This is DC Tyler Neish."

Logan gestured to Tyler, but the DC didn't immediately respond. He was peering up at the slightly taller Isaac, his eyebrows practically dancing up and down his forehead.

"Hmm? Oh. Aye. Sorry. DC Neish. Tyler," he said, shaking Isaac's hand. "Nice to meet you, Mr Young. Sorry about the circumstances."

"Isaac's fine. And it is what it is," he said. His accent was an odd one. A mix of a few different places, both north of the border and south.

"Do you have any ID on you?" Tyler asked.

"ID?" said both Logan and Isaac at the same time.

"Just, eh, for the notes," Tyler said, as if this explained everything.

Shrugging, Isaac fished in his pocket, produced his wallet, and slid out the driving licence. Tyler took it, checked both sides, and handed it back.

"Perfect. Thanks."

"Right. No problem," said Isaac, returning the licence to the wallet. "Please."

He motioned to the couch and took a seat in a battered old leather armchair across from it, which looked even older than he did.

"Obviously, we're here about what happened to your mother," Logan said.

"Aye, like she was ever much of that," Isaac said. "Our relationship was... Well. It was barely a relationship at all."

"You didn't get on?" Logan asked.

"Oh, she got on with me just fine. As soon as I was out fending for myself, I mean, and wasn't cramping her style. Once I was earning money, she was all over me. Before then?" He shrugged, one finger tracing a circle on the arm of the couch. "I mean, technically we got on fine then, too. But only because I hardly saw her. She was young when she had me, though. I suppose I should give her some slack."

"What about your dad?" Tyler asked. Logan shot him a slightly quizzical look, but the DC was too fixated on Isaac to notice.

"Not much better. He left when I was, I don't know. Eight. We were living down south at the time. He stuck around for a while. I went between his place and mum's, and then he got into some dodgy stuff and wound up inside. Drugs. He's out now, though. We keep in touch back and forth. Christmas. Birthdays."

"Right. Right. Fair enough," said Tyler, making a note in his pad.

Logan glared at him as if to ask if he could get back to his interview now, then continued with his own line of questioning. "When did you last see your mum?"

"Tuesday," Isaac said. "In the pub. She was making an arse of herself. No surprise. Up to her usual trick."

"Which was?"

"Trying to shag anyone who'd have her," Isaac said. He spat the words out like they burned the inside of his mouth, and the way he flinched told Logan that, despite the issues he had with his mother, Isaac didn't like seeing her that way. "It was like a ritual. As soon as a new bloke arrived on the island, she'd set out to have her wicked way with the poor bastard. It was a running joke." He shook his head, his lips drawing back over his teeth in disgust. "*She* was a running joke."

Louise came in from the kitchen then, drying her hands on an Edinburgh Castle tea towel. There were no other seats in the living room, so Tyler stood to give her his. Instead, she perched herself on the arm of Isaac's chair, and leaned her weight against him in a wordless show of support.

Tyler sat down again. He and Logan ran through their introductions, and then the conversation resumed.

"Was there anything unusual about Tuesday night?" Logan asked. "Anything that struck you as strange, or out of the ordinary?"

Isaac stuck out his bottom lip and shook his head. "No. Not really. I mean, I suppose it's a wee bit unusual for her to be in that state on a Tuesday night, but it's certainly not unheard of."

"Every night's a weekend night for Iona," Louise said, and the venom behind it made it clear there was no love lost between the two women. She shot her partner a look bordering on the apologetic. "Was."

"Aye, she had form for the weeknights," Isaac admitted. "In terms of her behaviour? Nothing out of the ordinary. She was pissed, tried to crack onto Bruce behind the bar and some tourist—practically put it on a plate for both of them—then she left when it was clear that nobody was going to buy her a drink."

"And you left soon after. Is that right?" Logan asked. He looked from one to the other, studying their reactions. Confusion was all he saw.

"No," said Isaac. "I mean, not right away. We had a couple of drinks first."

"Right. I see," Logan said. "It's just, a witness at the scene said you both left soon after Iona."

"What witness?" Louise demanded. Her voice was suddenly shrill. Fingernails-down-a-blackboard stuff. "And what do you mean? What are you getting at? Are you accusing us of something?"

Logan held up his hands for calm. "Relax, Miss Beaton. Nobody's accusing you of anything. I'm just trying to build up a picture of the night Iona died. That's all. You say you didn't leave early? Fine. Can you tell me what time you did leave?"

Neither of them jumped in to volunteer a reply.

"Roughly?" said Logan.

"We didn't really keep track," Isaac said, exchanging a fleeting look with his fiancée. "Mum had... she'd thrown us. We weren't really paying attention to the time. We were upset."

"Upset?" Logan said. "Angry?"

"I mean—" Isaac began, but Louise took over.

"Yes, we were bloody angry. I mean, I know I was," she spat. "She'd mortified him. Both of us. *Again*. I was furious. But did we kill her? No, of course we bloody didn't."

"To be clear again, nobody is saying you killed her," Logan said, but Louise wasn't having it.

"But you're implying it, aren't you? That's what you're getting at." She sat back against the armchair and took Isaac's hand in hers. "We should have a solicitor. If they're trying to stitch us up, we should have a solicitor."

"Miss Beaton..." Logan began, then he adjusted the severity of his tone, and tried again. "Miss Beaton. Louise. You can get a solicitor. Of course. If that's what you want. But nobody is under arrest here. Neither of you was a suspect when we walked in that door, and I've heard nothing yet to change that fact. We're just trying to get a clear picture of what happened so we can clear all this up and get out of your hair."

He smiled, first at Louise, then at Isaac. "We're not here to stitch anyone up. We're here to catch a killer. Your mother's killer, Mr Young. Any help you can provide will be hugely appreciated."

The couple exchanged glances again. Their interlocked fingers rubbed together. Time to seal the deal.

Logan sat forward on the couch. "But if you'd rather we do it in a more official capacity, then that can be arranged. We don't have facilities here, obviously, but we can get you brought to the station in Mallaig, and arrange for a solicitor to meet us there. We can talk more... robustly."

He produced a smile that everyone in the room understood wasn't really a smile, at all.

"It's up to you. Whatever suits."

The couple sat in silence for a few moments, and then Isaac quietly cleared his throat. "Here's fine," he said. "What do you need to know?"

Logan sat back. Tyler clicked the end of his pen.

"You said Iona had been trying to crack onto the barman. Bruce Anderson."

Isaac sighed. "Yes. Yes, she was. Not for the first time, either."

Tyler made a note. Logan made an encouraging motion with one hand. "Tell me, what do you know about Mr Anderson?"

"Bruce?" Isaac frowned. "Not a lot, really. He arrived, what...?"

"Couple of months ago," Louise suggested, although she didn't sound too confident. "Australian, but he's been around a bit. He's travelling, apparently. Working his way around the world. Been at it for a couple of years."

"Well, I don't know about all that," said Isaac, shooting his fiancée a sideways glance that suggested he hadn't been aware of how chatty she and Anderson had been. "But he seems friendly enough. Think he's staying out the back of the shop. That's where most of the staff Roddy gets in end up going. Have you spoken to Roddy, by the way? Him and my mum, they were close."

"We have," Logan said. "But anything we should be aware of there?"

"I don't know," Isaac said. "She said he was a bit clingy, sometimes. I got the impression he wanted more than she was offering. Which was pretty rich. He must've been the only guy on the island who wasn't a blood relative that she hadn't tried it on with."

"Were your parents married?" Tyler asked. The question came out of nowhere, and drew looks of confusion from the couple opposite, and a full-blown scowl from Logan.

"Do you mind?" he grunted, his expression making it very clear to the younger detective that they'd be discussing this later.

Logan held the look for a few emphatic seconds, then turned his attention back to Isaac.

"Sorry about that. He gets excited around new people. You were telling me about Iona's relationship with Roddy."

"I don't know much about it, if I'm honest," Isaac said. "I tended to keep my distance from her as much as possible."

"And yet, you've stuck to the same tiny island," Logan said. "You could've gone anywhere. You moved away, didn't you? If you were that keen to avoid her, you could've stayed away."

"This is his home, too," Louise said, jumping in again. "He did most of his growing up here. His grandfather's here. He's as much right to be here as she has. Had. Whatever. More, even. People like him, which is more than I can say for her."

"Louise." There was a pleading tone to Isaac's voice. He may not have got on with his mother, but there was still feeling there. "Please."

"Well..." Louise sighed, but she took the sentence no further.

"We spoke to your grandfather earlier," Logan said, changing tack. "He seems like an interesting character."

"He's that, alright," Isaac replied, and there was something cagey about it, like he didn't want to say too much. "Mum hated him."

"And you?"

"He has his quirks, but he's always been good to us," Isaac said. "Even though, us living together... It's not ideal, as far as he's concerned. He's made that pretty clear. But he's been supportive. Of us. Of the business."

"What is it you do again?" Logan asked.

"Soap. And candles," Louise said. "All handmade."

Logan raised his eyebrows and nodded slowly. "Right. Market for that, is there?"

"Not locally, really, but we send stuff all over the world," she continued. "Big demand for that sort of stuff worldwide, and the Scottish connection helps."

She sniffed and wriggled upright on the arm of the chair.

"We're building a brand."

"Right. Well... good for you," Logan said. "Well done."

Isaac turned away for a moment, and Logan caught the longing look he fired in the direction of the kitchen.

"One final question, and we'll let you get back to your dinner," he said. "We were told that Iona got into an altercation with a man named Dudley Brown on the night she died. Would you know anything about that?"

Isaac snorted. "Dudley Broon? Aye. She was having a go at Louise, effing and blinding. The usual. Dudley stood up and told her she should go, and she laid into him. Verbally, I mean. Called him a retard."

"And is he?" asked Tyler, then his eyes instantly widened in horror at what he'd said. "I mean, not a... Not a... Does Mr Brown suffer from any..." He gave a frantic wave of his pen, like he might be able to conjure up all the missing words he was looking for with it.

"Learning difficulties?" asked Isaac.

"Aye! Yes. Anything of that... nature," said Tyler. He winced, gave the tiniest shake of his head, then looked back at his notebook again, all the while avoiding the glare from the DCI beside him.

"He's a good man," Isaac said. "Is he the sharpest knife in the drawer? No. And sure, maybe he's got some difficulties, but he's one of the good guys. His parents and grandparents both grew up here, so he's as local as they come. I've never seen him lose his temper. I don't think he's even capable of getting angry. So, if you're suggesting he killed my mum, I think you're barking up the wrong tree."

"I've met a lot of people over the years, and in my experience, Mr Young, everyone has their breaking point," Logan intoned. He slapped his hands on his thighs and smiled thinly. "Still, there's a first time for everything, I suppose."

He moved as if to stand, then stopped. "Sorry, one final quick thing. The pub that night, who else was there?"

"Just the usual, really," Isaac said. He rattled off a few names of locals, which Tyler scribbled down. "They were still there after I left. Would've been there until closing, I'm sure. They'll be able to tell you at the pub."

"Right. Thanks. Anyone else?"

"There was that tourist fella," Louise said, nudging Isaac with her arm. "In the corner."

"Oh. Aye. I told you about him. Mum was offering it up to him. Poor bastard. He left pretty soon after. Can't say I blame him. He looked mortified."

Logan felt a frown begin to form, but managed to put a stop to it. "How soon after?"

"Twenty minutes, maybe," Louise said. "I don't think anyone really noticed. When I went to get another round, he was gone. That was about twenty minutes after Iona left."

"So, he could've been gone for a while?"

The couple shrugged in near-perfect unison. "Suppose so," Isaac said.

"Could he have left at the same time as Iona?" Logan asked.

The headshake was immediate. "No. I kept watching the door for a few minutes after she'd gone," Isaac said. "Kept thinking she'd come staggering back in. Thankfully, she didn't. I think your man probably just left after he'd finished his drink."

"Aye, makes sense," Logan agreed. He stood suddenly and jabbed a thumb in the direction of the kitchen. "Now, away you go before your tea's ruined."

Louise got up first, making room for Isaac to stand, too. "Thanks," he said. "If there's anything else, just ask."

Behind Logan, DC Neish flipped his notebook closed and got to his feet. Both detectives looked from Isaac to Louise and back again.

"We know where to find you," Logan said, and the words sounded less of a statement and more of a threat.

After a quick glance around the room, Logan shoved his hands in his pockets. "We'll see ourselves out," he said, then he turned on his heels and marched for the door, with Tyler hurrying along behind him.

CHAPTER TWENTY-SIX

"Kevin about?" Logan asked, as he and Tyler came trudging through into the lounge of the B&B. Norman was sitting by the window, gazing out at a sunset of pinks and oranges, lined with stringy strands of black and grey cloud.

"Hmm? Oh, sorry. Miles away," Norman said, jumping to his feet. "Stunning, isn't it? Never get tired of it." He shook his head and smiled. "Sorry. What did you say?"

"Kevin. From the other room," Logan said. His eyes went to the ceiling for added emphasis. "He around, do you know?"

"Uh, presumably, yes," Norman said. "I saw him earlier, but I'd imagine he's upstairs. Why? I mean, not that it's any of my..." He shook his head again. "Sorry. Want me to get him for you?"

"No, it's fine," Logan said. He gave Tyler the nod, and the younger detective retreated out of the room. His footsteps went thudding up the stairs as Norman continued the conversation.

"Have you eaten?" he asked.

"Eh, not in a while actually, no," Logan admitted.

"Pat did a steak pie. There's some left. Can I tempt you?"

Logan's stomach answered for him, and Norman laughed.

"I'll take that as a 'yes,' shall I?"

"I wouldn't say no. Thank you. But, what about bawchops?" Logan asked, pointing with a thumb to the ceiling. "DC Neish, I mean. There enough for him, too?"

Norman leaned in closer and put the back of his hand to his mouth, like he was revealing some big secret. "There's enough for the whole island, and half of bloody Skye!" he chuckled. "Pat cooks when she's anxious. It's her thing. And, well, I suppose all this murder business has got her wound up."

The footsteps came clumping down the stairs again. Logan turned to the door just as Tyler appeared from the hallway. "No answer, boss. Doesn't sound like he's in."

Logan faced Norman again. "Dinner would be lovely. Thank you. But before that... I don't suppose you've got a spare key to Mr Tillerson's room?"

Norman's face paled. "Argh. No, actually."

"No?" asked Logan. "You don't have a spare key to one of the rooms in your own house?"

"We had a couple in last week. They went away with it. Supposed to be posting it back, but with the ferries being off..." Norman smiled apologetically. "Kevin has the spare."

Damn. That wasn't ideal. It would've been good to get a poke around in Tillerson's room, but all Logan had at the moment was some contradiction. Tillerson had said Isaac and Louise left early, and they'd said the opposite. Conflicting accounts by two parties who'd been drinking alcohol. Easy to lose track of time. Easy to get mixed up.

Probably nothing. Not worth putting the door in for, anyway.

He wanted another chat with Mr Tillerson, but it could wait. Right now, there was more pressing business to attend to.

"Right then, Norman," Logan said. "About that steak pie..."

Pat had dished them up their dinner at the same table where they'd eaten their breakfast earlier in the day. The plates had come out practically groaning under the weight of the scoff piled on top.

As well as the steak pie (with extra pastry) there were boiled tatties, roasties, carrots, and parsnips. There were also a couple of pieces of broccoli, which Logan immediately scraped to the side of the plate so they didn't contaminate the rest of the meal.

"Bloody hell. This is going above and beyond," Logan had told her.

She'd smiled, a little embarrassed, and admitted that she'd made far too much, although she didn't directly mention the 'stress-cooking' thing that Norman had alluded to.

Once she was sure the detectives had everything they needed, Pat left them to it, before popping back in to tell them to leave room for dessert.

"Homemade banoffee pie. Best you've ever tasted," she promised.

The first five minutes of the meal were spent in silence, other than the scraping of cutlery on plates, and the occasional expletive of enjoyment. Pat made an excellent steak pie, they agreed. It was so good, in fact, that Logan was even prepared to overlook the broccoli, which was just about the highest praise he could offer.

It was only when the worst of their hunger pangs were satisfied that the detectives moved on to discussing the day's developments.

Bruce Anderson was the big headline, of course. They still had an hour and a half before the internet cut off for the night, so time yet to follow up with Hamza on that. The worst of the weather had passed, so hopefully they'd get news about support arriving, too. That would make life easier.

They both agreed that the Reverend Abraham Kerr was a certifiable head-case, and that he seemed perfectly capable of committing murder. Assuming God tipped him the wink and okayed it.

Did they think he'd done it, though? There was no physical evidence to tie him to the scene—although, there was no physical evidence to tie anyone else to the scene, either—and Logan was still convinced that, had the minister killed his daughter, he'd have taken some perverse pleasure in owning up to it.

The son and his partner? There was clearly little love lost there, particularly on Louise's part. Still, it was a stretch to imagine they'd killed her. They agreed that they couldn't see Louise losing any sleep over her future mother-in-law's demise, though.

And there was that inconsistency between the accounts of who'd left when. That was something they were going to have to get to the bottom of, Logan had said, as he'd torn off a big chunk of puff pastry and dunked it in the pie's thick gravy.

It was around then that the conversation had taken an unexpected turn. Since they'd sat down, Tyler had been edging to say something, but had bottled it every time, until Logan eventually got fed up with waiting.

"Well? What is it?"

Tyler glanced up from his plate, where he was loading up his fork with a wee bit of everything.

"Boss?"

"You've clearly got something you're building up to saying. What?"

"Oh. No. It's, eh..." Tyler fished around inside his mouth with his tongue, then shook his head. "It's nothing, boss."

"Bollocks, it's nothing. What is it? Spit it out."

Tyler brought the fork to his mouth, and held it there, ready. "Isaac Young, boss."

"What about him?"

"How old would you say he was?"

"I don't know. Late twenties?" Logan guessed. "Why?"

"I wasn't sure either, boss," Tyler said. He still had the forkful of food poised next to his mouth, ready to cram in. "That's why I asked to get a look at his ID. Pin it down, sort of thing."

"Aye, what the fuck was all that about?" Logan demanded. "I meant to jar you about that when we left."

"Like I say, boss, wanted to get his age. Thought it'd be a bit weird if I'd just come out with it and asked him."

"Why'd you want his age?" Logan asked. "What's his age got to do with anything?"

"Nothing. I didn't really. Want to know his age. I mean, I did, but..." Tyler began. He shot a longing look at his fork, clearly wishing he hadn't started this, and had just stuck to stuffing his face, instead.

"What are you talking about? You said you wanted to know his age, now you don't. Make your mind up, Tyler."

"It was his date of birth," the DC blurted out.

Logan blinked in surprise.

"His date of birth?"

"You're right. He is late-twenties, boss," Tyler said. "He's twenty-nine, in fact. Pushing thirty."

Logan drew in a breath as if about to speak, but nothing came out.

"Born in August. Nineteen-ninety."

Tyler shovelled his food into his mouth then, filling it before he could say any more. As he chewed, he watched the range of expressions that played across the face of the man sitting opposite. They each flitted by quickly, like the individual pages of a flipbook. The resulting animation was one of slowly dawning horror.

Logan placed first his fork, then his knife on the table.

He clasped his hands in front of his mouth and stared directly through Detective Constable Neish like he wasn't there.

"Oh," he muttered. He bit down on his bottom lip, then spat it out again. "Fuck."

CHAPTER TWENTY-SEVEN

He'd thought the lad had looked familiar. He'd put it down to him looking like Iona, but what if that wasn't it? Isaac had Iona's eyes, but that was about the lot. The facial structure... The profile... Those could feasibly have been someone else's. They could easily have been...

"Christ Almighty," Logan mumbled.

This particular "Christ Almighty" was the fourth "Christ Almighty" that had passed his lips in the last ten minutes. It was also, aside from a brief, "Thanks," aimed at Pat as she'd cleared the plates and brought dessert, the only words he'd spoken during that time.

He shovelled a big spoonful of banoffee pie in his mouth, hoping the sugar rush would take the edge off everything else he was currently feeling.

It didn't.

His head spun. His stomach churned. His heart alternated between racing like a humming-bird's and stopping completely.

A son. *His* son.

No. It couldn't be. Could it?

It could. He knew it could. The dates matched. He and Iona had gotten together after the Halloween Disco. Then, just a shade under ten months later, she'd had a bouncing baby boy.

And, God, Tyler was right. There was a similarity. It hadn't been immediately obvious to Logan, and you really had to look for it, but... maybe. Aye. Maybe.

"Christ Almighty," he said, and a half-chewed lump of toffee-coated banana fell from his mouth and went *thump* on the tabletop.

Tyler was already scraping the last few remnants of the pie's biscuit base off his plate. While Logan had been spending half his time staring blankly at the wall, shaking his head, and *Christ Almightying* over and over, Tyler had devoted all his attention to eating.

He felt it was best not to get involved in the DCI's mini-meltdown any more than he already was, and stuffing his mouth with dessert was the best way he could think of to keep it from saying anything stupid.

A glance at his watch told him he had no choice but to speak up now, though. He dabbed at the corners of his mouth with the napkin Pat had set out for him, wiped his hands on it, then set it down on the table.

"If we're calling back to base, we'd better get a shift on, boss," he said. "Internet's going to go off shortly."

"Hmm?" Logan stared uncomprehendingly at him for several long seconds, like the DC had just said something in Mandarin Chinese.

From another room, the cuckoo called nine. This seemed to kick Logan's brain back into gear, allowing Tyler's words to filter through. Blinking, Logan set his fork down on his plate, and wiped his mouth on the back of his hand. "Shite. Aye."

He stood up, the legs of his chair scuffing across the laminate flooring. "Listen, do me a favour, will you?" he said. "Not a word of this to the others. Not yet. Not until I know for sure."

If Hoon found out, he'd be off the case before he could say *conflict of interest*. And maybe that was right. Maybe that was all well and good. But he wanted to find Iona's killer. He owed her that much.

Now, more than ever.

"Of course, boss. Mum's the word," Tyler said. A smirk played at the corner of his mouth. "Or dad's the word, in this case."

The force of Logan's look almost pushed the Detective Constable backwards out of his chair. He cleared his throat, the smile falling away. "Sorry, boss," he said. "Too soon?"

THEY WERE at the bottom step when the doorbell rang. The door opened immediately, and Joy Bryden was ushered in by a sudden gust of wind that billowed the net curtain on the little hall window.

There was a brief flash of surprise when she saw both men standing at the bottom of the stairs, but then it was gone. To show surprise was to show weakness, Logan thought. At least, he guessed that's how the head of the Community Council would see it.

"Detectives," she said. "Just who I was looking for."

"Hello?" said Norman, appearing from the lounge. His eyes were ringed with red, and he had the look of someone who'd just been woken up from a very deep, very enjoyable snooze.

When he spotted Joy he stiffened, practically standing to attention. His eyes, now wide and alert, tried to peer backwards through his own head in the direction of the kitchen.

"Patricia!" he called, and there was a hint of alarm in it. "We've got a visitor!"

The way he said 'we've got a visitor' made Logan think that this was some sort of pre-arranged safe word, or warning. It was delivered in the same sort of tone as a sailor who'd just found a dirty great hole in their boat might sound a red alert.

Pat, sensibly enough, didn't answer. Joy waved Norman away before he could offer any words of welcome. Or possibly mutter any banishing curses.

"I'm not here to see you. I'm just here to show the officers this," Joy said. She thrust an iPad into Logan's hands and gave the power button a prod. "I was looking through the webcam footage, like you said. The night Iona..."

She turned to Norman, her face folding into a particularly sour look. "Do you mind, Norman? This is police business."

"Oh!" Norman said. "Right. Sorry. Yes."

He turned to his left, almost walked into the wall, then turned all the way around to the right until he was facing the kitchen. "I'll just... Right."

Joy waited for him to scurry off, rolled her eyes at Logan as if expressing some shared pain, and turned her attention back to the screen. "I looked through Tuesday's footage. There's not a lot. I mean, there's hours, obviously, but there's not a lot actually happens."

Given the nature of life on the island, this did not come as a surprise to either detective.

"I can send you it all, but this bit... I thought you'd want to see," Joy continued.

She leaned in so her head was briefly blocking Logan's view of the screen, then tapped the little triangle in the middle of an otherwise black rectangle.

It took a moment for the image to appear. When it did, it was immediately obvious what they were looking at. Most of the screen was still in darkness, with a few blobs of shapeless light dotted here and there.

"It's a bit blurry to start with," Joy said. "Give it a sec."

They gave it a sec. Sure enough, the blobs of colour and expanses of darkness sharpened to form a view of the island's main street, looking down from by the shop, past the pub, and out across the water to Rum.

The water was a gently undulating carpet of black, with the occasional waves cresting as white horses here and there.

"What am I looking at?" Logan asked.

Joy tutted. "Well, give it a minute," she said in a conspiratorial whisper.

They gave it a minute. Or rather, half of one.

"There. See?" said Joy, her finger pouncing on a sudden movement on the screen. A woman in a tight dress stumbled across the street from right to left, in and out of shot. It was hard to make out her face in much detail, but there was enough light to make a positive ID.

"That's Iona," Logan said. Judging by the direction she'd staggered, she was heading towards the pub. "When was this from? Earlier in the night?"

"No. Later. Shh," Joy said. "Watch."

Logan watched. He hadn't stopped watching, in fact, since Joy had started the footage playing, but now no force on Earth could tear his eyes away from it.

Behind him, standing on the first step of the staircase, Tyler craned his neck to see the screen, too.

There was no sound, so when Iona appeared on screen from the left again, it came as a surprise. What came next was an even bigger one.

Iona was not alone. She was hanging off the arm of someone else. A man. The angle they were walking meant his face was hidden from the camera, but that didn't matter. Logan recognised the orange cagoule immediately.

Slowly, solemnly, Logan's eyes crept to the ceiling.

"DC Neish?" he said.

"Yes, boss?"

"Go and apologise to Pat and Norman, will you?"

Tyler frowned. "What for?"

"We're about to kick one of their bedroom doors down."

CHAPTER TWENTY-EIGHT

The door to Kevin Tillerson's room was flimsy enough that one good dunt from Logan's shoulder did the trick. The DCI had been expecting more resistance, and swore loudly as he went freewheeling into the room, then almost broke his neck when he tripped over a rucksack.

"Everything alright?" called Pat from the bottom of the stairs.

She and Norman had assembled there after Tyler had told them the plan. Neither of them had looked particularly pleased at the thought of the door being forced open, but neither had voiced any strong objections, particularly once Logan had assured them that Police Scotland would cover the cost of the damage.

He didn't tell them it might very well take months to come through, of course. Some things, they were better off not knowing.

Joy had suggested she should probably stay, too, but Logan had sent her packing so she could email over the footage of Tillerson and Iona before the internet went down for the night.

He had hoped he could get her to keep the signal active after the usual ten o'clock shut-off, but she'd explained it was on a set schedule, and overriding it was a lengthy process involving calls to an IT support desk somewhere in India that she'd have to dig out the phone number for.

The room Logan now stood in didn't feel like it belonged with the rest of the house. There was no dated wallpaper, no horrible curtains with ancient, sagging pelmets. No chipped old furniture, or cracked switches.

There was just a lovely big bed with a driftwood frame, an ultra-thin wall-mounted TV, and a couple of nice scenic photographs to break up the crisp whiteness of the walls. The reason it felt like it didn't belong in the house was because this room, unlike the others, was genuinely nice.

"Modernised in here, alright. Eh, boss?" asked Tyler. He was standing out on the upstairs landing to reduce the risk of compromising any evidence that might be lying around.

"Yes, we couldn't put up with it anymore," called Pat from the bottom of the stairs. "Please don't say anything."

"Your secret's safe with us," Tyler assured her, as Logan poked around in Tillerson's room.

Aside from the rucksack, which had been sat by the door, there wasn't a lot in the room that looked like it might belong to the guest. The built-in wardrobe was empty. The bedside table had nothing sitting on it.

There was a toothbrush and toothpaste in the small en-suite, both sitting on the sink. Remove those, though, and there was very little sign that the room was actually in use. Even the bed had been meticulously made-up. It didn't look like anyone had so much as sat on it all day.

"Bag packed by the door, ready to leave in a hurry," Logan remarked. Squatting down, he pulled on a pair of blue vinyl gloves and had a rummage around in the bag's many compartments.

What was he looking for? He wasn't entirely sure. He didn't find it, though, whatever it was. All he found were a compass, map, and some camping cooking gear, a small multi-tool, a battered old pair of trainers, and a pile of neatly-folded clothes which, by the smell of them, had been recently laundered.

He vaguely recalled hearing the washing machine going when they'd been eating breakfast that morning. If Tillerson's clothes had all been washed and put through the tumble dryer, it almost certainly put the kybosh on getting any forensic evidence from them.

At the bottom of one of the side-compartments was a small hard-backed notebook. Logan didn't expect to find anything exciting written within, but was taken aback by just how right he was.

A good thirty or more pages of the notebook were full of detailed notes on what Logan guessed must be real ales and craft beers from across the UK. Each page was filled with phrases like 'hoppy and rich' or 'smooth, with bitter notes,' all written in the same fastidiously neat handwriting.

"Jesus Christ," Logan muttered.

"Got something, boss?" asked Tyler, leaning into the room.

"No. Just... Jesus Christ, he's a boring bastard," Logan said, returning the book to the bag, and zipping the pocket closed.

It was in the final section that he found something of interest. It was a small roll of cash, tucked into a Velcro pocket inside the main part of the bag. All twenties. All identical, aside from the serial numbers. Logan counted out eight notes—a hundred and sixty quid—then turned on his haunches and pointed to Tyler.

"Time?"

Tyler appeared momentarily confused, then checked his watch. "Shite. Nearly ten, boss."

"Phone Hamza."

"WhatsApp," Tyler said, before he could stop himself.

"Whatever! Just fucking get him. I need to know, the money found on Iona Wallace, what bank was it from?"

Tyler tapped Hamza's picture in the app, then touched the phone icon. He glanced at his watch again while he waited for the other DC to pick up.

"Cutting it fine," he said, dancing from foot to foot. "Come on, come on, come—" He stopped dancing. "Hamza? Aye. No. Shut up. Boss needs to know something."

He relayed Logan's question, and both detectives listened to the frantic tapping of keyboard keys coming over the speakerphone.

Hamza's voice, when it came, was a rushed garble that crackled from the handset on a cushion of static.

"Bank of England. Why?"

Logan looked down at the notes in his hand. All twenties. All issued by the Bank of England.

"Kevin Tillerson," Logan said, practically shouting the words at Tyler's phone. "Look him up, get me what you can on..."

The phone gave a *bleep* as the internet connection went off. The cuckoo called from down the stairs.

Logan cursed below his breath. Then he cursed again, but louder. Finally, he stood and pointed past Tyler at the staircase beyond.

"Get down there. Use the landline, phone the office and tell Hamza to get digging."

"Getting late, boss," Tyler pointed out. "Imagine they'll be knocking off soon, if they've been in all day."

"Well, have him give it to someone else, then. Jesus, do I have to think of everything?" Logan spat. "I want a full report on the bastard in my inbox for when the internet comes back on tomorrow morning. Got that?"

"Got it, boss," Tyler said.

Logan waited for him to move. When it was clear he wasn't going to, the DCI ushered him along with a wave of his arms. "Well, go on, then!"

While Tyler hurried down the stairs and asked Pat and Norman if he could use their phone, Logan took an evidence bag from his pocket and placed the money inside.

Then, after a moment's thought, he removed two of the notes, and placed those in another of the transparent bags.

He didn't have a bag big enough for Tillerson's rucksack, so he carried it carefully through to his and Tyler's room, and placed it out of sight between the beds.

That done, he shoved both the bundles of bagged money in his coat pocket and left the bedroom, locking the door behind him.

Logan was standing by the big window in the lounge when Tyler returned. The DCI acknowledged him with a nod, then went back to staring out at the water, and the sparse lights of Rum.

The rain had stopped, the wind had all but died away, and the sense of calm beyond the window was not one reflected within Logan himself.

"Hamza's going to find out what he can tonight, then get back in sharp in the morning," Tyler announced. "He did a quick search on HOLMES while I was on the phone. Nothing coming up on Tillerson, but it's not always the most up-to-date."

Logan felt a twinge of disappointment. A nice juicy history of violence would've been handy when it came to the interview, although he wasn't entirely surprised. Tillerson hadn't struck him as violent. Certainly not as a killer.

But appearances, as he had learned the hard way, could be deceiving.

"Also, something that might be of interest, boss. Ham went through Iona's social media. Apparently, she'd been ripping into that Dudley fella—the big lad—for the past few weeks. Nothing too major, but lots of little digs about him. Pictures of Mr Potato Head with his face Photoshopped on. Petty stuff, but not nice. Quite a lot of comments from folk on the posts saying they're out of order, but she seemed to enjoy the attention."

"Worth a word with him, then," Logan said. "Between that and the argument at the pub, he'd have motive."

"Deffo, boss," Tyler agreed. He shifted uncomfortably, glanced at the door as if contemplating making a run for it, then steeled himself. "Hamza. I, eh... He's..."

The rest of the sentence died away like the wind outside.

"He's what?" Logan asked, meeting the DC's reflected gaze in the window.

"I thought—and I hope you don't mind, boss—but I got him to look into Isaac Young, too. Didn't tell him why, obviously, just thought it'd be good to have a bit more background. For, you know, for you to have a bit more background."

Logan wanted to be furious at Tyler's interference. Annoyed, at least. Something. Instead, he just nodded, and pointed his gaze back out over the water again.

"Pretty mental stuff, boss," Tyler remarked. He closed the lounge door, so Pat and Norman wouldn't hear. "Your head must be spinning."

"Aye. No' half," Logan confirmed. "Mind you, we don't know that he's definitely... That we're... That he and I are..."

Logan aborted the sentence there and then. Technically, he didn't know. Technically, Isaac could've been someone else's son. Someone else's boy.

Realistically, though?

The timing fit. The face, too.

He exhaled through his nose, muttered another, "Christ Almighty," at his reflection, then went back to gazing out into the darkness.

The floorboards creaked as Tyler moved his weight from foot to foot, not quite sure what to do with himself, and even less sure of what to say.

Fortunately, Logan took it upon himself to do the talking.

"Always wanted a son. Back in the day. Aye, no' when I was fifteen. Later, I mean. When me and Vanessa got together."

Tyler lowered himself into one of the wingback chairs and listened as the DCI continued.

"We had Maddie, of course," Logan said. He was looking further than the lights of Rum now. Further, even than the mainland beyond. "And she was bloody marvellous, if I say so myself. Funny. Smart. Kind."

He tucked his hands behind his back, the fingers knotting together. It was the first time Tyler had seen the gaffer so ill-at-ease. He was used to Logan storming about, shouting his head off, or sitting quietly as a picture of calmness and control.

This, though? This was something new.

"I always thought kids made you vulnerable. Made you weak. And then, she came along. And, well... I realised that was a load of old bollocks." He let out a little snort. "I realised a lot of stuff that I used to believe was a load of old bollocks, in fact.

"I couldn't have loved her more. Couldn't have. Not possible," Logan continued. "But, I still wanted a son. Complete the set, sort of thing. You know? Like a Panini sticker album."

Both men smiled at that.

"Why didn't you?" Tyler ventured. The conversation was making him perhaps even more uncomfortable than Logan, but it felt like the DCI needed to off-load, and while Tyler very much doubted he'd be the boss's first choice, he was the only one around.

Logan looked deep into the eyes of his reflection in the window. When he spoke, his breath fogged the glass.

"Owen Petrie."

"Mister Whisper?" asked Tyler. His forehead furrowed as he thought this through. "I don't get it, boss."

"Aye, you and me both, son," Logan said, so quietly Tyler almost didn't hear it. Logan gave himself a shake, then carried on, louder this time. "I wasn't much older than you when he was doing the rounds. When he started taking the kids. We didn't know then what he'd go on to do. What he'd become. He wasn't 'Mister Whisper'. No' then. No' yet. He was some random child-snatching bastard, and I was on the team that was meant to catch him."

"And you did," Tyler said. "You got him."

Logan grunted. "Aye. Eventually. Years later," he said. "Years of following up on leads, acting on hunches, knocking on doors. Chasing bloody shadows."

He swallowed. It sounded unnaturally loud in the near-silence.

"Consoling parents."

"Couldn't have been easy, boss."

Logan shook his head. "No. No, it was not," he admitted. "But the bastard became an obsession. All-consuming. Not a minute of the day went by when I wasn't going over and over it all."

Still facing the window, he pointed to the side of his head and slowly circled his finger around. "Sitting at dinner, tick-tick-tick. School prizegiving, tick-tick-tick. Bloody... marriage counselling. Tick-tick-tick. Tick-tick-tick. *Tick-tick-tick*. Over and over. Non-stop. Only way I could stop it was through the drink."

Logan sniffed and rocked back on his heels. His voice, when it came, was an admirable attempt at sounding nonchalant. "She kicked me out in the end. Vanessa, I mean. My wife. Ex-wife. Don't blame her. The drinking was out of hand." He ground his back teeth together, clenching and unclenching the muscles in his jaw. "*I* was out of hand."

Neither man said anything for a while after that. Elsewhere in the house, the cuckoo clock called eleven.

"Still. Least you got him in the end, boss. At least you stopped him."

"But for what? So he can sit in a hospital, staring out the window? Cushy wee number that, given what he did."

"He's brain-damaged, isn't he? After the..." Tyler's hesitation was brief, but did not go unnoticed by the DCI. "...accident. After he fell."

A tension knotted the muscles in Logan's shoulders and stiffened his neck.

"Aye."

He thought back to all the silent phone calls over the past few weeks.

And all the whispered ones.

"Maybe."

And then, the spell was broken when a bright orange shape passed the window, waving at Logan as it came striding up the path.

The detective turned from the window just as the house's front door opened. The wistful, far-away look that had temporarily set up camp on his face was gone. In its place was a much more familiar grimace of grim determination, that immediately set Tyler more at ease.

"Talk about timing," he said, charging for the lounge door before the DC could scramble up out of the wingback. "I'm just in the mood to ruin some bastard's night."

CHAPTER TWENTY-NINE

The dining room of the B&B stood in for the interview room of a police station. Tyler and Logan sat on one side, while Kevin Tillerson sat across from them.

Between them, a caddy of tomato sauce and other condiments sat ready for breakfast service in the morning. There had been cutlery set out, too, but Tyler had moved it all out of grabbing distance before he'd sat down.

Whose grabbing distance he was moving it out of, he wasn't entirely sure. There was always a chance that Tillerson would try something stupid, but Tyler reckoned the safe money was probably on Logan.

"Everything alright?" Tillerson asked, still wrestling himself out of his waterproof jacket.

He looked concerned. Not curious, like someone who had no idea what this was all about, but worried, like someone who did. And who knew what was almost certainly coming next.

"Just got a few questions, Mr Tillerson," Logan said.

"Kevin, please," Tillerson said, smiling so desperately it made Logan's stomach churn.

"Kevin. Right. We've just got a few questions. Some things we're hoping you can help us clear up."

"Of course. No problem."

"I warn you, this interview is being recorded."

Logan paused momentarily, a silent signal for Tyler to take out his phone.

"For quality and training purposes?" Tillerson blurted, then he let out a panicky breathless cackle at his own joke, before momentarily looking like he might be about to burst into tears.

"Something like that," Logan said. "You're not under arrest, but if we decide to move to arrest, anything you say may be used in evidence against you in court. Is that clear?"

Tillerson nodded. He started to speak, but his voice became an unintelligible croak. He swallowed, inhaled slowly, then tried again.

"Should I have a solicitor?"

"That's up to you, Kevin. Although, obviously, that'll drag things out for you," Logan said. "My suggestion? Just answer honestly, we'll clear this whole thing up, and it'll never need to get to that stage. We're sure there's just been a misunderstanding. Aren't we, Detective Constable?"

"We're pretty confident, boss, aye."

Logan raised his eyebrows, waiting for a response from Tillerson. Despite having shed his big jacket, Kevin was sweating profusely. When he nodded his head, a drop fell from his forehead and onto the table. He wiped it away with the sleeve of his fleece, then clasped his hands in an obvious attempt to stop himself fidgeting.

"Right. Yes. Let's get it sorted," he croaked.

Logan clasped his own hands and leaned forward, mirroring Tillerson's body language. "On the night Iona Wallace died, you said her son and daughter-in-law left soon after her. Is that right?"

"I, uh, yes. I think so. I'm pretty sure they did."

"Pretty sure? How sure?" Logan asked.

Tillerson's face became an exaggerated picture of concentration. It gave him a cartoonish appearance, like his face was made of living rubber.

"Um. Let me think..." he said. "Maybe... fifty percent?"

"Fifty percent?" Logan repeated.

"Maybe. Yes. Thereabouts."

"Fifty percent isn't 'pretty sure,' Kevin. Fifty percent is, 'I don't have a clue.'"

"Is it?" Tillerson asked. "Uh. Sixty, then? Sixty. Yes. About sixty, I'd say. I can't be certain."

"You can't even be 'fairly confident' at sixty percent, Kevin," Logan countered. "That's a vague hunch, at best. Would you agree, Detective Constable?"

"That's barely an inkling, boss," Tyler said, neither detective taking their eyes off the other man.

"We spoke to the couple themselves, Kevin. They say they were in there much longer. They say they had a few drinks after Iona left."

Tillerson exhaled with relief. "Right. Well, my mistake then," he said, clearly under the impression that the contradictory statements were the reason for the interview. "Sorry. I wasn't paying too much attention. If they say they didn't, then they didn't. That's that. Apologies for the misinformation. Hopefully, no harm done."

Logan smiled and tapped both hands on the table, one after the other. "Well, glad we got all that cleared up. Thanks for your time, Kevin."

"No problem! And, again, sorry for any confusion caused."

"These things happen," Logan said. He began to move as if he was about to stand up, then stopped. "Oh. Just one other thing."

"Yes?" asked Tillerson. He was beaming from ear to ear now, believing he was safely through the worst of it.

For a moment, Logan almost felt sorry for him.

It didn't last.

"Do you mind telling us what you were doing with Iona outside the pub shortly before she was murdered?"

Tillerson's face froze. Every line. Every crease. Every atom of it became rigidly fixed in place. His body, too. Not a part of him moved. It was like all his life-force had been diverted to the panic centres of his brain in an attempt to come up with an answer. An explanation. An excuse.

He failed. Dismally.

"Hmm?" he cheeped.

"Shortly before ten on Tuesday evening, you were seen crossing the street away from the pub with Iona Wallace," Logan said.

"*With*?" Tillerson said. "I don't... I can't... *With*? I did leave the pub around then, but, but, if she was there at the time, then it was coincidence. That's all. I wasn't *with* her. We may have just been, just been, just been... We weren't together. Is my point. If she was even..."

"She was hanging onto your arm, Kevin," Logan said. "Draped from it, some might say."

"I'd say 'draped,' boss," Tyler chipped in.

Tillerson's head tick-tocked between them. "How did...? I don't..."

"When I said you were seen, I didn't mean by a witness, Kevin. I meant by the webcam," Logan said. He is voice lightened, becoming chatty. "Did you know there was a webcam? Looks along the street from up the hill, out over Rum to the mainland. It's nice. Nice view. And, well, the thing is, Kevin, they back-up all the footage. It all gets saved. Boats coming in. The weather changing. People coming and going."

Kevin sat in a stunned, anxious silence. His brain was working overtime, trying to formulate a plan. Trying to work out what to say and how to say it, to make it all stop and go away.

He'd realise he should have his solicitor with him soon, Logan suspected, and so he pressed on before the thought had a chance to form in Tillerson's head.

"So, going by the footage, Iona walked in the direction of the pub at around nine fifty-three, visibly intoxicated. Roughly a minute later, she crossed the street in the opposite direction. With you, Kevin. Not at the same time as you. Not near you. *With* you. *With*."

Logan's tone became markedly more serious again. "Now, does that, or does that not contradict your earlier statement?"

Tillerson swallowed several times, like he was fighting not to drown in his own saliva. "I, uh... Yes. Yes, it does," he admitted, having no other routes available to him. "I didn't kill her," he blurted. "I didn't. I swear. I swear to God."

"I'll be honest, Kevin. From where I'm sitting? It looks very much like you did," Logan said. "How about from where you're sitting, Detective Constable?"

"View's much the same from this seat, boss," Tyler replied. "And it's not looking good for Mr Tillerson here."

"Kevin," Logan said.

"Oh. Aye. *Kevin*," Tyler corrected, and the way he said it made it sound like a particularly nasty insult.

"So, if you've got another explanation—one that doesn't involve you raping and murdering Iona Wallace—now would be a good time to let us hear it," Logan suggested.

Across the table, Tillerson's eyes filled with tears. He seemed to be shrinking before their eyes, his shoulders sagging, his back stooping until it was only his forearms on the table holding him up.

"We... We had sex," he said. The words were a shameful whisper, sobbed more than spoken. "But I didn't rape her. I didn't. She... She invited me. Everyone in the pub heard. And they heard me say 'no!' I did! I said I wasn't interested, and... and... I wasn't. I'm married. I have a wife!"

"What changed?" Logan asked.

"Oh, I..." Tillerson closed his eyes, taking a moment to compose himself. "I was going to come back here. I was only in the pub making plans for when I head to Skye. Checking maps. All that. When I was done, I left. I went outside."

His eyes welled up again. A tear broke through and was quickly lost in the sweat-sheen on his cheek. "And there she was. She'd been, I don't know, hanging around or wandering about, I suppose. She saw me, and she came over, and she... Well, she... Her hand, she put it down my... into my pants, and she... she... *manipulated* me. Down there."

Tyler side-eyed the DCI. "He saying she touched his cock, boss?"

"Aye. I think that's what he's saying," Logan confirmed. "Is that what you're saying, Kevin?"

"Yes! Yes. She... she touched my... down there," he said, his face reddening at the very thought of it. "And, well, I succumbed. I'd had a couple of drinks. She told me we could go back to her place, and..."

He buried his head in his hands, his shoulders heaving with big, breathless sobs. "Oh, God. Oh, God, I knew I shouldn't have. I knew it was wrong!"

He straightened, and when his face re-emerged it was a deep crimson, and slick with sweat, tears, and snot.

"But she was so... so *insistent*. Kept telling me how good it would be. How much fun we'd have. And she wasn't unattractive, you understand? She wasn't half bad."

"I'm sure she'd be delighted by that review," Logan said. "So, she took you back to her house. What then?"

Tillerson shook his head. "No. We didn't go."

"I thought you said—"

"She invited me back, but we... we didn't make it. She said it was too far to walk, and so we went behind... the school, I think it was. It was dark, and she just... sort of... set about it. Doing it. She didn't mess around. We just got, I don't know, down to it, I suppose."

"Did you use any sort of protection?" Logan asked.

Tillerson looked away, chewed on his bottom lip, and shook his head.

"Right. So, to be clear, you're saying that you and Iona Wallace had unprotected sexual intercourse behind the school building on the night she died?"

Tillerson let out another involuntary sob. "Oh. God. When you say it like that... But, yes. Yes. We did. We did. But that was the last I saw of her. I swear. I *swear*. Once we were finished, she just sort of left."

"She left? Just like that? Without saying a word?" Logan asked. "Bit odd, that. Don't you think, Detective Constable?"

"Very unusual, boss," Tyler agreed.

Logan reached into his coat pocket. He produced the evidence bag containing two twenty pound notes and slid it into the centre of the table without a word.

Tillerson's eyes swivelled down and fixed on the money. He gritted his teeth, like he was fighting back the urge to start crying again.

"Take your time," Logan said.

Kevin continued to stare at the money on the table for a while, then tore his eyes from it and didn't look at it again for the rest of the interview. "She, uh, she remarked on my performance. Not positively. She was... quite cruel. Rather damning, really."

"And how did that make you feel, Kevin?" Logan asked, not unkindly.

"No more ashamed than I already felt. I just... Afterwards—right afterwards, I mean—I just wanted it over. I knew right away I'd made a mistake. That I shouldn't have done it. I was pulling up my trousers, and I felt sick. Properly sick, to my stomach. I just wanted her to go, to forget it ever happened, but she kept going at me. Laughing at me. Taunting me. Said it wasn't fair that I'd got something out of it, but that she hadn't."

"Did that make you angry?" Logan asked.

"Angry? No. Just... Humiliated. I tried to leave, but she followed. Kept asking what was in it for her? Kept going on about how I'd 'got my jollies,' but she hadn't. And that's when I realised."

"When you realised what?"

"Money. That was what she wanted. Money," Tillerson said, his voice little more than a whisper. "That was what she was really after. I had forty pounds in my wallet. I offered her twenty."

"Twenty?" said Tyler. "Christ, he drives a hard bargain, eh, boss?"

"She got angry. She did, not me. Demanded all of it. Said she'd tell everyone what had happened. Told me she'd make sure it got back to my family. Blackmailed me," Tillerson continued. "So, I gave it to her. I let her take it. Just to shut her up. Just to make it all stop. I gave her all of it."

"All forty quid," Logan said. "Very big of you."

"It wasn't a... a... *transaction*," Tillerson protested. "At least, I didn't think so when it... When we started. If I'd known she was a prostitute, I wouldn't have gone near her!"

For reasons Logan couldn't quite put his finger on, his heart skipped a beat.

"She wasn't a prostitute," he said.

Tillerson let out a little cheep of nervous laughter. "Well, she certainly seemed like one, from where I was standing."

"And where was that? With your pants around your ankles and your cock hanging out?" Logan asked.

His tone was a dangerous one. The knuckles of his clasped fingers had turned almost all the way white. Tyler spotted this, and stole a quick glance at the neighbouring table, making sure he'd moved the cutlery far enough out of grabbing range.

"So, what happened then?" the DC asked, taking the wheel while Logan wrestled his temper back under control. "You paid her the forty quid. Then what?"

"Then she left. She stuffed it in her... Down her cleavage, and she left. Said, 'Cheers,' winked at me, then left," Tillerson said. "That was it. That was the last I saw of her. I came back here. Got back before eleven."

"And Pat and Norman can vouch for that?" Tyler asked.

"Yes. Well, Norman. I didn't see Pat, but Norman was up. He was watching television. Newsnight, I think. We chatted for a while, then I went to bed. Well, I had a shower."

"What did you talk about?" Logan asked.

Tillerson puffed out his cheeks, drawing a blank. "I'm not sure. Nothing. The weather. Ferries. Nothing substantial."

"You didn't tell him about Iona?"

"Of course not!" Tillerson cried. "I'm hardly going to mention that, am I? 'How was your night?' 'Oh, not bad. Just fucked a local prozzie round the back of the school. How has your evening been?'"

He winced, taken aback by his own tone, and sat back, wrapping his arms across his chest. "Sorry. Sorry, that was... Sorry. It's just... God, if my wife finds out. My kids."

"I'd say that's the least of your worries right now, Kevin, wouldn't you?" Logan said. "Your DNA has been found on the body of a murder victim. You've admitted to having sexual intercourse with her, and to then being coerced into paying her for the pleasure. We've got camera footage showing you together shortly before she died. At this stage, we've been unable to identify anyone else who saw or was in contact with Iona after you were seen with her... Do you see what I'm getting at here?"

Tillerson's face had been turning paler and paler while Logan laid out the situation as he saw it. By the time the DCI was finished, Kevin looked like a literal ghost of his former self.

"I didn't kill her. I didn't," he whispered.

Logan leaned back in his chair and was about to reply when his phone rang. It was so unexpected, so out of the blue, that all three men sat exchanging looks of confusion, before Logan realised what was going on.

Reaching into his pocket, he pulled out the handset. The triangle of signal at the top showed one tiny bar tucked into the far-left corner.

Logan didn't notice this. Nor did he notice the notification at the top telling him he had new text messages.

All he saw were the green and red phone icons wobbling on the main part of the screen, and the text above it.

Unknown Number.

"Excuse me," he said, snatching up the phone and getting up from the table.

He was out in the hall before he thumbed the green button and pressed the phone to his ear.

"Hello?"

There was no reply.

"Hello? Who is this?"

Nothing.

Taking the phone from his ear, Logan checked the screen. The single bar was still holding steady. The seconds on the call timer ticked up, suggesting everything was still connected.

"Petrie?" Logan hissed.

There was a sound—a snigger—soft and muffled down the line. It was followed by a *beep*.

When Logan checked the screen again, the signal triangle was empty. The line was dead.

"Everything alright, boss?"

The sudden appearance of Tyler behind him made Logan jump.

"Shite. What? Aye. Aye, fine," he said. "Fine."

Tyler looked back over his shoulder into the kitchen. "Want to get back to it?"

Logan was still staring at his phone, like he might be able to force it to reconnect through sheer force of will.

"Boss?"

"Eh, no. No. Let's turn him loose for now," Logan said. "Not like he can go far. We should have Uniform coming in tomorrow. We can start back on him again then."

"Oh. Aye. About that," Tyler said. "Hoon's been a bit tight with resources."

"How tight?" Logan asked. "How many are we getting?"

"How many Uniforms?"

"What else would I be talking about? Aye. How many Uniforms?"

Tyler's lips moved silently, like he was doing some complex mathematical calculation in his head.

"One, boss."

The bottom half of Logan's face remained completely impassive, almost like he hadn't heard the reply. His top half, though, from the forehead down to the bridge of his nose, made his displeasure very clear.

"One?" he said.

"Aye."

"One? Fucking... one? He's sending one Uniform as support?"

"The DI tried to get him to up it, by all accounts, but he wasn't having it," Tyler said. "Also, he told Hamza to tell me to tell you that if you don't phone him soon, he's going to... Well, I don't really want to repeat the words he used, boss, but it involves his foot and your... well... vagina."

"Aye. I can imagine," Logan said. He huffed out a big breath. "Fucking *one*. Do we know who we're getting?"

"Not yet. Guess we'll find out."

"One bloody Uniform," Logan muttered. Then, he shook his head, ran his hand down his face, and pointed into the kitchen. "Go tell him we're done for tonight, but we'll want to talk to him again in the morning. Then, go get some rest."

"Right, boss," said Tyler. "Fair enough. What about you?"

"I'm going to sit in the lounge and stare at some alcohol," Logan said. He caught the concerned look on Tyler's face, and arranged his mouth into something close to a smile. "I'll be fine. I'll be up soon."

Tyler nodded. "Right. If, eh, you want to talk, or whatever... About anything."

"Thanks," Logan said. He put a hand on the younger man's shoulder and drew himself up to his full, terrifying height. "But I absolutely will not."

CHAPTER THIRTY

The lounge was in darkness when Logan wandered through. He clicked on the light, drawing a gasp from Pat, who was curled up on the couch nursing a large glass of red wine. She was wearing a pair of button-up pyjamas, the top two buttons undone.

"Shite. Sorry," Logan said. "Didn't think anyone was here."

"It's fine. My fault. Guest lounge," said Pat, uncurling her legs and making a move to stand.

Logan stopped her with a wave of his hand. "It's fine. Don't be daft. It's your house."

"Thanks," said Pat, smiling. She reached over and tapped an ugly lamp on the table beside her. The light activated at her touch. "Stick the big light off, then, will you? If you don't mind, I mean?"

As Pat moved, Logan caught a glimpse of a bruise where her shoulder met her neck. It was a pungent sort of blue, yellowing around the edges.

"What happened to your neck?" he asked, with typical levels of polis tact.

"Hmm? Oh, nothing, nothing," Pat said, adjusting her pyjama top to cover the mark. "Slipped in the shower, that's all."

Logan nodded, but he wasn't buying it. He thought of Norman. Older. Stronger. He didn't seem the type, necessarily, but then they often didn't.

"You sure?" Logan pressed.

Pat mustered a smile. It was a sparse, paltry thing, and the sadness in her eyes betrayed the emptiness of it. "I'm sure," she said. "Promise."

She wasn't going to talk about it. Maybe later, but not right now. Not to him. Logan switched off the overhead light, and the stark brightness darkened to a dim, comforting glow.

"That's better. Hate that big light," Pat said, relaxing a little in the gloom.

From elsewhere in the house, the cuckoo began to call twelve. Pat's lips thinned until they showed her teeth.

"Not as much as I hate that bloody clock, mind you," she said, then she washed the words down with a swig from her wine glass.

"Thought you said you'd stopped hearing it?" Logan asked, taking a seat in one of the uncomfortable wingbacks.

Pat snorted. "Yeah. That may have been a fib."

She reached down the side of the couch, and there was a clinking of glass. Lifting a bottle, Pat gave it a shake, found it empty, then returned it and pulled out another. This one still had half the contents left in it. She sloshed it around, then offered it across to the DCI.

"Sorry. Manners. Wine?"

"I'm fine, thanks," Logan said. "Never really been a wine drinker."

That wasn't quite true, of course. It had never been his drink of choice, but by God, he'd put his fair share away over the years.

"There's other stuff. Gin? Think there's some lager in the fridge. Belgian stuff in little bottles. I could get you a couple of those, if you like?"

Logan gave a polite but firm shake of his head. "I'm fine. Thank you."

"You don't mind if I do, do you?" Pat asked, refilling her glass with an unsteady hand.

"Not at all," Logan said. He turned to the window, partly to admire the night-time view, but mostly to limit his exposure to the smell of the wine. It was cheap stuff. Supermarket own-brand. High alcohol content, low class.

Just his vintage.

"Quite a view you've got," he remarked.

Pat finished filling her glass, deposited the bottle on the floor beside her, then shrugged. "Suppose. It's like anything though, I suppose."

Logan turned back to her and raised an inquisitive eyebrow.

"The novelty soon wears off," Pat clarified. "Especially when the weather turns and you're stuck here."

"Aye. I'd imagine that takes some of the shine off it, right enough," Logan said.

"Eighteen months we've been here. Shine wore off about a fortnight in. And then you've got Joy, with her beady eyes everywhere. That bitch sees bloody everything. Christ knows how. I swear the woman's bloody omniscient."

She swirled the wine around in her glass, stared at her reflection in the darkened window for a moment, then blinked as if coming out of a trance. "Sorry. Just moaning. Pretend you didn't hear all that. It's a lovely place. Really."

"Just no' your cup of tea?" Logan asked.

It took a long time for Pat to pick her words. "It's not what I hoped for. Put it that way." She drew in a big breath, then fixed Logan with an intense stare. "It's my own bloody fault, though. Me that pushed for it. Have you ever wanted something? *Really* wanted something, I mean, but then, once you get it, you realise the thing you wanted isn't actually the thing you wanted at all?"

Logan replayed the sentence in his head. "Um, aye. Aye, I think so."

"Right! Well, it's like that, I suppose," Pat said. She pulled her legs up higher on the couch and motioned to the big window with her glass. "We were so excited. Before we came, I mean. New start. New adventure. And then, once we were here..." She smiled, but there was nothing but sadness in it. "The magic went. Poof. Gone. Just... gone."

Logan didn't really know what to say, so settled for keeping his mouth shut. Sensing his awkwardness, Pat drew her sleeve across her eyes, cleared her throat, and switched her tone for one much more decisive, if not exactly upbeat.

"I think we'll sell up, ultimately. That's the plan. Or, we'll try to. It's not easy getting people to move out here, but if we're lucky we'll find someone." She leaned in closer and whispered. "I haven't told Norman any of this yet, though. So, please keep it to yourself. He'll be bloody furious."

Logan nodded his understanding. "Well, best of luck, whatever you decide. And, if there's anything you want to tell me about Norman... Anything you want to talk about?"

Pat's hand slipped to her shoulder where the bruise was now hidden by her pyjamas. "Honestly, there's nothing. I promise. Just an accident. Norman is many things, but he isn't violent."

"Right. Well, I'm very glad to hear it," Logan said. He checked his watch, groaned quietly at the time, then stood up.

"You off to bed?" Pat asked. She picked up the wine bottle again and tilted it towards the detective. "Sure I can't twist your arm? You look like you've got plenty on your mind. Might help."

"Trust me, it won't," Logan said. "But thank you for the offer."

"Was it him?" Pat asked, the words tumbling over each other in their rush to get out. "Kevin. Mr Tillerson. Room one. Was it him?"

She watched the detective closely, silently appraising his response. Or his lack of one. "If there's a murderer staying in this house, I should know."

Logan's answer, when it came, was an honest one. "I don't know. We're following up on a few different leads, and I'm afraid I can't say much more than that at this stage."

"He fucked her, didn't he?" Patricia spat, and the venom of it took them both by surprise. "Had sex with her, I mean. I overheard."

Logan skirted around the question completely. "He said he came back here before eleven on Tuesday. Do you know if that's right?"

"I don't know," Pat said. "I would've been in bed. Norman didn't mention anything, though."

"I'll ask him in the morning," Logan said.

He started to say his goodnights, but Pat wasn't finished yet.

"Probably shouldn't blame him too much. Kevin, I mean. For... You know. She had a reputation for it. Jumping on the tourists. 'Fresh meat,' she called them."

"Aye. Well. Takes two to tango, I suppose," Logan said.

Pat's eyes became two circles of surprise, then she gave a satisfied nod and raised her glass. "Exactly! That's what I say," she said, then she glugged down the rest of her glass and filled it from the bottle again.

Logan took that as his cue to leave. "Well, goodnight. I, uh, I hope it all works out."

"Thanks," said Pat. She raised a glass and winked. Co-ordinating both these actions required quite a lot of concentration. "You, too."

TYLER WAS SNORTING and grunting like a pig in heat by the time Logan made it up to bed, and the DCI knew immediately that there'd be no sleeping through it. Not yet, at least. Not until exhaustion came creeping over him sometime in the wee small hours.

Instead, he rummaged in the box they'd taken from Iona's house until he found the diary from nineteen-ninety.

From the year Isaac was born.

Kicking off his shoes, Logan settled himself on top of the bed, and switched on the bedside lamp.

Tyler hissed and groaned in his sleep, like a vampire getting a face full of tanning lamp.

Muttering to himself, Logan switched the light off, then got up and checked in his coat until he found the small pocket torch he carried.

That done, he settled down to read, bracing himself for what he might find out.

It was the tail end of February when Iona realised she was pregnant. The date—the twenty-third—was marked by a full page filled from top to bottom with the words, 'Oh shit,' over and over again, in handwriting that became increasingly deranged as it continued down the paper.

The twenty-fourth was more of the same.

The twenty-fifth and twenty-sixth formed a double-page spread. On these, Iona had written an elongated, upper case version of the word, 'fuck,' with the letter U repeated forty or fifty times. In the bottom corner, she'd drawn a picture of a pregnant woman—herself, presumably—hanged from a tree, with her tongue sticking out and crosses where her eyes should be.

The rest of the week was blank. So was most of the following month, and the month after that, too. In fact, aside from a few scribbled pictures of freakish-looking babies with two heads and frog-like legs, and some low-level bitching about her father and brother, Iona didn't write much for the entire first half of the year.

Logan skipped on to August. Like July, the majority of the pages were empty. But then, he turned a page to reveal two short lines of text.

Isaac Donovan Kerr.

Seven pounds five ounces.

And below that, more telling than anything she could've written, was a neatly-drawn love heart that took up most of the page.

It was a few weeks later—the thirteenth of September, nineteen-ninety—when Iona first wrote about her plans to kill herself.

CHAPTER THIRTY-ONE

Norman handled breakfast, explaining that Pat was having 'a bit of a lie-in.' The food wasn't to the same standard as the day before, but the effort was a valiant one. What it lacked in finesse, it more than made up for in quantity.

Tillerson didn't show face in the dining room, so Logan went back upstairs and made it very clear what would happen were he to attempt to get off the island before he'd been given permission. Tillerson listened with widening eyes, and then vowed on his mother's life that he'd stay in the house until further notice.

Logan chose to believe him, and arranged for Norman to lend the guest some clothes, as the detectives were holding onto his rucksack for the moment.

All that done, Logan gave Tyler the keys to the Land Rover, tasked him with finding and talking to Dudley Brown, then set off walking to the office.

Down at his side, Iona's diaries sat nestling in an evidence bag.

Logan reached the school building at just after nine. He was passing it, fishing the office key from his pocket, when a side door opened and a young man in an offensively yellow shirt sprang out in front of him.

"Hi! Are you... Are you the policeman?" he asked. He had a strong Western Isles lilt to his voice. That sing-song quality you didn't get many other places.

"One of them," Logan said. "Why?"

The man shot a glance back into the building behind him, then stepped out and quietly closed the door.

"Fergus. McDougal. Fergus McDougal," he said, giving a little wave. "I'm the teacher here. At the school." He winced. "Obviously at the school. Where else would I be...?"

He caught the impatient look on Logan's face and got to the point.

"The kids... They're... With the murder. They've heard stories. They're really anxious."

"Right," said Logan. "That's understandable. We're doing all we can."

"Oh, I know. God, yes. No. I wasn't saying..." Fergus picked at the skin around his fingers and danced from foot to foot. If this guy was saying the kids were anxious, Logan thought, they must be in a hell of a state. "I just thought, maybe, since you were here..."

Fergus's features screwed up and his shoulders raised, as if he was bracing himself for a haymaker straight to the face.

"I thought you might have a word. Settle them down a bit," the teacher suggested. "Two minutes. That's all it'll take. I swear. Two minutes."

Logan groaned. His gaze went a few paces ahead of him to the door of the Community Council office. It was so close.

And yet, so far.

"Two minutes," he grunted. "That's your lot."

Eleven minutes later, Logan stood in front of a whiteboard, completely dwarfing the six children sitting cross-legged on the floor in front of him.

They were of varying sizes and ages, all seven Primaries being taught by the one teacher in the same classroom. The little ones were down the front. They'd started a few feet from where Logan stood, but had shuffled incrementally closer while he spoke, so they were now gathered around him like lepers around Christ.

A couple of older kids—nine or ten, the DCI guessed—sat at the back, playing it marginally cooler than their younger classmates.

Most of the original two-minutes Logan had promised had been taken up by the teacher introducing Logan to the class, then introducing the class to Logan, then encouraging the class to introduce themselves to Logan, then—for reasons Logan wasn't entirely sure of—getting them up out of their seats to sit on the floor.

After that, Fergus announced he was, "Just quickly going to do the register," and Logan stood in impatient silence while the teacher read out the names, and the children confirmed what was already perfectly clear—that they were in the room.

Talking to children had never really been one of DCI Jack Logan's strong points. Not really.

He liked kids. In general. Some of the wee bastards he'd met over the years, he'd have gladly throttled, but broadly speaking, he had nothing against them *in theory*. Children were great *as a concept*, and while he absolutely understood the importance of putting their minds at ease, he didn't really think he was the right man for the job.

And, all things considered, he was probably right.

While listening to the register being taken, he'd decided that he wasn't going to talk down to them. He was going to accurately explain the situation, albeit in simple layman's terms, and not make any false claims. He'd be honest, but reassuring. Calm, but accurate.

The next six minutes were spent listening to the younger children crying, as Fergus tried desperately to console them.

The two minutes after that were spent reassuring each of them in turn that no, they weren't going to be murdered, and no, their mummies and daddies weren't going to be murdered, and no, nobody was coming to kill their pets.

The following minute was spent listening to them listing the types of pets they had, and their names. It was round about this point that Logan started to think it was all starting to get away from him.

"Right, so... Any questions?" he asked, looking down and around at the children.

Three hands went up near the front.

"That aren't about pets," he clarified.

Three hands went back down.

"Well, then—" Logan began, then a tentative hand at the back slowly raised. It was attached to a girl who looked to be the oldest child in the class. The other kids around her whispered in anticipation of what she was about to say. Logan pointed to her and nodded. "Yes?"

"Was it the Tattiebogle? Did the Tattiebogle do it?"

A worried murmur rippled through the small audience.

"The...? Oh. The scarecrow? No. I can definitely say—"

"There's a Tattiebogle near my house," announced one of the younger boys. He was a particularly dishevelled looking specimen, with a finger jammed up one nostril. "Mrs Bryden says it's keeping an eye on me to make sure I behave. Will it kill me?"

"No, it—"

"Will it kill his mum?" asked a girl of around the same age. This suggestion made the boy yank his finger out of his nose with an audible *pop*.

"It'd better not try to kill ma mum. Or ma wee granny," he announced. "Or it'll get... boof!"

He mimed throwing a punch, which drew excited gasps from some of the other kids.

"Do you know the Tattiebogle song?" asked the oldest girl, raising her hand but not waiting for Logan to acknowledge her.

Logan shook his head. "Um, I don't…"

"Great idea, Doris!" the teacher exclaimed, clapping his hands with barely constrained glee.

Doris, thought Logan. *Who the fuck calls a wean 'Doris' in this day and age?*

"Why don't we all sing the Tattiebogle song that Mrs Bryden taught us? I'm sure Mr Logan would love to hear it!"

Logan cleared his throat. "Well, I mean, I'm not sure I—"

"And a-one, and a-two, and a-one, two, three, four…" chimed Fergus, waving his hands like a conductor and completely ignoring the DCI's protests.

The kids all launched into the song at the same time. Or approximately the same time, anyway. Logan felt he should offer a smile of encouragement as he stood listening, but the best he could do was a sort of fixed grimace that made him look as if he was suffering a minor stroke.

"Tattiebogle, Tattiebogle, standing on its own," they sang. Or more chanted, really. "Tattiebogle, Tattiebogle, waiting all alone. Tattiebogle watches, Tattiebogle sees."

Their voices rose for the last part, getting steadily louder until they were practically shouting the words.

"Tattiebogle, Tattiebogle, don't take me!"

"Or ma wee granny," the nose-picker down front added quietly.

"What about your big granny?" asked another.

"Ma big granny's deid," the boy replied.

"How's she deid?" the girl beside him chipped in. "Did she get killed by a killer?"

The nose-picker's brow furrowed. "I don't know," he said. He raised his eyes to Logan's again. "Did ma big granny get killed?"

"How the f—" Logan began, then he caught himself in the nick of time. "I doubt it. I'm sure she…"

"Was it cancer?" one of the other children asked. "I bet it was cancer."

"What's cancer?" enquired another.

They all gazed at Logan, expecting him to provide the answers. He shot a sideways look at Fergus, but the teacher was looking even more expectantly at him than the kids.

"It's, uh, it's a disease that people get," Logan said.

"Old people?" piped up a voice from near the back.

"No. Anyone," Logan replied. "Anyone can get it."

There were a couple of whispers from the audience.

"Even people who're the same age as us?" a boy asked.

"Uh, aye," Logan said, although a nagging little voice in his head was starting to ask him questions of its own. "Aye. Anyone can get it."

The whispers became a concerned mumbling that rippled through the class. A few bottom lips started to go.

I told you, said the voice in Logan's head. *I tried to fucking warn you.*

"I don't want to get cancer and die like Michael's big granny," a girl with a blue ribbon announced. Then she, and another girl beside her, simultaneously burst into tears.

"I miss ma big granny!" the nose-picker wailed, as the tears began to spread like a virus, infecting everyone from the front of the class to the back.

Logan regarded the crying children in silence for a few moments, then he turned to the teacher, puffed out his cheeks, and raised both eyebrows.

"Right, then," he announced, jabbing a thumb in the direction of the classroom door. "I'd best be shooting off."

"Um, thanks for that," said Fergus, stepping out after Logan and shutting the door so you really had to strain to hear the anguished wailing from within. "That was... very helpful."

"No bother. Anytime," Logan said, safe in the knowledge that there was no bloody way he was ever being invited back. "Sorry if it went a bit... off-course."

"My fault. Should've reined them in a bit. They just don't get many visitors, so they get a bit excited if it's not me or Joy."

Logan looked down at the office key he now held in his hand again. "Joy Bryden? Does she teach here?"

"Oh. No, no. Not officially. She just comes in and works with the kids. Neighbourhood Watch type stuff. Security, safety..."

"Creepy scarecrows," said Logan, adding to the list.

"Haha! Yes! She was behind the Tattiebogle Trail. You might have come across it?" Fergus said, then he shook his head. "What am I saying? Of course you have. I think she made up the song to stop the kids messing about with them. Keep them at bay, sort of thing. Worked, too. They're blinking terrified of the things!"

"Aye, well—" Logan began, shooting a very deliberate look in the direction of the office, which went unnoticed.

"Surprised Joy hasn't told you who the killer is yet," the teacher said.

Logan's eyebrows came together above his nose. "Sorry?"

"Oh. Sorry. I don't mean she knows! I'm just surprised she doesn't," Fergus said, quickly clarifying. "She always knows what's been going on around the island. She's got eyes everywhere, that woman!"

Pat's words from the night before replayed themselves in Logan's head.

"*That bitch sees bloody everything*," he muttered.

"Sorry?" said the teacher, taken aback.

Logan shook his head. "Oh. No. Nothing. Just... something someone said."

He swung the key around his finger on its metal loop. "I'd best get on. Good luck with that lot."

"Thanks! I'll need it!" Fergus said, then the sounds of sobbing rose as he opened the door. "Oh, and good luck. Iona had her differences with... well... everyone, but she didn't deserve that."

"No. They very rarely do," Logan said, then the teacher slipped back into the school and the door swung closed.

Logan was at the door of the office when he stopped, the key held poised in front of the lock.

That bitch sees bloody everything.

She's got eyes everywhere, that woman.

"Webcams," Logan whispered.

She'd said, 'Webcams.'

Plural.

It had been raining. Pouring. *Pishin' doon.*

Had been for days.

Logan turned away from the door.

"So, why was she watering the bloody plants?"

CHAPTER THIRTY-TWO

THIS WAS THE OPENING TO A HORROR MOVIE. TYLER WAS SURE OF IT.

Dudley Brown lived alone, down near the water on the Skye-facing side of the island. The Land Rover had coughed and wheezed its way along the narrow single-track road, then struggled up something that might have been a driveway, could've been a footpath, but equally might have been none of the above.

Eventually, he'd arrived at a low white building with a corrugated iron roof that was surrounded by the decaying relics of old farming equipment. Bits of old tractor lay scattered around like dinosaur bones, lengths of fishing net draped between them in a way that made the DC think of giant cobwebs.

Knowing his luck, the giant spider who'd made them would be lurking somewhere nearby.

He cut the engine on a patch of vaguely flat ground around thirty feet from the building. The place didn't look like a house, exactly. It was more like a large garage or workshop, with a set of peeling wooden doors, and half a dozen high, narrow windows clustered around near the uneven roof.

Hamza had found the address, but it was possible he'd given him the wrong one. It certainly didn't look like anyone was home, but the boss would kill him if he didn't properly check it out.

"Mr Brown?" Tyler called, preferring to draw the man out, if he could. "Dudley Brown? I'm Detective Constable Tyler Neish. I just need to ask you a couple of questions."

There was silence from the house. The only sounds were the gentle crashing of water on rocks, and the strangled cries of the seabirds circling somewhere overhead.

"Mr Brown?" Tyler tried again. "Dudley? Anyone home?" He listened for several seconds, before adding, "Yoo-hoo," as much to calm his nerves as anything else.

The windows were too high for him to reach without a stepladder and a brass neck. Even if they hadn't been, they were too caked with dirt and grime to be able to look inside.

The double-doors were each the width of two normal-sized doors, side-by-side. Presumably, they would once have allowed tractors or animals through, but they had been fastened together by long straps of wood that were nailed across where they met in the middle.

It took another half a minute of exploring before Tyler discovered the other door tucked around the back of the building, on the water side. There was a wooden box fixed to the wall beside it with a hinged lid. The words, 'Dudley Broon,' had been painted on the top in white.

It was the right place, then. Tyler didn't know whether he should be happy about that or not. Had it belonged to someone else, he could've turned around and blamed Hamza for the mix-up.

As it was, though, he had no choice but to persevere. His arse would be out the window if he came back empty-handed again.

Tyler knocked on the door. "Hello? Mr Brown? Police. We'd like a word."

He gave it a minute.

Nothing.

"Oh, bloody hell," he muttered, looking along the building in both directions.

This side was in an even worse state than the front, exposure to the wind and rain coming in off the water having taken more of a toll.

Tyler knocked again and gave the same spiel. Then, when he received no reply, he tried the door handle.

He'd have quite liked it to have been locked, if he was completely honest. He had no reason to kick it in, and no warrant permitting him to do so.

But an unlocked door? It wasn't exactly an invitation, but it wasn't a refusal, either.

What would the boss do? he wondered.

He didn't have to wonder for long. There was no doubt what Logan would do, were he here. No doubt, at all.

And so, with the waves crashing at his back, and the wind nudging him on, Tyler opened the door to the darkened building, and stepped inside.

Logan rummaged around in the hanging basket, pushing aside the plants and buckling their thin branches. It hadn't rained in hours, but the compost, or soil, or whatever the container was filled with was still absolutely sodden. There would've been no reason for Joy to be watering it during the height of the storm, but Logan found nothing that might explain what else she could have been doing.

Plant food of some kind? That was a thing, wasn't it?

He'd have said she was just being a prying bastard and using watering the plants as an excuse to check out the new arrivals, but she'd been at it when they'd pulled up in the Land Rover. So, unless she was both nosy *and* psychic, that didn't explain it, either.

"Everything alright?"

Logan looked up and found himself face to face with Isaac Young.

Iona's son.

Isaac stood on the pavement right outside the pub, a small bundle of parcels all stacked up in a cardboard box that he was carrying on both forearms, and a quizzical look on his face.

"Lost something?"

Logan removed his hands from the basket, saw they were covered in wet muck, and quickly brushed it off.

"Eh, no. No, just... The baskets. Community Council, aye?"

"That's right," Isaac said.

Logan nodded for a long time. Too long. "Right. Right. Aye," he said. "And they're all over the island?"

"Just on the street here. Couple down at the dock. Why?"

"Nothing. Just interested, that's all," Logan said. He gestured to the pub behind the other man. "Listen, Isaac..." he began, but he couldn't find the end of the sentence.

"Listen to what?" Isaac asked.

"Have you got a few minutes?" Logan said. "We could grab a coffee. There's something... It'd be good to talk to you."

"I've told you what I know," Isaac said, becoming defensive.

"No, I know. I know, it's not about... Well, I mean, it *is* about..." He tutted, annoyed at himself, then pulled himself back together. "Doesn't have to be now. But I think you and me should sit down for a chat once everything's settled down."

Isaac's confusion was clearly written all over his face. He looked from the DCI's dirty hands to the hanging basket, then shrugged.

"Aye. Sure. Once it's all settled down," he said. "But for now, I need to go get this stuff posted off."

"Of course. We'll talk soon," Logan said.

From the corner of his eye, he watched Isaac continue along the street, then vanish inside the shop.

Then, he turned, scanned the street until he spotted the next hanging basket, and set off to investigate.

The second basket was closer to the school than the first, which was almost slap-bang level with the pub's front window. Like that one, this basket hung from a limb attached to a streetlight.

Unlike that one, there was something odd about it. On the inside wall of the plant pot there was a circle of sticky residue, roughly the size of a five pence piece. It was part of a foam pad—the kind of thing used to hang pictures when the landlord won't allow holes in his wall, or if you can't be arsed digging out a hammer.

Something had been stuck to the inside of the basket, pointed in the direction of the school window.

Backtracking down the street, Logan returned to the first hanging basket, and carefully checked around the inside of the plant pot contained within it.

It took him three runs around the pot before he felt a slightly raised circular outline. He tapped a finger on it. It wasn't particularly sticky, but there was a slight suggestion of tackiness there on the third and fourth tap.

There had been something in both baskets. Something stuck in place, which had now been removed. One facing the school window, the other pointing directly at the front of the pub.

"Well, now," Logan remarked. Then, he turned in the direction of the dock, shoved his hands in his pockets, and trudged down the hill.

THE OVAL of light from Tyler's phone torch projected mishappen shadows onto the bare stone walls of the... what? It wasn't a house. It couldn't be. Surely, nobody lived here?

Workshop, then? Barn? Some sort of storage facility for old machine parts and long-past-its-best animal feed?

Whatever the place was, it reeked of mould and motor oil, and the scattering of straw strewn across the floor was home to lots of scurrying shapes that rustled around beyond the edges of the torchlight.

A face appeared from nowhere in the torch's beam. Its eyes were empty hollows, its mouth a twisted leer, and Tyler came dangerously close to soiling himself when he clapped eyes on it.

He gave the face a poke. Dried grass or straw rustled inside the hessian sack of the scarecrow's head. The whole thing teetered then, with a *creak* and a *clack*, the wooden frame supporting the figure hit the stone floor.

"'*Go talk to Dudley Brown, Tyler,*'" he muttered, sweeping the light across a row of ancient metal shelving stacked with old paint cans and glass jars full of mysterious liquids. "'*See what you can find out.*'"

He jumped and ejected a noise he was grateful nobody else was around to hear when he caught his reflection in a cracked mirror that stood propped against a wall.

"I found out I don't like creepy fucking buildings," he grumbled. "Does that count, I wonder?"

Tyler pressed on through the creepy fucking building as, behind him, a shape detached itself from the shadows.

LOGAN WAS POKING around in the dockside hanging baskets when he heard the buzzing of an outboard motor that signalled an approaching boat.

He couldn't see the boat at first, and the open water made it difficult to pinpoint which direction the sound was coming from. He figured it out just as the prow of a manky old dinghy appeared around the curve of the island.

It was barely ten feet long, and dipped and rolled on the water, apparently at the full mercy of the waves cresting beneath it. It was made of rubber, dirty and scuffed, and its outboard motor stuttered and spluttered, and occasionally belched out balls of oily black smoke.

It was being steered by a man who, at this distance, appeared to be a hundred years old. He had a long grey beard that blew out behind him in the wind, and sat hunched over at the back of the boat. Up front, a uniformed officer clung to a narrow bench with both hands and, it seemed, tried not to throw up.

Logan finished checking the hanging baskets. By the time he'd determined that one of them had the same circle of sticky residue as the two up the hill, the boat was coughing and wheezing the last few feet to the dock.

"Well, Constable, you sure know how to travel in style," the DCI remarked, turning to the new arrivals.

PC Sinead Bell—who was looking substantially greener than she had the last time Logan had seen her—attempted a shaky smile.

"It was this or swim, sir," she said. The boat bumped to a violent stop against the dock, almost throwing her off the bench. She swore below her breath. "On reflection, I might've made the wrong choice."

CHAPTER THIRTY-THREE

Tyler didn't know what hit him, only that it hit him hard, and fast, and came out of nowhere.

It was a shove, he thought. Or a shoulder. The impact sent the world into a sudden spinning lurch. He hit the shelves, grabbed for them, but his weight and momentum toppled them like dominoes.

His phone went bouncing across the hard floor—*crick-crack-clack*—the torchlight swinging wildly, sending shadows scurrying like spiders up the walls.

And then, darkness, as the torch went out, leaving only the faint light from the grime-encrusted windows to pick faint, silvery lines from the shadows.

Tyler twisted on the wreckage of the shelves, trying to get up, find his feet, get moving. A punch hit him like a sledgehammer, slamming him back down, and his mouth was filled with spit and copper.

A foot connected with his chest, hard and heavy, a battering ram with a rubber sole. The air left him in one sudden gasp. His lungs tightened, refusing to refill. Refusing to breathe. Refusing to respond.

He kicked out, weakly, pathetically, his foot skiffing the side of his attacker's leg. Doing nothing.

"S-stop," he managed to wheeze, but then two hands were on his throat. Tightening. *Tightening*. Grip too strong. Wrists too thick.

His attacker's face swam in the dim light, his features blurred by blood and tears as, from all corners of Tyler's vision, a checkerboard of darkness came creeping in.

ONCE SINEAD HAD CLAMBERED out of the boat and onto dry land—an undignified, shambolic process which had twice almost ended in soggy disaster—Logan had given the old fella in the boat a very clear, very concise set of instructions. These had started with, "Right, then," and finished with, "fuck off."

The last thing he needed was a boat hanging around the place. Particularly with Bruce Anderson still on the loose somewhere. Nobody was getting off the island until Logan said so, which meant anything that could conceivably be used as a means of anyone doing so wasn't welcome.

They'd waited until the boat had chugged its way back around the headland, then set off up the hill towards the main street.

"Rough crossing?" Logan asked. Sinead's colour was marginally better, but she still had a wee touch of the living dead about her. She had a slight stagger, too, like she'd just got the hang of being on the water and was now finding it difficult to adjust to being back on dry land.

"You could say that, sir," she replied. "Still, at least the company was good."

"Aye?" said Logan, stopping outside the front door of the pub.

"Not really. Crotchety old bugger didn't say two words the whole time." She watched as Logan knocked on the pub's closed door. "Bit early in the day for this, isn't it?"

"Hmm? Oh, aye. No. Just want to ask the landlord something," Logan said. He glanced back at her. "So, whose idea was it?"

"Whose idea was what?" Sinead asked.

"To send you? Yours or Ben's?"

Sinead smiled. "Bit of both."

"Aye, well. If I'm only getting one, might as well make it a good one," he remarked, before knocking on the door again.

"Thanks, sir. Oh, and DI Forde asked me to tell you—"

"To phone Hoon. Aye, I'll get round to it," Logan said. He stepped back, cupped his hands around his mouth, and shouted at the upstairs window. "Mr Mackay? Roddy? It's DCI Logan. I need a quick word."

A curtain twitched at the window. There was a creak as the window was opened. "Sorry. Sorry, be right down," Roddy said, and then the window closed over with a *thunk*.

"Nice place," Sinead observed, looking around them.

"Has its moments, aye," Logan said.

"Is that the school? It's tiny."

"I was in there this morning, actually," Logan said. "Teacher asked me to have a word with the kids. Help set their minds at rest, sort of thing."

"Oh. How did that go?"

Logan puffed out his cheeks. "Well, they were all greeting their eyes out when I left, so it probably could've gone better."

Sinead gave a chuckle. "I'd have liked to have seen that," she said. She skirted around the edges of the next question, before coming out with it. "Tyler around?"

"That useless gobshite?" Logan grunted. "He's following up on a lead. Should be back soon."

There was the clunk of a bolt lock sliding across on the other side of the door, and it opened to reveal Roddy standing in a dressing-gown. His gaze flitted from Logan to Sinead and back again several times, getting more and more concerned each time.

"Hello. Um, hi. Morning," he said, his throat dry. "Is there... Is everything alright?"

"Morning, Mr Mackay," Logan said. "This is my colleague, PC Sinead Bell."

"Hi," said Sinead, offering a brief wave.

"Hello," Roddy said, managing a sort of half-smile. His eyes darted back to Logan. "Was there...? Is there some sort of problem?"

Logan looked back over his shoulder at the closest hanging basket, then faced the pub landlord again. "I think it'd be best if we discussed it inside."

Tyler's brain screamed at him. His lungs burned, begging for air. His feet kicked out, but the weight of his attacker had him pinned in the wreckage of the shelving, the hands constricting around his throat like a boa constrictor.

He swung a punch. Again. Again. Each one made contact, but may as well not have for all the good they did. The hands kept squeezing. The weight kept pressing. The eyes of his attacker blazed down, and a thought slammed into Tyler harder than any shoulder, harder than any punch.

This was it. This. Now. This was the last sight he would ever see. Those eyes. These hands. This bastard.

Bollocks to that.

He grasped around him. His fingers found the handle of a paint pot. He swung it, and there was a satisfyingly solid *thunk* as it whanged off the skull of the man pinning him down.

His attacker sprawled sideways. Air—sweet, precious air—flooded Tyler's lungs. He coughed it back out in three big choking gulps, then kicked himself free of the shelves, the paint pot swinging for another direct hit.

"Ah! Ah!" squealed his attacker. "Stop! Help! Murderer! Police! *Police!*"

"What the...? What are you...?" Tyler wheezed, the paint pot raised and ready to swing again. "I am the fucking police!"

Down on the floor, his attacker cowered behind his raised hands. "What?" he asked, after a moment's pause.

"I am the police!" Tyler repeated. He snatched up his phone and tapped at the cracked screen. The torchlight returned, drawing a hiss from the man on the floor.

Tyler recognised him as the giant they'd seen at the church the day before. The man he'd come looking for.

Dudley Brown's eyes were wide with shock and horror. His hulking great hands, which were raised in front of his face for protection, trembled as he lowered them. A trickle of blood ran from his hairline and was in the process of filling up an ear.

"You're the police?" he whimpered.

"Aye! And you, sunshine..." Tyler spat a wad of blood onto the floor between them. "...are bloody nicked."

THE FLAT ABOVE the pub was relatively spacious compared to most of the other living accommodation Logan had seen on the island. Roddy had led them up the stairs, through a good-sized, if sparsely-furnished living room, and into a kitchen-diner with a small circular table at one end, and a draining board teetering with dishes at the other.

They'd been offered a cup of tea. Logan had initially declined, but Sinead was quick to accept, so he decided he might as well join her.

He waited until the kettle had boiled and the mugs were placed down on the table, before throwing Roddy for a loop.

"I think you've lied to me, Mr Mackay."

Roddy stood, his mug clutched in one hand, his face tight with worry.

"What? What do you mean? Lied? About what?"

Logan took a sip of his tea before replying. "Tell me about the cameras."

Roddy tried to sound like he didn't know what the detective was talking about. It was an admirable effort, but the rising inflection and the shake of the mug in his hand gave him away.

"Cameras? What... What cameras?"

Logan held his gaze over the rim of his mug.

"I don't... What cameras?" Roddy asked. He was practically sweating already. This wouldn't take long.

Logan took another sip of his tea. He smacked his lips together. He very slowly and deliberately set the mug on a coaster on the table.

"You know what cameras I mean, Roddy," the DCI said. "You're going to tell me sooner or later. Save us all a lot of bother and make it sooner, eh?"

Roddy's legs wobbled, and he flopped down into the chair across from Logan, sloshing tea up over his hand.

"She... she used to borrow them sometimes. Couple of cameras and a tripod. Microphone. One of my laptops. Basically, the set-up we used for her music videos."

Logan frowned briefly, but chased it away before the other man could spot it.

"Go on," he urged.

Beside him, without a word, Sinead took out her notebook and began to write.

"I don't… I don't know much more. She asked me to show them how they worked, how to transfer the footage to my laptop, and always brought the kit back next day."

"Sorry," said Sinead, looking up from her pad. "Is this Iona we're talking about?"

Logan let Roddy do the confirming. "Aye. That's right."

Sinead smiled appreciatively and went back to writing.

"What was she doing with it?" Logan asked.

"She didn't tell me. But… I mean, it's not exactly a big leap of the imagination." He shot a slightly embarrassed look in Sinead's direction and dropped his voice to a whisper. "Sex stuff."

"She was making pornography?" Logan asked.

Roddy recoiled at the word. "Yes. I mean… Yes. I think so. I didn't… I didn't *see* any of it, obviously. But there were a lot of… People talk, you know?"

"They do," Logan agreed. "Doesn't mean it's true, of course. Did she ever tell you that's what she was doing?"

"No, never."

"And you never saw it for yourself?"

"No. I never saw it."

"Did you know what she was doing with it? Was she uploading it somewhere? Storing it?"

"I don't know."

"So, if you've never seen it, and you don't know what she was doing with it —" Logan began, before Roddy jumped in and cut him off.

"But I know Iona. Or… knew her. And, while I don't want to believe that's what she was doing, while I don't want to believe she was selling herself for money, or selling videos of herself doing things with men, or whatever it was she was doing… I do. I do believe it. What else could it have been? And she'd say things."

"What sort of things?" Logan asked.

"Not… Nothing specific. Little things. Or little looks she'd give when I asked what she was doing. 'Nothing for you to worry about,' she'd said. 'Nothing you'd be interested in.' But it was the way she said it." Roddy shook his head. "It's hard to explain."

Logan nodded slowly. He took another drink of his tea, then smacked his lips together before continuing. "How many laptops do you have, Mr Mackay?"

Roddy tried very hard not to let the impact of the question register on his face. He searched for a response, his tongue flicking across his lips, which were suddenly sandpaper dry.

"Sorry?" was the best he was able to come up with.

"You said she used to borrow one of your laptops. I took one away. How many others are there?"

Sinead's pencil stopped scratching on the pad. She joined the DCI in staring expectantly at the man sitting across from them.

"Um, two. My main one—that's the one you have—and a, and a backup. Which I'd loan Iona." He cracked a smile, trying to lighten the moment. "Wasn't that I didn't trust her with the main one, or anything, it was just... Better safe than sorry."

"Very wise," Logan said. "Is the other one here in the flat?"

Roddy's gaze flicked momentarily to the door leading into the living room. "Uh..."

"Is it through there?" Logan asked. "Mind if we have a look?"

"The, uh... I mean... No," Roddy said. He shook his head. Or maybe it was shaking all on its own. "Help yourself. I don't mind. I just..."

"Just what?" Logan asked.

Roddy swallowed. "Nothing. It's in the bedroom, actually." He began to stand. "I'll go get it."

"You're fine," Logan said, stopping him with a raise of his hand. "Constable Bell will go get it and take a look."

Sinead pushed her chair back and stood. Logan kept his gaze fixed on the squirming Roddy Mac.

The DCI's eyes shone, like a cat that had found a mouse to play with. "You and me can carry on our little chat."

CHAPTER THIRTY-FOUR

Dudley Brown perched on a rickety wooden stool in the now brightly lit workshop, his hands fastened behind his back by a set of plastic zip-tie restraints, his eyes practically bulging out of their sockets in distress.

After securing the big bastard, Tyler had gone in search of something to clean himself up with, and had settled on a big stack of supermarket-brand toilet paper piled up at the back of a walk-in store cupboard.

He stood before Dudley now, dabbing gingerly at his bloodied face while trying to look suitably like he was in charge. The stool the other man was sitting on wasn't very big, but even seated, Dudley had a couple of inches height advantage over the DC.

"Right, then," Tyler began. The vibrations of his voice made his nose ache sharply. "Mind telling me what the bloody hell all that was about?"

"I thought you were the murderer," Roddy said.

The direct simplicity of the answer, and the wide-eyed innocent way in which it was delivered told the detective to go easy. Duty of care, and all that. Although, he had to admit, he wasn't sure how that extended to his whanging the bastard with a paint pot.

"You broke in. I thought you were going to kill me like you killed Iona."

"OK, first of all, I didn't kill Iona," Tyler said. "Like I said, I'm with the police. Detective Constable Neish."

Dudley's brow furrowed, like he was struggling to store all these new details.

"You can call me Tyler."

"Tyler," said Dudley. He said it tentatively, like he was checking it for traps.

"That's right. And I didn't kill Iona. Also, I didn't break in. The door was unlocked."

"Door's always unlocked," Dudley said. "That's the good thing about living out here. Everyone knows everyone. It's very friendly. You can leave your door open."

The way he said it suggested he'd learned the sentences by rote. Tyler smiled and nodded, trying to further reassure the man that he wasn't the enemy.

"Aye. It's nice. Although, I'm not sure 'very friendly' is how I'd describe the welcome I got."

Dudley blushed and looked down at the floor. "I thought you were—"

"The murderer. Aye. You mentioned," Tyler said. He stepped in a little closer and indicated the red staining down the side of Dudley's face. "How's the head?"

"Bit sore."

"We'll get it looked at," Tyler told him.

"Thank you. And we'll get you looked at, too," Dudley said.

His smile was open and child-like. Tyler didn't reckon it was any sort of calculated attempt to get him on-side, but it had that effect.

"Some right hook you've got," he said.

"Thank you very much," Dudley said.

There was no point questioning him here. None of it would stand up. He'd need a support worker with him at the very least.

There was one thing Tyler had to know, though. He gestured to the scarecrow he'd knocked over earlier. When he'd found the switch and the lights had come up, three more of the things had been revealed propped against the far wall.

"What's with all the scarecrows?"

Dudley, who had been looking increasingly relaxed over the past couple of minutes, suddenly tensed again. His eyes widened. His mouth dropped open. There was a gasp as he sucked in a mouthful of air.

"Oh. No. I forgot!"

"Forgot what?" Tyler asked.

"No comment."

Tyler blinked. "Eh?"

"I'm supposed to say that. No comment."

"Why are you supposed to say that? Who says?"

"Joy says. She said..." Dudley's face crumpled. He let out a low groan. "No comment."

"Joy? Joy Bryden?" Tyler asked.

"No comment."

"From the Community Council?"

"No comment."

Tyler approached the prisoner and flashed his most charming smile. Although, it had to be said, the swollen nose and the mask of dried blood that covered half his face took some of the appeal out of it.

"Dudley. Mate. I'm trying to help you here," Tyler said. "Why did Joy tell you not to talk to us? What is it she wants you to keep quiet about?"

Dudley shifted on his stool. His eyes darted in all directions, searching for somewhere to settle. His bottom lip grew fatter, like he was holding back tears.

"No comment," he said in a whisper. "No comment, no comment, no comment."

"OK. OK," Tyler said, keeping his voice measured and calm. Those restraints were tough, but they weren't unbreakable. The last thing he needed was for Dudley to Hulk-out on him and break free. Next time, he might not be able to reach the paint pot. "Just you... Just you sit there, alright?"

"No comment," Dudley said.

"Aye, that wasn't really a question. You don't have to no comment that."

"No comment."

"Right. Fair enough," Tyler sighed.

He turned his back on Dudley, decided that this might not be the best idea, and half-turned back. It had been the mention of the scarecrow that had turned him uncooperative, so Tyler sidled over to the one he'd knocked over and squatted next to it.

In the stark glow of the overhead lights, it wasn't nearly as terrifying as it had looked in the beam of the phone's torch. It just looked a bit... naff, in fact. A canvas bag packed with dried grass and sawdust, fastened to a skeleton made from a simple wooden cross.

It was dressed in a mishmash of old clothes—checked shirt, denim dungarees, and two boots that weren't even remotely similar, much less from the same pair.

The dungarees had a patch on one knee, and a few other holes had been repaired by some clumsy stitching.

There was a square pocket in the front of the denims, roughly the size of a cigarette packet. It bulged like there was something inside. Tyler started to reach for it, then stopped himself, found a pair of rubber gloves in his pocket, and tried again.

At first, he found himself fumbling with the pocket's shiny round button. It was only when he couldn't get it to unfasten, that he discovered it wasn't a button at all.

"Well now, Dudley," Tyler said. He whistled through his teeth. "What do we have here?"

PC BELL SAT in Roddy Mackay's living room, tapping away at the laptop's keyboard. It was a clunky old thing, that whirred and chugged after every click and keystroke, and she was rapidly losing patience with it.

There was no email account set up on the machine, from what she could gather. No passwords stored in the browser. Nothing incriminating on the desktop, or any of the obvious folders. Nothing much of anything, really, incriminating or otherwise. It was all a bit of a blank canvas.

The only thing of obvious note was the desktop wallpaper, which showed Roddy with a woman in her forties. From the looks of her, she'd had her hair done nicely, but maybe thirty-six to forty-eight hours before, and she'd done very little with it since. Her burgundy lipstick was slightly smeared, and there was something about the leering grin on her face that suggested she wouldn't pass a breathalyser test.

The woman had her arm wrapped around Roddy's neck, pulling him in close to her chest. He was smiling. It was one of genuine warmth. Genuine happiness.

Sinead recognised Iona from the photo Hamza had shown her while she'd been reviewing the case back at base the previous night. She'd looked dour and trashy in that picture. She was still looking trashy in this picture, but there was a joyfulness about the desktop image that had been missing from the other one.

Sinead double-tapped the trackpad to open another folder. At first, the laptop audibly baulked at the idea, and the cursor arrow became a little spinning egg-timer. But then, with a real sense of begrudgement, the folder expanded to fill the whole screen.

Twenty or more other folders were revealed, all laid out in rows.

Sinead sighed. "Balls to this," she muttered, then she clicked the magnifying glass icon in the bottom left corner of the screen and began to type.

"WHAT ABOUT THE OTHER CAMERAS?" Logan asked, setting his mug down on the coaster again.

"Other cameras? What... I don't... What other cameras? I don't have any."

"In the plant pots," Logan said. "I'm assuming Joy Bryden asked for your help to install them?"

"Plant pots?" Roddy parroted, and there was a real look of bewilderment on his face. "What...?"

"Aye. You know. The cameras hidden in the hanging baskets. Keeping watch. Poking their noses in. You helped set those up, didn't you?"

"No!" Roddy protested. "I didn't... I mean, *what*? Since when? She had cameras in the *hanging baskets*? I knew nothing about it. Let me see."

"They're no longer there," Logan said. "But they were."

"Well... how do you know?"

"I've a nose for that sort of thing," Logan said, giving it a tap to emphasise the point. "I think she removed them soon after we got here, so we didn't find them. But they were there, alright. Watching everything. Everyone. How did it make you feel, by the way?"

Roddy blinked. "The cameras? I don't—"

"Iona. Doing those things. Other men," Logan said. He paused momentarily. "Not you."

"What? No. She wasn't... She and I, we never..."

"I know. You said. And I believe you, Roddy. I do. You were friends. Just friends," Logan said. "But, I mean, come on. You must've thought of it, surely? Bachelor like yourself, all alone here. And her. No' bad for her age. You were close, too. It must've gone through your head once or twice. You must've thought about it."

"I... No. No, that's not fair," Roddy protested. "We were... She was my friend. That was all."

"You weren't jealous, then?" Logan asked. "Of the other men? It didn't make you upset? Angry?"

"No!" Roddy yelped. A vein throbbed on the side of his forehead, getting more pronounced with every word he said. "I mean... Honestly? Did I like it? No. Because she was better than that. I hated that she felt the need to do it. To have that... that contact. With strangers. With people whose names she barely knew. Did it make me upset? Yes! Because she was worth more than everyone thought she was. More than *she* thought."

He had been leaning further and further forward across the table during his speech, and now slowly sat back again, wringing his hands together in his lap.

"Come on, Roddy," Logan said, eyeing the man across the table. One corner of his mouth pulled up into a boorish smirk. He winked. "Don't tell me you never thought about it. You and her. Not once? Don't tell me the thought of her choosing to do those things with strangers—choose them over you, her friend—didn't get you riled up."

The kitchen door opened before Roddy could reply.

"Uh, sir?" said Sinead. Her eyes went from Logan to Roddy. The pub landlord swallowed and shrunk further in his seat. "There's something you really need to see."

Logan sat on the couch, the laptop open in front of him, two naked bodies writhing and heaving on the screen. The sound had been on when Logan had first hit the play button, but the grunting and squealing and the *slap-slap-slap* of flesh on flesh had quickly led to him turning it down.

He looked over at Sinead, who stood in front of the kitchen door. She'd pulled it mostly all the way closed, but left it ajar just enough that she could listen out for Roddy doing anything stupid, like trying to climb out of the window, or slit his wrists with a bread knife.

"And there's a few of these?" Logan asked as, on-screen, arms and legs and assorted other body parts entangled.

"About a dozen, sir," Sinead said. "Maybe more. Obviously, I didn't sit and watch through them all."

"No," Logan grunted. "You'd want to get settled in with popcorn for that, I suppose. And they're all the same?"

"Broadly similar, sir, aye," Sinead confirmed. "I mean, not always the same people, but you get the gist. There are photos, too. Pretty, eh, full-on. I can show you, if you like?"

"Tempting as you make that sound, Constable, I'll take your word for it," Logan said.

He craned his neck so his head was sideways, his forehead furrowed into deep troughs of confusion. "The hell's he planning to put...?" he wondered, then his eyes widened. "Jesus. He's flexible. I'll give him that."

Standing, Logan picked up the laptop and, with the video still playing, took it through to the kitchen. He plonked it on the table in front of Roddy, who was shaking from head to toe now, purposefully facing away from the screen.

"So then, Mr Mackay," the DCI urged. "You mind telling me what all this is about?"

CHAPTER THIRTY-FIVE

"Your car smells horrible," complained the voice from the back seat.

"I told you, it's not my car," Tyler said, chugging the Land Rover up the last hundred yards of the narrow dirt track, and onto a road that could, at best, be described as 'marginally less awful.'

The surface of this one had been tarmacked at some point, but was so pock-marked with potholes it looked like it had recently come under heavy military assault.

They were halfway back to the main street area now. A couple of minutes of driving. That was all. Then, Tyler would take his prisoner into the office, and Logan could figure out what the hell to do about him.

A couple of minutes. That was all. A couple of minutes, and this was no longer his problem. Or not exclusively his problem, at least.

"I feel sick," Dudley said.

"We're nearly there. We'll be stopping in a minute. You'll be fine," Tyler told him.

"What if I'm sick?"

"Jesus. You won't be. We're nearly there," Tyler said.

Dudley went quiet.

It was nice while it lasted.

"My hands are sore from sitting on them."

Tyler sighed and looked at the man reflected in the rear-view mirror. "Well don't sit on them, then. Angle yourself sideways a bit."

"Then my seatbelt might not work," Dudley pointed out.

"Your seatbelt will still work."

"It might not, though."

Tyler's fingers tightened on the wheel, as he steered the Land Rover towards a tight, right-hand bend in the road.

"It will. And besides, we're in the middle of nowhere. It's not like we're going to crash, is it?"

"Look out!"

Tyler swore and swerved as the Land Rover rounded the bend to reveal a man crossing the road directly ahead of them. The brakes screeched. The suspension clunked. The tyres churned up a spray of loose chippings and gravel, which rattled around the inside of the wheel arch.

The vehicle thumped to a stop in a pot-hole just a few feet from the man outside.

The man carrying a rucksack on his back, a six-pack of toilet rolls under one arm, and a four-pack of beer in his hand.

The man with the blond hair and the surfer's tan.

Tyler stared at Bruce Anderson, who stood frozen like a rabbit in headlights.

Bruce Anderson stared back.

"Fuck me," Tyler muttered. He unclipped his belt. He opened his door.

And with that, Bruce Anderson ran.

"What do you want me to say?" Roddy asked, the words coming out as a series of hoarse, throaty sobs. He looked from the detective to the uniformed constable and back again. "What...? I don't know what you want me to say."

Logan sat down across from the landlord. He tapped the pause button on the video currently playing on the laptop. On-screen, two glistening naked men froze, mid-thrust.

"So, I suppose that explains why you and Iona never got together," Logan said.

Roddy blushed and looked down at his squirming hands. His shoulders were hunched over, his breathing was shaky, and he looked to be one wrong word away from a full-scale breakdown.

"You could've just told us, you know? It would've saved a lot of pointed fingers."

"*Told you*?" Roddy asked, practically spitting the words out. His head snapped up, his eyes blazing with emotion. "How could I have told you? What if it got out? What if everyone knew? Hmm? What then?"

"Would that be so bad?" Sinead asked.

Roddy snorted. "Yes! Yes, of course! Maybe anything goes where you're from."

"I'm from Fort William," Sinead said. "It's no' exactly Las Vegas."

"But it's still better than here, I bet. Now. With this lot," Roddy said, sweeping an arm in the direction of the window. "I might as well tell them I'm a kiddie-fiddler."

Panic flashed across his face. "Which I'm not, by the way! It was... I was just making a point."

"I know, Roddy. And, I understand your concern. But I can assure you, nothing you tell us gets into the public domain. We're good at confidentiality. If you don't want anyone to find out..."

"Of course I don't!"

"...then they won't. Not from us. I give you my word on that," Logan told him.

He caught Sinead's eye, then indicated Roddy's empty mug. Sinead nodded and clicked the kettle on.

"How long have you known?" Logan asked.

Roddy puffed out his cheeks. "Forever. I've always known."

"And Iona?" Logan asked. "Did she know?"

The response took several seconds to come. When it did, it was in the form of a slow, weary nod. "She did. Yes," he admitted. "I didn't... I didn't tell her. I didn't have to. She just knew somehow."

"Did she maybe find all the videos of lads shagging each other on your laptop?" Logan asked.

For a moment, Roddy just stared back at him in horror, then he laughed. It wasn't big, or boisterous, or even particularly audible, but it was a laugh, all the same.

"I suppose it might've been that, right enough," he admitted.

"Kind of gives the game away," Logan agreed, and both men shared a thin smile.

"You really won't tell anyone?" Roddy asked.

Logan sniffed, looked up at the ceiling as if thinking it through, then shook his head. "No. No, we won't tell anyone," he said.

Sinead set a mug of coffee down in front of Roddy, and Logan took that as his cue to stand up.

"But I think you should," the DCI said.

Roddy shook his head. "People will... react."

"Fuck them. Let them react," Logan said. He pushed the chair in under the table and leaned on the back of it. "I... we, PC Bell and I, we had a colleague. A friend. She was... something else. Miserable cow, most of the time, but she found someone. A partner. Female. And she was happy. It was a strange bloody sight, actually, but she was happy."

Roddy reached for his coffee. "That's... I'm very happy for her. But, again, though, she doesn't live here."

"Doesn't live anywhere," Logan said, his fingers flexing on the back of the chair. "She died. In the line of duty. Came out of nowhere. Nothing anyone could've done."

The muscles on his jaw tensed as he clenched his teeth, crushing the croak he could feel building at the back of his throat.

"And between you, us, and these four walls, Roddy, some nights I lie awake and I think... Why didn't she find it sooner? Happiness, I mean. Why then? Why not years before? Decades before? Why just a few days before she...?"

Logan glanced down, just for a moment, composing himself.

"How is that in any way fair?" he asked.

He straightened, smoothed down his coat, then stuck his hands in the pockets. "I'm not going to pretend to talk for her. For Caitlyn. She'd be able to say it all much better than I can."

"She could do most things better than you can, sir, to be fair," Sinead chipped in.

Logan didn't look at PC Bell, but he pointed in her direction. "She's no' wrong," he admitted. "So, I won't be able to do it justice, but if she was here, I think she'd be telling you to get your bloody finger out, Mr Mackay. None of us know how long we've got left on this side of the ground."

He patted the seated man's shoulder. "So, what the bloody hell are you waiting for?"

"I FEEL SICK! I FEEL SICK!"

Tyler hissed through his teeth as the Land Rover's shock absorbers failed once again to absorb any of the shock that jolted up his arse and along the length of his spine.

"Jesus fucking Christ, Dudley, will you shut up?!" he bellowed, thundering the rust bucket across a series of bone-rattling dips and bumps. "Just hold on!"

"I can't hold on! You've tied me up!" Dudley protested.

Tyler groaned. "Aye. Fair point, right enough," he conceded, then he jammed a foot to the floor and powered the Land Rover up an incline towards the peak that Bruce Anderson had just disappeared over.

The dashboard was a bonanza of warning lights. Some flickered. Others flashed. Most just stayed on. At last glance, he reckoned he needed another three for a full house. At the rate the terrain was slamming into the vehicle's underside, it was only a matter of time until...

"Bingo," Tyler cried, as the Land Rover crested the hill to find Bruce

Anderson stumbling off-balance down the other side. "I've got you now, you bastard!"

From the back-seat came a loud *hurp* as Dudley vomited. It came blasting from his mouth with not an unsurprising amount of force, given the size of him, splattered against the headrest in front, then cascaded down the back of Tyler's neck.

"What the fuck?!" the DC yelped, shoving his shoulders up to his ears in an attempt to stop the warm vomity sludge from oozing all the way down his back.

Dudley puked again. Tyler threw himself forward in the chair as the hot spray hit him for a second time.

"Jesus Christ! Stop it!"

"I told you!" Dudley sobbed. "I told you I felt sick!"

Outside, Bruce Anderson hung a right across the wide-open wilderness, trying to dodge the pursuing 4x4. Gagging at the stench of Dudley's spew, which was currently plastered all down his back, Tyler wrenched the wheel to the right and gunned the accelerator.

The Land Rover shot forward like a sprinter off the blocks.

There was a *thud*.

There was a scream.

And Bruce Anderson vanished, out of sight, beneath the front of the vehicle.

CHAPTER THIRTY-SIX

Tyler slammed down on the brakes, but a gulley stopped the vehicle first, the front bumper smashing against the side and shearing off several centimetres of soil.

Driver and passenger were both flung forward. Dudley chose that moment—or perhaps the moment chose him—to empty the rest of his stomach contents in a predominantly forward direction, fully dousing the detective in front.

On the dashboard, the final few lights illuminated, like Tyler had just struck the jackpot.

Behind Tyler, Dudley gave a little groan. "Oh. That feels a bit better," he mumbled.

"Speak for yourself!" Tyler hissed, before ejecting a sentence made up entirely of swear words.

Gagging, dripping, and ever-so-slightly steaming, he hooked the door handle with a pinkie finger, prised it open, and almost fell out onto the hillside.

He waddled around to the front of the car like some sort of wind-up toy, desperately trying not to let any part of his body touch any other part, and wishing his vomit-caked clothes would levitate a couple of inches off his skin.

Tyler had no idea what sight would await him at the front of the vehicle. He'd wanted to catch Bruce Anderson, yes, but not to mash the poor bastard into a paste.

He was relieved, then, when Anderson subjected him to a torrent of abuse the moment he squelched around to the front.

"The fuck you think you're doing, you bloody maniac?" the Australian bellowed, his voice easily drowning out the chugging of the still-running engine. "You could've flaming killed me!"

"Well, you shouldn't have run away then, should you?" Tyler snapped. "Come out."

"I can't come out, can I? Bloody stuck, ain't I?" Anderson protested.

Sure enough, while the Land Rover hadn't exploded his insides outside as Tyler feared it might've, the position the vehicle had stopped in meant Anderson's lower half was pinned between the front of the chassis and the ground below.

"Can't you jiggle sideways?" Tyler asked.

"Jiggle sideways? What are you talking about? If I could jiggle sideways I'd have jiggled bloody sideways and legged it, wouldn't I?" Anderson snapped. He shook his head. "Jiggle sideways."

"Alright, alright," Tyler muttered. He started to move in closer to investigate, but stopped when Anderson retched.

"Jesus fucking Christ, mate! Did you throw up on yourself, or something?" he demanded.

"No, I didn't throw up on myself," said Tyler, witheringly. "Someone else threw up on me."

"Right, well... I mean, what? Well done, I guess," Anderson said. "Now hurry the hell up and get me out of here!"

Tyler reached a hand out. Anderson shrank back.

"Don't come near me! Christ! I don't want to get covered in puke, do I?"

"Well, what do you want me to do, then?" Tyler asked.

"I don't know. How about *not* hit me with a big bloody car?" Anderson suggested. "Oh, wait. Scratch that. Bit fucking late!"

"Wait there," Tyler told him.

"Good one. Funny," Anderson replied, but Tyler was already penguin-walking back around to the driver's side of the Land Rover.

He recoiled at the smell as he reached the door. "Fuck."

Turning away, he raised his head like a werewolf howling at the moon, drew in a deep breath, and clambered into the driver's seat.

"Everything alright?" asked Dudley from the back.

Tyler gritted his teeth and crunched the gearbox into reverse. "Just fucking peachy. Thanks for asking," he said, then he depressed the accelerator and raised the clutch.

The engine died immediately. One moment, it was chugging and rattling away, the next there was nothing but silence. Something whined for a few seconds. Something else went *ping*, like metal cooling.

"Great," Tyler groaned. "Just... great."

"What's wrong?" asked Dudley.

Tyler turned in his seat. He regretted this at once, as it gave him a close-up view of his headrest, which looked like the epicentre of some sort of gaseous swamp eruption. Smelled like it, too.

"What's *wrong*? What's fucking..." he began, then he shook his head in disbelief. "What's *right*, Dudley? That's the real question here. What's bloody right?"

"Did you kill Bruce?" Dudley asked. His eyes shone, wide-eyed and innocent, through the mask of vomit that was currently plastered across his face.

"No. I didn't kill him. He's just... he's trapped under the front. I need to get him out."

"How are you going to do that?"

Tyler said nothing.

"How are you going to get him out?"

"Jesus Christ, Dudley! I'm thinking," Tyler barked.

In the back seat, the harsh tone of the DC's voice seemed to make Dudley shrink. He went from being a giant of a man to a slightly less gigantic man.

Tyler looked him up and down. Big. Strong. Caked in his own spew, right enough, but that was neither here nor there.

"Sorry, Dudley. I shouldn't have snapped," Tyler said. "Listen, you're a big lad. Fancy giving me a hand?"

Dudley looked unsure. "If I say yes, can I get the handcuffs off?"

"Course you can."

There was a *snap* and Dudley brought both hands out from behind his back. Tyler stared, struck dumb, as the big man rubbed the two bright red welts that marked his wrists.

"OK," Dudley said, smiling cheerfully. "What do you want me to do?"

It didn't take long to get Sinead up to speed on the case. It never did, which was why Logan had pegged her for a future career in plain clothes within minutes of meeting her.

After everything with Caitlyn, he'd offered Sinead a job—Detective Constable with the MIT. Perfect match for her, he'd said. Be right up her alley.

She'd said no. Aye, she'd been very grateful and respectful, and all that stuff. But she'd said no. It wasn't right for her current situation. Wasn't the right time. Wasn't the right choice.

Logan had rarely been more impressed with anyone in his life.

There had been no footage of Iona Wallace on Roddy's laptop. The only porn there had been of the man-on-man variety—or, occasionally, the men-on-man variety—and meant for his own personal consumption.

They'd had to take the laptop for further study, of course, and Logan was secretly looking forward to making Tyler comb through every last minute of the video content. All four-plus hours of it.

After leaving Roddy's flat, Logan and Sinead had headed out back to where the scarecrow stood watching over the beer garden. The DCI had hoped that he might find a camera tucked into the stuffing somewhere, but if there was one, then it was microscopic.

Still, he was sure there had been one, but that it had been removed. Joy Bryden, the one-woman Neighbourhood Watch, had reported people smoking in the beer garden in the latest meeting minutes.

Logan was sure that, if he went back through them, he'd find the locations of all her hidden cameras, and all the things they'd seen.

No wonder she was so keen to get wireless internet access for the whole island. Without it, she wouldn't have been able to spy on the place.

On the way back to the office, Logan had sent Sinead to borrow a whiteboard from the school. He'd have done it himself, he said, except he felt the kids might spontaneously combust through fear just at the very sight of him.

She'd come back ten minutes later with a flipchart on a rickety metal frame, which was the best the teacher had been able to rustle up. There was only one classroom, the teacher had pointed out, so they weren't exactly overflowing with spare equipment.

Logan had written while he'd explained, the Sharpie darting across the page as he'd told Sinead about Iona's background, her relationship with the other islanders, and filled her in on Bruce Anderson, Kevin Tillerson, Joy Bryden, and the "utter fucking delight" that was the Reverend Abraham Kerr.

He'd made only the most basic reference to Isaac Young. He hadn't gone into any great detail. Not yet. It would all come out, soon enough, of course—the diaries would make sure of that—but now wasn't the time.

When he finished, they had three pages of A3 paper filled with barely decipherable scribbles. They found some tape, and stuck them to the wall of the office, side-by-side. It wasn't a Big Board, and, if Logan was being completely honest, it objectively made very little sense, but it would do the job.

They were discussing next steps over tea, when the office door opened. The smell of vomit came wafting in, followed a moment later by the source.

"Christ Almighty. What happened to you?" Logan asked, burying his nose in the crook of his arm.

"Sinead!" said Tyler, when he spotted the uniformed officer sitting across from the DCI. He opened his arms as if to move in for a hug, but was promptly told he could get that idea right out of his head.

"Is that... Is that spew?" she asked, her nostrils clamping shut of their own accord. "And what happened to your face? Is that blood?"

"Aye. It's been an eventful day. Had a wee..." Tyler began. He spun on his heels as a thought struck him, started in panic, then ran back outside. "Shite!"

Logan and Sinead swapped glances across the desk. Sinead shrugged. There was something vaguely apologetic about it, like she felt the need to take some sort of responsibility.

"It's alright. I had him," droned a voice from outside. Its deep resonance suggested a very large man, or perhaps a mid-sized bull. It was affable, too, though, and gave the impression that even if the owner of it was about to gore you to death with its horns, it'd be nothing personal. "He wasn't going anywhere."

"Cheers, Dudley," Tyler said, then he reappeared sandwiched between two other men, both larger than he was.

Even with the vomit pebble-dash effect covering him from head to toe, Logan recognised Dudley Brown from the church service. It was the sight of the man Dudley was holding by the arm that got him up on his feet, though.

"Where the hell did you dig him up from?" Logan asked, looking Bruce Anderson up and down.

"From under the front wheels of the Land Rover, boss," Tyler said.

Logan and Sinead both regarded him quizzically.

"Long story," he said.

"He hit me with his fucking ute!" Anderson spat. His hands were behind his back, wrists bound together with another zip-tie.

Tyler shrugged. "Alright. Turns out it's not that long," he said. "Fortunately, no harm done. To him, I mean. Land Rover's knackered. Luckily, Dudley here was on hand to help me lift it enough to get him out."

Anderson snorted. "*Help?* You did fuck all, mate. Dud lifted it, you just made groaning noises and went red in the face."

"Shut up," Tyler told him. "I told you, anything you say can be used in evidence. This is all character stuff. I'd be careful what you say."

"Stick it up your arse, you dickhead."

Tyler patted his shirt pocket. The squelch it gave immediately made him regret this, but he tried not to let on. "You want me to write that down? Because I will."

"Ooh, you'll write it down? Shit, mate, you've got me on the bloody ropes now, alright."

Tyler squared up to the much bigger Anderson. "Look, pal, I'd be very careful what you say to me right now."

"Why?" Anderson asked.

Tyler hesitated. His reply, when it eventually came, was disappointing for all involved. "Just... because. Alright?"

"Right, well, that told him," Logan said. "You've read them both their rights?"

Tyler stepped back from Anderson and nodded. "Aye. Arrested this one on the suspected murder of Iona Wallace, and Dudley on assaulting a police officer. Although, that was a misunderstanding, and he's been a big help."

Dudley straightened proudly. Tyler shot him a sideways look.

"Apart from no commenting me about the scarecrow stuff—on the orders of Joy Bryden, no less—and repeatedly vomiting on the back of my head."

Tyler reached into one of his trouser pockets. "Which reminds me. One of the scarecrows, it had—"

"A camera," Logan said.

Tyler produced a plastic evidence bag with a flourish. He'd presumably been going for some big dramatic reveal, so the fact that Logan beat him to it caused him some visible disappointment.

"Right. Aye. A camera," Tyler said. He handed over the evidence bag. "Check the thickness of the wiring, boss. I'd say we've got a match for our murder weapon."

"Check out Sherlock bloody Holmes," Anderson sneered. "Good job, mate. Pat on the head for you."

Logan spoke before Tyler could open his mouth. "PC Bell?" he said, fixing Bruce Anderson with a cool stare that just bordered on being mildly amused. He was going to very much enjoy interviewing this one.

"Sir?"

"Why don't you take DC Neish and Mr Brown here to get cleaned up? I'm sure Pat and Norman at the B&B will be able to help you out. DC Neish will show you the way. Get them cleaned up, then bring them back."

"Ooh, can you clean me up, too, sweetheart?" Anderson asked, leering down at her. Tyler lunged, but Logan blocked his path with an arm like a steel girder.

"Go, Detective Constable," he ordered. "Now."

Tyler's frustration was written all over his face, but he bit his tongue and followed Sinead when she stepped past him and headed for the door.

"Come on, Dudley," the DC urged.

"Coming! Bye Bruce, bye... Mr Policeman," he said. Then, with a clumsy wave, he turned and left with the others.

Bruce Anderson snorted and shook his head. "Fucking cabbage," he remarked, although he waited until the door was safely closed first.

He turned to find Logan standing very close to him. The mildly-amused expression was gone. In its place, a granite impassiveness had been chiselled into the lines of the DCI's face.

"Mr Anderson," he said, indicating the chair tucked in behind Tyler's desk. "Please, take a seat."

"You going to make me?" Anderson asked.

Logan didn't move, yet he seemed to get closer to the other man. Anderson was tall, but he had nothing on the DCI.

"I can if you like, son," he said. "Middle of nowhere. No cameras watching. No one to dispute my account of you going mental on me, trying to escape."

He clapped his slab-like hands together and rubbed them. The *bang* of them meeting made Anderson jump.

"So, if you want us to go down that road, just you go ahead and say the word."

Logan could almost see Anderson's bravado seeping out of him, taking most of the colour in his face with it. There were no sarky comebacks. No snidey remarks. None of the cockiness that had previously been on display.

"Right then," said Logan, indicating the chair again. "How about you take a seat and we can talk this over like grown-ups?"

CHAPTER THIRTY-SEVEN

Pat's voice was the first thing Tyler, Sinead, and Dudley heard when they arrived at the Bed and Breakfast. It was impossible not to hear it, in fact, the way it shrieked out through the ancient windows.

"No, *you* piss off, Norman! *You* piss off! I've had it up to bloody here, with—"

"Look, I said I'm sorry, alright?" That was Norman's voice. Angry, yes, but cowed, too. Whatever the argument was about, he knew he'd already lost it. "It was a mistake. A stupid mistake."

"A *mistake*?" Pat yelped. Tyler could see her through the net curtains, throwing her arms up as she turned away from her husband. "You ruined my life, Norman! You ruined my bloody—"

She stopped when she saw the three figures standing frozen in the middle of the path. Tyler gave her an awkward wave. She returned it as a nod, then turned her back on the window and hurried away from it.

"That the owners?" asked Sinead.

"Pat and Norman. Aye," Tyler confirmed, leading the way up the path. "They're usually less... shouty."

The door opened before they reached it. Pat was flushed red, either with anger or embarrassment. She shot Tyler an uncomfortable smile as way of an apology.

"Sorry about that," she said. "We were just..."

"It's fine," Tyler said. He stopped on the step and looked past her into the house. "Everything OK, though?"

"What? Oh. Yes. Fine. Just a domestic," Pat said. "I mean, not in that sense... Just an argument."

"About what?" Tyler asked, his polis instincts spitting out the question before he could stop himself.

Pat shifted her weight from one foot to the other. "Uh..."

"Sorry. Force of habit," Tyler said, smiling at her. "None of my business."

"No. It's fine," Pat said. "We were just arguing about this place, actually. About coming here. All Norman's idea. Can't believe I went along with it. That was all."

She gave herself a shake, then looked the group up and down. She gave Sinead a welcoming nod.

"Hi. I'm Sinead."

"Hello, Sinead. Nice to meet you," Pat said. She turned her attention to the big man looming behind the officers. "Dudley."

"Hello, Pat," Dudley said. "Sorry you had an argument."

Pat started to smile, but then her nostrils flared as the breeze brought the smell inside.

"Jesus, what's that? Is that... Is that spew?"

"Aye, afraid so," Tyler confirmed. "Dudley had... an accident."

"I was sick on him," Dudley said.

"Yes, that pretty much—"

"And on myself."

"She can see that, Dudley," Tyler sighed. He half-rolled his eyes for Pat's benefit, then smiled. "We were hoping we could..."

Pat stepped aside. "You can use the one in your room, and Dudley can use the shower room downstairs."

"Cheers, Pat," Tyler said. "You're a lifesaver."

Logan sat in silence, reading over his notes. He hadn't been able to figure out how to connect to the office's printer, so he'd hastily jotted much of the information down longhand from Hamza's emails, then added his own thoughts and observations below.

Bruce Anderson was sitting in Tyler's chair, wedged in between the desk and the wall. The only way out of the room was through Logan, and they both knew that there was no way that was happening.

Logan's phone sat between them, the voice recorder app open and running. It had been going for almost five minutes so far, but had recorded nothing but the sound of pages turning, the occasional clearing of the DCI's throat, and an angry, "Can we get on with it?" from Anderson.

That last one had resulted in a long, oppressive glare from Logan, and a promise that they'd get on with it when he was good and bloody ready.

And now, the time had come. He was ready.

Good and bloody.

"Sorry to keep you there, Bruce," he said, flipping back to the first page of his notes.

"I'd prefer you to address me as 'Mr Anderson,'" the man on the other side of the desk sneered.

"Aye, well, I'd prefer you no' to be a thieving smart-arse, Brucie. Looks like we're both going to be disappointed," Logan replied. He continued before Anderson had a chance to object. "You saw Iona Wallace the night she died. Correct?"

Anderson shrugged.

"What was that?" Logan asked. "Yes or no, son? It's not a difficult question. Did you, or did you not—"

"Yes. I was working," Anderson spat. "She was in the pub. She left. I didn't see her again. Happy?"

"Ecstatic," Logan told him, although his face offered nothing to back that statement up. "What time, exactly, did you last see her?"

"I don't bloody know. What am I, her fucking biographer, or something? She had a few drinks, got into a fight with... well, everyone, then she left. What happened to her after that? How the hell should I know?"

"You'd had sex with her before though, yes?" Logan asked. It was a stretch, but he said it with enough authority to make it sound like he knew more than he did.

As it turned out, Anderson didn't need the truth teased out of him. He looked positively gleeful as he spilled the beans.

"Course I did. Show me anyone between the age of twenty and fifty who hasn't." He snorted, amused at the thought. "Listen, mate, if shagging her's enough to get you found guilty, you'd better lock up most of the men on this island, and half the flaming visitors who come here every year. You'll need to build a whole new prison just to hold us all."

"Yes. Thank you," said Logan. "I get the point. When did you sleep with her?"

"Which time?" Bruce asked. He grinned at the brief flicker of surprise that flitted across the detective's face. "Island's dull as shit. You got to take your jollies where you can. Know what I'm saying?"

Logan slid a blank sheet of paper across the desk and placed a pen on top of it.

"Write the dates."

"Dates? You expect me to remember the dates? I got no idea. Last time was about, maybe, what? Four weeks ago? Five? There were two times before that. Two nights in the same week."

"When?" Logan asked.

"Christ, I don't know. Two weeks before, maybe? Maybe a couple of months ago, in total. Not like I kept a diary."

"Iona did," Logan said. "Maybe you'll be in there."

"Ha! Maybe I will," Anderson said, but the way he shifted in his seat suggested he sincerely hoped he wasn't.

"How did it end between you?" Logan asked.

Anderson laughed. Properly, this time. "Will you listen to yourself? Nothing ended, mate, because nothing started. It was sex. That was all. She knew it, I knew it. Just sex."

"Did you pay her?" Logan asked.

Anderson's hesitation was fleeting but telling. "Not like that. I mean, it wasn't a bloody *transaction*, if that's what you mean. She just... She was broke. I gave her a tenner to help her out."

"Each time?"

"Fuck off. I'm not made of money! A tenner. Total."

Logan felt his insides sink a little. He had a little flashback of Iona Wallace in her school uniform, bold and brassy, and taking no shite from anyone. What an ending to her story. *Three Rides for a Tenner,* like a big wheel or a roller-coaster at a funfair. A one-woman *Irn Bru Carnival.*

"What was with the cleaning gear?" Logan asked.

"What cleaning gear?"

"You bought a load of cleaning supplies from the shop the day after Iona Wallace was murdered. Why?"

"Because I was told to," Anderson replied.

"Told to? By who?"

"By Roddy. In the pub?" Anderson said. It sounded like a question—both sentences did, in fact—but then, so did most things the Australian said.

Stupid bloody accent.

"You bought the cleaning supplies for the pub?" Logan asked.

"Yeah. Paid for out of the petty cash. I put the receipt in, and everything."

"Very conscientious of you," Logan said, his voice if not dripping, then at least moist with sarcasm. "Used them on your own place first, though."

"Perks of the job. Landlord's been bitching at me for weeks to get it cleaned up. Figured I might as well do it on Roddy's tab."

"Again," said Logan. "How very conscientious of you."

"Hey, I'm a bloody good member of staff, I'll have you know."

"That why you had your hands in the till, is it?" Logan asked. "Hardly screams 'Employee of the Month' that, does it?"

"I was just taking my wages," Anderson said. "I'd earned it. That money was mine, fair and square."

"I don't run a business, so I can't be sure, but I'm pretty confident that's no' how the payroll system works," Logan said. "You don't just grab a handful of notes and run. Roddy agrees with me, by the way. He says you nicked that money, no question about it."

"Well, that's not how I see it," Anderson said.

Logan pressed the tip of an index finger against the tabletop. "Well, that's very much how I see it, Brucie, and I'm the one with the polis badge. I know a bad bastard when I see one, and I see one sitting in front of me right now."

"Is that supposed to be scary?" Anderson asked.

"Scary? No. Not scary. Not yet," Logan said. "But how about I give it a try? I and a fellow officer both witnessed you stealing money from the pub till. As did the landlord. You attempted to evade arrest. You're in the country illegally, and you're wanted in a country that we will be *only* too happy to extradite you to. A country where the prison system isn't as jovial and carefree as our own. A country where, if you go down—and you will go down, Brucie—you don't get back up again."

He spread his hands, palms upwards. "In those circumstances? With what you're facing? Pretty boy like you? I'd be *wishing* I'd killed Iona Wallace, so I could spend the next fifteen years eating mince and tatties in a Scottish jail, instead of getting passed around in the showers of a prison in one of the... *less refined* nations, and coming out with an arsehole like the entrance to the Clyde Tunnel."

Logan nodded down at the pad and pen that still sat, unused, in front of the prisoner. "So, how about you go ahead and write your confession now?"

Anderson's eyes crept down to the paper and stayed there, but the rest of him made no move towards it.

"On you go. Don't overthink it," Logan instructed. "Doesn't have to be long or complicated, just write down the *whats*, the *whens*, and the *whys*, and we can make sure you do your time in this country, not in some underground Vietnamese dungeon."

Anderson's fingers twitched. His gaze remained fixed on the pen and paper.

"I hear they're clamping down hard on sex offenders over there, Bruce. Really making an example of the bastards. Foreigners especially."

He smiled thinly. "How'd you reckon you'll cope with that? Being made an example of, I mean? I wonder just what that will entail? Nothing good, I'm sure. I'll tell you this, I don't bloody envy you, son."

Bruce Anderson inhaled slowly through his nose, held it for several seconds, then exhaled through his mouth. He tore his eyes from the notepad just long enough to glance at the ceiling, then he was back to staring again.

"I'll be honest here. You're going to do time, Brucie. That's inevitable. But, do you do it here, or do you do it over there? Have you seen the conditions in some of these places? I wouldn't keep a bloody animal in them." Logan's finger tapped the edge of the paper. "Tell me how you killed Iona. Tell me *why*. And you can stay here. You'll serve your time in this country. I guarantee it."

The DCI let out an incredulous laugh. "They've even got Sky TV in the prisons now. Would you believe it? Sports package. Movies, I'm told. Over there, you'll be lucky to even catch a glimpse of the *actual* fucking sky ever again. Here? It'll be all catch-up, and Premier League, and HD On Demand. You'll be Live Pausing to your heart's content. Food's good too, these days. I mean, don't get me wrong, it's nothing spectacular. But it's no' bloody crickets, or grasshoppers, or whatever it is they make you eat in those Vietnamese places. It might no' be haute cuisine, but at least you can identify what's on your plate without a degree in entomology."

Logan picked up the pen. He clicked the button on the end, extending the point, then he held it out for the other man. "Go on, son. Get it off your chest. You'll feel better."

Bruce reached a hand out. His fingers wrapped around the pen's plastic casing, and his eyes met Logan's. A nod of encouragement passed from detective to prisoner, and then Anderson took the pen and began to write in big, angry strokes.

It didn't take him long to finish. Not nearly long enough.

Once he was done, he held the pad up for Logan to see. On it were five words, written in the middle of the page in block caps:

I WANT A FUCKING LAWYER.

"Come on now, Bruce. You don't want to hold all this up any more than we have to, do you?" Logan asked.

"Cut the shit, mate," Anderson said. He jabbed a finger against the notebook a few times, then waved it in Logan's face. "And do as you're bloody told."

CHAPTER THIRTY-EIGHT

"Hello, Jack. It's yourself!"

DI Forde squinted at the screen of the phone propped up on his desk, tried his reading glasses on to see if that helped make it any clearer, then took them off again and shook his head.

"Is that Sinead with you? She arrived, then."

"Aye, made it, sir," Sinead said. "Bumpy ride, but got here."

She was sitting to the right of DCI Logan, the phone pushed back a bit to fit them both in. Sinead's head was down near the bottom of the screen, while everything of Logan's, from the eyebrows upwards, had been cut off at the top.

"What's the news?" Ben asked. He glanced up as Hamza sat a cup of tea next to him, and smiled appreciatively. "Cheers, son."

Hamza sat down and rolled his chair closer, so they could both see the screen.

"We've found Bruce Anderson," Logan said. "Well, I say 'found.' Tyler hit him with a Land Rover."

"Jesus!" Ben exclaimed. "Is he hurt?"

"Sadly not," Logan said. "Refusing to talk without a solicitor present, though. We're going to have to get him brought back to the mainland. Thought I'd get him up to Inverness for you two to take a crack at him."

"Aye, be good to get our teeth into something," Ben said. "It's been a lot of internet and phone calls up this end, and I think we could both do with stretching our legs."

"Watch your hips," Logan suggested. "Man of your age."

"Don't you worry about me, Jack. I'm no' the heart attack waiting to happen," Ben replied. "I'm sure we can get a boat out to you from Mallaig today. Get a couple of Uniforms from Fort William to transport him."

"Want me to arrange that, sir?" Hamza asked.

"Aye. Good. Thanks," Logan said. "We've got him locked in the storeroom at the shop. No windows, one door. Tyler's keeping an eye."

"Nice bit of improvisation," said Ben.

"Aye, well, the more temporary the better. I want him off the island and in an Interview Room by this afternoon."

Ben nodded. "No problem. I have to ask, though, Jack... If he's our main suspect, why are you no' coming to interview him yourself?"

Logan shifted his weight in the chair. "I've a few things to tidy up here first. I'll send Sinead and Tyler back on the boat, so make sure there's enough room. I just need to..."

He thought of Isaac Young. He had to know the truth.

However hard that might be.

"...deal with a couple of outstanding issues."

Ben smirked. "Sure you're no' just hiding from Hoon, Jack?"

"I wish I was, Ben," Logan replied, his voice one long, heavy sigh. "I really wish that was it."

THE INTERVIEW with Dudley Brown was slow going at first, but it helped when Tyler said they weren't going to charge him for leathering shite out of the detective.

There was still a lot of *no commenting* from the big man, but Logan had quickly realised that the only questions he replied with 'no comment' on were those that he would otherwise answer with 'yes.'

Ask him why he made scarecrows, and he'd recite his reasons at length—it was fun, he was good at it, it gave him something to do, the local children loved them. That sort of thing.

Ask him if someone had given him the cameras to hide in the scarecrows:

"No comment."

Ask if that person was Roddy from the pub:

"Of course not! Why would Roddy want to put cameras in the Tattiebogles?"

Ask if that person was Joy Bryden:

"No comment."

Within twenty minutes or so, Logan had got the whole thing worked out. Dudley was thanked for his time, warned to stay out of trouble, and then he and Tyler went off to find the big man a lift back home across the island.

After that, Logan had Sinead bring in Joy Bryden. He'd taken great pleasure in seeing the expression on her face when she'd been led into her own office to find him holding court from behind her desk. She looked like she had a mouth full of wasps, and was under strict orders not to let any of them escape.

"Joy. Nice to see you again," he said. He gestured to the smaller, more rickety of the office's two seats. "Please. Sit down."

Joy regarded the seat with displeasure and distaste, then lowered herself onto it. She sat perched forward, like she thought she might catch something if she positioned herself too far back.

"Did PC Bell explain why I wanted to see you?"

Joy shook her head. "No. Nothing. I asked, but she was *not* forthcoming," she complained. "I have to say, the timing was not good. I was in the middle of some important paperwork, which I'm having to do at home, I should add. Any idea yet when I'll be able to get my office back?"

"Oh, not long now," Logan assured her. He pulled open one of the drawers of her desk and reached inside. "Just got a few matters to clear up."

There was a rustling sound and a soft *thack* as Logan placed an evidence bag on the desk between them. The beady eye of a camera gazed upwards from within a nest of wiring.

Logan sat back and folded his arms. "I'm going to leave you to do the explaining," he said.

Joy regarded the bag for a long, long time. She swallowed. She cleared her throat. She shook her head and had a stab at forming a nonplussed sort of smile.

"What's that?"

Logan's only reply was through his body language. It didn't change much—a slight adjustment of the shoulders, an incremental leaning forward of the head—but made it clear that he was not impressed by that answer. Not impressed, at all.

"Is it a camera, or something?" Joy asked.

"It is."

"Right. Well, what does it have to do with me?" she asked.

"I know what you've been up to, Joy," Logan said. "Do us both a favour and stop wasting my bloody time."

Now, Joy did sit back. Her lips drew tightly together, saying nothing, but her gaze went skittering around the room, like she might find a plausible explanation or excuse tucked away in one of the corners.

"Look, tell you what I'll do, Joy. I'll make it easier for you," Logan said. "I've got a boat coming over. Couple of officers on it. You know what they'll be bringing with them? A warrant to enter and search your premises, and to seize all your computer equipment."

He let that revelation sit there for a moment.

"So, here's what I want you to do for me, Joy," he continued. "I want you to think about what's there in your house right now. What's on your computers. What's lying around. Picture it for me. Because that—all that stuff—will be gone over with a fine-tooth comb.

"You might think you've deleted everything, but let me promise you, you haven't. We've got teams that can work wonders with that stuff. I've seen them reconstruct files from hard drives that had been smashed to pieces. I've seen them dig out stuff deleted years back. Had convictions on it, in fact."

He looked at his watch. "By my reckoning, they'll be here within the hour," he said, then he tapped the bag. "If I were you, I'd start talking."

Throughout the DCI's speech, Joy had tried valiantly to remain stoic and calm. By the time he reached the end of it, though, the effort of maintaining her composure was taking a visible toll, ageing her ten years in ten seconds.

"I was just... It was for the Neighbourhood Watch," she said, the words blurting out of her despite her best efforts to keep them inside. "It was for security!"

"You don't have a Neighbourhood Watch, Joy," Logan said.

"We do! Me! I'm the Neighbourhood Watch!"

"You're not. You're a nosy bastard. That's not the same thing," Logan told her. "You know what the law says about spying on people, Joy?"

Joy shook her head.

"No, nor did I. I mean, I probably should've, but it's no' really my area of expertise," Logan said. He tapped the screen of his phone. "Luckily, I had a colleague look it up. Apparently, it's covered under general Human Rights laws. You know, everyone's basic right to privacy, that sort of thing?"

He scrolled for a moment, then tapped the screen again. "Here we go." He cleared his throat, then rattled through a few lines in quick succession. "'It is illegal to fit spy cameras to a business or residential property that you do not own or in which you don't have legal occupancy.' That's one. 'All CCTV systems recording in public must be registered with the Information Commissioner's Office, and must be accompanied by signs that alert members of the public that CCTV is in operation.'"

Logan pointed at the screen. "They're apparently quite strict on that one," he said, before reading the final bullet-point in Hamza's email. "And, 'It is illegal to use spy cameras in areas where subjects may have a reasonable expectation to privacy. For example, you may breach the Human Rights Act if your CCTV camera is pointing directly into a neighbour's bedroom.'"

He set his phone down again and looked across the desk to the woman now practically cowering opposite. "Or a school. That's another example for you."

Joy's voice was trembling now. Her eyes were wide, imploring, tears welling up at the bottom. "I was just keeping an eye on things. Making sure everything was safe!"

"Didn't keep Iona Wallace safe, did it?" Logan said. "There was a camera in the scarecrow next to where the body was found, wasn't there, Joy?"

"It… it didn't see anything," Joy said. "It was late. Internet was down. It didn't see anything."

"No. But you did," Logan told her, and the breathless sob that forced its way out of her told him he was right. "See, I don't really care too much about you sticking cameras around the place. I mean, it's out of order, obviously, but it's not my department. But here's what I do care about, Joy…"

He sat forward and picked up the evidence bag. "Whoever killed Iona used the cable of one of these things to strangle her with. It wasn't this particular one, of course. I think, given the damage to the scarecrow itself, the killer spotted the protruding wire, grabbed it, and used it to finish Iona off. That's my theory."

Joy said nothing, just sat sobbing hot, silent tears of guilt, or shame, or a flavour not dissimilar.

"But here's the thing, there was no trace of it at the scene. No sign at all. No camera, no wiring, no battery pack, nothing," Logan said. "And you think, aye, fair enough. Killer took it. Makes sense, right? Except… next day was Wednesday."

Logan turned in his chair and indicated the calendar behind him, with all its little stickers. "Battery change day. That's what you said. For the 'webcams.' Plural."

He turned back, fixing the woman with a glare that could've punched a hole through concrete.

"You found her, didn't you?" he said. It was a question, yes, but it didn't sound like one. "Either when you went to change the battery, or when you realised the camera feed was down. You found her body, and instead of telling anyone, you removed all evidence of the camera having been there. Then, when that was done, you left her. Just left her there, in the mud. Dead. Didn't you, Joy?"

Joy continued to choke back her silent sobs. She and Sinead both jumped when Logan slammed a hand down on the desk and roared the question again.

"Didn't you? You left her!"

Joy's mouth formed the words, but her throat had tightened to the point it was almost impossible to hear them when they came out.

"Yes," she wheezed. "I'm sorry. I'm sorry."

Logan nodded. "Aye. I'm sure," he said, standing up. "Joy Bryden, I am arresting you on suspicion of attempting to defeat the ends of justice and on…" He glanced momentarily at his phone on the desk, realised there was no way he was going to remember the details, and gave a vague wave of his hand. "… various privacy-related breaches of the Human Rights Act still to be determined."

"I didn't kill her. I didn't. You have to believe me," Joy babbled. "Please. I didn't. I didn't."

"Aye, well, it'll all come out in the wash," Logan said, motioning for Sinead to put her handcuffs to good use. "It'll all come out in the wash."

CHAPTER THIRTY-NINE

Logan, Tyler, and Sinead stood on the dock, the engine of a motorboat chugging away in the water beside them.

Joy Bryden and Bruce Anderson were safely aboard, and now under the watch of two of Fort William's brightest and best uniformed officers. Or, the two who happened to be available, at least.

"You sure you're going to be alright, boss?" Tyler asked. "We could hang off with you."

Logan shook his head. His hands were deep in his pockets, and the breeze coming in off the water was swishing his coat around his knees.

"No. You two go. Get us underway with Anderson. He should have a solicitor waiting when you get him to Inverness. I want him singing by the time I get back."

"When are you coming back, sir?" Sinead asked.

Logan glanced back up the hill. "Soon. Just... got a matter to attend to."

Tyler met his eye, and a look of understanding passed between them. "Good luck with that, boss," the DC said.

"Aye. Thanks," Logan told him. "Whatever happens, I'm just pleased I don't have to listen to your bloody snoring."

"He says I snore," Tyler told Sinead. "I don't snore."

Sinead blushed a little, then smiled. "No comment."

"Right, off you go," Logan instructed. "Tell the boat to come back in an hour." He checked his watch. "Make it two, actually."

"And you're sure you don't want us to stay, boss?" Tyler asked.

Logan shook his head. "No," he said, sighing wearily. "This one is all on me."

"Right, well, if you head back to the B&B, you might want to wear a crash helmet," Tyler said. "Norman and Pat were having a right set-to earlier."

Logan frowned. "Aye? What about?" he asked. "Wasn't violent, was it?"

"No. Nothing like that. Mostly Pat raging at him," Tyler explained. "Think she's angry that he dragged them out here. All his idea, apparently."

"Was it? That's interesting," Logan said, after a momentary pause to consider this information. "Right. Well, I'll be sure to keep my head down."

HE'D ARRANGED to meet Isaac in the pub in an hour. Iona's son had seemed cagey when Logan called, but the DCI had stressed the importance of it, and Isaac had eventually agreed.

Between then and now, Logan was at a bit of a loss. He'd sent most of the evidence they'd gathered off on the boat, then had returned to the B&B to tell Kevin Tillerson that, provided he didn't leave the country, he was free to head home on the first ferry that turned up.

That done, Logan said his goodbyes to Norman and Pat, assured them Police Scotland would be in touch to cover everything, then asked if he could sit in the lounge and wait for his meeting.

They readily agreed, of course, and provided tea and biscuits to help him while away the time.

He sat in one of the wingback chairs, a single evidence bag down on the floor beside him, mug in hand, plate of biscuits balanced on his lap.

The view, which had been mostly obscured since he'd arrived, was finally clear. And Christ, it was worth the wait. He sipped his tea and gazed out at the world, lost in the cresting of the waves, the glacial movements of the clouds, and the circling of the birds above the rocks.

If he squinted, he could just make out the motorboat chugging towards Mallaig in the distance. There'd be transport waiting to whisk Joy and Bruce to their respective destinations. Joy Bryden was being handed over to CID in Fort William, while Bruce would be taken to Inverness to be met by an eager DI Forde and DC Khaled.

Anderson would likely prove to be a tough nut to crack, but Ben could handle it, particularly with the threat of the international warrant and life in a Hanoi prison to barter with.

He went back to admiring the scenery. It was the kind of view you could get lost in. The sort of vista a man would never tire of just gazing at. Admiring. Drinking in.

Four minutes later, his tea finished and all the biscuits eaten, Logan had seen enough of it to last him a bloody lifetime.

He took out his phone and, on a whim, typed in the address of one of the bigger porn sites, then he thumbed Iona Wallace's name into the search box.

No results.

He shut down the browser, clicked the button that put the phone onto standby, then set the device on the armrest of the chair.

He drummed his fingers.

Outside, waves crested and birds circled.

Somewhere in the house, that bastard of a cuckoo clock called three.

He picked the phone up again.

He opened the browser and typed in the address for another porn site.

He searched 'Iona Wallace.'

Nothing.

He searched 'Iona.'

Thousands of results. A quick scan through the thumbnail images didn't reveal anyone who resembled the particular Iona he was looking for.

He shut down the browser.

He set down the phone.

He sighed and scowled at the scenery, like it was really starting to get on his tits.

Logan moved in the chair. His foot hit the evidence bag on the floor beside him.

A thought crept in—slowly, tentatively, like it might be startled off at any moment.

He unlocked his phone. Opened the browser. Went back to the first site he'd checked and tapped in the search box.

He could see the front of the diary through the clear plastic of the evidence bag. The name there, written all those years ago. Her nom de plume. Her alter ego.

Logan typed.

Desiree Shanelle.

He hit return. The page went blank for a moment, and then the results loaded.

And there, in all her glory, she was.

There were nine videos. The thumbnail images of each one showed Iona—Desiree—either fully naked or in a state of undress.

Logan clicked on the first. The title was simply 'Desiree Shanelle 9' which, he assumed, made it the most recent.

The screen changed to show a video window. Logan got up, closed the lounge door, then returned to his chair before hitting the play button.

It jumped straight into the action. Iona lay on her front on the bed, while a naked man ground against her from behind, groaning and wheezing like he was a horse on the final furlong at Aintree.

Disappointingly, his face had been blurred out, which would make identifying him difficult. There might be something the tech bods could do, but Logan wasn't going to hold his breath.

He didn't recognise the room, either. Quaint. Old-fashioned. Like most of the houses on the island.

He reached for the back-up button so he could check through the other videos on the list. Somewhere, the cuckoo called.

"Stupid bloody clock," he muttered.

And there, in that moment, was when it all made sense.

CHAPTER FORTY

Logan found Norman in the garden shed at the back of the house. The detective knocked twice on the open door, then stepped back as Norman wheeled around in surprise.

"Mr Logan. Uh, hi. Sorry. I thought you were gone," Norman said. He had a screwdriver in one hand, held low at his side. A long screw hung from one corner of his mouth, like a cigarette. It bounced up and down when he spoke. "Is... is everything alright?"

"Could you come out here a moment please, Mr Dawson?" Logan asked.

A frown creased Norman's brow at this sudden use of formality. He moved to step out of the shed, but Logan indicated the screwdriver with a nod.

"Can you leave that, please?"

There was a pause as Norman looked down at the screwdriver, but then he set it down on the workbench and emerged onto the neatly-cropped lawn.

"Is everything alright?" he asked again, more tentatively this time.

"What was your relationship with Iona Wallace, Mr Dawson?"

Norman's Adam's Apple bobbed all the way to the bottom of his throat.

"Relationship? We didn't have... We didn't have a relationship."

"But you'd had sex," Logan said. Not a question. A statement of fact.

"What?" Norman half-laughed, his voice disintegrating around the edges. "Why would you...? What makes you...?"

Logan held up his phone. The image on-screen was frozen and showed a naked man, his face blurred, with Iona Wallace's legs wrapped around him.

With a tap of a finger, Logan pressed play, and the figures began to writhe and moan.

"I'm not... I don't know what—" Norman began, but Logan held up a finger for silence.

They waited, the only sounds in the garden the twittering of birdsong and the grunting of the people in the video.

And then, it came. The call of the cuckoo clock they both knew all too well.

Logan paused the video and returned the phone to his pocket.

"That was uploaded ten days after you and Pat arrived on the island," Logan said. "I checked."

He sighed, but seemed more annoyed with himself than with the other man. "People have been telling me since I got here that she was quick to jump on any new arrivals. I thought that meant tourists. Didn't occur to me that you were a new arrival, too."

Logan turned and looked at the upstairs windows of the house. The smallest window was open, the textured glass coated white with steam.

"I had a poke through the other rooms in the house. Except the bathroom. I think your wife's in there. Thought best not to disturb her until you and I had this wee chat. The décor in the video doesn't match anywhere. But that's because you redecorated, isn't it? The one room in the house you changed is the room you had sex in. The room you knew she had video footage of."

Norman said nothing, but half-stepped, half-fell backwards until he thudded against the side of the shed. He leaned there, using it for support, his face melting into sorrow and shame.

"I was... I was drunk. I didn't know she'd filmed it until weeks later. She asked at the time, and I said no. Of course, I said no, but she must've... She..." He buried his face in his hands. "Oh, God! How did you find it? She said she hadn't shared it. She promised me. It's not online, is it? Oh, God, it's not online? I paid her! She asked for money, and I paid her! What more did she bloody want?!"

So, she was blackmailing him, then. That was it.

"You wanted to keep her quiet. Newly arrived in the community, struggling to fit in, you want to make a good impression. Video footage of you rodgering Iona Wallace isn't going to help your case," Logan said. "You wanted to make sure she stayed quiet, so you killed her."

Norman opened his mouth, but Logan spoke before he could.

"Except... you were home. Kevin Tillerson saw you. Spoke to you. The night Iona died. You were home," Logan muttered.

"Yes! Exactly!" Norman confirmed. "I was home. All night. I didn't kill her, I swear!"

"Shh. Shut up." Logan's eyes widened. He took a big step closer to Norman, pinning him to the shed with the sheer weight of his presence alone. "Pat. Did she know? About you and Iona? Did she know?"

"She wouldn't—"

"*Did she know, Norman?*" Logan demanded.

"Yes! Yes, Iona told her. But she didn't... She wouldn't..."

But Logan had already spun on his heels and was thundering across the grass. Behind him, Norman slid down the shed wall, the tears of shame he'd been holding back for months finally bubbling to the surface.

Steam was seeping from beneath the bathroom door when Logan arrived at it.

"Mrs Dawson?" he said, knocking. "Pat? Can you come out, please?"

There was no sound from within besides the faint whirring of the extractor fan. Logan knocked again, making sure to rattle the door this time in a way that suggested it wouldn't hold him out for long.

"Mrs Dawson, I need you to get dressed and come out. We need to talk."

A door creaked open along the hall. Kevin Tillerson poked his head out. "Everything OK?"

"Get back in your room, Mr Tillerson," Logan ordered.

Tillerson didn't need telling twice. The door closed again immediately, and was followed by the *clack* of a lock sliding into place.

Logan rattled the handle of the door. Locked, of course, but there was something oddly violating about a bathroom door handle being turned from the outside that tended to force those inside into some kind of action.

Sure enough, he heard movement. A creak. A sob. A faint rattling sound.

"Fuck," he spat, then he drove a shoulder through the door, throwing it wide.

Pat stood naked in the corner, tears streaming down her face, blood oozing from raw, gaping gouges in her wrists.

Logan crossed the room in two big steps, wrenched the pill bottle from her hand, and tossed it into the bloodied water of the bath.

She tried to fight him off. Screamed as she slapped at him. Howled as she pushed, and shoved, and kicked with her bare, water-wrinkled feet.

"She was going to tell everyone," Pat sobbed. Her legs gave out and Logan had to wrap his arms around her to keep her on her feet. Her weight pressed against him, hot and wet and shaking from head to toe.

The words that tumbled out of her were all tangled up in tears, and snot, and raw, throaty sobs.

"She ruined our marriage. She was going to ruin our lives! We gave her money, but it wasn't enough. It was never enough!"

Logan checked the woman's wrists. The gouges looked painful, but they hadn't gone deep enough to do any serious damage.

"She was evil!" Pat whispered. "She was *evil.*"

"She wasn't evil. Just damaged," Logan said. He listened to the muffled sobs of Pat as she buried her face against his chest. "But then, aren't we all?"

CHAPTER FORTY-ONE

Logan sat in the Canna Come Inn, a tepid cup of coffee on the table in front of him.

The boat had been quick off the mark coming back over. One of the Uniforms from Fort William had been aboard, and Logan had handed Pat Dawson over into his custody, then given instructions to wait at the dock for him to return.

He hadn't managed to get the full story from Pat yet, but he'd pieced together enough. Iona had been blackmailing them for months, demanding more and more money to keep secret the fact that she and Norman had done the dirty deed.

She'd threatened to release the video. They hadn't known that it was already online, albeit with Norman's face blurred out. She'd said she was going to send it to the couple's parents. To their siblings. To their nieces and nephews.

The local community would've shunned them, Pat said. Everything they'd built would've been taken from them. They'd have been ruined, if she'd gone through with it.

It was Iona's fault, Pat had insisted. She had left Pat no option. Murder was the only road left open.

Any other details could wait for now. He had his killer. He'd nabbed two other bastards, into the bargain.

Aye, he might not still have a job by the time any of it came to trial, but he'd done it. He'd brought them in. He'd given Iona a justice that, he had to admit, she may not even have deserved.

But there was one injustice he could still put right. One that she did deserve.

Logan looked up from the coffee cup as Isaac Young arrived at the table.

"Sorry, I'm a bit late," Isaac said. "Got caught up with a few errands."

"No bother at all," Logan said. He indicated the seat across from him. "Can I get you anything?"

Isaac shook his head as he sat. "I'm fine, thanks. I don't have much time."

"Right. Well," Logan said, getting down to business. "First up, I want you to know that we've arrested someone for your mother's murder."

"I heard. Bruce. The barman from here."

"Eh, no. There's been a new development," Logan said. "We've had a confession from Pat Dawson."

Isaac blinked. "What? At the Bed and Breakfast? *That* Pat?"

"Aye," Logan said.

"Why?"

"It's a long story," Logan said. "And one that, to be honest, you'd be better off not knowing for as long as you possibly can. We don't have the full story yet ourselves. But we will. We'll get it."

Isaac stared down at the table in front of him, like he was trying to will a stiff drink into existence.

"Bloody hell," he muttered. "That's... Bloody hell."

"Aye. Understandable reaction," Logan said. He took a swig of his cold coffee, grimaced, then sat up straighter in his chair. "There was... There was something else, too. Something I found in your mum's old diaries."

Isaac looked up, frowning. "Mum kept diaries?"

"Aye. Sometimes," Logan said. He cleared his throat, not quite sure how to say what he needed to say. "And, well... the thing is, Isaac..."

He inhaled, held it, then breathed out.

"It's about your dad."

Isaac sat and listened in silence as Logan told him. Told him how his life had been a lie. Told him how the man he'd thought was his father was not. Told him, for the first time ever, the full truth.

And then, when it was all out in the open, Isaac Young fell forward onto the table, buried his head in his arm, and sobbed in anger and in shame.

"Is Isaac OK?" asked Roddy, glancing over at the younger man. He was still sitting at the table, now nursing a hot cup of tea which he'd shown no signs yet of drinking.

Logan stood by the bar with his wallet open, ready to settle the bill. He glanced back at Isaac, then gave a single shake of his head.

"No. No' really," he admitted. "What do I owe you?"

"Nothing. On me," Roddy said.

Logan thought about protesting, but what was the point now?

"Thanks," he said, returning the wallet to his pocket.

"No. Thank you, Mr Logan," Roddy said. "I've been thinking a lot about what you said. About happiness, and not knowing what's around the corner. About what happened to your friend. And... you're right. It's stupid. I've been stupid, hiding away, pretending I'm someone I'm not."

He inhaled deeply through his nose, and his chest seemed to double in size. "I'm going to do it. I'm going to tell them all," he vowed. "If they don't like it, tough. It's my pub. If they don't want to drink here, fine."

"No' like they've got a wealth of other places to choose from," Logan said.

Roddy laughed. It was a giggle of relief. "Exactly! Yes! What else are they going to do? Go to the cinema? Go bowling?"

He looked around at the patrons of the bar. There were three of them, not counting Logan or Isaac, all sitting at different tables, reading, doing crosswords, or just staring blankly into space.

"I'm going to do it," Roddy whispered. "I'm going to bloody do it."

"Good for you, Mr Mackay," Logan said. "You could even consider a name change for the pub."

Roddy's smile remained in place, but a frown troubled his brow. "Eh?"

"The 'Canna Come Out?' has a nice ring to it," Logan said. He reached across the bar, shook the landlord's hand. Then, with a final look at Isaac—a look filled with every different shade of sadness and regret—he turned to the door.

He'd just pushed it open when the bell behind the bar rang. Logan stepped through, but waited and listened as Roddy cleared his throat, then spoke in a loud, clear voice.

"Sorry, everyone. Sorry. It's not last orders, don't worry. I just wanted to tell you all something," he said.

He drew in a breath. All eyes turned his way.

"I'm gay," he announced.

There was silence. Lengthy. Pregnant. Contemplative.

"Oh," said the man with the crossword. "Right. Fair enough, then."

And then, Logan let the door close, and headed for his final appointment of the day.

"Do you mind? We are in the middle of a reading."

Logan stood in the doorway of the church, a dark silhouette against the pale blue sky.

The Reverend Abraham Kerr stood at the front, scowling up the short aisle. Four elderly parishioners sat on the front-most pews. They shuffled around, craning their necks to look in the direction of the door.

"No. Don't mind at all. You carry on," Logan said, strolling into the church and letting the door swing closed with a *thunk*.

"What do you want, Mr Logan?" the minister asked.

"Detective Chief Inspector," Logan reminded him. He arrived at the front, and looked down at an old woman perched near the end of the pew. "Budge up, sweetheart," he told her, and she and the skeletal man beside her both slid a few feet along the bench.

Logan flopped down onto it, folded his arms, then gave the minister a nod. "Crack on, then."

"This is a private Bible study group," Kerr said. "I'd appreciate it if you—"

"Do you do requests?" Logan asked.

Kerr's hawk-like features frowned. "I beg your pardon."

"Requests. Bible's greatest hits. Feeding of the five thousand. Water into wine. All that shite," Logan said. "Do you do requests?"

"What are—"

"Matthew, Chapter One, Verse Two," Logan said. "That's a favourite of mine. Love to hear it."

Reverend Kerr did not reply. His features locked together in place, frozen and immobile.

"Come on. Out with it, then," Logan urged. He waited for a response he knew wouldn't come, then shrugged. "Well, fortunately, I memorised it on the way up here. Wasn't difficult. It's very short."

He stood, drawing himself to his full height. "Matthew, Chapter One, Verse Two," he began. "Abraham begat Isaac."

There was some murmured confusion from the elderly parishioners, but there was no confusion on Kerr's face. The truth, he knew, was finally out.

"Abraham Kerr," Logan said. "I am arresting you on suspicion of the rape of your daughter, Iona Wallace."

THE BOAT JOURNEY to Mallaig was, Logan had to admit, an absolute belter. At one end, the Uniform from Fort William was trying his best to keep Pat Dawson from throwing herself overboard, while Logan sat at the back with Reverend Kerr, glaring at him whenever he tried to open his mouth.

They didn't need a confession. They had Iona's diaries and, more importantly, they'd get Isaac's DNA. No matter how much the minister wriggled and squirmed, it was concrete. The twisted bastard was going away.

Isaac had taken it hard, of course. No surprise there. He told Logan he'd suspected the man he thought of as his dad wasn't his actual father, but he'd clung to it because he wanted to believe it. He didn't want to believe the alternative, that his dad was some random teenage hook-up down a dark alley somewhere.

Although, given what he now knew, Isaac had wished, more than anything, that were the case.

And Logan, to his surprise, had too.

The DCI watched the foaming waters breaking past the starboard side, losing himself in the churning bubbles.

They'd passed Rum now, where he'd watched stags go darting along the beach, almost like they were challenging him to a race. Mallaig was a few minutes ahead. The mainland. Normality.

And all the consequences and complications it would bring.

Still, four collars in one day. Not a bad way to end it.

There were three polis cars waiting at the harbour at Mallaig. Uniforms had jumped out of two of them when the boat came in, their jackets zipped up against the unforgiving winds.

Pat and Abraham had been separated, one in one car, one in another.

"Mind if I cadge a lift back to the Fort off you, son?" Logan asked the constable who'd landed the job of driving the minister.

The DCI had already opened the passenger door when the other Uniform piped up from the next car over. The only one not to have a prisoner in the back seat.

"Actually, sir, I've been asked to take you," he said. Logan spotted the sergeant stripes on the man's shoulder and closed the door with a soft *thunk*.

"Aye. Right. Makes sense," he said. "You want me in the back or the front?"

"Up to you, sir," the sergeant replied.

"In that case, if you don't mind, I'll call shotgun," Logan said, opening the front passenger door.

He looked out across the water, to the islands sitting out there by the horizon. He inhaled, breathing in the salt, and the fish, and the freedom.

"Right then," he said, climbing into the car. "Let's get this over with."

THE JOURNEY PASSED IN SILENCE. Logan's choice. The sergeant tried to strike up a conversation a couple of times, but the DCI wasn't in the mood.

The convoy of police vehicles slowed as it approached the roundabout next to the Fort William station. Logan watched the first two cars hanging a left, caught glimpses of Pat and Abraham through the side windows as they turned onto the station road.

But then, the car he was in continued straight across the roundabout without turning.

"We no' going in there?" Logan asked. "They've not got you taking me all the way to Inverness, have they? Can I stop for a pee first?"

"Not to Inverness, sir, no. West End car park," the sergeant replied.

"West End... Why? What's at the West End car park?" Logan asked.

The sergeant shrugged. "Dunno, sir. Just doing what I'm told."

They cruised through the sparse, off-season traffic. Logan gazed out of the side window, watching familiar landmarks slide by. There was JJ's café. The High School. The bridge he'd raced across in Sinead's car the first time he'd met her, when they'd thought her brother was in danger.

Onwards, past the turn-off to the pizza shop that didn't take card payments.

Past the leisure centre, past the supermarket. The hotel he'd stayed at with Ben and the rest of the team was down there somewhere, hidden by the golden arches of the MacDonald's.

Caitlyn had been with them then. It was the first night Logan had seen her truly happy.

And the last.

A black BMW was waiting at the West End car park. The door opened as the polis car pulled in off the roundabout, and Logan saw the bulky frame of Detective Superintendent Hoon step down from inside.

"Fuck," he muttered.

"Aye. Good luck, sir," the sergeant said. He pulled them into a space directly across from the Beamer, keeping a safe distance. "Think I'll just drop you here, if that's alright?"

"Don't blame you, son," Logan said. "Cheers for the lift."

He unclipped his belt, puffed out his cheeks, then stepped out to face his fate.

"Well, well, look who it is. The one-man clusterfuck," Hoon spat, when Logan approached.

Behind the DCI, the sergeant's car went speeding out of the car park. Probably trying to escape the blast radius, Logan thought.

"Sir," Logan said. "Wasn't expecting a personal visit."

"My toe should be paying a personal fucking visit to the crack of your arse, sunshine," Hoon told him. "Where the fuck have you been?"

"Canna, sir, it—"

"Don't come the cunt wi' me, Jack. You know what I fucking-well mean!"

Logan flashed the DSup an apologetic smile. "Aye. Sorry, sir."

"I appreciate that being a smart-arse is a force of fucking habit, Detective Chief Inspector, but now's no' the time or the fucking place. Got it?" snapped Hoon.

Logan nodded. "Got it." He shoved his hands deep in his pockets and rocked on his heels. "So, I'm guessing this is about what happened at Bosco's."

"Bosco? That clown? Fuck me, Jack. What do you take me for? Only mistake you made there was no' tying the prick to a fucking chair before lighting the match," Hoon said. "Bosco? Fuck off. I don't give a flying fuck about that Russian bastard."

Logan's brow furrowed into lines of confusion. "What? So... What's this about, then?" he asked, gesturing around them.

Detective Superintendent Hoon rolled his tongue around in his mouth for a moment, like he was having to manhandle the words out.

"You were right, Jack," he said, and it visibly pained him to say the sentence aloud. "You were right."

"Right? About what?" Logan asked.

There was something about the way Hoon was acting that made the fine hairs on the back of Logan's neck stand on end. The wind coming in off the loch beside them seemed colder than it should be.

"Sir?" Logan pressed. "What am I right about?"

Hoon sighed. It was heavy and weary, full of trepidation about what had happened.

Or what was about to.

"It's Owen Petrie," he said. "It's Mister Whisper."

Logan's heart fell into his stomach. He knew what was coming. He knew, beyond a shadow of a doubt, what the man standing across from him was about to say.

"He's free."

AFTERWORD

(AND A NOTE ON CANNA)

Thank you for reading this book. At the time of writing, most of the world is in a state of lockdown as we do our collective best to combat the Coronavirus situation we find ourselves in.

I hope this book - murder, betrayal, and all - has given you some respite from the worry, stress, and drudgery of our new normal.

It's a frightening time. But, like DCI Logan always does, we'll find a way to overcome it. We'll get through. It might not be easy, but by supporting each other and accepting help when we need it, we'll get through this together.

Now, I'm afraid I've got something I have to admit. The Canna featured in this book does not exist. It is a completely fictionalised version of the real island, which currently has a population of around seven people.

It also has no pub.

I decided to make up my own version of Canna for a number of reasons. There are other Scottish islands much more similar to the one in this book, but that is part of the problem.

Setting a crime novel in Inverness, or even Fort William, is one thing, as both have reasonably large communities. Setting one in a small island community, using actual locations, is more problematic, and I was worried I might inadvertently paint real islanders in a bad light.

I could have completely made up a new island, but the other locations in the books have all been real places, so I didn't want to break that continuity.

And so, I compromised - a real island, with a false reality laid over the top.

Once the current lockdown has passed, and we're all free to travel again, I urge you to visit Canna and the rest of the Scottish small isles. No, you won't be able to drink at the Canna Come Inn, or take part in the Tattiebogle Trail, but the scenery is incredible, the locals are friendly, and you're very unlikely to be murdered. So, swings and roundabouts, really.

Thanks again for reading the book. If you have time to leave a review on Amazon, Goodreads, or anywhere else you fancy, I'd massively appreciate it.

As I'm sure you can gather from the ending of this story, book six is on the way, so you haven't seen the last of DCI Logan and his team.

Until then, stay safe, stay sane, and look after yourself and each other.

Best wishes,

JD Kirk

A WHISPER OF SORROWS

DCI JACK LOGAN BOOK SIX

CHAPTER ONE

THE ROOM WAS MOST NOTABLE FOR ITS MISSING BASTARD.

At least, to DCI Jack Logan it was. To anyone else, the most comment-worthy aspect of the room would likely be the tape outline across the threshold of the door, marking the shape of a person.

Or, perhaps it would be the stain on the floor, once red, now dried to a shade of rusty brown, or the similarly coloured spattering across the walls on either side.

If someone was looking very closely, the thing they passed remark on might be the missing leg of the chair, the rigid plastic sheared off at an angle to create a long sliver of a point.

Logan had noticed all of that. Of course, he had.

But it was the missing bastard that disturbed him most.

"You alright, Jack?"

Detective Superintendent Hoon's voice was uncharacteristically soft. It was also the longest sentence Logan had heard the man say without swearing, which spoke volumes about the gravity of the situation.

"No. No, I am not," Logan muttered. His eyes went from the tape, to the bloodstains, to the broken chair. Finally, it swung a right and stopped on the unmade bed that the room's former occupant had slept in for most of the last decade. A gush of blood had stained the clinical white sheets down near the foot of the bed, but it was the man-sized indent in the mattress that Jack focused on.

He glared at that imprint. Glowered at it, like he could summon the bastard back through sheer bloody force of will. He couldn't, of course. Not like that. But he would get him back.

One way, or another.

"Talk me through it again," Logan said, turning away from the bed and addressing the man standing out in the corridor.

DCI Samuel Grant—*Snecky* to pretty much everyone who knew him—had been stationed in Inverness until Logan had requested a transfer earlier in the year. Snecky had been quick to jump on it, believing he was destined for the Central Belt Big Time, despite having predominantly attained his rank by showing up often enough, as opposed to through any sort of actual aptitude.

He looked thinner than he had when Logan had last crossed paths with him. It had been nine or ten months since then, but Snecky had lost some of the excess weight he was carrying, and his already-receding hairline had started to beat an even hastier retreat.

The weight-loss didn't suit him. It made him look ill and gaunt. There was a haunted look to him, too, like he was screaming behind the eyes, and Logan felt a pang of guilt for throwing the poor bugger into the lion's den of his old stomping ground.

A flash of irritation flitted over Snecky's face that immediately eradicated Logan's guilt. The other DCI glanced briefly down at a stack of notes he carried, but it was done through habit, and he recited the information from memory.

It wasn't hard. There wasn't a lot of it.

"Orderly turns up to give him his medication on Friday afternoon. Checks through the slot, Petrie's in his bed. Opens the door, steps in, crosses to the bed, and Petrie stabs him with the sheared off chair leg," Snecky recited. He sounded bored of the details now. Resentful of having to go over them all again. The Invernesian accent that had earned him his nickname was less pronounced now, hidden by the Glasgow accent he was trying very hard to affect. "Blood, blood, blood, scream, scream, scream, he staggers back, falls in the doorway. Voila."

Snecky stepped back out of the tape outline he'd been standing in and gestured down at it.

"Dies a couple of minutes later, but Petrie's already well on the move by then," Snecky continued. "Grabs a nurse, threatens to kill her, too, unless they buzz him out. So, they buzz him out."

"And the twisted fucker kills her, anyway," Detective Superintendent Hoon concluded.

Logan nodded, recalling the other person-sized outline of tape down in the hospital foyer.

"Why was the door open?" Logan asked. "Why didn't the orderly shut it behind him?"

DCI Grant glanced down at his notes again. "I don't know. Should it have been?"

"Yes. I want to know why it was left open," Logan told him.

Snecky nodded and started to turn, then stopped himself. He faced front again, pushing back his shoulders like a soldier on parade. "Aye, well, it's not your case, Jack," he said.

Hoon answered before Logan could open his mouth. "Less of your fucking lip, you jumped-up wee fuck, and do as you're fucking telt," he barked, stabbing a finger out the door and along the corridor.

Snecky literally sprang into the air in fright, almost dropping his notebook. "Aye. I mean, aye. Right. Aye, I was going to say I'd... Aye," he babbled, then he turned and scurried away, his tail tucked so far between his legs he was almost choking on it.

"Thanks," Logan grunted.

Hoon shook his head. "Tell you, Jack, swapping you for that clueless sack of shite was the best thing I've ever done," he remarked. It was, Logan thought, far and away the nicest thing the Detective Superintendent had ever said to him. "I mean, don't get me wrong, you're a useless bastard, but you're no' *Snecky* useless. And that's something."

"Aye. I suppose it is," Logan agreed.

Hoon had been waiting for Logan when the DCI returned from a case out on one of the Small Isles, and had broken the news then about Owen Petrie's escape.

They'd made the trip south to Carstairs State Hospital in Hoon's car. Most of the journey had been spent in silence, aside from a few dozen foul-mouthed outbursts from the Detective Superintendent whenever they came across another driver who had the audacity to be travelling at any speed not exactly matching his own.

It wasn't until they'd pulled screeching into the car park that Hoon had asked the question that had clearly been preying on his mind.

"Well?" he'd demanded. "Aren't you going to fucking say it?"

"Say what?" Logan had asked.

"You know full fucking well what I mean. 'I fucking told you so.'"

Logan had shaken his head and said that no, he wasn't.

What would be the point?

He *had* told them so, of course. Scores of times. Hundreds.

Owen Petrie might have fooled the doctors. He might have convinced everyone else that the head injury he'd sustained during his arrest had left him irreparably damaged, but not Logan. Logan had seen through it. Logan had known the truth, that the bastard was just waiting. Biding his time until he was ready.

Until now.

"Who was he?" Logan asked, looking down at the outline on the floor.

"Hm? Oh," Hoon said, following the DCI's gaze. "New guy. Another Jack, as it happens. Wright, I want to say. Twenty-fucking-six. Poor bastard. Got a wee one at home."

Logan met the DSup's eye, an unspoken concern passing between them. "Aye. We've got Uniform keeping watch, but I doubt the bastard'll head there. To paraphrase that Australian bint, *you should be so fucking lucky*."

"Never pegged you as a Kylie fan, sir."

"Aye, well I'm a man of many fucking mysteries, Detective Chief Inspector," Hoon replied. He dragged a hand down his face, and Logan got the impression it had been a few days since the DSup had slept. "You know the sick bastard's going to come after you, don't you?"

Logan looked around the room, nodding slowly. "Aye. Probably."

"No fucking *probably* about it," Hoon said.

He turned, leaned out of the door, and roared, "SNECKY!" at the top of his voice.

There was a bustling from out in the corridor, then the hurried clatter of footsteps as DCI Grant came rushing back to the cell.

"Sir?"

"The fuck've you been?" Hoon demanded.

Snecky blinked. "You said—"

"Jesus fucking Christ. Do you no' recognise a rhetorical question when you hear one?" Hoon indicated the stack of notes in DCI Grant's arms. "Show him."

Snecky looked down at the bundle, winced, then raised his head again. "Show him what, exactly, sir?"

"Fuck's sake. The photo. The fucking picture. It's no' difficult. It's no' a big leap of fucking logic. Show him the photo."

"Right. Aye. Sorry," Snecky replied, fumbling through the stack of paperwork.

Hoon shot Logan a sideways look, rolled his eyes, then sighed. "Just you fucking take your time, son. No rush," the DSup said, in a tone that made it very clear he meant the exact opposite of everything he'd just said.

"Sorry. Just... Aha."

Snecky tugged a glossy A4 photo from the pile and presented it to Hoon with a flourish and a hopeful smile.

"The fuck you giving it to me for? I don't want it. Him," Hoon said, pointing to Logan with a jerk of his head.

Snecky's smile lost some of its shine as he shuffled a half-step in Logan's direction and handed him the photo, instead. Logan took it and studied it in silence for a few moments.

The picture showed the very spot where they were standing, albeit with a body filling most of the frame.

As corpses went, it wasn't the worst one Logan had seen. Not by a long shot. The eyes were open, rolled back in the head, the face frozen forever in a rictus of horror and shock.

There were multiple stab wounds in the stomach, although the amount of blood staining the lower half of the orderly's white tabard made it impossible to tell how many just from the photograph alone. Going by the ravaged state of the material, though, 'a lot' would be a reasonable guess.

The sight of the blood on the lower half of the dead man's uniform didn't really disturb Logan, though. He'd seen it all before, too many times to count.

The blood on the top half was another story.

There was much less of it, and what there was had been daubed onto the otherwise unblemished material. Smeared into the fabric.

Six letters, crudely finger-painted across the man's upper chest.

HIJACK.

"This cretinous jizz stain reckons it means the bastard escaped to carry out a fucking terrorist attack," Hoon said, indicating Snecky with a look that didn't so much border on contempt as fully muscle in on its territory.

"Well, I mean, it does say, 'Hijack!'" DCI Grant protested.

Logan shook his head. "It doesn't," he muttered.

Snecky leaned in and pointed to the letters. "I think you'll find—"

"It says, "Hi Jack,"" Logan said, cutting him short.

Snecky hesitated, his brow lightly furrowing. "Aye. So..."

"For fuck's sake. Were you dropped on your coupon as a wean, son? Is that the issue here?" Hoon snapped. "It's hi-fucking-space-fucking-Jack. No' *hijack*. He's no' going to bring down the twin towers."

There was a moment of silence, during which Snecky's lips moved, like he was testing out his next question before voicing it.

"Who's...?" he began, then his gaze flitted across to Logan. "Oh. Shite. Aye."

Hoon pointed at one of his ears. "Fuck me. You hear that? The clang of that penny dropping?" he asked, then he gave DCI Grant an appraising up-and-down look that found very little worth praising.

"Where's his badge?" Logan asked, still looking at the photo.

"Badge?" asked Hoon.

Logan tapped the left of the man's chest, just above the letter 'K'. "They've got badges, haven't they? Where's his?"

Hoon ripped the photo from Logan's hand, considered it, then practically threw it at Snecky. "His badge. Why has no one else mentioned his fucking badge?"

"I, uh, I don't—" Snecky stammered, before Hoon silenced him with a glare.

"Then how about you fucking find out?" the DSup suggested. "And speaking of which, you find out why the door was open yet?"

"Uh, not yet, sir," Snecky admitted.

"Then why are you standing here with that glaikit look on your face? Away you fuck! Get out of my sight."

Logan almost felt sorry for the other DCI as he went scuttling off along the corridor again. Although, on the other hand, it was nice not to be the direct focus of the Detective Superintendent's temper for once.

"Looks like the shitestain's got a stauner for you, Jack," Hoon said.

Logan frowned. "Snecky?"

"No. No' fucking Snecky. Jesus Christ." Hoon stabbed a fingertip against the photo, almost knocking it out of Logan's hands. "Petrie."

"Oh. Aye. Well, hardly surprising," Logan said. His eyes widened a fraction. "Shite. I should—"

"Uniform's already watching them," Hoon said. "Your daughter's at work. Your wife's at home."

"Ex-wife," Logan corrected.

Hoon scowled at him. "Do I look like your fucking marriage counsellor? Do you want to piss about discussing your marital problems, and your *cock*-handed attempts to fire it up that Irish Pathologist bird—aye, don't think I don't know about that, by the way—or do you want to go out and catch this prick?"

Logan felt a prickly heat creeping up his neck and across his cheeks. He looked down at the photograph in his hand. "I want to go out and catch this prick."

"Aye. That's more fucking like it," Hoon said, then he spun around and roared out into the corridor again. "Snecky! Get your finger out your arse and get back here!"

The Detective Superintendent turned back to Logan, tutted loudly, then let out a long, weary sigh. "Seriously, that bawbag manages to make *you* look good," he said. "And believe me, that is some fucking achievement."

CHAPTER TWO

Logan, Hoon, and Snecky stood in silence, watching the fuzzy black and white security camera footage of Petrie's escape on four different screens. Each screen showed a different part of his route through the hospital, and their attention switched from monitor to monitor as Petrie dragged his prisoner through the corridors and down the stairs.

She hadn't cried. The victim. She'd stayed calm. Complied. Did everything you were supposed to do. No sudden movements. No heroics. Nothing that might increase the danger she was in.

And then, he'd killed her anyway.

There was no big finale for her. No moment of high drama. The security camera that showed her death was fixed in the foyer, and the low resolution meant the detectives could barely make out what was happening once Petrie had hauled her outside into the drop-off zone.

"Watch this bit," Snecky urged. He said it in a hushed whisper, like they were all watching a film together at the cinema. All that was missing was the rustle and crunch of his popcorn.

Still, had he not said it, Logan might not have noticed the knife going in. Upper chest, he thought. Base of the throat. Two stabs, or maybe a stab and a twist.

Petrie dragged her out of frame then, her hands grasping at her throat. Right at the edge of the image, there was a bigger movement. A sliver of something—a suggestion—appeared at the bottom left corner of the screen, and Logan realised that's where she'd been dropped. That was where Petrie had dumped her, if not already dead, then dying.

"That's it," Snecky said. He jabbed a button on the control deck and all four images paused.

"Where did he go from there?" Logan asked.

Snecky winced like he'd been bracing himself for that question. "We, uh, we don't know."

The pressure in the security room altered a fraction, as if the walls themselves were holding their breath.

"You don't know?" Logan said, his voice taking on an eerie echo in the confined space. "What do you mean, you don't know?"

"There was a car waiting for him," Snecky said. The heat from the equipment had been making him sweat, and there was an anxious sheen across his brow as Logan loomed over him. "Blue Renault Megane. Five-seven plate. He, eh, he jumped in the back and it drove off."

"So... what are you saying, Snecky?" Logan demanded. "This was all planned? He had an accomplice?"

"Well, unless he's yer man from *Knight Rider* and the fucking car drove itself, then aye, I think it's safe to say he had an accomplice," barked Hoon.

"But don't worry. We're one step ahead," Snecky said. He looked all puffed up and proud, like this was his big moment. "We think we know who it was."

"The doctor," Logan said. "Dr... Ramesh, was it?"

Hoon snorted and pointed to DCI Grant. "Aw, look at his wee face there. He was pure fucking buzzing to tell you that."

Snecky smiled. It was supposed to be a relaxed, nonchalant sort of smile, but his disappointment was written there, plain for all to see.

"Aye. Dr Manan Ramesh. He's been in charge of Petrie's case for... well, nearly a year," Snecky said. "He was off sick the day Petrie escaped. Didn't report back afterwards, and there's no sign of him at any known address."

"I knew there was something about him," Logan muttered.

"You'd met him?" Snecky asked.

"Once or twice, aye," Logan said. "Wasn't a fan. Seemed very protective of Petrie."

"Aye, well, you hit the fucking nail on the head there," Hoon said. "Turns out your man was tugging it over Mister Whisper even more than you were, Jack."

"Ramesh did his PhD—aye, his second one, like—on Petrie," Snecky explained. "Or, on... I don't know, the primal urges that drive a man to torture and murder kiddies, or some shite. He interviewed him dozens of times, starting seven or eight years back and continuing up to about six months before he got the job here."

"This was planned," Logan said. "They've been working on this for a while."

Snecky nodded. "Aye. We checked out Ramesh's house. Nice place. He's no' short of a bob or two. He wasn't there, but he knew we'd be coming. He'd burned a load of old notebooks out back."

"Anything survive?" Logan asked.

"We had Forensics go over it. Got a couple of scraps, but nothing of interest. I can get photos over to you, if you like?"

Logan shook his head. "No. It's fine. I'll take their word for it."

He glanced around at the pokey wee room, then at the bank of security monitors showing the clinical but slightly decaying insides of the hospital. "You found Ramesh's body yet?" he asked.

The other DCI blinked in confusion. "Body? Why would he...? We don't think he's dead. We think they're working together to—"

"He's dead," Logan said, cutting him short.

"How the fuck d'you know that?" Hoon asked.

"Because I know Petrie. Ramesh is dead. And, if we're right, and Petrie is going to make this about me, then I think I might know where we'll find him." He held a hand out to Hoon. "Can I borrow your car, sir?"

Hoon's pock-marked features contorted in horror. "Give you my car? I'd sooner be gangbanged by the fucking *A-Team*. No, you cannot borrow my car." He fished the keys from his pocket and spun them around a pudgy finger. "I'm driving."

Logan remembered the smell of the place like it was yesterday.

The multi-storey car park on Cambridge Street was not particularly noteworthy in its design. It was an ugly bugger of a thing, all cracked concrete and metal mesh, and would've slotted right into any other part of Glasgow—or any industrial area anywhere in the world, in fact—without anyone batting an eyelid.

And aye, to pretty much anyone else, the smell would be equally as unremarkable. Diesel fumes and jakeys' pish for the most part. Maybe a wee whiff of Dettol garnishing the top of it, depending on what day of the week it was.

To Logan, though, the smell of the place was like a fingerprint. Once smelled, never forgotten. And, just like a fingerprint on a phone screen, the stench of the place unlocked everything as he stepped into the stairwell. The memories. The anger.

The fear.

He'd asked Hoon to hang off down in the car. The DSup, to his surprise, had agreed with only a moderate outburst of personal abuse.

Snecky had been sent back to base and told to wait on the call. It was a call Logan still hoped he might not have to make, but one he knew, deep down, that he would.

As he made his way up the stairs—two-at-a-time at first, then one-at-a-time, then with a moment's rest after each fourth or fifth step—he desperately wanted to believe that he was wrong. He wanted to believe that Owen Petrie wasn't targeting him. Wasn't about to single him out, and turn his life into a living nightmare.

He wanted to believe that. He really did.

But Jack Logan was no fool.

He emerged onto the uppermost level of the car park and gulped down a few gallons of fresh air, cleaning the smell of the stairwell from his airways and his memories. Behind him, the door closed with a *clack*. Ahead of him, twenty or more cars sat parked in bays, noses pointing out at all four corners of the city.

Logan took another breath, enjoying this moment of not knowing. Not for sure, anyway. This calm before the storm. This one moment, after which everything would change.

He exhaled.

He stepped forward.

It took him six seconds to spot it.

Renault Megane. Five-seven plate. Blue.

It was parked directly across from where he was standing, like it had been deliberately placed to be as visible as possible. Which, of course, it had been.

He fished a pair of gloves from the depths of his coat pocket. Pulled them on. *Snap-snap*.

The car was neatly positioned between the lines of the bay. Unlike most of the others, it had been reversed in. Textbook parking. Meticulous. Nothing that would make anyone look too closely.

His feet felt heavy as he approached it, as if the closer he got to it, the more of his bones were turning to lead.

By the time he was standing in front of the car, he had doubled in weight, each onward step requiring all his strength and effort.

The doors were locked. This was unexpected. The car had clearly been left here for him to find, so why lock it?

Cupping his gloved hands against the tinted back windows, Logan peered into the vehicle. There was a small bundle of blood-stained clothing bunched up on the back seat—Petrie's hospital gear, presumably—but nothing else of note.

The front seats were empty, too. That left the boot.

He ran his fingers along the underside of the metal ridge at the back of the car until he found the release button, then pressed it.

Locked, like the rest of the car.

The parcel shelf was down, meaning he couldn't see what was inside by peering through the glass. Bending, he tried a sniff test. If there had been a body in there for a day or two, he should be able to get a whiff.

Nothing.

Squatting, Logan checked behind the car's tyres, then ran his hands up under the wheel trims, searching for keys but finding none.

He stood up, plodded his leaden legs around to the front of the car again, and then stood there considering it, the honking and revving of the city rising from the streets on all sides.

The car was a message. That was why, of all the places in the country it could be, it was here. Now. On top of this car park.

Or... no. Not on top. Not quite. Not yet.

Logan turned, following the direction the Megane's nose was pointing. Following it all the way over to the door that led to the stairwell.

His eyes went to the roof above it. Something that had been coiled up in his gut for a decade slithered as it drew itself tighter together.

"Aye," he muttered, and there was a waver in his voice that he didn't think he'd ever heard before. "Of course."

CHAPTER THREE

He remembered this, too. Every rung. Every pitted indent in the metal. He could feel them through the rubber of gloves, and through all the years that had passed since he'd last climbed this ladder.

He hadn't been alone then, of course. He'd known who was waiting for him —*what* was waiting for him—at the top. He'd known his duty. Known his job. And he'd known, in those moments, that he wanted to ignore them both. That he wanted to make the bastard suffer, like those kids had suffered. Their parents, too.

He'd wanted to end it, once and for all.

And now, here he was. Climbing that ladder, ten years later. Older, certainly. Wiser?

Time would tell.

There were nine rungs. His feet were on the fifth when he was high enough to see over the edge and onto the roof.

There was a sheet of blue tarp there, weighed down with bits of broken brick. The sniff test wasn't necessary—the smell presented itself almost as soon as Logan's head had drawn level with the rooftop.

He should climb down, call it in, get Scene of Crime out to comb it all over.

But he had to know.

A few more steps took him up onto the roof. It wasn't big—about half the size of a tennis court, maybe—and well overlooked by the much taller hotel across the street. That's what the tarp would be for. Petrie wouldn't have wanted anyone but Logan to find what lay beneath.

He kept his distance at first, scanning the area around the plastic sheet for anything obvious.

It was no distance at all from this roof to the upper floor of the car park below, and yet the din of Glasgow had softened, like the city was holding its breath. Like it remembered what had taken place here last time, and was now watching and waiting to see what would happen next.

A breeze swirled around Logan, nudging his coat around his knees, and crackling the tarpaulin. Even that—even the whistling of the wind—was familiar.

No, not familiar. The same.

He closed his eyes, and the world was ten years younger. Shapes heaved in the darkness behind his eyelids. Figures thrashed and fought.

And fell.

Logan snapped his eyes open, shook his head, and focused his attention on the here and now.

It had rained since the tarp had been placed down. Water gathered in its crinkles and crevices, and pooled in puddles on the uneven tiles of the roof.

Very little for him to accidentally compromise, then.

He approached the tarp quickly, the earlier leaden feeling replaced by an urge to just get this over with. Get it done, and find out what he was dealing with.

Carefully, he moved aside one of the bricks that pinned down the tarpaulin, then took hold of the material's edge.

He took a breath. Held it. Exhaled.

And then, he lifted the plastic sheeting away, and stared into the unblinking eyes of horror.

Logan leaned against the bonnet of Detective Superintendent Hoon's BMW, sipping a disappointing coffee from a paper cup.

The whole of Cambridge Street, where the car park stairs were, and Hill Street, where the vehicle entrance was, had been cordoned off. Flashing blues painted the grey rendered walls of the multi-storey, and danced in the windows of the hotel opposite.

The Scene of Crime team were up there now, doing their thing. Getting what they could from the site, and from Ramesh's body.

Or what was left of it, anyway.

He had been tortured. Extensively. His eyelids were missing. Most of his teeth and fingernails, too.

Pathology would have to confirm, but Logan was putting the cause of death as the bloody great indent in the doctor's skull, just above his hairline. The positioning of it wasn't coincidence, Logan knew. The injury was in the exact same spot as the one Petrie had sustained the night Logan had caught him.

The night he fell.

The torture couldn't have been done at the scene—someone would have seen or heard—and it was a safe bet that he'd been killed elsewhere, too. Which meant Petrie had somehow managed to get his body up onto the roof.

Presumably, he'd done it under the cover of darkness, so as not to risk being spotted by someone in the hotel. It wouldn't have been easy, but then the bastard had never exactly been lacking in conviction.

The SOC lot would do their best, but it was pointless, really. They knew who the killer was, and there would be nothing up there that would point to his whereabouts.

And, besides the body, the only other thing of interest at the scene was currently tucked out of sight in the inside pocket of Logan's coat.

"How's the coffee, Jack?" asked Snecky, appearing around from the back of the Beamer.

"Shite."

The other DCI appeared mildly offended, like he'd ground the beans himself, rather than just sending the nearest Uniform to the closest available petrol station.

"Aye, well. Better than nothing," Snecky replied.

This, Logan thought, was debatable.

Snecky joined Logan in leaning against the bonnet. The moment his backside touched the metal, a horn blasted, and he leaped forward like he'd been fired from a catapult.

"Get your fat arse off my fucking car!" Hoon ordered, sticking his head out of the driver's side window. He had a phone pressed to his ear, and a scowl fixed to his face.

Snecky glanced around, hoping no one had seen him throwing himself skyward like he'd been electrocuted. Half a dozen Uniforms and a couple of detectives all looked away as his eyes swept over them, little smirks tugging at the corners of their mouths.

"Sorry, sir," Snecky said, lowering his head in a show of deference and submission that obliterated any last shreds of respect Logan might have had for the man.

The other DCI made a point of glaring at the point where Logan's body met the front of Hoon's car, but the Detective Superintendent had pulled his head back inside the vehicle now, and the window was sliding back up with a faint electronic hum.

"I must be in his good books," Logan said. He used his sleeve to wipe the spot on the car where Snecky had attempted to sit. "If it's any consolation, it won't last."

Going by the look on Snecky's face, this wasn't much consolation at all, but he said no more about it, and instead indicated the roof of the car park with a jab of a thumb.

"How'd you know?" he asked. "Where he'd be, I mean."

Logan's eyes pointed up at the spot where he'd found the body, but he wasn't looking there. Not really.

Or, maybe he was looking *there*, he just wasn't looking *then*.

"It's where I caught him," he said, although it wasn't immediately clear if he was talking to Snecky or just reminiscing out loud. "I chased him down. He ran up to the roof. Aye, where the cars are, I mean. Thought he was going to jump off. Thought he had, in fact. There's a drop into bushes on the far side. We assumed he'd gone over."

"But he hadn't?"

Logan shook his head. "Hid himself up on the very top. Lay down flat. Don't even know what made me look. I didn't check the cars, didn't wait for Uniform to check the bushes, I just... knew. Like a fucking homing beacon. I knew the bastard was up there."

"Then what happened?" asked Snecky.

Logan blinked and looked away from the roof. He drained his coffee, winced, then stood up. "Then he attacked me, and then he fell, mashed his skull, and had everyone convinced that he was a turnip." He grunted. "Almost everyone. And now, here we are."

The Beamer rocked as Hoon got out and shut his door. He joined the DCIs up front, checked the hood of the car for damage, then nodded vaguely at the organised chaos surrounding them.

"All in hand?"

DCI Grant practically curtsied as he delivered his report. "Got my team over at the hotel talking to staff. Once we've got a solid idea of time of death, we can see about getting a list of guests in the overlooking rooms. See if anyone saw anything."

"I assume no bastard's getting in or out of the car park until our boys have had their fucking way with it?" Hoon asked.

"All cordoned off, sir, yes," Snecky confirmed. "It'll ruffle a few feathers when folk realise they can't get their cars out, but we'll deal with that when we have to. A wee bit of inconvenience is a small price to pay when a man's life has been—"

"Aye, aye, I wanted an update, no' a message from fucking Hallmark," Hoon snapped, cutting off the end of the sentence. "I spoke to the Assistant Chief Constable. She's going to try to get the jump on the press. She says she'll stick her foot down their fucking bile-ducts and out their collective arses if she has to. I mean, no' in so many words. I'm paraphrasing, but that's the general gist. This does not get out into the fucking wild until we say so. None of it. Ramesh. Petrie. Fuck all. Understood?"

Snecky nodded obediently. Logan didn't bother. The question hadn't been aimed at him. He and Hoon shared very similar views on the men and women of the media, although only one of them had ever threatened 'a fucking press genocide' on live TV.

The fact that the Detective Superintendent hadn't lost his job after that press conference was testament to how highly his superiors thought of him. Or, as he himself insisted, how shit-scared they were.

"You can count on me, sir," said Snecky, overcompensating for Logan's lack of response. "And I've taken the liberty of adding Jack to the team inbox. His knowledge and experience will come in handy. Aye, just on this particular case, I mean," the DCI added, lest anyone should think for one second that he wasn't up to the job.

"No need. I'm not hanging about," Logan said.

He crumpled up his coffee cup, looked around for somewhere to dispose of it, then handed it to Snecky. The other DCI accepted it, stared at it in confusion for a moment, then shoved it into the pocket of his jacket.

"You're... what? You're not? I thought... You know, given the circumstances?" Snecky said.

"No. I'm going to head back up the road," Logan replied. "I'll take a lift, sir, if it's going."

Snecky's face was all crumpled up with concern. He side-eyed Hoon, but found no support lurking there.

"You're... you're heading up the road?" he asked. "But, I mean, I thought you'd be sticking around to... assist. I thought you'd want to help collar the bastard."

"I do. And I will," Logan said. He turned to Hoon. "You said it yourself, sir. He'll come after me. And if that's going to happen, I'd rather it happened on my home turf."

"Thought this was your home turf, Jack?" Hoon replied.

Logan looked up at the car park, then around at what he could see of the city's towers and spires.

"Once-upon-a-time," he admitted. He thrust his hands into his pockets and pulled his coat tighter around himself. "But no' anymore."

CHAPTER FOUR

There were two things Logan insisted he had to do before starting the journey north. This had earned him a barrage of abuse from Hoon, and several comments along the lines of how the Detective Superintendent was, "No' a fucking taxi service."

But Logan had held firm, and Hoon had eventually relented to the DCI's requests.

The first stop was the easy one. Logan just wanted to put his head round the door and look into the eyes of Hoon's counterpart while he broke the news about Dr Ramesh. He wanted to see the reaction, up close and first-hand.

Of course, the bastard already knew by the time Logan got to his office. Snecky had gone scuttling into his office the moment the call had come through.

Detective Superintendent Gordon Mackenzie—the Gozer, to pretty much everyone on the force this side of Hadrian's Wall—was sitting back in his chair, fingers steepled in front of his mouth, when Logan went barging in without knocking.

There was a tiny freeze-frame of alarm on the Gozer's face when Logan came striding in, then it was swept away by a look of distinct disapproval.

"The general idea is you knock and wait until I tell you to come in, Jack," he said. "It's sort of traditional."

"Your old golf buddy's dead," Logan told him, wasting no time. "Dr Ramesh."

The Gozer's chair squeaked as he adjusted himself. Or, given the circumstances, it may have been his arse.

"Yes. I'm aware of that," he said. "And, he wasn't my 'old golf buddy.' I mean, yes, he was, but… I barely knew him."

"He had your phone number, didn't he? Was quick to come running to you after I'd been in to see Petrie."

"My personal number, yes. Not work. I'm the club secretary. Everyone has my number," the Gozer said. "Manan was no different."

"First name terms, though," Logan said. "Cosy."

"For Christ's sake, Jack. We knew each other socially. I'm hardly likely to call him 'Ramesh.' That's generally considered rude out in the real world. Maybe if you visited it once in a while, you'd know."

The Gozer leaned forward, his expression hardening. "Look, if you've come here to accuse me of something, spit it out. But if I were you, I'd be careful of what I said, Jack. I'd be very fucking careful, indeed."

Logan ground his back teeth together, the muscles in his jaw clenching and unclenching as he stared the older man down. The Gozer, to his credit, didn't blink. Not once.

"We found him on top of the car park. Cambridge Street."

From the look on the Gozer's face, Snecky hadn't considered this detail important enough to share.

"Jesus," the Detective Superintendent whispered. "How bad?"

"Bad. Tortured. Head caved in." Logan tapped a spot on his skull. "Here."

"He couldn't have known what he was getting himself into," the Gozer muttered. "He couldn't possibly have known."

"He knew only too fucking well," Logan snapped. "Your pal was playing the long game. He'd been talking to Petrie for years prior to working at Carstairs. Did a PhD on the bastard. He knew him better than most, and he helped him escape. So, forgive me if I don't shed a tear for him."

The Gozer nodded, albeit with some reluctance. "No. No, you're right, of course," he said. "The ACC was in here earlier. She'd been talking to Bob Hoon…." A look of concern briefly creased the lines of his face. "…for some reason. Not really his patch, but… Anyway. The thought is to keep it low profile for as long as we can. Hopefully, catch Petrie before the press can get wind of it. Last thing we need is to drag it all back up with a fresh barrage of Mister Whisper headlines."

That thing lying coiled in Logan's gut tightened again at the mention of Owen Petrie's nickname. He hadn't chosen it himself. The tabloids had come up with it, based on the description of his voice one of the kids who'd managed to get away from him had given. But, it had become so indelibly linked to the bastard that even now, the merest mention of it still made parents run off to check where their kids were.

"Aye. Makes sense," Logan said, although he wasn't entirely comfortable with it. The last thing he wanted was to get the press involved—to give them the bloody satisfaction of whipping the country into a state of panic.

But, maybe the country should be in a state of panic. Maybe parents should be keeping their kids inside. Maybe going public would help stop him sooner. Maybe it would save lives.

"We'll review it in a day or two," the Gozer said, as if reading the DCI's mind. "See where we are. With any luck, we'll have caught him by then."

"Aye. Maybe," Logan said. He shoved his hands deep down in his pockets and, for a moment, considered mentioning the thing that was tucked in the inside of his coat.

If anyone would understand, it was the man sitting across the desk. He'd been there, after all. He'd been there on the ladder when Petrie fell.

"Was there something else, Jack?" the Gozer asked.

And like that, the moment was gone.

"No. Nothing else," Logan said. He turned for the door, opened it a fraction, then stopped. "Wait."

The door closed again. Logan turned back to the Detective Superintendent.

"Ramesh. When did he join? The golf club, I mean."

The Gozer's nose wrinkled as he thought back. "Couple of years. Two and a half, maybe."

"And how was he? Any good?"

"Not particularly. Think he was pretty new to it when he joined up. He paid for quite a lot of coaching to get his game up to..."

The DSup's voice tumbled away into silence. He ran a hand through a hairline that wasn't so much receding as beating a full-scale retreat.

"You don't think..."

"That he joined the club to get access to you?" Logan finished. "Like I said, looks like he was playing the long game, so I wouldn't put it past him."

He stepped closer, the floorboards creaking beneath the carpet tiles. The Gozer's eyes darted left and right, like he was scanning through his memories of Ramesh, looking for clues as to his motive.

"I told you Petrie was phoning me," Logan said. "And not just the mobile. He got office numbers. Direct lines. No way he could do that without someone on the inside."

The Gozer's head snapped up. "What the hell are you implying, Jack?"

"Implying? Nothing, sir," Logan said. He took another step closer, forcing the Gozer to lean back to maintain eye contact. "I'm coming right out with it. Someone on the force fed Owen Petrie details of where to find me. The only viable way they could do that—that we know of—is via Dr Ramesh. Your golf buddy."

"I told you, he's not my..." the Gozer objected, but the protest got off to a weak start, and quickly died away.

"I'm not accusing you of anything, sir. Not yet. Not without evidence," Logan said.

"Oh, well that's very bloody generous of you," the Gozer spat.

"What I'm saying is, is it possible that Ramesh compromised you in some way? Got into your computer somehow? Maybe your phone?"

"No. No, can't see it. Got the impression he was a bit of a Luddite. Always forwarding on those bloody round robin things. 'Share this with six people to help cure this kid of cancer.' That sort of thing. That and bloody jokes. YouTube videos. Pain in the arse, if I'm honest." The Gozer shook his head. "So, no. He's far from a computer genius. I mean, half the links he sent to things didn't even work."

The silence that followed that sentence was deafening.

Logan didn't know much about technology, beyond what he needed to. He knew that switching things off and back on again was usually a safe bet. He knew that phone batteries didn't last nearly as long as he wanted them to.

And he knew never to click a link from an untrustworthy source. And Dr Manan Ramesh, as far as Logan was concerned, was up there among the least trustworthy sources of all.

"With all due respect, sir," he groaned. "You're a fucking idiot."

"I beg your pardon! What did you just say?"

"Turn it off. Your phone," Logan instructed. "Turn it off. Now!"

A number of emotions went swooshing across the face of the man behind the desk, starting at *fury* and progressing through to *horrified realisation.*

"Shite!"

Springing to his feet, he hurried over to where his coat was hanging behind the door and searched the pockets until he produced a phone in a slightly battered wood-effect case. He turned it over in his hands, fumbling for the button, then pressed it down until the freshly illuminated screen went dark again.

The Gozer tossed the phone onto his desk, then stepped back, like it might explode at any moment. "Fuck. Shit. *Fuck*," he said, ejecting each word with more passion than the one before. "You don't really think...? Fuck!"

"Give it to the tech boys. They'll be able to tell," Logan said. "But aye, if you clicked the links he sent, then I think there's a very good chance that he's put something on there."

"Oh, shit. *Shit*," the Gozer hissed. He clutched his head in his hands, like he was trying to stop it blowing itself to bits.

"It's your personal phone though, right?" Logan said, indicating the handset on the desk. "You said he had your personal number. Not work. That's what you said."

"Yes. Yes, my personal number. Not..." the Gozer began. He chewed his lip and swallowed, visibly building up to something. "But there were emails, Jack. And I..."

His eyes went to the PC sitting on his desk, then came darting back to the Detective Chief Inspector. Logan groaned.

"Oh," he said. "Well, is that no' bloody marvellous?"

THE SECOND STOP Logan wanted to make was far less enjoyable than the first, and that hadn't exactly been a barrel of laughs.

Still, give him a barney with the Gozer any day over this.

Dylan Muir had been the first of Owen Petrie's three victims. The first child to be taken by the bastard, and the only one whose remains had never been found.

Logan now knew why, of course, but the couple sitting on the couch across from him didn't know. Would *never* know, if he had anything to say about it.

They were in hell wondering what had become of their son, but even that—even the endless misery of not knowing—would be better than the truth.

But he had to tell them this. And he had to tell them in person.

"Escaped? What do you mean, 'escaped'? How can he have escaped?"

It had been twenty years since Aisling Muir had lost her son, and every second of that time had been carved into the lines of her face.

She'd been a young mum—just eighteen when Dylan had been born—which made her... what? Forty-one now? She looked older. A decade older, maybe more. Her hair was greying at the roots, and cut into a shapeless sort of bob that sat flat against the sides of her head.

Logan had stopped in a few times over the years, delivering updates—or a lack of them—to Aisling and her husband, Jerry.

Dylan's dad was a couple of years older than his wife, and was holding up no better. He'd been a larger-than-life type when Logan had first met him—tall and broad, and with a vigour that had driven him to spend hours on end searching the streets for his boy, rallying neighbours, organising awareness-raising events, and generally doing anything and everything he could to bring Dylan home.

His energy had seemed limitless. His drive, remarkable. It took a lot to impress Logan, even back then, but Jerry Muir had done it day in, day out.

The shape slouched on the couch across from Logan now was like a shrunken version of that man. A memory of him that had been fading further every time the DCI had visited, and which was now little more than a ghost.

"Jack?" Aisling prompted. She had a cigarette clutched between two boney fingers. Smoke circled her head like a wreath. "What are you saying? Escaped?"

Logan set his cup down in his saucer. They'd made him tea when he'd turned up, like they usually did, but he hadn't touched it. He wasn't sure, given everything, that he'd be able to keep it down.

"He killed an orderly. Took a nurse hostage, and killed her, too," Logan said. There was no point in sugar-coating it. Not to them. "We don't currently know his whereabouts, but we're making a concerted effort to—"

"Don't fucking talk like that," Aisling snapped. She sucked on the end of her cigarette like it was a blast of pure oxygen. "Not to us. Not after everything."

Her face had hardened, but that didn't last. It couldn't. Her eyes softened first, becoming wide and pleading.

"Please. Don't. Just tell us straight."

Beside her, her husband gave her hand a squeeze, but said nothing. He'd spoken less and less each time Logan had visited, and now the DCI got the impression that Jerry didn't tend to say very much.

"We're looking for him. Everyone. We're not going to the press yet, but it's a full-scale manhunt," Logan said. "We're telling the other parents, but I wanted to tell you personally."

"But... but how the fuck could he escape?" Aisling demanded. "He was a vegetable. You all said he was a vegetable! That's why he couldn't tell you where our Dylan's body was. That's what you all said!"

"I know, Aisling, but—"

"Then how the fuck can a vegetable escape from a secure hospital? Hmm? Tell me that, Jack!"

Logan placed the cup and saucer down on the coffee table. Through the glass top, he could see the shelf below, still stacked with kids' books and colouring pencils.

They'd told him during a visit six or seven years ago that they hadn't changed Dylan's room. They hadn't mentioned it again since, and he'd never been able to bring himself to ask.

"I know this must be difficult for you. Both of you," he said. "But we're going to catch him. We're going to get him, and we're going to put him where he belongs."

"You can get him to tell you what he did with Dylan," Aisling said. Her voice shook as she said it, a blend of anger and grief. "You can make him. Can't you? You can let us bury our boy."

Logan glanced down at the floor by his feet. The carpet was the same one he'd first walked on when he made his first visit. The couch was unchanged, too, and the same pictures of Dylan Muir smiled down at him from the walls.

The house had been frozen in time, while its occupants had withered and aged.

"I'm going to do everything I can. I'm going to stop him. You have to trust me on that."

Jerry spoke then. His voice was flat. Detached. His eyes, which had been glassy and distant, came briefly into focus.

"Like we trusted you to bring our boy home, you mean?" he said.

"Jerry, I—"

"I think you should go, Jack," Aisling interjected. Her face had hardened to solid steel. Jerry squeezed her hand like he was feeding her his strength. "Please. Just go."

CHAPTER FIVE

Hoon was impatiently drumming his hands on the steering wheel of the Beamer when Logan emerged from the Muir's block of flats and came plodding along the pavement through the orange puddles thrown down by the streetlights.

The DSup spoke even before the DCI had reached to open the door, raising his voice to be heard through the glass. "Well, going by the state of your face, I'm guessing that wasn't a roaring fucking success?"

Logan said nothing until he was sitting in the car with his belt on. "No, but I had to tell them. They deserve to know."

He looked back at the flats. There were eight of them in the block. The Muirs lived second up on the left. Aisling watched him from the window. He raised a hand, giving her a wave. She reached a hand up, and for a moment, Logan thought she was going to wave back. But then, she pulled the curtains closed with a jerk, shutting out him and the rest of the world.

"I want Uniform keeping an eye," he said. "Low profile."

"Think the fucker'll come here?" Hoon asked.

Logan shook his head. "No. But no harm in keeping watch."

"Well, you can phone it in," Hoon said. He pushed a foot down on the clutch and jabbed at the button that started the engine. "I want to get us the fuck up this road before midnight."

Logan cleared his throat. "Uh, aye, about that, sir," he said, turning in his seat.

Hoon's hands gripped the wheel. His bottom jaw locked into place, lower teeth protruding in front of the upper set. He turned his head. Slowly. Dangerously.

Logan offered up a hopeful smile and raised his eyebrows. "Any chance we could make a couple more quick stops first?"

Vanessa's face went through its entire emotional repertoire in the first two seconds after opening the door, before settling on something halfway between anger and fear.

"What?" she demanded, looking the man on her doorstep up and down. "What's happened?"

Their marriage had been a good one, right up until it wasn't. He wished he could blame her for it. Or that he could say it was a mutual thing. *Two people, just falling out of love.*

But it was his fault, of course. All of it. Him and—

"Petrie," he said. "It's... it's Petrie. He's out."

The anger slipped away, leaving only the fear behind. A hand went to her mouth. Tears came to her eyes. She stepped aside without a word, and Logan stepped over a threshold he hadn't crossed in a very long time.

Given their history and the circumstances, the conversation went better than Logan had been bracing himself for. Vanessa listened. It had been a while since that had happened. She just listened, not interrupting, not shouting him down, not calling him out on any of it. She just sat there on her big leather couch, listening as she worked her way through a sizeable glass of red wine.

And, with everything she heard, her fear grew.

"You think he'll come here?" she asked, once Logan had brought her up to date. "Why would he come here?"

"To get at me," Logan said. "To hurt me."

Vanessa snorted. "Christ. He's well off the mark then, isn't he?"

"Don't say that," Logan told her. "I got that call. Remember? The one I phoned you up to warn you about. He asked how you were. No one believed it was him—"

"How could we?" Vanessa asked.

"But, I knew. I knew," Logan said. "And if he asked about you then, there's a good chance he'll come for you now. And, well, differences aside, I'm not having you get hurt. I won't." He swallowed. "I can't."

"So, what are you saying, Jack?" Vanessa asked. There was no aggressiveness in it. Nothing confrontational for once. "What should I do?"

"I want you and Maddie to come with me to Inverness. We'll put you somewhere safe. Just until this is over."

"Jesus, Jack," Vanessa sighed. "Why Inverness? Isn't there somewhere down here we can go?"

"Because… Because I want you both close," he admitted. "If anything happens, I want to be there."

"Christ Almighty." Vanessa looked to the ceiling, shook her head, then faced him again. "Fine."

Logan straightened a little in the armchair, not quite believing what he was hearing. "Fine? What… just like that? Just… fine?"

"What the hell else do you expect me to say?" Vanessa asked him. "You know Petrie better than anyone. You know what he's capable of. If you think we're in danger, then I've got no choice but to believe you, have I?"

She drained the last glug from her wine glass, swished it around in her mouth, then swallowed it as she got to her feet. "Give me ten minutes to pack some things and phone Maddie. Will I tell her you'll pick her up on the way?"

"Aye. Good. Aye, do that," Logan said, also standing. He glanced out of the window at the black BMW parked along the leafy suburban street. "Although, I should point out, it won't be me driving."

Eighty-odd minutes later, Detective Superintendent Hoon was practically growling as he powered the BMW up Loch Lomondside, his full-beam headlights driving the darkness away from the narrow, twisting road.

Occasionally, another car would appear around a bend ahead. Hoon gave the oncoming driver approximately a fifth of a second to dip their lights, before ejecting a, "Fuck's sake!" and furiously flashing the high-beams.

It had taken a bit more convincing to get Maddie to drop everything and head north, but Vanessa had done much of the heavy lifting, and she'd eventually seen sense. Both women sat in the back of the Beamer, hands gripping the handles above the doors, and occasionally reaching down to check that their seatbelts were fastened correctly.

Even without Hoon there, conversation would likely have been awkward. Given the DSup's presence, though, and his frequent foul-mouthed outbursts, much of the journey had been spent in a solemn, stilted sort of silence.

The rain started at the Crianlarich bypass, an inoffensive smir at first, that was a downpour by the time they stopped for a pee at the Green Welly in Tyndrum.

Technically, the toilets were closed at that time of night, but after Hoon unleashed both barrels of his persuasive charm at the poor bugger behind the counter in the petrol station, a key was quickly sourced.

Realising he hadn't eaten since leaving Canna that morning, Logan grabbed a sandwich, a bag of crisps, and an iced coffee from the petrol station, only for Hoon to make it very clear that he wasn't 'eating any of that shite' in the Detective Superintendent's car.

While Hoon sat revving the engine on the forecourt, Logan wolfed down two big bites of the sandwich, forced it down with the cold coffee, then shoved the crisps in his coat pocket for later.

That done, he jumped back in the car, and Hoon screeched off up the hill towards Rannoch Moor and the darkened hills and valleys of Glen Coe.

THEY ARRIVED in Inverness a little after one in the morning. Logan wanted to keep the safe house as secret as possible from the rest of the force—it was likely that the Gozer had been the one inadvertently leaking information to Petrie, but the DCI wasn't ruling out the possibility of other rats—so the fewer people who knew, the better.

Unfortunately, this meant arranging it all himself, and that would take hours.

He'd invited Vanessa and Maddie back to his flat, although had warned them that they'd have to share the bed, and that the place hadn't been aired in a few days.

They had, unsurprisingly, declined, and Hoon had taken them to the Premier Inn out by Raigmore Hospital, where they'd managed to book a twin room for the night. Logan had insisted that he pay for it. Vanessa had insisted that he didn't.

After thanking Hoon, and receiving an ear-bashing in response, Logan had accompanied his daughter and ex-wife up to the room and started to talk them through what they could expect to happen the next day.

Hotel check-out was at eleven. He'd have the safe house sorted out for them by then, he promised. It wouldn't be a palace, but it would only be for a few days. Petrie would show himself before long. It would all be over soon.

"Dad," Maddie said, during his second run-through of all that information. She covered her mouth as she yawned. "We get it. You're going to sort it out. Can we sleep now?"

Logan nodded. Smiled. "Aye," he said. "Aye. Get some sleep. We can talk about it all tomorrow."

He opened the door and stopped there, half in the room, and half out in the corridor.

"And I'm sorry. About all this," he said. "I know it's..."

"A pain in the arse?" Vanessa said.

"I was going to say 'difficult,' but aye. Yours is more accurate," Logan said.

He looked back at them both, standing there together. There was so much he wanted to say to them. So many words tumbling around in his head. Too many for him to be able to choose.

"Goodnight," was the one he settled on, and then he stepped all the way out into the hotel corridor, and pulled the door closed behind him.

Logan was paying for the taxi outside his flat when the front door of the building opened, and a young woman came hurrying down the steps, a rucksack swung over her shoulder, a look of grim determination fixed on her face.

"Tanya?" Logan said, stepping into the path of his downstairs neighbour. "What's the matter?" He looked past her to the front door of the close, and the steps leading up to the flats above. "Has something happened? Has he done something?"

Tanya blinked a few times, like she was struggling to recognise the bear-sized figure towering above her.

"Jack," Logan said. "From upstairs. With the polis."

"Oh. Aye. Aye," Tanya said. She wiped her nose on the sleeve of her denim jacket and tried to arrange her mouth into the shape of a smile. Judging by the result, she'd forgotten what one was supposed to look like. "Fine. I'm just... I'm getting out."

"But it's your flat. If..." Logan clicked his fingers a few times, searching for the name. "What's he called?"

"Bud."

"Bud," Logan said, his nostrils flaring like he resented having to dirty his mouth with the word. "If you want me to get him out, I can. It's no bother."

It would be a source of tremendous personal pleasure, in fact, but he stopped short of saying so.

Tanya shook her head. She was in her early twenties, but looked younger. Much younger right now, in fact, with the rings of red around her eyes, and her hair tied back in a ponytail.

She had a pyjama top on under her jacket. A fluffy pink thing with a unicorn on it. She wore a pair of dirty combats on her bottom half, but the waistband of her pyjama bottoms stuck up over the top, and the bottom of one leg had fallen out at her left ankle and snagged on the heel of a trainer.

"I've just... I'm sick of it. Him coming in pissed. Bringing randomers back every night. He's drinking with some new mate of his in there now, and I just looked at him, and I thought... fuck this. I'm done. I've had it."

Logan looked up at the flat below his own. Lights burned in all the windows, and he could hear a series of muffled noises that were presumably meant to be music.

"You shouldn't have to leave your own flat, Tanya," he told her, positively itching to go up there and kick off on her behalf. "Come on, away back inside."

Tanya pulled away from him, like she was worried he might try dragging her back up the stairs. "I've spoken to my mum. I'm going to go there," she said. She gritted her teeth, fighting off the cracks that had appeared in her voice. "I just... I want my mum."

There was a *clunk* as the taxi driver put the car into gear. Logan turned and slapped the flat of his hand on the roof. "Hold up," he said.

"I've no' got money. I'll just walk," Tanya said. "It's not that far."

Logan opened the back door. "You're fine," he said, urging her inside with a nod.

She eyed him warily for a moment, then swung her bag down off her shoulder and got into the back of the car.

"Tenner cover it?" he asked.

She nodded, and watched in silence as he took the money from his wallet and held it out to her.

"Why are you doing this?" she asked, regarding the folded-up note with suspicion.

"Because I'm a mug," he said. He stretched forward with the money until she took it. "Now, away and get a hug off your mum."

Tanya scrunched the note up in a fist, then looked past the DCI to the light in the windows above. "You're not going to hurt him, are you?" she asked.

"Only if I have to," Logan said, then he closed the door, knocked on the taxi roof, and watched it until it vanished around the corner.

It had been a long, unpleasant day. One of the longest and most unpleasant he could remember, actually. It had been a succession of low-points, with very few highlights to speak of.

Until now.

"Right then, *Bud*," Logan said, rubbing his hands together. "Let's you and I have a little chat."

CHAPTER SIX

Bud yanked the door open after the third round of hammering, letting the god-awful din of his music flood out onto the landing. He stood there, eyes blazing in the dark hollows of their sockets, greasy hair plastered flat against one side of his head, and sticking up like *Oor Wullie*'s on the other.

He was drowning in a big black jumper that trailed down to his knees, food-stains down the front, thumbs sticking out through holes in the sleeves. His teeth were turning so yellow they'd started to come out the other end into brown. They were so squint, so higgledy-piggledy, that it looked like they'd been scattered into his mouth at random, and probably from a great height.

It had been a few months since Logan had first introduced himself to Bud. The wee scrote still had a kink in his nose to remind him of it, and he instinctively traced it with a fingertip when he saw the DCI looming out on the landing.

Given that so much time had passed, Logan was immensely satisfied by the flash of panic that made itself known as it passed across Bud's face. Obviously, he'd made an impression on the lad beyond the physical one.

"The fuck you want?" Bud demanded, but there was no conviction in it. No venom. He was playing the role he expected of himself, no doubt against his own better judgement.

"I saw Tanya," Logan said.

Bud turned and looked back over his shoulder towards the source of that bloody music. Logan clicked his fingers a couple of times, drawing his attention back.

"She's no' there. She's gone."

This appeared to be news to Bud, but he shrugged and carried on. "And?"

"And, I'd much prefer her as a neighbour than you. So, tomorrow morning, you're going to gather up your stuff, you're going to clean the place from top to bottom, and then you're going to go."

Bud opened his horrible little mouth to object, but Logan wasn't done.

"I don't care where you go. Ideally, it'll be a long way away. But you're going to go." He laid a hand on the smaller man's shoulder. The weight of it almost buckled Bud at the knees. "One way or another, you're going to go. Is that clear?"

Bud regarded the hand like it was a poisonous spider for a few seconds, then he pulled away and squared up to the man in the doorway.

"That a fucking threat, like?"

Logan smiled genially and shook his head. "No. No, son, I wasn't threatening you," he said. The shape of the smile didn't change, yet it suddenly became something much more dangerous. He leaned forward, bringing himself closer to Bud's height. "Would you like me to?"

He waited for an answer, knowing he wouldn't get one but hoping he would.

"No, thought not," he finally said, straightening. "Tomorrow morning," he reiterated. "Get up and get cleaning."

Bud started to close the door, but Logan slammed a hand against it, easily holding it. "And turn that fucking racket off," he barked. "Or I'll turn it off for you."

And with that, he stepped back and let the door swing shut. He stood there, hands in his pockets, counting down from twenty in his head. He reached thirteen before the music stopped. Then, with a nod of satisfaction, he turned and plodded up the stairs.

His flat was exactly as he'd left it, aside from a smattering of mail on the front mat, and the smell which was noticeably worse. He'd forgotten to open the curtains the morning he was called over to Canna, and the living room felt like it was withering through lack of sunlight. Still, no point in opening them now.

He checked his watch. Ten to two. He should eat, he knew, but it was late, and the worst of the smell was coming from the bin in the kitchen, so he didn't much fancy the idea of going in there to cook.

Instead, he flopped down into his armchair, leaned left a little to compensate for the slouch in the base, and took the bag of crisps from his coat pocket. He tore the top of the bag open without paying too much attention, and shoved a handful in his mouth.

He was two chews in when he winced at the taste, and checked the front of the bag. "Tomato and basil?" he read out loud. The packet was a near-identical red to the *Ready Salted* he'd been aiming for.

He peered inside the bag and gave the crisps a look that suggested they had personally betrayed him in some way, then grabbed another couple and horsed them down.

Logan made sure he'd eaten every last crumb before he allowed himself to think about the other thing in his pocket. Some part of him hadn't stopped thinking about it since he'd found it there, placed neatly in the cold, dead hand of Dr Ramesh. Left there for the DCI to find.

He folded up his crisp packet, rolled it into a thin strip, then tied it in a knot and sat it down on the coffee table beside a mug that was growing a wee furry blue lifeform at the bottom.

That done, he got up, went to the bathroom, and washed his hands. The little box of rubber gloves he kept in his pocket was empty, so he was forced to venture through into the kitchen to get the spare box he kept in the drawer.

The smell was pungently sweet, with rich notes of rot and decay that coated the lining of his nose and oozed down the back of his throat. He remembered the chicken he'd burned the arse off the night before his Canna trip and recalled how he'd chucked the inedible bits—most of it—in the kitchen bin, fully intending to take it out next day.

Holding his breath, he lifted off the plastic lid of the bin, unhooked the top of the bag, and scrunched it together to trap the stench inside.

"Right," he grunted, and he headed for the door, kicking the mail aside so as not to trample on it.

He was back in the kitchen a minute later, cracking open a window to try to air the place out.

The landing had been quiet when he'd passed the downstairs flat. Just as well for Bud, or the bastard would've found himself the recipient of an all-you-can-eat chicken buffet.

With the window open and fresh air tentatively making its way inside, Logan rummaged in the kitchen drawers until he found the box of gloves, then returned with it to the living room.

He sat in the sloping armchair, pulled on a pair of the gloves, then reached into his inside pocket for the rectangle of card he had tucked there.

It had been a message, in the most literal sense of all. A postcard, written in handwriting he'd recognised at first glance. Handwriting he would *always* recognise, and which would always make his mouth go dry, and the hairs on the back of his neck stand on end.

The message was simple. Direct.

'Jump,' it read. 'And I'll turn myself in.'

There was a smiley face below that, and then another sentence further down still.

'Don't, and everything that happens next is on you.'

He'd signed it 'M.W.'

Not 'Owen.' Not 'Petrie.'

M.W.

Mister Whisper.

Logan turned the postcard over. There, on the front, was a photograph of Loch Ness, with a badly Photoshopped head and neck rising from the water. He recognised it from a dozen different racks outside tourist shops all through the city. A bright red caption emblazoned across the sky above it read: 'Look Out For the Monster!'

He placed the postcard back in his pocket and rubbed his eyes with the thumb and forefinger of one gloved hand.

Poor Snecky had looked like someone had pissed on his chips when Logan had told him he wasn't sticking around. Had it not been for the postcard, he probably would have.

But what would be the point of staying there now? Petrie wasn't in Glasgow. Petrie was coming here. Coming for him.

And there was no way Logan was going to hide from the bastard.

He checked his watch again, groaned at the time, and got up from the chair, pulling off the gloves as he stood, and tossing them onto the table with the rest of his life's debris.

It took him less than five minutes to get ready for bed—an eminently satisfying slash, a cursory brush of the teeth, and then he headed through to his bedroom, kicking his clothes off on the way.

The bed was made. Or as close to 'made' as it was ever likely to get, anyway. After he'd last woken up in it, he'd hooked the fitted sheet back on at that one corner the bloody thing kept pinging off at, and thrown the top of the quilt roughly in the direction of the pillows. It was far from hotel standard—and he'd kipped in some ropey hotels in his time—but he'd at least made an effort.

Albeit, not a very big one.

He had just pulled off the second of his socks and tossed it into a corner with the first, when he pulled back the covers and saw what had been left for him.

A badge.

A name.

Jack Wright.

The orderly at Carstairs.

The twenty-six-year-old with the wee one at home.

The dead man in the doorway.

CHAPTER SEVEN

Logan was in his office at the Burnett Road station before the rest of the team started to show up. His early arrival was no real surprise, of course, given that he hadn't slept a wink. How could he, knowing that bastard had been in his house? In his damn bedroom.

"Jesus, Jack, you look like death warmed up," DI Ben Forde called through from the Incident Room, as he took off his jacket and hung it over the back of his chair.

Ben jabbed the button that turned on his computer monitor, then came strolling into Logan's office and sat himself down in the seat across from the DCI.

"And here I thought the fresh island air would've taken years off you," Ben said.

An evidence bag *clonked* onto the desk between them. Ben reached for it, turned it over in his hands, then read the name on the front of the badge. "Jack Wright. Who's that?"

"That, Benjamin, is Owen Petrie's fourth victim," Logan said, then his jaw tightened and he gave a barely noticeable shake of his head. "Or... third, technically."

Ben looked from Logan to the badge and back again. "Petrie? What are you talking about?"

"Hoon didn't say?"

Ben shook his head. "Say what?"

Logan sighed, ran a hand down his face, then sat forward in his chair. "Four days ago, Owen Petrie murdered an orderly and a nurse at Carstairs. He got in a car, and he escaped."

"Escaped? How could—?"

"It was an act. Like I've been trying to tell everyone for years. His whole loss of memory thing, his whole, 'Look at me, I'm a cabbage,' act was just that. A sham," Logan said. "Petrie got a doctor at the hospital on side. A Dr Ramesh. He helped the bastard set up the escape. Then, Petrie tortured him and smashed his skull in."

"Charming," Ben muttered. He set the evidence bag down between them again. "But... *Petrie*?" he said, still not convinced. "The medics had him written off."

"They did, but I knew, Ben. I knew. This? Now? This was always coming. This was always just a matter of time," Logan said. "The badge there. Petrie took it off the man he killed. Took it with him."

Ben peered down at the bag over the top of his glasses. "How'd you manage to get your hands on it?"

"Because he left it for me," Logan said. "In my bed."

Ben's gaze snapped up and met the DCI's. "In your *bed*?"

Logan nodded. "Got home last night and found it. He'd been in my flat."

"When?"

"I don't know. It's no' like he clocked-in," Logan replied. "But recently, obviously. Yesterday at some point, I'm guessing."

"Jesus. You should get SOC in there, get them going over it."

"No point. He won't have left anything useful," Logan said. "Besides, I'm fucked if I'm having Sex Pest Palmer going through all my stuff."

"Aye. Fair point. But still..." Ben said. He picked the badge up again, studied it for another few seconds, then replaced it on the desk. "Bastard, eh?"

"Aye. He's that, alright," Logan said. He thought about the postcard in the pocket of his coat, hanging by the door. "There's something else, too."

"Christ, what now?" Ben asked.

Before Logan could answer, there was a *thunk* from out in the Incident Room as the door swung open and closed.

"Morning!" called DC Hamza Khaled. "Anyone for tea or coffee?"

"I knew there was a reason I missed you, Ham," said another man's voice, as the door swung open again. Logan could practically hear the grin on the face of DC Tyler Neish. "Tea. Milk and two."

"Doesn't matter. We'll talk later," Logan told Ben, then he raised his voice and shouted through to Hamza. "Aye, cheers, I'll have a coffee, if it's going."

"Better make it a strong one," Ben added, looking the DCI up and down. "And maybe ask them if they can do it as an IV drip."

"So, you're not sacked then, boss," Tyler observed, once Hamza had returned with the teas and coffees. DC Neish's voice was a little more nasal than usual, the beating he'd received on Canna having now blackened his eyes and swollen the bridge of his nose.

They were all sitting out in the Incident Room, chairs turned to face the middle. The fifth chair stood at another desk, its back to them. Logan had barely been able to bring himself to look at it since it had become empty.

"I wish," Logan said.

"Sacked?" asked Ben. "What would you be sacked for?"

"Burning down Bosco Maximuke's office," Tyler announced. His gaze darted to the DCI. "Shite. That's probably not meant to be common knowledge, is it?"

"Bit late for that. Every bugger knows," Ben said. "CID's probably arranging a whip-round for you as we speak."

"Thought the Detective Superintendent might have a few things to say about it, though, sir," Hamza said.

Logan shook his head. "Other things on his mind," he said, then he took a swig from his coffee, set the paper cup down on the desk beside him, and broke the news. "Owen Petrie—Mister Whisper—has escaped from Carstairs."

Tyler, who had been mid-sip of his tea, coughed hot liquid out through his nose. "Fuck," he wheezed, drying his face on his sleeve.

"How's that possible, sir?" Hamza asked. "Is he not meant to be...?"

"A cabbage. Aye. Key phrase there, 'meant to be,'" Logan said. "Turns out, he's been putting it on."

"Didn't his head get caved in though, boss?" asked Tyler. He was still recovering from the tea-down-nostrils ordeal, and his voice was far higher-pitched than usual.

"Obviously, not enough," Logan said. "But aye. I'm no' saying he's in the prime of his life or anything, but he's been exaggerating the damage for years. Bastard's been biding his time. And now, he's out."

"Shite," said Hamza, and there was a general consensus in the room that this was an accurate summary of their feelings on the matter.

Logan decided to steer them off the subject of Petrie for now. The bastard was consuming enough of his own head without infecting the others, too.

"What's the latest on our haul from Canna?" he asked.

"Oh aye! Meant to say, quite the bloody haul you brought us yesterday," Ben remarked. "Well done, Jack."

"Aye. Well, I couldn't have done it without Detective Constable Neish," Logan said.

Tyler perked right up at that. "Seriously, boss?"

"No. No' really," Logan said. "I mean, you nearly killed a man by running him over, and I seem to recall you spending much of your time covered in vomit. So, all things considered, you were probably more of a hindrance."

"Wait, wait, wait," said Hamza. "What's all this? Nobody said anything about him being covered in vomit."

"I'd say 'covered,' is a strong word..." Tyler objected.

"Dripping with it, he was. Head to bloody toe," Logan said. He turned to Ben. "How did you get on with them all?"

"Mixed bag," Ben said, wrinkling his nose. "But dealt with. We got the murder confession pretty much right away. No real prompting required. Everything else was proving a bit trickier, but it's all CID stuff, so we've passed it over. They'll be extraditing your man with the international arrest warrant. The rest, they'll sort in-house."

"Bloody hell. You can be efficient when you want to be," Logan remarked.

"True. But such talent brings its own problems," Ben said. "Alice wasn't happy." He looked across at the Detective Constables. "The wife."

"Aye, we know, sir," Hamza said. "I've, eh, had the pleasure of her on the phone before, checking when you'd be home."

"You have my condolences, son," Ben offered.

"What's up with her this time?" Logan asked.

From way back when, he and Alice had never exactly seen eye-to-eye. Their relationship had taken a further turn for the worse when Logan had accidentally smashed a ceramic hedgehog called Harry Pricklepants, which Alice had been particularly fond of, despite the fact that it was a hideous bastard of a thing.

"Royal visit yesterday, wasn't it? Opening the castle after the refurb," Ben explained. "And not just any royal visitor. Oh no. None of your Dukes of... whoever. The Queen. Her Majesty herself. Queen Elizabeth the Second, scissors in hand, cutting the ribbon. Waving. The works."

Logan frowned. "She wasn't happy that the Queen was here?"

"On the contrary, Jack. She was bloody delighted that the Queen was here. What she was less delighted about was me no' turning up to drive her in to see said Queen in action," Ben said. He winced at the thought of it. "She had to get the bus. All dressed up in her nice outfit, too. By the time she arrived, it was chock-a-block. She tells me she caught a glimpse of a hat, and that was it."

"That's all you need, surely?" Logan said. "You ask me, the hat's the best bit."

Ben sucked in his cheeks. "Aye. Well, I maybe wouldn't go saying that to Alice when you next see her, eh? For both our sakes."

A phone rang on Ben's desk. His face fell.

"Christ, see if that's her..." he whispered, his eyes darting around the room as if searching for a bugging device.

He signalled for Hamza to take the call, then took a big swig of his tea while the DC leaned over and picked up the handset.

"Major Investigation Team. Detective Inspector Forde's desk. How can...?"

He reached for a notepad as the person on the other end spoke. It was a woman's voice but not, to Ben's relief, the short, clipped tones of his wife. He, Logan, and Tyler sat in silence, watching Hamza scribble down the details as they came down the line.

"Right. Aye. Thanks. We'll follow up," he said, once the message had been conveyed. Then, he hung up the phone and sat back in his seat, still writing the end of the message in the notepad.

"Well?" Ben asked. "What's up?"

"Body found behind the Premier Inn," Hamza said.

Logan was on his feet in an instant. "What? Where? Which one? Who?" he demanded, all in one breath.

"Uh, out at the West End. The one with the Beefeater," Hamza said, startled by the DCI's reaction. "Junkie, by the looks of it. Probably an OD, although they say he's a bit of a mess."

Logan's legs gave way and he thumped back down into his chair. "Right. Good," he said. "I mean, not good, but... Doesn't matter. Forget it." He looked between Hamza and Tyler. "You two get over there, check it out. Ben, get Scene of Crime rounded up and dispatched, and warn Shona Maguire at Raigmore that she's got incoming."

Ben smirked. "You no' want to give her a call yourself?" he suggested, but Logan wasn't in the mood.

"I've got to see a man about a house," he replied cryptically. "But tell her I'll come see her this afternoon to see what she's got for us."

"What about Petrie, boss?" Tyler asked. From the way Hamza and Ben both looked at the DCI, it was clear they'd been wondering the same thing.

"Petrie..." Logan began. He thought about the postcard in his pocket in the office next door. "He's not our concern. Central Belt's after him. He won't get far. This," he said, pointing to the notepad in Hamza's hand. "This is our case. We'll let someone else worry about Owen Petrie."

Tyler nodded. He and Hamza both got to their feet. "Right, boss. Sounds good."

"We'll give a shout when we know what we're dealing with," Hamza added, then both DC's gathered up their jackets, drained the last of their drinks, and hurried out of the Incident Room.

It was only then that Logan turned to Ben. The DI had been watching him for several long seconds, a curious look on his face.

"Got something to say, Benjamin?"

"You're letting someone else worry about Owen Petrie, are you?" Ben asked.

"Aye. Well," Logan said, getting to his feet. "There's a first time for everything, I suppose."

CHAPTER EIGHT

"I MEAN, I'M NO EXPERT," SAID TYLER, GAZING DOWN AT THE BODY IN THE grass. "But I'm going to go out on a limb and say I'm not pegging this one as an overdose."

"You reckon? What was your first clue?" asked Hamza.

Tyler gestured down to the lifeless lump sitting propped against the back of the hotel. His head was angled sharply backwards, so the top of his skull was jammed against the wall.

"Take your pick," he said.

Most of the man's face was missing. Some of it—a lot of it, in fact—was stuck to the roughcasting over on his right, suggesting he'd been repeatedly dragged along it until most of the flesh had been torn off.

It didn't need an X-Ray to tell them that his jaw was broken. It hung open, as if stuck mid-scream, revealing a series of black and bloody chasms where his teeth should have been.

He was dressed in what would have been a pretty nice suit, were it not for all the dirt and the blood. The top button of the shirt was done up, but he was missing a tie. Although, all things considered, that was the least of his problems.

They spotted the tie a moment later. It was red, so had blended in with all the many other red patches that covered the body like varying shades of camouflage. The tie was wrapped around the man's wrists, pulling them tightly together. This would have made it difficult for him to get his hands out, were it not for the fact that he no longer had any.

"Pretty fucked up this, eh?" Tyler remarked.

"Aye," Hamza concurred. "That's one way of putting it."

They were keeping their distance from the body until SOC turned up, and while they couldn't see the missing hands sitting in the grass nearby, there was no way of telling if he was sitting on them until the body was moved.

Thankfully, neither of them would have to get involved in that part.

Chances are they wouldn't be there, of course. Missing teeth, missing hands, and a face that had been mangled almost down to the bone suggested someone had been determined to hide the man's identity.

The smell of all the assorted bodily fluids at the scene had started Tyler's saliva glands working overtime. He turned away to get a breath, just in time to see a female uniformed officer climb out of one of the four squad cars currently gathered at the scene.

Constable Sinead Bell smiled and waved at him, and Tyler let out an involuntary little yelp of delight. She started to make her way over, but he held a hand up and shook his head.

"I wouldn't. He's honking," Tyler advised, wafting his other hand in front of his face. "And the dead body stinks, too."

"Haha. Funny bastard," Hamza said. He rolled his eyes, gave Sinead a wave, then turned his attention back to the corpse.

Taking out his phone, Hamza snapped off a couple of pictures while Tyler headed over to meet Sinead. He checked them over, winced at some of the gorier close-ups, then sent the whole lot over to the team inbox.

The lack of face made it difficult to judge the man's age. He had a decent head of hair, and none of it was grey, so probably not very old, but anything beyond that would require a closer look than he was prepared to give.

The length of the sleeves made the suit look a little on the large side for him. Although, they might well have appeared shorter had he not been missing everything below the wrists.

Hamza's eyes went to the man's shoes. They were battered trainers, not in keeping with the rest of the outfit. Size twelve or thirteen, he guessed. Big buggers of things. Well worn on the sole. Badly scuffed on the one side that he could see from where he was standing.

He snapped off another couple of pictures, mailed them to the inbox, then turned and headed for the cordon tape, where Tyler stood talking to Sinead.

"Was filling her in on the state of our boy over there," Tyler said, as if justifying the conversation.

"No hands, I hear," said Sinead.

"Largely missing a face, too," Hamza said. "Hi, by the way."

Sinead smiled. "Hi."

"I mean, technically he's not exactly missing a face," Tyler said. "It's all there. It's just that it's spread out across several feet of wall beside him."

Sinead gave an involuntary shudder. "Who the hell does something like that?"

Tyler puffed out his chest. "That's what we're going to find out," he said. "That's why they pay us the big bucks."

"They don't," Hamza reminded him.

Tyler deflated. "Oh. Aye. Fair point. 'That's why they pay us an absolute bloody pittance' hasn't got quite the same ring to it though, does it?"

There was a honk from a horn as a large white van pulled into the car park at the rear of the building and crunched to an abrupt stop at the cordon tape. A red-faced man in a white paper hood wound down the driver's window and leaned his head out.

"Bloody shift, will you?" the Scene of Crime team's Geoff Palmer bellowed at the closest uniformed officer. "Some of us have got jobs to do."

Logan marched along the hotel corridor, an overnight bag in each hand, enduring the ongoing flashback that was the sound of his ex-wife complaining.

"Good Night Guarantee, my backside," she said. "That traffic goes on all night. And the heat. We couldn't get the heat turned down, could we, Maddie?"

From right behind him, Logan heard their daughter eject the tiniest of sighs. Had he not been listening for it, he wouldn't have heard it. The fact that he did gave him immense pleasure. That sigh, barely audible as it was, was the highlight of at least the past forty-eight hours.

"It was warm, Mum, yeah," Maddie agreed.

"We should get our money back," Vanessa said. "That's what they offer, isn't it? The guarantee? If you don't sleep?"

Logan gave a non-committal sort of grunt and shouldered open the door that led to the stairs. He held it long enough for Maddie to take the weight of it, then continued on. Vanessa barely missed a beat as she ducked under Maddie's arm and followed Logan down the stairs.

"How much was it, anyway? I mean, it can't have been much, but still. It's the principle, isn't it? 'Good Night Guarantee.' I know I didn't have a good night. Did you, Maddie?"

"Definitely not," Maddie muttered, although the way she said it suggested that wasn't so much the fault of the hotel as the company.

"There you go, then," Vanessa said. "We can ask for our money back. It's in their adverts."

"We're not asking for the money back," Logan said without turning.

He reached the bottom of the stairs. The door here had a pull handle, so he stepped aside to make room for someone else to open it.

"Why not?" Vanessa asked.

Logan indicated the door with a nod. She grabbed the handle and yanked it open, eliciting a little scream from the hinges.

"Why not?" she asked again, as Logan, then Maddie trudged into the hotel's reception area.

A woman in her fifties rose from behind the front desk and smoothed down her purple uniform with a smile. "Good morning!" she chirped, and Logan felt a pang of sympathy for her over what was to come. "Checking out?"

"They are, aye," Logan said, hoping he might be able to keep Vanessa quiet if he just jumped in quickly enough.

No such luck.

"Yes, that's right," she said, slapping the plastic card keys down on the desk as if disposing of a losing poker hand. "And not a minute too soon, I'm sorry to say."

The woman behind the counter's face fell. "Oh! Was there a problem?"

"Problems. Plural," Vanessa said.

Logan closed his eyes and whispered a, "Christ's sake, here we go," beneath his breath.

"Mum..." began Maddie, clearly sharing her old man's sentiment, but Vanessa wasn't for backing down.

"For starters, the traffic. I know it's not your fault. But, I mean, who builds a hotel between a dual carriageway and a busy hospital? Without triple glazing?" Vanessa complained. "And then there was the heat. How do you switch it off? *Can* you switch it off? Is that possible? We were cooking in there, weren't we, Maddie?"

"That's a bit of an overstatement," Maddie said. She shot the receptionist an apologetic look. "It was just a bit warm."

"You do the guarantee thing, don't you?" Vanessa demanded. "I've seen it in the adverts."

Logan side-stepped in front of his ex-wife and addressed the receptionist directly. "Could you give us a minute?" he asked, indicating the office behind her with a nod of his head.

The woman behind the counter blinked, frowned, and smiled all at the same time. "Uh, yes. Of course," she said, then she retreated into the room like she was backing away from a wild animal, and closed the door with a *click*.

"Do you bloody mind?" Vanessa hissed. "I was in the middle of—"

"Shut up, Vanessa," Logan said. He took no pleasure from it, or for the look of shock that spread quickly across her face.

OK, maybe a *little* pleasure.

"What did you say?" she asked him, hackles rising. He knew the warning signs. He knew this could turn explosive. But, right at that moment, he didn't care.

"Do you know what the words 'low profile' mean, Vanessa?" he asked. He was still carrying both overnight bags, and the handles *creaked* as he tightened his grip. "Do you understand the concept of hiding?"

"Don't patronise me, Jack," she spat.

"I wouldn't dream of it. It's a serious question. Do you understand what I mean when I say that you—the pair of you—weren't here for a wee holiday. This isn't a pleasure break."

"You don't have to tell me that!" Vanessa bit back.

"This was for your safety. That's why I paid in cash. That's why, when I filled in your details on the wee machine there, I didn't use your real names. Low profile. That's what we're aiming for."

He glanced to his right, where Maddie was saying nothing. From her expression, though, she had grasped all this already, even if her mother hadn't.

"Low profile does not mean kicking up a fuss at reception," Logan continued. "It does not mean complaining about the heating, or the bloody windows, or anything else for that matter. And, it certainly doesn't mean filling out a form to get me my money back."

Vanessa had no response to that beyond a tut and a shake of the head. Both those things used to wind Logan up no end, but he ignored them now, and his voice took on a softer edge as he spoke again.

"I don't want my money back, Vanessa. I want both of you safe," he said. "That's all that matters." He smiled hopefully. "Alright?"

Vanessa held his gaze for a few seconds, then sighed. She picked up the keycards. "Fine," she muttered, then she dropped both cards into the return slot on the desk, and gestured towards the hotel's sliding front door. "Lead the way."

"No, after you. And good. Great. I'm glad you saw sense," Logan said. He waited until Vanessa had passed him, then winked at their daughter as they both shared a smile. "Besides, if you think this was bad, just wait until you see the next place."

Despite the warning, the safe house wasn't too shocking. It was a two-bedroom mid-terrace on Murray Road, in the Smithton area of the city.

From the outside, it could be generously described as 'functional,' and was unlikely to win any design awards. There was a small garden at the front from which you could look out across the Moray Firth. Aye, you'd need a sturdy ladder and a decent pair of binoculars, but it was out there somewhere.

The back garden was slightly larger and well enclosed on all sides by tall fence panels. There was a wee shed at the far end, but even if Logan had known where the keys for the padlock were, the mechanism had rusted shut long ago.

Inside, the house was basic, but functional. Couch. TV. Assorted cooking appliances. Everything they could possibly need, Logan had told them. Which, Vanessa had replied, spoke volumes about how he chose to live his life.

The beds hadn't been made up, but the bedding was all there in bags in one of the upstairs cupboards. There was one double, and two singles. Vanessa, of course, had claimed the double without actually saying so. She'd just placed her bag in that room, right behind the door, and the message was understood.

There was no food in the place, but Logan had stopped in at Tesco before picking them up at the hotel. He'd brought in four big bags of shopping from the car. He'd got staples like bread, milk, eggs, and cheese, mostly, but there was some chocolate, a multi-pack of *Wotsits*, and a couple of bottles of wine in there, too.

"Who the hell were you catering for?" Vanessa had asked, standing with a bottle of Merlot in one hand, and a three-pack of *Freddos* in the other. "Alcoholic toddlers?"

Logan had suggested she make him a list for next time. Not that there'd be a next time, he'd quickly added. The Petrie thing would be cleared up in no time. This would be a temporary inconvenience, nothing more. He was certain of it.

Or he hoped he'd sounded certain, at least.

The place was used as an Airbnb. Different people came and went all the time, so the neighbours wouldn't think twice about them staying there. Still, probably best not to talk to them. Or anyone, for that matter.

"You're lying low," he stressed, mostly for Vanessa's benefit. "No shopping trips. No nipping to the pub. No long walks in public. You need something, tell me, and I'll get it."

"Actually, Dad, you could get me, um, sanitary products," Maddie said.

Logan's face didn't know what to do with itself. The eyes widened, narrowed, then blinked, while the mouth attempted a sort of parted-lip smile that wandered dangerously close to grimace territory.

"Right. Aye. Of course. Is it... uh... urgent?" he asked.

"No. I'm fine for today," she replied. "I'll send you a photo of the box so you know what to get."

"Aye. OK. Good," Logan said, nodding on each word like his head was connected to his voicebox by a pulley system. "You do that."

He said his goodbyes then, and headed for the door. He was just stepping out onto the front path when Vanessa appeared in the hallway behind him.

"Jack?"

He tried very hard not to sigh, and instead turned to her, all smiles. "Vanessa."

Vanessa stayed inside the house, but looked both ways along the street before focusing her gaze on her ex-husband. "Thanks," she said.

Of all the words Logan had expected to come out of her mouth, that one had been way down the list.

"Thanks? For what?" he asked.

"Well, for this. Obviously. Maddie. Both of us," Vanessa said. "I know you wouldn't do it if we weren't... If you weren't worried. I know all this... with Petrie... it must be hard on you. But, well, I appreciate it, is what I'm saying. You looking out for us."

"Aye. Well," said Logan, not quite sure of what else to add. "Uniform will keep an eye. They won't know who you are, but they'll keep a watch on the house. You'll be safe. You'll both be fine."

"I'm sure we will," Vanessa said. She smiled. It was, he thought, the first time she'd smiled at him in a very long time. "I mean, we've got cheesy *Wotsits* and wine. How could we not be?"

"That's the cornerstone of any nutritious diet right there," Logan said. He looked past her into the house. "I know I don't need to tell you, but look after her."

Vanessa nodded. "You're right. You don't need to tell me," she said. "And good luck. With Petrie. I'm sure you'll get him."

"Not me," Logan said. "Petrie's no' my case."

Vanessa snorted. "Oh, yes. Sure, Jack," she said. She smiled at him as she started to edge the door closed. It was a thin and sad-looking thing. A smile not so much for the here and now, but for a life that could have been. "Just you go ahead and keep telling yourself that."

CHAPTER NINE

Music was playing behind the door of the downstairs flat when Logan passed it. It wasn't blaring out. Had it been anyone else, in fact, he might not even have noticed it, but as it was, he gave the door a dunt and shouted, "Turn that racket down!"

There was no response at first, then a sullen voice replied with a, "Fine," and the music dropped in volume.

Three black bags were stacked up outside the door to the flat. Logan poked one with his foot and was able to tell that there were clothes inside.

Logan was about to shout a reminder that he expected Bud to hurry up and fuck off, when a hoover coughed into life somewhere further inside the flat. He decided to leave him to it, and trudged on up the stairs to his own place.

He found his old holdall in the cupboard next to the bathroom, and spent the next few minutes gathering up the essentials—underwear, socks, a couple of shirts, and his shaving gear—and bundling them into the bag.

He'd had a good look around after finding the badge, of course. Checked all the obvious spots for cameras or microphones. Chucked out everything in the fridge, in case Petrie had poisoned it, and binned his toothbrush in case the bastard had shoved it up his arse.

But even as he'd given the place the all-clear, he'd known he couldn't stay there. Not now. Not knowing that Petrie had been there in his bedroom—that he'd come and gone without smashing a window or breaking the lock.

It wasn't even the thought that he might come back that bothered him. God knew, he *wanted* him to show face again. It was the thought that he'd been here. The thought that he'd contaminated the flat with his very presence. He'd haunt the place until he was caught, and that was one flatmate Logan was not prepared to put up with.

He'd bed down at the office for a few nights. Wouldn't be the first time, and probably wouldn't be the last. If Petrie was caught in the next few days, then great. If not, he'd sort out something longer term. That Premier Inn had seemed alright.

The thought of the hotel led onto another one. After zipping up his bag, Logan checked the shared team email inbox from his phone, and was immediately presented with a close-up of a faceless corpse in a suit.

"That's one hell of an overdose," he muttered, swiping through the other images.

Once he'd gone through them all, he sighed, picked up his bag, and cast his gaze around the flat.

"Never rains but it pours, eh?" he asked of nobody in particular, and then he turned and left, and locked the door behind him.

"Well?" asked Tyler, when the man in the white paper suit had come striding over to the cordon line where he and Hamza were waiting. "What have we got?"

"The hell happened to you?" Palmer asked, practically recoiling in horror at the sight of Tyler's bruised and swollen face. "Plastic surgery go wrong, did it?"

"Something like that, aye," Tyler said.

Geoff Palmer looked both DCs up and down, his displeasure written on the pudgy circle of his face that stuck out through the hole in the paper hood. "Look at the pair of you. Where's Logan? He sending the bairns in to do his dirty work now, is he?"

"Bit rich that, Geoff," Hamza said. He made a circular motion with his finger, indicating Palmer's face. The elasticated seam of the hood was tight and squeezed in on both his cheeks. "Considering you look like you're in the process of being born before our very eyes."

Tyler held a fist low at his side. Hamza bumped it without looking.

"Aye, very good," Palmer tutted. "Have your wee jokes. I'm sure Big Chief Shitting Bull will be very impressed. You're both a chip off the old block."

"Who's Big Chief Shitting Bull?" Hamza asked.

"And is that no' a bit racist, Geoff?" Tyler wondered. "You'll want to be careful saying stuff like that. Cultural appropriation. Maybe even hate speech. You'll want to watch yourself."

Palmer sighed. "God Almighty. I think you might actually be worse than he is. Do you want to know the story, or don't you? No skin off my nose." He tipped his head back in the direction of the body, which was in the process of being covered up. "No pun intended."

Hamza took out his notebook. "Aye. Go for it. What have you got?"

"A lot more than he's got, let's put it that way. No teeth, no hands. No sign of either laying around the scene. We're going to extend the search around the perimeter of the hotel, but beyond that, it's on you. You might need to bring the dogs in. See if they can sniff out the missing bits."

"Right. Aye. What else?" Hamza asked. He held his pencil poised, ready to start writing just as soon as Palmer said something worth taking note of.

"The suit's not his. Or, I suppose it is now, no other bugger's going to want it. There's a charity shop label on the tag, though. British Heart Foundation. Four quid."

"Bargain," Tyler remarked.

"Not his trainers, either. Far too big. I'd put him about a size seven. They're thirteens. Laces were around his feet to hold them on. Even then, they were hanging off."

"Probably couldn't have walked far in them, then," Hamza reasoned.

"No. Feet were manky, too. Bruised and cut. There were a lot of wee stones sticking to them and insides the shoes, so he walked barefoot for some distance before the shoes were put on. We're having a look for fingerprints on the trainers, but nothing turning up so far."

"And on the rest of him?" Tyler asked.

"Nothing yet. With all that blood, I'd expect to see stray prints somewhere, but nothing showing up at all so far. Killer probably wore gloves," Palmer continued. "Also, before you ask, there was no wallet, no keys, no ID of any kind."

"But then where would be the challenge in that?" Tyler asked.

"Killed at the scene, do you think?" Hamza asked.

"Looks like it, given the amount of blood, aye. There's a puncture wound to the neck that would've sprayed. That matches the spatter on the wall and ground. Can't say if the face was done before he bled out, during, or after. Hands were done after, though, I'd say. Teeth, I've got no idea. Pathology will be able to tell you more. We'll take the clothes and shoes for testing. We've also taken a cast of a print that's been left in the grass."

"Fingerprint?" Tyler asked. It was out of him before he could stop it, and he fully accepted the withering looks the question earned from both Hamza and Palmer.

"Footprint, obviously," Palmer said. "Doesn't match the trainers, so might be your killer. It was near the scene, as opposed to at the scene, though, so it could be from anyone."

"Great," Hamza said, scribbling in the pad. "Anything else?"

"Nothing startling. Obviously, the death was violent. There's bunching on the back and front of his clothing that suggested he was dragged, probably when they mashed his face into the wall," Palmer said. "The guy's probably nine stone soaking wet, so it could've been one attacker, and most likely was, given how little the ground around him was disturbed. Killer took the weapon with him, or disposed of it somewhere we haven't been able to find it yet."

"What about time of death? Any idea?" Hamza asked.

"Recent. Very recent," Palmer said. "He wasn't warm when we got to him, exactly, but not stiff enough to have spent the night here. Blood was still wet, too, and hadn't fully soaked into the grass."

He bent his wrist back and glanced at the watch he had tucked between where his paper sleeve ended and his rubber glove began.

"What are we on now? Quarter past one? I'd say... Six this morning? Thereabouts. Obviously, there's a bit of leeway in that either way."

"He was found just after half seven," Hamza said. "Young lassie on her way into work found him. Poor thing."

"Sinead's with her in one of the hotel offices," Tyler told the other DC. "I said I'd go in and have a chat."

"No bother. We're nearly done," Hamza said. He raised his eyebrows and looked over the top of his notepad to Geoff Palmer. "Anything else?"

"Jesus Christ, son. What else do you want?" Palmer asked. "The killer's name and address?"

"That'd be handy, if you've got it," said Logan, ducking under the cordon tape and striding over to join them. "Save us a bit of time and effort."

"Alright, boss?" Tyler asked.

"Got my emails, then," Hamza added.

"Aye. Bit of warning next time would be nice. Lucky for both of us, I hadn't bothered with breakfast," Logan replied. He turned his attention to the man in the paper suit. "So, what have we got?"

Palmer scowled and gave a dismissive wave in Hamza's direction. "Your man here's got it all. We'll finish up in the next couple of hours and I'll get the full report sent over. But, I think we can all safely agree that you're looking at a homicide. You'll need to get a move on, Jack," he said, with a self-satisfied smirk that was crying out for a belt in the mouth. "You'll be building up a backlog soon, between here and Canna."

"Canna's done," Logan said.

Palmer's forehead furrowed beneath the hood. "Done? Already?"

"Full confession," Logan said.

He watched the expression settle on Palmer's face. The bastard actually had the brass neck to look annoyed.

"Well... good work, I suppose," the Scene of Crime man said.

"Aye, well, I only do it to earn your praise, Geoff, so thanks. That really means a lot," Logan replied.

Palmer looked from Logan to the two DCs who now flanked him on either side. With a tut, a sigh, and a shake of his head, he pulled off a crisp about-turn and announced he was getting back to it.

"Right, so, what have we got?" Logan asked, once Palmer had joined the rest of his team over by the body.

Hamza opened his mouth to reply, but Tyler interjected before he had a chance to speak.

"I'm going to go talk to the lassie that found him. Sinead's waiting inside with her," he said.

Logan regarded him with something treading the line between confusion and disbelief.

"Unless... Do you want to do it, boss?" Tyler asked, unable to miss the look the remark had earned him.

"No. It's fine," Logan said. "You go. Shout if you need us."

"Will do. Cheers, boss," Tyler replied, all smiles again. He ducked under the cordon tape, fired off a finger-gun at a passing Uniform, then went strutting around the side of the hotel in the direction of the front door.

Logan waited until he was out of sight before turning to Hamza. "Did he just...? Did he just use his initiative?"

Hamza glanced in the direction the other DC had gone. "He might've done, sir. Aye."

"Bugger me. Wonders will never cease," Logan mumbled. He tapped Hamza's notepad with the end of a finger. "Now, talk me through it, and let's see where we are."

CHAPTER TEN

The girl was upset. But then, who wouldn't be?

She was sitting hunched in a wooden chair in something that might have been an office, but equally could have been a storeroom. Packs of toilet paper were stacked six high at one end, while reams of other—probably much less vital—paper overflowed from an in-tray that stood on a desk at the other end.

Constable Bell was perched forward on another chair, saying soft, soothing things when Tyler knocked and entered. Both women looked up at him as he stepped through the door, although only one of them looked even remotely pleased to see him.

"Detective Constable. We've just been talking about you," Sinead said.

Tyler visibly struggled with where to pitch his comeback. On the one hand, there was a young woman in the room who'd just found a dismembered corpse. On the other hand, his natural instinct around Sinead was to flirt for all he was worth.

In the end, he settled for something that erred on the side of professionalism without, he hoped, making him sound like a humourless twat.

"Thought my ears were burning," he said. He reached a hand out to the young woman in the chair. She looked squarely in her teens. Seventeen, maybe? "Hi. I'm Detective Constable Neish. Call me Tyler."

"Kerri," she said in a voice that was just a half-decibel or so above a whisper.

"With an 'i'," Sinead added.

"Nice," said Tyler, smiling at the girl. "Fancy."

He looked around for another chair but found none. Sinead started to get up, but he motioned for her to stay seated, and instead grabbed a couple of packs of toilet paper, placed them on the floor in front of Kerri, and sat on those.

"You've had a rough morning, I hear," he said.

Kerri drew in a breath through her nose. Her eyes widened a little, like she'd just managed to forget what she'd seen, and had now had it brought rushing back.

"Not the best," she said. Her accent was local, not the Eastern European that Tyler realised he had been expecting.

"I'm sorry you had to see that. Must've been rough."

"Not the best," she said again. "What happened to your face?"

"Hmm? Oh," Tyler said. He very carefully traced the bump in his nose with his fingertips. "Got into a fight. You should see the other guy."

"He's largely unharmed," Sinead said.

"Key word 'largely,'" Tyler said. "He's not *completely* unharmed."

"Just mostly."

"Aye. Just mostly," Tyler confirmed, and Kerri managed half a smile at that.

Even smiling, she had a haunted look about her. One of the worst Tyler had seen, in fact. He'd have said she looked like she'd seen a ghost, but it was more than that. She looked like she'd accidentally spilled a ghost's pint, and it was now drunkenly threatening to kick her teeth in. It was the mask of the shell-shocked, and she was wearing it well.

"Did we call her parents?" Tyler asked Sinead.

"There's just my mum," Kerri said, answering before the constable could. "She's in Glasgow all week. Training."

"Oh. Right."

"She's a dog groomer," Kerri said.

"Wow. Cool."

Kerri rolled her eyes, and for a moment looked a bit more like a normal teenager, and a bit less like someone who was going to need therapy for the rest of their life.

"It's really not."

This was clearly a conversational route she was more comfortable with. Tyler indulged her, wandering along it with her. They chatted about dogs for a while. Then about jobs. Then about parents, and their many embarrassing qualities.

"You think your mum's bad? My dad's a doctor. A GP," Tyler said. "When I was in... I think second year in high school, maybe? Guess who came in to do the sex talk in SE."

Kerri sat up straighter in her chair. "No way!"

"Yep. There he is, front of the whole class, banana in one hand, condom in the other, and I'm sat up the back looking at the window thinking, 'It's only four floors. Maybe I'll survive the impact.'"

Kerri slapped a hand over her mouth and groaned. "Oh, God. I can't imagine," she said, then she turned to PC Bell.

Sinead felt her heart plunge into her stomach. She battled valiantly to keep her smile fixed in place, but she knew what was coming. She could see it approaching, like a set of headlights powering along a darkened road towards her. Unavoidable. Inevitable.

"What about you? What do your mum and dad do?" Kerri asked.

"They, uh..." Sinead could feel Tyler's gaze on her. Could feel his sympathy burning into the side of her face. "You know, this and that. Nothing much."

Kerri's brow creased into the start of a frown, like she was about to press the constable further. Tyler quickly steered the conversation back onto more pressing matters before she had the chance.

"So, do you mind taking me through what happened this morning, Kerri?" he asked. "Just in your own time. There's no hurry."

The girl's body language drew itself tighter again. She pulled the heels of her feet up onto the chair, her bent legs like a barrier between her and the officers.

"Eh, yeah. OK," she said. Then, after a few deep breaths and a couple of false starts, she took them through it.

She usually got a lift in from her mum, but had walked that day, due to the aforementioned dog clipping training down in Glasgow. She'd left sharp, to be on the safe side, and so had turned up almost half an hour early for her morning shift, which was due to start at eight. She'd nipped around the back of the hotel for a fly blast of her vape before she clocked in.

And that was when she'd found him.

At first, she'd thought it was another staff member on a smoking break. Then, as she'd got closer, she'd thought it was someone lying drunk.

It was only when she'd put on her glasses, that she'd realised the full terrible truth of what she was looking at.

"Did you go over to it? The body?" Tyler asked.

Kerri's expression made it very clear that no force on Earth would've been able to drag her over to that man propped up against the wall.

"No. I just turned and ran inside and found Cathy."

Tyler side-eyed Sinead.

"Assistant night manager," the constable clarified.

"She called the police. I didn't go back out," Kerri said. She wrapped her arms around her legs, hugging them. "I didn't want to see it again."

"That's understandable. And you absolutely did the right thing, Kerri. Well done," Tyler said. "Now, I need you to think, was there anything else you saw that seemed... out of place, maybe?"

Kerri shook her head. "No. Just... that. Him."

"Take a minute. Don't rush," Tyler urged. "Think. Could there have been anything else, anything at all, that struck you as odd? Or not even odd, necessarily, just different?"

Kerri's eyes flitted left to right, like she was rewinding and replaying film footage of the event inside her head.

"No," she finally said. "No, I don't think... wait."

Tyler straightened on his stack of toilet paper. Kerri looked from him to Sinead and back again.

"Now that I think about it, there was one thing."

"A van?"

"That's what she said, boss. Small transit. No markings on the side that she noticed, but she can't be sure," Tyler said. He turned his chair away from his desk so it was facing Logan's, then sat in it. "Passed her coming out of the car park about quarter past seven. She went inside, dropped her stuff, then went around the back for a smoke and found the body."

"Hotel car park. Could've been workmen staying," Logan reasoned. "Not uncommon for vans to be coming and going."

"No, I know, boss. But..." Tyler sat back and gestured for Hamza to take over.

"Guests have to log their vehicle reg at reception. I got the list for last night and ran through them."

Logan sat forward in his chair, becoming more interested. "No vans, I take it?"

"No vans," Hamza confirmed.

DI Forde had been prodding away at his keyboard while the conversation had taken place, but leaned out from behind the monitor now to chip in. "Delivery maybe?"

"I thought about that, too," Tyler said. He exchanged a look with Hamza, then shrugged. "Alright, technically Sinead thought that, too. So, we checked. Nothing."

Logan drummed his fingers on the desk. "So, we've got a van. What's the camera situation around there? I know there's nothing at the hotel, but anything nearby?"

"Afraid not, sir," Hamza said. "CCTV's mostly just city centre. We could put out an appeal on the radio for dashcam footage. Paper's out late tomorrow night, too. We could get something in there."

"Aye. Do that. Maybe someone saw something," Logan said. He sucked air in through his teeth. "Still, pretty thin, though. A van."

"Better than nothing, boss."

"Aye. Barely," Logan said. He stood up. He hadn't bothered to take his coat off since coming in last time, and his hands instinctively found their natural home in his pockets. "But keep at it. I'm heading to the hospital."

"No' the prostate exam is it, boss?" Tyler asked. He grinned, despite the thoroughly unamused expression that had settled on Logan's face. "Man of your age, and all that."

"Did anyone ever tell you you should've been a comedian, son?"

"No' yet, boss."

Logan shook his head. "No. Didn't think so," he said. "Ben, hold the fort. Call me if anything comes in. I'm going to go check in on the post-mortem."

"Right, Jack. No bother," Ben said. "And for God's sake, be careful."

Logan stopped by the exit. "Aye. Well, you know me, Detective Inspector," he said, then he pushed through the swing doors, and was gone.

"I do," Ben muttered. "And that's what bloody worries me."

"Haw! Fannybaws!"

Logan stopped a pace or two past Detective Superintendent Hoon's open office door, then backtracked until he was filling the doorway.

"Sir?"

"Don't fucking, 'sir,' me. Come in," Hoon urged.

Logan contemplated objecting, then stepped into the office.

"Were you born in a bastarding barn?" Hoon asked.

Logan closed the door behind him without a word.

"Good. Right," Hoon said, indicating the chair across from him. "Got some reports in from the fuckers down the road. Petrie case. Thought you'd want to be kept up to date."

"Honestly, sir?" Logan began. "I'm not sure that—"

"Just shut your fucking piehole and listen," the DSup snapped. He clicked his computer mouse, and his eyes went to the top right corner of the screen. "Right. Hang on. It's... fuck. Hang on."

He clicked a few more times. Each time he did, something else on the monitor caught his attention, until his gaze was moving left, right, up, and down like he was following the ball in a game of *Pong*.

"Jesus Christ. They make these things so fucking complicated. How do I get back?"

"Back where?" Logan asked.

Hoon shot him a foul look. "I was thinking out loud, for fuck's sake.

Was that no' obvious? I don't expect you to fucking know what I'm... Aha. Here we go," he said, double-clicking something and then sitting back in his chair. "Post Mortem report on the doctor. Best estimate is he was killed within five or six hours of Petrie escaping Carstairs. Judging by his injuries, those five or six hours would not have been pleasant ones."

"Aye. He was a mess," Logan said.

"You don't know the fucking half of it," Hoon said, staring at the screen. "Eyelids cut off. Teeth and fingernails pulled out. Not all of them, but enough that you'd well and truly fucking smart."

He continued to read, turning the mouse wheel with a fingertip as he scrolled down the page.

"Signs of strangulation. Burns to chest and stomach from some fucking corrosive material they've yet to identify. In the mouth and stomach lining, too, so he made the poor bastard drink it," Hoon continued. "Ribs cracked. Fingers and toes broken. Thumbs completely fucking detached."

His face screwed up and he tucked his own thumbs into his palms. "Ooyah bastard," he remarked, before turning his attention back to the report. "Rectal damage suggests something was forcibly rammed up there. Doesn't say if it was implement or cock."

He scrolled down a little further.

"No. Tell a lie. Wasn't a cock. Don't know if that's better or worse," he muttered. His eyes went to the next paragraph and he flinched. "Fuck me! Worse. Something hooked or barbed, they reckon."

"Aye. That's worse," Logan agreed.

"Long and the short of it is, he might've had a stiffy for Mister Whisper, but the feeling clearly wasn't mutual. Petrie fucked him over the first chance he got."

"No great surprise there," Logan said.

Hoon grunted, neither in agreement nor disagreement. He sat back until he was almost reclining in his chair, and rested his hands on his stomach, fingers interlocked.

"They've got their eyes peeled down the road, checking his old haunts, likely places the fucker might hide. The usual," the DSup said. He pinned Logan to his seat with a sharp, piercing stare. "No sign of him. But then, they probably won't find him, will they?"

"I hope so, sir," Logan said.

"Cut the shite, Detective Chief Inspector," Hoon told him. "You and I both know, that if you thought Owen fucking Petrie was knocking about in Glasgow, there's no' a snowball's chance in Hell you'd have fucked off back up here so soon."

Logan said nothing. He didn't have to.

"You think he's up here, don't you?" Hoon asked. "No, you fucking *know* he's up here."

"He might be. He's hard to predict."

"Fuck off! 'Hard to predict.' Who the fuck do you think you're talking to, son? I was doing this job while you were still hanging off yer mammy's tits."

Part of Logan wanted to point out that the Detective Superintendent was barely more than ten years older than him, but another part—the part that concerned itself with his personal welfare—thought it best not to mention it.

"If you want to fuck around obsessing over that sick bastard, fine. I don't care. Let him cut your eyelids off and shove whatever pronged devices he likes up your arse," Hoon said. "But I'm sure I don't need to remind you, Jack, that you've already lost one good officer recently."

Logan's chair gave a low, ominous groan as the DCI adjusted his position.

"If I find out you're putting anyone else at risk by withholding information, I will engulf you in a whirlwind of shit. I'll be the vengeful fucking Thunder God of Faeces. A maelstrom of steaming hot excrement, and you'll be at the eye of the fucking storm. You won't have to worry about Petrie ramming stuff up your arse, because I'll be in front of him in the queue wi' an electric whisk and a foot pump. Is that clear?"

"I wouldn't do anything to put my team in harm's way," Logan said.

"Aye, well. They're my fucking team, too, and believe it or not, I care about their welfare," Hoon said. "I mean, maybe no' the mouthy wee prick wi' the hair. I'd gladly punch his fucking mouth loose. But the rest of them. Understood?"

Logan nodded. "Understood."

"Good. And, I mean, maybe I've got it wrong. Surely you can't be too fucking concerned about him coming up here, or you wouldn't have brought your daughter up here, would you? The ex, aye. That I can see. But your wean? What kind of monster'd do something like that? Eh, Jack? Knowing what we know?"

Several seconds passed, both men staring the other down. It was Logan who eventually broke.

"I brought them here to keep them safe," he said.

"Right. And I should hope so, too. Now, go. Fuck off and get back to it," Hoon said. "And, if you think of anything—any reason you might have for believing that fucker's somewhere up this way—then you be sure to let me know."

"I'll rack my brains, sir," Logan said.

"I'll rack your balls, if you're no' careful," Hoon warned. He waved a hand, dismissing the DCI. "Now, get out of my fucking sight."

CHAPTER ELEVEN

It wasn't fair!

The first day—maybe the only day ever—that he'd been allowed to go out by himself, and nobody else was coming out to play. Not Michael upstairs, not Adam from the flats next door. Not even Lisa from the houses round the corner, which he was secretly a bit relieved about, because she always talked about kissing and wanted to hold his hand when they walked round to the park.

He had no one to hold his hand when he walked round to the park today.

Him and his mum always went to the park together at the same time, but he'd been excited about the idea of going out on his own one time. He'd harped on about it for weeks, in fact.

"Michael's already been out *twice* by himself," he'd said. "And he's nearly a whole month younger than me!"

She'd said, "No way," at first. A lot of times, actually. Sometimes laughing about it, sometimes serious.

Once, after she'd been working late the night before, she'd shouted at him so sharply that he'd burst into tears on the spot, and gone running into his bedroom. She'd come in a few minutes later with a bar of chocolate and an apology, snuggled up with him on his bed, and told him she just worried about him. Told him he was still very young, and that she'd be scared if he went out on his own. Told him she hoped he understood, and that one day—someday—he'd get to go out by himself.

That had been yesterday. This morning, when he'd asked, she'd sighed, shaken her head, and told him he could go, but only if he didn't go further than the park so she could at least watch him from the window.

He'd tried to protest, but it was that or nothing, she'd said. Take it or leave it.

"My way, or the highway."

He knew better than to argue. This was the best deal he was likely to get. And so, he'd given in. Fine. She could watch him if she *had* to, but she wasn't allowed to shout over and embarrass him in front of his friends.

No chance of that now.

The park was empty. The swings creaked and groaned on their chains as they were nudged back and forth by the breeze, all swinging at different times.

He'd seen the bigger kids play games like that before, where they'd start the swings going, then try to run through the middle of them without getting hit.

He'd always thought the whole thing looked scary, and when Alice Something-Or-Other from the other side of the estate had misjudged a run and had her nose smashed open by one of the baby swings, he'd made the decision never to try it for himself.

He went to the roundabout first, put one foot on the wooden base, and pushed himself around with a series of drawn-out screeches of metal on metal. It had never turned properly since Wee Sid had got the front wheel of his bike stuck under it that time, and after four slow revolutions his legs were aching too much to keep pushing.

Cupping his hands to his eyes, he looked over at his block of flats. He counted the windows—three from the bottom, two in from the left—and squinted to try to see his mum. The sunlight was reflecting off the glass, so he wasn't sure if she was there. He waved, anyway, and in that moment felt a little pang of regret and wished she was here with him.

He trudged over to the swings, jumped up onto the rubber seat, and reached with his feet to try to touch the ground. Some of the other kids could get themselves started just by swinging their legs, but he'd never been able to manage it.

Groaning with the effort, he stretched his legs as far as they would stretch, pointed his toes straight out until the tips of his shoes brushed against the safety mat. It was half-covered in stones, and most of the little holes were clogged up with weeds. He wasn't sure just how safe it would be to land on if he fell, but he wasn't planning on going high, anyway.

Just a wee swing. Just for a minute, so he could say he'd done it, then he could go home. His mum might play a game with him. Maybe she'd do hot-dogs for lunch.

Clinging to the chains with both hands, he slid his bum to the edge of the seat. His toe touched the ground. He tried to kick back, but instead just sort of hopped and finished in the exact same position, poised like a ballerina.

He tried again. Push. Hop. *Thump.*

He really hoped his mum wasn't watching. She'd never let him out on his own again if he couldn't even get a swing started.

One more try. That would do it. One more big push, and...

He cried out with the effort of the kick, clutching the chains and throwing himself backwards as he put his full weight into the shove.

For a moment—a glorious, perfect moment—he felt the swing start to climb. But then, he buckled. His nerve gave out, and he slipped forward off the seat, pain jarring up his legs as both feet thudded flatly onto the mat.

Shame burned at his cheeks and pricked at his eyes. He couldn't look over at the window now, in case he saw her looking back. He hoped she wasn't there. He hoped she hadn't seen him failing so spectacularly. He hoped nobody had.

"Hello there."

The voice came from behind him, making him jump.

A man was there, smiling at him. He had a woollen hat pulled down low on his head, but not quite low enough to hide the bottom of the scar that was above his eye.

The man stepped forward and spoke again. His voice was soft and gentle. A murmur.

A whisper.

"Would you like me to give you a push?"

CHAPTER TWELVE

Dr Shona Maguire wasn't in her office when Logan turned up. The lights were on through the back, though—the room where all the post-mortem unpleasantness took place—and he could hear her singing Alice Cooper's *School's Out* to herself as she went about her work.

Logan shuffled from foot to foot in the outer office doorway for a few seconds, not quite sure if he should interrupt. He certainly didn't want to go marching into the back room unannounced. His constitution was pretty rock-solid, but the body had been in a grim state even before Shona had got at it. He wasn't sure he wanted to wander in there and find him with his stomach pinned open and his intestines piled up on a set of scales.

He settled for announcing his presence with a cough and a shout of, "Hello. Just me. Take your time."

The singing stopped. "Me who?" came the reply.

"It's, uh, just... Jack."

"Jack who?"

Logan felt like he'd taken a punch to the chest. Before he could reply, the door swung open enough for Shona's head to appear through it. She wore a visor over the top part of her face, and a mask across the bottom, but he could tell she was grinning at him.

"Just kidding. Hiya. Give me a couple of minutes," she said, then she vanished back into the mortuary, only to appear again a second later. "And stick the kettle on."

Logan looked around the untidy outer office until he found the kettle. It was tucked behind a stack of paperwork on a stainless steel countertop, the cable trailing to a bank of sockets on the end of a long extension.

A spaghetti of wires ran from the other plugs connected to the extension. At least three of them were charges for various electronic devices, and the other stretched up to a smart speaker that teetered ominously on the edge of a shelf.

Logan picked up the kettle, swished it around to gauge if there was enough water in it, concluded there was, then set it back down and switched it on.

He conducted a cursory search for cups, but found only one sitting beside the PC. As it was crawling with enough mould to repopulate Mars, he decided to leave it be. No point disturbing it. That might make it angry.

Turning away from the boiling kettle, Logan caught sight of his reflection in the glass of the office's outer door. Christ, he looked tired. Old, too. He ran a hand down his face, like he might be able to magically wipe away the five days of stubble and the two decades of bags under his eyes.

No such luck.

The kettle had just clicked off when the mortuary door opened. Shona pointed to a box that sat on the closest table. "Masks and gloves are in there," she said. "If you fancy taking a wee swatch at your man?"

Logan couldn't say he did particularly fancy it, but he grabbed the protective gear anyway, and pulled it on before squeezing past Shona into the much colder room beyond.

The faceless figure had looked bad in the photographs, but was even more unsettling up-close and in person. He was mostly covered by a sheet, with only his head and feet poking out at either end.

"OK, victim was a Caucasian male, mid-to-late-twenties, best guess. And, well, I'll say this about you, Jack, you keep things interesting. You bring me some crazy stuff," Shona remarked. "I mean, you see a lot in this job—too much, some might argue—but this is a first for me."

"How so?" Logan asked.

"Well, I'm not sure if you've noticed, but someone's gone and scraped all his face off," Shona said. She stood at the head of the body and cupped her hands at either side, as if presenting the prize-winning entry in a baking contest. "Ta-daa."

The face was mostly sinew and gristle, but worn down enough that patches of skull showed through on the cheeks and forehead. The jaw hung impossibly wide, making the face look even more monstrous than it already did.

The teeth had been removed. "Smashed in and ripped out," Shona explained. "While alive, I'd say. There's clotting around some of the front sockets, which were probably the first to go. There's also bruising on his arms and shoulders that would suggest he was held down, and that he tried to put up a fight. Someone, it is safe to say, was not a big fan of this gentleman."

"Jesus Christ," Logan muttered.

"Nah. I doubt he's the culprit," Shona said. "He's more the 'turn the other cheek' type than the 'grind both cheeks against a roughcast wall until they fall off.'"

"That must've taken a lot of force," Logan remarked, flicking his eyes down to the victim's face. "Before or after he died, you think?"

"Hard to determine," Shona said. "Either right before, or immediately after. Given that it's a reasonably public place, and there'd be a *lot* of screaming involved, I'd say after. Or, at least, that he was unconscious during it."

"That's something."

"Yeah. Although, that said, he was stabbed in the back. That's what killed him. Multiple downward strikes with a reasonably short blade. Four, five inches maybe. Hard to be precise on the number of times he was stabbed, but somewhere between twelve and fourteen. They were clustered tightly together, so there's a lot of overlap."

"How tightly together?" Logan asked.

"About that," said Shona, using the forefingers and thumbs of both gloved hands to indicate a circle the size of a small orange. "I've got pictures I can send you."

"Doesn't suggest someone panicking and just stabbing wildly, then," Logan said. "That's controlled."

"Yeah, that fits," Shona said. "And, in the back, downward strikes suggest the killer was standing over him."

"So, he could've had his face against the wall then. Down on his knees," Logan said. He thought back to the photos Hamza had sent him. "Pretty sure there were grass stains on the knees of his trousers, now I think about it."

"Right. Well, that's what makes me wonder if maybe the face was..." She gestured down at the body, at a loss for words. "*...rubbed off* while he was still alive."

Logan looked at her over the top of the corpse. "Best guess?" he asked.

Shona scratched the back of her neck. "If you're putting me on the spot, it was done after. I think it went teeth—done elsewhere, not at the scene, judging by the clotting and the whole *scream factor* I mentioned—then he's shoved up against the wall on his knees, stabbed repeatedly, and then, while he's still bleeding, the face is dragged back and forth across the wall."

"Then his hands are cut off?" Logan asked.

Shona looked a little disappointed behind her mask. "Aw, you knew about that? I was going to leave it as a surprise. Just, like, whip the sheet away and... Boom. No hands." She stared in silence at the DCI for a few seconds, before clearing her throat. "Which, now I say it out loud, would've been inappropriate. But yes. Hands last. He'd lost a good percentage of his blood before then."

Logan nodded and looked the body up and down, focusing more on the feet-end, and less on the face, which was like something out of a nightmare. "Anything else?"

"I'd say you're looking at more than one attacker. At least two, probably more. The shape of the bruises on his arms and shoulders would suggest a couple of people held him," Shona reasoned. "If it was while his teeth were being pulled, then someone else would've had to have been on pliers duty. Strong, too. The ones holding him, I mean. Big hands."

"Anything in his system? Drink? Drugs?"

"Too early to say. I've already sent samples off to Toxicology, but it'll take a while. He's a habitual drugs user, though. Track marks on his arms, and a couple on his legs and feet. Varying ages, going back a few weeks up until the last few days."

"How long's a while?" Logan asked.

"For the full report? Days for preliminary. Could be a month waiting for the full spectrometry at the minute. I'm told there's a backlog at the lab. Funding cuts."

"Great," Logan grunted.

"If it helps, I did a basic alcohol blood test—not easy, given the amount of blood loss—and he'd definitely been drinking. I can tell you that, at least. How much or when? Can't say for sure. But there was alcohol in his system."

"Right. Hopefully, the full Toxicology report will clarify," Logan said.

"It should. Oh! I almost forgot," Shona said. She pulled back the sheet to reveal the victim's left arm. There was a deep gouge that ran almost from his shoulder to the crook of his elbow, the skin hacked away until only the flesh beneath it remained. "He also had this."

Logan joined her on the other side of the table, and leaned in for a closer look at the wound. The edges were neat, so whatever had been used to carve out the chunk of flesh had been sharp. The exposed muscle was a sickly pale shade of pinkish-grey, not the meaty-red Logan would've expected.

"Done after he was dead," Shona said. "Big chunk of skin and flesh just cut right out of him. Another trophy, I'm guessing."

Logan straightened and shook his head. "My money's on a tattoo," he said. "Common placement for one, and if you're going to the trouble of taking the hands and teeth to hide the guy's identity, you don't want a distinctive tattoo to make it all pointless."

"Of course. Yeah. Should've seen that," Shona said, and she seemed genuinely irritated that she hadn't.

"It's an educated guess. I could be talking shite," Logan told her. "Only mentioned it because I've seen the same thing before."

"No, it makes sense," Shona said. She bumped him with her hip. "On another note... It's good to see you, by the way. You're looking well."

Logan snorted. "I am bloody not."

"Well, I mean, forty percent of your face is covered, and the only thing I've got to compare you to is him," the pathologist said, indicating the body on the table. "So, I guess it's all relative."

She smiled at him behind her mask. "You hungry?"

Logan glanced down at the mutilated corpse. "Not particularly," he admitted.

"Oh," said Shona, a little crestfallen.

Logan shrugged. "But, I'm sure I could eat. You know, just ideally not in this room."

"Excellent!" said Shona, brightening immediately. "Because... You know how we've been talking about lunch, or dinner, or whatever for... Well, forever?"

"Aye," said Logan. "We may have mentioned it once or twice."

"Right. Well, I was fed up of it never happening, so I decided to take matters into my own hands," Shona said. She headed for the door, already pulling off her rubber gloves. "Come with me. I've had a bit of an idea."

It wasn't the lunch date Logan had been hoping for. Not by a long shot.

He'd never admit it, of course, but he'd had a plan for it. A nice restaurant. Some wine for her, a soft drink for himself. Music, maybe, not so loud that it interfered with their conversation, but a nice accompaniment.

That was the lunch he'd been hoping for. That would've been perfect.

What he got fell short of that ideal by some distance.

His *Pot Noodle* sat steaming on the stainless steel worktop beside him. It was chicken tikka flavour. "A new one!" Shona had excitedly announced, as she'd ripped the foil lids off both pots and poured in the boiling water with meticulous care and precision.

"You don't want it runny," she'd explained. "Too much, and you've got chicken tikka noodle soup, and who wants that?"

She'd slid Logan's to him along the worktop, like an Old West barman sliding whisky along the bar. He'd caught it with only the most minimal sloshing of scalding hot liquid, and had begun jabbing at it with his fork to break up the still hard-packed noodles.

"What are you doing?" Shona had demanded, practically snatching the pot back out of his hands. "Leave it two minutes, *then* stir. Jesus, what are you, some sort of Philistine?"

"Oh. Sorry," he'd replied. "I generally just bash it into submission."

Shona had smirked at that. "Interesting insight into your psyche there, Detective Chief Inspector," she'd said, her amusement evidenced in the musical lilt of her Irish accent. Then, she'd set his pot down next to her own on the counter and hopped up onto the stool beside his.

"Well, this is—" Logan began, but Shona held a finger up for silence.

"Alexa!" she barked, with such sudden ferocity that Logan nearly jumped off the stool. Shona smiled apologetically and lowered her voice to a whisper. "Sorry. I'm sure the bitch ignores me on purpose."

She glanced back over her shoulder to make sure the top ring of the smart speaker was glowing blue, then spoke again.

"Play *Come on Eileen*."

There was a momentary pause, before an electronic voice replied: "Playing *Come on Eileen* by Dexy's Midnight Runners on Spotify."

She turned to Logan and grinned as the opening bars of the song played from the speaker.

Not too loud. A nice accompaniment.

"Good choice," Logan said. "You remembered."

"I did. And don't say I'm not good to you. Sure, it's an awful bloody song."

Logan leaned back on the stool in a show of mock outrage. He pointed to the smart speaker. "This?"

"Aye."

"What are you...? Are you even listening? Do you have ears?" Logan asked. "This is the greatest... Well, no, it's no' the greatest song ever written, but it's up there. Top ten. Top five, maybe."

"You're deluded," Shona laughed.

"Shh," said Logan. "Appreciate."

They listened, holding eye contact through the first verse and into the chorus. Shona shook her head. "Nope. Not getting it," she said. "You know who I feel sorry for?"

"Eileen?" Logan guessed, which brought a snort of laughter from the pathologist.

"Well, yes, obviously. Poor cow. But no. Duran Duran."

Logan frowned. "Eh?"

"Duran Duran. *Save a Prayer*. Clearly a better song by any conceivable standard, but this shite robbed it of getting to number one."

"It's not a better song!" Logan countered. "It's dreary guff."

"It's a far better song. There's not a metric available by which it isn't. And it was kept off number one by this and by... and I'm going to guess that you'll approve of this... *Eye of the Tiger*."

"A classic," said Logan, very much approving. "From *Rocky*."

Shona shook her head. "No."

"It bloody is," Logan told her.

"It's from *Rocky* 3," she told him.

She picked up her *Pot Noodle*, stirred it, and indicated for Logan to do the same.

"Oh. Is it? I always thought it was the first one. Is three the one with the big Russian fella?"

"That's *Rocky 4*. Dolph Lundgren. Three's the one with Mr T." She scowled and adopted her best Mr T voice. "I'll kill you, sucka!"

"Aye. So it is," Logan said. "And that was eerily accurate, by the way. Well done. Shut your eyes, and maybe, you know, cover your ears nearly all the way, and you'd swear it was him."

"I thank you. I'm a woman of many talents," Shona said, taking a little bow.

Logan finished stirring his noodles, then began twisting them around his fork.

"Jesus Christ," Shona sighed. "You've still to put the sauce in and leave it another two minutes. Seriously, have you never had one of these before?"

"Plenty," Logan replied. "But I'm no' a big one for following instructions."

Shona shook her head reproachfully. "There's nothing big or clever about slapdash *Pot Noodling*," she told him. She pointed to the little square sachet sitting on the counter next to the container. "Sauce."

Logan obediently tore open the sachet and stirred in the sauce.

"Now, leave it be," Shona told him. "Let it mature."

Logan chuckled at that. "*Mature*. It's no' a fine wine."

"No, it's better," Shona said. She shot the pot a slightly worried look. "Although, new flavour. This could all go horribly wrong."

Logan wanted to reply that, as lunch dates went, it hadn't exactly gone particularly right so far, but he couldn't. The fact of it was, this was... nice. Good.

Not perfect, obviously but how could it be? When had anything in his life ever come close to perfection? When had anything in anyone's?

The final few bars of *Come on Eileen* echoed around the office, then faded into silence.

"Right. You want to hear a real song?" Shona asked. She raised her voice without waiting for his response. "Alexa! Play *Then You Can Tell Me Goodbye* by Bettye Swann."

The smart speaker replied to confirm, then an acoustic guitar began to play. They both listened as a simple, sultry female voice started to sing. Logan watched Shona as she first hummed, then quietly sang along with the lyrics.

"Come on," she said, stepping down off the stool. She held a hand out, but he baulked at it.

"What? No."

"You don't dance?" Shona asked, her hand still outstretched.

"Not if I can possibly avoid it."

She reached over and took his hand. "Well, you can't," she told him, and he gave a resigned little grunt as he let her pull him up onto his feet.

The fingers of her right hand interlocked with his left, and her other hand went to his chest. Logan tensed at her closeness, suddenly filled with the type of self-consciousness he hadn't felt in years. Decades, maybe.

He began to shuffle in time with the music, one hand on her waist, her eyes gazing up into his.

"Wow," she whispered, staring up at him.

Logan felt himself blush. "What?"

She bit her bottom lip, fighting back the urge to laugh. "You really can't dance, can you?"

He spun her around with one hand, then caught her as he leaned her back. "Who says I can't?" he said, his face close to hers, breathing the same air.

"Well, aren't you just full of surprises?" Shona said. Her smile fell away, as her eyes searched his face.

Logan held her there, nestled in his arms, as the music continued to play.

He maintained that this wasn't the perfect lunch date. How could it be?

But it was, he reckoned, close enough.

His phone rang. Of course, it did.

He saw his own disappointment mirrored on Shona's face, and for a moment he considered ignoring it. Just letting it ring.

At any other time, he would've. But not today. He couldn't today.

And like that, the moment was gone.

He straightened, lifting Shona back up onto her feet.

"Sorry," he told her, reaching into his pocket.

"No. It's fine," she said. "Duty calls."

He took out the phone, and Ben Forde's name flashed up at him from the screen. Logan sighed. Never a bloody cold caller when you needed one.

"Ben?" he said into the handset. "What's up?"

"Where are you? You still at the hospital?"

"I am. Just... looking over the pathology findings. Why?"

"We've had... an incident. It's, eh... We think it's Petrie. There was a boy at a park. You should come in."

Logan turned and looked at Shona. She was back on her stool now, stirring her *Pot Noodle*. She read the meaning in the look without him having to say a word.

"It's fine," she whispered. "Go!"

Logan managed a thin-lipped smile, silently mouthed a, "Sorry," then turned and marched towards the door. "I'm on my way," he said into the handset. "What is it? What's happened?"

Shona watched the door swing closed behind him, then looked down at the steam rising from the abandoned plastic pot on the countertop.

"Alexa! Stop," she said.

The music cut off, and silence flooded the office.

But only for a moment.

"Playing *Stop* by The Spice Girls," Alexa announced.

"No, I don't..." Shona began, but then she rolled her eyes and shook her head. "Fine. Whatever."

As Ginger, Scary, Baby and the others began their tuneless caterwauling, Shona twisted her fork around in her noodles, blew on them to cool them, then slurped them down.

Alone.

CHAPTER THIRTEEN

Logan sat at one end of a corner couch, talking to the anxious, drawn-out looking woman perched at the opposite end.

He could hear Sinead rattling around through in the kitchen, hunting for mugs as the kettle came rolling to the boil.

"Miss Thomas... Louisa. I know you've already spoken to my officers, but if you could just take me through it again one more time, that would be really helpful," the DCI said.

Louisa Thomas was sitting forward, balanced right on the front edge of the cushion. One leg bounced up and down, shaking the couch all the way around to Logan's side.

"I don't know what... What else can I tell you?" she asked.

"I know it's upsetting to go over it again, but if you can go from the start, that would really help me out," Logan told her. "You were watching your son... Jaden. You were watching Jaden out of the window?"

Louisa nodded. She was young—mid-twenties or so—and lived alone with her boy. Her lips stretched out, becoming thinner as her eyes shimmered behind a wall of tears that had been building since Logan's arrival.

"He'd never been out on his own before," she said, her eyes going past Logan to the room's only window. "I'd told him no, but he kept going on and on. Everyone else did it. 'It's fine, Mum. It's safe.'"

She pressed a crumpled tissue to her mouth, cleared her throat a few times, then exhaled slowly and continued.

"So, I let him. I let him go. Told him not to go any further than the park. You can see it from the window."

Logan got up, crossed to the window, and looked out. The playpark was roughly two hundred yards away. Two squad cars were parked on the grass beside it. Their flashing blue lights reflected off the slide, and the swings, and the cordon tape that billowed on the breeze.

"I was watching him. I swear, I was keeping an eye on him," Louisa said behind him. "I just looked away for a couple of minutes. That was all."

"You can't blame yourself," Logan said, turning his back on the window. He returned to the couch, sitting a little closer this time. "None of this is your fault, Louisa."

She sniffed into her tissue and nodded, but she clearly wasn't convinced.

"Any sign of that tea, Sinead?" he called into the kitchen, giving her a moment to compose herself.

"We're working on it!" Sinead replied. "Just a sec."

Logan turned his attention back to the woman on the couch. "You looked away," he said. "Then what?"

"I looked back and... I couldn't see him. Not at first," Louisa said. "The sun was... It was bright, it made it tricky to..."

Her voice cracked. She sat up straight, drawing in a deep breath that pushed her chest out.

"You're doing brilliantly," Logan assured her. "I know how difficult this is."

"And then... And then..." Louisa pressed on, like she had to get it out now, had to be free of it. "I saw him on the swings, and there was a man there, and... and... he was grabbing Jaden by the... He had him by the arm. And he was pulling him. He was pulling him towards the exit! He was taking my son!"

The words were like an exorcism for all the fear and hurt churning around inside her. She sagged in the middle and flopped back onto the couch like her spine could no longer hold her upright.

"Davey saw it all. His front window looks out onto the park," she said.

"Davey?"

"Neighbour. Across the way," Louisa explained. "If he hadn't seen... Well, it doesn't bear thinking about."

"Tea's up," Sinead announced, opening the door to the kitchen and letting a boy go through first, proudly carrying a plate of chocolate digestives. "Jaden helped sort out the biscuits. He tells me he knows all your hiding places, Mum."

Louisa sat up as Jaden carefully placed the biscuits on the table.

"Oh, I know he does!" she said.

She beamed at the boy and pulled him onto the couch beside her. He snuggled in, wrapping an arm around hers and clinging to it like it was all that was anchoring him in place.

"Jaden had a big scare today, sir," Sinead said, handing Logan his tea and sitting on the couch beside him. "He's been telling me all about it. Haven't you, Jaden?"

Cooried up beside his mum, Jaden gave a quick single nod of his head.

"I've been hearing all about it," Logan said. "But he's back safe with his mum. No one's going to hurt him now."

"That's what I said, sir," Sinead replied. "And you'll never guess. Jaden's only done a picture of the man he saw at the park."

"Brilliant!" said Logan. He smiled at the boy. "Can I get a look, Jaden? You gonnae show me?"

Jaden looked up at his mum for reassurance, and she gave it with a nod and a smile. "Go get it. It's really good."

"It'll be a big help, Jaden. It'll help us to catch the bas—" Logan stopped short just in time. "It'll help us to catch the bad man who grabbed you."

Jaden slid off the couch like he was melting onto the carpet. He rummaged under the coffee table until he found a sheet of A4 paper. Logan watched as the boy clutched it in both shaking hands and stared at the drawing he'd done. Fear blazed behind his eyes, the image representing the worst, most terrifying moment of his young life.

"Mind if I see, son?" Logan asked. He held a hand out, and Jaden was only too eager to be rid of the thing.

Logan studied the sheet for a moment, then flicked his gaze to the boy still sitting on the floor. "You never did this! It's really good," he said, which brought a flighty, tentative smile to Jaden's face.

The image wasn't going to be hanging in any galleries anytime soon, but for a five-year-old, it was a solid effort. It showed a man with dark rings around his eyes, and a vile, twisted leer that contorted the lines of his face.

There was something on the ground next to him that looked like a bobble hat. The head that the hat should have covered had hair on one side, and a jagged, angular dent on the other, which the boy had added zig-zag red lines to.

"What's this bit?" Logan asked, pointing to the lines.

Jaden squirmed on the floor, like he didn't want to think about it again.

"Tell him, pet," his mum urged.

"He had a sore bit," Jaden said.

"Was he bleeding?" Logan asked.

Jaden shook his head.

"Was it an old-looking sore bit?"

Jaden nodded.

"And did he speak to you, Jaden?" Logan asked. "Did he say anything?"

"Sort of."

Logan frowned. "Sort of? How do you mean?"

"He said stuff, but he didn't speak properly," Jaden said.

The boy took a biscuit from the plate, then climbed back up onto the couch and tucked himself in at his mum's side. He was so far back that Logan could barely see him.

"How did he speak?" Logan asked.

Jaden took a bite of his biscuit and chewed it before replying.

"He whispered."

Logan stood at the Big Board, Jaden Thomas's drawing held in one hand, a photograph of Owen Petrie in the other.

Even without the additional details the boy had provided, the resemblance was there. The big dunkle on the skull was the biggest giveaway, but the boy had nailed the bastard's eyes, too. Dark. Soulless. The eyes of evil itself.

He pinned both images close together on the otherwise unmarked board, then turned to face the rest of the room. Ben, Hamza, and Tyler were sitting at their desks, chairs angled to face him. Sinead had joined them, but sat slightly apart from them, like she felt she didn't quite belong.

It was also, Logan thought, a deliberate attempt to put distance between herself and Tyler, because she was too professional to do otherwise.

They all watched him in silence, waiting for him to deliver some words of wisdom, or genius insight that he didn't possess. He couldn't give them those things, but there was one thing he could give them.

The truth.

Or, most of it, at least.

"Owen Petrie—Mister Whisper—is in Inverness," he announced. "I have... suspected he might be since yesterday evening, after I found this."

He deposited an evidence bag on Ben's desk with a *thunk*. Everyone except Ben himself leaned in for a closer look.

"It's a badge," Logan explained. "It belonged to the orderly Petrie killed while making his escape from Carstairs."

"Where'd you get that, sir?" Hamza asked.

Logan rolled the response around in his mouth, like it was resisting him.

"In my flat," he eventually said. "In my bed."

"What the fuck, boss?" Tyler gasped. "He was in your flat? In your *bedroom*?"

Logan nodded. "Aye. Looks like."

"How did he know where you live?" Sinead asked.

"From what we can tell, he was working with a doctor at the hospital. That doctor compromised the phone and PC of a senior officer down in Glasgow," Logan said. "I think that's most likely where he got the information."

"He was in your room last night, and you're only telling us now, sir?" asked Hamza. There was a touch of outrage about it, like the DCI had betrayed them in some way. "Why didn't you say anything earlier?"

"He did to me," Ben said, shooting the DC an admonishing look. "The Detective Chief Inspector is not obliged to share every piece of information with junior officers."

"No, I know that, sir, but this is—"

"That's enough, Detective Constable," Ben warned.

"No. He's right, Ben," Logan said. "On this, I should've said."

He took a deep breath, gave a shake of his head, then tapped the photo of Petrie with a knuckle. "You've all heard of Owen Petrie. You all know what he did. Only... you don't. No' really," Logan said. "Without being there, without seeing it, you couldn't possibly comprehend what the man is capable of. The things he did. To them kids."

Logan shook his head again, more firmly this time, like he was trying to chase away the mental pictures that were gathering there like hungry wolves.

"Just be grateful you weren't there. That you didn't see," Logan muttered. "And pray to God that you don't."

"What's the plan, boss?" Tyler asked. "How are we going to catch the bastard?"

"*We're* not. I am," Logan said.

"Eh?" Ben ejected. "What you talking about, Jack?"

"Petrie's here for me. He's after me, and he will kill anyone he thinks stands in his way," Logan explained. "I can't put you at risk."

"At risk?" Ben said, his voice climbing higher.

"Your job—all of you—is to focus on the body found this morning. Someone somewhere has lost a son, or a father, or a husband, or whatever he may be. We need to find out who he was, and then—"

"Hold on just a minute, Jack," Ben said, pushing back his chair and standing up. "Obviously, we're going to work on the murder. That's a given. But you're not going after Petrie on your own."

"I didn't say I was going after him," Logan said. "He'll come to me."

"Well, he'll find us all bloody waiting for him," Ben replied.

Logan looked the Detective Inspector in the eye. How many years had they known each other now? Eighteen? Twenty? Ben had just been out of the army when they'd met—older than Logan, but newer to the force. They'd hit it off almost immediately, and their friendship had only grown since.

Which was why he couldn't let him get involved. Not in this. Not Owen Petrie.

"I'm perfectly able to look after myself, Benjamin. But thank you for your concern," Logan said.

"Bollocks to 'concern,' Jack!" Ben protested. "Anyway, this isn't just about you. A wee lad was nearly taken today. We both know what would've happened to him, you and I better than most. This isn't just about you now. It's about the kids out there. It's about his next victim."

"I'm going to take care of it," Logan assured him. "There'll be no more victims."

"How the hell can you possibly know that?" Ben demanded. "He could be out there grabbing a kiddie off the street right now for all we know!"

"You'll just have to trust me."

"I trust you on most things, Jack. I'd trust you with my life. But, you've never seen straight on Petrie. The bastard's always gotten under your skin. On your own, you'll make mistakes. You might not see him coming. Together, with all of us, we can—"

"That's enough, Detective Inspector," Logan said, raising his voice to silence the older man.

"Enough? I've no' even got started—"

"I said, that's enough!" Logan roared. The ferocity of it took the whole room by surprise. "I am the senior investigating officer here. I decide what resource is allocated where, and you—the lot of you—are working on this morning's homicide. Is that clear?"

He glowered at them—Ben in particular—daring any of them to object.

"I said, *is that clear*?"

"Clear, sir," said Hamza.

"If that's what you want, boss," Tyler added.

Sinead just gave a nod, while Ben stood eyeballing the much larger man standing before him.

"Crystal, Jack. Just crystal," DI Forde said through gritted teeth, then he more or less threw himself back into his chair and folded his arms across his chest.

Turning, Logan tore down the pictures he'd stuck to the Big Board and tucked them under his arm. "Petrie's mine. He's nothing to do with you. You're not involved. None of you. I'll take care of him myself. DI Forde's lead on the homicide, reporting directly to me. I want the body ID'd, then I want to know who killed him."

He glared around at them, making sure there were no further objections, then went storming towards his office.

"Good," he said. "Now, get on with it."

IT WAS three whole minutes before one of them knocked on his door. Logan had expected Ben to follow him into the office for an almost immediate round two, but he hadn't. Nobody had, and Logan was just starting to think they'd gotten the message when there was a rapping on the glass on the other side of the blinds.

"What?" he called.

The door opened, revealing Sinead in her uniform. "Got a minute, sir?"

Logan sighed, deliberately suggesting he very much did not have a minute, but he motioned for her to enter and sat back in his chair, waiting for her to speak.

There was a *click* as she closed the door behind her.

"What can I do for you, Constable?" Logan urged. "As you know, we've a lot to be getting—"

"That was out of order, sir," Sinead told him.

Logan blinked in surprise. His chair let out a low moan as he shifted forward in it, leaning his elbows on the desk as he fixed Sinead with one of his better glares.

"It was, was it?"

"Yes, sir," Sinead said, not flinching. "They all care about you. *We* all care about you. We want to help."

"Ben put you up to this, did he?"

Sinead shook her head. "He told me not to. But, I thought, if anyone's going to fire me for it, it'll be you, not him."

She sat on the chair across from him, the rubbing of one finger against her thumb the only indication of her nervousness.

"I don't know about the Petrie case. Not really. Only what I've heard. But I know how it affected you, sir. Your relationships. You told me yourself, how it made you drive everyone away. Your wife. Your daughter."

Logan's face remained impassive as he listened in silence.

"And, well, I know I'm out of line, sir, but it seems to me like that's what you're doing again. Pushing people away. People who care about you. And, well, I don't think you should. If you ask me, that's the last thing you should be doing." She smiled sympathetically. "I know you don't believe it, but you need people around you. People you can trust. Now, more than ever, sir."

Logan ran his tongue across the back of his teeth, then clicked it against the roof of his mouth. "You done?" he asked.

A look of shock flitted like a shadow across Sinead's face, then was gone. She nodded. "I've said my bit, sir."

"Good," Logan said. "Then get out of my office and get back to work."

She was hurt by that. He saw it in her eyes. But, she nodded, stood, then pushed the chair in and headed for the door.

"Sinead," Logan said, as her fingers touched the handle.

She turned. "Sir?"

Logan contemplated his next sentence for a long time before coming out with it. There were so many things he wanted to say.

But so many things he couldn't.

"I appreciate the concern," was all he said in the end. "Please close the door behind you on your way out."

CHAPTER FOURTEEN

"Told you," said DI Forde, as Sinead emerged from the office. "He's a stubborn bugger. Although, I have to say, I'm impressed you made it out in one piece. He must think very highly of you."

Sinead gave a thin-lipped smile. "I said my bit, sir. All I could do." She cleared her throat and straightened her back. "And sorry for disobeying your order. I understand if you want to start disciplinary action."

"Och, away you go," Ben told her. "All that paperwork? How about you just help us out here? Reckon that should be punishment enough for you."

"Sounds good, sir," Sinead said. "And thanks."

She glanced back at Logan's closed door, then looked from Tyler to Hamza. Tyler was rocking back in his chair, twiddling a pencil, while Hamza was staring at his computer screen, eyes flitting left to right as he read.

"Anything you want me working on?" Sinead asked.

"I'd say you can help Tyler, but he appears to be doing bugger all," Ben replied. "What *are* you doing, DC Neish?"

Tyler stopped twiddling his pencil, then reached over and clicked his mouse a couple of times. "I'm, eh, just..." He knew the charade wasn't standing up to scrutiny. "Nothing yet, boss. You didn't give me anything."

"Jesus Christ, son. How about you try using your initiative for once?" Ben sighed. "There's plenty needs doing. Pick one and get on with it."

"YES!" Hamza roared, thrusting both hands into the air. All eyes turned his way, and he quickly dropped his arms again. "Shite. Sorry. It's just... the road-works being done at the new roundabout on the A82, they've had a load of stuff nicked off site recently."

"Magic!" Tyler cried, emulating Hamza's upwards arm thrust. "But in what way is that good news?"

"Because, ya fanny, they installed CCTV on-site three days ago."

Tyler still had his hands held above his head. He lowered them and frowned. "Still not getting it."

"The new A82 roundabout," Hamza began, turning his monitor for the other DC to see. "Is right by the entrance to the Premier Inn where the body was found."

"The van!" Tyler exclaimed.

"The van," Hamza confirmed. "If the van headed into the city, their camera will have got it. Hell, depending on where it's set up, whichever way the van went, the camera might have got footage."

"Bloody hell, nice find, Ham."

"Let's not get too excited yet," said Ben. "One of you go over and check it out. Get them to show you it."

"They sent a link to the footage with their reply, sir," Hamza replied. He clicked to download, then clicked again to confirm. A timer appeared in the middle of the screen. "I'm getting it now. Be done in five, ten minutes."

He reached for his mug, looked disappointed when he found it empty, then held it out for Tyler. "Your turn on tea run."

"What? How is it my turn?" Tyler asked.

"Because you didn't find the CCTV footage," Ben told him. "And because you're doing nothing else."

Tyler tutted. "Aye. Fair enough," he said, reluctantly dragging himself to his feet. "Boss?"

"Don't mind if I do," Ben said, offering up his mug. It *chinked* against Hamza's as Tyler threaded his fingers through both handles.

"Want a hand?" Sinead asked. She turned to Ben. "Unless you need me here, sir?"

"I'm sure we can spare you for five minutes," the DI told her. He raised a finger and pointed to them both. "But no funny business."

Tyler headed for the fridge while Sinead put water in the kettle and switched it on to boil. The DC squatted down, recoiling from the smell of an egg sandwich some selfish bastard had decided to contaminate the place with.

"Shit," he said, after checking in the shelf on the inside of the refrigerator door. "We're out of milk."

"What's that there?" Sinead asked, pointing to a tall plastic bottle with a green lid.

"That's CID's. They go batshit if we take that," Tyler said. He tapped the top of a smaller bottle. Blue lid, this time. "And that's Detective Superintendent Hoon's. Apparently, we're welcome to use it, but he gobs in it. He made a point of telling us that *after* we used it last time."

He closed the fridge, leaned past Sinead, and clicked off the kettle. "There's the vending machine. We can try that. Boss won't be pleased, but if it's that or Hoon's saliva, he'll take the machine."

Tyler brushed his hand against hers, then quickly stepped back when the door to the staff canteen opened and one of the Detective Sergeants from CID came in.

She stopped just inside the doorway, regarding them both with suspicion.

"Alright, Sarge?"

The DS looked them both up and down. "Yous'd better not have touched our milk."

"Haven't been anywhere near it," Tyler replied. "Scout's honour. We were just heading to the vending machine."

The Detective Sergeant pulled a mildly horrified face. "Aye. Well. Good luck with that," she said, then she held the door open and motioned for them both to go.

A FEW MOMENTS LATER, Tyler stood pumping coins into the vending machine, with Sinead by his side.

"You think Logan's going to be OK?" she asked as she passed him another pound coin.

"The boss? Oh. Aye. He's pretty much indestructible by this point, I'd have thought. Like the Terminator, but bigger, and with less emotional range."

"Ha. Aye. Maybe," Sinead said.

"What time you finish?" Tyler asked, feeding more money into the machine's slot.

"Eh, not sure. Thought I'd hang on until the DI kicked me out. So, whenever, really."

"Nice one. What about your brother? Who's getting Harris from school?"

"Auntie Val. She's picking him up and watching him until I'm done," Sinead said. "Or maybe overnight, depending on when I get done."

"He'll be alright with that, will he?"

"Alright? Aye. You can say that again."

"AUNTIE VAL? Can I get another drink?"

Harris lay on his front on Val's big leather couch, fingers frantically prodding at the controllers on the side of the Nintendo Switch console. Val had bought it especially for his visits, along with a stack of games that Sinead had complained must've set her back a fortune.

"Another one?" chuckled Val, poking her head around the doorframe. "Your bladder's going to burst at this rate. Coke?"

"Yes, please!"

"Right you are," Val said. She smiled as she watched him jabbing furiously at the buttons. "And I'll see if I can rustle up a wee slice of cake."

Tyler finished putting in the money, then thumbed one of the buttons. A red light flashed up on it, indicating the dispenser was empty.

"Oh, for fuck's sake," he grumbled, pressing the button several more times in case the machine just wasn't looking hard enough.

"What's it out of this time?" Sinead asked.

Tyler leaned in closer to check the position of the light. "Water, apparently."

"How can it be out of water? Is it not plumbed in?"

"No idea," Tyler said. He jabbed in the button that was supposed to spit his money back out.

It didn't.

"What a heap of shite," he complained, giving the thing a dunt with his shoulder. "This is what happens when you use your initiative. You get your money nicked."

"Want me to go across the road and get takeaway?" Sinead suggested.

Tyler winced and smiled. "Would you mind?" he asked. "I'd go, only..."

"You can't be arsed."

"Basically, aye."

She grinned at him, then they leaned in and kissed so quickly Tyler wasn't quite sure it had actually happened. He decided to try for a second helping, but Sinead blocked him with a hand on his chest.

"Go. Detect," she told him, then she wheeled around and set off along the corridor. "And if you're lucky, I might bring you back a cake."

"And a coffee, please," Sinead said. "Black, two sugars."

The man behind the counter at the takeaway barely qualified as a fully-grown man at all. He was sixteen or seventeen, she guessed, and while his fingers flew across the touch screen till with a speed and grace that suggested he'd been born for the job, any part involving anything resembling conversation seemed to be beyond his grasp.

He'd already addressed her by three different titles – miss, ma'am, and—a bit worryingly—sir. She'd have said it was the uniform that made him nervous, but she'd been three back in the queue when she arrived, and he'd been just as awkward with the other customers, too.

"Thanks," he said, once he'd finished tapping her order into the touchscreen.

She waited for him to say more. He stared back at her with a blank, vacant sort of expression that suggested his mind was an open book. And probably a picture book, at that.

"Something wrong?" he asked her.

"How much is that?" she replied.

"Oh. Aye. Sorry," he said, looking down at the screen.

He had just formed the first syllable of the price when a thought hit him. Physically, given the way his head snapped back and his eyes widened in shock.

"Wait. Are you with the police?" he asked.

Sinead resisted the urge to look down at her uniform, or the word 'Police' on the Velcro badge above her left breast.

"I am. Why? Everything alright?"

"No. I mean, yeah. It's just, there was a guy who wanted to pay for your coffee."

"What guy?" she asked. "What did he say?"

"Just... a guy," the boy said. "He might still be in."

Sinead turned her attention away from the counter. The takeaway was attached through an archway to a small family restaurant. Most of the tables were empty, but a man in a flat cap sat hunched at one in the far corner, his back to the counter.

"Is that him?" she asked.

The boy scrutinised the man's back for a painfully long time, then nodded. "I think so, aye. Maybe. He said he wanted to buy coffee for the next police person that came in."

"Officer," Sinead said, still staring at the man in the hat.

"Eh?"

"Police officer. Not person," she said.

"Right. Sorry. Want me to take it off his money? He left twenty quid."

Sinead stepped away from the counter. "Give me a minute, will you?" she said.

Then, before the cashier could answer, she squeezed past a woman with a buggy and headed through the archway into the restaurant.

The man was gazing out of one of the big windows at the police station across the road. There was a large coffee on the table in front of him, steam rising from the tall glass mug. The hair she could see below the back of his hat was a salt and pepper of whites and greys. It stopped just above the collar of his battered-looking beige raincoat.

There was background music playing in the restaurant—Radio 2, Sinead thought—but she could hear him humming to himself as she approached, his fingertips dancing on the table like he was practising the piano.

"Uh, hello?" she said, when she was right behind him.

His fingers stopped. The humming died in his throat. He turned slowly in his chair and looked up at her from below the peak of his cap.

"Hello?" he said. His voice was dry, like Autumn leaves being crushed underfoot. "Is there a problem?"

"Did you... Did you leave money, sir?"

"Money?" He flitted his tongue across his lips, wetting them. "How do you mean?"

"Someone left money to buy us coffee. The police, I mean. The cashier thinks it might have been you."

"Ah. Yes. That was me," he said. "I thought... they do such an important job, and they just don't get the thanks they deserve. It's not much. A gesture, that's all."

"Right. OK. Well, thank you," she said. "It's very much appreciated."

"And you're very much welcome, Constable," the man replied. "You and all your colleagues."

"Yes. Well... thanks again," she said.

She started to turn away, but then stopped, her eyes drawn to the man's cap.

"Was there something else?" he asked her.

He was about the right age. Similar build, from what she'd seen of him. The peak of the hat was shadowing his face, making it difficult to make out clearly.

The hat would reveal the truth, of course. Or, what lurked beneath it would.

"Uh, odd question. Your hat, sir. Would you mind removing it?"

The man tilted his head to one side and peered up at her through the veil of shadow.

"Removing it?" he echoed. "My hat? Why?"

Sinead was suddenly aware of all the children in the restaurant. Laughing. Playing. Colouring in their menus.

She was also painfully aware of the knife and fork on the table, well within easy grabbing distance for the man sitting before her.

"We're looking for someone who matches your description, sir," she said. "If you take off your hat, I'll be able to confirm."

"I don't like to take my hat off if I can avoid it," the old man told her. He shifted his gaze around at the parents and children dining in the restaurant, then dropped his voice into a low, hushed whisper. "It's rather embarrassing, you see."

"Please remove your hat, sir," she said, more forcibly this time. "You can do it here, or you can do it at the station."

"I'm no lawyer, Toots, but I'm fairly confident you can't arrest me for wearing a hat," the man said. His eyes seemed to twinkle in their deep pools of shadow. The only part of his face that was clearly visible was his smirk.

She could feel the eyes of the other diners on her now. The low murmuring of conversation had faded into an expectant hush.

Sinead stole a look out the window at the station, hoping to see back-up sauntering over, but nobody was coming. She was on her own.

She stared back into those shadowy depths.

"Sir, I'm going to ask you again one more time. Please remove your hat."

"This is the thanks I get, is it?" He sighed. "Try to do a nice thing, and this is the thanks I get."

He got up slowly, his movements careful. Meticulous. He wasn't as tall as Sinead, but there was a presence about him that made him seem larger than his physical frame suggested.

The man dabbed at his mouth with his napkin, cast his gaze around at the other diners, then gave a resigned shrug. "Fine. Whatever you say, officer."

Sinead felt the world go into slow motion as his hand came up and caught the peak of his cap. Her eyes remained trained on it, but she stepped back, buying herself space in case he tried to make a grab for her.

And then, with a self-conscious cough, he lifted the hat, revealing a perfectly smooth, undamaged skull. His hairline had receded all the way up his head and set up camp there in an unflattering straight line that crossed the summit on a slightly diagonal angle.

It was, Sinead thought, the most unfortunate case of male pattern baldness she'd ever seen.

"Happy?" he asked, eyes darting around with shame and embarrassment. "Can I...?"

"Sorry. Yes. Sorry," Sinead said. "Sorry, I just... Sorry. I'm really sorry."

The man gave an unhappy little scowl, then pulled his hat low on his head and sat back down at the table. Turning his back on her, he reached for his coffee with a shaking hand.

Sinead turned, and the eyes of almost everyone in the building darted down to their food, or across to the person sitting opposite. Her journey back to the counter was accompanied by hushed words and murmured whispers which she did her best to ignore.

"Here's your drinks, sir." The lad behind the counter tutted and shook his head. "Miss. Ma'am. Sorry."

"Thanks," said Sinead. She reached into the front pocket of her vest and took out a bank card.

"I thought the old boy was paying for it?" the cashier said.

Sinead glanced back at the old man at the table. "Yeah," she said with a wince. "I think he'll probably be asking for his money back."

CHAPTER FIFTEEN

Tyler regarded the stack of printouts the uniformed officer who stood over him had deposited on his desk. It was about half a ream's worth of paper, divided into about fifteen card folders.

"Eh, what's this?" he asked, looking up at the female officer. She was in her mid-forties, with a fierce look about her that suggested she didn't suffer fools gladly. Or, at all, for that matter. "Sarge," he hastily added when he saw the stripes she wore.

"Missing persons," she told him. "You wanted to see if anyone matched the description of your body."

Tyler sized up the pile on his desk. "Oh. Right. Aye," he said. He leaned past her and looked over at DI Forde. "Initiative. See?"

"It doesn't count if I have to tell you to do it," Ben replied, not looking up from his PC.

Tyler tutted, then fixed on his most winning smile—the one he saved for special occasions—and took aim with it at the sergeant. "Thanks for this. It's just... I thought you were going to go through it for me."

The sergeant let out a derisory snort. "Aye. Well, you thought wrong. Keep dreaming, son," she said. "They're all yours."

She gave Ben a nod of recognition and left the Incident Room before Tyler could offer any further objections.

"Shit," Tyler muttered.

He shot a sideways look at Hamza. DC Khaled was sitting back in his chair, watching the CCTV footage on his monitor and crunching noisily on a packet of *Polos*.

"Want to swap?" Tyler asked.

"Nothing ventured, nothing gained, eh?" said Hamza, not turning. He shook his head. "But no. Definitely not."

Tyler tutted and sighed. "Can I have a Polo, then?"

Still not taking his eyes off the screen, Hamza tore the paper and silver foil of the packet just enough for a single mint to protrude, then offered it out to Tyler.

"Cheers," Tyler said, taking the mint and popping it in his mouth.

"They're the sugar-free ones," Hamza said.

Tyler physically recoiled, like the other DC had just told him the sweets had been dipped in dogshit.

"What? *Why*?" he asked.

"Calories," was Hamza's only explanation. He gestured to the screen. "Now, shut up, I'm trying to concentrate."

Tyler moved the sugar-free Polo around in his mouth with the tip of his tongue, bouncing it from tooth to tooth like he was deliberately trying not to taste it.

With a groan, he reached for the uppermost folder on the pile and opened it on the desk in front of him. A woman in her thirties stared sullenly up at him from the page. She had a haunted, hunted look to her, and Tyler immediately concluded that she'd killed herself.

"Nope."

He placed the printout to one side, then looked into the eyes of a man who'd gone missing seven years previously. Considering he was in his late-eighties at the time of his disappearance, Tyler reckoned the chances of finding him fit and well now were slim.

"Not you..."

"You're not going to say something for every single one, are you?" Hamza asked. He still had his eyes trained on the screen, watching black and white traffic go trundling by.

Tyler sniffed. "I might."

"Can you say it silently, then?" Hamza asked. "Because you're only two in, and it's already getting on my tits."

Tyler rattled the Polo around inside his mouth. *Clack-clack-clack.*

"Fine," he said. He glanced at the pile of reports, then rolled his chair closer to the other DC's and groaned. "Aw, come on, just swap."

Hamza looked back over his shoulder at Tyler. "No. I'm not swapping. I came up with the lead. I got the footage. I'm going to sit here and watch it until—"

"There," Tyler said, stabbing a finger past him at the screen.

Hamza's head snapped back to the screen. "What? No. What?" he yelped.

The footage showed a car and a bus go trundling south on the A82. "You winding me up?"

"No. Rewind. Honestly," Tyler urged.

Hamza eyed him suspiciously, then scrubbed backwards through the footage a few seconds.

"Play from there," Tyler said.

"Aye, I know," Hamza said, suddenly defensive. "I've been watching that for bloody ages, see if you've come swanning in and..."

"There. See it?" said Tyler, pointing to the screen again.

Hamza tutted. "Of course, I see it. It's a big van."

"You would've missed that, if it wasn't for me," Tyler crowed, sitting back in triumph.

"Would I bollocks! It was your fault I turned around. I'd have been looking right at it if you hadn't come trundling over."

Tyler patted the other DC on the shoulder. "Aye. Keep telling yourself that, Ham. You've got to help me with the missing persons files now, by the way. Fair's fair."

"How's that fair?!" Hamza protested. "You literally looked over my shoulder for two seconds!"

"Fair's fair, Detective Constable. Come on," Tyler said, adopting a smug expression and superior attitude that would, in almost any other company, have earned him a smack in the mouth. "I helped you, you can help me. I scratch your back, you scratch mine. *Mi casa, su casa.*"

"I don't think that means what you think it means," Hamza said.

"Whatever. Which half do you want?"

Hamza glowered at him, then turned away and straightened to look over the top of his monitor. Ben sat at his own computer, pecking at the keys with two fingers.

"We've got the van, sir," he announced.

"Well, 'we' is being a bit generous," Tyler added, then he wheeled back in his chair and narrowly escaped getting a dead leg.

"Can you get a plate off it?" Ben asked.

Both detective constables looked at the screen. "Bit fuzzy," Hamza reported. "But I could maybe try to sharpen it up, only DC Neish wants me to help go through the missing persons files."

"DC Neish is perfectly capable of going through those on his own," Ben said.

"But I found the van!" Tyler protested.

"Right. Well, do you want to try using your technical wizardry to sharpen up the CCTV footage, then?" the DI asked him.

Tyler looked from Ben to the image on screen, then to Hamza. Finally, he tutted and rolled his chair all the way back to his own desk. "Fuck's sake," he muttered. "I'll go through them myself."

"Go through what yourself?" asked Sinead, appearing by his desk with a cardboard tray laden with paper cups.

Tyler grinned up at her. "Ah, Constable Bell," he said. He picked up roughly half of the folders and set them down beside the rest. "Just the very woman I was looking for."

"Come in."

Sinead eased open the door to Logan's office, the cup of coffee held in front of her like a shield.

"Brought you a drink, sir."

He was sitting behind his desk, his sleeves rolled up, a notepad beside him cluttered with increasingly frantic-looking scribbles.

"Oh. Thanks," Logan said. He pressed on his eyes with finger and thumb and rubbed, then blinked a few times, clearing his vision. "Bloody computer screens."

Sinead searched the desk for a clear path to put the cup down on, then decided it was safest just to hand it to him. "Anything I can help with?" she asked, as he took the drink from her.

"No. Just going over some old stuff. Jogging the memory on a few details," Logan replied. "That's all."

"Right, well, if you do need anything, you know where we are."

"Aye. I know," Logan said. "And thanks for the coffee."

"There was only Detective Superintendent Hoon's milk in the fridge," Sinead said, and Logan pulled back from the drink like it was a cup of poison. "No, I mean... I went and got them across the road. So that we didn't have to use his."

"Thank Christ for that," Logan said, then he frowned. "Hold on. What am I saying? I stopped taking milk months ago. And now, you know why."

Sinead laughed. "Makes sense," she said. "Well... bye for now, then, sir."

"The suit," Logan said, as the constable turned to leave.

"Sir?"

"The suit came from a charity shop."

Sinead nodded. "Aye. DI Forde's got Uniform..." She looked down at how she was dressed herself. "I mean, he's got some officers checking the British Heart Foundation, where it was bought, to see if anyone remembers anything."

"He kept the tag on," Logan said.

"I believe he did, sir, yes."

"Why would someone keep the tag on their clothes?" he asked. He said it like a teacher might who already knew the correct answer.

It took just a second or so for Sinead to work out what that answer was. "So they could return it."

"Right. They buy it, they wear it to some party or event, and then they return it and get their money back," Logan said. "So, what sort of one-off event might a fella with a history of drug abuse find himself having to attend that would require the wearing of a suit?"

"Court! A court date."

Logan raised his cup to her. "Worth a look, I'd have thought."

"Definitely. I'll get checking," Sinead said.

"Do that. And take the credit for it," Logan urged. "You practically worked it all out, anyway. I just nudged you along."

Sinead shook her head. "No, sir, it was you who—"

The phone on Logan's desk rang. He reached out and grasped the handset, but made no move to lift it yet.

"Please. Take the credit, Sinead," he said, and there was a note to his voice that made it sound less like a request and more like a direct order. "You deserve it."

His eyes went to his ringing phone, then to the door, but she'd already taken the hint and was halfway through it. "OK. Well... will do, then, sir. Thanks again."

Logan waited until the door had closed before lifting the handset. "DCI Logan."

There was silence from the other end, but it was soft and muffled, like someone had accidentally dialled his number from their pocket.

"DCI Logan. Who's this?" he asked.

The silence shifted at the other end of the line. Definitely a pocket-dial, he thought.

He was about to hang up when the voice came creeping out of the dark.

"You didn't jump, Jack," it whispered. "On your head be it."

"Petrie!" Logan hissed. "Owen, listen to me, you need to—"

There was a click, then a hum and the line went dead. Logan squeezed the handset until his knuckles went white, then replaced it on the base unit.

Then, after a moment, he picked it up again and slammed it back down three or four times in rapid succession until there was a *crack* of breaking plastic.

"Fuck!" he spat at the world in general.

Grabbing the phone's base unit, he dragged it closer and fumbled through the menu options until he found the list of incoming calls. The latest was listed simply as 'unknown'.

Of course, it was.

He added to his previous *fuck* with a couple of *shits* and a particularly venomous *bastard*.

Then, the phone rang again and he pounced on it like a tiger on its prey.

"Petrie?" he hissed.

"Aye, in your fucking dreams, ye cock-thumbed bawbag," snarled the voice of Detective Superintendent Hoon.

He usually sounded angry—it was pretty much his default setting—but he was positively foaming-at-the-mouth-level seething now.

"Get your fat, useless arse through here to my office," he ordered. "Right. Fucking. *Now*."

CHAPTER SIXTEEN

"THE FUCK'S THIS I'M HEARING, JACK?"

Logan stood in Hoon's office, making a point of saying nothing until he knew exactly what had driven the Detective Superintendent into such a rage.

He had been standing at the window when Logan had entered, bent low, furiously trying to suck the fresh evening air in through the narrow opening allowed by the window's safety catch. He'd spun with surprising speed and grace, given the size of him, and had it not been for the desk blocking the way, Logan was sure the DSup would've come windmilling at him, fists flying.

Instead, he'd kicked his chair aside, slammed both hands on the desk, and asked the question again.

"Eh? What am I fucking hearing, Jack?"

Logan thought of the postcard in his coat pocket.

At least, he hoped it was still in his coat pocket. It had been a while since he'd checked.

His gaze did a quick sweep of the desk but saw nothing incriminating there.

"Is it all your blood whooshing about, sir?" Logan asked. "Because your face has gone quite red."

A stapler clattered against the wall on Logan's left.

"Do I look like I'm in the fucking mood for jokes here?"

Logan had to admit that no, he did not.

"Who's Jaden Thomas?" Hoon demanded.

"Jaden Thomas is a boy we spoke to earlier today," Logan said, trying very hard to hide his relief. This was fine. This, he could deal with. "He was at the park, and someone tried to grab him."

"Someone," said Hoon. It wasn't a question. It was more like he was drawing the DCI's attention to the word and inviting him to circle back to it.

"A man, sir. He... matched the description of Owen Petrie."

"And there it fucking is," Hoon said. "There's the topsy-fucking-turvy world we find ourselves in. Mister Whisper gets up to his old shite in my fucking town—in broad daylight, no less—and my own DCI doesn't feel that it's worth his bastarding time to tell me."

"I was compiling a report, sir. It would all have been—"

"Close that toothy fucking wound in your face until I say you can speak, Detective Chief Inspector," Hoon seethed. "Or maintenance'll be Vaxing you out of the fucking carpet."

He flexed his fingers in and out like he was counting up in tens, rapidly at first, then slower as he breathed in through his nose and out through his mouth. He made Logan think of Dr Jekyll trying to hold back Mr Hyde. Bruce Banner struggling to contain the Incredible Hulk.

Finally, he stopped flexing, clasped his hands together, and sat in his chair.

"Tell me the boy's alright, at least."

"He's alright. Freaked, obviously, but safely back home. Parents are split, but his dad's coming to stay over for a few nights," Logan said. "We've got Uniform checking in and keeping an eye."

"How'd he get away?"

"Neighbour intervened," Logan replied. "We spoke to him. Same description. He tried to give chase, but Jaden was upset and clung to him, so he couldn't. Petrie—assuming it *was* him—disappeared into the housing estate that borders the swing park. Uniform did a sweep, but he'd have been long gone by then."

"Well, obviously," Hoon said. "He's hardly going to hang about."

His voice was a lot softer following his breathing exercises, and the redness of rage had faded from his face. It wasn't gone completely—it never went completely—but he no longer looked like he was about to pop open like a pimple and fill the room with brains and pus.

"You want to know how I know about Jaden?" Hoon asked. He was smiling. This, Logan knew, was rarely good.

"How, sir?"

"Because I know fucking everything, Jack. That's important. I want you to remember that. I want you to keep that at the forefront of your fucking mind from here on in. *Hoon knows everything*. That's what I want you to be thinking at all times. Morning, noon, and fucking night," the DSup said. "And I'll know if you're not. Because, to reiterate, I know everything. Where this place is concerned, I am fucking omnipotent. Got that?"

"Got it, sir," Logan said.

"Specifically, though, you want to know how I found out about wee Jaden's run-in with the most notorious fucking child-killer in this nation's modern history, Jack? Because this'll surprise you. This'll blow your shrivelled wee brain out through your arsehole."

Hoon's smile was wider now. Bordering on manic. This did not bode well.

"How did you find out?" Logan asked.

"Because Louisa—Jaden's mum? She's my fucking niece, Jack," Hoon said, his eyes just about bulging out of their sockets with the effort of containing his rage. "Wee Jaden's my great-nephew. And he *is* a great nephew. I mean, I wouldn't fucking want him on my team at a pub quiz, but he's a great wee lad, so he is. Kind. Thoughtful. And now, oh-so-fucking-terrified."

Logan's head was spinning. Petrie trying to snatch one of Hoon's relatives couldn't be a coincidence, could it? What were the chances?

"I can see you and I are of a similar train of thought, Detective Chief Inspector," Hoon said, reading Logan's mind through his expression alone. "Of all the weans knocking about up here, what are the fucking odds he goes after the only one of the snottery-nosed wee bastards that's directly related to me? Not high, I'd have thought. No' unless it was fucking deliberate."

"Seems unlikely, sir, aye," Logan agreed.

"I'm glad we're in agreement, Jack," Hoon said. His hands were still clasped together, but the white spots forming at each of his knuckles revealed he wasn't as calm as he was trying to make out. "Now, keeping in mind what I said a moment ago about my all-seeing, all-fucking-knowing omnipotence.... Is there anything else you'd like to tell me?"

Logan stood his ground, uncowed and unblinking. He should tell him about the orderly's badge, of course. That was bound to get back to him before long. But, if he found out Petrie had been in Logan's room—that the bastard was acting on the vague threat scrawled across the poor bastard's chest back at Carstairs—then he might take him off the case before he was even officially on it.

And Logan wasn't about to let that happen.

"No, sir, I don't—"

Hoon leaned forward sharply a finger raising to silence the DCI.

"Wait!" he said, the word ejecting out with enough kinetic force to shift the paperwork around on the desk. "I want you to think very fucking carefully about the next words out of your mouth, Detective Chief Inspector. *Very* fucking carefully, indeed."

Logan's lips parted to speak. Hoon jabbed the finger at him again.

"At-at! *Very fucking carefully*, I said," Hoon reminded him. "And, just to make it a wee bit easier on you, if your answer doesn't contain the words, 'the bastard left a badge in my bed,' you'll be on immediate fucking suspension."

Logan's heart sank. *Shite*. So much for that plan.

The Detective Superintendent eyeballed him for a few lingering seconds, then lowered his finger, clasped his hands across his belly, and reclined in his chair.

"Now, on you go, Jack," he said, that dangerous smile twisting up the corners of his mouth and showing an uncomfortable number of teeth. "In your own time."

Logan's explanation took just a couple of minutes. The bollocking he received for it lasted considerably longer.

Eventually, though, Hoon's rage burned itself out. He dropped back into his chair, surrounded by scattered paperwork and broken stationery, ran through his breathing exercises again, then muttered something that might have been a calming mantra, but just as easily might have been a voodoo curse.

"Right. So. The badge. We've got that. Tick," the Detective Superintendent said. "You say you showed it to the team, and it's being logged. Fine. Would I have liked you to have told me about it sooner? Too fucking true, I would."

He took a breath again, catching himself before his temper could escalate. He pressed a finger against a spot on his wrist, taking his pulse, then continued.

"But, realistically, would me knowing have made any difference to anything? To wee Jaden? No. It probably wouldn't," Hoon said. "What it would've done was made me happy. And believe me, Jack, you want to keep me happy, if at all fucking possible. So, one more time—is there anything else I should know about?"

Logan thought of the postcard in the pocket of the coat currently hanging behind his office door.

He thought of the phone call that had come right before Hoon's own.

You didn't jump, Jack.

On your head be it.

"No, sir. Nothing else."

Hoon glowered at him, his stare so sharp it threatened to stab the DCI's eyes clean out of their sockets.

Logan held it. Calm. Composed.

A stark contrast to everything churning around inside him.

"One more time, Detective Chief Inspector," Hoon said, leaning forward in his chair. "Is there anything else you'd like to tell me?"

Logan couldn't tell him about the postcard. No way. He'd taken evidence from the scene of a crime. He wouldn't just be off the case for that, he'd be off the force.

"No, sir," he said again. "There's nothing else I'd like to tell you."

Hoon's gaze kept boring into him for a few more seconds, before the DSup grunted and sat back.

"Right. Good," he said. "Well, as it happens, I've got a fairly fucking juicy piece of gossip for you."

"Oh?"

"Dr Manan Ramesh. The prick who helped Petrie escape?"

"What about him?"

"Nonce."

Logan frowned. "Ramesh?"

"Computer's fucking overflowing with the stuff. Dates back years. Taskforce down the road has gone through some of it, but the sick fucker had tens of thousands of images on there. Abuse. Posing. Torture. You name it."

"Jesus."

"Aye. Taskforce has seen some of them before. Stuff that's been circulating a while. Kids who've already been identified," Hoon said. He had taken a pencil from the pot on his desk and was rolling it around between finger and thumb with enough force to make the wood groan under the pressure. "But there are images in there they've never seen before. New stuff. Recent, going by the fucking... codes. Whatever it's called. Data. In the picture. I don't fucking know."

The pencil snapped. He looked down at both halves in surprise, like he hadn't realised he'd picked the thing up in the first place, then returned them to the pot.

"There are other pictures there, too, Jack," Hoon continued, and he sounded almost apologetic. "The kids Petrie... took. Ramesh had photos of them. New ones. Well, not new, obviously. Unseen."

"Petrie shared them? How?"

Hoon shook his head. "No, not Petrie. Not directly. There's a suggestion that he and Petrie might have been part of the same group. A fucking ring of the dirty bastards. From what they can glean from his computers, Ramesh has been in with the fuckers for four or five years."

"Petrie could've told him about it when he was in doing his interviews," Logan said.

"Aye. Very possible," Hoon said. "We're hoping to get more, but they've hit a bit of a dead-end, tech-wise. There are no direct connections to other members of the ring, it was all done through... fucking... I don't know. The dark web. Fuck knows. However these fucking nonces do their thing."

"What about the other kids? Have they been identified?"

"I said we've got a taskforce working on it, Jack, no' fucking Batman. These things take time," Hoon said. His tone softened. "But they're working on it. They'll keep us updated.

"Well, anything I can do to help..."

"You can help by getting the fuck out of my sight and back to work," Hoon said. "Oh, and from now on, I want to know everything that's going on in that Incident Room of yours. I want every fucking iota of information you have."

"I'll make sure we keep you in the loop, sir."

"Fuck keeping me in the loop. From here on in, I *am* the fucking loop, Jack.

Every decision gets run through me. Every choice you're faced with, I'll be the one doing the choosing. I don't want you taking a shite without my prior fucking approval. Got that?"

Logan said nothing. There was no point trying to argue with Hoon when he was like this. Easiest just to ignore his orders and hope he didn't find out.

"I've got a call scheduled with the Gozer in the morning. I'll see what Snecky's come up with. Probably a big heap of fuck-all, knowing that useless bastard, but you never know," Hoon continued. "Oh, and we're getting CID in on this. The more the fucking merrier. And, we need to get a warning out to parents, pronto."

Logan would've gasped, but he wasn't really a gasping sort of man. Instead, he mostly just glowered, with a single eyebrow raised in surprise.

"You can't be serious, sir? We're not going public on Petrie, are we? We'll be hoaching with the bastards of the mass bloody media before we know it. They'll be crawling all over the place."

Hoon blew out his cheeks and shook his head. "I don't like it either, Jack. You know me. The only time I want to hear the words 'mass' and 'media' in the same sentence is when the words '*murder of every fucker working in the*' is jammed between them."

He gestured to the window, and to the darkening city beyond.

"But, funnily enough, much as I hate those wankers in the press, I dislike children being kidnapped and murdered even more. I mean, don't get me wrong, it's a close-run thing, but that one just takes it by a nose."

"What if we don't say it's Petrie? Not yet. Just say someone's making a grab for kids. Buy us some time before the vultures descend."

Hoon drummed his fingers on the desktop, considering this.

"You know what'll happen, sir. It'll be a zoo. It'll slow down the investigation, and put more kids' lives at risk," Logan said. "And, knowing Petrie, we'd be giving the bastard exactly what he wants. It'll be 'Mister Whisper' front pages on every rack. He'll be revelling in it."

The thought of Petrie basking in his notoriety was clearly too much for the Detective Superintendent. He threw himself back in his chair and stabbed a finger up at Logan.

"Fine. No names, just the warning. For now," he said. "But we both know, we can't contain this for long, Jack. Some bastard'll get wind of it. We've got to find that fucker and get him banged up before it all kicks off."

"Aye. Agreed, sir," Logan said

"Then why the fuck are you still standing there? Hoon asked. "Go. Find him. Do your fucking job while you've still got it."

"I have a request first, sir."

"A fucking *request*?!" Hoon said, almost choking on the word. "You winding me up?"

"Vanessa and Madison."

"Your wife and daughter? What about them?"

"Ex and... Aye." Logan cleared his throat. "With Petrie up here. I'd like to get them protection. Someone to keep an eye."

"I bet you fucking would," Hoon said. He leaned forwards in his chair. "But first, I want you to answer me a question. Honestly."

Logan shifted his weight from one foot to the other. "What's that then, sir?"

"Your family. Your ex and your daughter... You didn't know he was going to come after you when you brought them up here, did you? Beyond the 'Hi Jack' message, I mean?"

Hoon was scrutinising the DCI, watching every movement of his face, every flicker of emotion that passed there.

"You didn't know they'd be in more danger up here than they were down the road when you packed them into my car? Did you?" he asked.

Logan's hesitation was fleeting, but it was there. He couldn't tell if Hoon had picked up on it or not.

"No, sir," he replied, with an emphatic shake of his head. "I did not."

Hoon's glare lingered for several long, uncomfortable moments, then he sat back. "I can arrange Uniform to keep an eye on the house." He checked his watch. "But it'll be tomorrow, now."

"Tomorrow?"

"Take it or fucking leave it, Jack."

Logan nodded. "Thank you, sir," he said. "Tomorrow will be fine."

CHAPTER SEVENTEEN

Ben Forde looked up from his computer when Logan returned to the Incident Room.

"Well, you've no' got your balls in your hands, so unless he's made you eat them, I'd say that must've gone pretty well," the DI remarked.

"Not the best. Not the worst," Logan conceded. "He wants all decisions in the Petrie case to go through him first. He is the loop, apparently."

"Aye. Well. Might be good to have a more objective viewpoint," Ben said. "Or... detached viewpoint, maybe. Aye. Detached. I'm no' saying you're no' objective, I'm just—"

"I get it, Benjamin, thank you," Logan said, cutting him off. "And aye. Maybe. He wants to bring in CID now that Petrie's made a move. Also wants us to put word out to the public."

Ben's eyebrows crept higher up his forehead in surprise.

"We're not naming him. Not yet, anyway," Logan explained. "But he wants parents aware that there's someone trying to nab kids off the street. The wee one who was nearly grabbed... Jaden."

"What about him?" Ben asked.

"He's Hoon's great-nephew. The mother's his niece."

Constable Bell and DC's Neish and Khaled all turned in their chairs at that.

"Bloody hell," Hamza remarked.

"I didn't think he had any relatives," Tyler added. "I thought he'd just been, like... *made* at some point. Like... built by the government."

"Coincidence?" asked Ben, ignoring both comments.

"Highly doubt it," Logan replied.

"Well, looks like we'll be getting involved whether you like it or not, Jack," Ben told him. "I mean, if he's getting CID to chip in..."

"We'll see," Logan said.

"Jack..."

"For now, your priority's the homicide."

"Aye. Well, we thought we had a bit of a breakthrough with that, actually," Ben said. "Sinead came up with a pretty clever theory about why the fella had the tag in his suit."

"Did she?" Logan asked, turning to the room's only uniformed officer.

Sinead blushed. "Didn't pan out, sir," she said. "Dead end, unfortunately."

"Well, worth a try though, I'm sure," Logan told her.

"Aye, it was solid detective work, alright," Ben confirmed. A knowing smile curved the lines of his mouth. "Worthy of yourself, even, Jack. She'll go far, this one."

Avoiding Ben's gaze, Logan looked over to the Big Board. It stood off to one side, like an unwelcome guest at a party, bare and untouched.

"You not putting anything up?" he asked.

Ben and the others exchanged glances.

"Didn't have the heart to, sir," Hamza said. "Didn't think we'd do it justice."

"I mean, we tried with the Canna case," Ben added. "But it just... It wasn't the same."

"No. You made an arse of that, right enough," Logan said. "No offence."

"None taken," Ben said. "I just don't have the knack for it."

Over at her desk, Sinead quietly cleared her throat. "I, eh, I could have a bash at doing it. You know, if you want." She looked across their faces. "It won't be as good as DS McQuarrie's. I mean, obviously. But..." She looked to Tyler for help. "I know you said having it laid out visually helped you. Didn't you?"

Tyler nodded. "Yeah. It did. It does. It's handy to have."

Logan gestured to the board. "If you think you can do it justice, by all means, have a bash."

"Right. OK. I will do then, sir," Sinead said.

Nobody moved.

"I'll, eh, maybe not do it with everyone watching, though," she said, her face reddening. "I'll hang off a bit and get it set up tonight."

"And then, we can all take the piss out of it in the morning," Tyler said, rubbing his hands together in gleeful anticipation.

Sinead gave him two fingers, but it was good-natured. Mostly.

Logan checked his watch. "Unless there's anything urgent you're waiting on, I'm going to suggest we call it a day," he announced. "Tomorrow could be a big day, and if Petrie tries anything, we might all be called in tonight. Best get some rest while you can."

Tyler quickly flipped closed the missing persons folder he'd been working through and got to his feet, already reaching for his jacket. "Sounds good to me, boss."

Hamza clicked the refresh button on his email inbox, and watched as absolutely nothing whatsoever happened.

"I'm waiting on word from DVLA. Got a partial plate match for a van seen near the hotel around the time we're interested in. Hoping they can give us something." He shrugged. "It'll come to my phone, if there's anything. I'm sure the wife won't complain if I'm home early."

"No doubt mine will," Ben said. He switched off his screen, then got to his feet. "But she'll just have to like it or lump it."

Logan nodded. "Good. Right. Well, I'll hopefully see you all in the morning, and not before."

"Night, boss," Tyler said, and the others chipped in with their own farewells before Logan retreated into his office to get his coat.

DC Neish hung back with Sinead while Ben and Hamza left the Incident Room.

"Sorry about the dig earlier," he said. "Force of habit."

"Aye, well, you won't be laughing when you see how good my Big Board is," Sinead teased. "You'll be blown away."

"Want me to stay and give you a hand?"

"No chance," Sinead said. "And have you take all the credit?"

"I wouldn't!" Tyler protested. He maintained the lie for three-fifths of a second, before conceding with a nod. "No, you're right, I totally would do that."

He stole a glance at Logan's door, then quickly leaned in and kissed her. It lingered for a second or two, before the squeak of the door opening made them both spring apart.

"Want me to come over later?" Tyler asked, as Logan came trudging towards them.

Sinead shook her head. "Better not tonight. By the time I get Harris back from Val's, it'll be late. I'll see you tomorrow."

"This man annoying you, officer?" Logan asked

"Constantly." Sinead grinned. "Don't know how I put up with it, sir."

"Either you've the patience of a saint, or you're filled with self-loathing. I haven't quite decided yet," Logan told her.

He looked over at the Big Board and let his gaze stare there for a long time.

"Right. Good luck," he eventually said, then he turned to Tyler and motioned towards the door. "After you, Detective Constable. Let's let the lady work."

Sinead watched them go, Logan walking behind Tyler, ushering him out the door with the weight of his presence alone.

Once they'd left, she turned to the Big Board, and perched herself on the edge of a desk, sizing it up. The blank emptiness of it seemed to look back at her, taunting her, daring her to cover it. Daring her to try.

She held her gaze on it, like she was trying to stare it into submission, and took her phone from her pocket. Her fingers moved on instinct, navigating to the phone screen and tapping on the face of her Auntie Val without breaking eye contact with the Big Board.

The Big Board, for its part, remained just as defiant as before.

The phone rang six or seven times before Val answered.

"Sinead. Hello! How you getting on?"

"Aye, not bad, Val. How's you two?"

"We're fine," Val replied down the line. "I mean, I'm run ragged, but you know me. I wouldn't have it any other way."

Sinead bit her lip before asking the next question. "Any chance he could stay over tonight? I think it's going to be a late one."

"Of course! I already told you, it's no problem," Val said. "It's a pleasure, actually. He'll probably eat me out of house and home by the morning, but he's a growing lad."

"Thank you so much, Val. I really appreciate it," Sinead said. "Is he there? Can you stick him on?"

Val's voice became simultaneously louder and quieter as she leaned away from the handset and shouted. "Harris! Sinead wants a word."

There was a shouted reply that Sinead couldn't quite make out.

"He's coming," Val said, her voice closer again. "What about you? Have you eaten?"

"I'm fine, aye. Thank you," Sinead said.

"Make sure you get plenty to eat and drink. And take your breaks. You're entitled to them," Val said. "Oh. Here he is. Hang on."

There was some rustling as the phone was handed over, then Harris's voice was right there in her ear.

"Hiya. What's up?"

"Hey. How's it going?"

"Good. Auntie Val got me *Let's Go Pikachu* on the Switch."

Sinead heard an urgent mumbling in the background, and Harris quickly retracted his previous statement.

"Wait. No. She didn't."

Sinead smiled. "Tell her she's too bloody good to you. You OK staying there tonight?"

"Yeah. But my homework's at home, so I can't do that. You'll have to do me a note."

"Aw. You must be gutted. I know how you love your homework."

Her gaze hadn't shifted from the Big Board throughout the call. She could feel it pulling at her now, asking her to show it what she'd got.

"Right, I'd better run. I'll get you after school tomorrow. Be good, OK? Tell Auntie Val just to phone if there's anything."

"OK. Night."

"Night, Harris. Love you."

"Eugh," was Harris's disgusted reply, then the call was ended.

Sinead slipped the phone into her pocket and slapped her hands on her thighs.

"Right then," she announced. She grabbed a stack of *Post-Its* from Hamza's desk, and the sharpest pencil she could find. "Let's give this a bash."

CHAPTER EIGHTEEN

DC Neish whistled to himself as he made his way across the car park to where he'd left his car. Logan, who held one of the cherished reserved spaces close to the entrance, had already gone sweeping past in his Volvo, blasting his horn right as he passed Tyler, and subsequently almost causing the detective constable to lose bladder control.

"Cheers for that, boss," he'd called after the car, earning a quick flash of the hazard lights in reply, before Logan hung a left onto Burnett Road and was absorbed into the evening traffic.

Tyler's car *chirped* happily as he tapped the button on his key fob. He was still whistling when he reached the driver's door and opened it, but spun suddenly on his heels when another vehicle skidded to a stop behind him, gravel crunching beneath its wheels.

"Fuck's sake, Ham," Tyler spat, lowering the fists he had instinctively raised. "I thought I was about to be abducted."

"Who'd want to abduct you?" asked Hamza, his side window gliding down. "I can't think of anything worse."

"Shut up. I'd fetch a pretty penny on the black market, I'll have you know," Tyler insisted.

"Aye, well, good luck with that." Hamza held up his phone and waved it at the other DC. "Just got an email from DVLA with a possible match for the van."

"Did you?" asked Tyler making very little effort to hide his almost total lack of interest. "Cool. Well done."

"You not going to ask what they've come back with?"

"I hadn't planned to, no," Tyler said. "But, I'm guessing you're going to tell me, anyway."

"Bosco Maximuke," Hamza blurted, unable to keep it to himself any longer.

Tyler perked up at that. "What? Seriously?"

"Aye. Van belongs to him. Registered to his company. I mean, that's if the plate says what I think it says, but I can't see what else it could be. So, yeah."

Tyler closed his car door and leaned against it, considering the ramifications of this new information. Bosco Maximuke was well-known to the team, and to Logan in particular. Bosco and the DCI went back years. Logan was the reason the Russian had moved his business out of Glasgow and up the road to Inverness.

Maximuke was a big player in the Scottish drugs scene. Everyone knew it. Finding a way to prove it, however, had thus far escaped them all. The man was either 'coated in Teflon' or 'a slippery fat bastard'. It depended on who you asked.

To say there was no love lost between Logan and Bosco was a fairly substantial understatement. Logan held the Russian at least partly responsible for the death of DS McQuarrie, and it was only a few days ago that he'd taken matters into his own hands and burned Bosco's Portakabin office to the ground.

Had Maximuke made an official complaint, Logan might well have been looking at the end of his career. Fortunately, given his understandable reluctance to have the polis snooping around his business, Bosco wasn't likely to be picking up the phone to the Complaints Commission anytime soon.

"So... what do we do?" Tyler asked. "Think we should forward it on to the boss tonight?"

Hamza shrugged. "Not sure. Which one? Ben, maybe. Think the DCI's probably got enough on his mind. And, if he thinks Bosco's responsible, he might go storming round there, and given everything that happened recently..."

"Probably not the best idea, no," Tyler agreed. "Maybe just sit on it until the morning? I mean, Bosco's not going to up sticks and leave town, and the victim's unlikely to get any deader overnight." He nodded like the decision had been made. "Aye. Leave it. Do the big reveal in the morning."

Hamza smiled with relief. "Great. I thought the same, but wanted to run it by you. Promised Amira I was on my way home. If I got dragged into something else..."

"God, no. Leave it. It'll keep until the morning," Tyler urged. "Get home. Tell her I said 'hello.'"

"What, and spoil her night?" Hamza replied. He chucked his phone into the dooket beneath the stereo. "See you tomorrow."

"Aye. Night," Tyler said, waving him off.

DC Neish got into his car, shoved the keys in the ignition, then pulled on his belt.

He looked back at the station, at the window of the Incident Room, where Sinead would no doubt be stressing over the Big Board, thinking she'd bitten off more than she could chew.

Come tomorrow morning, she'd blow them all away with it, of course. He had no doubts whatsoever.

Tyler drummed his hands on the wheel, beating out a tuneless rhythm. Beyond the car park, night was creeping in across the city. He should go home, grab a bite to eat on the way, maybe. Get some rest.

And yet...

"I'll show you bloody initiative," he muttered, then he turned the key, crunched the car into reverse, and pulled out of the parking space.

MADDIE STOOD in the hallway near the front door, not yet reaching for the handle. There was a creak from behind her as Vanessa crept out of the kitchen, and Maddie motioned for her mother to stay back.

"Hello?" she called, adjusting her grip on the weapon in her hand. "Who is it?"

"It's me," came the reply, and both women sighed with relief.

"I thought you were going to phone ahead?" Maddie said, opening the door to reveal Logan standing out there on the step. Her brow creased when she saw his expression. "What is it? What's wrong?"

"Nothing. Nothing, it's... Can I come in?"

Maddie looked down at the threshold, as if only just realising she was blocking it, then stepped aside for him to enter.

"Nice frying pan," Logan remarked. "You'd do some damage with that."

"Don't tempt me," Maddie replied. She stole a glance out at the darkened street, then closed the door and turned the snib to lock it.

"Jesus Christ, who were you expecting?" Logan asked, noticing the long, serrated knife that was currently in the clutches of his ex-wife. "Jack the Ripper?"

Vanessa glanced down at the knife, then passed it from one hand to the other. Her face reddened, either through embarrassment or anger, it was hard to say which.

"It's late," she said. "You didn't phone ahead. We didn't know who it was."

"Aye. Well... good. Better safe than sorry. Well done." He eyed Vanessa warily. "But, eh, you can put it down now."

Logan headed for the living room while both women returned their respective weapons to the kitchen. He sat on the arm of the couch, decided it was better if he stood, and was barely back on his feet when Maddie appeared in the doorway.

"Want tea? Kettle's on?"

"Eh, no. No thanks."

"Bloody Hell," called Vanessa from the hallway behind her. "Must be serious."

"Can you... Can you both come in? I need to talk to you about something," Logan said.

Vanessa followed Maddie into the living room. Concern was etched across her face. "Shit, it is something serious, isn't it?" she asked.

She folded her arms and leaned all her weight on one leg, pushing out her hip. It was a stance Logan knew only too well. It meant she was anticipating an argument, and that she was bloody well ready for it.

"Well?" Maddie asked. Her body language was less aggressive than her mother's. More worried than soon-to-be-angry. "What is it?"

Logan had rehearsed the speech all the way over in the car. Or... no. Not *speech. Confession.* He'd carefully picked the right words, honed their order to minimise the fallout and the number of casualties. It had been right there in his head as he'd come striding up the path, on the tip of his tongue when he'd knocked on the door.

Now, though, it was nowhere to be seen. Now, all he had was a head full of nothing, and a weight in his coat pocket that he swore was dragging him down at one side.

"Oh, for God's sake, Jack, don't leave us in suspense!" Vanessa urged. "You're not announcing the winner of the bloody *X-Factor*. Spit it out."

"It's, eh..."

He had to tell them. They had to know what he'd done. To know how he'd put them at risk.

The postcard in his pocket felt hot against his chest, like it was spewing out radiation that was rotting away his insides.

He had to tell them. They had to know. They deserved that much, at least.

"It's, eh... It's nothing, really," he said, and the weight in his pocket almost pulled him to the floor. "It's just... We've got reason to believe Owen Petrie's in Inverness."

"Jesus," Vanessa whispered.

"How do you know?" Maddie asked.

Logan rubbed the back of his neck and angled his head back, unable to hold his daughter's gaze. "He tried to take a boy from a swing park. A neighbour intervened. The description we got... Well, it's Petrie."

"How sure are you?" Maddie asked.

"We're sure."

"Well, so much for us being safe up here!" Vanessa spat. "We'd have been better off down the road!"

"He didn't know, Mum," Maddie said. "He couldn't have known this would happen."

Logan continued to stare up at the ceiling, his fingers massaging the back of his neck. He could say it. Now. Right now. He could just come out with it. Tell them the truth. Tell them what he'd done.

How he'd used them as bait.

"No," he said. "You're safe here. I'd never let anything happen to you—either of you, believe it or not—but, now that we know he's here, maybe we should think about getting you back down the road."

"Home! Yes! I agree," Vanessa said. "Let's do that."

"Not home," Logan told her. "You can't go home yet. He's up here now, but the road goes both ways. He could be down there in a few hours." He shook his head. "No, if you go down the road, you're going to another safe house."

"Then what's the point?" Maddie asked. "I mean, if we're going to be stuck in another safe house, then why not stay in this one?"

"Because Owen Petrie's here," Vanessa said. "You might not remember him, but I do, and—"

"I remember him. Of course, I remember him," Maddie said, and there was an accusing tone to her voice. "How could I not remember?"

She stared at her mother, almost daring her to speak, then turned her attention back to her dad.

"It's like you said, road goes both ways. If he wants to get to us, he will. And, honestly? I feel safer knowing that you're around."

Logan hadn't been prepared for that. "You do?"

"Of course, I do."

"I don't. Just for the record," Vanessa was quick to add. She winced at how the comment sounded. "Meant to be a joke," she clarified. "I suppose, on balance, all things considered... So do I. A bit. A tiny bit."

Under any normal circumstances, Logan would've enjoyed the moment. Enjoyed his family—broken as it was—telling him he made them feel safe.

But how could he enjoy it now? When he knew the real truth of it.

When he'd deliberately put them in harm's way.

"Aye, well... I want you both to be careful," he told them.

"I almost clanged you with a frying pan, and she nearly fucked you up old school with a bread knife," Maddie pointed out. She smiled at him. "I'd say we've got 'being careful' pretty much covered. Wouldn't you?"

He conceded that she had a point but stressed the importance of keeping the place locked down, and only opening the door to him, to Ben, who they both knew, or—at a push—to a uniformed officer.

He was going to arrange extra patrols, he told them, try to get Uniform to keep a close eye on the place. Their safety was his number one priority. Not Petrie. Not this time. He'd learned that lesson, he said.

They didn't believe him. He could see it in their eyes.

He couldn't blame them.

CHAPTER NINETEEN

The stairwell leading up to Logan's flat had a clinical, bleachy sort of smell to it when he entered and started up the stone steps.

Tanya, the downstairs neighbour, was digging around in her pocket for her keys outside her front door, a holdall slung over her shoulder.

"Hey. You're back," Logan remarked. "He gone, then?"

Tanya nodded, smiled, and brushed a strand of hair back over her ear. "Yes. Thankfully. He texted this morning, said that was him out. Said he'd cleaned the place from top to bottom. He mentioned you'd... had a word."

Logan gave a non-committal tilt of his head. "I mean, I may have *gently* suggested he consider moving on."

"Thanks. Really," the girl said. "Mum was totally doing my nut in."

"Aye, they do that," Logan said.

"Aha!" Tanya cried, finding her key in the back pocket of her ripped jeans. "Got it."

"Right, well, I'll leave you to it. Good to see you back. If he turns up again, I probably won't be upstairs, but you've got my number."

"You going away somewhere?" Tanya asked, suddenly concerned. "You're not leaving, are you?"

"No, just... work-related. Be back in a day or two. But I'm around. So, if there's anything..."

Tanya exhaled with relief. "I'll call you. I'm sure it'll be fine, though."

"I'm sure it will be," Logan agreed. "So, I'll just—"

She flung herself at him, arms wrapping around his broad chest and barely meeting at the back. Her head pressed against him, and she squeezed for a moment, then quickly released and stepped back, all bluster and embarrassment.

"Sorry. Sorry, I just... Thanks. For everything you've done. It's good to have someone looking out for me."

"Aye. Well. You're welcome," he said, then he gave her a nod and headed for the next flight of stairs.

He was halfway up them when he turned back. The girl had the key in the lock, and the door ajar.

"Oh, Tanya," he called down to her.

"Yeah?"

"Do me a favour, and don't open the door to any strange men."

Tanya blew air out through her mouth, making a sound like a horse. "No worries there. I've had enough of strange men to last me a lifetime!"

"Good. Well, if you see anyone... odd poking around, call me. OK?"

That look of concern fell like a veil over Tanya's face again. "Sure. OK," she said.

And then, with a final nod, Logan continued up the steps, stopped outside the door to his flat, and pulled on a pair of rubber gloves.

He'd checked the place over at the time, but mostly for camera and microphones. Given the amount of adrenaline that had been flooding his system at the time, and the gnawing urge he'd had to get the fuck out of there as quickly as his legs would carry him, it was possible he'd missed something.

He could've ordered a full forensic sweep of the place—and it might come to that—but for now, the thought of Geoff Palmer poking around in his pants drawer was almost as bad as the thought of Petrie doing it.

There were a couple of other letters sitting on the mat near those he'd kicked aside on his last stop by the place. Both looked like marketing shite, and he swept them into the corner with his foot to join the others.

The flat felt stuffier than it had last night, having had another seventeen or so hours to stew in its curtained-off lack of sunlight.

The smell of the bin was no longer the first thing you noticed when you stepped inside, though. It was still lingering, but it was background noise now, not the full-scale assault it had previously been. That was something, at least.

"Right, then," Logan said to the empty hallway. "Let's see what we've got."

Hamza dropped his bag in the hallway, hung his coat on the peg, then followed the smell of Mexican food into the kitchen.

"Well, well, wonders will never cease," said his wife, Amira. She turned away from the stove to give him a peck on the lips, then got back to stirring the contents of the pan. "Live case, and you're home before midnight? That DCI of yours must be losing his touch."

"It was his idea, actually," Hamza said. "He sent us home."

"Wow. Really a day of miracles, then," Amira said. "We're having fajitas, by the way."

"I noticed," Hamza said. "Want me to do anything?"

"You could get out of my road," Amira suggested.

Hamza raised his hands and backed away. "Consider it done," he said.

"Kamila and I made lemonade. It's in the fridge."

"Oh? Nice one," Hamza said. He opened the fridge and there, standing proudly in the centre of the meticulously organised shelves, was a plastic bottle of a very faintly yellowish liquid.

He took the bottle out, gave it a shake, opened the lid, then sniffed it tentatively. There was a definite scent of lemon in there, and so he brought the bottle to his lips and sipped.

"I wouldn't," Amira told him, glancing back over her shoulder.

Hamza's cheeks almost collapsed inwards into his head, even as his head jerked back, desperately trying to get away from the liquid in the bottle.

"We forgot to put sugar in."

"Oh... fuck," Hamza wheezed. His face was scrunched up like a ball of paper, and he was sure he could feel the enamel being stripped from his teeth. "What did you use instead? Nitric acid?"

"She wanted to leave some for you to try," Amira said.

"Does she hate me? Is that it?" Hamza asked, screwing the top back on the bottle.

Amira laughed. "Count yourself lucky. She gave me a whole cup of the stuff."

Hamza turned to face her, eyes wide. "A whole cup? You'll be dead by morning! You'll dissolve."

"I didn't drink it, obviously. Turns out, you don't need a lot of sleight of hand to fool a three-year-old."

"That's a relief," Hamza said. "I couldn't face having to mop you up first thing in the morning." He held the bottle over the sink. "Down the drain?"

Amira nodded. "Might clear them."

Hamza glugged the liquid down the sink, being careful not to spill any of it on the wooden worktop, in case it burned clean through.

Once it was empty, he swirled the bottle under the tap a couple of times, then set it on the draining board to dry out.

"She sleeping?" he asked, wiping his hands on a piece of kitchen roll.

"Yes. Just down. She didn't nap today, so she was exhausted." Amira turned, wooden spoon raised like a weapon. "If you go in, *don't* wake her up!"

"I won't."

"I mean it! She's been a headwreck all day. I just want us to be able to sit down and have a nice dinner for once."

"I won't wake her up," Hamza said. He dodged around the spoon and kissed his wife on the forehead. "Promise."

The door to Kamila's room was two along from the kitchen. It was mostly in darkness, aside from the strip of light that came in through the gap where Amira had left the door ajar.

Hamza tiptoed the last few steps, edged the door open just enough to peek through, and looked down at the bed where his daughter lay.

Should've lain.

His body reacted before his brain could, heart fluttering into a higher gear, stomach clenching, like it was bracing itself for the worst. His blood became hot in his veins. His breath froze in his lungs.

The bed was empty, the covers pulled back.

She was gone. Kamila, his daughter, was—

"Daddy!"

Hamza pushed the door all the way open, and the light flooded in. Kamila ran to him from the window, arms wide, pyjamas so long they were almost tripping her, smile brightening the room better than any lightbulb ever could.

He dropped to his knees and caught her, pulling her in close. She felt so tiny against him, so vulnerable. The feeling of her in his arms—and the adrenaline of those few terrifying moments—brought tears springing to his eyes.

"I made you juice," Kamila told him. He felt her little hand patting against the back of his neck.

"I know. And it was delicious!" he said. "I drank it all."

Kamila leaned back and looked at him, delight widening her already big brown eyes. "Every single drop?"

"Every single drop," Hamza said.

"So much for not waking her," sighed a voice from the doorway. Amira stood there with a plate of food in each hand.

"Mummy!"

"Hello, you. You're meant to be sleeping."

"It wasn't my fault. She wasn't in bed," Hamza was quick to explain. He turned back to their daughter and wagged a finger. "Why weren't you in bed, young lady? Hmm?"

"I was talking!"

"Talking?"

Kamila nodded. "To the man."

Hamza glanced up at his wife, then back to their child. "What man?"

"That man," Kamila giggled. "The man out there."

And then, she turned and pointed to the gap where her bedroom curtains hadn't quite met. Her other hand rubbed against her forehead, just above her left eye.

"The man with the boo-boo."

"Don't be silly, Kamila—" Amira began, but Hamza was already on his feet, already racing to the window, already throwing the curtains all the way open.

The back garden was empty. The open gate *clacked* gently against the latch, shifting back and forth on the breeze.

"Stay here," Hamza said. Storming to the door and pointing to their daughter. "Watch Kamila. Don't open the door to anyone but me."

"What's going on?" Amira asked. "There's nobody there. She probably imagined it."

"Amira, please," Hamza said. He stopped in front of her, just for a moment, and the look on his face told her everything she needed to know.

"Kamila, come here. Come with Mummy," she said, setting the plates down on the bed and taking her daughter's hand. "How about we go play Hide and Seek with Daddy? We'll hide. Together. OK?"

Kamila danced with excitement, her grin showing off the big gap between her two front teeth. "Yay! Don't come until we're ready, Daddy!"

"I won't," Hamza said. He shot his wife another look, then hurried out into the hallway and headed for the door.

He made a brief detour via the kitchen, grabbed the dirty chef's knife from the countertop where Amira had left it, and headed outside to face the darkness.

CHAPTER TWENTY

THE SMELL OF SMOKE STILL HUNG IN THE AIR AROUND BOSCO Maximuke's yard.

Tyler had seen the old Portakabin over the fence on the drive down the hill that led to the yard's entrance. There wasn't a lot left of it, and under the insipid glow of the streetlights, the blackened frame made him think of dinosaur bones.

The big vehicle gates at the front of the yard were locked, but he blasted his car horn on the street outside until a stony-faced skinhead in a black bomber jacket emerged through a smaller gate a few yards along from the main two, and came storming over to the vehicle.

"What is problem?" the skinhead demanded. He leaned in through the open side window, slapping his hands on the door of the car with such force he made the whole vehicle shake.

His face was bruised, like he'd recently taken a kicking, and his accent was either Russian, Latvian, or—because Geography had never really been Tyler's strongpoint—from any country remotely in that neck of the woods, none of whose names he could remember.

"What you want?" he barked. "Why you fucking *beep-beep*?"

"I'm here to see Bosco," Tyler said.

The skinhead's sneer remained fixed in place.

"Maximuke," Tyler added, just in case there was more than one Bosco knocking around inside the yard's high fences. He didn't think there was, but it'd be embarrassing if he ended up being brought to the wrong one, so no harm in specifying.

"We're closed," the skinhead replied. He jabbed a thumb back over his shoulder. "See? Closed."

Tyler produced his warrant card and held it up like it was a party invitation. "DC Tyler Neish. Police Scotland, Major Investigations."

"So?"

Tyler side-eyed his ID, making sure he was showing off the right thing. "So... I'd like to ask Mr Maximuke a few questions."

"You have warrant?"

"Warrant?" Tyler snorted. He leaned back against the car's headrest and laughed. "Do *I* have a warrant?"

"Do you?"

"Well, I mean... Not on me, no," Tyler said. "Look, I'd just like—"

"Shh."

"Sorry?"

"Shut fuck up."

The skinhead straightened and held a hand up for silence. A finger of his other hand pressed against one ear, and Tyler spotted the coil of wire running down the side of the man's thick, sinewy neck.

"Wait," he ordered, firing a look of utter contempt in the DC's direction. He turned and entered the yard again via the same gate he'd come out through.

Tyler sat in the car, the engine running, waiting to see what would happen next. This had all seemed like a good idea back at the station. A solid demonstration of using his initiative.

He'd become less convinced of it on the drive over. And now that he was sitting there alone outside the lion's den, he was starting to think it was up there with the worst ideas he'd ever had.

Thankfully, it wasn't too late to back out. The skinhead seemed to have gone, and the road behind Tyler's car was clear of vehicles. He could turn around. Go home, maybe via KFC. He could come back tomorrow with back-up.

Aye, that made much more sense. Back-up. Daylight. Even just someone somewhere knowing where he was.

That sounded like a plan.

He'd just slipped the gearstick into reverse when the double gates opened. At first, Tyler thought he was looking at some sort of mirror system, as both gates were being pulled back by the same hulking, baldy-headed bastard. It was only when they both caught the full-beam of his headlights that he realised they were two different, albeit near-identical-looking, people.

A third man came striding into the space left by the gates. Tyler thought he was the guy he'd been speaking to a few moments before, but they all looked so bloody similar, it was hard to be sure.

"Bosco says you can come in," he shouted. He made an urgent beckoning motion with one hand. "Hurry up."

Tyler sat there with the car in reverse for a few long, uncertain seconds. Then, with a quiet sigh and a plastered on smile, he slipped the gearstick into first and went crawling in through the open gates.

The skinheads on both sides glowered at him as he eased through the gap and passed them. Tyler watched as, reddened by the glow of his tail lights, they pushed the gates closed behind him, and slid the large metal latch closed with a *clunk*.

Logan had searched through most of the rooms in turn, starting with his bedroom and working through to the kitchen via the bathroom and living room.

In each room, he'd stand as close to the middle as furniture allowed, and slowly turn on the spot, searching for anything that looked out of place.

In each room, he'd seen nothing.

Then, he went through them all more thoroughly, checking under the bed, in the drawers, in the toilet cistern, inside the washing machine—anywhere Petrie might feasibly have left something for him to find.

Still, he'd found nothing.

By the third time around, he was growing more impatient. He yanked up the sofa cushions and tossed them on the floor so he could dig down the sides. There was only one picture on the wall—a bland-looking winter landscape that had been there when he'd moved in. He unhooked it, checked behind, then removed the back in case there was anything hidden away in there.

Nope.

The fourth pass of the flat essentially just involved him kicking random pieces of furniture and swearing at them.

He shoved the couch cushions back into place, then slumped onto them, lay back, and stared up at the ceiling.

What had he expected to find? He had no idea. Something. That was all he'd hoped for. Something, anything, that might point him to Petrie's whereabouts, or give him some clue as to what he was planning to do next.

But there was nothing. He was no further on than he had been an hour ago, and there was no saying what the bastard had been up to in that hour.

"Hoon's bloody nephew," he spat at the light fitting above him. He'd ransacked that bloody thing, too, but there had been nothing hidden in it.

What were the chances of Petrie targeting Hoon's nephew by accident? It *could* be a coincidence, of course, but it felt unlikely. Although, that said, Logan hadn't even known that Hoon had siblings, let alone other relatives. If someone had deliberately targeted the kid, then it would've taken a lot of dedication and research.

And why Hoon? He'd been around at the time of the original case. He'd even pitched in from time to time, but he hadn't been involved enough to warrant a revenge play from Petrie.

The Gozer? Aye, he could see him being a target. The Gozer had been right there with Logan all the way through it, but Hoon? It didn't make sense.

He let his mind go for a wander, skirting around the edges of the case, where sometimes the view was clearer.

Dr Ramesh had been closer to Petrie than they'd first thought. A 'nonce,' Hoon had called him, but he was something even worse than that. He hadn't just collected those images. It wasn't just a case of him having enjoyed them, in whatever sick and twisted way he had—although, that was bad enough.

More than that, though, he'd sought out and helped the man responsible for some of the worst of them. He'd deliberately helped him escape, so he'd be free to do those things again.

Petrie was a monster, no doubt, but Ramesh was almost as bad, and in some ways even worse. Logan would not be mourning the bastard's death, only the loss of opportunity to question him. Ideally, in a soundproof room with no cameras.

But Ramesh was just the tip of the iceberg, it seemed. There was a ring of them out there, sharing that stuff, egging each other on.

That was hardly news, of course. Rings like that popped up all the time. But to have Petrie as a member? That had to be the nonce equivalent of having DeNiro join your drama club.

How long had he been a member? Pre-arrest, obviously. Which begged the question, how much did the rest of his little group know about what he was up to? He wouldn't have needed much egging on, but if they had, then weren't they an accessory to everything that happened to those boys?

Logan pushed the thought away. One thing at a time. Catching Petrie was the main priority. After that, they'd have a long chat about his circle of friends.

He smiled grimly at the thought of having Petrie sitting in an interview room, all that pretence of his brain damage stripped away, so there was only the two of them and the truth between them.

As he lay there on the couch enjoying that thought, the exhaustion of the last few days came creeping up on him. He caught his eyes closing and forced them open again.

No. No time for that. Not tonight.

Swinging his legs down from the couch, Logan stood, gave himself a shake, and retrieved his coat from the corner where he'd chucked it.

As he pulled it on, he felt the weight of the postcard in the pocket. He thought about taking it out to look at it again, but what would be the point? The message was etched there—*burned* there—on his brain. Indelible. Permanent.

Jump, and I'll turn myself in.

Don't, and everything that happens next is on you.

Logan took one last look around the living room from over by the door, then clicked the light off and went stomping along the hall.

He had just turned the latch and started to pull the front door open, when his toe brushed against one of the marketing letters that had been waiting for him earlier.

A sweep of his foot sent it skidding across the carpet, and Logan left the flat.

Then, a few seconds later, there was a rattle of keys and the door opened again. The DCI leaned inside, and his eyes crept down to the several days' worth of mail that lay piled up in the corner.

CHAPTER TWENTY-ONE

HAMZA PAUSED IN THE SHADOWS AT THE GABLE END OF THE HOUSE LONG enough to swallow down a couple of steadying breaths, then he peered around the corner into the back garden.

Light spilled out in overlapping rectangles onto the neatly tended lawn, but the area by Kamila's bedroom window was cloaked in darkness.

The tall back gate groaned at him as it shifted incrementally on its rusting hinges. Hamza listened for any other signs of movement—anything to indicate someone else was there with him in the garden—then crept across the grass, avoiding the pools of light as best he could.

The shed stood between him and the gate. He checked the door, but the padlock was in place, and there were no signs of forced entry.

He had a better view of Kamila's window from there, and with his eyes adjusting to the gloom he saw the patch of garden outside her bedroom was empty.

Hamza had just started to make for the gate when the light in his daughter's bedroom flicked on. The curtains were pulled aside, revealing a figure silhouetted on the other side of the glass.

His grip tightened on the handle of the knife.

The figure raised a hand, knocked on the window.

"See anything?" Amira asked, shouting to be heard through the glass.

Hamza breathed. "Fuck," he whispered, then everything inside him clenched as the bedroom door edged open behind his wife.

"Amira!"

She turned at the sound of footsteps, then bent and picked up Kamila.

Hamza let out a sob of relief as he watched his wife reprimand his daughter, and watched his daughter hold her own. Their voices were too muffled for him to hear, but he could imagine them.

"You were supposed to be hiding."

"But, Mummy, so were you!"

The gate *clacked* behind him, and he turned knife raised as a man came stepping from the gloom of the footpath that ran between the back of the house and the one across the way.

"Wait, wait! It's me! It's me!"

"Shite. Jim. Sorry," Hamza said, hurriedly lowering the knife.

His neighbour—the other half of the semi-detached—stepped back, eyeing him with concern. Jim was pushing eighty, but he had more energy and drive than most people half his age.

He'd cut Hamza's grass an embarrassing number of times, and had even fixed a couple of tiles that had slipped loose in a storm a few months back. Hamza had only been aware of the problem when he'd returned home from work one day to find Jim teetering atop a ladder with tools in hand.

"Everything alright, Hamza?" Jim asked.

Hamza forced a smile. "Fine, Jim. Aye. Fine."

"Right. It's just... you've got a big knife."

Hamza looked down at the knife, then tucked it out of sight behind his back. "Sorry. Yeah, it's... There was—"

"Is it about that fella who was hanging about?"

Hamza took a step closer. "Fella? What fella?"

"Saw him from the kitchen window," Jim said. "Coming out of your garden a couple of minutes ago. Thought to myself, 'That's strange,' I thought. 'Who's that, and what's he up to?' Looked shifty, see?"

"You got a good look at him?"

Jim's nod was a firm, definite one. The way he wrinkled up his nose lessened his air of certainty, though.

"Yes. No. A bit. I mean, it's dark, isn't it? I've been onto the council umpteen times about getting a light for the alleyway. They could stick it on the side of Sandra's house, if they didn't want to put a pole in. It'd make a right difference to—"

"Jim," Hamza implored.

"Oh. Right. Yes. Well, he had a hat on. He was about my height, I'd say, based on... well, the size of him. Came strolling out, too, casual as you like. Not a care in the world."

"You didn't see his face?"

"No," Jim admitted. "Now, if we'd had a light..."

While Jim continued to bemoan his lack of response from the Highland Council street lighting officials, Hamza looked past him along the alleyway. It branched off in the middle, joining a maze of other passages that ran through the whole estate. Given his head-start, finding him in there would be almost impossible.

"...had no idea what he was up to, and then he got up again and hurried off."

Hamza blinked, snapping back to the present moment. "Sorry? What?"

"I was just saying how he stopped and bent down," Jim said. "And I thought to myself, I thought, 'Hello. What's he up to now? Odd, that,' I thought. And so, when he was gone, I came out, and looked, and that's where I found it."

"Found what?" Hamza asked.

Jim held up a soft toy. It was a ragged, threadbare looking teddy-bear. An envelope had been stapled to its paws.

"This ugly bugger of a thing. It's hard to read what it says on the front—again, a light would be handy—but I was able to make it out. It says, 'Open me,'" said Jim. "Surprise inside."

Bosco Maximuke sat in a high-backed leather chair, naked from the waist up.

The office Tyler had been brought to was in another Portakabin, with the window looking across to the burned-out remains of the old place. The room was stiflingly hot, and rivulets of sweat trickled through the forest of curly hairs on the Russian's sagging chest.

There had been a young girl sitting in the corner of the office, staring at an iPad screen with headphones on. Bosco had sent her out of the room when Tyler had been brought in, and she'd glared at the DC as she passed, like she despised him for this tiny interruption to her arduous viewing schedule.

"My daughter. Olivia. Apple of my eye, light of my life," Bosco said, once the girl had slammed the door behind her with enough force to shake the whole hut. "She is charming girl, really. So I hear, anyway. Please, excuse her manners."

"It's fine," Tyler said. Bosco's Russian accent was thicker than the DC had been prepared for, and he was having to recalibrate his hearing to pick up what the other man was saying.

"And, excuse my bareness," Bosco continued, indicating his upper half with a wave of both hands. "Fucking heater is stuck on. Crazy, yes? Run fucking building company, can't get electrician to come fix heater."

"Aye. Well, we've all got our problems," Tyler said.

"Ha!" Bosco ejected. He waved a finger in Tyler's direction. "This, you can say again, my young friend. From you? Now? This is... what is word? Apt. Apt? That is word, yes?"

"It's *a* word, yes," Tyler confirmed, although he chose not to dwell too much on what it meant in the context of him or his being here.

He glanced back over his shoulder at the two hulking skinheads who flanked the door. They weren't blocking it, exactly, but then they didn't have to. The way they loomed there in silence made it very clear that he wasn't going anywhere until the semi-naked Russian behind the desk decided he was.

If he survived this in one piece, Tyler thought, he was never using his initiative again.

"What is it you want, *Detective Constable*?" Bosco asked. The way he spoke Tyler's rank made it sound like he found it amusing. Like it was the punchline to some private joke he wasn't prepared to share. "It is late. Business hours are over. And—maybe I am wrong—but I do not think you here for construction work. Yes?"

"One of your vans was spotted leaving the scene of a crime this morning."

Bosco's brow furrowed, as if in concern. He ran a hand down his chest and over the ripples of his naked belly, smearing the sweat into polish-like sheen.

"Oh? This is most concerning," the Russian said. "What van? What crime?"

"It's, eh..."

Shit, shit, shit. What was the reg? Why hadn't he written it down?

"We ran the registration, and it's one of yours. Transit-type. Unmarked. Was seen leaving the Premier Inn at the West End early this morning."

"Going to hotel is not crime. Unlimited breakfast buffet." Bosco slapped his stomach, making everything from his neck to his waistband wobble. "Is good."

"A body was discovered at the scene. We have reason to believe foul play was involved."

Bosco chuckled at that. "You have *reason to believe*? So, you don't know for sure?"

"No, we know," Tyler said. "I just—"

"And what van? Tell me registration. I have many vans, going many places. All the time. In, out, roundabout. You check CCTV across city, across country, there I am. My vans."

"Well, yes, that might be the case, but—"

"Who was body? Dead man. Who?"

Tyler picked up on the Russian's mistake and jumped on it.

"I didn't say it was a man."

"You didn't say it was not. And... how do you say it? Numbers?" Bosco shook his head. "Statistics say, murder victims most likely men. By three to one. In Russia, four to one. It says much about us, does it not? Men."

"I mean—"

"Am I wrong? Was victim woman?"

"I'm not at liberty to disclose that information," Tyler said.

Bosco waved a hand in irritation.

"Then, you have come here to bother me with nothing, *Detective Constable*." He said Tyler's rank in that same amused way, and this time both skinheads let out single, simultaneous snorts of laughter at it. "You have come to tell me a van—a van you say is mine, but that you cannot identify for me—was seen near a hotel that serves delicious breakfast buffet."

Tyler said nothing. He wished he could argue. He wished he could pull out some firm piece of evidence that would wipe the smile off the bastard's face.

Then again, if he did that, he might well not walk out of there alive.

Bosco slapped out a rhythm on his belly. It wobbled hypnotically, and Tyler found his eyes briefly drawn to it.

"What are we to do with you?" the Russian wondered aloud. "Hmm? What are we to do?"

Bosco jammed a finger in his belly button, wiggled it around, then brought it out and gave it a tentative sniff.

"Did Logan send you?"

Tyler shook his head. "No."

"But he knows you are here?"

Tyler was about to shake his head again, when he thought better of it. "Yes."

Bosco cocked his head to one side and studied the DC. A smile spread, tooth-by-tooth, across his face.

"Liar, liar, pants are on fire," he said. "He would not let you come here alone. Not after what he did. You see my old office? Burned. Ruined. He did this. And now, I stuck here in too-fucking-hot other office, sweating like a... like a..."

He grasped for an appropriate word or phrase, then gestured to one of the men behind Tyler.

"Valdis?"

"Like a fat whore?" suggested Valdis, the man who had met Tyler at the gate.

"Yes! Perfect! I sit here, and I sweat like fat whore, because our mutual friend burn my fucking office to the ground."

There were no amused tones woven through Bosco's words now. His smile had gone, replaced by a cold, menacing scowl.

"Cannot even open fucking windows. So here I sit, and boil like a pig. Because of Jack Logan."

The back of Tyler's shirt was sticking to him with sweat, and only partly because of the temperature in the room.

"I don't know anything about that," he said. "You'll have to take it up with him."

"Oh, I will. I will get own back, yes?" He glanced at the chunky gold watch on his wrist, and his mouth curved upwards at the edges again. He winked and lowered his voice until it was a conspiratorial whisper. "In fact, maybe I already have!"

"What does that mean?" Tyler asked.

"You think you know him. Jack Logan. You do not. Not like I do," Bosco said. "You have not seen him as he truly is. You see... fake news. You see disguise that he hides behind. Mask that he wears. You think he is good man? He is not good man."

"Again, you'll have to take that up with him," Tyler said.

"How is Ruth?" Bosco asked, changing the subject with a carefree smile.

His hands tapped out a beat on his belly again. This time, Tyler didn't look.

"Ruth?"

"Yes. You know. Ruth. Your mother. How is she?"

Tyler tensed his jaw, only just managing to stop it falling open.

"Her and your father still separated?" Bosco continued. "Must be a worry for you. For her. Living all alone."

Tyler's fingers curled inwards, forming fists. Behind him, the floorboards of the Portakabin squeaked as both men shifted their weight.

"What is she? Fifty-eight. Attractive woman, for her age. Fine, handsome woman. Looks after herself. Jogging. Every morning. Without fail. Up and down road. Always the same."

"Shut your fucking mouth," Tyler hissed, which drew a booming outburst of laughter from the man across the desk.

"I am just being... what is word? Complimentary, *Detective Constable*. That is all." Bosco wiped the sweat from his chest, then flicked it onto the desk between them. "You see, I know everything that happens in this city. Top to bottom, side to side. I have eyes and ears beyond those you see here on my face. Out there. Everywhere."

Tyler's whole body was trembling now, as he fought the urge to dive across the table and smack the fat Russian bastard in the mouth. It would be suicide, of course, but it would be a thoroughly satisfying one.

"This is why our friend, Logan, he comes to me over the years. Asks me for favours. Turns a blind eye if one of my men should accidentally find themselves in trouble. We go back, he and I. Way back. We have been mutually scratching for a very long time."

Bosco opened his arms like he was offering up a hug. "And I can scratch your itches, too, *Detective Constable*. My nails are very sharp. And maybe, once you are older and a grown-up, you can help me, too. Win-win. Scratch, scratch."

His eyes darted to Valdis. Tyler uncurled his fists as he heard the door opening behind him.

"Please, see yourself out," Bosco urged. His smile crept higher on his face, becoming something twisted and wrong. "And, please, give my regards to Ruth when you next see her."

He curled his forefinger and thumb together, then smacked his lips off them in a chef's kiss. "Tell her she is looking very beautiful."

Hamza stood in his kitchen, well back from the countertop where the teddy bear sat nursing its dirty envelope.

Jim had been spot-on with the words of the message, although he'd got the order of the sentences themselves jumbled up.

'Surprise inside,' had been typed first, the letters varying in weight and darkness, like they'd been hammered out on an old manual typewriter.

'Open me,' was a couple of line-spaces below it, indented so it was almost but not quite centred beneath the previous sentence.

It was eerily similar to the bear and the envelope that had been left on the doorstep of Connor Reid's parents back in Fort William all those months ago.

And to the bears and the envelopes that had been left for the parents of Petrie's original victims so many years before that.

He heard footsteps beyond the kitchen door. "Stay there! Don't come in!" he barked. An order, not a request.

Usually, Amira would have given him an earbashing for talking to her like that, but these were not normal circumstances.

"Just... shout if you need me," she replied, then the footsteps receded along the hall.

"I will," he replied, but he knew his wife couldn't help him. Not with this.

Only one man could help him with this.

Still eyeing the bear like it might be about to explode, Hamza slipped a hand into his trouser pocket and took out his phone.

CHAPTER TWENTY-TWO

LOGAN DESCENDED THE STAIRS FROM HIS FLAT WITH A BAGGED-UP envelope clutched in one hand, all the colour missing from his face.

The door to Tanya's flat was closed, but he could hear music playing quietly from one of the rooms beyond. It was light and poppy. Some boy band or other. Shite, in other words, but a far cry from the thunderous din her ex had been pumping out at top volume.

He had just left the close and was marching back to his car when his phone rang. He fished in his pocket, saw DC Khaled's name on screen, and answered with a tap.

"Hamza? What's up?"

A couple of paces later, he stopped walking. He stood there, in the middle of the darkened pavement, listening to the words coming rushing at him down the line. Listening to the fear and the worry in the DC's voice.

"Text me your address, son. I'm on my way," Logan said.

And the postcard in his pocket felt heavier than ever.

FOURTEEN MINUTES LATER, Logan stood in Hamza's kitchen, glaring down at the teddy bear like he was trying to intimidate a suspect.

Hamza himself had backed away so he was leaning against the opposite worktop. He sipped a glass of water he'd poured himself from the tap, washing down a couple of painkillers he'd had Amira bring him for the headache he could feel building behind his eyes.

"And it was left on the window?" Logan asked, not turning away from the stuffed animal.

"No. In the alleyway. My neighbour found it," Hamza said. His voice shook as he said the next sentence, the breaths coming in all the wrong places. "Petrie was at the window. At my daughter's window. She... she spoke to him."

Logan turned at that. "What did he say?"

Hamza shrugged. "Amira asked, but didn't get much. He said he liked her room. And he said..."

The DC's voice failed him completely, and he necked a big gulp of water while he tried to steady himself.

"He said she was pretty."

The crags and furrows in Logan's face deepened. "I'm sorry, son. How is she?"

"Kamila? She's fine. She doesn't understand." Hamza looked at the vile thing on his worktop. "How could she?"

Logan nodded. "It's probably overkill, but I think maybe—"

"Amira's already packing," Hamza said, anticipating the rest of the DCI's suggestion. "They're going to go to her brother's. Big family, mostly grown-up. Lot of adult nephews. She'll be safe there. Her and Kamila will share a room."

"Good. You going to take them?"

"No. Her brother's coming over. Be here shortly."

Both men turned their attention back to the soft toy. One of its glassy black eyes dangled from a loose thread, so it was resting on a threadbare cheek. The other stared defiantly back at them, like it was urging them to follow the instruction on the envelope.

"What do we do with it?" Hamza asked.

Logan bent forward, bringing his head to the same level as the bear. The moment he'd stepped into the kitchen and seen it, his every instinct had told him to run. To go. To get out. To not go back to this. Not this.

Anything but this.

He'd seen too many bears with too many envelopes. Too many children lost to a monster.

Too many.

But no more.

"Do you have a knife?" Logan asked.

Hamza picked up the knife block from the counter behind him and offered it out to the DCI. Logan gloved himself up, then picked the smallest handle from the block.

He approached the bear cautiously as if it were a real wild animal that might attack at any moment.

Holding the top of the envelope, he inserted the blade of the knife and slid it sideways, creating an opening.

Sitting the knife down, he prised the envelope open, and felt a bubble of panic rise in his throat when he saw a small stack of Polaroid photographs inside.

His brain rebelled. Screamed at him. He shouldn't look at those images. *Please, God, don't look.* Not this. Not again.

But, his legs were now tree trunks, their roots buried in the floor. He was going nowhere.

Taking great care, he teased the photographs out of the gap at the top of the envelope. There was a moment of relief, that was quickly replaced by confusion.

The first image was not one he'd expected. He'd been braced for another child in another chair, tears cutting grooves through the blood and the filth on his face.

Instead, the image showed the window of a house. The curtains were drawn, blocking all but a thin gap at one side, where a strip of the room could just about be made out.

Beneath the image, on the thickest part of the white border, the word 'driveways' had been written in black pen. Whoever had written it—presumably Petrie—had pressed so hard and gone over it so often the word was practically carved into the glossy paper.

He fixated on the word for a few moments, contemplating its possible meaning. A connection was made in his head. A confirmation of something he'd been almost, but not quite, certain of.

Logan turned the photograph over, found nothing on the other side, then placed it in an evidence bag and set it on the counter next to him.

Hamza stepped closer and leaned over so he could see the image.

"*Driveways?*" he said, but Logan was already focused on the next picture.

It was of the same window, but taken closer, so the gap was more prominent. It was just about possible to make out part of something that might have been a couch, but could have been a bed. The word 'toast' had been written beneath this one, in the same demented, scratched-in style.

Logan flipped quickly to the third and final image. This one was taken from right outside the window, the lens pressed up to the gap so only a suggestion of the curtain and the window frame could be seen at opposite edges of the photograph.

It was a couch. That much was clear now. Someone lay on it. Young, Logan thought, judging by how far their feet reached.

Their arms were up like they were holding something, but whatever it was had been cut off by the edge of the window frame, along with their head and neck.

Logan's gaze flitted momentarily to the word 'nature' which was etched into the border, then back to the unknown child in the unfamiliar house.

"Who's that?" asked Hamza, looking over his shoulder. "Is that... is that a kid?"

Logan said nothing, just stood there staring at the image.

"That's... shite. Who is that? We need to get this out. If he's going after that kid, we need to stop him, sir. We need to warn... whoever."

"It's too late."

The words hung there in the air between them, surrounded by the stifling silence of the kitchen.

"Whoever it is, it's too late. Petrie's already got them."

"Auntie Val, can I get something for supper?"

Harris lay on his back on the couch, gaze fixed on the screen of the Nintendo Switch he held directly above him, his fingers frantically jabbing at buttons and flipping the little joysticks.

It had only been a few minutes since Sinead had phoned, but he'd been quick to settle into the idea of spending the night at Val's. She always had the best sweets, and didn't ration them out like Sinead did.

Supper back home was toast or cereal. At Val's, it was cookies, or cake, or freshly-baked scones with butter and jam. Sometimes, if he was hungry, she'd make chips, even if it was after ten o'clock!

She wasn't as strict on bedtime, either. She was far more relaxed and laid back about it, like Sinead had been after their mum and dad had died. She'd let him stay up nearly all night once, and they'd quite often just fall asleep on the couch together, watching stuff they'd recorded off the telly.

Yes, it was fun spending the night at Auntie Val's, and he couldn't wait to see what she was going to serve up for supper tonight.

She hadn't replied to him, so he shouted again, louder this time.

"Auntie Val?"

He jabbed at buttons for a few more seconds, waiting for the response, then glanced over at the living room door to see if he could see her out in the hall.

When he didn't, he paused the game, swung his legs down onto the floor, and sat on the edge of the couch.

"Auntie Val?" he called again.

Somewhere in the house, a floorboard creaked.

Harris set the console down on the coffee table, got up, stretched, and went padding through to the kitchen. The lino floor was cold on his bare feet, and he tiptoed over to the big drawer where Val kept the biscuits and chocolate.

She was probably in the bathroom, he thought. She'd be out in a minute.

His eyes fell on the kettle, and he decided he'd surprise his aunt with a cup of tea. She'd been running about after him for most of the day, making sure he had everything he could possibly need.

A cup of tea and a biscuit. That's what he'd get her. When she came out of the bathroom, he'd tell her to go put her feet up, and he'd bring it through to her.

He lifted the kettle off the base, filled it at the tap, set it back on the base, then wiped up all the water that had sprayed onto the worktop around the sink when the tap had come blasting on like a fire hose.

He pressed the button that started the kettle boiling, then searched in the cupboards until he found the cups. If he stretched, he was *just* able to get a finger to a big red mug and with a bit of effort, he was able to pull it close enough to the front of the high cupboard for him to be able to lift it out.

Harris stood swinging the mug by its handle on one finger, his other hand scratching the top of his head.

"Teabags," he muttered, looking across the rest of the worktop. "Teabags, teabags, teabags..."

He spotted three metal canisters tucked in under the windowsill, and was just reaching for one when he heard the whispering of the wind outside. It seemed loud in the otherwise quiet kitchen, and he assumed the window must have been left open.

Crinkling the metal blinds, Harris reached through them and felt for the window handle. To his surprise, he found it closed. Shut tight, against the darkness outside.

The whispers came again. Louder, this time.

For a moment, he could've sworn they said his name.

But, if they weren't coming from outside, then...

Slowly, his bare feet slapping on the cold lino, Harris turned around.

And the big red mug shattered against the floor.

CHAPTER TWENTY-THREE

Logan indicated the teddy bear on Hamza's kitchen worktop, while the other hand tapped his phone awake and swiped to his contacts.

"Bag it up. I'll get Ben, tell him his night off's just been cancelled," Logan said. "Yours, too, I'm afraid."

"Of course," Hamza said, making for the door. "I've got bags through in the spare room."

Logan nodded, then winced at the voice that answered the phone. "Alice? Hello. I was, eh, I was looking for Ben."

"I'll bet you bloody were," said the voice from the other end. "He's barely in the door. He's away for a shower."

"Could you get him to call me when he's done?" Logan asked.

Alice's sigh was so loud and forceful it made the line crackle. "I don't see why I should. You know there's a law about working hours, don't you? How long you can work in a day, and how many days. How many breaks you need. That sort of thing. You know that, don't you, Jack?"

"I do, but—"

"And, let's be honest here, he's no spring chicken," Alice continued. "He's knocking on now. Sure, he'll tell you he's fine, but you don't see him when he comes home. Exhausted he is, some days. Can barely put one foot in front of the other, so—"

"It's a child, Alice," Logan said. She stopped talking at that. "There's a child's life in danger."

Alice sighed again, but this one wasn't for his benefit.

"I suppose I'd better go make him a flask of coffee, then," she said, and then there was a *beep* in Logan's ear as she hung up the phone.

Hamza grabbed gloves and an evidence bag from the computer desk in the spare room and turned to leave. Amira stood in the doorway with a sleeping Kamila in her arms. They both had jackets on, Kamila's so puffy it made her upper body look twice the size it actually was.

A small wheeled suitcase sat patiently in the hallway behind them.

"You all set?" Hamza asked.

Amira gave a tiny tilt of her head. "Yes. I mean... I think so. We might have to send for more things. Depends how long we'll be away for."

"Not long," Hamza said. "We'll get him. I promise. It won't be long."

He leaned in and kissed their daughter on the forehead. She rumbled in her sleep, peeled open one eyelid, then gave a half-smile before flaking out again.

He kissed Amira, too. His wife put a hand on his face, holding him close to her, even after the kiss had broken off.

"Be careful," she whispered. "Please."

"I will," Hamza said. "I promise."

There was a knock on the front door. "Amira?" a concerned voice called. "Everything OK?"

"That's Usman," Amira said. "We'd better go."

Hamza reached past her for the suitcase, but she beat him to it. "It's fine. It's on wheels. I've got it."

She kissed him again, then trundled the case over to the front door and opened it. Her brother smiled warmly and hugged her, being careful not to crush the sleeping Kamila between them.

"Thank you for this," Amira said, but Usman dismissed it with a shake of his head and the wave of a hand.

"Shut up, sis. We're all looking forward to it. We can't wait to have Kamila running about the place," Usman said. "You, we can take or leave, but her..."

Amira kicked him playfully with the side of her foot. "Hey, watch it. You might be bigger, but I can still kick your arse."

"Ha! I don't doubt it," Usman said.

He looked past his sister to where Hamza stood in the hall. A look passed between them. A nod. A moment of understanding. And Hamza knew that his family would be safe.

"Thank you, Usman," he said. "I'll call you in the morning, Amira."

And with that, he headed into the kitchen to join his DCI.

Logan had just hung up the phone when Hamza returned, and let out a big breath as he swiped back to his contacts.

"Jesus, that woman can fair give out an earbashing," he remarked. "Don't know how Ben copes with it."

"Love, sir, I suppose," Hamza said. He picked up the teddy bear and slid it into the evidence bag, then listened to the sound of Usman's car driving off. He thought of his wife and child, and what they'd gone through tonight. "It makes you put up with a lot of shit."

"Aye, so I hear," Logan said. He pointed to the bagged up bear and the Polaroids. "Can you take that into the office? Ben'll meet you there, and I'll try to get hold of Tyler. Tell Ben I said to get cracking. Better notify Hoon, too. See if there's been any reports of kids going missing. If not, work on trying to identify them from the photos. Go public, if you have to."

Hamza sat the bear down beside the photographs. "What about you, sir? When are you coming in?"

"I'm not," Logan said.

Hamza's eyes widened. "What?"

"I'm following up another lead," Logan told him. "On Petrie."

"What other lead?" Hamza asked. It snapped out of him, not a request for information but a demand.

"Another lead. That's all you need to know for now," Logan said.

"Bollocks it is, sir," Hamza said. "That bastard was here. He was at my house. He was talking to my daughter in her bedroom! I've never met the man, never been involved with him, but he's targeting me. My *child*."

"I know it feels that way, Hamza, but this is to get at me. I'm the target."

"You? Then why the fuck was he outside *my* daughter's window?!" Hamza demanded.

His voice had been growing louder, the tone turning more and more sour. He took a breath and brought it all down a notch.

"I think I deserve to know what's going on," he said.

"You're right. You do," Logan conceded. There was no anger in his reply, just a heavy sort of weariness that almost made Hamza regret his outburst. "And you will. If it turns out to be anything concrete, you will. But for now, your focus is on finding that child."

"And what about you?" Hamza asked, and the venom was back in his voice again. "What's your priority, *sir*?"

DC Neish sat behind the wheel of his car, watching as the identikit skinheads heaved open the big double gates of Bosco's yard.

He glanced in his rear-view mirror, saw the semi-naked Bosco watching him from the window of the Portakabin, and quickly averted his gaze.

"Come on, come on," he muttered, as the Russian's men slowly walked the gates into the fully wide position.

Just as they got them all the way open, and Tyler put the car into gear, there was a sharp knock at his window. Valdis, the first man he'd encountered, signalled for him to wind the window down, and Tyler slid it down a few inches, then stopped.

"You want advice?" Valdis said. "Stay away. You come back here, we will not be as welcoming. Yes?"

He banged a hand on the top of the car, making the DC jump. A toothy grin cracked open the bottom half of his face.

"Get fuck off our property, little mouse," he hissed, then he stepped back from the car, and Tyler quickly drove out through the open gateway.

He was halfway along the street, heading back up the hill, when his phone rang over the car speakers, making him jump again. He spat out a, "Shit!" as he corrected his jerk of the wheel, then stabbed at the button on the radio that answered the call.

"Uh, yeah? Hello?" he said, and his voice sounded different, like it had lost something.

"Tyler?"

Logan sounded confused, like he wasn't sure he'd come through to the right person.

"Eh, aye. Aye, it's me, boss," Tyler said.

"You sound weird."

"I'm... I'm in the car."

This seemed to satisfy the DCI.

"That's handy. We need you back into base. There's been a development."

Tyler checked his mirrors, half-expecting to find an unmarked van following him up the hill. The road, to his relief, was empty.

"You there?"

"Aye. Sorry, boss. Here," Tyler said. "Development? Which case?"

Logan's reply was short and to the point. "Petrie."

Tyler indicated right at the next junction and turned in the direction of Burnett Road. "Right, boss," he said. "I'm on my way."

Sinead stepped back from the Big Board and was just weighing up her next move when the door to the Incident Room opened. She turned to see Tyler come shuffling in. He smiled at the sight of her, but it was a thin, hollow thing that she saw through immediately.

"What's wrong? What's happened?" she asked, hurrying over to him.

"Eh... nothing. Nothing," Tyler said. "Just... the boss phoned. Wanted us back in here. Some sort of development in the Petrie case. Ham's going to fill us in."

"Right." Sinead looked the DC up and down. "You sure you're alright? You look shellshocked, or something."

Tyler shook his head, and diverted more energy to the smile, trying to make it more convincing. "Honestly, I'm fine. Was just looking forward to putting my feet up." He gestured past her. "Big Board's looking good."

The hasty change of subject did not go unnoticed, but Sinead decided to go with it for now. "It's getting there," she said. "It's harder than I thought. I was half-thinking of scrapping it and starting over again."

"Don't you bloody dare."

Tyler and Sinead both turned to see Ben Forde standing just inside the doorway. He had a small rucksack on his back, and a big Thermos in one hand. His thinning hair was light and fluffy, and stood up as if full of static electricity.

"It's good work. It'll come in very useful. You've done Caitlyn proud," Ben said, plodding over to his desk.

Swinging the rucksack down, he dumped it on the desk and pulled open the zip. With a bit of effort, he wrestled two large Tupperware boxes out, sat them down one beside the other, then pulled the lid off one to reveal a large stack of assorted sandwiches.

"Anyone for a piece and ham?" he asked. "There's cheese spread and tuna, too. Alice was worried I might get hungry."

"What does she think you are, sir?" asked Sinead, looking down at the mound of bread and fillings. "A horse?"

Ben's eyes twinkled mischievously, but then he gave a curt shake of his head. "Was going to make a joke there, but realised it would've been inappropriate," he said, clearing his throat. "Aye, she's a feeder alright. You think that's bad?"

He pulled off the lid of the other box to reveal a hefty Victoria sponge with an inch-thick layer of jam and cream.

"Check out this brute of a thing."

"Ooh, very nice," Sinead said. "I'll be happy to take a bit of that off your hands, sir."

Ben turned to DC Neish. Tyler hadn't spoken a word since the DI had arrived. That was over a minute now, which had to be some sort of personal record.

"Fancy a bit of sponge, son?" Ben asked.

"Eh, maybe later, boss. I'm no' that hungry."

A frown troubled DI Forde's brow, but before he could ask the younger officer what was wrong, the door swung open for the third time in almost as many minutes.

They could tell right away from Hamza's expression that something had happened. Something serious. Something awful.

"What is it, son?" Ben asked. "What's going on?"

Without a word, Hamza sat the evidence bags he was holding down on the desk next to the one with the cake and sandwiches. All three of the other officers stared down at the threadbare teddy bear, and its one good eye stared back.

"Oh God," Ben whispered. "Oh God, no."

LOGAN STARED at the darkened screen of his phone, willing it to light up.

"Come on, come on," he muttered, drumming a finger on the steering wheel of the Volvo in time with each word.

He tapped the phone awake, and saw his own message sitting there on the screen:

Just checking in. Everything OK?

It had been sent almost a full minute ago now. How long did he wait for a response? How long could he afford to give it?

Logan looked out through the windscreen at the terraced house a hundred yards along Murray Road, squinting like he might be able to see right through the walls.

There was no sign of anyone outside. The lights were on in the living room and an upstairs room. Hallway, too, he thought, judging by the glow through the mottled glass in the door.

He checked the phone again.

Nothing.

"Damn it, Maddie," he muttered, reaching for the door handle.

His phone buzzed just as he got the door open.

Fine, thx. U?

He closed the door again, texted out a quick reply and wished her goodnight, then plugged the phone into the charging cable and set it in the holder on the dash.

Reaching into the carrier bag beside him, he took out the sandwich he'd picked up at the Tesco petrol station on the drive over. It was cheese and onion —not something he'd normally go for, but at this time of night the range had been pretty limited—and the smell of it filled the car almost the moment he broke the seal on the packet.

Next out of the bag came a four-pack of Red Bull. He tore one from the cardboard, cracked the ring-pull, and gulped the liquid down. His face contorted at the taste of it, but it wasn't the flavour he'd bought them for, it was the caffeine.

He took a bite of his sandwich, fixed his gaze on the safe house door, and settled in for a long, uncomfortable night.

CHAPTER TWENTY-FOUR

Ben and the others stood in a vague semi-circle around the teddy bear. To anyone walking in at that moment, it would've looked like the soft toy was holding court, telling its audience of some horrendous tragedy that had befallen it.

Certainly, that would explain the long faces of the officers, and the looks of trepidation in their eyes.

"It was in the alleyway behind my house," Hamza said. His voice was low and flat, like he was afraid he might scare the teddy bear away if he spoke loudly or with too much inflection. "Petrie had been talking to Kamila. My little girl."

Tyler put a hand on the other DC's back for a moment, saying nothing.

"I called the DCI. He came over and opened it. There were pictures inside. Polaroids."

The sound Ben made at the back of his throat was quiet, but it was raw and primal, like an animal in pain. He picked up the evidence bag containing the photographs, and fanned the glossy squares out inside their plastic protector, but didn't look at them yet. He gave himself a moment to prepare first.

Over the years, Ben Forde had seen things that would have broken most other men.

Teenage rape victims. Bruised and bloodied, but too afraid to let anyone near them to help.

Murder victims. Beaten, burned, bludgeoned, stabbed, strangled, sliced from end to end.

Car accidents. Parents sobbing up front, demanding to know why they couldn't hear their littles ones crying in the back, but in no right mind to hear the answer.

And that was just since joining the polis. Before that, when he'd been serving in Northern Ireland during the Troubles, he'd seen worse still. Far worse.

He'd thought he had faced the darkest aspects of humanity. He thought he had seen the worst.

And then, he'd seen the Mister Whisper photographs, and he'd realised how wrong he was.

He took a breath and forced himself to look at the images in the evidence bag.

They were not, to his relief, what he'd been expecting. The Mister Whisper photographs of old had been close-up, post-abduction images that showed his young victims tied to a chair, faces twisted in agony and terror.

He had hand-delivered them to the parents, leaving them on the doorstep in the arms of a threadbare teddy bear not unlike the one that sat glaring up at them all now.

The words scratched into the bottom of the pictures was a new touch, too. *Driveways, toast, nature*. Christ knew what all that was about. Not his immediate concern, though.

There was a child in the last picture, although—mercifully—not bound to a chair.

Not yet.

"Who is this? Do we know?" Ben asked, looking across at Hamza.

"No, sir," Hamza said. "DCI reckons he—or she, it's hard to tell—will already have been taken."

Ben handed the photographs to Tyler, then looked past him to Sinead. "Anything come through about kids being taken, do you know?"

"I've been flat-out on the board, sir," Sinead replied. "Want me to go check?"

"Please," Ben said.

Sinead turned away just as Tyler moved to hand her the photographs. He held onto them, instead, staring blankly down at the kid on the couch.

"What do you make of it?" Ben asked.

Tyler looked up from the images, then back down. "It's... I don't know, boss. It's a kid."

"Astute observation, Detective Constable," Ben said. "Identifying this child is top priority. Maybe Logan's right and Petrie's already nabbed them, and maybe he isn't. We need to know, and we need to know now. Hamza, go through and talk to CID. We'll need to bring them in on this."

Hamza nodded. "Yes, sir. The DCI wanted me to keep Hoon informed, too."

"Christ. Did he?" Ben said, wincing. "Aye. Aye, I suppose so," he conceded with a sigh. "I'll do that. Don't you worry about him. Tyler."

DC Neish was back to looking at the photographs again. Ben had to say his name a second time before his head snapped up.

"Hmm? Sorry, boss. What?"

Ben motioned for Hamza to leave. "Go see CID, will you?"

"On it, sir," Hamza said, heading for the door.

Sinead was talking on the phone, her back to the two men. Ben dropped his voice so she wouldn't hear.

"Look, I don't know what's up with you, son, but you need to shake it off. A child's life is at stake here. I need you firing on all cylinders, not moping about." He glanced over at Sinead. "If you two have had a falling out, then leave it at the door."

"What? No. It's nothing like that, boss," Tyler said. "It's..."

He wanted to tell him. About Bosco. About everything the Russian had said. Even about how scared he'd made him feel.

But now wasn't the time. Now wasn't about him.

"I'm fine, boss," he said, straightening his shoulders. "Just tell me what you need me to do."

Ben tapped the evidence bag in Tyler's hand. "I want you to find the child in that photograph," he said. "Because I'm afraid I don't have the first bloody clue as to how we're going to do it."

LOGAN WAS two cans of Red Bull down, but he could still feel sleep prowling around him like wolves around a campsite, searching for a gap in his defences. He contemplated cracking open the third can, but that would leave just one to see him through the rest of the night, and so he opened up the family-sized bag of *Maltesers* he'd brought along and got ripped into those, instead.

The street was quiet. A few cars had come and gone. A dog walker or two. A woman on a bike. Nothing out of the ordinary.

As he watched, his mind kept drifting back to Hamza's kitchen. To the look of fright on the face of his wee girl when Logan had been let inside.

And to the fear in Hamza's eyes when he thought of that bastard being right there at his home.

Logan drew in a sharp breath, and almost choked on a Malteser. He hacked and coughed it back up as he opened the Volvo's glovebox. An evidence bag slid out, and he caught it just as he managed to crunch the sweet between his back teeth and swallow what was left of it.

Sitting upright, Logan spread the evidence bag across the steering wheel, flattening its contents. With all the drama at Hamza's, he'd almost forgotten what he'd found in his flat.

There was no saying it had come from Petrie. It wasn't his style. It was a plain white envelope with Logan's name and address printed neatly on a rectangular sticker on the front. He'd barely have glanced twice at it, were it not for the fact that it didn't have a stamp or a postmark on it.

He'd opened it carefully, and had found three separate sheets of paper inside. Each one contained just a single word, printed in a sans-serif typeface in the middle of the page.

Mentions.

Idealist.

Info.

Three words, apparently all random. It hadn't been until he'd seen another random word—*driveways*—scribbled onto one of the photographs that had been left at Hamza's that he became sure of the Petrie connection.

This wasn't like him, though. Riddles were never his thing. Mind you, ten years in a secure mental hospital pretending to be brain-damaged would no doubt change a man. He'd certainly have had plenty of time on his hands.

Logan took pictures of the pages on his phone, then emailed them to the central team inbox.

Less than a minute later, Ben Forde's name flashed up on the phone's screen, and Logan swiped the button to answer.

"Ben."

"Jack. Where the bloody hell are you?" DI Forde demanded.

"Following up on another Petrie lead," Logan said.

"Aye, Hamza said something along those lines," Ben replied. "What lead?"

Logan thought about pulling rank and giving Ben the brush-off, but he knew the older man would never let him get away with it.

"I'm watching the safe house. Where Maddie and Vanessa are," he said. "I'm thinking Petrie might try something."

"What makes you think that?" Ben asked.

Logan adjusted his position in the seat. Half his arse and most of his left leg had been falling asleep for the past ten minutes, and it had reached the point where he had to do something about it.

"Just a feeling."

"A feeling? How would he even know where it was?" Ben asked. "I don't even know which one you're using."

"I don't know. Because the bastard knows things. He's been in at the Gozer's phone and computer."

"The Gozer wouldn't have that information though. It's held locally. There are very few people with access, and Owen Petrie certainly isn't one of them."

"Aye. I know. It's just... I've got a feeling. I can't explain it. I think he'll come here. I think..."

"You think what?" Ben asked after Logan let the sentence die away.

Logan almost spoke the terrible truth of it. *I think I hoped he'd come here. I think that's why I brought them.* But how could he say it? How could he confess to using his daughter and ex-wife as bait? How could he admit that to Ben? To anyone?

"I just think he's going to turn up," he said in the end. "That's all."

"And what? You're just going to hang around and catch him in the act, are you? That's your big plan?"

"It's the best one I've currently got, aye," Logan admitted. He sighed, and the warmth of his breath fogged the edges of the cold windscreen. "I brought them here, Ben. I can't let anything happen to them. Hoon's going to get surveillance sorted for tomorrow, but I can't leave them tonight. And, if he does show up, this is our chance to nab the bastard."

The grunt Ben gave suggested he wasn't happy with any of it, but knew better than to push too hard.

"What's this in the inbox?" he asked.

"Found it in my flat tonight. Put through the door. I wasn't sure it was Petrie, but the random three words thing ties it to the photos left for Hamza to find. See if anyone makes anything of it, and I'll get the originals in as soon as I can for Forensics to go over," Logan explained. "You given them the other stuff yet?"

"Not yet," Ben said. "We want to go through it all with Hoon and CID first, see if it sparks anything, then we'll hand it all over. Sinead's checked the nine-nine-nine logs. No reports of missing kids tonight, so we're hoping it's a warning or something, and that he hasn't actually nabbed anyone."

"Aye. Maybe," Logan said. "But I wouldn't count on it. Keep me posted."

"Will do," Ben said. "Oh! Jack!"

"Still here. What's up?"

"Not the Petrie case, but thought you'd want to know. Hamza ID'd the van."

"Van?"

"The one CCTV caught driving away from our murder scene," Ben said. "At the hotel."

"Oh. Aye. And?"

"You'll never guess who it belongs to."

Logan wasn't in the mood for guessing games. He puffed out his cheeks and shrugged. "Pass."

"Bosco Maximuke."

Normally, Logan would've had some sort of reaction to that. Tonight, though, with Mister Whisper on the prowl, his family sitting in a safe house just along the road, and half a litre of Red Bull buzzing around in his system, his focus was elsewhere.

"Interesting," he said. "I'll follow that up once all this has settled down."

"Aye. Well. Just thought you'd want to know," Ben said. "Keep in touch."

The screen lit-up as the call was ended, then dimmed again.

Ben hadn't sounded happy. No surprise there. Logan would have to go some to make all this up to him later. Hamza, too.

He fished out another handful of Maltesers and turned his attention back to the safe house. Almost the precise moment he did, his phone rang again. An incoming video call this time. The name on the screen made him sit up straighter, despite the protests from his dead arse.

He caught himself checking his hair and teeth in the rearview mirror, reprimanded himself with some muttered swearing, then answered the call.

Shona Maguire's face filled the screen. Logan couldn't see anything of the background, but he could tell by the way her hair was hanging in loose ringlets that she wasn't at work.

"Hey!" she said, all smiles at first, then frowning. "Where are you? You're all dark?"

"In the car," Logan said.

"Shite, you're not driving, are you?" she teased. "I don't think you're allowed to video call and drive. You could get into trouble, and I hear the police in this town are a right bunch of dicks."

"Aye, I've heard that a few times myself," he agreed. "I'll keep my eyes peeled."

"You do that," Shona said.

There was an awkward silence as Logan tried to decide if it was his turn to speak.

"Is, eh, is everything alright?" he asked, filling the void with the first thing that came into his head.

"Fine, aye. Just relaxing after a hard day's cutting people into wee bits. That Pot Noodle was pretty rank, by the way," she said. "You didn't miss much."

"Oh, well. That's good to know," Logan said. "But it was... fun. Lunch, I mean."

"It would've got way more fun, too," Shona said, then her face fell. "I don't mean... I'm not saying... I had chocolate eclairs in the fridge."

"Those weren't a weird flavour too, were they?"

"What, like Spaghetti Bolognaise? No, cream, chocolate, and that pastry stuff. What's it called."

"Choux?"

Shona smirked. "Bless you."

It wasn't a funny joke. Not by a long-shot. Logan found himself chuckling, anyway.

"You get the report on our mystery man?" Shona asked.

"Uh, yeah, I saw it," Logan lied. "Haven't had a chance to go over it properly yet."

"It's pretty much what we discussed," Shona said. "Any luck IDing him?"

"Not yet. It's sort of slipped down the list of priorities a bit. We've had something come up."

"Ah. Is that why you went running out on me earlier?" Shona asked. She gave a little shake of her head. "Sorry, none of my business."

"No. Aye. I mean, it was just a..."

He wanted to say 'work thing.' He wanted to play it down, to avoid her being soiled by Owen Petrie like everything else in his life had been.

But that wasn't fair.

He took a deep breath, looked her in the eye, and told her the truth.

"Owen Petrie. Mister Whisper. He escaped from Carstairs a few days ago. He's up here now. He's targeted the kids of two officers I work closely with."

"Jesus. He's taken them?"

"No. Didn't manage. Got disturbed both times. But he's sent pictures of another kid, taken through a window. Like he was watching them."

"Christ Almighty, that's creepy," Shona said, visibly shuddering. "Another officer's kid?"

"No. I mean, I don't know. But none of the others I work with have..."

The rest of the sentence stuck in Logan's throat. He choked, coughed, and sat forward, grabbing for the phone.

"Shona, I have to go. I'm sorry."

The look of surprise on her face was only there for a moment before he terminated the call and frantically swiped to recent calls.

"Come on, come on," he muttered, as he waited for Ben to answer. The line clicked. Logan spoke before Ben had a chance to. "Has Sinead seen the photos?"

"Sinead?" Ben sounded confused. But, when he said the PC's name a second later, Logan could hear the same dawning horror in the DI's voice as he felt himself. "Sinead. Shite."

"Show her. Put me on loudspeaker so I can hear."

There was some clunking and clattering from the other end. Logan set the phone back in the cradle on the dash and stared at it his leg bouncing on the clutch pedal.

"Sinead, do me a favour, will you?"

"Sure, sir. What do you need?"

Logan bit down on his bottom lip, eyes still fixed on the phone.

"Take a look at these."

There was a rustling of the evidence bag. Sinead's voice came again.

"Are these the photos that..."

Her words fell away into a chasm of silence.

"Sir?" she said, and the breathless whisper of it told Logan everything he needed to know before she said it. "That's Harris. That's my brother!"

"What? What's happening?"

That was Tyler, his voice growing louder as he approached the phone.

"These photos! They're Harris! That's Val's house!" Sinead said, the words coming out as a series of throaty sobs.

"What's the address?" Logan asked.

There was silence from the phone. A sniff. A sob.

"Sinead, what's the address?" Logan asked again.

This time, she gave it. Logan's knowledge of Inverness still had big gaps in it, but he knew roughly where that address was. Close. He could be there in minutes.

"Shite," he spat, shooting a look along the road in the direction of the safe house. He fired up the engine, and the Volvo roared like a lion. "I'm on my way."

CHAPTER TWENTY-FIVE

He was too late. That much was obvious.

The front of the house had been all locked up, but the back gate was open. The back door, too. Logan hurried towards it, not sneaking, or creeping, no thought for his own personal safety. If the bastard was lying in wait in there, he'd deal with it. Let him jump out. Let him spring his fucking trap. See how far it got him.

Logan was halfway along the path when he saw the body of a woman slumped over beside the bins. Somewhere in the distance, sirens wailed.

He hurried over to the motionless woman. Several thin lines of blood ran down her face. They were uneven, unsteady, like they'd been painted on by someone with a shaky hand.

Logan felt her neck. There was a pulse there. Weak, but steady. He fired off a text to Ben, telling him to send an ambulance, and then copied in Tyler and Hamza to be on the safe side.

Removing his coat, he draped it over the unconscious woman and tucked it in underneath her as best he could.

With that done, he pressed on into the house, more cautious this time than a few moments before, the discovery of poor Auntie Val a stark reminder that it wasn't just his life that he was putting on the line by barging in.

The back door led into a utility room off a good-sized kitchen. The internal door was open, and through it, Logan could see the debris of a broken mug on the floor.

He poked his head around the doorframe, but found the kitchen empty.

The kettle was cool to the touch. If someone had been making tea, then it had been a while ago.

Logan moved on into the hall. He stopped there and listened, but all he could hear was the coming of the sirens. The house itself was silent and still.

The light was on in the living room. Logan entered, and recognised it from the photographs. Same curtains. Same couch. All that was missing was the child.

Blue lights lit up the room, flashing across the walls.

Logan met two Uniforms at the front door, flashed them his ID, then sent them around to the back of the house to look after Val until the ambulance arrived.

His phone rang as he was dishing out the orders, and he reached for it without looking. He automatically swiped the answer button while the Uniforms went hurrying around the back, and it was only as he was bringing the phone to his ear that he realised there was no name on the screen.

The sound down the line was echoey, like the person on the other end of the line was far underground.

"Hello?" Logan said.

He'd expected Petrie to reply. He'd been ready for the bastard's voice.

He wasn't ready for the voice he actually heard.

"H-help me."

A child.

A boy.

Harris.

"P-please."

And with that, the line went dead.

Logan looked along the path, beyond the gate at the front, as another car came skidding to a halt. Sinead was out of the passenger door before the vehicle had fully stopped, leaving the door open as she raced up the path, shouting her brother's name.

"Harris? Harris!"

Logan caught her at the door. "Sinead. Sinead, stop," he said.

Sinead's eyes were wide and blazing with panic and fear. She looked from the DCI into the hallway behind him, her thought process written in the anguished lines of her face.

"Oh God. Is he...? Is he...?"

"He's not here," Logan said. "But he's alive. I spoke to him."

Tyler ran up the path behind Sinead, the wailing of an approaching ambulance accompanying him like a soundtrack.

"You spoke to him?" Sinead gasped. "How could you speak to him? Where is he?"

"I don't know," Logan said. "I got a phone call just a few seconds before you got here. I'm pretty sure... I'm *sure* it was him."

"Well, what did he say?!" Sinead demanded.

Logan shifted uncomfortably. "I'm not sure..."

"Tell her," Tyler interjected. "What did he say?"

Logan tightened his grip on Sinead's shoulders, readying himself in case he had to hold her up. "He said, 'Help me.'"

Tyler was at Sinead's side in one step, an arm around her waist, a hand grabbing for hers. He met Logan's gaze dead-on.

"I've got her," he said. "It's fine."

Sinead twisted, shrugging them both off. "Where's Val? What happened to Val?"

"She's out back. She's hurt, but she's alive. Ambulance is on its... It's here," Logan said, just as the paramedics arrived in a blaze of sirens and lights. He looked from Sinead to Tyler and back again. "I'll take them round, then I'll check the rest of the house."

"You haven't checked it yet?" Sinead asked. She forced past him, voice rising as she projected it into every corner of the building. "Harris? Harris!"

"We should try not to disturb the place if we can—"

"Aye. I know, boss," Tyler said. "Can I get in?"

There was something off about the DC. Something had changed in the way he was looking at Logan, and not for the better.

"Aye. Just be careful," Logan said, stepping aside.

Tyler entered without a word and hurried after Sinead, who had gone running up the stairs, two at a time.

Logan glanced after them, then jogged along the path to meet the paramedics as they climbed down out of the ambulance. "She's round back," he said, pointing them towards the alley that ran around to the back of the house. "And please..." His gaze went to the upstairs bedroom window, where a light had just clicked on. "...hurry."

Sinead hadn't expected him to be up there. Not really. She'd had to check, though. She'd had to know for sure.

His room—and it *was* his room, Val had repeatedly told him, any time he wanted to use it—was empty. A pair of new pyjamas had been sat on his pillow for him, and a hot water bottle—now lukewarm—had been slipped between the quilt and the sheet.

The bedroom spun, the floor rocking like the deck of a boat. Sinead grabbed for the doorframe to support herself, missed, and was caught by Tyler before she lost her balance completely.

"He's gone," she sobbed. "He's gone. He's taken him. Oh, God, Tyler, he's taken him."

"I know, I know. Shh. We'll get him back. It's OK, we'll get him."

"How?!" Sinead demanded, her grief shifting gears into an explosive burst of anger. "How will we get him? *How?*"

"We'll..." Tyler began, then she collapsed against him and buried her face against his chest. He held her as her body was wracked by big silent sobs. "We'll get him back," he said, holding her close. "We'll get him back."

"The fuckity fuck's going on, then?" asked Detective Superintendent Hoon, appearing in the Incident Room like a demon summoned from the fiery depths of Hell.

His gaze swept across the room like a searchlight, alighting briefly on the faces of DC Khaled and DI Forde.

"You both look like you've recently shat out a walrus. What's happened?"

"A lot, sir," Ben said. "Not one bit of it good." His phone rang. He grabbed it from the desk and checked the screen. "It's Logan," he said, tapping the answer button and putting the handset to his ear. "Jack?"

Ben listened. Hamza and Hoon both watched him, and both saw the way the colour left his face.

"OK. We'll be here."

The DI hung up the call. He dropped the phone back onto the desk like it was dirty, somehow. Infected.

"What happened, sir?" Hamza asked.

Ben felt behind him until he found his chair, then lowered himself into it. "The, eh, the boy's gone."

"Shite," Hamza whispered.

"What boy?" Hoon demanded. "What the fuck's going on?"

"Sinead's... Eh, Sinead Bell. From Uniform?" Ben said.

"What about her?"

"Her brother. Harris. Petrie's taken him."

"Fuck. *What?*" Hoon spat. He looked from one man to the other, his expression darkening with every moment that passed. "Well?" he snapped, at neither one in particular. "Is someone going to explain to me just what the fuck is going on?"

And so, they did. They tag-teamed it, in the end, Hamza filling the DSup in on everything that had happened at his house, and Ben taking over to explain how the photos had led them to discover that Harris was missing.

Once it was all over, Hoon sat heavily in Logan's chair, spun it around once, then loudly announced: "Well, what an almighty clusterfuck this is," before jumping back to his feet and dishing out orders. "Ben, get the press. All of them. Round up every last one of the parasitic wankers you can find. No point trying to fucking contain this when that boy's life's at risk."

"We're going public, sir?"

"Too fucking right we are. Name and shame. Let them all tug each other off in a foamy-mouthed Mister Whisper frenzy. Let's shine a spotlight on the fucker, make sure he's got nowhere to hide. I want pictures of him on every front page tomorrow morning, and every news bulletin within the hour. Wall to wall coverage. I want to see the bastard's ugly mug everywhere I look. Papers, telly, internet. Commemorative fucking tea towels, if it comes to it. I want his face everywhere. Got it?"

Ben nodded. "Right, sir."

"In fact, no. Forget that," Hoon said. He spun on his heels to Hamza. "You. Tweedle-fucking-dum. You do all that stuff I just said. DI Forde, you're going to help me round up the cavalry. Anyone who's off-duty is now officially back on fucking duty as of right now. If they're sleeping, I want them woken up. If they're having a shite, I don't even want them wasting their time wiping. We get them in, and we get them in now. I want all fucking hands on deck for this."

The Detective Superintendent's face had been turning a deeper, richer shade of purple with every word he spat. Now, his whole head resembled a particularly nasty bruise.

"Mister Whisper is not getting up to his old fucking tricks again. Not in my town!"

He looked around at both men, neither of whom had yet moved.

"Well?" he screeched. "What are you fucking waiting for? Jump to it!"

Logan pulled his coat on, patted his inside pocket to make sure the postcard was still there, then watched as Sinead climbed into the back of the ambulance beside the unconscious Val.

The paramedics had done what they could to stabilise her at the scene, then loaded her onto a spinal board and into the back of the ambulance. She was breathing, which was good, but she was still unresponsive, which wasn't. The longer she remained out, the more chance there was for lasting damage, and she'd been out for a while already.

The house and gardens had been cordoned off with tape as soon as the paramedics had taken Val out, and half a dozen Uniforms were standing guard at various points, because they hadn't been dismissed, and they weren't entirely sure what else to do.

Geoff Palmer's Scene of Crime team was on the way. Logan was hoping to be gone by the time they showed up.

The rear ambulance doors closed, and Logan watched it go speeding off, sirens screaming. He kept watching until it had rounded the corner and vanished out of sight at the end of the road, then turned to find DC Neish standing on the path behind him.

"Tyler," he said. "Didn't see you there. You OK, son?"

"Petrie's nothing to do with us."

Logan frowned. "Eh?"

"That's what you said. Petrie's nothing to do with us. Any of us." Tyler was shaking, like he might be about to burst into tears, or start swinging punches. There was also a very good chance he might do both. "And now look what's happened. Harris. Hamza's wee one. Fucking... Hoon's nephew. You told us to keep away. You told us it wasn't our case, but it looks like nobody bothered their arse to tell Petrie that. Looks like we're all up to our necks in it, whether you like it or not."

"Look, Tyler—"

"And what next? Who next?" Tyler asked. He thought of his mum, and of a semi-naked Russian grinning up from his office chair. His voice came out as a high-pitched croak. "Who else is in danger?"

Logan sighed. It wasn't aimed at the DC. It wasn't even aimed at himself, really. It was just a brief lapse of strength. A sagging of the shoulders. A lowering of the head.

"I don't know, son," he admitted. "I honestly don't know." He looked back over his shoulder in the direction of the fading sirens. "You going to head in to the hospital?"

Tyler shook his head. "No. She doesn't want me there. She wants me out looking for Harris. So, that's what I'm going to do."

Logan looked up at the light burning in the bedroom window of the house. He felt the weight in his inside pocket and thought of the safe house just a few streets away.

At last, he looked DC Neish straight in the eye. He smiled. It was an apology. A peace offering. "Mind if I give you a hand?"

CHAPTER TWENTY-SIX

Logan closed the door to Hoon's office, allowed himself a tiny moment of relief, then set off in the direction of the Incident Room.

They were going to be OK. It had taken some persuasion on his part, and two-thirds of a full-scale bollocking on Hoon's, but the DSup was authorising the resource required to put the safe house on twenty-four-seven surveillance.

Aye, that was just a grand way of saying there'd be a Uniform in a car parked along the street keeping watch on the place, but it would do. If Vanessa and Maddie kept their wits about them, then that should be enough.

Please, let that be enough.

He entered the Incident Room to find the place alive with activity. Ben was talking to a couple of officers from CID—a DS and a DC, if Logan remembered correctly, although there was no chance of him recalling their names—while Hamza and Tyler spoke into their phones. Both men were animated, their hands gesticulating as their voices rose, like they were giving serious grief to whoever was proving to be an obstacle on the other end of the line.

Good for them.

The press conference had been scheduled for first thing in the morning. Photos and quotes had gone out to the major media outlets and the locals, and they'd been scrambling to be the first to break the news online.

Hamza had seemed genuinely delighted when the first 'Mister Whisper Strikes Again!' headline had appeared on one of the red tops' websites. Logan had felt a sickness deep in his gut.

Harris's photo would soon be everywhere, sat right next to Petrie's mugshot, forever linking the two in people's minds. Tyler had given Sinead a call to prepare her, but she hadn't answered, and there had been no further updates from her on the condition of her aunt.

Logan sat at his desk and looked over to the Big Board that Sinead had been working on. It was good. Different to how Caitlyn would've done it, but a solid effort. Clear, informative, easy to follow—everything he could've asked for.

He swept his gaze across it, taking in the bigger picture, then something drew him back to the start where Sinead had stuck half a sheet of A4 paper with the words 'Premier Inn' printed on it. To the paper, she'd added a Post-It that simply asked 'Why?'

Logan read both notes again.

Why?

Why there? On the one night in his life that he'd put his own family in an Inverness Premier Inn, a body turns up at another branch at the opposite end of the city.

Connected? Almost certainly not.

But maybe.

He rose slowly from his chair. The others were all still engaged in their conversations. Ben seemed to be about to finish up with the CID lot, but he had a habit of remembering things at the last moment, so it might drag on yet.

Logan approached the Big Board. He touched the 'Premier Inn' sheet, like physical contact might somehow impart more information, then went over the other information that Sinead had pinned in place.

The photographs of the victim looked like a make-up test for a low-budget horror movie from the eighties, where buckets of blood and visceral gore compensated for god-awful acting and a complete lack of plot.

Sinead had added a Post-It for every notable thing about the body—the missing teeth, the mashed-up face, the lack of hands. That sort of thing.

Below those was another note that listed a few less-interesting details, like his suit with its charity-shop tag.

Logan turned to ask Hamza if anything useful had come back from the British Heart Foundation stores, but he was still fully invested in his phone call. It could wait.

The bottom note also referenced the victim having walked in his bare feet, and his shoes, which were too big for his feet. Logan had been dimly aware of that detail, but his head had been full of Owen Petrie, and it was only now that something about it nagged at him.

Logan stared into the mangled face of the victim. He picked at the skin around his thumbs with his forefingers, the cogs in his brain clanking and whirring into life.

"The shoes," he muttered.

The shoes.

"Do we know what—?" he began, before a wave from Tyler caught his eye.

"Boss. Sinead," the DC said, holding up his mobile phone. He was still on the landline, and he tossed the smaller handset to Logan, who snatched it from the air and brought it immediately to his ear.

"Sinead. Hello. It's Lo... It's Jack. What's the latest?"

Constable Bell sounded shaken. Probably the understatement of the year. Val was in a bad way. Her skull had been fractured, and there was a bleed on her brain. Whoever had hit her had done so with tremendous force.

The next few hours would be critical, the doctors had told her. She was in surgery now, but the damage was severe, and Sinead had been primed to prepare herself for the worst. Even if Val woke up, there was no saying she'd be anything like the person she was before.

Another life destroyed by that bastard.

How many more?

Logan filled her in on the progress so far. It made for slim pickings, so he focused on the effort, rather than the results. They were pulling out all the stops. Officers were being drafted in from across the country. They were going to find him, the DCI promised. They were going to bring Harris home.

"You want me to send Tyler to you?" Logan asked, once he'd brought her up to date.

"No. I want him there helping."

"You shouldn't be on your own, Sinead. Not at a time like this."

"Nor should Harris," Sinead said, and he heard her break as she spoke his name. "So bring him home, sir. Please."

"I will. *We* will," Logan said.

Sinead sniffed and cleared her throat. "I better get inside," she said, and the strain of holding it together was obvious in her voice. "I'll call back."

The line went dead before Logan could reply. He held onto the phone until it went dark, then set it on Tyler's desk.

"One sec," the DC said into the landline, then he pressed the handset to his shoulder.

"Val's in surgery. Sinead is... doing fine, considering."

"Does she want me over?"

Logan shook his head. "She wants us all focused on getting her brother home."

Tyler looked down at his mobile, nodded, then returned to his call.

"Sorry about that. Can you send the link through to my email?" he asked. "Have you got a pen?"

Logan headed over to Ben, the Big Board and the victim whose face was plastered across it forgotten for the moment.

"Call it twenty minutes, will we?" Ben was saying to the CID officers. "Briefing room won't be big enough, so we'll use the canteen. Can you get on that?"

The Detective Sergeant—a thirty-something man with a rugged, outdoorsy sort of look to him—gave a confident nod. "Not a problem, sir. We're on it. Fifteen minutes."

He and the younger DC he'd brought with him about-turned in near-unison and went striding out of the Incident Room.

"What was all that about?" Logan asked, as the doors swung closed.

"Hoon wants a full staff briefing. As many bodies as we can cram in. He wants to bring them all up to speed. Stress the importance of getting the boy home safe," Ben said. "Only, he swore a lot more when he was explaining it."

"Obviously," Logan agreed. "Does he have everything he needs?"

Ben raised a quizzical eyebrow.

"For the briefing," said Logan. "Does he have all the information?"

"Oh, no. You misunderstand, Jack," Ben replied. He gave the DCI a bump on the arm, and smiled. "He's no' giving the briefing. You are."

A SHADE over fifteen minutes later, Logan stood in the canteen, looking out at a sea of officers. Most of them were Uniforms, but there were half a dozen plain-clothes officers dotted around, as well as Tyler and Ben sitting in the front row.

Any other day, he'd be bracing himself for the pair of them to start heckling him as soon as he stood up to talk, but not tonight. Everyone's sense of humour had long-since deserted them.

Hamza sat behind Logan and off to the side, the back of his chair pushed up against a stack of trays. Technically, the canteen was still open, but the food had all been covered over, and the lights had been switched off at the serving area for the duration of the briefing.

Detective Superintendent Hoon stood at the very back of the room, directly across from Logan and very deliberately in his eyeline. There was a low murmur of chattering from the audience, but mostly they were staring at him, too.

God, Logan hated doing these things.

He had never been what you might call a motivational speaker. Not unless you counted the threat of a boot up the arse as an acceptable form of motivation.

Even then, that worked much better on a one-to-one basis. In a room this size, with this many people, there were just too many arses to kick. And that meant finding a way to motivate them without the threat of physical violence. Inspiring through words alone.

It had never been his strong point. Fortunately, given what he was about to tell them, it shouldn't take much to get them motivated.

He looked out at the sea of expectant faces. He hardly recognised any of them, and very few of them knew him other than by reputation. A few of them—a lot of them, actually—looked young. Stupidly young. Too young for what they might be about to face.

God, Logan hated doing these things.

But then, he only had himself to blame. It was all his fault.

He had a postcard in his pocket that told him so.

Pushing that thought away, Logan turned and gave the nod to Hamza. With the press of a remote, a boy's face—all dirt and smiles—filled the projector screen beside the DCI.

"Harris Bell. Brother of Constable Sinead Bell, who I'm sure most of you know. He was staying with his aunt tonight in the Viewhill area when she was badly beaten, and he was taken, we believe, by this man."

Hamza picked up on his cue. He moved to the next slide. Logan didn't have to look to know this had happened. The ripple of recognition and horror that spread through the audience told him that the image on screen had changed.

"Owen Petrie. Maybe better known to some of you as 'Mister Whisper.' For those of you fortunate enough to be unfamiliar with him, he abducted and murdered three young boys in and around Glasgow over a decade ago," Logan explained. "He was, until last week, a patient at Carstairs State Hospital. But he got out. And he came here."

"Why?" asked a senior uniformed officer. A Chief Inspector, if Logan remembered correctly. "Why here? What ties him to Inverness?"

Logan briefly met Hoon's eye at the back of the hall.

"I do," he said, in answer to the question. "I was the arresting officer in the original case. I brought him in. He's here because I'm here. I believe he targeted Constable Bell's brother to hurt me and the people I... know.

"But, right now, the why isn't important. We need to know the where. Where is Harris? Where would he take him? Petrie's new to the city, fresh out of Carstairs. We have reason to believe he had access to information on the inside through a doctor who worked there, but he's on his own now. No money, no friends, nowhere to go. But he's gone *somewhere,* and we need to find where."

Logan frowned. A thought darted through his head, then was gone. He tried to grab for it, but it slipped through his fingers like a dream in the moments after waking.

"He, uh... Historically, he's kept his victims alive for around seventy-two hours," Logan continued. "But in those three days he put those kids through hell. So, we find Harris quickly. Tonight. Even if it means turning the city upside-down. We find that boy. We bring him home. If we can catch Petrie while we're at it, that's a bonus, but the safe return of Harris Bell is our number one focus, and we..."

Is he on his own, though?

The question popped unbidden into Logan's head, throwing him off his stride.

The audience watched in silence as the DCI turned and looked at the projector screen. Owen Petrie's face leered out at him from ten years ago. The scar on his head was still fresh, the skin puckered where the sutures pulled it tight.

This wasn't the face Logan remembered, though. That had been pre-scar. Pre-arrest. Pre-fall. Back when he was leering at him, laughing at him, telling him of all the terrible things he'd done to those kids.

Telling him how much he'd loved it.

"Eh... Jack?" Ben prompted him from the front row.

"Hmm? Oh. Sorry. I just..."

There was a ring of them. That's what Hoon had said. A ring. A network.

A support group.

They'd been assuming he was working alone now, like they'd assumed he was working alone then, but what if he hadn't been? What if he wasn't?

What if he had help?

Shoes.

That word also made itself known without warning or fanfare.

Shoes. The murder victim's shoes had been too big.

How big?

"What size were those trainers?" Logan asked, turning to DI Forde.

Ben frowned. "Trainers?"

"On the victim. At the hotel."

"Oh. Them. Eh... I'm no' sure."

"What the fuck are you two wittering about?" bellowed Hoon from up the back. "Now's hardly the time for a cosy fucking chat. Get on with it."

"Tyler? Hamza? The shoes, any idea?" Logan asked, ignoring the Detective Superintendent. There was some confused murmuring from the audience, as the Uniforms and CID tried unsuccessfully to follow what was going on.

"Not sure, boss. Big, though," Tyler said, which was no bloody help at all, quite frankly.

"Thirteens, sir," said Hamza.

Thirteens.

Thirteens.

No. Couldn't be.

Another coincidence, that was all.

Logan looked down at his feet, and the scuffed boots he wore on them.

"Fuck it," he ejected, then he turned and ran out of the canteen, with the roaring of Detective Superintendent Hoon chasing him along the corridor.

Logan was out of breath when he threw open the doors of the Incident

Room. He thundered over to the exhibits desk, where the evidence they'd gathered in the case was stacked in sturdy storage boxes.

He found the trainers in the second box and lifted them out by the corner of their sealed plastic bag. They were battered old Nikes, the rubber of the sole well-worn, the leather, or plastic, or whatever the hell they were made from nowadays, all coated with flecks of dried mud.

Logan hadn't run in years. Not unless he had to. But, somewhere at the back of his mind, he'd harboured the idea that he might again someday. That he might find the time and the inclination to get out there into the wilderness like he used to do.

And so, he'd kept his old running shoes. He'd taken them with him when he and Vanessa had split up, and they'd moved with him whenever he'd relocated to a new place. A new house. A new flat.

Even a new city.

The door opened at Logan's back. A slightly breathless Tyler hurried in and let the door close again behind him. "Hoon's on the warpath, boss. He's charging over, and he's not happy," the DC said. He swallowed, then puffed out his chest. "And, well, I'm not happy, either. We're meant to be discussing Harris and Petrie. What's more important that you go—"

"These trainers," said Logan, holding the bag up for the younger detective to see.

Tyler flicked his gaze to them, then back to the DCI. "What about them?"

"They're mine."

CHAPTER TWENTY-SEVEN

THE MAN HAD GONE. THAT WAS GOOD. HE SCARED HIM. TERRIFIED HIM. Made him cry, even though he tried so hard to hold it back.

The man had laughed at him. He'd stood over him, and he'd laughed. Then, he'd caught one of his tears on the tip of his finger and he'd tasted it, moaning with pleasure like it was something delicious.

After that, the man had squatted down in front of the chair and put his icy-cold hands on his knees. The man had just stared at him for a while, like he was memorising his face. There had been no expression on his own, just a blank, lifeless stare from eyes that felt cruel and judgemental.

Harris had sat there, saying nothing, his hands tied behind him, his face glistening with tears and snot. A minute had passed. Two. The man just watched him, and watched him, and watched him, until the tension of it all became too much, and Harris sobbed into the rag that had been rammed into his mouth and taped over.

He had wanted to be sick. He had gagged and boaked as the material was forced into his mouth back at Auntie Val's. He had thought he was going to die, right there and then, unable to breathe. But the man had told him to breathe through his nose. He'd guided him, demonstrating with his own breaths.

In. Out. In. Out.

He'd almost seemed kind, but then he dragged the boy out into the garden, and Harris saw Auntie Val lying by the bins. Her eyes were staring. Her mouth moved, making gurgling sounds as bubbles of blood burst on her lips.

Harris had kicked and struggled, tried to scream, but then he was inside the back of van, and the door was sliding shut, plunging him into total darkness.

An engine had roared. A voice had spoken as a whisper in his ear.

"You and I are going to have a lot of fun together."

Everything after that was a blur of panic and fear. A bag had been put over his head. Voices had spoken, muffled and quiet. There had been arguing, he thought, but whispered so he didn't hear it.

And then, there had been hands, and dragging, and carrying, and movement.

And then, there had been the ropes, and the chair, and the man standing over him, waiting to taste his tears.

He was gone now, but Harris wasn't alone. He'd left the woman to watch him. She sat in a chair in the darkened next room, only half-visible through the open doorway.

The man had said she was going to watch him, and Harris could see the light reflecting off her eyes. She hadn't said a word since he'd been brought in, but her gaze was fixed on him, pinning him to the spot and daring him to make a sound, to try to escape.

The man was bad, but something about her told Harris that the woman would be even worse.

And so, he lowered his head to hide his shame, and cried big heaving sobs into his lap.

CHAPTER TWENTY-EIGHT

"This had better be fucking good, Jack!" Hoon spat, throwing open the double doors of the Incident Room like a gunfighter entering a Wild West saloon. "What's with the fucking vanishing act?"

"The body found behind the Premier Inn was wearing a pair of trainers that were too big for his feet," Logan explained, wasting no time. "They were my trainers. They came from my flat. Petrie must've taken them."

Hoon's forehead furrowed as his brain worked to process this.

"So, what are you saying? Petrie killed that guy?"

"Aye. I think so."

Tyler shot Hoon a sideways glance to make sure he wasn't about to incur the DSup's wrath by speaking over him. "Didn't the Pathology report say he was held down by two or three people when the teeth were being yanked, boss?"

"It did," Logan confirmed, not taking his eyes off Hoon. "You said it yourself, sir. He was part of a ring. He's not working alone on this. He's got help."

"Oh, well that's fucking marvellous news," Hoon ejected, in a tone that suggested it very much was not.

"Bosco."

Both senior officers turned to look at Tyler, and he had to resist the urge to run away.

"*What*?" Hoon asked.

Tyler cleared his throat. "Eh, Bosco Maximuke, sir. His van... one of them... was identified as being at the scene around the time the body was dumped."

Hoon blinked several times, like this information was causing some sort of short-circuit in his brain. "Bosco and Owen Petrie? I can't see it. Bosco's a fucking pain in the arse, but... a paedo? No. Doubt it."

"Bosco goes where the money is," Logan said. "And there's money in filth."

"I just can't see it," Hoon said, shaking his head. "Drugs, prostitution, whatever. Aye. That's Bosco. But him and Petrie working together? No."

"Worth a follow-up," Logan said.

"I don't think it is," Hoon said. "I think we need to focus on finding the missing boy. Forget Bosco for now."

Logan noted that Hoon had gone several sentences now without swearing once. Surely a new personal best?

"With all due respect, sir, this is our only lead on the boy."

"You fucking deaf, Detective Chief Inspector?" Hoon spat, breaking his swear-free run. For a moment, it looked like he was about to launch into one of his usual tirades, but then his shoulders dipped, and he ran a hand down his face from top to bottom. "Fine. No, you're right. Worth a look. Ben can finish the briefing. I think it's a waste of time, but I've been wrong before."

"Very big of you to admit it, sir," Logan said.

"Aye, well. It was once, when I accepted your fucking transfer request," Hoon replied.

"We all make mistakes."

Hoon nodded. His head seemed heavy, like he was struggling to hold it up. "Aye. That we do, Jack. That we do." He drew himself up to his full height and headed for the door. "And remember, I am the fucking loop. Alright?"

"Got it, sir," Logan replied, just as Hoon vanished out through the double doors again. He watched them for a while, wondering what the hell all that was about, then turned to Tyler. "Fancy a trip to see Bosco Maximuke?"

Tyler shifted on the balls of his feet. "I, uh, I'd better check in with Sinead, boss. I mean, I would, but... I should probably..."

"Aye. Makes sense. If she needs you there, go," Logan said. "Soon as I know anything, I'll be in touch.

"Cool. Good. That's..." Tyler's tongue flicked across his lips, which had gone dry. "I mean, you two know each other, anyway. Don't you? Bosco and you, I mean. You go... back. A while."

"We're no' exactly best pals," Logan said. "I did recently burn down his office, you might recall? But aye, for better or worse I've been dealing with the Russian bastard for a while."

"You never pegged him as being connected to Petrie?"

Logan shook his head. "No. Not a pair I'd have put together, but... Christ knows. We'll see."

"Yeah, boss." Tyler nodded. "I guess we will."

Logan made a quick diversion via the safe house on the way to Bosco's yard and was satisfied to see a squad car parked just along the street, a burly male Uniform watching the house from the driver's seat.

One less thing to worry about.

When he reached the Russian's yard, it was locked up. Hardly surprising, given the time of night, but a few long blasts of his horn brought an irritated looking skinhead scuttling out through the front gate.

The smell of burning Portakabin still lingered in the air, but the rain—never far away—had started to fall on the drive over, and it dampened the odour down. The steady downpour did nothing for the demeanour of the skinhead, though, who scowled up at it like he was angry with the gods themselves.

Logan recognised Valdis, mostly from the bruising the skinhead had sustained when the DCI had elbowed him in the face just a few days earlier. Judging by the way Valdis's mouth curled into a sneer, he had no problem recognising Logan, either.

"It's you. Should have guessed," Valdis spat. "What now?"

"I'm here to see Bosco," Logan said. He pointed at Valdis's bruises and twiddled his finger around in a circle. "How's your face, by the way? On the mend, I hope."

"Face is fucking not your business. And Bosco is not here."

"Where is he?"

"Not here. That is all I know." Valdis held up a finger. "Wait. No. I know something else, too."

"And what's that?" Logan asked.

"I know you are not fucking getting into yard without warrant," Valdis said. There was venom in it, and he looked Logan up and down like he was a giant cockroach who'd just come climbing out from behind the fridge. "You fucking police pigs. I am sick of you coming here, throwing weight around. If it up to me, you go fuck yourself."

"That's no' very friendly now, Valdis," Logan said. He nodded back in the direction of the gate, and a droplet of rainwater fell from the end of his nose. "How about you run along and tell Bosco I'm here? Be a good lad."

Valdis squared his shoulders. He gave the DCI another once-over with his eyes, sizing him up this time.

"I wouldn't, son," Logan warned. "Or have you forgotten what happened last time?"

"Fucking take me by surprise last time," Valdis said.

Logan chuckled. "I took *you* by surprise? If memory serves, son, you were the one trying to jump me from behind. I just defended myself."

The DCI's smile remained fixed in place, but the look in his eyes became a sharp and dangerous thing.

"How do you fancy your chances face to face?" he asked.

"No problem," Valdis said, after just a moment's hesitation. His sneer became a grin far broader than Logan's own. "How you fancy chances three against one?"

Over the sound of the rain, Logan heard the scuffing of a footstep behind him. He looked back, first over his left shoulder, then his right, and realised he was in the centre of a triangle of angry bastards.

"Now, here is my advice," Valdis said. "Go. Get fuck out of here. Bosco is not here. I will—if I fucking feel like it—tell him you came when I see him tomorrow."

Logan nodded slowly. "And if I choose not to follow that advice?"

"Then... This would be regretful for you," Valdis replied, and there was no mistaking the meaning behind it.

Logan glanced around at all three men again, calculating his chances. He came to the conclusion that they weren't great. He might be able to take down one or two of them, but the men were younger than he was, faster than he was, and no doubt had come tooled up. It was not a fight he was going to win.

"Maybe you can pass on a message for me, then?" Logan asked.

Valdis seemed annoyed by the suggestion. "What is message?" he demanded.

"Tell him I hadn't put him down as a nonce. Tell him I know he's helping Owen Petrie. Tell him if either of them harm a hair on that boy's head, I will hunt them down, I will find them, and I will turn them inside-out. Slowly. Along with anyone else who helped them. And I will enjoy every fucking moment of it."

He looked from face to face. The men behind him were stoic and impassive, but there was a subtle shift in Valdis's expression that he couldn't quite identify.

"You got that?" Logan asked. "You want to write it down, maybe, so you don't forget?"

Valdis tapped the side of his head to indicate that the message was locked in, then gestured to the Volvo abandoned outside the yard's double gates.

"Now, get in car and fuck off."

"You don't want to get involved in this, Valdis," Logan said. "Child abduction. Child murder. This isn't what you signed up for. If you know where the boy is, tell me, and we can make sure you—none of you three—get the rap for it."

There was an exchange of looks between the points of the triangle surrounding the DCI, and Logan almost let himself believe the skinheads were going to take him up on the offer.

But then, Valdis had to go and open his mouth and ruin it.

"We know nothing about any boy," he said. "Now, get fuck out of here before we make you."

Logan thought about just going for it. Taking a kicking would almost be worth it, if it meant getting another crack in at Valdis. That smug fucking look wasn't going to wipe itself off.

But, no. He needed to be in one piece for whatever came next. He couldn't find Petrie from a hospital bed, or worse, the bottom of the Moray Firth.

He settled for eyeballing all three of the baldy-headed bastards in turn, then muttered an, "I'll be back," that was worthy of the Terminator himself, before climbing back into the Volvo and getting the hell out of there.

CHAPTER TWENTY-NINE

HAMZA WAS ONTO SOMETHING. HE WAS SURE OF IT.

It would require a spreadsheet, though. And, ideally, a few people with some data entry experience.

Granted, it was a bit of a stretch, and Hoon had made it very clear that until such times as he had evidence that backed up his theory, he was on his own. By then, of course, there would be no point in the additional manpower. He'd have cracked it.

He opened a spreadsheet, typed the numbers one, two, and three in the top left columns, and was about to start working his way through the next hundred or so rows when Logan returned to the Incident Room.

From the look on his face, his meeting with Bosco had not gone well.

"Uh, alright, sir?" Hamza asked. He was the only one in the Incident Room, and felt like he should extend some sort of greeting. "How'd you get on?"

"Shite," Logan said. "No sign of Bosco at the yard. I'm going to pull a home address for him, if we've got one. Last I checked, his address was still registered as being in Glasgow. Don't think we've got a new one for up here, but worth a look. My gut tells me we won't get to speak to him until tomorrow, though, and even then we might be lucky. If he's involved, he may well have done a runner already."

"I think CID went round to speak to his ex-wife at one point, sir. They should have an address for her. She might know where to find him."

"Good to know. I'll get that checked out," Logan said. He looked around. "Where's everyone else?"

"The DI's in with the Detective Superintendent, and Tyler's off to the hospital."

Logan stopped with his coat half on and half off. "What's happened?"

"Nothing. Nothing bad, anyway. Sinead's aunt's stable, they reckon. They're keeping her in an induced coma to give her brain a chance to heal," Hamza said. "So, Sinead doesn't see the point in sitting around there."

"Makes sense. Best to get home and get some rest."

"Aye, you'd think, sir," Hamza said.

Logan finished taking off his coat this time before replying. "She's not coming in, is she?"

"Apparently, aye. Wants to help. Understandable, I suppose."

"Still an' all," Logan said. "This could get rough. Very rough. I'm not sure she should be on the front line for it."

"Good luck trying to stop her, sir," Hamza said, to which Logan could only grunt and nod.

"Fair point," he conceded.

Sinead was young, but she'd had to grow up fast. She was determined to the point of stubbornness, and a bloody good officer to boot. If she wanted to be at the coal face on this one, then someone else would have to discourage her, because Logan wasn't prepared to.

"I've, eh, I've maybe got something," Hamza said. "But it's... tentative at the minute."

Logan hurried over to the DC's desk. "Tentative? I'll take 'almost impossible' at the moment. What is it?"

"It's the words, sir. On the photos and in that envelope he left for you. I've been thinking about them," Hamza said. He glanced down at his notepad. "Mentions, idealist, info. Driveways, toast, nature."

"And?"

"I was trying to think of a way they linked together. Or to see if they made a message. Like, 'driveways toast nature,' could be some sort of environmental message, or whatever."

Logan side-eyed the younger detective. "He's a child killer, Hamza, no' fucking Greenpeace. I mean, I know you said it was tentative..."

"Aye, I know. I decided against that, and started thinking about what else it might be," the DC continued. "You heard of an app called 'what3words,' sir?"

The creases on Logan's forehead made it clear that he had not.

"Right, well, it's like a map thing. Every square metre on Earth is represented by three random words. You put a location into the app and it spits out three words that you can share with people so they can find you. RAC is using it, I think. There was a mountain rescue case down in Fort William recently where a climber was—"

"I don't need the backstory," Logan interrupted. "So... did you try?"

"I did, sir," Hamza replied.

"And?"

"I started with the first three words. From the photos left at my place. Driveways, toast, nature."

"And?" Logan urged again. "Did it work? Is it a place?"

"It's a place, sir, aye."

Logan flopped down into the nearest chair, wide-eyed. "Bloody hell! Seriously?"

"But it's in Alaska."

"Jesus Christ," the DCI sighed, his sudden surge of optimism leaving him like air from a shrivelled balloon. "What about the other one?"

Hamza winced, ever so slightly, before replying. "Switzerland, sir."

"Great," said Logan slapping his thighs and standing up. "So, either he's in Switzerland, or he's near the Arctic bloody Circle."

"Aye, but... they might be jumbled up, sir," Hamza said. "They might not be in the right order. Nature, driveways, toast, for example. That's Norway."

"I highly doubt he's there, either," Logan said. "But... How long to go through them all?"

"A wee while, sir. By my reckoning, there are about a hundred and twenty combinations, if we use all six words. I'll go through them as there original groups of three first, and... I mean, it might turn out to be nothing, obviously, but..."

He ran out of steam then, and finished with a shrug and a vaguely embarrassed look.

"Worth a try," Logan told him. "And good thinking. It's not something I'd have ever come up with. Crack on, and see what you get." He looked at the door and puffed out his cheeks. "I suppose I'd better go rescue Ben."

DI Forde was not in Hoon's office when Logan knocked and entered. The Detective Superintendent sat alone, gazing out of the office window at the city beyond.

It wasn't much of a view, really. From Hoon's seat, it was all car showrooms and dual carriageways. Aye, if he got close to the window and got the angle right, he might be able to get a glimpse of the building that housed *Iceland* and *Home Bargains*, but that hardly seemed worth the effort.

"Sorry, sir, I was expecting Ben to be here," Logan volunteered. He wondered if he could just leave now without any fuss. From the look of him, Hoon would probably quite like to be alone. Maybe he could just back out into the corridor again and close the door.

"Sit down," Hoon said, not yet turning.

Damn it.

Logan wheeled one of the other chairs out from the DSup's desk and took a seat across from him. Hoon still hadn't turned away from the window, the lure of the Longman Industrial Estate clearly proving too much of a temptation.

"I sent Ben home," he said.

Logan repeated that last word, but in a higher, somewhat incredulous register. "Home?" he said. "Why did you send him home?"

"Because he's dead on his bloody feet," Hoon said, finally walking himself around in his swivel chair to face the DCI. "He's no' as young as he once was, and I know what a nebby cow that wife of his can be."

Logan had to admit that Ben had looked exhausted. And he couldn't really argue with the 'nebby cow' part, either. Still, given what they were facing, he'd have expected the DI to hang it out a little longer.

"I gave him a choice," said Hoon, appearing to read Logan's mind. "He could go home and rest for a few hours, or he could be suspended. He did not go willingly."

Logan nodded, pleased to hear this. "No. I wouldn't imagine he would've."

"Exhaustion breeds mistakes. You're tired, you miss things. We've all seen it," Hoon said. "And look at the state of you. When did you last sleep?"

Logan had absolutely no idea when he'd last slept. Not without grabbing a bit of paper and a pencil and doing some sums.

"Not too long ago, sir," he lied.

"Then see a fucking doctor, man, because you look like a sack of shite," Hoon told him.

The swear words jumped out at Logan. Usually, the Detective Superintendent poured on the cursing like salt on a chip shop fish supper. It was rare for him to make it through a sentence without effing and blinding at least once. It was how he expressed most of his emotions—anger, rage, fury, contempt, and, very occasionally, begrudging respect.

For the second time tonight, though, he was being oddly subdued with his language, and it made Logan uneasy.

"What happened with Bosco?" Hoon asked. His fingers were drumming on the arm of his chair. Fast, too. Another odd change in behaviour.

"Couldn't find him. He wasn't at his yard," Logan said.

Hoon nodded, like this had confirmed something. "Well, it's late. Got a home address?"

"No, sir. But we're digging up one for his ex-wife. They have joint custody of the daughter, so she'll likely know."

"Right. Right. Good," Hoon said. "And what's your gut telling you about him and Petrie? You think that's a thing?"

"I do, sir," Logan said.

Hoon frowned. "You sound very confident."

"Aye. I know the shoes were in my cupboard before I went to Canna. I saw them when I was packing. Petrie was in my flat when I was away—or someone was in there for him—leaving the name badge. Presumably, they took the shoes at the same time, and stuck them on the victim."

"But we don't know Bosco had anything to do with that," Hoon said. "The murder. Do we?"

"We don't know very much, no. But we can put one of his vans leaving the scene just after the time we believe the victim was done in. And we know he's a dodgy bastard who's had people killed before, even if we've never been able to make anything stick."

"But this? Petrie? That's different," Hoon said. "I mean, aye, we know he's big in the drugs scene, but if he's killed anyone before it's been some other shady bastard. Crooks killing crooks. I'm no' saying I approve, but... it isn't kids."

"I still hold Bosco responsible for Detective Sergeant McQuarrie's death," Logan said, and the tone of his voice suggested that, senior officer or not, Hoon was skating on some very thin ice.

"I'm no' saying he's one of the good guys," Hoon said. "And believe me, I'd love to take the bastard down. I've tried often enough. But, my point is... Bosco. Petrie. I just... I don't see it."

"Well, I do, sir," Logan said. "And I think it would also go some way to explaining what happened with your nephew. Jaden."

Hoon's head snapped up at that. "What the fuck are you talking about?" he asked, some of his usual fury spluttering into life behind his eyes.

"It's how Bosco operates, isn't it? Threaten the family. Usually veiled enough that we can't charge him for it," Logan said. "He tried it with mine a few years back."

"What happened?" Hoon asked.

"I stabbed him through the hand with a fountain pen," Logan said, matter-of-factly. "The point is, I don't think Petrie was ever going to take Jaden. I think it was a warning. Same with Hamza's wee one."

"Then why take the other kid? PC Bell's brother?"

"That, I'm not sure of," Logan said.

Hoon leaned forward and clasped his hands on the desk. "So, then maybe Petrie is working on his own, like we first thought. Maybe he did try to grab Jaden and DC Khaled's daughter, but was interrupted. Maybe you're over-thinking all this."

"How would he know where to find everyone?" Logan asked. "If he was on his own?"

Hoon shrugged. "The Gozer's phone and computer were hacked, you said. Maybe—"

"They were, but he wouldn't have got Hamza's address from that. Or your niece's, for that matter," Logan reasoned. "I mean, aye, maybe he's working with someone else—someone who's not Bosco, I mean—but I think it's a safe assumption that Petrie is not on his own. He's only been out a few days, nowhere near long enough to get this established on his own. And Bosco knows everything that's going on in the city. He's got eyes and ears everywhere. We know there's got to be at least one leak in this building."

"What makes you say that?" Hoon asked.

"The stuff he knows. When he ran me off the road on Loch Ness-side a while back. Only way he could've got set up for that is if someone told him where I was going." Logan said. "The man is bloody everywhere. He'd know where to find your niece's kid. He'd know where Sinead's aunt lives. And he'd know..."

Logan stopped. There had been a knot building in his stomach for the past few hours. A niggle worming its way around inside his brain that only now popped to the surface.

He knew everything. How to find everyone.

He threatened families. That's what he did.

He'd threatened Logan's own.

Logan was on his feet in an instant. He looked out of the window at the city, like some sort of telescopic vision might let him see all the way to the Smithon Area.

To the house on Murray Road.

And to his ex-wife and daughter hiding away inside.

CHAPTER THIRTY

Vanessa lurked in the corner behind the door, the handle of the frying pan held tightly in both hands. She gave the nod to Maddie, confirming she was ready, then braced herself for whatever was coming next.

Maddie, for her part, held the kitchen knife low at her side, but angled so she could stab upwards should the need arise. She hoped it wouldn't. God, she hoped it wouldn't. But if it came to it, she'd do it.

Wouldn't she?

Edging closer to the door, she peered through the peephole, but the darkness outside made it impossible to tell who was out there. The knocking had roused them both from their rooms, although neither of them had been able to sleep.

There was a light on the porch, but switching it on would alert whoever was out there to their presence. Still, better that than opening the door to a serial killer.

Holding her eye to the peephole, she reached for the switch and clicked it on. A uniformed officer on the front step was momentarily taken aback by the sudden illumination. The rain had been pooling on top of his flat cap, and it came pouring off as he leaned in a little closer to the door.

"Hello? Is someone...? I just got a call from base. DCI Logan believes the location of the house has been compromised. He thinks you're in danger. I'm to take you to him at the station."

Maddie shot a sideways look at her mother. Vanessa's only response was an unhelpful shrugging of her shoulders.

"Give him a call to verify, if you like," the officer said. "I can wait until you've spoken to—"

From outside came a short screech of tyres skidding to a stop, and a muttered, "Shite," from the policeman on the step.

Maddie pressed her eye to the peephole again, and saw headlights blazing just beyond the garden gate. Three doors opened then slammed. A trio of figures appeared silhouetted in the glow of the full beams.

The officer grabbed for the radio on his shoulder, but he fumbled with it, unable to find the button in his growing panic.

"Shit," Maddie hissed, then she unlocked the door, pulled him in, and slammed it again.

The constable almost jumped out of his skin when he saw Vanessa hiding in the corner. His eyes, like most of his face, were in shadow beneath the brim of his cap, but they darted anxiously to the knife in Maddie's hands.

"Uh, best watch what you're doing with that," he began, then a hammering on the door became a bigger priority for all of them. "Is there a back door?" the officer whispered, as they all backed off along the hall.

"There is," Maddie confirmed.

"Right, then let's use it, get to my car, and get the hell out of here."

The Volvo screeched to a stop nose to nose with the squad car on Murray Road, its headlights flooding the inside of the smaller vehicle.

Empty.

Logan jumped out without switching off the engine and ran to the car. The driver's side window had been lowered, and there was blood on the glass and down the white paintwork of the door.

A man lay slumped in the back seat, naked apart from a blood-soaked shirt and a pair of boxer shorts. There was a gaping hole where his throat should have been, the flesh there pinkish and raw.

His eyes were open and staring at the seat in front of him, like he'd known it would be the last thing he'd ever seen, and he'd wanted to memorise it, hang onto the image for as long as he possibly could.

"No, no, no," Logan said, each one louder than the one before. He threw himself in the direction of the safe house, top half leading the way, legs pumping furiously as they tried to keep up.

He had his phone in his hand by the time he reached the gate, was calling Maddie's number before his shoulder connected with the front door. It held firm, and pain went rattling through his skeleton as the sound of Maddie's voice came tinnily through the speakers.

"Hi, this is Maddie."

"Maddie!" Logan cried, but his daughter's voice spoke over him.

"I can't come to the phone right now..."

Shite!

He hung up, hammered on the door with one hand, while scrolling to Vanessa's name in his contacts with the other.

"Maddie! Vanessa! Open up, it's me!" he bellowed.

There was no movement from the windows. No twitching of curtains, or switching on of the lights.

He put his shoulder to the door another couple of times, then brought his foot up and kicked it. Once. Twice. Vanessa's voicemail greeting played from his phone's speaker.

"No, no, no!"

Sirens approached. He'd put the shout out on the way over, hoping someone was close enough to beat him there, but most of the station was focused on Harris, and doors were being knocked on all around the area he'd gone missing from.

Logan searched the garden for a rock, or a bit of loose paving—something light enough for him to lift, but heavy enough to obliterate the window at the side of the door.

He found nothing, but spotted the smiling wee face of a garden gnome peeking over the wall at him from the garden next door. A big concrete bastard of a thing it was, with a jolly red hat and a chin like a baby's arse.

That'd do it.

He vaulted the wall, grabbed the gnome, and was halfway back to the front door when the neighbour shouted at him from an upstairs window.

"Put that back! What do you think you're playing at?" he bellowed, but Logan wasn't listening.

Charging for the door, he raised the gnome above his head and launched it at the glass. Both window and garden ornament exploded into shards of glass and concrete, and the neighbour exploded into a foul-mouthed tirade that Logan barely caught any of.

He was inside the house a handful of seconds later, charging along the hall, calling out for his daughter and her mother as he searched the downstairs rooms.

Empty.

He was headed for the last of the downstairs doors when he felt the draft blowing through the gap beneath it.

Throwing the door wide, Logan stumbled into the kitchen. The toe of his boot collided with something heavy on the floor, and sent it skidding across the lino. It hit a kickplate with a metallic clang.

A frying pan.

And there, on the counter by the open door, a knife. Blood dotted the metal of the blade, like paint on a non-porous surface. More of it pooled on the worktop beneath it, and a bloodied handprint was smeared on the wall next to the door.

The postcard in his pocket howled at him, screamed at him, as he pulled the back door open all the way and went racing out into the garden.

"J-Jack?"

Vanessa lay on the grass, blood marking her face like camouflage. Her breathing was fast and shallow, each breath accompanied by a whimper or a sob.

He was at her side in an instant, and immediately saw the hands she held pressed against her thighs, and the blood that came pumping up between her fingers.

"Vanessa! What happened?"

Aside from the vibrant red of the blood, Vanessa was sepia-toned, like she'd stepped out of a photo in some old book. She was shivering, her body wracked with violent shudders as it went into shock.

"It was him... It was Petrie. He was in uniform, he... he..." Tears choked her, forcing her to gulp and gasp for breath. "He took her," she sobbed, when she could speak again. "Maddie. He took Maddie. He stabbed me. My legs. And he... and he... he said I should wave. He said I should wave goodbye."

Logan looked over to the back gate. It stood open, creaking gently as it was nudged back and forth by the breeze.

"When? How long ago?" he asked.

"I don't... Ten minutes. Fifteen. I don't k-know.

She hissed, as pain radiated through her. The cuts in her legs were deep, the one on the right worse than the one on the left. She had a dressing gown on, so Logan pulled out the belt cord and wrapped it around the right leg, a few inches above the wound.

"What are you d-doing?" she demanded. "Go. Get her. Not me, get her."

"Vanessa, if we don't stop this bleeding—"

She lashed out at him, slapping at his arm, her hands leaving bloody prints wherever they made contact. Her face was all twisted up with grief and rage.

"Fucking... go! Go, get her. Not me! I don't c-care!"

Pain tore through her again, arching her back on the grass. When it passed, all the venom had left her, and her voice was a pleading wheeze.

"Save our baby girl, Jack. Please."

"Police. Don't move!" barked a voice from inside the house, and Logan felt a surge of relief when he saw a surly-looking female constable glaring at him from the back door.

"DCI Jack Logan," he replied, turning and blinking in the beam of the officer's torch. She held the light on him for a couple of seconds, then angled it away.

"Sorry, sir, didn't recognise you in the dark," she said.

Logan jumped up and pointed to Vanessa. "Get an ambulance. Apply pressure to her injuries until it arrives. And put a call in, Owen Petrie is in this area. He may be wearing a uniform. There's a dead constable in a car out front."

The officer stared at him, her torch angled limply down at the grass. Her mouth moved, like she was reciting everything Logan had told her over again in her head, not quite able to process any of it.

"Get a fucking move on, Constable!" the DCI barked, which jolted the officer into life. He met Vanessa's wide-eyed look of terror again. "You're going to be OK."

"Just go, Jack. Hurry," Vanessa whispered. "And bring her back safe."

CHAPTER THIRTY-ONE

Logan's lungs burned as he raced along the path that led past the back of the safe house. It was flanked on both sides, gardens to the right, a high wall and a small forest of trees on the left. Pools of weak orange spilled from the streetlights dotted along the way, the night sky overhead too choked with cloud to offer any light of its own.

"Maddie!" he called as he ran, forcing what little breath was left in his lungs to carry her name ahead of him into the gloom. He spat *his* name out, too —"Petrie!"—but neither one brought any response.

And so, he ran. Ran faster than he'd ever run before. Ran like his daughter's life depended on it.

Some time later—probably not long, but it felt like a lifetime—he came stumbling into a car park beside a modern-looking church.

There were no cars there. No signs of life. No Owen Petrie.

No Maddie.

"Fuck!" Logan roared, just as a clap of thunder went rolling across the sky. He shouted her name again. Screamed it. "Maddie!"

What had he done? God, *what had he done*? This was his fault. He'd brought them here. He'd known this might happen, that it was at least a possibility.

An ambulance whizzed past, lights flashing, headed for the safe house.

What was he going to tell Vanessa? How could he break it to her?

How could he say he'd lost their little girl?

No. He wouldn't. He couldn't.

He'd find her. He'd get her back. That was what he did.

Logan ran in the direction the ambulance had gone, reaching for his phone as he did. Hamza answered on the third ring.

"Sir?"

"Bosco's ex-wife's address," Logan said. "Did you get it?"

"Aye. Are... are you alright, sir? You sound out of—"

"Text it to me," Logan ordered, then he hung up.

He reached the Volvo after a few minutes of running, stared at the ambulance parked outside the safe house for a few moments, then yanked open the driver's door of the car and jumped in.

His headlights filled the interior of the squad car parked in front of him. He muttered an apology to the dead officer in the back, then crunched the car into gear and floored it.

As he went speeding along Murray Road, he caught a glimpse of one of the paramedics moving through the house, and then he was turning onto Tower Road, tyres squealing in protest at his cornering speed.

Hamza's text arrived with a *bleep*. The address was in the Crown area. Close to the city centre, but plush. Made sense for a gangster's ex-wife.

It wasn't the sort of place the polis got called to frequently, and Logan wasn't overly familiar with it, but he knew it was near the Eastgate Centre enough for him to be able to find his way there. The night traffic was thin, so he didn't need to announce his arrival by sticking on the lights or siren.

If Logan was lucky, Bosco would be at the house. He doubted that, though. At best, he'd get a home address for the bastard, or some insight into where he might be.

One way or another, whatever it took, Bosco would lead him to Petrie, and Petrie would lead him to Maddie and Harris.

One way or another.

Whatever it took.

HAMZA GOT up from his chair and hugged Sinead. She leaned against him, grateful for the temporary support, then flopped down onto a chair when he stepped back and let her go.

"Stupid question, I know, but... how you doing?" he asked her.

Sinead shrugged. Her mouth formed a variety of shapes, testing out several possible responses. In the end, she settled on, "I don't know."

"You want coffee, or tea, or...?"

"Tyler's getting it. Thanks."

"No, no. Don't... It's fine," Hamza said, turning his seat to face her before sitting down.

She was still wearing her uniform. Its short sleeves showed crisscrossing red lines on her forearms, where she'd been anxiously scratching while waiting for news.

"How's your aunt?"

Sinead shrugged again. "Not great. But still with us." She looked down at the floor, took a breath, then forced herself to look up again. Her eyes were filled with some new emotion, some mix of dread and hope. "Anything on Harris?"

"Uniform's doing a huge push. Door to door across the whole area," Hamza said. "Got a press conference scheduled for tomorrow, but it's already out on the web and social media."

"So, no, then."

Hamza could only offer a sympathetic smile. "We'll find him. I'm looking into..."

He thought better of saying more. No point getting her hopes up. So far, the three-word combinations he'd tried had taken him all over the world, but none of them had brought him even close to Scotland, much less Inverness. He was barely a third of the way through, but he was starting to suspect he was wasting his time.

"You're looking into what?" Sinead pressed.

"It's probably nothing. I shouldn't have—"

"Hamza." The hope was draining from Sinead's face, leaving only the dread behind. "Please."

"Right. OK. But, like I say, it's probably nothing," Hamza began, and then he launched into the explanation he'd offered Logan earlier.

Unlike the DCI, Sinead was familiar with the what3words app, and was already reaching for her phone by the time DC Khaled was approaching the main thrust of the explanation.

"Have you got a list?" she asked, tapping the App Store icon with her thumb.

"Spreadsheet, aye," Hamza said.

"Let's see it, then."

Hamza spun his chair back to his computer, clicked back to the spreadsheet, and showed Sinead the list of all the possible alternatives he'd compiled.

"I can share it with you," he said.

"Tyler, too," Sinead instructed. "We'll split up what's left and work through it."

Hamza nodded. "OK. Just... like I say, it might not work."

"But it might," Sinead said. She bit on her bottom lip, like she was stopping tears from coming. "I have to do something."

"Right. Well, let's get it done, then," Hamza said, clicking the 'share' icon.

He had just filled out Sinead and Tyler's email addresses when the door to the Incident Room opened and a shocked-looking DC Neish came charging in.

He hadn't brought any coffee with him. Probably just as well, given how much his hands were shaking.

Announcing his arrival with a cry of, "Fucking Hell," Tyler stopped by the first available desk and leaned on it, supporting himself.

"What? What's wrong?" Sinead asked, already on her feet, already fearing the worst.

"Just heard. Boss's daughter's been taken. Wife's being rushed to hospital," Tyler said, tripping over the words as they came tumbling out of his mouth. "Constable who'd been watching the safe house was murdered. Fucker took his uniform. A PC Lindsay?"

"Ross Lindsay?" Sinead gasped.

"Maybe, I'm not sure. Little fella, I think. Aye, I mean, no' a dwarf, but..."

"We were at Tulliallan together," Sinead said. "Fuck. Nice guy, too."

"Where's Logan now?" Hamza asked.

Tyler shook his head. "No idea. Nobody seems to know."

Hamza glanced down at his phone sitting on the desk beside his computer. "Eh... I might," he said. "And he might be going to do something stupid."

The former Mrs Bosco Maximuke lived in a mock-Tudor place with a garden you could've held a five-a-side tournament in. There was a set of iron gates at the front, but the wall that surrounded the grounds was barely waist-height, so Logan abandoned the Volvo in the street and vaulted over it.

A downpour had accompanied the latter half of his drive over, but it had dialled back enough that only the occasional fat drop of rain went flecking off him as he hurried across the damp grass.

Spotlights illuminated high on the walls, and around the path as the sensors detected his approach. From an extension on the right that had probably once been a garage, a couple of large-sounding dogs began to bark and growl.

Shielding his eyes from the glare of the lights, Logan ran the last few yards to the front door. It was a heavy old wooden thing, with enough ironmongery bolted to it to build a Spitfire. He rattled the heavy round knocker, hammered on the wood with a fist, and then gave the doorbell half a dozen jabs for good measure.

After almost a minute of this, and with an increasing number of lights appearing in the windows of the houses across the street, a lock *clacked*. The door opened, and Logan found himself staring into a hallway with a sweeping staircase, yellowing wallpaper, and shelves laden with enough tacky ornaments to put Alice Forde's collection to shame.

What he did not see was a person. At least, not until he adjusted the angle of his gaze.

Bosco's daughter stood on a 'Please Wipe Your Feet' mat just inside the door. She was bare-footed, dressed in Christmas-themed pyjamas, and carried a sizeable axe in a way that suggested she wasn't only prepared to use it, she was actively looking forward to it.

Logan had not been prepared for this. He'd been expecting Bosco's wife, or some other adult he could shout at or threaten. He couldn't exactly threaten a ten-year-old, though. Axe or no bloody axe.

"What do you want?" she asked.

Christ, what was her name? Bosco had mentioned it a few times...

"Olivia," Logan said, trying not to make it sound like a question. She did nothing to confirm or deny the name, so Logan pressed on. "I'm looking for your dad. Bosco."

"I know what my dad's name is," Olivia replied. She looked the DCI up and down. "Why?"

"I just... I need to talk to him," Logan said. He looked past her into the house. "Is your mum around? Or someone else I can talk to?"

"Mum's sleeping," Olivia said. "She took her pills. She won't wake up until about lunchtime tomorrow."

"*Lunchtime*? What did she take, a horse tranquilliser?"

Olivia frowned, not getting the joke. "No. Sleeping pills."

"Aye. Fair enough. So... what? You're on your own?" Logan asked.

Olivia rolled her eyes and hefted the head of the axe onto her shoulder. She kept her grip on it, though, and it wouldn't take much for her to throw the blade forward and hack a chunk out of Logan's crotch.

"No, my mum's here. She's just sleeping," Olivia said. She spoke slowly and deliberately, like she'd come to the conclusion the DCI had learning difficulties. "And I don't know where my dad is."

"You know his home address, though."

Olivia looked him up and down. She took her time about it, not even remotely unnerved by the towering detective on the front step.

"You're the one who beat up Valdis and set my dad's office on fire," she said.

Logan fumbled for a response to this, ideally one that wouldn't immediately make her slam the door.

"That was... There was a misunderstanding," he said. "I shouldn't have done what I did."

"It was pretty awesome," Olivia said. "I liked watching it burn." She rubbed her cheek idly against the side of the axe's blade. "Fire's cool."

She gave him another once-over with her eyes, then sighed and dropped the axe to her side. "Wait here."

The door closed. Logan turned and looked up at the neighbouring houses. Three faces watched him from three different windows. At least one of them was talking into their phone, probably calling nine-nine-nine. He waved, then turned back to the door as it opened.

Olivia thrust a torn-out notebook page into his hands. "There. That's where he lives."

Logan looked down at the address. Out of town, but not too far.

"Thank you," he said. "I won't tell him you gave it to me."

The girl shrugged. "I don't care. It'll be funny," she said, then she slammed the door, and Logan heard the *clunk* of the lock sliding back into place.

"Jesus. She's going to be one to watch," he remarked, then he turned and jogged back across the grass.

He was just vaulting over the wall when a car pulled around the corner and onto the street. The headlights blinded him, forcing him to shield his eyes with an arm. He stuffed the address in a coat pocket, freeing both hands up for what might come next.

"Boss?"

Logan peered through the glare and saw a well-maintained head of hair emerge from the driver's side window of the car, followed by the head itself.

"Turn the fucking lights off," he growled.

"Shite, aye. Sorry, boss."

The lights went out, leaving only the spots they'd created swimming in the air before Logan's eyes.

"What are you doing here?" the DCI demanded, as Tyler stepped out onto the street.

It was hard to tell with all the glowing yellow orbs still dancing in front of his face, but DC Neish had a shady look about him, like he was hiding something.

"Just, eh, wanted to check if you needed back-up, boss," he said.

"Bollocks. You thought I was going to tear the place apart looking for Bosco," Logan replied.

Tyler smiled warily. "I, eh, we heard what happened. With your daughter. I'm sorry, boss. We just thought... We didn't want you burning this place to the ground, too."

"Aye, well, no need," Logan said. He produced the piece of paper from his pocket. "I got the address. I'm going to go check it out. If I need support, I'll call for it."

Tyler clicked his fingers a couple of times, playing out an anxious little rhythm. "Aye. Right. Just... don't do anything stupid, boss. I mean, not that you would... Just..."

"Thanks for the advice, Detective Constable," Logan said, pulling open the driver's door of the Volvo. "But I've got this. Does Hoon know?"

"I, eh, don't know, boss. I'd imagine so, given that he seems to know pretty much everything, but I haven't seen him."

If Hoon knew that Petrie had Maddie and that Logan was on the warpath, he'd be duty-bound to intervene. Whether he actually would or not, Logan wouldn't like to speculate. Best not give him the opportunity.

"If he asks where I am, you don't know," Logan said.

Tyler hesitated, wrestling with something, then he gave a nod. "Right. OK. But, I don't like this, boss. It feels... I don't know. I've got a bad feeling about it all."

"Aye. You and me both, son," Logan said. "You and me both." He started to get in the car, then stopped with one hand on the roof. "How's Sinead?"

"She's coping," Tyler said. "Her and Hamza are going through some spreadsheet of... like addresses, or something? It's keeping her busy, which is what she needs."

"It is," Logan agreed. "Keep an eye on her. She's strong, but... Keep an eye."

"I will, boss," Tyler said. He looked down at his feet, took a breath to compose himself, then came right out with the question that had been gnawing at him over the past few hours. "We're going to get him, aren't we?"

"Petrie?"

"Harris," Tyler said. "I mean... You know Petrie better than most. If we find him... *when*... Harris is going to be alright, isn't he? Sinead's already been through so much, boss. With her parents. And now Val, and... If anything happens to Harris..."

"He'll be fine, son," Logan said. He had nothing to base this on, of course. Whatever game Petrie was playing now, it wasn't the same rules as before. But he knew what the DC needed to keep going, and so he gave him it. "Harris will be fine, if we catch this bastard soon."

Tyler seemed to grow an inch or two. "Right, boss. Best get to it, then," he said.

"Aye. Best had," Logan said. He tapped the roof of the car a couple of times in farewell, then dropped the rest of the way into the driver's seat.

Before he could even start the engine, his phone rang. It wasn't the usual ring, and it took him a moment to recognise it.

Video call.

Bringing the phone from his pocket, he saw Shona Maguire's name emblazoned across the screen. He hesitated with his thumb over the answer button, then swiped to reject the call.

She'd be checking on him, that was all. A friendly social call, to make sure he was OK after he'd ended things so abruptly last time.

The phone was halfway back to his pocket when she called him back. This time, he tapped the other button.

This time, he answered.

And there and then, in that car, in that moment, everything changed.

CHAPTER THIRTY-TWO

Petrie was there. Logan couldn't see him, but he could hear his voice. That hoarse, scratchy rasp that had earned him his nickname. That same voice that had been goading him on the phone of late.

"Is that him?" Petrie said. "Has he answered?"

On screen, Shona nodded. There was blood on her top lip, and her cheeks shone with tears and thin black rivulets of mascara that she hadn't got around to taking off.

"J-Jack," she said. Her voice was shaking, but she was doing her best to hold it together. "It's him. It's Petrie."

"You don't have to tell him. He knows it's me. Don't you, Jack?"

Logan flashed his headlights several times, then held up a hand, signalling for Tyler to wait.

"Owen. You need to stop this," Logan warned. "You need to stop before you make it worse for yourself."

"Worse? This isn't worse, this is *great*. I'm loving life again, Jack," Petrie hissed from the other side of the phone. "After all those years locked up, these last few days... well, I'll be honest, they've been a bit of a dream come true. And, the best part is, we're just getting to the good bit!"

The footage was handheld and shaky, and Logan caught a glimpse of a movie poster on the wall at Shona's back.

They were still at her place. Logan thumbed the microphone mute button and beckoned Tyler over, as Petrie's voice continued to seep from the phone's speaker.

"Rule one. You come here, and you come alone," he said. "If you want her to live, you come alone. If you call it in, I'll know about it."

"Wait," Logan told Tyler, signalling for him to stop.

"Jack? I can't hear you. Do you understand rule number one?"

Logan activated his phone's microphone again. "I understand, Owen. But, why are you doing all this?"

"Why am I doing this?" Petrie asked, and his tone, which had been light and taunting so far, took a darker turn. "Why do you fucking *think* I'm doing it, Jack?"

"We can talk about this, Owen. We can sort—"

"Rule number *two*," Petrie declared, shouting him down.

The video footage swept across the walls and ceiling as the phone was turned around. A quarter of Petrie's face filled the screen—an eye, part of his scarred forehead, and a direct line of sight up one flared nostril.

"Get here quick," he urged. He kept the camera on himself as he walked behind Shona and caught her by the hair. He yanked her head back with enough force to make her cry out in pain, then lowered his head so they were side by side, like lovers in a photo booth. "All that time rotting in that hospital you put me in means I have a tendency to get bored easily." He ran a hand through Shona's hair and grinned. "And, believe me, neither of you wants that."

And then, before Logan could say a word, the call was ended.

"Shite!" Logan spat, tossing the phone into the dooket beneath the dash.

"Boss?" Tyler asked, cautiously approaching the car. "What's going on?"

"It's Petrie. He's got Shona."

Tyler looked at him blankly, then realisation registered on his face. "The Pathologist? Where?"

"Her place," Logan said.

"I'll call it in," Tyler said, reaching for his phone.

"No! If we call it in, he'll kill her," Logan said. "I'm going. Alone."

"Jesus, boss..." Tyler began to protest, but a look from the DCI cut it dead.

Logan jumped out of the Volvo, fished in his pocket, and thrust the notebook page into Tyler's hands. "Bosco's house," he explained. "Go, see what's what. But quietly."

"Bosco's house?" Tyler repeated, looking down at the address.

"Drive by. That's all," Logan instructed. "Scope the place, but do not engage with the fucker if he's there. Don't even let him see you. Drive past, look, drive on. Repeat, if necessary. Do not approach without backup. That clear?"

Tyler was still staring down at the address. A shout from Logan kick-started him again.

"*Is that clear*, Tyler?"

"Yes, boss. Sorry, boss. I'm on it," the DC said. "Bosco's place. Drive by only. Don't engage."

Logan clapped him on the arm. "Don't fuck this up."

Tyler smiled grimly. "Aye," he said. "You, too, boss."

A TEXT HAD COME through a minute or so later, Shona presumably having explained that Logan didn't have her address. He'd been vaguely aware that it was somewhere near the Kessock Bridge, but he'd assumed it was on the Inverness side.

He'd also assumed it had been a flat, so when he pulled up outside a ramshackle whitewashed cottage looking out onto the Beauly Firth, he had to double-check to make sure he had the right place.

There were four windows visible from the front, two downstairs and another two which looked like relatively recent additions in the loft space. The curtains were drawn in all of them, and all but one were in darkness.

Logan spent a few seconds staring at the upper left window, where the light had been left on. Were they in there? Was it a trap?

Of course, it was a trap. Petrie was hardly going to confront him one-on-one. But, trap or not, he had to go in and face whatever was waiting for him.

The front door was unlocked. It was an old, heavy thing, and badly in need of a coat of paint. He'd expected it to creak ominously when he opened it, but it glided smoothly on its hinges, and he clicked it quietly closed again behind him.

The hall was oddly shaped, with three doors leading off it and a steep set of wooden stairs leading to a landing above. The ceiling was not so low that Logan bumped his head, but low enough that he felt sure he was going to. He ducked a little as he approached the steps, and listened from the bottom.

There was no sound from upstairs. No squeaking of floorboards, no chattering of voices, no sobs, or cries.

Nothing.

The steps were essentially a large wooden ladder with elongated rungs. Theoretically, it was probably possible to go up them without using your hands, but given his size and the width of the hatch above, Logan felt it best not to try.

While the well-oiled door hinges had been a pleasant surprise, the steps completely betrayed him. Each one creaked out a different note as he placed his weight on it, and any hopes of keeping the element of surprise completely evaporated.

He stopped with his head just below the hatch and looked up and around at the darkened landing, in case Petrie was waiting to brain him. Seeing nobody lurking near the edge, he hurried up the last few steps and found himself in a space not much bigger than a large cupboard. It would hold two people at a push. One, if they were both Logan's size.

A poster promoting the film, *Lethal Weapon 2*, hung from one wall. It was in a frame, and had two signatures in silver pen below the names of the main stars at the top of the image.

Beside it was the door that led to the only room with the lights on. The door stood ajar, letting the light seep out through the gap.

Logan edged it open cautiously, eyes darting up and down to check for traps or tripwires. He doubted Petrie would bother with such things, but he'd rather not find out the hard way.

The room he entered was a small bedroom, with a neatly-made single bed along one wall, a small bookcase against the other, and not a lot else to write home about. It didn't strike Logan as being to Shona's taste at all. Spare bedroom, he guessed.

Not only was it lacking Shona's design taste, it was also lacking Shona herself.

Logan was about to leave, when he spotted the glossy squares spaced regularly on the bed. At first, he'd thought it was just the design of the quilt cover, but as he turned towards the door, he saw them more clearly.

Polaroid photographs. Dozens of them, neatly presented for him to find.

His legs wouldn't move. Not at first. They rooted him to the spot, unwilling to take him closer, unwilling to let him see.

But he had to look. He had to know.

They relented at last, and he went stumbling over. He didn't see any one particular image, but rather got an impression of them all. Pain, suffering, and fear emanated from the display. The pictures ranged from garish, wide-eyed close-ups with too much flash, to wider shots filled with deep pools of darkness.

They showed Harris.

They showed Maddie.

Both tied up. Both in different locations, he thought.

Both crying. Both bleeding.

But both alive.

There was a thump from downstairs. Logan spun around and raced for the steps. He slid backwards down them—a clumsy descent, followed by an even clumsier landing that drew a hiss of pain through his teeth.

The sound he'd heard had come from directly below, so he turned to the door on his right, placed his palm flat against it, then pushed it open.

From the darkness, there came a muffled sob. *Shona.*

Logan found the light switch and clicked it on. Shona winced in the sudden brightness of it, recoiling and screwing her eyes shut in shock, which meant she didn't see the look of horror that crossed Logan's face before he could chase it away again.

Shona sat in the centre of the room, tied to a chair. This was bad, but it was not the worst part.

She had been beaten, her face already bruised, her bloodied nose crusting on the gag that was tied tight across her mouth.

This was not the worst part, either.

The worst part, by some considerable margin, was the bomb.

"Oh," muttered Logan, as the device on Shona's chest gave a *whirr* and a *click*. "Shite."

CHAPTER THIRTY-THREE

DI Forde lay on his side with the covers pulled up under his chin, listening to the toilet flushing for the third time that night.

"Sorry, but I've a weak bladder," was Alice's go-to excuse whenever her midnight micturitions roused her sleeping husband. Ben had tried suggesting she maybe not neck those six cups of tea in the two hours before turning in, but Alice was having none of it. It was a genetic condition, she insisted. Her mother was the same.

Tonight, though, she hadn't disturbed him, because he hadn't been to sleep. He'd been trying since Hoon had sent him home, but it continued to evade him. How could he sleep when that boy was out there somewhere? How could he sleep when the others were still trying to bring him home?

"Did I wake you up?" asked Alice, sliding into the bed behind him. She snuggled up to him, siphoning off some of his warmth. "It's my bladder. You know what it's like."

"Aye, I know," Ben said, his voice partly muffled by the pillow. "But, no. I wasn't sleeping."

"Well, you should be," Alice said, raising her head to look him in the eye. "You'll do nobody any good if you're knackered. And they'll all be done-in tomorrow morning. You can go in brand new. Fresh pair of eyes. It'll be useful."

"And what if the boy's dead by then, Alice?" Ben asked, half-turning to look at her.

"Then that would be tragic. Horrible. Just... horrible," she said. "But he's not my concern. You are. Besides, Bob Hoon sent you home. There's no arguing with him. Unless you'd rather get suspended. Which, I'll be honest, I'd be in favour of."

She lay back down again. Ben faced front. The alarm clock sat next to the bed, but he'd turned it around so he wasn't just lying there watching the minutes tick by. Somehow, lying there *not* watching the minutes tick by felt better.

"You've given half your life to that place. You can have a night off. I thought I'd stop worrying when you left the forces, but I worry about you more now, if anything," Alice continued. She yawned, then smacked her lips together a few times as if tasting it. "You're not as young as you used to be, Ben. It's high bloody time you started keeping that in—"

The sentence ended in a snore, and Ben was grateful for it. The last thing he needed now was a lecture on how old and useless he was, even a well-meaning one.

Reaching for the bedside table, he turned the alarm clock around, pulled his covers more tightly under his chin, and went back to watching the minutes creep slowly on.

Bosco Maximuke's gaff was on the north side of the city, and the sight of it made Tyler sick to his stomach.

There were a number of reasons for this. He wasn't going to lie and say that anxiety wasn't one of them. His last encounter with Bosco Maximuke had not exactly gone well for him, and it wasn't something he was in a rush to repeat.

The main reason, though, was the size of the bloody place. It sat on its own, surrounded by high fences on a patch of land he'd need a compass and map to navigate across. Half of the house looked old, but painstakingly restored. That part was all sandstone and pillars, while the other half was a metal and glass L-shape that had been built onto the side and wrapped around the back.

Turf had been laid on the roof of the extension. This had presumably been done in an attempt to make the thing look less conspicuous, but in reality, had the exact opposite effect. Who the hell had grass on the roof?

It was all a bit *Grand Designs* for Tyler's tastes, but he resented it, anyway. The place had to be worth a fortune. A million, easy. Far beyond anything Tyler could ever hope to achieve.

He had driven around it twice now, but had seen no sign of life inside. The windows were all in darkness. The gates and doors were all closed. The house had a driveway out front that could've held a dozen cars, but it stood empty.

The house, as far as he could tell, was deserted.

Tyler stopped his car around the side of the building, at the point where it was closest to the fence. There was a gate there. Unlike the big double set at the end of the driveway, this one didn't have a camera above it, or an intercom button fixed on a pole beside it.

It was... just a gate. Tall, yes, but climbable.

He shook his head, admonishing himself. No. He couldn't go in. He had no warrant, for one thing. Logan had told him not to—that was another very valid reason.

And then there was Bosco himself. If Bosco caught him sneaking around, there was no saying what the Russian would do to him, but he could be fairly confident it would be nothing pleasant.

And, what if he did something to his mum?

No.

It was dangerous. Reckless.

Insane.

But Harris might be in there.

And how could he live with himself if he didn't check?

With a turn of the key, Tyler switched off the engine, unbuckled his seatbelt, and opened the door.

"What are you doing? Don't fucking touch it!"

Logan whipped his hand back in fright at the sharpness of Shona's outburst. "Jesus! Don't do that!" he told her. "I wasn't going to touch it."

"You bloody were. You had your hand out," Shona hissed back.

Logan had been expecting her to start crying when he removed the gag, but she'd been remarkably composed, and had mostly just snapped at him whenever he tried to examine the device more closely. He was almost starting to regret taking it off.

"I was looking, that's all," he said.

"Look with your eyes! Don't go pissing about with it unless you know what you're doing."

Logan very much did not know what he was doing.

Sure, he'd come across explosive devices before, but they were usually bodge-jobs with less explosive potential than a disposable barbecue. This one, though? This one looked serious.

It was all metal plates and wires, with a canister taped on either side of a plastic box in the middle, where the *clicking* and *whirring* sounds were coming from.

"Take me through what he said again," Logan urged.

"He said there were new rules," Shona repeated for the third time now. "Rule one, you're not allowed to call the bomb squad, or he blows this thing up. Which, in case there's any confusion, I definitely don't want. Rule two is the same as last time." Her eyes flicked down to the device, then back to Logan. "*Hurry*."

Logan straightened and stepped back a couple of paces. "And he definitely said 'new rules'?"

"Yes."

"And he definitely said 'bomb squad'?"

"Yes! He definitely said 'bomb squad'!"

"You're sure? It's important."

"I got a sense that it was fucking important, Jack," Shona spat, her Irish accent coming through thicker than ever. She shot the bomb on her chest an anxious look, then lowered her voice to a whisper. "Believe me, I'm not underestimating the importance of any of it."

"Sorry. Aye," Logan said. "Just... just try to stay calm."

"I'm calm," Shona told him. "I'm perfectly calm. Given the circumstances, I think I'm the Sea of fucking Tranquillity, don't you?"

Petrie had shaken her badly, Logan could tell. That was hardly surprising, of course. It was to her credit that she wasn't a gibbering wreck.

The injuries on her face seemed mostly superficial, and she'd dismissed Logan's attempts to check her over more thoroughly, at least until such time as there wasn't an explosive device ticking away on her upper torso.

Logan ran a hand down his face, his fingers rasping across his stubble as they passed over his mouth and down to his chin. He sighed then, shot the window a glance, and laid out the options.

"OK, assuming the bomb squad warning is right, and we can't call them, we've got two choices," he said.

"And they are?" Shona asked, sounding like she didn't like any of them already.

"One, I cut this off, chuck it out the window, and we both hope for the best."

"I'm not a big fan of that one," Shona said, after a nanosecond's contemplation. "What's option two?"

"Ben," Logan said.

Shona frowned. "Ben?"

"DI Forde. He's ex-military. Worked with bomb disposal for a big chunk of that time. Landmines, mostly, I think, but he might be able to have a crack at this."

"Might? What the fuck's *might*?"

"Will. He'll know what to do," Logan said.

Shona bit her lip. Aside from the blood and the bruising, there was no colour left in her face.

"Shit. I don't know, Jack..." she said.

"He's not the bomb squad. That's Petrie's rule. I can't call the bomb squad. Well, I wouldn't be. I'd be calling Ben."

"But he said you couldn't call for back-up," Shona reminded him. It was clear from her expression that she wasn't a fan of this plan, either. Unfortunately, there were no others left for her to choose from.

"'New rules.' That's what he told you. That means the old rules don't apply. If I call Ben, I'm sticking to the rules," Logan said. He gave a slightly uncertain tilt of his head. "Technically."

"So... it's a loophole?" Shona asked, her voice rising again. She caught it, this time, before it climbed too high. "How is that a good idea?"

"I'm not saying it's a good idea, but it's the least bad idea we've got," Logan said. "I mean, unless you've got anything better up your sleeve?"

By the looks of her, Shona would dearly love to have something better up her sleeve. Also by the looks of her, she didn't.

"Right, then," Logan said. He turned and raised his voice, addressing the house at large. If Petrie had bugged the place, the DCI wanted to make it very clear what he was doing. "I'm not calling the bomb squad. Like you said. I'm calling DI Ben Forde. He's not involved with any counter-terrorism or explosives-related departments. He's on my team."

There was nothing to indicate that Petrie was even listening, much less that he'd heard. Logan waited a few seconds in case some sort of confirmation came, then turned back to Shona and reached for his phone.

"Right, then. I'm calling Ben," he said, keeping his voice as light and worry-free as possible. "We'll have you out of that thing in no time."

Ben answered the phone within two rings, jumping on it before it woke his wife up.

"Jack?" he said, after a glance at the caller ID.

"Thank Christ! Ben, I'm at Shona Maguire's. We've... got a situation here. I need you up and dressed and over here, fast as you can."

Ben looked down at his trousers and half-buttoned shirt. He'd concluded that sleep wasn't going to be coming any time soon, and that what Alice didn't know wouldn't hurt her.

"What's the situation?" Ben asked.

"Eh... we've got a bomb."

Ben blinked. "You've got a bomb?"

"Aye."

"Well... can you get rid of it?"

"No. That's what we need you for," Logan explained.

"Then it's no' me you want, it's the bomb squad," Ben said, fastening up the remaining buttons of his shirt.

"Can't. Petrie said if I call the bomb squad, he'll blow it. He must have some sort of remote control on it. But he didn't say anything about calling you."

Ben grimaced and looked back at the door to the bedroom. He could hear Alice in there, snoring away. She'd be up for another bathroom break soon, and would notice he was gone.

She'd worry.

But then, she always did.

"Text me the address," Ben said, flattening down his collar. "I'm on my way."

CHAPTER THIRTY-FOUR

TYLER RAN, DOUBLED-OVER, ACROSS THE GRASS IN THE DIRECTION OF THE house. It was, to his dismay, further than it looked.

Each scurried step was accompanied by a breathless, "Oh shit," as he scrambled for the cover afforded by the pools of shadow around the darkened building.

After what felt like an inordinately long time, he slammed himself against the sandstone side of the house, and stood there with his back flat against it, gulping down the cool night air.

This was stupid. What was he bloody playing at? He was trespassing at least, but a good solicitor could get that upped to housebreaking without too much difficulty. He could lose his job for this. His freedom, maybe.

Or, if Bosco caught him, his life.

And for what? There was nothing to suggest that Harris was in there. If it came to it, it was allowable to enter a property without a warrant, provided there was evidence that someone inside was in danger.

But, he had no evidence of that. None. And he didn't think, 'Frankly, I just don't trust the shifty Russian bastard,' was likely to stand up to a whole lot of scrutiny.

He was getting his breath back from the awkward, bent-over run. In hindsight, he should've come striding over confidently. If anyone saw him sprinting furiously with his head at waist height, it was likely to arouse some suspicions.

"Walk in like you bloody own the place," Logan had once told him. "Make them feel like they're the ones who shouldn't be there."

That was easy to say when you were DCI Jack Logan. His size alone made most folk sit up and take notice, and his glare would soon grab the attention of those who didn't.

For Tyler, here and now, stealth was the key. He'd find a way to look inside, and then slip out unnoticed. If Harris or the boss's daughter were in there, then...

Well, he'd cross that bridge if he came to it.

For now, the important thing was to find a way inside.

Sliding along the wall, Tyler stopped at the first window he came to. It was a sliding sash design, but firmly locked so he couldn't budge it.

"Not to worry," he whispered. It was comforting to hear the sound of his voice. It meant he hadn't yet been horribly killed.

Or, it would've been a comfort, had he not sounded quite so terrified.

"Plenty more where that came from," he said, then he squatted, did an ungraceful side-shuffle under the window, and straightened up again on the other side.

It was a big house. There were a lot of windows.

This was going to be a very long night.

Hamza leaned back in his chair, grabbed a wrist with the opposite hand, then stretched until his back gave a deeply satisfying *clunk*.

He buried his face in his hands as he yawned, then turned his chair to the desk where Sinead was sitting. Her head was raising and lowering as she compared the words on the computer screen with those on her phone.

"Getting anywhere?"

Sinead gave her phone's screen a tap, watched it hopefully, then tutted and shook her head. "Ukraine," she said. "You?"

"Nowhere close yet, and we're over halfway through," Hamza said. As time had ticked on, he'd started to lose faith in the whole idea. He was beginning to see why Hoon hadn't wanted to waste resources on it. "This might be a waste of time."

"Maybe," Sinead said. "But we won't know until we go through them."

Hamza rubbed his eyes with finger and thumb, then stood up. "I'm going to get coffee. You want some?"

Sinead was already back to her computer screen, clicking and scrolling to the next set of possible word variations.

"Hmm?" she asked, when she realised Hamza had spoken to her. "Sorry, I was... What?"

"Coffee," Hamza said. "Want some?"

"Uh, yes. Please," Sinead replied, her eyes pulling back to the screen.

"Any word from Tyler yet?" Hamza asked.

Sinead's gaze flicked to the clock on the wall, then to her phone. "Uh, no, actually," she said. "Should've heard something by now. Shouldn't we?"

"He'll be helping the boss with something. That's all," Hamza assured her.

"Maybe I should phone him."

"I'm sure he'll call when he can," Hamza said, but this didn't reassure Sinead at all. She rubbed her thumb slowly back and forth across the phone's screen like she was stroking it. "Or... maybe give it twenty minutes. If he hasn't turned up then, give him a call."

Sinead gave a nod and set her phone down on the desk. "Aye. Makes sense. I'll do that," she said, then she turned her attention back to her list of words.

There were over twenty-five combinations left on her screen. Checking them wasn't difficult, but it took time.

Time that Harris might not have.

No. She pushed the thought away. They were going to find him. They were going to bring him home.

They had to.

Sinead studied the words on screen, then picked her phone up again.

This was going to be a very long night.

"I'll give you this much," said Logan. "It's a hell of a second date."

Shona didn't laugh. Not quite. She still had a fuck-off great explosive device strapped to her chest, after all. But she smiled, and that, as far as Logan was concerned, was good enough.

"Always knew I'd get you back to my place someday," she replied. "Granted, it's not quite what I had in mind..." She let out a sigh. "God, I'd love a cigarette."

Logan turned and scanned the room around him. It was the sort of place an estate agent would describe as 'cosy, with character and charm.' Tiny, in other words, and cluttered with a lot of weird shit.

"Where are they?" he asked.

"Where are what?" Shona asked.

"The cigarettes."

"Oh. No, I don't smoke. I've never smoked," she said. "It's just, I always thought about trying it to see what all the fuss is about. And I reckoned, if I'm going to be blown to bits anyway, lung cancer's probably the least of my concerns."

"You're not going to get blown to bits," Logan said.

"Yeah, well..." she replied, unconvinced. "I'm making a bucket list, just in case."

"'Have a fag,' hardly seems bucket list material," Logan replied.

Shona tutted. "Well, I can hardly go bungee-jumping in my current condition, can I?" she pointed out. "I'll take what I can get."

She had a lop-sided old armchair in the corner of the room, the covering a Frankenstein's monster of different fabrics, where she'd patched it, either through necessity or—and Logan felt this was more likely—by choice. He wrestled it closer to the middle of the room so he could sit facing her.

"What else is on the list, then?" he asked. "Not that you'll need it," he hurriedly added.

He'd hoped Ben would be here by now, but there was still no sign. Keeping her talking was keeping her calm, though, so he was quick to head along this new avenue of conversation.

Who was he kidding? Shona had already managed to get a handle on her panic and was coping well. The conversation was keeping *him* calm. Keeping him distracted from all the thoughts and fears that gnawed hungrily at his insides. Thoughts of what Maddie and Harris might be going through. Thoughts of what Petrie might have done to them. Be doing to them, right now.

Thoughts that, if he surrendered to them, would have him curled up in a ball on the floor.

So, he pushed those thoughts down. Stomped them into the ground.

"Bucket list top five," he urged. "Go."

Shona pursed her lips and moved them from side to side, thinking this through. "In general, or based on the current situation?"

"Either."

"OK. OK. Current situation, then," she said. "We'll call having a smoke number five."

"That can't be top five. Seriously?"

"Who's bucket list is this?" Shona asked, shooting him a reproachful look.

"Sorry. Go on. Number four," Logan urged.

"Right. Four. And this is a biggie. I would fecking love to go for a pee," she said.

The sombre tone she adopted and the intensity in her eyes brought a burst of laughter from Logan that he wouldn't have thought himself capable of. Hysteria, probably, but he'd take it.

It proved infectious, and Shona joined in, too, much to her apparent dismay. "Christ, don't make me laugh, or I'll be ticking that one off the list right here and now. And I've just cleaned this carpet."

There was also a chance she might explode, Logan thought, although he decided against saying it out loud.

"Right, number three?" he asked, pressing on.

"Number three...?" Shona clicked her tongue against the roof of her mouth. "A comfier chair. This one's got a wicker seat. I don't know what possessed me. That's a lie. I do know. It was cheap."

Logan looked down at the wooden chair she was sitting on. The wiring of the bomb ran around to the back and wrapped around her wrists, holding them together perhaps even more effectively than the wrap of silver tape Petrie had also applied.

"I'd give you this seat, but I'm not sure moving's the best idea," he told her.

"Moving? I'm trying not to bloody breathe, never mind move," Shona replied. "I've accepted I'm not going to tick too many of these off, by the way. Don't you stress yourself. Although..."

Logan raised an eyebrow. "Although what?"

"You could maybe help me with number two." Her eyes widened in horror. "I don't mean... Jesus. On the list, I mean. Number two on the list. You could help me with that."

"What is it?" Logan asked, neatly glossing over any possible misinterpretation of what she'd said in a remarkable show of self-restraint.

"You could scratch my nose for me. Sure, it's driving me up the wall," Shona said. She scrunched her face up, presenting the offending item to him. "Just right on the end there."

Logan leaned closer. "Where? Here?" He reached out a finger and scratched. "That it?"

"Up a bit," Shona said. "Up a—There! Right there!"

She moaned with relief as Logan took care of the offending itch.

"That got it?"

"That got it," she confirmed. "Oh. God. That's better. I so should've made that number five."

Logan sat back. He stole a glance at his watch, then the window, before turning his attention back to Shona.

"Right. The big one. What's top of the list?"

There was some colour coming back to Shona's cheeks now. A slight reddening beneath the blood and the bruises.

"Kiss me," she said.

Logan snorted. "What?"

"Christ, you going deaf in your old age?" she asked with a smirk. Her eyes searched his face. "Kiss me."

"Me? Kiss *you*?" he blurted. "Now? With..." He gestured to the bomb. "...everything?"

"Well, it might be my last chance," she pointed out. "So, yes. Kiss me. Unless..." Her face fell. "Shite. Unless you don't want to. Have I been...? Oh, God. I've been totally misreading things, haven't I?"

"No. No. I mean, you haven't. I mean, I do. Want to," Logan said.

Shona drew in a big breath of relief, then shot the bomb a worried look, turned her head and let the air out slowly again.

"Then, kiss me," she said. "It's number one on the bucket list. You can't say no to a dying woman's last request."

"You're not dying," Logan told her. "We're going to get this sorted."

"Well, whatever," Shona said. "You going to kiss me or what?"

For a moment, Logan didn't move. He wanted to kiss her. He did. He had for a long time.

But now? Like this? With Harris and Maddie out there somewhere? With everything that was going on?

Not to mention the dirty great bomb.

"Bucket list," she reminded him. "Jump to it."

At that, Logan sat forward in the chair. It didn't bring him close enough, so he got down on his knees and shuffled to her. With her sitting and him kneeling, they were at about the same height.

Heads level. Face to face.

"Right, then. Here goes," he said, in what surely qualified as one of the least romantic build-ups in modern history.

He leaned in.

Shona shut her eyes.

There was a knock at the door before their lips could meet. A solid hammering. A polis knock.

"Jack? Jack, you in there?" called DI Ben Forde. "Open the door, it's pishing down out here!"

"Ben," Logan said, holding Shona's gaze.

She smacked her lips together, smiled weakly, and sighed through her teeth. "So close," she lamented.

Logan got up clumsily, using the patchwork chair for support. "I'd better let him in."

"Yeah," Shona agreed. "I suppose you'd better had."

Despite the urgency of the situation, Ben spent a couple of seconds wiping his feet on the mat outside the front door before he stepped inside. Logan closed the door behind him, and shot his friend a grim smile.

"Thanks for coming. I didn't know who else to call."

"Not a problem." Ben indicated the only downstairs room with the lights on. "She in here?"

"Aye." Logan lowered his voice to a whisper. "There's something else you should know."

Ben groaned and raised his eyes to Logan. "God. What now?"

"It's Maddie," Logan said. "He's... Petrie. He's got Maddie."

"Oh, Jack." Ben gripped the DCI's arm. "Oh, Jack. I'm sorry. When? How?"

"Got her at the safe house."

"And Vanessa?"

Logan shook his head.

"Oh, shite. Jack, I'm so sorry," Ben whispered.

"What? Oh, no. She's no' dead. I meant she wasn't taken. She was stabbed in both thighs, though. Not life-threatening. Uniform got her taken into Raigmore."

There was the sound of a throat being cleared from the room next door.

"Uh, hello?" Shona called. "Big bomb in here. Remember?"

"Just coming," Logan replied. He lowered his voice again. "She doesn't know. About what's happened to them. She's got enough to worry about."

"Makes sense," Ben said. He released his grip on Logan's arm and offered a supportive smile. "Right, then. Let's go see what we're dealing with."

CHAPTER THIRTY-FIVE

Tyler had done almost a complete circuit of the house when he found the open window. He cursed himself—had he gone left instead of right at that first window, he'd have found this one in under a minute. Instead, he'd spent the best part of half an hour creeping and crawling his way around the outside of the building, checking every possible entrance he came to.

He'd looked inside most of them, too, shining his torch in through the glass when he was sure nobody was lurking within. He'd seen nothing incriminating, unless you counted the ninety-inch curved TVs, and the artworks that probably cost twice Tyler's annual salary.

Bastard.

The open window was another of the sash types, and the gap at the bottom was large enough for him to slide his hands in. The space beyond, from what he could gather, was some sort of utility room, although it had enough washers and driers in it that it might well be a fully-operational laundrette.

The rain rattled on his back and the backs of his legs. He was already soaked to the skin, and the thought of getting into shelter—even in the house of a Russian gangster, which he had illegally entered—made him throw caution to the wind.

He pushed up on the window. At first, it didn't budge, but a bit of shoving and a fair amount of grunting, and it finally succumbed. The window shot up inside the frame with a high-pitched screech, and banged against the top.

Tyler spun on his heels, pressing himself flat against the wall beside the window, listening for any signs of movement.

Nothing.

The only sounds were the pattering of the rain and the thumping of his own heart inside his chest. As his panic subsided, even his racing heart quietened, until the rainfall was the only sound left.

The house had to be empty. Somebody would've heard that, surely?

He inched out from behind the wall and risked a glance in through the open window. The utility room was still in darkness. The door remained closed.

"This is fucking... nonsense," Tyler whispered to himself, then he reached in through the window, found a handhold on the radiator fixed to the wall beneath it, and slid clumsily inside.

He hit the lino floor with a *thack*, and sat there for another few terrifying moments, listening for any movement within the house.

Satisfied that there was nothing, he got up, dusted himself down, and crept to the door. He opened it just a crack at first and put his eye to the gap. There was a hallway outside the room. Long and narrow, he thought, although he couldn't be sure from that angle.

Nobody moving around, though, so he opened the door enough that he could lean out, quickly glance in both directions, and lean back in.

Empty.

Thank Christ.

Tyler stepped out into the hall, keeping close to the wall. To the left of the door, the corridor ended at a window that looked out onto the grounds at the front of the house.

To the right, it led to a T-junction. A left there would take him through to the rest of the building, he figured, so that was the way he went, tiptoeing along the wall to remain as silent as possible.

It occurred to him a few steps in that he should've worn gloves. He'd have left fingerprints everywhere, and what he was doing was technically illegal.

OK, not even 'technically.' It was fully illegal. He had broken into a man's home on a whim. Even Logan had told him just to drive by the place. Even Logan wouldn't be this reckless.

Would he?

Tyler briefly contemplated going back to the car for gloves, but the damage was already done. Best to press on, do a sweep of the place, and see if Harris or Maddie were here. A quick look, then out. No harm, no foul. No one would ever even know he had been there.

At the T-junction, he looked to the right first. That branch led to another door, much like the one he'd just come through. A bathroom, maybe.

He looked along the branch to the left. The hallway led into a large open-plan living space. The kitchen area, from what he could tell, was bigger than his whole flat, and he could only see part of it.

"Bastard," he said, out loud this time.

He was halfway along the hallway when he heard movement. He froze. There were no doors on either side of him, nothing for him to hide behind. He strained to hear the sound again, but his heart was hammering inside his chest, and all he could hear was the blood surging around inside his head.

Tyler had just taken a backwards step when the dog appeared from around the corner at the end of the hallway ahead. It was, he noted, quite a big dog. As dogs went, this one was exactly the size of a large Doberman. Exactly the same shape and colour, too.

"Oh, shit," Tyler whispered, as the dog's mouth became a showcase for its teeth and gums. It growled, its ears stood up. The short fur on the back of its neck did the same. "Good dog," said Tyler, raising a calming hand.

And with that, the animal launched itself at him, snarling and barking. Tyler spun on the spot and ran, skidding on the polished wooden floor as he threw himself around the corner and powered back towards the utility room.

He caught a glimpse of car headlights approaching through the big window at the end of the corridor, but that felt like a problem for another time. He could hear the dog right behind him now, could practically feel its breath on the back of his legs.

The door was still ajar. He shouldered through it, already turning, and closed the door with a *slam*. There was a thud and a yelp from the other side, then the barking resumed, more furious than ever, as claws scraped and scratched at the door.

From out front, Tyler heard the sound of a car door closing. No, wait. Doors. Plural. Multiple.

Fuck.

"Shh. Shut up," he hissed through the door, but this just made the dog bark louder still. At the rate the animal was tearing at the wood, it would get to him before whoever had just pulled up made it inside.

Time to abort.

Tyler hurried to the open window, stuck a leg through, and sprackled out. He ducked, as another set of headlights swept up the driveway, their glare licking across the lawn ahead of him.

The dog was still barking, but he could hear other sounds from inside the house now. Voices. Raised. Angry.

Shit, shit, shit.

There was nothing else for it. The moment the headlights had passed, Tyler ran, throwing himself towards the gate he'd clambered over. His legs powered like pistons, propelling himself across the endless expanse of grass, putting as much distance between himself and the house as he could.

And then, when he was just past the halfway mark, the inevitable happened. The door to the utility room was thrown open, and the barking of one extremely pissed-off Doberman began to grow exponentially louder as it leaped through the open window and gave chase.

Tyler wasted a lungful of air on a selection of hasty expletives, then he fixed his gaze on the gate, and begged his legs to move faster.

"How you doing there, Shona?" Ben asked. "Holding up alright?"

"I'll be honest, I've had better days."

Ben was already studying the device on her chest, and only half-heard the reply. "Hmm? Oh. Aye. I can imagine. Well, let's see about getting this thing off you, will we?"

"Can you do it?" asked Logan. He was hovering behind the DI, peering over his shoulder and watching him work.

"Maybe if you gave me a bit of room..." Ben suggested.

"Right. Sorry."

Logan took a backwards step. Ben rolled his eyes.

"How about you go get me a cup of coffee?" the DI suggested.

"Is caffeine a good idea?" Logan asked. "Steady hands, and all that."

"Just get me the bloody coffee," Ben instructed, then he turned back to Shona and gave an exasperated shake of his head.

Shona managed a solid three-fifths of a smile. "And I'll have an Earl Grey, while you're there."

Logan's lips drew back in distaste. "Fucking Earl Grey," he muttered, expressing his long-held resentment for a drink he considered nothing more than watery Potpourri.

With a final look at the bomb, he turned and stomped off to find the kitchen. Shona lowered her voice to a whisper once he'd left.

"I don't have Earl Grey," she told Ben. "That should keep him busy for a bit."

Ben chuckled. "I can see why he likes you." He pulled on his reading glasses, balancing them on the end of his nose. "Now, try to keep still, I'm going to have a closer look at this thing and see if we can figure out what we're dealing with."

He brought an ear closer to the device, and listened until it gave its *whirr* and *click*.

"Uh-huh," he said.

"Is that a good 'uh-huh'?" Shona asked.

It didn't sound like a good 'uh-huh.' It didn't sound like a good 'uh-huh,' at all.

"Still figuring it out," Ben said. "You're doing well."

He very gently tapped the canister attached to the left of the device's central hub, then did the same with the one on the right.

"Hmm."

The 'hmm,' sounded even less promising than the, 'uh-huh,' Shona thought, but she didn't say anything. If the news was bad, she wasn't sure she wanted to know. Not just yet.

Ben straightened, then walked around behind her. He knelt down, getting low enough to study the wires that were wrapped around her wrists. One red. One blue. He followed them, and found they connected into the base of the canisters, joining both together.

He returned to the front again, and looked more closely at the canisters. They were both metal, and both had lids on top. The same red and blue wiring set-up ran from inside each lid to the *whirring* and *clicking* central hub of the device.

"Well, well, well," Ben muttered, and this time Shona couldn't help herself.

"Well, well, well, what?"

"What's happening?" Logan asked, appearing in the doorway behind them with a conspicuous lack of coffee and tea. "What is it? What have we got?"

Ben half-turned so Logan was on his right, and Shona was on his left. His head tick-tocked between them as he told them his findings.

"I've seen a fair few IEDs in my time. All sorts. Nail bombs. but this...? This is a new one on me. I've never seen anything like it."

"Shite," Logan spat.

Shona's eyes were wide with worry again. "Then, what do we do? How do we get it off?"

"Easy," Ben said. "It's fake."

The DCI and the Pathologist both blinked simultaneously. Logan was the first to respond.

"Fake? Are you sure?"

"As sure as you ever can be," Ben replied.

"Which is how sure, exactly?" asked Shona.

"Ninety-five percent," said Ben.

"So, that's one in twenty *not* sure," Shona hurriedly pointed out.

"Ninety-nine percent, then. Ninety-nine-point-nine-nine-nine. It's a fake. I'm certain of it."

"Almost certain," Shona corrected. "*Almost*."

Ben took off his glasses and tucked them into his shirt pocket. "PIES," he said.

Logan and Shona exchanged glances.

"Pies? What the fuck's 'pies'?" Logan asked.

Ben sat on the arm of the patchwork chair and began to list on his fingers.

"Power, initiator, explosive, switch. The four components of a functioning explosive device. PIES. It's a… what do you call it?"

"Acronym," said Shona.

"Yes. Thank you. It's an acronym. PIES."

"And how does it help us?" Logan asked.

Ben gestured to the device strapped to Shona's chest. "At a stretch, let's say those canisters are full of explosives. They're not—I'm sure of it—but for the sake of argument, let's says they are. That's one element. The ticky thing in the middle? That could be the switch. Two. It's got power, because it's making a noise. Three. Is there an initiator? Maybe."

"What's an initiator?" Shona asked.

Logan knew this one. "Like a detonator."

"Right. Basically. It's usually a small amount of explosive that triggers the bigger explosion," Ben explained.

"So… what? It doesn't have one of those?" Logan asked.

"Oh, it might well do," Ben said. "Could be in one of the canisters, or this plastic bit in the middle.

Ben and Shona exchanged another look. This one was even more incredulous than before, and considering that had come after Ben had inexplicably said the word, "Pies," out loud, that was saying something.

"You've lost me," Logan said. "You said it wasn't real, but now you're saying… what? That it is?"

"No, I'm saying it appears to have all the right components," Ben said. "It's meant to fool the layman. No offence, Jack. But it's no' a bomb. It's no' an anything."

Logan remained unconvinced. If the DI was wrong, then things would get very messy, very quickly.

"He said he'd detonate it if you called the bomb squad. Right?" asked Ben.

Logan nodded. "Right."

"How? There's no phone connected. No receiver. How's he going to send the detonate signal?" Ben asked. Logan was almost convinced by that, until the DI continued. "I mean, aye, maybe he's got a small SIM device in the switch. That would work. The key components of the phone without the phone part. I've seen that done."

"For fuck's sake, Ben," Logan cried, throwing his hands up in the air. "Make your bloody mind up. Is it a bomb or isn't it?"

"It isn't. And I'm prepared to stake my life on it."

"You might be staking all our lives on it," Shona pointed out.

"Relax. Trust me. There's more chance of me exploding than that thing," Ben said. He turned back to Logan. "Besides, think about it. Petrie brought you here. He knows you wouldn't leave. Do you really think he'd let you off that easily by blowing you to kingdom come?"

That thought had not occurred to Logan, but it made sense. Petrie was out to torture him. To make him suffer. This would be too quick a death. Too easy a way out.

He took a breath. He met Shona's eye. Something unspoken passed between them, then she nodded. "Just get rid of it," she said. "I just want it done."

Ben clapped his hands so suddenly and loudly that the other two occupants of the room both jumped.

"Jesus Christ!" Logan hissed. "What are you trying to do, give us a bloody heart attack?"

Ben smiled sheepishly. "Sorry." He clapped his hands again, more quietly this time, then rubbed them together, warming up his fingers. "Right, then, m'dear. Let's get this thing off you."

THE BARKING SEEMED to come from behind and on both sides as Tyler thundered across the grass. He could hear voices shouting further back, but the dog was a far more pressing concern.

Tyler tried not to think about its slavering jaws and huge, pointy teeth. He tried, but failed, and a vision of his own grisly death propelled him on.

The dog was close. The gate was closer. He was just a few seconds from it now. A few seconds to prepare. A few seconds to hope the four-legged bastard behind him didn't sink its teeth in at the last moment.

With a banshee yell, Tyler threw himself at the top of the gate, hands grasping for the metal bar. If he caught it, he had a chance. If he missed it, he was done for.

He caught it. Somehow, he caught it. He heaved himself upwards, legs bicycling as his feet tried to find purchase on the narrow metal mesh.

The dog arrived in a fanfare of snarls and barks. Tyler felt its teeth graze against the back of his leg, caught a glimpse of it lowering itself to the ground as it prepared to leap, and then he was tumbling over the top of the gate, and plunging towards the other side.

Just as he registered his concern over the approaching concrete slabs, he hit one, upside-down. The impact fired hot streaks of pain through his shoulder, then his leg flipped over his head and both knees crunched against the neighbouring slab.

Every part of him complained as he bounded to his feet, already fumbling in his pockets for his keys.

He was at the car when he saw the headlights of another vehicle come racing up behind him.

He was in the driver's seat when a van came screeching to a halt in front of him, blocking him in.

"Shite," Tyler hissed.

He grabbed for his phone, opened the contacts, and found Logan's name. Before he could tap it, the window beside him exploded, showering him with diamond-like fragments of glass, and sending his phone tumbling into the passenger footwell.

The business end of a shotgun poked in through the broken window. Tyler looked along it and saw the bruised face of a familiar-looking skinhead.

"Well, now," said Valdis. "Take a look what we have here."

CHAPTER THIRTY-SIX

"And you're absolutely sure about this?" Logan asked. He was looming behind DI Forde, his hands buried deep in his coat pockets.

"Can we ever be absolutely sure of anything?" Ben asked, glancing back over his shoulder. "I'm as sure about this as I've been about anything in my life. Is that good enough for you?"

"Good enough for me," Shona said. "I'm about three minutes away from wetting myself. One, if you do that thing with your hands again."

Ben looked momentarily offended. "What thing with my...? Oh. Clapping. Right. Aye. No, I won't do that." He shot Logan another look. "How's that coffee coming along, by the way?"

"Aye, getting there," Logan replied, showing no signs of moving.

Ben tutted, then turned his attention back to the device. With a click, he slid out the blade of a craft knife Shona kept in a drawer in the kitchen, alongside forty double-A batteries, two screwdrivers, and a head torch.

For a man so confident that the bomb wasn't real, he moved awfully slowly. The top of each canister had been attached with strips of tape. There were three that Ben could see on each one, and probably more around the back of the containers.

He wouldn't be able to reach those without disturbing the device, and an embarrassing amount of hand-to-breast contact, but if he could get the front and side pieces off, those on the back should act like a hinge.

The tape was thin, and the blade was sharp, and he was through them all in a matter of seconds.

Shona's breath came faster as Ben started to slowly jiggle the lid from side to side, working it upwards.

"Here. Look at me," Logan told her, sensing her distress. "Real bucket list. Top five. Go."

Shona's mouth opened and closed, but no words came out. "Um... I don't..." Her eyes were pulled back down to the movement of the canister.

"Pyramids," Logan suggested, drawing her gaze back towards him. "Everyone wants to see the pyramids, don't they?"

Shona gave an absent sort of nod that was sorely missing an accompanying smile. "Suppose."

Ben muttered something quietly below his breath, which earned another worried look from the Pathologist.

"I mean, I don't want to see them personally," Logan continued. "No' really my cup of tea. Just pointy hills, aren't they? And it always looks roasting over there." He shook his head definitively. "No. Not my scene. Always fancied Venice, though. I quite like a wee boat. You fancy Venice?"

"Is... is that an invitation?" Shona asked. Her voice was hoarse, and she was fighting a losing battle against the shakes.

"Almost got it..." Ben remarked.

"Oh, fuck," Shona hissed.

Logan appeared behind her and put his hands on her shoulders. "You're alright. You're doing great."

"Y-you should go," she told him. "Get out. Just in case."

"I'm going nowhere," Logan told her. "DI Forde has my full faith."

Ben glanced up briefly. "Christ. First time for everything," he said, then the canister lid sprang open, and all three of them made involuntary noises in fright.

"See?" said Ben, after a pause. "Nothing to worry about."

He peeked into the canister, then poked around with the craft knife at the contents.

"What is it?" Logan asked.

Ben leaned in closer to the canister and took a sniff. He gave a gentle downwards tug on the wire at the bottom of the container, then pulled upwards at the top.

"It's salt," he said. "And the top wire's just taped to the side. The other end's probably taped inside the bottom, too."

He sat back on his haunches, looking pleased with himself. Had he not known the DI for so long, Logan wouldn't have noticed, but Ben also looked more than a little relieved.

"You can horse it off her now," he said, indicating the harness. "It's fine."

"What about the other one?" Shona asked, looking down at the second container.

"There's not a complete circuit," Ben said. "Even if that one's packed full of explosives—and it won't be—there's no power getting to it. You're fine. If it makes you feel better, though..."

He grabbed the wire at the switch and gave it a sharp tug. It came free without much resistance, and this time Ben looked all-the-way smug.

"Nicely done, Ben. Never doubted you for a minute," Logan said, holding a hand out for the knife.

"Can I get that in writing?" Ben asked, passing the blade over.

Logan unbuckled the straps of the harness and—still being careful—set the device down on the floor. Shona bounced in her chair, agitated, as Logan bent and cut the tape holding her hands, and unwound the rest of the cable.

"There. That's you—"

She was up out of the chair like a sprinter off the starting blocks. "Bathroom. Be right back," she announced, haring out of the room.

Ben flopped down onto the armchair. He'd been hiding it since he'd arrived, but now that the drama was over, Logan could see that Hoon was right. The DI looked exhausted. The kind of exhaustion that penetrated the bones and switched out the marrow for lumps of lead.

"You OK?"

Ben gave himself a shake. "Me? Aye. What about you? I mean, Jesus, Jack..."

"Trying not to think about it," Logan said. "Or... not dwell on it. I'm no use if I'm a basket case."

"That's what he's aiming for," Ben said. "That's what all this is about. He's targeting people close to you. He knows that's how to hurt you."

Logan lowered himself onto the wicker seat of the chair. Shona was right, it was an uncomfortable bugger of a thing.

"How did he know about her?" he asked, gesturing to the door through which the Pathologist had gone running. "I mean... Nobody knows about her. Hell, *I* don't even know what's..."

He sighed and sat back, eliciting a squeak of complaint from the chair's wooden back. "My relationship with Shona is hardly going to be on the Gozer's phone. I mean, it's hardly even a relationship. There's barely anything about it on *my* bloody phone."

"Bosco?" Ben guessed.

"Christ, that reminds me. I'd better check in with Tyler. He's scoping out Bosco's house," Logan said.

Ben frowned. "That sensible?"

"He's keeping his distance. I mean..." Logan shrugged. "I suppose it has to be Bosco feeding Petrie the info. But how would *he* even know? It's not like I've been popping round here. I've seen her out of work once, months ago, and we both got called away a few minutes into it. The man would have to be bloody psychic or..."

He looked past Ben, his eyes darting back and forth, like he was seeing some explanation written there on the wall.

"Or what?" Ben asked.

"Or... Jesus."

"What? What is it?"

There was the sound of a door opening elsewhere in the house, and Shona returned, looking just as bruised and battered, but far more relaxed than she'd looked when she'd left.

"That's better," she said. "Sorry about that."

Logan and Ben both stood up. "No, you're fine," Ben said. "Understandable. Between you and me, I may have had some light leakage of my own when I was lifting the lid of that container.

"Lovely image there," Logan said. "Thanks for that."

Ben gestured to the armchair, and Shona didn't argue. Her legs practically gave way as she got close to it, and she collapsed into its multi-coloured cushions.

"I'll go get that tea," Logan told her. "Give you a chance to get your breath back before we bombard you with questions."

Shona nodded. "Thanks. I'll tell you everything I can."

Logan took a step towards the door, then stopped when Shona spoke again.

"I don't get it, though," she said.

"Don't get what?"

"Why me? Why come here and do this to me? What have I done?"

Logan backtracked until he was looking directly down at her. "You've done nothing. We think Petrie is targeting people I... have a close working relationship with. It's me he's trying to get at. Not you. He's already targeted the children of three colleagues."

"Bloody hell, that's horrible," Shona said. She turned her gaze to Ben. "Has he done anything to you?"

Ben shook his head. "No. Not me."

"Right. Good," Shona said. She looked between the two detectives. "Because you go way back, don't you?"

"Aye," said Logan. The word came slowly, bringing with it a little knot of dread in the hollow of his chest. "We go way back."

"Decades," Ben agreed. He shifted his weight from one foot to the other. Clearly, he had that same niggling concern that Logan had. "Why hasn't he targeted me?" he wondered aloud.

Logan's heart was in his throat now.

Don't call the bomb squad. That had been the instruction.

But he knew. Petrie knew. About Ben. About his past.

And he knew he'd be the first person that Logan would call.

Logan pulled out his phone, started dialling Hamza's number.

"Oh God," Ben whispered, working it all out just a second or two behind Logan. "Alice!"

CHAPTER THIRTY-SEVEN

Even at that time of night, it was a twenty-five-minute drive from Shona's to Ben's. Logan had done it in under fifteen.

Ben was out of the Volvo before it had fully come to a stop. He ran the rest of the way along his street, blue lights spinning through the darkness around him.

He saw the faces of officers he'd spoken to a dozen times before avert their gazes as he went stumbling on towards his house.

Towards his wife.

As he ran, his head was filled with thoughts of her. Memories. Experiences they'd shared.

Their wedding day, the sun filtering through her veil.

Their first house together. Barely a cupboard, but she'd been so proud of it.

Her face when he'd come home from the service for the final time. The hug she'd given him. The touch of her cheek against his, and the tears they had shared.

Their life together.

There was an ambulance right at the end of the driveway, the back doors open, the bed inside empty.

A uniformed sergeant called after him as he clattered past. "Detective Inspector..."

It sounded like an apology.

Ben ignored it. Ran on. Chest heaving.

He saw it on the faces of the Uniforms he passed, in their eyes, in the way they didn't know how to look at him, much less what to say.

He ignored them. Ran on. Heart breaking.

He heard Logan calling to him from somewhere far away. Too far back to stop him. Too far back to intervene.

He was under the tape now. The house was right there. *She* was right there.

He was through the gate.

He was up the path.

He was at the open door.

And then DC Khaled was there before him, eyes wide, hands shaking. "Sir," he said, planting his feet in the doorway. "You can't."

"Get out of my way!" Ben spat, throwing his full weight at Hamza, shouldering, and pushing, and elbowing at him. "Hamza, move!"

"You can't, sir," was all Hamza could say. "I'm sorry."

He jammed himself against the door, absorbed the furious pushing and shoving of the senior officer.

"Get out of the way!" Ben roared, punching and slapping at him now. "Hamza, get out of my way, or—"

He collapsed against the DC, grief hitting him like a hammer-blow. Hamza wrapped his arms around the older man and held him there. Held him close.

"I'm so sorry, sir," he said. "I am so, so sorry."

Logan stood frozen at the end of the path. His head was shaking like he couldn't believe it—like he refused to believe it.

But he knew, of course. He'd known before they'd left Shona's. Petrie was out to hurt him in the most painful ways possible. He'd taken his daughter. And now, he'd broken the heart of his oldest friend.

And he'd made Logan the one who'd called him away. The one who'd made Ben leave Alice alone and unprotected. The bastard had made him responsible.

The flashing blues made the house look different—almost unrecognisable from the place he'd had dinner shortly after he'd relocated up north. Alice had spent much of that night giving him grief about... well, everything.

In hindsight, he'd probably deserved it.

"Ben," Logan said, forcing his feet to carry him along the path. There should have been more after that, he knew. Some words of comfort. Of support. Of *something*. But nothing would come.

What could he possibly say?

"I want to see her," Ben said, pulling away from Hamza and rubbing his eyes on his sleeve. "I'm fine. I'm fine. I want to see her."

Hamza met Logan's gaze over the DI's shoulder. Everything that Petrie had done was written in that look, and Logan felt the hot prickling of tears at the backs of his own eyes.

"Maybe best not, Ben, eh?" Logan said. "Maybe now's not the time."

"I've seen plenty of bloody bodies before!" Ben spat, spinning to face the DCI. "More than you, Jack! A lot worse nick, too!"

"She's no' a body, Ben," Logan said. Softly. Kindly. "She's your wife. She's Alice."

An agonised sob burst from Ben's lips. He leaned a hand on the wall, supporting himself.

He looked past Hamza into the hallway. It had been their hallway when he left the house. His and Alice's. It would never be theirs again. It would never be *his* again. The hallway, like the rest of the house, now belonged to some past version of himself. To the Benjamin Forde who existed before this moment, and who had died along with his wife.

"What am I going to do now?" he asked of nobody in particular, then he cleared his throat, straightened his shoulders, and looked Hamza in the eye. "Where was she?"

Hamza looked uncomfortable with the question. "You should probably try not to—"

"Hamza!" Ben barked. He sighed, his shoulders sloping like that short outburst had drained him of the last of his strength. "Sorry. I just... I need to know where it happened."

Still unsure, Hamza looked to Logan for guidance and received a tentative nod in reply.

"She was... still upstairs, sir. In bed."

Ben tried very hard to put a brave face on it. Tried very hard to pretend that this was normal. That she was some other victim, at some other scene.

"Right," he said, the word barely making it through his constricted throat. "Thanks."

Logan put an arm around Ben's shoulders and beckoned a Uniform over. "We'll get you sat down. Get you that coffee I've been promising."

Ben tore his eyes away from the door. "Aye," he said. "Coffee. That's..."

And then, he ran, pulling away from Logan and catching Hamza off-guard. They both tumbled into the hallway, Hamza thrown off-balance while Ben managed to hold onto his own.

In a second, he was passing the living room. Two Paramedics in there looked up from where they were packing up their equipment as he went charging past, with Logan hot on his heels.

"Ben, no!"

And then, he was on the stairs.

And then, he was at the bedroom door.

And then...

And then...

He stopped, a hand hovering above the handle, not yet touching it. Not yet daring.

Logan clumped to the top of the stairs but came no closer.

"Ben, I know what you're thinking."

"You've got no idea what I'm thinking," Ben snapped back, more savagely than Logan had ever heard him. "This was to get at you. He did this to get at *you*. Not me. Not her. She'd done nothing. Nothing, Jack!"

It was another one of those times where Logan had no reply to offer. Nothing beyond an admission of guilt, anyway.

"Aye," he said. "I know. And I'm sorry, Ben. I'm so sorry. And if you have to go in there, if you have to see her for yourself, then I'm not going to stop you. You're a big boy, you make your own decisions."

Ben's hand rested on the handle, but didn't yet move to turn it.

"I didn't know Alice anything like you did, but I do know that she wouldn't want you seeing her. Not now. Not like this," Logan said.

The house—no, the whole world—hung there in silence around them. Like it, too, didn't quite know what to say.

Ben sniffed and wiped his nose on the back of his hand. He spoke directly at the door, not looking at Logan once.

"She'd... she'd put make-up on. In the morning. Before I was up. Said she didn't want me seeing her looking old." Tears tripped down his cheeks. "But I... I told her. I *loved* seeing her old. Her crow's feet. The grey. Because they were all *ours*. Hers and mine. We were growing old together. The two of us. Me and her."

He leaned forward until his head was resting against the wood. His shoulders heaved. His hand slipped from the door handle and fell to his side.

"I'm sorry, darling," he whispered, and Logan looked away, shamed by his friend's grief. "I'm so sorry."

Logan and Hamza stood in Ben's front garden, watching him being led away by a uniformed sergeant, a blanket draped over his shoulders, a cup of coffee from the petrol station along the road clutched in one hand.

"Think he'll be OK?" Hamza asked.

Logan watched Ben getting into the passenger seat of the Volvo, then shook his head. "No. I don't," he admitted.

"He got any family locally? Kids?"

"No. Never had any. Was just him and Alice. Always has been."

He watched Ben for a few more seconds, until the sight of him sitting there staring emptily ahead became too painful, then turned towards the open front door of the house.

"Right. I'm going in before Palmer and his lot get here. One wrong word from that bastard tonight and I'm liable to add to the body count."

Hamza glanced at the upstairs window. "Mind if I... stay here, sir?"

"That bad?"

"It's bad. Not really any worse than some, I suppose, just... knowing who she was..."

Logan patted the DC on the shoulder. "You're fine, son. Stay out here." He turned, then a thought struck him. "Any progress on your three-word thing?"

"Sinead's still on it, back at base," Hamza said. "We're getting through it."

"How is she?"

"She's keeping busy. But about what you'd expect," Hamza said. "How are you doing?"

Logan smiled thinly. "About what you'd expect."

"Did, eh, did Tyler catch up with you?"

"Tyler?" Logan frowned. "Didn't he check back in?"

"Not yet, sir. I mean, maybe. With Sinead. I haven't spoken to her since I left. So, aye. He probably has."

"Phone him, will you? Find out where he's got to," Logan instructed, then he fished a pair of rubber gloves from the pack in his pocket, said "Right, then," for nobody's benefit but his own, and headed back in through DI Forde's front door.

The stairs seemed to go on forever. The closer he got to the top, the more like quicksand they became, pulling him down, trying to get him to stop, to go no further, to turn back before it was too late. Before he saw.

But there was no turning back. There had been no turning back for a while now.

He stopped at the door just as Ben had done, but only for long enough to pull on his gloves and slide shoe protectors on over his boots.

The room was in darkness, but the light from the upstairs landing picked out the thing that had been Alice Forde. It lay on the bed, a torn nightdress exposing its nakedness. It had slashes across its throat, and several others across its breasts and stomach. Its arms, too.

Alice had tried to defend herself. She'd been awake, then. Aware. She'd have looked into the bastard's eyes. She'd have known what was coming.

And she'd fought. Of course, she had. She was Alice Forde. She'd never backed down from an argument in her life.

The bedclothes and mattress had absorbed most of the blood, but some of it had trickled over the edge and onto the floor. A crimson waterfall against the pale blue valance.

There was some spattering on the headboard, less on the wall above it. A bloodied handprint had clutched at the bedpost at one point. Forensics would have to determine whose, but given that the hands of the thing on the bed were smeared with red, he guessed the prints would be Alice's.

He looked around the room, grateful to no longer be looking directly at the remains.

What else? What else?

The clock had been knocked off the bedside table on the empty side of the bed. The duvet had been thrown off in that direction, and probably clipped the clock on the way over. It hung off the side of the bed now, most of it on the floor, but one corner still trying to cling on.

How had he got in? Window was open, but still on the latch, so he couldn't have come in that way. Through the door, then. He'd have to ask about signs of forced entry downstairs.

What else? What else?

He crossed to the far corner of the room and looked back at the door, taking it all in from another angle. He squatted to see under the bed, and saw the knife there, the blade the colour of a fine red wine.

There were a pair of slippers tucked underneath the bed, too. They were thick, comfy, tartan things, with a white woollen stripe across the front. A single splash of blood pinkened the white at one corner—the only flaw on the otherwise untouched pair.

He left the knife where it was for the Scene of Crime team. The room gave up no further secrets, and Logan headed for the door.

Before he left, he stopped and turned back to the thing on the bed. The thing that had been Alice Forde.

The love of his best friend's life.

"I'll look after him," he said. "I promise."

And with that, he stepped out onto the landing and closed the door.

CHAPTER THIRTY-EIGHT

BEN DIDN'T LOOK UP WHEN LOGAN CLIMBED INTO THE DRIVER'S SEAT OF the car. His eyes were instead fixed on the cup of coffee he was nursing in both hands. He'd got as far as removing the lid, but hadn't drunk any of it, for fear of throwing it all back up.

It would only have been a waste, anyway. His senses felt dead. He wouldn't have been able to taste it.

"Well?" he asked.

Logan pulled on his seatbelt before replying. It was a fine line, he knew. Give Ben too much information, and it would haunt him forever. Give him too little, and the images he created in his head would be much, much worse.

"Her throat was cut," Logan said, staring straight ahead at the flashing lights of the various polis vehicles.

Ben nodded slowly, but remained focused on the now-cool liquid in his cup. "And?"

"She fought back. No doubt got a good few licks in."

"Did he rape her?" Ben asked. It was blunt and direct, and he took a big steadying breath after it, like it had taken physical effort to get the question out.

"No. No, nothing like that," Logan said. He wasn't sure of that. He didn't think so, but he couldn't be sure until the post mortem. As he said the words, though, he made damned sure to sound as certain of it as he could.

A tear *plipped* into the cup. Ben's breathing came fast and sudden, like he was hyperventilating. Relief, Logan knew. He'd seen it before under very similar circumstances. All that pent-up fear and dread releasing itself in one go.

"We'll take you back to the station," Logan said. "You can bed down in one of the rooms there. We can talk. Or, you know, there's... support. Mental health."

Ben shook his head. "I've already booked myself into a hotel."

Logan turned in his chair. "A hotel? On your own? I'm not sure that's—"

"I've booked it, Jack. I'm going. You can take me back to my car, or you can drop me off and I can get a taxi out there tomorrow."

"It's tomorrow now," Logan pointed out. "There's no point paying for a hotel for a couple of hours. Come on back—"

"I've made my mind up. I'm booked in. That's that."

"Ben, you're in shock. You shouldn't be in a hotel. You should be with people you know. People who can help."

"People who can *help*? How in God's name can anyone help, Jack? Can they bring Alice back? Can they rewind time?"

"No. They can't," Logan admitted. "Maybe not 'help,' then. Not yet. But you should be with people who care about you."

Ben laughed drily. "People who care about me?" he said, sounding incredulous. "Seems to me, the people that *you* care about all end up hurt. Or dead."

He winced, hearing how the words sounded as they came out of his mouth. His face softened.

"Jack..." he began, and it seemed like an apology was about to be forthcoming. But then he stole a glance back at the house that was no longer his, and the window of the room where his wife's body lay, and his expression firmed up again. "Just take me to the bloody hotel."

THE FIRST FINGERS of sunlight were grasping across the sky when Logan returned to the Incident Room. Four Uniforms and a couple of CID officers sat at desks, talking into phones or typing on computers. They all looked up as Logan entered, nodded to him, then went back to whatever they'd been doing.

Hamza emerged from the DCI's office at the back of the room, and carefully pulled the door closed. The blinds were drawn—something he usually reserved for those occasions where he had to give someone a bollocking.

"Sinead. I told her to get some sleep," Hamza whispered. "She's dead on her feet."

"I know the feeling," Logan said.

Both men asked their next questions at the same time.

"How's Ben?"

"Where's Tyler?"

The look on Logan's face more or less answered Hamza's question, so he volunteered an answer of his own.

"Can't get him, sir. Phone's switched off."

"Sinead's not heard from him?"

"No, sir. I played it down, though. Don't want her getting worried."

"Good thinking. Get a pen, I'll give you Bosco Maximuke's address. Get Uniform round there to suss the place out. See if Tyler's car is anywhere nearby."

Hamza already had pen in hand and notebook open by the time Logan had reached the end of his instructions. He jotted the address down as the DCI relayed it, then went off to arrange the drive-past.

He stopped at his desk. When he turned, there was an apologetic look on his face. "Oh, I almost forgot. Detective Superintendent Hoon wants to see you."

"Does he, indeed?" Logan asked. He shrugged his coat off and tossed it onto the nearest available desk. "That's handy. I want a wee word with him, too."

Hoon jumped to his feet the moment Logan appeared around his door.

"When the fuck were you planning on telling me about your daughter?" the DSup demanded. "Jesus fucking Christ All-bastard-mighty, Jack! You can't be fucking swanning about like—"

"Sit down, Bob."

Hoon's brow became a series of interlocking lines. His eyebrows met so hard in the middle they practically fused together.

"What did you fucking say?"

Logan's voice had an icy edge to it. "I said: Sit. Down."

Hoon stood his ground. Logan unbuttoned one cuff of his shirt and began to roll up the sleeve.

He was on the second sleeve when Hoon finally caved and sat in his chair.

"I've had quite the bloody night, Bob," Logan told him. "Maddie, you've heard about. Ben's Alice, too, I'm sure. That's bound to have filtered through to you by now. Yes?"

Hoon said nothing, but his head dipped forward to confirm that he had.

Logan finished rolling up his sleeves, then wheeled one of the other chairs back from the desk like he was going to sit on it. Instead, he rolled it over to the corner of the room, out of the way.

"What about Shona Maguire? Did you know about that?" he asked, moving the other chair to the opposite side of the room.

It was clear from the expression on Hoon's face that the Detective Superintendent didn't know about that one, so Logan elaborated.

"Petrie got to her. Strapped a bomb to her chest. Fake, it turned out. She's fine. More or less. But, that's what drew Ben away from home. He used my relationship with her to get me to call Ben. It's thanks to me that Alice was left alone. Which means, it's partly thanks to me that she's dead."

"You can't go blaming—"

"I wasn't finished," Logan said, cutting the Detective Superintendent off.

He glowered at Hoon across the desk. Under any normal circumstances, the DSup would have bitten Logan's head off by now. Possibly literally.

But then, these were far from normal circumstances.

"All through this, I've thought, 'How does he know?'" Logan continued. "How does he know where I live? How does he know where Hamza lives? About Harris? How could he know all that?"

"You said it yourself. If he's working with Bosco, then—"

"But how does Bosco know? To get all that—everything he's had in the past—he'd need half the bloody force on his payroll. Or one very high-up officer with a lot of connections."

Logan left that statement hanging there for a few moments, then leaned forward and placed his clenched fists on the desk.

"How was it you described it, Bob? Your 'all-seeing, all-fucking-knowing omnipotence.' That's what you said, isn't it?"

Once again, Hoon said nothing.

"Until we were in Carstairs, I thought there were four other people who knew about my relationship with Dr Maguire. And then you mentioned—and I'm paraphrasing here—my attempts to 'fire it up that Irish Pathologist bird' and that number grew to five. Four of them, I'd trust with my life. The fifth one? Well..." Logan straightened again. "I'm sure you can figure out who that is."

"If you're saying what I think you're fucking saying, Detective Chief Inspector..." Hoon began, but his heart wasn't in it. The fire was gone.

"Cut the shite, *Bob*," Logan told him. "You owe me that much."

Hoon stared up at him for a few seconds, then opened the bottom drawer of his desk and took out a half-empty bottle of Lagavulin malt. He produced a glass and clunked it down, then raised his gaze back to the DCI.

"You still off it?"

Logan gave a nod, and Hoon grunted his disapproval. He unscrewed the top of the bottle and glugged a couple of fingers into the glass, briefly contemplated replacing the lid, then tossed it onto the desk beside the glass.

"I didn't know," he said, raising the liquid to his lips but not yet drinking. He wasn't meeting Logan's eye, either. "About Petrie. That he and Bosco were... I didn't know. I had no idea."

"Aye. Well. That one came a bit out of left field for all of us."

Hoon took a sip of his drink. His lips drew back over his teeth as the liquid burned down his throat. "I dug into it. After you told me. Couldn't find a link, though. I tell you, I was fucking relieved. I thought... 'That's it, then. It's bullshit. Coincidence, or...' Ach. I don't fucking know."

He gave a little shake of his head and looked up at Logan for the first time since taking out the bottle.

"It isn't, though. Is it? They're connected."

"Aye. I mean... aye. They're connected," Logan said. "I don't know how, exactly, but there's something there. I'll find out what."

There was a knock at the door. It opened half-way, and a secretary popped her head in.

"Give us a minute, will you?"

The look on Logan's face made her hurriedly beat a retreat, and the DCI turned back to the senior officer sitting in the chair. He looked smaller than before, like he was shrinking.

Or like Logan was outgrowing him.

"How did it start?" Logan asked. "Money?"

"No. No, not... Not to start with, Jack. I want you to believe me on that," Hoon said. "Threats. Blackmail. Fucking... photos of my niece. Videos."

"Louisa?"

Hoon took another sip of his drink, and this one burned less than the last. "One of them—Bosco's guys—had got her to do all fucking sorts on a webcam. And I mean *all* sorts. Some of the stuff they got her doing..." He swallowed, like he was resisting the urge to throw up. "Stupid cow."

"What are you saying? You threw us all under a fucking bus so your niece didn't get herself shared around online?"

"It wasn't just that. I mean... it was a part of it. You don't know her, Jack, it would've fucking destroyed her. That girl has been through... Well, she's been through a whole fucking lot."

Logan banged both hands on the desk. "My *daughter* could be going through a whole lot right now, *Bob*. Sinead's brother. How much do you think Alice Forde went through in her final few moments? Eh? Let me tell you, it was a *whole fucking lot*!"

"It wasn't just that," Hoon protested. "The fella. The guy. He'd been chatting to her for weeks. Found out fucking everything. About her. About the wee man. Where he went to school. Who his pals were. The whole fucking shebang. They were threatening all sorts."

"You're a Detective Superintendent of the fucking polis, Bob. Or had you forgotten that? Have them arrested!"

"Oh, come on, Jack!" Hoon spat, jumping to his feet. "How many times have you tried to nail that Russian bastard's fat hairy balls to the fucking wall? How many times have you brought him in? Or one of his guys? They're coated in fucking chip fat, the lot of them. They slide right through our fingers. Every bloody time.

"What, you think they were fucking open about who they were? You think he signed off, 'PP Bosco fucking Maximuke'? They did what they always fucking do, gave me just enough that I knew who they were, but not so much that I could prove it."

He sat down again, the snake that had uncoiled itself in his gut going back to sleep.

"And I tried. Believe me, I fucking tried everything. But I couldn't bring the lot of them in, could I? And if I bring in one or two, what then? What happens to Louisa then? To Jaden?"

"You could've talked to us," Logan said. "Told us."

Hoon waved a hand dismissively. "This goes way back. Before you were on the scene."

"Snecky, then."

"Fuck off! Snecky? I wouldn't tell that bastard the fucking time."

He polished off the last of his drink, then refilled it, glugging more into the glass this time.

"You said, 'Not to start with.'"

Hoon frowned, the glass halfway to his lips. "Eh?"

"I said, 'Money?' You said, 'Not to start with.'"

The Detective Superintendent flinched. He gulped half of the glass's contents, exhaled, then replied.

"I didn't ask for it. Never. And I didn't spend it, either. He just... It started turning up. Wee bundles. Through the post. In the glovebox of my car."

He opened the top drawer of his desk and pointed into it.

"In there, one time. A grand, just sitting there in an envelope with my name on it." Hoon shook his head as he continued to stare into the drawer. "I mean, how the fuck...?" he asked, more to himself than to Logan.

He closed the drawer again. "It's all at home. In shoe boxes. I never touched it. And I told him, I told him I didn't fucking want it. But he said I'd earned it," Hoon continued, and the disgust Logan felt was mirrored by the look on the DSup's face. "And, the worst thing is? He was right. I had."

Logan could feel his back teeth grinding together. He'd heard enough. More than enough.

He'd hoped he was wrong. He'd hoped he'd come in here, throw his accusations around, and Hoon would chew him up and spit him out, and prove him wrong on every one.

But this? This was pathetic.

"Enough with the sob story, Bob. I thought Jinkies was a fucking liability down in Fort William, but at least he was just a useless bastard. But *you*? You knew full well what Bosco Maximuke was. You knew what he'd do with the information you gave him."

"I didn't know he'd do this, Jack. I didn't know he'd do anything like—"

"Shut your fucking mouth!" Logan roared. "I haven't finished talking."

Something flickered behind Hoon's eyes. Some ingrained angry bastard stirred.

But then, it was gone. The fight had left him. The fire had been extinguished.

"You knew what he was capable of. You knew he had it in for me."

"Not to start with," Hoon said, grasping at straws. "He said you'd helped each other. In the past."

The floorboards beneath Logan's feet squeaked as he shifted his weight from foot to foot.

"Aye. Know what? Cards on the table? I turned a blind eye to a couple of Bosco's boys in the past. Nothing major. Nothing we could've put them away for," Logan admitted. "And I called in those favours a couple of times. You know why? To aid me in fucking investigations, Bob. To get bad bastards off the streets. To put killers behind bars. No' for a stack of cash and to save my niece's tits from being plastered all over the internet."

"He didn't ask me for much, either," Hoon said. "Mostly just... wee things. About other bastards we were investigating, half the time. Dealers. Traffickers. Just names and addresses, mostly."

The whole station seemed to go silent then. The air between Logan and Hoon *hummed* like it was alive.

"Was one of those addresses the house where DS McQuarrie was shot?" Logan asked.

"What?" Hoon shook his head. "No. No, it... No. Definitely not. You think I could just fucking sit here if I'd given him that?"

"Aye, Bob. I do. I think you're that much of a coward," Logan replied.

Hoon started to offer up some other objection to that, but Logan raised his voice and spoke over him, cutting him short.

"All I want to know is where to find him. We've got Uniform headed to his house, because DC Neish went round there earlier, and now he's nowhere to be found."

Hoon seemed to shrink another few percent at that news.

"I don't know, Jack. I don't," he said. "I know his yard. That's it. I didn't even know his home address. I swear. He'd always contact me. Well, one of his boys. Never him."

Logan said nothing. He just stared.

"I don't know how to find him. I mean it," Hoon insisted. "Listen, if I did, I'd fucking tell you. I would. I'd spill my guts. What the fuck do I have to lose now?"

"We're a couple of bright lads, Bob. I'm sure, if we put our minds to it, we could think of plenty," Logan said, his voice low and menacing. He leaned forwards again, the knuckles of his clenched fists resting on the table. "If anything has happened to Tyler, I'll start with your fingers. And, if I find out you were even *remotely* involved in Caitlyn's death... Well, you'll wish I'd started with your fucking fingers."

He pinned him there in the seat with his glare for a few moments, then turned and headed for the door.

Hoon cleared his throat. "Aren't you... Aren't you going to arrest me?"

"I'll get Uniform to notify the Procurator Fiscal," Logan said. He turned and gave the shell of Detective Superintendent Robert Hoon one last look of contempt. "You're no' worth my time."

CHAPTER THIRTY-NINE

Ben sat in the dark on the foot end of the room's single bed, his hands clasped limply together, his elbows resting on his thighs.

He hadn't got undressed. He hadn't even kicked off his shoes. What was the point? He wouldn't sleep. Not tonight. Maybe not ever again.

But he'd needed to be alone. Away from Jack and the others. Away from the polis, from the station, from the well-meaning words, and the sympathetic looks. Away from any suggestions of help, or counselling, or support.

Maybe there'd be time for all that. Someday.

Or, maybe there wouldn't.

There was already a hole where she should have been. He could feel it in the space where his heart had been. It tempted him to prod at it, like he might with a newly-removed tooth, but the hole was too raw, and the pain was too great, and even the thought of her name inside his head made his whole body ache.

Alice.

All those happy memories from earlier came rushing back. Their first meeting. Their first date. Their first home.

But, they brought others with them, the pain in his chest dredging up the worst of times, too.

The day they'd lost their unborn baby.

The day she'd started her chemotherapy.

The day they'd found out that she could no longer bear children.

All those tears. All those years. Together.

And now...

He slid off the end of the bed and onto the floor, grasping his head in his hands, the hole where Alice had been threatening to consume him, to swallow him down into the dark.

She must've been so scared. Had she called out for him? Had she wondered why he wasn't coming?

Did she think he'd abandoned her? Left her to die.

Or, God. Worse.

In the dark, did she think it was him? Did she think he was hurting her? Killing her?

"No, no, no, please, no. Please, no."

He rocked back and forth, knees up at his chest, head jammed between them. Pictures came crashing unbidden into his head. Images of Alice. Of a knife. Of a terrified look of betrayal on a face he had forever loved.

'No, Ben! Stop! Why?'

"Please, no, please, no, *please no!*"

He shouted that last one into the darkness. It echoed around the cramped single room and rattled a teaspoon in a mug on the tray by the television.

Ben scrambled onto his hands and knees, grabbed the mug, and hurled it at the wall. It exploded into fragments, but he didn't see. He wasn't looking by then. He was grabbing for the cheap flatscreen TV, pulling on it, tearing the cables out of the wall.

He threw it to the floor, but it wasn't enough, so he stamped on it, drove his heel into the screen—again, again—lashing out, finding an outlet for his pain and his grief.

Alice stared back at him from the bed, her face a finger-painting daubed in blood.

Why hadn't he been there?

Why hadn't he saved her?

Why was he hurting her?

"It wasn't me!" he sobbed, dropping to his knees beside the bed. He buried his face in the floral patterned quilt, muffling the roar that erupted from somewhere deep within him. Somewhere deeper than he had ever thought possible.

There was a knock at the door. He ignored it and just knelt there, face down on the bed, hands twisting knots in the covers.

"It wasn't me, sweetheart," he whispered. "I'd never hurt you. I'd never hurt you."

The knocking came again, more insistent this time. Ben straightened and looked around at the broken TV and shattered mug.

"I'm fine," he croaked. "It's... Everything's fine."

"Sir?" said a male voice, muffled by the door. "Please, open up."

Sighing, Ben got to his feet. He wiped his eyes and his nose on his shirt sleeve, briefly contemplated putting the telly back, then decided not to bother. What were they going to do, call the polis?

He got his warrant card out of his pocket, just in case, and opened the door.

Two skinheads in bomber jackets stood there in the corridor. Ben hesitated for half a second before starting to close the door. But that was all it took.

A fist hit him. A battering-ram. He tasted blood, felt his brain rattle inside his skull as his head snapped back.

And then, the world lurched sideways, and Ben fell straight through the floor, and into a smothering void of absolute black.

CHAPTER FORTY

Hamza and the three CID officers sat in a semi-circle around Logan, their jaws practically in their laps.

They had seemed sceptical when Logan had first started telling them about Hoon, but as more details had emerged, they'd become increasingly shaken. They believed him now, alright, he could tell by the slack-jaws and the numb expressions.

They'd trusted him. They all had. They hadn't liked him, obviously, nobody *liked* him, but they'd believed in him. They'd put their faith in him, time and again.

And he'd sold them all out, just as often.

When he'd finished filling them in, he asked a female DI to get in touch with the Procurator Fiscal's office. Hoon would do time for this. Assuming he didn't top himself before that, of course.

"You sure you want me to do that, sir? Assistant Chief Constable will be here any minute for the press conference. Might be worth kicking it up the line to her."

"What? Shite." Logan checked his watch, then shot a glance out the window at the brightening city beyond the glass. It was going to be a nice day. Weather-wise, at least. Everything else was still up in the air. "Aye. Bugger it. Let her handle it. Might as well get her working for her money."

Logan waited until everyone had returned to their stations before asking Hamza for an update.

There was still no word from Tyler. No sign of anyone at Bosco's, and no trace of the DC's car. Uniform was keeping an eye out for it, and for any vehicles registered to Maximuke, but there had been no hits so far.

"Anything from the web and social media appeals?"

Hamza gestured to the other officers seated around the Incident Room. "That's pretty much what this is. Following up on a lot of tips, but mostly all junk so far. Nothing that's panned out, anyway."

"What about building sites?" Logan asked. "Bosco's company must've been working on a few projects. The legitimate side of his business, I mean."

"A couple. We checked. Nothing doing," Hamza said.

The door to Logan's office opened, and Sinead emerged. Half her face was a swirl of lines from where she'd been sleeping on her folded arms. Her eyes darted fitfully from Logan to Hamza and back again. "Anything?"

Logan shook his head. "Not yet."

Sinead's expression remained mostly neutral, like she'd been braced for bad news and hoping for good, and the lack of fresh information had landed squarely in the middle.

"We finished going through those words yet?" she asked.

Hamza glanced back at his computer. "I haven't had a chance, I've been—"

"Right, then," Sinead said, heading for the desk she'd been using earlier in the night. "I'll crack on."

Logan almost told her to go home. Almost told her to go and get more rest.

But he knew he'd be wasting his breath. She dealt with things the same way he did. She got on. She kept busy.

"Grab yourself a coffee and a bite to eat first," Logan told her. She started to object, but he was having none of it. "That's a bloody order, Constable."

Sinead relented. "Right, sir," she said, then she went plodding out of the Incident Room.

Logan stood in his office, trying to give himself a skoosh of deodorant without removing his shirt. This was proving difficult, and he knew the icy-cold burns he inflicted on himself by blasting the spray from too close range would come back to haunt him throughout the day.

It was a token effort before the arrival of the Assistant Chief Constable, done out of courtesy more than any sort of professional deference. He was, not to put too fine a point on it, honking. The deodorant barely made a dent. What he really needed was a hot shower, a scrubbing brush, two good meals, and twelve hours sleep.

Maybe a haircut.

Then, and only then, he might start to feel human again. But none of it was possible. Not while Maddie and Harris were missing.

And Tyler, too. Where had that daft bastard ended up? 'Drive past.' That's what Logan had said. Don't make contact, don't get involved. Drive past, scope it out, leave. If he'd followed that, there shouldn't have been a problem.

So, where was he?

There was a knock at the door, and Logan hurriedly disposed of the deodorant in his filing cabinet, and tucked himself in.

He'd expected to find the Assistant Chief Constable there, but instead, Sinead held out a disposable cup and a small paper bag. A pleasing amount of grease was soaking through the bag, turning the paper shiny and transparent.

"Breakfast, sir," she said, offering it out to him. "That's a bloody order."

He accepted both gratefully. "Thank you. How you holding up?"

"Shite. You?"

"Much the same," Logan told her. "Quite the night."

"So I've been hearing," Sinead said.

She stepped forward and hugged him. It came out of nowhere, and he could only stand there, hot cup of coffee in one hand, bag of something deliciously greasy in the other, until she'd finished.

"Right, then," she said, with a slightly sheepish smile. "Back to it."

"Back to it," Logan agreed. He held up the cup and the bag. "Thank you again."

"No problem. Oh!" Sinead said, half-turning then turning back. "Any word on Tyler?"

"He's... around," Logan said. He regretted the lie immediately, but went with it, anyway. "I'm sure he'll check in soon."

"Aye," Sinead said. The lines on her brow deepened momentarily, before fading again. "I'm sure he will."

She left, then, and Logan closed the door. He devoured half of the roll before he made it over to his chair. It was bacon and fried egg. The bacon was a bit too well-done, and the egg was dry and rubbery, but it was up there with the best things he'd ever eaten.

His stomach growled, wanting more. He tried to appease it with a couple of breadcrumbs from the corners of the bag, but by the sounds it made, it was largely unimpressed.

Wiping his hands on his shirt—because he couldn't really make it any worse at this point—he took out his phone and tried Tyler's number. Unsurprisingly, it went to voicemail.

After that, he called the hospital to check-in on Vanessa. She was recovering well, the nurse told him, although there was talk of some minor surgery on the right leg. She'd offered to transfer the call through to Vanessa herself, but he'd been quick to decline.

She knew he'd be in touch when he had news on Maddie. She might not trust him with much, but she'd trust him on that.

He checked the time before making the next call. It was rapidly approaching nine o'clock. The press conference was in just under forty minutes. The bastards would already be assembling downstairs, no doubt rubbing their hands with glee.

The next call was the hardest. It rang eight or nine times before he heard the voice on the other end offer up a croaky, "Hello?"

"Sorry. Did I wake you?"

"Wake...? What?" Shona gave a sleepy groan down the line. "Shit. Yes. No. What time is it?"

"Just about nine," Logan said. "I, eh, I owe you an apology. We ran out, and I didn't get back to you."

"No, it's fine. It's fine," Shona said, although she wasn't entirely convincing. "How was everything?"

"Not good," Logan said. "Alice—Ben's wife—she was dead by the time we got there."

He heard Shona sitting upright. All the sleepy slurriness left her voice in an instant. "Oh, God Almighty. Oh, Jesus. I'm sorry, Jack. Oh, God. That's... That's... Oh, God. How is he?"

"He's... rough. He's taking it hard."

"Well, of course, he is. I mean... Jesus. What a world," she said. "Give him a hug from me, will you?"

"Eh, aye," Logan replied, thinking of Ben's empty desk sitting out there in the Incident Room. "Aye, I will do. I'm going to arrange for Uniform to come over and take a statement from you this morning, if that's OK?"

"Yeah. Sure. Of course," Shona replied. "I'll have to get into work, obviously, but—"

"Work? I don't think you should be going into work," Logan told her. "Not after what you went through."

"Ben's wife will be coming in," Shona said. "I should be the one to look at her. I owe him that much."

"Ben would understand. Let someone else do it," Logan insisted. "What you went through... You could still be in shock."

"I'm fine, Jack," she said. "I'm dandy."

There was a knock at his door, and Hamza poked his head inside. "She's here," he whispered.

Logan gave him a thumbs up in acknowledgement, then turned his attention back to the call.

"Listen, I have to go. Sorry. Big press conference coming up, and I need to brief the Assistant Chief Constable. I'll get Uniform over there in half an hour, and I'll call you back when I can. OK?"

"Grand," she replied, and he could hear the forced smile in her voice. "And I'm fine. Honestly. Bye for now."

She hung up the call before he could. Logan swept the crumbs from his desk, necked a big glug of his now-lukewarm coffee, then dumped the cup and the bag in the wastepaper basket beneath his desk just as sharp knuckles rapped on his door.

Years ago, Logan had first come to know of Assistant Chief Constable Michaela Haldane by her nickname—'The Impaler.' The name had been given to her due to her elongated features and pale white skin, which gave her a certain vampire-like quality. Hence, 'Vlad the Impaler,' had become the more phonetically pleasing, 'Michaela the Impaler,' before being shortened to just the second and third word for brevity's sake.

Unlike the creatures she resembled, she entered without being invited and closed the door behind her. She wore the full dress uniform, minus the cap, which she carried tucked under one arm. Her expression suggested she was either sooking on a soor ploom, or wasn't impressed by what she saw.

"You look like a sack of shite, Jack."

Not a soor ploom, then.

"Ma'am," he said, standing. He looked down at himself, then conceded her point with a nod. "Aye. Well, you know how it gets in the trenches. Maybe you remember?"

"I do. Very well. And I never looked like that," she said. Her nostrils flared. "I saw victims that didn't look like that. Quite a mess you've got here."

Logan glanced around the office. He'd seen it worse.

"Not the room. The situation," Haldane said, sighing. "Still, you always did say Petrie was faking. Maybe we should've listened to you."

It was the closest Logan was likely to get to an apology, he knew. May as well take it.

"Aye. Maybe you should," he agreed.

She took a seat, then indicated for him to do the same.

"You'll have to fill me in on where we're at. I'll lead the press conference, you can answer any direct questions I specifically defer to you," she instructed. "That means no jumping in. No adding your tuppence worth unless I tell you to. I lead, you follow. Yes?"

Logan would've been happy not attending the bloody thing at all, so he had no problem with keeping his mouth shut.

"Sounds like a plan."

"Yes. Well. I get the sense 'a plan' is something you're often lacking," Haldane said. She took Logan's notepad from his desk, removed a silver pen from her breast pocket, and clicked the button. "We don't have long, but from the start, please. Tell me what's happened."

And so, he did. Her face remained largely impassive for most of it, as her hand scrawled and scribbled like it had been possessed.

Logan told her everything, from the badge in his flat onwards, right up to the disappearance of DC Neish, and the death of Alice Forde.

"OK. Well, then," Haldane said, clicking the button on her pen and returning it to her pocket. "I'll have DCI Grant brought in to relieve you."

"Snecky? What the hell for?" Logan demanded.

"Come on, Jack. Your daughter has been taken. You're hardly going to be thinking objectively on this. You're too close. Far too close. DCI Grant will take point, you can offer your insight as and when requested. I'm aware you and Petrie have your little history, and so your guidance might prove useful at points."

"Bollocks," Logan spat.

The Assistant Chief Constable fixed him with a dangerous glare. "I beg your pardon."

"Sorry. Bollocks, *ma'am*," Logan said. "No disrespect to the man, but Snecky couldn't catch VD in an African brothel, let alone Owen Petrie. The man's a total fucking clown. Again, no disrespect meant."

"DCI Grant will lead. You will advise," Haldane reiterated. "You will still accompany me to the press conference, then Detective Superintendent Hoon will supervise until Grant can offload his cases and head north."

"Oh. Aye. I didn't tell you that bit, did I?" Logan said. He sat back in his chair, getting comfortable. He might even enjoy this part.

"Which bit?" Haldane asked, priming her pen again and holding it ready above the paper.

"Before you hand things over to Hoon, there's something you might like to know..."

CHAPTER FORTY-ONE

Logan peeked through the door into the room where the press conference was being held, and immediately felt his hackles rise.

They had swarmed into the place, filling it from front to back with their cameras, and their recording equipment, and their smug-as-fuck wee faces. The ladies and gentlemen of the national press.

Bastards, one and all.

The stage had been set at one end of the room. Four tables had been set out in a long line, with just two chairs behind them. One of the chairs was just off-centre enough that the person sitting there wouldn't have to straddle the legs of tables two and three. That one was the Impaler's, Logan reckoned, judging by the way the second chair was tucked away near the far end of the fourth table.

She'd remained pretty stoic when Logan had told her about Hoon. She'd pointed out to him that he was making a very serious accusation and then, when he'd made it clear he understood, she'd gone to speak to the man himself, although not without instructing Logan to find himself a new shirt and to 'do something' with his 'bloody hair'.

A Uniform had tracked him down a spare shirt. It was a size too small, but he'd just about get away with it if he avoided any sudden large movements.

As for the hair, he settled for dampening it down with water and brushing his fingers through it a few times so it didn't appear to be plastered to his head.

He'd managed another blast of deodorant during the shirt change procedure, so he no longer smelled like some sort of farm animal. He smelled like some sort of farm animal that had been dunked repeatedly in cheap antiperspirant.

He wasn't convinced this was better.

"You ready?" asked Haldane, appearing in the corridor behind him. Her cap was on her head now, and where it had been tucked under her arm there was now a clipboard with her notes.

"You see Hoon?" Logan asked.

"I did. It's being dealt with," she said. "For God's sake, don't bring it up in here. And if any of them have somehow gotten wind of it, leave the talking to me. Yes?"

"Aye. Whatever you think, ma'am."

She gave the curtest of nods. "Yes. Good. So, I'll go on, make my prepared statement, then I'll bring you on for questions. You will wait until I ask you a question directly before answering. You will answer through me, and I will add anything I feel is necessary. Yes?"

"Like I said. Whatever you think."

"Yes. Good. Watch for my signal. It will be this." She made a very clear and obvious beckoning motion with one hand. "Got that?"

Logan was tempted to ask her to show him again, just to be on the safe side, but resisted. "Got it."

"Good. Yes," Haldane said, then she touched her hat to check the angle, checked her tie in much the same way, and went striding through the doors and up the steps at the side of the stage.

Logan could see and hear the flashes going off already, each *pop* projecting an animated shadow of the Assistant Chief Constable on the *Police Scotland* backdrop at the back of the stage.

"Vultures, the bloody lot of them," he muttered to himself as he watched Haldane take her seat and pour herself a glass of water from the jug in front of her.

She set her notes out on the table, unrushed and uncowed by the sense of urgency radiating off the members of the media. The air was positively humming with anticipation. Logan recognised a few of the print journos. Some bastard from *The Sun*. Some other bastard from *The Daily Record*. Assorted other bastards from various other rags. They were all practically slavering down themselves at the thought of what was to come.

"I want to thank you all for coming out this morning," Haldane began. "I'm going to start by reading a prepared statement, then I'll be joined on stage by Detective Chief Inspector Jack Logan, who has—until now—been leading the investigation I'll be discussing. I'll take a few questions at that point, but I'm sure you all appreciate that we don't have a lot of time."

Logan's attention drifted in and out as she read through her statement. As he'd expected, at any mention of the name 'Owen Petrie,' a murmur of excitement rippled through the audience. This was big news. Front-page stuff. A nice fat bonus, maybe, if he remained at large for a few weeks and killed a couple of kids.

Bastards.

The statement gave the basics, but was light on detail. Petrie had escaped Carstairs. Two members of staff had been killed. He was now in Inverness, and had taken Harris Bell.

While she did go into some detail on Harris, and said she'd be providing additional photographs to those the force had already sent out, she didn't mention his connection to Sinead, or her role in the polis.

She didn't mention Maddie or Alice, either. That was no surprise. Keep the message clear and to the point. 'A very bad man took an innocent young boy.' That's what got attention. That's what had people keeping their eyes open. Muddy the message, and people switched off.

The Assistant Chief Constable was nearing the end of her statement when Logan felt a tap on his shoulder.

"Got a second, sir?" Hamza asked.

Logan glanced back at the stage, then motioned for Hamza to join him a few steps away from the door.

"Aye. What's up?"

"The three-word thing, sir. We've cracked it. Well, one of them. Sinead's working on the other one, but it shouldn't be long now that we've got this one figured out."

Logan's heart missed a beat. "Where is it?"

"Off the A862. Near Bunchrew House."

Unlocking his phone, Logan handed it over. "I got the app. Punch it in."

Hamza took the phone, opened the *what3words* app, and typed in 'idealist.-mentions.toast.' The map zoomed in to show a location to the northwest of the city. A ten-minute drive. Probably less.

"Right. Thanks. Go back. Help Sinead with the next one. I'm going to check this out."

Hamza looked past him into the press conference room. "Aren't you supposed to be on stage soon?"

"Supposed to be, aye," Logan confirmed, but in a way that suggested he wouldn't be.

"You shouldn't go alone, sir. You should take back-up."

Logan shook his head. Enough people had been put in danger because of this thing with him and Petrie. Too many.

No more.

"I'll call if I need support. In the meantime, keep it to yourself." He stole a look into the next room. Haldane was saying his name now. She'd be giving the hand signal at any moment. "Oh, and if there's a chance to hide somewhere before the Impaler comes looking for me, you're probably going to want to take it."

THERE WAS a can of Red Bull rolling about in a bag in the passenger footwell. Logan managed to snag it while keeping the car going in a straight line, and guzzled it in a couple of big swigs. The caffeine should take the edge off his tiredness and help keep him sharp.

Or sharper than he currently felt, at least.

The road heading into Inverness was pretty slow-moving at this time of the morning, but traffic flowed freely as he headed across the Telford Street bridge.

Telford Street became Clachnaharry Road, which in turn became the A862. The houses on his left were large and grand. They stood on the rise of a small hill, looking out across the final stretch of the Caledonian Canal at the less affluent Merkinch on the other side.

The journey took just over seven minutes. As he neared the spot marked on the map on his phone, he slowed until the Volvo was crawling along the quiet stretch of road.

To the right of the road was a large, well-tended field. To the left was a barbed wire fence, a lot of jaggy bushes, and about an acre and a half of stinging nettles.

"Aye, figures," Logan muttered, pulling off the road onto a grassy verge and cutting off the engine.

The red dot on his map showed him the spot he was looking for was over the fence, through the jaggies, and deep into the nettles. Nothing was ever bloody easy.

He looked both ways along the road. Nobody watching, as far as he could tell.

The barbed wire fence wasn't too great an obstacle for a man of his stature and inside-leg measurements. There was a wee worrying moment in the middle when the ground on the other side turned out to be an inch or two lower, but some quick thinking and the judicious application of fingers in just the right places kept the pointed metal barbs from doing any real damage.

The jaggy bushes were more problematic. They stood in a line like a military regiment, the last line of defence between the road and the sea of stinging nettles. Logan had to backtrack a good thirty or forty yards until he found a gap big enough to squeeze through without tearing first his trousers, then the flesh from his legs.

Once through, he skirted close to them until he was back level with his original starting point and turned so the wee blue arrow on his phone that represented him, was facing the wee red dot that represented whatever surprise Petrie had left for him to find.

The nettles were evil bloody things, and he was grateful he was a boots guy and not a shoes guy. A shoes guy would, not to put too fine a point on it, be royally fucked right now. But, as a boots guy, he was able to make his way freely through the field of nettles, sustaining only the occasional sting through his trousers and socks from some of the larger specimens.

After a minute or so spent picking his way around the denser patches, and another few seconds pointing himself in the right direction again, he arrived at the spot marked on the map.

Idealist.mentions.toast

At first, he saw nothing. Nothing more than the same big patch of nettles he'd just waded through, at any rate. He checked the map, looked around like this might somehow help him get his bearings, then bent over and checked the ground in front of him.

He found it a couple of paces to the right, hidden under a canopy of nettle leaves. It was an Aldi Bag for Life. One of the good ones. Sturdy.

Logan pulled on a pair of gloves, partly for evidence handling purposes, and partly to ward off the bloody nettles.

He prised the top of the bag open. There was a shoebox inside. There was also, he noted, a lot of flies.

The smell hit him a half-second later, almost knocking him onto his arse. Christ. It was ripe. There was something dead in the box. Something on the turn.

Reaching into the bag, he raised one corner of the box, waited to make sure nothing was going to come scrabbling through the gap, then opened it all the way.

"OK," he muttered, peering down into the box. "What the hell is this now?"

"YES!" Sinead exclaimed. "Got it."

Hamza looked up from his computer just as Sinead held her phone up for him to see. It showed a map of Inverness. A little location marker was positioned out to the east of the city.

"Old Military Road. Behind the airport."

"Nice work," Hamza said. "I'll text it to the DCI."

"Right. Right, yeah," said Sinead.

She sat back in her chair.

Her fingers tapped out an impatient rhythm on the desk.

She sat forward again.

"Or, we could go scope it out."

Hamza stopped tapping at his phone screen. "What, not tell Logan?"

"Oh, no. Tell him. Send it over. I'm just saying, once you've done that... We could go."

Hamza looked unconvinced. "We should probably wait until—"

"Harris could be there," Sinead said, her eyes pleading. "And... I know something's happened with Tyler, and you don't want to tell me. They could both be there."

Hamza beckoned for her to show her phone again. He squinted at the screen, figuring out exactly where the marker was. "That's just a big field, isn't it? Hit the satellite overlay."

"Where's...? Oh."

Sinead tapped a button at the bottom right corner and the map image was overlaid with a bird's eye view of the same area. It showed a large, empty field to the north of Inverness Airport.

A big, wide-open space. Broad daylight. How dangerous could it be?

From out in the corridor, he heard a woman's voice shout.

"Where the bloody hell did Logan get to?"

"Guess the press conference is finished, then," Hamza said. He grabbed his car keys from his desk and gave Sinead the nod. "Right, then," he whispered. "Let's go."

Logan hadn't reached into the box itself, and he had no great urge to do so.

Inside, sitting on a stack of plastic bags, was a human hand. It lay on its back, fingers curling upwards like the legs of a dead spider. The wrist was a grisly stump of sinew and bone that suggested it hadn't been removed with any great care or precision, just rather a lot of elbow grease.

It wasn't particularly big, but it had belonged to an adult, judging by the general condition of it. A man, he thought, although he couldn't be certain. Not Maddie's, though. He could say that much.

That had been his first thought when he'd seen it, but it hadn't lasted more than a second or so before he concluded it wasn't hers.

It had probably come from the victim behind the hotel. He hoped so, at least. One handless guy was enough to be dealing with right now.

He replaced the lid on the box and stood up, the constant goading of the nettles starting to get uncomfortable.

This didn't make a lot of sense. A victim who had been mutilated to hide his identity. A clue leading here to his hand. The fingerprints were intact, which meant there was at least a chance of getting an ID, assuming the victim had been known to them.

If that was the case, then Petrie wanted him to know who the body belonged to.

If it wasn't the case, and the fingerprints didn't help identify him, then...

He had no idea. What would be the point?

He called it in and arranged for Uniform to come out and cordon off the scene, and for SOC to come out and take the hand away. Let's see how Geoff bloody Palmer liked the jaggies and the nettles.

It'd be run for prints. If they got a hit, then at least they'd have something else to pursue. Some other way of getting closer to Petrie.

Although, since Petrie had given them the lead himself, just how reliable could it be?

A text came through on his phone. He saw Hamza's name, and tapped to open it.

Found it, it read. And then, there was a link which, once clicked, opened a map on Logan's screen. Near the airport. Opposite end of the city.

He found a stick in the nettles and jammed it into the ground near the box to act as a marker.

That done, he set off back towards his car, his fingers tapping away at the screen in response to the message.

On my way.

CHAPTER FORTY-TWO

Hamza pulled across Old Military Road and brought his car to a stop on the right-hand side of the road, roughly level with where the icon on the map pointed. Two trucks, which he had been holding up for a while as he'd crawled along scoping the field out, went thundering past, horns blaring, slip-streams shaking the car.

"This looks about right," Sinead said from the passenger seat.

"Aye. Think so," Hamza agreed. "See anything?"

Sinead shook her head. "No. You?"

"No. Just a field."

Another truck passed them in a cloud of diesel fumes. Over on the right, behind the field, an EasyJet plane took to the air.

Sinead watched it. Since moving to the city, she and Harris had made a game of trying to guess where each plane they saw taking off was heading. It had started normal enough—France, America, Australia—but the suggestions had gradually become more ridiculous until they verged into the surreal.

The last one they'd seen, Harris had decided was going to, 'The Nexus of All Things.' When Sinead had asked for clarification as to where that was, he'd said, "Your face," then erupted into wild, uncontrollable laughter that had reduced them both to fits of happy tears for reasons neither of them could explain.

The thought of it proved too painful. She flicked her eyes from the plane to the field, then unbuckled her seatbelt. "Let's scope it out. Did you text the DCI?"

"Aye. Before we left the station. Gave him a map link," Hamza replied. He shot a glance in the rearview mirror and put a hand on Sinead's arm. "Wait. Don't open the door. Truck coming."

Sinead turned in her seat and saw the truck approaching. It would pass in the left-hand lane, Hamza's car blocking two-thirds of the right-hand lane, facing the wrong way.

The truck slowed as it passed, and Sinead was about to open her door when it swerved in in front of them, its brake lights turning solid red.

She shot Hamza a wary look as the truck stopped with a *hiss* of hydraulics.

It was a large box-truck, the kind of thing used for transporting cargo long distances. Supermarkets used them all the time, but this one was unmarked. Hamza's eyes automatically went to the number plate, but it had been obscured by a spray of mud.

"I don't like this," he said, putting the car into gear. Sinead hurriedly clipped her belt back into place and instinctively grabbed for the handle above the door.

Before Hamza could pull away, the truck's back door opened, revealing four men wearing black balaclavas. Two of them held shotguns, and Hamza bellowed at Sinead to, "Get down!" as he floored the accelerator and pulled out onto the other side of the road.

The second truck came out of nowhere. Neither of them saw it, but they felt the impact as it ploughed into them, sending Hamza's car into a tornado-spin that threw them around like ragdolls.

The inside of the car was filled with dust, and noise, and glass, and airbags. The interior lights came on. The horn blared.

And then, with a *crunch*, the movement came to a sudden, jarring stop.

The car was upside-down, although Hamza didn't realise this at first. It was only when he saw the feet approaching the side window that he was able to grasp it, and even then it took a bit of working out.

His arms ached. His hands positively *screamed.*

There was blood on his airbag. There was more spattered across the thousands of pieces of glass that sat on the inside of the roof like a stack of uncut diamonds. Was that his blood, or...?

Sinead.

He turned to her, the movement sending shockwaves of pain down his spine. She was hanging upside-down, like him. Her face was cut. There was a lot of blood. She wasn't moving.

Hamza tried to say her name, but the words sounded distant and far away.

Something crunched beside him. Footsteps on glass.

His door was opened with a *screech.*

A shotgun appeared.

A face.

A smirk.

There was a bang. A pain. Excruciating.

And then, there was nothing at all.

Logan was halfway back to his car, through the nettles but not yet around the jaggy bushes, when he spotted the van.

He'd been expecting them to start turning up, but not yet, and not any that looked like this. Those would have blue lights on top. This one was white and unmarked. It slowed as it passed, and Logan caught a glimpse of a black bomber jacket sitting behind the wheel, and then it was off again, continuing its journey along the road.

Logan watched it until it rounded the bend and drove out of sight. It was one of Bosco's. Had to be.

He took out his phone, swiped to his contacts. Four rings later, Shona Maguire answered.

"I'm still fine!" she insisted, before he could say a word. "No one from the police has turned up yet, if that's what you're calling for?"

"Actually, it isn't," Logan said. He had his eyes fixed on the spot where the van had disappeared. He'd passed the turn-off for Bunchrew House on the way here. It was maybe forty seconds up the road. Add in fifteen seconds to turn...

"Social call, then?" Shona asked.

"Eh, no. Not quite that, either."

The van reappeared, slowed as it passed in the opposite direction, then continued on again. He pretended not to notice this time, but kept track of it until it was out of sight again.

"I've got a bit of a favour to ask you," he said. "It's a big one, too. I'd say feel free to say no, but... well, you can't. Sorry to put this on you."

"Is it dangerous?" Shona asked, after a momentary pause.

"No. Well... No, it shouldn't be," Logan said.

He heard her take a breath down the phone, composing herself.

"Right, then," she said. "What do I need to do?"

Logan explained as quickly and efficiently as he could, recited the information she needed, then answered her questions as he climbed over the fence and plodded up the marshy incline that led to the road, and the Volvo parked on the verge.

He stressed the importance of it again, wished her good luck, then they said their goodbyes. He had just taken his car keys from his pocket when he heard the van approaching again, the engine giving a guttural grunt of complaint as the driver shoved the pedal to the floor.

Logan stepped in behind the car, as if making room for the van to pass, but then it screeched to a halt beside him, the side door sliding open even as he adjusted his grip on the keys so they stuck out through the gaps between the fingers of his clenched fist.

He saw three men, got the impression of more, all masked up. All moving quickly. Voices shouted in Polish, or Latvian, or whatever it was. Hands grabbed for him. Eyes blazed and mouths sneered through the gaps in the balaclavas.

The first of the grabby bastards howled and spluttered as Logan drove the key to his flat's front door into the fleshy part at the bottom of the man's jaw. It pulled away with a satisfying *schlop* sound, spilling blood onto the tarmac at their feet.

The man stumbled back, gagging and gasping, but Logan was already moving, shifting his weight, throwing another punch.

A cheek was torn open through the woollen mask. A man screamed and swore. Logan didn't understand the language, but he got the gist of it, all the same.

Something hit him on the back of the legs, right across the knees. His legs went from under him. He hit the ground hard.

He saw a shotgun. He saw an iron bar. He didn't know which of them hit him, just that pain exploded across the side of his head, making his eardrum sing and his vision go white.

Jesus Christ. One of these days, someone was going to give him brain damage.

The ground rolled. He reached for it, trying to stabilise himself, but it wasn't there. Nothing was there but empty space.

As he fell sideways, he saw the eyes of the men staring down at him from behind their masks.

He tried to speak, but whatever part of his brain controlled his mouth was clearly still reeling from the impact.

A boot connected with his ribs. Another with his lower back.

He tried to get up, but a foot stamped on him, smashing him down onto the road. He coughed wetly. Something ground against something else in his ribcage.

Hands grabbed at his hair, pulling him backwards, forcing him to scrabble up onto his knees. A bag was pulled down over his head. He swung a punch, but it was a limp and useless thing, and whoever was on the receiving end laughed it off.

He felt movement. Impact. Heard the van door sliding shut.

And then, from nowhere, something connected hard with the side of his face, and he lost his slippery grip on consciousness.

CHAPTER FORTY-THREE

PAIN.

That was his first thought.

Or no, not thought, exactly. It was too early in the process of coming round to form thoughts yet. The subconscious part of his brain was stirring. The conscious part, ironically, was still anything but.

Pain.

That one had been a thought. Not fully-formed, but heading in the right direction.

His legs twitched, the animal part of his brain doing what it could to jolt the rest of it into life.

Instincts propelled Logan upwards before his eyes were even open. More pain—one of the many—tore at his wrist. Metal rattled. He was jerked back to the floor by the chains that shackled him in place.

His eyelids felt sticky, like something wet had dried there, fusing the eyelashes together. He forced them open, then hissed in the blinding glare of a spotlight that stood on a tripod, pointing his way.

He could feel the heat of it on his face. Not burning, but hot enough to be uncomfortable. Even behind his eyelids, he saw a shadow move across the light, passing from left to right.

A voice whispered in his ear.

"Look who's awake."

Logan twisted, ignoring the fire the movement ignited in his ribcage. He swung with a fist, but the chains snapped him back.

For a moment, he saw a figure looming just beyond the edge of his pool of light. He saw a smile. He saw eyes that had been burned into his brain a decade before. Cold. Cruel. Callous.

"Petrie!" he hissed, just that glimpse of the man sending a much-needed jolt of adrenaline buzzing through his system. "Where are they? What have you done with them?"

The reply came from elsewhere in the shadows. That voice, the hoarse whisper of a former sixty-a-day man who'd done his throat irreparable damage.

"If you'd been paying attention, I already told you where the boy is. But the rest? All in good time, Jack. All in good time."

Logan pulled on his chains. They were attached to an old-style radiator. A great big brute of a thing that wasn't going anywhere.

The floor beneath him was a mess of plywood and loose carpet tiles, like the place was in the middle of being ripped up and packed away.

The light was still too dazzling for him to see much of anything beyond the edges of its beam, but he thought he got the impression of shapes behind it. People, he thought. Watching him.

"I swear to God, Petrie—"

"Oh, please, Jack. I don't think God's listening. Do you?" Petrie replied. He was over on the left now, moving just beyond the border where light fell away into darkness. "And I'd rather you called me by my real name."

"Owen?"

"No. You know the one I mean."

"Aye, well you can get that idea right out of your fucking head," Logan spat. "You're no' a supervillain, Owen. You're a sad wee bastard with a big ego. That's it."

In the shadows, Petrie snorted. "Aye, well. Could a sad wee bastard do this?"

There was silence.

Stillness.

Nothing.

"That's your cue to hit the fucking lights," Petrie whispered, his voice even lower than usual and clearly not meant for Logan's ears.

Logan would've laughed at him—made a point of it, just to piss him off—had the lights not come on then, and knocked the bottom right out of his world.

They were there on the floor, kneeling, hands behind their backs, tape across their mouths. He'd lined them up, Ben on the left, then Hamza, then Tyler, then Sinead.

And there, right at the end...

"Maddie!" he gasped.

His daughter. His little girl. Her eyes were two bulging spheres of panic. They were fixed on him, begging, pleading, desperate.

"It's going to be OK. It's going to be OK," he assured her.

Petrie laughed at that. A theatrical, throwing-the-head-back guffaw that rang around the room.

"No, Jack," he said. "It really isn't."

Logan didn't so much as glance at the bastard. Didn't give him the satisfaction. Instead, he looked along the line of kneeling figures on the floor. Sinead and Hamza were in bad shape, and were struggling to hold their heads up. Tyler looked more or less fine, although one of his eyes was all but swollen shut, and the fear on his face... Christ. The fear.

And then, there was Ben. Ben may have been on his knees, but he held himself upright and rigid. While the others all stared at Logan, DI Forde's gaze remained fixed on Petrie. Burned into the murderer's back. He followed the bastard's every step as Petrie approached the spotlight, picked up the cable, and turned the beam off with the click of a switch.

Spots swam before Logan's eyes, big fat blobs of white that slowly cleared to reveal Bosco Maximuke and two of his men leaning against the wall at the back of the room. Bosco gave him a cheery wave as Logan's gaze fell on him. To the Russian's right, Valdis shoved his hands in the pockets of his bomber jacket and looked along the line of hostages.

"Surprise!" Bosco called.

"No' really," Logan spat back. "We've had you two pegged together for a while."

Bosco's smile remained fixed, but his brow furrowed in the middle for a moment. "Bullshit."

It was Logan's turn to frown. Of course they'd known about the two of them. Why wouldn't they have known? They'd made it obvious.

Hadn't they?

"Do you mind?" Petrie asked, stepping between them and derailing Logan's train of thought. "This is my part. We agreed."

Bosco gave a wave of a hand, giving Petrie the floor. He gave a grateful nod, then turned his attention back to Logan.

Petrie was standing right behind Tyler, slap-bang in the middle of the line-up. DC Neish tried to turn to see what he was doing, but Petrie clamped a hand on his head and turned him to face front again. He made no attempt to turn Ben's head, though. Watching Petrie strut around would be causing the DI more pain than if he wasn't watching, and the fucker knew it.

"Well," Petrie said, smiling broadly. It was a little squint, the mouth pulled down at the side where his head was dented. If anything, it just added to his overall effect. "Here we are. Do you have any idea how long I've dreamed about this, Jack? This moment, or one like it? I mean, I had no idea who'd be filling these roles..."

He moved from Ben down to Sinead, bonking them all on the head and saying, "Bing," or, "Bong," like he was playing musical notes.

"But, I knew there'd be someone. You always find someone to reel into your web, don't you, Jack? Someone to corrupt with your influence." He looked along the line. "But my, you've been busy."

"Let them go, Owen."

Petrie's smile fell away. "You will speak when I tell you to speak, Jack." Reaching to the back of his belt, he produced a kitchen knife. It wasn't particularly long, but it was plenty big enough to do serious damage to anyone on the receiving end. He wrapped an arm around Hamza's throat and wrenched him back, his face all twisted up in rage as he pressed the blade of the knife against the DC's cheek. "Or this one loses an eye. Got that?"

Logan didn't dare reply. Not out loud. He nodded his understanding, and Petrie threw Hamza forward onto the floor. His already badly-injured face hit the plywood, and he let out a grunt of pain.

Petrie gestured to the two skinheads flanking Bosco. "Our guest fell. Pick him back up, would you?"

Both men looked to Bosco for confirmation. He gave it with a nod, but Valdis hung back for a second or so before following his fellow bomber-jacket. Together, they hauled Hamza back up onto his knees, then retreated to the back of the room and took their places at Bosco's side.

"See, this is the effect you have, Jack," Petrie said, ruffling Hamza's hair. "This one and the girl there. They came alone. Would you believe that? The two of them, out to the middle of nowhere, following a clue I'd left for them. Alone. I mean... What's up with that?"

He put his hands on his hips and shook his head like a parent who wasn't angry, just *disappointed.*

"Couldn't believe how well it worked out, though. You going one way, them the other. We've been watching those sites for... Well, a while now. I really thought you'd crack it sooner. Some of the lads were starting to get pretty bored waiting for someone to show up." Petrie jabbed a thumb back over his shoulder at Bosco and his men. "They were getting frustrated. Me? I was just excited to see who'd turn up where. And, honestly? It could not have worked out better."

His expression turned back to one of admonishment. "But they came alone. The two of them. Did you tell them to do that, Jack?"

Logan said nothing, just stared at the bastard and subtly felt around the edges of his handcuffs.

"That was a direct question. You can speak," Petrie said. He waved the knife vaguely above Hamza's head. "You *will* speak."

"No," Logan replied. "I did not tell them to do that."

"Aha! So, why do you think they did it? Rhetorical question, don't reply," Petrie said. "I'll tell you. Because they wanted to impress you. Oh, sure. They'll say they had other reasons. Urgency, maybe. Desperation. But you and I both know the truth. They wanted to make DCI Jack Logan proud. They wanted to be more like you."

He caught Sinead by the hair and bent down so his face was next to hers. She whimpered with the pain it brought. "Well, they will be just like you, Jack. At the end. In fact, it'll be difficult for anyone to figure out which bit belongs to who. That's how alike you'll all be."

Petrie planted a kiss on Sinead's cheek—a big, rubbery, cartoonish smacker complete with a *mwah* sound effect—then released his grip on her. Tyler shot her an anxious look, but Petrie spotted it and manhandled his head to the front again.

"This one, too. Broke into Bosco's house, would you believe? I mean… he's got balls, I'll give him that much."

"Not for long," Bosco chipped in from the back of the room. "Fucking show him what happens to sneaky little bitches who get in my business."

Petrie patted Tyler on the shoulder. "He means it, too. He brought pliers specially. I'm not even sure I'll be able to watch, and… well. As you know, I've got a high tolerance for that sort of thing."

He wandered along the line and stopped at Ben. The DI was still glowering up at him, bloody murder in his eyes.

"They all followed your lead, except DI Forde here, who ran away to a hotel after… Well, after his wife tragically passed." He laid a consoling hand on Ben's shoulder, but it was promptly shrugged off. "Ironically, we followed him. Both of you, actually. Right to the hotel's front door using a…?" He clicked his fingers a few times.

"GPS tracker," said Bosco.

"Yes. Thank you." Petrie smiled and shook his head. "Amazing how much technology can change in a decade, eh? Bosco's been keeping tabs on you for months."

Logan could feel all their eyes on him now. His colleagues. His friends. His daughter. They were all looking at him—looking *to* him for some sort of solution. Some sort of way out. This was a nightmare, and they were waiting for him to wake them all up.

He didn't look back at them. He couldn't. Instead, he kept his gaze on Bosco, and continued to fiddle with his handcuffs. Maybe there'd be some sort of weakness there. Something he could exploit.

Maybe, this wouldn't be the end. Maybe it didn't have to be.

But the cuffs were solid. The chain was strong. Even if he could get free, there was no way he could get to Petrie in time. No way he could fight him, Bosco, and the two skinheads in his current condition.

As he watched Owen Petrie—Mister Whisper—pace back and forth behind the line of kneeling figures, his knife swinging freely in his hand, Logan couldn't shake the feeling that maybe this *would* be the end, after all.

CHAPTER FORTY-FOUR

"Ask me why I'm doing this," Petrie instructed, pointing the knife at Logan.

"Jesus fucking Christ, Owen—"

"Ask me why I'm doing this," Petrie said again, the words slithering out of him, cold and dangerous things.

Logan sighed. "Why are you doing this?"

"Ooh! Good question," Petrie replied. "I mean, you and I both know why I'm doing it, don't we? But, for the benefit of the audience..."

He cleared his throat several times, coughed into his hand, then opened and closed his mouth, drawing his lips back over his teeth like a singer doing warm-up exercises.

Then, when he was finished, he began.

"Detective Inspector Logan, as I knew him—congratulations on the promotion, by the way. Very well deserved. See, he and I had quite the unique relationship dynamic. I tortured and killed children, he tried to stop me."

He held both hands up and chuckled, like he was reciting an amusing anecdote.

"I know, I know. Hardly the great love story of our time, and yet... Jack was *obsessed*. Weren't you? Relentless. I had people on the inside at the time, and they told me that I was just all-consuming for you. I was all you spoke about. It was flattering, if I'm honest. OK, maybe a *touch* creepy, but... you know. Flattering."

Petrie wandered along the line until he reached Maddie. He looked at her apologetically. "I hear your obsession even broke up the family." He rubbed the back of a hand lightly down Maddie's face. She shuddered and whimpered through her tape-gag at his touch. "I'm so very sorry to hear that. I was really rooting for the three of you."

"Get away from her," Logan barked.

"Uh-uh, Jack," Petrie snapped, waving his knife. "Careful, or the Paki loses an eye." Petrie looked back at Bosco and the others. "Can we still say that? 'Paki'? Is that still allowed?"

The Russian shrugged. "Fuck knows. Let's hurry this up."

Petrie turned back to Logan and pulled a face. "Getting impatient, isn't he? Where was I? Oh! Yes. So, to cut a long story short, he found me, eventually. I have to admit, I was impressed. That was proper detective work.

"Anyway, like in all the best stories, there's a chase. He's nippy for a big lad, I'll give him that. I try to hide. He finds me. We're up on top of a car park. I've got nowhere to go. Caught, fair and square." He held his hands out, wrists together. "'Slap the cuffs on, officer. Take me away.' But no. Oh, no. DI Logan had other ideas. He was getting me down off that roof, alright, but he was sending me via the most direct route."

Petrie pointed with a finger and moved it downwards as he whistled through his teeth, the note getting lower and lower, until...

"Bang. Impact. Next thing I know, I'm in hospital, full of tubes, and wires, and Christ knows what else. I'm pissing and shitting into a bag. But I don't really know any of it. Not clearly. I've got an impression of it, that's all," Petrie continued. "What I do remember—the only vivid thing in my head—is the last thing that I said to you, Jack, before you pushed me over."

Logan opened his mouth to respond, but Petrie pointed the knife at Hamza, silencing him. Instead, the detective just shook his head, pleading with his eyes. Not this.

Please, God, no. Not this.

"Anyway, I go under again. Next thing, it's three months down the line. I'm somewhere else. Still all tubes and wires. And everything's... slow. Like black treacle. I try to move my hands. Nothing. Then... I don't know. A minute later? An hour? They move.

"But I'm not worried about it, for some reason. It's just... the way it is. It's a nagging background concern. See, the front of my head is still full of those last words I said. They're written there, in big shiny gold letters, hanging there in the air." Petrie shrugged. "It was probably the drugs, I suppose."

At the back of the room, Valdis looked at his watch, then whispered something to Bosco. The Russian made a swatting motion, like he was batting away a fly. Valdis crossed his arms sullenly and went back to watching the show.

Logan's mind was whirring, searching for a way out. The handcuffs were solid, but maybe there was another weakness he could exploit. Bosco didn't know that Logan was already aware of his team-up with Petrie. Why? They'd signposted it with the shoes on the body.

He must've known they'd clocked one of his vans leaving the scene. Hoon would've passed that little nugget of information on. So why was he surprised?

The more Logan thought about it, the less it made sense. Petrie might have nothing to lose with a stunt like this, but Bosco had spent decades skirting around the law, never revealing too much of his hand, always avoiding prosecution.

This was a risky play for him. This could bring him down for good. So, why put everything he'd worked for on the line? Did he owe Petrie in some way? Was there some loyalty there that Logan didn't know about?

Or, was it something more obvious?

Before he could think any more about it, Petrie launched back into his monologue. Logan desperately wanted to tell him to shut the fuck up, but it would be Hamza who would pay the price. And, by the looks of him, the DC had already paid more than enough.

"After that, I get flashes. Glimpses of memories," Petrie said. "I'd close my eyes, and months would go by. Years. I'd blink, and there'd be a different face there, looking down at me. Poking at me." He pointed the knife at Logan. "And yours, Jack. Always yours. Popping up. You and me in rooms together. You and your photos. You and your questions. Just the two of us, over and over again."

He resumed pacing and tapped all five people in front of him on the head with the flat of the knife blade.

"See, you tell yourself that you've got people. You've got friends. Family. You tell yourself that you care about them. But deep down, you know the truth. It's me and you, Jack. It's always been me and you. It's pathetic, I know, but I'm the love of your bloody life."

"Holy shit," Bosco spat from the back of the room. "Just do what fuck you are doing so we can get out of here."

Petrie sighed. "You know your problem, Bosco? No flair for the dramatic." He shot Logan a look that bordered on apologetic. "I've known him since he was a lad, fresh off the boat. He worked for me. My building company. I gave him his start, introduced him to some friends of mine. Influential ones.

"We've been keeping in touch these last couple of years, and when he mentioned you. When he expressed his deeply-held feelings for you, well..." He put a finger to his head and turned it, like the spinning of a cog. "Let's just say, a plan started forming. You've cost him a lot of money over the years, he tells me. Personally, I'm not fussed about money. You know me, Jack. You know me better than anyone. I take my pleasures elsewhere."

He stopped near Ben, gave him a cheerful little wave, then turned his back and started to walk slowly back along the line. He turned the knife over and over in his hands, his lop-sided smile playing across his face.

"Getting back to the point. Those words that were in my head. Shining there. Those words I said to you. The thing that made you push me off that roof. You remember them, don't you? You remember what I said."

Logan didn't reply. He fought the urge to look at Maddie, overpowering as it was.

"Come on, Jack," Petrie urged. "You remember. I know you do. What was it I said I was going to do? You can speak. You can say it."

He couldn't. The words wouldn't come, *refused* to come.

Petrie huffed out a big breath. "Fine. I'll say it, then." He laid a hand on Maddie's head. "I told you that I was going to rape your daughter, and that I was going to make you watch."

Maddie let out an inhuman sound beneath the tape. It was like nothing Logan had ever heard before, and it pierced his heart like an icy spike. She tried to shuffle away, but Petrie twisted his fingers through her hair and held her in place. His eyes were blazing now, his face knotted up into a vicious sneer.

"After that, Jack. After I'm done. Once I'm *spent,* you're going to pick which one of your friends here is going to be the first to die. Refuse, and he rapes her," Petrie said, pointing to Bosco. "Refuse again, and it's your man there's turn." He pointed at Valdis, who shifted uncomfortably and glanced down at the floor. "And so on, and so on. There's a truck full of big strapping Polish lads downstairs. They'll all take their turn on her until you choose. Until you look one of these fine folks here in the eye, and you say, 'That one. That one dies first.'"

"Petrie, don't," Logan pleaded.

"You knew this was coming, Jack. That's what I mean about me being the love of your life." He reached into a back pocket and produced the postcard that had been weighing Logan down since he'd found it. "I gave you an ultimatum. Jump off that roof, or everything that happened next was on you. You didn't jump."

"I'll do it now. I'll jump. I'll do it. Just let them—"

"Oh, stop. Stop. We're way past that now," Petrie said. "Look at you. It's disappointing, I'll be honest. You knew I was coming. You knew how to stop me. But you didn't. And why?"

Petrie walked around the kneeling group and stopped just beyond Logan's reach. He squatted down and smiled, not unkindly.

"Because deep down somewhere, you wanted this. You wanted it to come down to me and you. The two of us, face to face. That was how it was always going to end, Jack. I mean, aye. You probably hoped you'd be the one holding the cards, but you can't have it all ways."

He stood up, ignoring Logan's shouts as he went strolling back over to Maddie.

"Petrie, don't. Don't do this. Don't." His eyes flitted desperately to the back of the room. "Bosco. Bosco, please, this isn't you. This isn't you!"

"What you fucking know about me?" Bosco hissed, launching himself from the wall and charging forwards. "For years, you fucking in my way. You interfere. You throw weight around. You burn my fucking office to ground!"

He barged past Petrie and stopped in front of the kneeling DCI. "Well, fuck that shit! It is over. You'll be gone. Done. No more. Maybe then, I get some fucking business done. Yes? Yes. Maybe then, things go back to normal."

"What are you talking about?" Logan asked.

He didn't know. He seriously didn't know.

"It's no' going back to normal for you now, Bosco. We know. The whole bloody force knows. You and him. Petrie. Your photos were all over the press conference today. Kill me if you like, but they're coming for you, Bosco. It's over."

A look of concern flitted across Bosco's face, then was gone. He snorted and wagged a reproachful finger at Logan. "Good try. Sow seeds of doubt. Clever."

"I'm no' sowing anything, Bosco. It was the shoes. The shoes the dead guy was wearing. They were mine. From my flat."

"Yes. Of course. That was point..." Bosco said. He looked across to the man with the knife for confirmation. It was clear that the plan had been Petrie's, and that Bosco wasn't quite up to speed with some of the finer details.

Shite. Logan had hoped that one would catch the Russian off-guard.

But, if he knew the shoes had been Logan's, and that his van had been seen leaving the scene, why didn't he know the polis had linked them together? What was Logan missing?

Wait.

"The badge," Logan said.

Bosco frowned. "Badge? What badge?"

"We're wasting time here," Petrie said. "This was meant to be my big moment. Can we—?"

Bosco ignored him. "What badge?" he asked again.

"In my bed. Petrie left it. A calling card, letting me know he'd been in the flat," Logan said. "You thought he'd gone in, grabbed the shoes, and left, didn't you? I mean, what were you trying to do? Set me up? Or... Or...?" He shook his head. "Doesn't matter. The point is, Owen couldn't resist leaving a wee calling card. We knew he was in my flat. We knew your boys dumped the body wearing my shoes, which could only have come from my flat. So, two and two together, that's how we knew about you and Petrie, Bosco. That's how the whole fucking world now knows."

Logan saw the change in Bosco's expression. There was a storm coming, but Logan wasn't going to be the one to take the brunt of it. Instead, the Russian turned to Petrie. His voice, when it came, was perfectly calm. Troublingly so.

"What the fuck is he talking about?"

"It's... He's..." Petrie shrugged. "OK. Fine. I thought it'd be funny. Wind him up. You know? The thought of me being there in his house. In his bedroom. I bet that wormed its way in there, didn't it, Jack?" he said, tapping the injured side of his head. "I bet the thought of me in there was eating you up from the—"

"You left fucking *clue*?" Bosco hissed. "What the fuck are you thinking? You say you need into his place, need shoes, you don't tell me why. All part of your stupid game you play with him. Your revenge mission. Fuck it, I help. You say you want us to get rid of your fucking friend you cut to pieces? To mess up his face? To finish him off? Fine. We do. But we are not meant to be connected, you and me. Us? We two? There meant to be no fucking link."

"In my defence," Petrie said. "Your men couldn't tell east from west. He wasn't meant to be left at that Premier Inn. He was meant to be at the one where the wife and daughter were staying. That was the whole point of the exercise. That was meant to freak him out. And there are no cameras there. Nobody would've figured it out."

He indicated Valdis and the other skinhead at the back of the room. Valdis glowered back at him, his arms still folded.

"So, really, if the police have linked us, then that's those idiots' fault, not mine. They messed up, not me. I mean, don't shoot the messenger, but that's the truth of it."

Bosco glared at him for a long time, muttering below his breath in Russian. Finally, with a wave of his hand, he relented.

"Just fucking get it over with. Then I sort out your mess."

Petrie's smile returned, broader than ever. "Make sure he watches," he instructed, pointing the knife at Jack.

There was a *crack* as Petrie hit Maddie with a backhanded slap that sent her spinning to the floor.

"Don't you dare! Don't you fucking dare!" Logan howled, the chain clanking as he heaved on it, slamming it against the underside of the old iron radiator.

Tyler struggled to his feet, but Bosco was at him in two big paces. The Russian drove a headbutt into the DC's nose, dropping him like a stone.

Hamza threw himself at the Russian's legs, driving a shoulder against them. The attack was weak and limp, though, and Bosco felled him with a knee to the side of the head.

Logan heaved against his chains, clanking them against the radiator. Bosco bent and drove a punch into Logan's already burning ribs, then the Russian was behind him, wrapping an arm around his throat, holding his head in place.

"He wants you to watch. So, you watch," Bosco said. "Front row seat. Best view in the house."

Maddie was squealing, screaming beneath the tape, bucking and thrashing as she fought to fend Petrie off. He had her on her back, side-on to her helpless father, her legs pinned beneath him, the knife in his hand.

"During everything that's about to happen, I want you to keep something in mind, my dear," Petrie told her. "Your daddy there knew I was coming. He knew I was coming, and he brought you here, anyway. Keep that in mind for me, will you?"

He turned to Logan, winked, then he hacked at the neck of Maddie's jumper with the knife until it split enough for him to tear it the rest of the way, revealing her bra and the flesh of her stomach.

"*Petrie!*" Logan howled, struggling against Bosco's grip as Petrie pushed his daughter's bra up, exposing her breasts.

"She's a wild one, I'll give her that," Petrie said, grinning back at Logan as Maddie continued to struggle and fight. He beckoned the two skinheads from the back of the room. "Come here. Hold her shoulders and help me get her legs open."

Valdis looked from Petrie to Maddie, then over at Bosco, even as his colleague trotted over to Petrie's side. There was a brief conversation in Russian between Valdis and his boss. Harsh words spat back and forth, crackling in the air between them, before Valdis relented and, with a sigh, went to lend a hand.

Valdis took the shoulders, pinning them, while the other man helped Petrie with Maddie's legs. She kicked out frantically. Desperately. Hopelessly.

Petrie undid the buttons of her jeans with one big pull, exposing her underwear. Maddie's eyes met her father's, begging him to help her. To save her. To make this stop.

Please. God. Make it stop.

"Now, make sure he watches every second. Cut his fucking eyelids off, if you have to," Petrie said, forcing her jeans and her underwear down to her knees. "I've waited a very, *very* long time for this."

CHAPTER FORTY-FIVE

SHE WAS ALL BUT NAKED NOW. JEANS AND UNDERWEAR DOWN AT HER ankles, bra pushed up almost to her throat. Petrie was laughing and whooping with excitement as he undid the button on his trousers. The other skinhead—the one Logan didn't know was holding Maddie by the thigh, his fingers digging into her soft flesh. He was sniggering, too, eyes darting hungrily across her naked body.

Valdis had a hand on each shoulder, but he was staring straight ahead, not at Petrie but past him to the wall beyond.

Logan struggled in Bosco's grip, but the Russian's arm was tight across his throat, and the bulk of his weight was too much to fight back against.

"Bosco, Bosco, please," Logan whispered. "Stop this. Please."

"Shut fuck up and watch show," Bosco said, his voice a growl in the detective's ear. He tightened his grip further, cutting off Logan's air supply.

Logan choked, wheezed, tried to swallow, but there was nowhere for anything to go.

And then, with a little hiss of laughter, Bosco eased back a little, and Logan gasped in a series of frantic breaths.

"Turn her over," Petrie commanded. "Make her face her old man. Make him look into her fucking eyes."

Valdis and the other man helped flip the squirming Maddie over. Petrie bent over and punched at her, like he was trying to get a pillow into just the right shape.

Beside him, Sinead heaved herself onto her feet. She threw a kick at him that caught him in the side of his stomach, and then the second skinhead caught her with a right hook that put her down. Her head hit the floor and she lay there, unmoving.

"Maybe she is next, yes?" he suggested, which drew a choking whine of rage from beneath Tyler's tape. The skinhead cackled at him, then went back to holding Maddie.

"You can't trust him, Bosco," Logan whispered. "He's right. I know him. Better than anyone. He set you up with the badge. He wanted us to know you were working together. He wanted you exposed."

"I sort that shit out after you are all dead," Bosco told him.

"Fuck's sake, Bosco. Think about this. Think about what he is," Logan hissed. "You don't know what he's capable of."

Bosco lowered his head, bringing his mouth closer to Logan's ear. "I guess your daughter is about to find out."

This was it, then. His Hail Mary. His only chance. He had to play this just right.

"And what about yours?" he asked.

He heard the hesitation. The tiny grain of doubt in Bosco's response.

"What you fucking talking about?"

"Your daughter, Bosco. He's got her."

"Bullshit."

"He has. He's taken her."

"Olivia is at home with her mother."

"She isn't. She won't be. She's stashed away somewhere. Tied up. Crying her fucking eyes out."

Bosco pulled his grip tighter again. "How the fuck would you know this?"

"Because I know him. I know how he works. How his mind works," Logan told him. "You want to kill him, don't you? For exposing you. You're planning to kill him. And what, you think he didn't anticipate that? You think he didn't want a contingency plan? He's got your daughter. He's got Olivia."

"What are you two whispering about over there?" Petrie asked. He stood above Maddie, one leg either side of hers, his trousers hanging from one ankle. "I want you paying attention, Jack. Not chit-chatting."

"If you think this is bad, wait until you see what he does with her," Logan whispered. "Kids are his thing, Bosco. You have no idea."

"What did he say?" Petrie asked, waving his knife in Logan's direction.

"He says you have my daughter," Bosco replied.

Petrie laughed. "Your daughter? Why would I have your daughter?"

Bosco looked from Petrie to Logan and back again. There was the faintest easing of his grip.

"You tell me," the Russian said.

Valdis stood up, placing himself directly behind Petrie. Bosco's other man continued to hold onto Maddie's leg, his gaze now fixed on her bare arse.

"He's lying, obviously. Jesus, Bosco, you think I'd be that stupid?"

"You were stupid enough to leave fucking badge."

"Why would I have any interest in your fucking daughter?" Petrie demanded. He sounded impatient. Irritated. The bulge that had been forming in his underwear waned. This was really taking the edge off his big moment.

"Because you are sick fuck," Bosco said.

Petrie gave a little shrug. "Aye, well, you've got me there, right enough. But I don't have your daughter. He's filling your head with shite to try to turn you against me. It's pathetic, really. Don't be a bloody idiot."

Bosco released his grip on Logan's neck. "I am idiot?"

"That's not what I'm saying," Petrie replied. "I'm saying—"

"Phone Olivia," Bosco said, tossing his mobile to Valdis.

"Jesus Christ." Petrie sighed. "Fine. Phone her. Maybe then, we can get back to business."

While Valdis phoned, Petrie leaned past Bosco and pointed the knife at Logan.

"Always one last trick up your sleeve, eh, Jack?" he said. "Well done. You've bought your daughter a few more seconds. Whoop-de-fucking-doo."

"She is not answering," Valdis announced.

Bosco's gaze flitted to Petrie. "She always answer. She always have fucking phone in hand. Try again."

For the first time since Bosco had mentioned his daughter, concern creased the lines of Petrie's face. Bosco was squared up to him now. With a clicking noise and a jab of his thumb, the Russian instructed his other man to get to his feet.

The three of them surrounded Petrie, all three of them eyeballing him. In the silence, they all heard the ringing from Valdis's phone.

Eight rings.

Ten.

Twelve.

A click of someone answering. Logan's stomach tightened. His heart stopped.

"The number you are calling is not available to take your call..."

"Bosco, think about—" Petrie began, but the Russian cut him off.

"Call her mother. Put it on speaker."

It took sixteen or seventeen rings for the phone to be answered. The woman on the other end sounded annoyed when she finally answered. Her accent was English. Essex, maybe.

"Bosco. You're a fucking dick," she barked. "She's not meant to be picked up until two. I've got her until then. We were going to have lunch. I bought fucking Lunchables in, and everything."

"What are you talking about?" Bosco asked, his gaze still fixed firmly on Petrie.

"Olivia. What the fuck else would I be talking about? When did you come get her, the middle of the bloody night?"

"She is not there?"

"No! She's not..." The penny dropped. "Wait. She's with you, isn't she?"

Petrie opened his mouth to speak, but Bosco raised a finger to silence him.

"I joke," the Russian said. "She is here. On iPad, as usual."

"Oh, fucking hilarious. Yeah, you got me there, alright. Proper laugh, that—"

On a signal from Bosco, Valdis terminated the call.

"Where is she?" Bosco demanded.

Petrie rolled his eyes theatrically. "Oh, for Christ's sake, Bosco. I don't know. This is him, isn't it? He's done this."

"I'm no' the one with a history of it, Bosco," Logan said. "Where is she, Petrie? What have you done with her?"

Bosco looked from Valdis to the other skinhead, then gestured angrily to the hostages. "Watch them. They fucking move, you kill them."

A meaty hand caught Petrie by the back of the neck and bundled him towards a door at the side of the room. Petrie tripped and stumbled, his trousers trailing behind him.

"Ow. Ow, fuck's sake, Bosco. Don't be so bloody stupid!" Petrie spat, and then he was thrown through the door into what looked like a stairwell beyond, and the room echoed with the sound of Bosco's roar.

"Where is she?!"

Logan heaved on his chains, but the radiator was heavy, and securely fixed to the wall.

"Cut that shit out," the second skinhead warned. He side-eyed Valdis, muttered something in a language Logan didn't understand, then looked down at Maddie.

She had rolled herself onto her back, and was trying desperately to wriggle her jeans and underwear back up.

"Ooh. Look at her go. She look so fucking hot. Yes?"

"Shut the fuck up, Olek," Valdis hissed.

The other man—Olek—sniggered and dropped into a squat beside Maddie. She froze, cowering as he reached a hand out and grabbed one of her breasts.

"Leave her alone!" Logan cried, hauling on the radiator again.

Olek squeezed her breast hard, making her whimper in pain. He raised his eyes to Logan and grinned. "I think she enjoy." He stopped squeezing and traced a hand along the length of her stomach. "I wonder what else she—"

Valdis grabbed him by the back of the jacket and hauled him to his feet. Angry words were exchanged. Harsh. Clipped.

Olek shoved Valdis in the chest, forcing him back a couple of steps. He turned back to Maddie, hunger in his eyes. "Maybe I take a go first. Yes? Give Petrie sloppy seconds."

He reached for the buckle of his belt. Valdis caught him by the shoulder, swung him around, then drove a headbutt into the centre of his face. Olek's nose exploded. He stumbled back, gasping, then went down in a flurry of frantic punches from Valdis.

Valdis followed him to the floor, raining blows on Olek as he spluttered and choked on his blood.

He let up only when the other man's eyes were rolling in his head, and his chances of getting up without medical intervention were close to zero.

Valdis sprang back to his feet then, spent a few seconds staring in horror at the gasping wreckage he'd left on the floor, then turned to face Logan.

"This is... This is not me," Valdis said, indicating Maddie. "I do not rape women. I do not hurt children. This is not me."

"I know, son. I know," Logan said. He shot a glance to the door. He couldn't hear raised voices now. They'd have worked it out. They'd be back any second. "Help us. Get me out of these."

Valdis shook his head. He shrugged off his jacket. "I... I can't. I'm sorry."

"Valdis, please!"

The skinhead draped his jacket over Maddie, covering what he could of her. "I'm sorry," he said again, aiming it at her this time.

He took a Stanley knife from his back pocket and extended the blade. Logan felt a surge of hope, but then he tossed it onto the floor. It landed near Tyler, but with his hands bound behind him, there was almost nothing the DC could do about it.

Without a backwards glance, Valdis turned and ran for the other door at the far end of the room, and went barrelling through it.

"Shit. *Shit!*" Logan cursed. He looked at Maddie, then across the faces of his colleagues. His friends. Hamza was barely with it. Sinead was rousing, but slowly. Tyler and Ben's heads were tick-tocking between him and the door, clearly having come to the same conclusion that he had.

There wasn't much time.

"It's going to be OK. We're all going to be OK," Logan promised.

He pulled on the chains. Gritted his teeth and *heaved*. His muscles burned. Metal groaned. Pain ignited in his broken ribs and he collapsed with a gasp, his head spinning as darkness crept in from the edges of his vision.

He couldn't do it. It was too hard. Too solid.

"I'm sorry," he sobbed, bent over. Broken. "This is all my fault. I'm sorry."

He thought of everything that had happened. Harris. Vanessa. Alice.

God, *Ben*. What he must be feeling. What he must be going through.

He thought of Harris. Alone somewhere. Tortured. Terrified. Was he even still alive?

Would it be better for him if he wasn't?

He thought of Maddie. Of what had happened to her. Of everything that might be about to.

His little girl. He made her feel safe, that's what she'd told him. Despite everything, despite all those failures over all those years, he made her feel safe.

He saw her as a baby, felt her weight in his arms.

As a five-year-old, over his shoulder, giggling.

As an eight-year-old, snuggled against him, falling asleep as he read her a story.

His daughter. His princess. His everything.

Slowly, like Atlas himself rising, Logan placed one foot on the floor, then the other.

He closed his eyes.

He clenched his jaw.

And he pulled with everything he had.

The pain tore through him. Through his ribs and through his wrists. It licked across his skin and buried through his insides, pouring into him, filling him up.

He thought of Harris.

He thought of Alice.

He thought of Maddie.

And he pulled, and he pulled, and he pulled.

CHAPTER FORTY-SIX

Logan held his daughter while she sobbed against him. While her body shook. While shame and relief and everything in between came tumbling out in her tears. He'd never felt her so fragile. So afraid.

He still wore the chains, but the radiator was on the floor now, and water was pooling beneath the buckled pipes that bent outwards from the wall.

"Ambulance and back-up on the way," Tyler said, his voice slurred, throat croaky. "ETA five minutes."

Ben was kneeling over Sinead, holding her hand. She'd insisted she was fine, but she hadn't let him go yet, and her grip was tight.

Hamza coughed. There was a rattle to it that Logan didn't like the sound of. The DC was on his feet, but it didn't look like it'd take more than a strong gust of wind to knock him on his arse.

There had been no movement from the door yet. No Bosco. No Petrie.

But, it was only a matter of time.

"I have to go get him," Logan said. Maddie's arms tightened around him. She shook her head. More than anything, he wanted to stay there, to hold onto her, to keep her safe.

To do his job.

But he had another job, too. And there was still one victim unaccounted for.

"I'll be back. I'll be right back," he whispered.

Reluctantly, she released her grip on him. She was dressed again now, Valdis's jacket zipped up in place of her torn jumper.

"Please, be careful," she urged.

"I will," he told her, then he hissed in pain as he stood up. "Tyler. You fit?"

"I am, boss," Tyler replied. His face was a mess of blood and bruising, but he was up, and he was standing, and that was the best they could hope for right now.

"Ben, you OK here?"

"Just go get them, Jack," Ben said. "We're fine. I've got them."

Logan twisted the chains around his arms, making them short enough to use as a weapon. "Good. Tyler, let's go nail these bastards."

THEY FOUND Bosco one flight of stairs down, blood pumping through his fingers where he clutched at his gut. He was leaning on the bannister, a red trail behind him suggesting he'd dragged himself up a dozen or so steps before stopping for breath.

"Oh... fuck," he spat, when he saw Logan and Tyler hobbling down the stairs towards him. "How the fuck are...? Shit, shit, fuck, shit!"

"Where's Petrie?" Logan snarled.

"Where you fucking think?" Bosco spat. "Piece of shit stab me. Piece of fucking traitor shit."

Logan cursed, then went hurrying down the steps past the bleeding Russian. "Tyler, watch him. I'll get Petrie."

Tyler fixed Bosco with a cold glare. "Got him, boss. You go."

The DC and the gangster held eye contact as they listened to Logan go clumping and clanking down the rest of the steps.

"What the fuck you waiting for, *policeman*?" Bosco spat through his blubbery lips. "Do your job. Call me fucking ambulance."

Tyler drove a punch into the spot Bosco was clutching, drawing a yelp of pain.

"Where's Harris?" he demanded.

"Ow, fuck!"

He hit him again. Harder. His face twisted into a mask of fury. "Where is he? Where's Harris?!"

"Fuck you!" Bosco snapped.

Suddenly, Tyler's hands were on his throat, forcing him backwards until he hit the wooden railing at the top of the bannister.

Another punch slammed into his stab-wound. The hand still on his throat forced him further back, until he was leaning over the stairwell, six or seven storeys above the ground.

"Where is he?" Tyler hissed. "What did you do with him?"

"Fuck. Jesus. I don't know! OK? I don't fucking know!"

Tyler yanked Bosco's hand away from the wound and jabbed his fingers into it, drawing a guttural roar of pain from deep in the Russian's throat.

"I'm going to ask you again, and then I'm going to throw you over this fucking drop," Tyler warned. His face was next to Bosco's. The look in his eyes said he was telling the truth. "Where. Is. Harris?"

"I swear. I swear, I don't know. He wouldn't tell me where he was, even if I wanted to fucking know. I never saw the boy. Not once. Not once!"

"You're lying!"

Bosco's eyes went to the drop, and the ground far, far below.

"No! No, it is truth! Why the fuck would I protect Petrie now? After this? After he took my Olivia?" He shook his head. Or as much as the hand on his throat would allow, at least. "No. I do not know. I do not know. I swear! I swear!"

Tyler's lips drew back over his teeth. He pushed, and Bosco scrabbled for the railing, his bloodied hands slipping as his fingers failed to grip the wood.

"Tyler."

DC Neish turned at the sound of his name. DI Forde stood there at the top of the stairs, a rectangle of red across his mouth marking where the tape had been. He looked old. Tired.

But he was standing. And that was the best they could hope for.

"Don't, son," he urged.

"But... but everything he's done," Tyler spat. "Everyone he's hurt. Why shouldn't I? Logan did it. Why shouldn't I?"

The reply came from down the stairs.

"Because you're a better copper than I am, son."

Tyler looked in the direction of the voice just as Logan rounded the corner of the next flight down.

"Petrie?" Ben asked.

Logan shook his head in response, not taking his eyes off Tyler. "Gone."

"He was just going to watch it all," Tyler said. Bosco was teetering on the bannister, his eyes almost popping out of their sockets. "He was going to watch what Petrie did. He was going to kill us."

"Aye, he's an arsehole. You'll get no arguments there," Logan said. "But you're not, son. Well, I mean... Aye, sometimes. Often, actually." He looked up at Ben. "Where was I going with that again?"

Tyler looked momentarily confused, then caught the grim smile on Logan's face. "Funny, boss," he said, very much not laughing.

"You're no' a killer, Tyler," Logan continued. "I don't say it enough, but you're a good officer. You've got a bright future ahead of you. Don't blow that on this waste of space. Do your job. Bring him in. He'll no' wriggle his way out of this one."

Tyler's grip tightened on Bosco's throat. His muscles tensed. He looked first at Logan, then up at Ben standing above him.

He'd hurt so many people.

He'd been about to kill them.

He'd threatened Tyler's *mum*.

The DC's muscles tensed. His eyes blazed with barely-contained fury.

"Bosco Maximuke," he said, spitting the words out in disgust. "You're under arrest."

"OK, OK, yes. Yes. But my daughter. Please. Olivia. Save Olivia."

Logan clicked his tongue against the back of his teeth. "Aye," he said. "About that..."

Olivia sat on the couch in Shona's living room. For once, she had no headphones on, and while her eyes were fixed on a screen, it was Shona's TV, and not an iPad.

She perched there transfixed, hand fishing around in an almost-empty bowl that had, until recently, been full of popcorn.

"OK, this is an oldie," announced a young man on the TV. He had a guitar strapped to his chest and was looking out across a sea of teenage faces. "Well, it's an oldie where I come from..."

Shona appeared from the kitchen, a can in her hand. "More Coke?"

"Please," Olivia said as, on screen, Marty McFly launched into the opening bars of *Johnny B. Goode*. She took the can, cracked it open, and slurped. "For a kidnapper, you're pretty nice."

Shona shifted uncomfortably. "Please stop calling me that. Like I said, I'm a... friend. Of your mum's. I'm just—"

"Yeah, yeah," Olivia said, shooing her out of the way of the TV.

"Enjoying the film?" Shona asked, taking her seat beside the girl.

Olivia nodded in reply. "Yeah. For something so old, it's pretty solid."

"Well, if you think this one's good," Shona said, picking up another Blu-ray box from the coffee table. Her phone rang, flashing up Logan's name. She sighed with relief and reached for it, before tossing the box into Olivia's lap. "Just wait until you see the sequels."

CHAPTER FORTY-SEVEN

Logan sat in his office, swallowing a couple of Ibuprofen and hoping they worked some sort of miracle.

He'd refused the hospital, but had insisted the others were taken in and checked. They'd been taken in a convoy, a police escort topping and tailing the procession of ambulances.

Shona was taking Olivia home. Persuading the girl to come with her had been surprisingly easy, she said. Olivia had come along without asking too many questions and hadn't seemed remotely worried. She'd seemed oddly excited about it, in fact, like it was nice to get the attention.

They'd watched *Ghostbusters* and *Back to the Future* back to back, then Shona had driven her home, laden with DVDs and Blu-rays. Olivia had said she would call next week.

Shona wasn't quite sure how to feel about that.

After Logan had finished the call, he'd cadged a lift back to base with one of the CID boys. There, he'd taken a short but thorough bollocking from the Assistant Chief Constable who, to his dismay, was still knocking about, and then he'd briefed her on everything that had happened and retired to his office to process the morning's events.

It had taken him just a few minutes to conclude that he couldn't process them right now, and possibly never would.

What Petrie had almost done...

He shook his head, forcing the image away. The bastard was still out there. He still had Harris.

But where?

I already told you where the boy is.

What had he meant by that? What had they missed?

He got up, went to the door, and addressed the various officers sitting at the desks in the Incident Room. "The boy. Harris. Any update?"

There was some reluctant murmuring. No. No update. No word. No sign.

Logan closed the door and returned to his seat.

If you'd been paying attention...

When? To what?

He sat back in his chair, rocking it from side to side. Even that movement was enough to make his ribs grind together. For now, he welcomed the pain. It was keeping him awake. Keeping him sharp.

Not sharp enough, it seemed. He had no idea what Petrie had supposedly told him. He had no idea where Harris was.

He grabbed a pen and flipped open his notebook. Maybe if we went back to the start... Or, no. Would it be better to work backwards from the end?

Or...

He sat forward.

Both.

He was on his feet again in an instant, throwing open the door almost as quickly.

"The hand. In the field. Did we get prints back yet?"

A uniformed sergeant turned in her chair. "Aye, sir. It's in your inbox. It came through about half—"

Logan was back at his computer before she'd finished the sentence. He saw the mail there, waiting for him. Double-clicked. Scrolled until he found the name.

He staggered back from the desk.

Oh, Christ.

Of course.

Bud Vance.

The scrote from the flat downstairs.

Logan heard Petrie's slow clap as the door flew open on the third kick.

"I'm sure you used to be able to do that in a oner, once upon a time," he called from through in the living room.

The smell in the flat was choking. Emptied bladder. Emptied bowels. The coppery tang of blood in the air.

He saw the girl, Tanya, propped up in a chair in one of the bedrooms, her throat cut, her eyes wide-open and staring at nothing.

Another victim. Another life lost.

"Bad timing on her part," Petrie said, and Logan turned to see him standing in the living room, Harris held in front of him like a shield. "Had to be done, though. If it's any consolation, I took very little pleasure in it."

Harris was gagged, just like the others had been back in the abandoned office building. He didn't look scared. Not really. There was almost no emotion on his face at all, like his brain was shutting everything down, blocking everything out.

Petrie had the knife to his throat. Bosco's blood still clung to the blade.

"Thought it might come down to this in the end," Petrie said. "This was the contingency plan, in case you slipped by us. That's why I gave you a hand." He chuckled at that, almost fondly. "I couldn't trust you to find the place yourself, even though... Keep your friends close, but your enemies closer, eh, Jack? Don't get much closer to home than this. If it's any consolation, he said some pretty horrible things about you. Bud, I mean. The way he spoke, you'd think the two of you were arch enemies!"

Petrie snorted out a staccato laugh, but it died away quickly and his face darkened. "And, well, for obvious reasons, I couldn't have that."

"Let the boy go, Owen. It's over."

"Oh, you're absolutely right, Jack," Petrie said. "It is over. This is the end. And, might I say, thank you for remaining as reliable as ever."

"What's that supposed to mean?" Logan asked.

Petrie gestured to the hallway behind the DCI. "Well, where's the clomp of running feet? Where are the Uniforms, or the negotiators? If I look out that window, will I see a big circus of flashing lights and polis?"

Logan didn't respond, and Petrie let out a triumphant little laugh.

"Aye. Thought so. You couldn't resist, could you? You and me, Jack. That's what it always comes down to, doesn't it? You and me. Just the two of us."

"If it's just the two of us you want, Owen, then let the boy go," Logan said.

He took a step closer, but Petrie moved back, tightening his grip on Harris.

"Ah-ah. Not so fast there, Jack," he hissed. "See, I need the boy. For this. For the end. I knew I wasn't going to get away anywhere. Not in the long run. I knew someone would spot me sooner or later, and I'd be brought in. But I wasn't having that. I wasn't having some fucking nobody catch me trying to sneak out of the country with a fake passport and a false moustache. Fuck that, quite frankly. That's now the finale either of us wanted. We wanted this. All this. Me and you, together at the end."

"You're a fucking headcase, Owen. Has anyone ever told you that?" Logan asked. He took another step. Petrie backed further away.

"I will cut his face off, Jack. Stay where you are," Petrie hissed.

"Alright. Alright. Easy, Owen. Easy," Logan urged.

"This was all for you. For *us*. For the dance we've danced all these years. For the game we've played."

"It's not a game, Owen."

"That's what Bosco kept saying, when I was setting things up. He was an idiot. You? I expected better of. Of course, it's a game! It's always been a game! And here's how the game ends," Petrie said, in that rasping whisper of his. "You watched my son die. And, while it's not the same as your daughter—I'd rather have fucked her in front of you and listened to you both screaming for me to stop—I know you care about this boy. That's why you came here. To plead for his life. Or to throw your weight around and try to scare me into letting him go."

Logan began to reply, but Petrie wasn't done talking.

"That's why you *think* you're here, Jack. But it's not. You're here because I want you here. Because I *brought* you here. You're here so you can watch him die, like you watched my son, die."

"He wasn't your son, Petrie," Logan said. "He was a wee boy you tortured and brainwashed."

Petrie shrugged. "Aye, well, is that not what all parents do to us, in the end? Maybe I just took it a bit further than most."

"I'll give you this. You were right about something, Owen," Logan said. He shuffled forwards, just a few centimetres. Petrie noticed and shifted back, maintaining the distance between them.

"What was that, then?" he asked.

"It was an obsession. Me and you. I can see that now. I wanted to be the one to stop you. To bring you in. To make you pay for what you'd done." Logan blew out his cheeks. "And, Christ, it cost me everything. Or... nearly."

Another shuffle. Another step back.

"See, when you had me chained to that radiator today. When you were going to... hurt my daughter. When I looked into the faces of my friends. Well, let's just say I re-evaluated a few things. Considered my priorities. And I realised something very important. Would you like to know what it was?"

"Indulge me," Petrie said. "I'm all ears."

"I realised that you're just no' worth the bother, Owen," Logan said with a disinterested shrug. "The game's not over because you say it is, it's over because, well, I can't be arsed playing. It's no' about you and me anymore. I've realised that. I don't have to be the one to take you down. Hell, I don't even want to be."

"What the fuck's that supposed to mean?" Petrie demanded.

"I didn't come here to plead for the boy's life, Owen. I knew you'd never let him go. So, my job wasn't to come barging in here to try to rescue Harris," Logan said. He took another step. Petrie retreated further, his knuckles going white as he gripped the knife harder. "My job was just to get you to stand near the window."

Petrie had just started to frown when one of the panes of glass behind him shattered. His hand went limp. The knife slipped from his fingers.

Logan caught Harris before the boy could fall, and pulled him in close so he didn't see the body slumping to the floor behind him, or the hole where its right eye had been.

"You're OK, son. You're OK," Logan told him. Through the window, on the rooftop of the building across the road, sunlight reflected off a lens. "You're safe now. We've got you."

CHAPTER FORTY-EIGHT

It rained. Of course, it did. It was only fitting.

Alice Forde was laid to rest in a small, private ceremony, attended only by family and close friends. It was nice, as funerals went. Wee bit too much about Jesus in it for Logan's taste, but Alice had always been a believer, and it was what she would have wanted.

Ben said a few words. Nothing much, just a minute or so about their time together, how he was going to miss her. The usual.

Logan had sat up the back on an empty pew, standing and sitting whenever the Minister told them to. He didn't join in with the singing, though. He may not have seen eye to eye with Alice on a lot of things, but even she didn't deserve that.

And then, they were all at the graveside.

And then, Ben was shaking all the offered hands, accepting all the hugs, reminding them about the do at the community centre. Tea and sandwiches. Plenty to go around.

And then, it was just him and Logan, and a hole in the ground.

They stood at opposite ends of it, both looking down at the coffin, with his smattering of dirt on top.

"Thanks for coming," Ben said.

"Of course."

"Just wanted to make sure the bugger was really dead, didn't you?" Ben asked. He tried a smile. It didn't sit comfortably.

"Aye. Something like that," Logan said. "I really am sorry, Ben."

Ben nodded, but didn't meet Logan's eye. "You and me both, son," he said, then he sniffed and wiped his eyes on the back of his hand. "You spoken to the others?"

"On the mend," Logan said. "Keen to get back to it."

"More bloody fool them."

Logan gave a grunt of agreement. "You can say that again. They're a good team, though. They'll do you proud."

Ben looked up, a questioning look on his face.

"I'm done, Ben. I've had enough. I told the Impaler."

"When?"

Logan shrugged. The rain pattered off the shoulders of his overcoat. "Now. I wanted to wait until after..."

His eyes flitted to the grave between them.

"I've done enough damage. It's time I moved on."

"Back to Glasgow?"

Logan shook his head. "No. Somewhere new, I think. Just for a while."

"Thought you'd want to be closer to Maddie."

"Aye, well. Eventually, maybe. She's..." He looked up at the sky, blinked in the rain, then sighed. "She's back to blaming me. And quite bloody right, too. That postcard. I should never have brought them up here, knowing what it said."

"They'd have been in just as much danger elsewhere, Jack," Ben said.

"Aye. Maybe," he said. "But best not to be around her or Vanessa right now. Give them space. They need it."

Ben swallowed. "Right. Aye." He turned and looked in the direction the other mourners had gone. They were clustering under brollies, as they made their way back down the hill towards their waiting cars.

"There's sandwiches made," he said.

Logan followed his gaze. The corners of his mouth turned up a fraction. It wasn't a smile. Not really.

"Another time, maybe," he said. He pulled his collar up against the rain. "Tell the rest of them I said cheerio, will you?"

Ben nodded. "Take care, Jack."

"Aye, you too, Benjamin," Logan said. He shoved his hands deep into his coat pockets. "You, too."

Another graveside. Another time. Logan propped the flowers in the little holder by the headstone, spent a few seconds trying to get them to stay together, then gave up and just let them splay apart.

They were a bit past their best, curling up at the edges, but they were the best the local shop had to offer, and he wasn't exactly spoiled for choice up here.

"I wish you'd been there, Detective Sergeant," he said, addressing the headstone directly. "You'd have kept us on track. Stopped it getting as far as it did."

There was a chill wind blowing in off the water. Logan shivered in it and stamped his feet on the frosty grass.

"Still, we got them," he told her. "Everyone responsible. We got them. I just... I wanted you to know."

He rubbed his hands together and blew on them, then looked across the graveyard. He was the only one in it, every other bugger having more sense than to come out in this cold.

"Don't suppose you know when the next ferry is, do you, Caitlyn?" he asked. When he got no reply from the headstone, he shook his head reproachfully. "Some bloody help you are."

He said his goodbyes then, rejoined the path, and headed for the gate. The roads were surprisingly busy, despite the time of year. Or maybe because of it. He had no real grasp of how Orkney's tourist seasons worked. Summer would be hoaching, he'd imagine, but maybe there was some draw to the place in the winter, too.

"No' the bloody weather, that's for sure," he muttered to himself as he crossed the road and headed for a hotel with a pub attached at the front.

A log fire welcomed him as he entered. The smell of lager and spirits swirled through the place, giving a faint blue edge to the flames in the hearth.

It was a smell that would've proved too enticing at one time. Challenging, at others. Now, he barely noticed it.

There were ten or eleven other patrons in the place, some drinking alone, but most in groups of two or three. A couple of them glanced his way as he entered, but they mostly paid him no heed.

An old man in a shirt and tie stood on the other side of the bar, leaning on it for support. He smiled as Logan approached, but it was an effort for him.

"You alright, there? What can I get for you?"

"Uh, hi. I was actually just looking for the ferry times heading back. Forgot to take a note."

"I've a winter timetable here. Hold on," the barman said.

He bent to look under the bar, and Logan caught his own reflection in the mirror that ran along the back wall. His beard was coming in. Not on purpose, he just hadn't bothered shaving in a while. He could do with a haircut, too.

"It's down here somewhere," the old man muttered.

Logan looked along the bar a little and saw the hand-written notice stuck to the mirror.

Staff wanted. Accommodation provided.

"No, can't see it, sorry," the barman said. He straightened with some difficulty. "I think I can remember, though..."

"Actually," said Logan. "It's fine."

He looked around the bar, with its fire, and its bare stone walls.

He looked through the window, to where the shore of the island gave way to the shimmering North Sea.

He turned back to the barman. To the sign. To a new beginning.

"I've just had a better idea."

EPILOGUE

TEN MONTHS LATER

There was nothing in the local paper. Nothing of interest, anyway. There had been a roof leak at the supermarket. The ferry prices were going up. The food bank had too many beans and not enough baby milk.

That sort of thing.

It had been a quiet day. Most days were at this time of year, after the summer rush, but before the winter season had started to kick in. It was the third time that week he'd read the paper. It somehow got no more or less interesting, regardless of how often he read it.

His record was nine times. That had been a fortnight ago. At the rate he was going, this week he was on track to break double figures.

The fire was getting low. He took a wander over, poked at it until the arse was about to fall out of it, and laid on a couple more logs.

There were a couple of dirty glasses on a table. He thought about leaving them for a bit, giving himself something to do later, but decided to treat himself by grabbing them now.

He returned to the other side of the bar, plunged one glass in the sink to wash it, but left the other sitting at the side. No point overindulging. There were still plenty of hours left in the day to fill.

He'd just returned to the newspaper when the door opened. The story was about the revised bin schedule, and he'd read it twice already, and yet something about it was so hypnotically fascinating that he didn't look up until he'd reached the end of the second paragraph.

"Alright, boss?"

Logan gawped across the bar. That hair. That grin.

"Jesus Christ."

"No' quite," Tyler said. "Although, you... With the beard and the hair. That the look you going for, boss?"

"Just Jack's fine, son. I'm no' your boss now," Logan told him. He looked Tyler up and down, like he couldn't quite believe what he was seeing. "What brings you out here?"

"Thought we'd take a wee jaunt over," Tyler said. Behind him, the door opened, and Sinead came in, laughing with Harris.

Logan's heart soared at the sight of them. Fit. Well. Happy.

Not that he let on, of course. That wouldn't do at all.

"Alright, sir?" Sinead said.

"Hi, Jack!" Harris said.

"See? He gets it," Logan said, pointing to the boy. "Alright, son? Look at the bloody height you're getting."

"I'm the second tallest in my class," Harris told him.

Logan glanced surreptitiously around, then leaned in closer. "Let me know who the tallest is, and I'll have him taken care of."

Harris laughed, although it was a little uncertain, like he wasn't sure if Logan was being serious or not.

"What can I get you all?" he asked. "On the house."

There was a knocking from the other side of the mirror at Logan's back. He rolled his eyes and tutted. "On me, then. No' on the house."

Tyler eyed the selection of drinks on offer warily. "Is... Is this not a struggle? All the... You know, with...? Temptation, and that?"

Logan looked around at the pumps and the optics, as if only now seeing them for the very first time.

"Well, I hadn't actually thought much about it until now," he replied. "So, thanks a lot."

He sorted them out with drinks, then joined them at the big table in the corner. They talked about everything and nothing. About Bosco's conviction. About how Ben was doing. About Snecky's not-so-triumphant return to MIT North.

"Hamza made Detective Sergeant," Tyler said.

"Aye? Good for him."

"Yeah, it was going to be one of the two of us," Tyler said. "But since Sinead's now officially out of uniform and on the team, we didn't want me outranking her."

"Plus, Hamza's better," Sinead added.

Logan snorted into his Coke.

"Aye," Tyler agreed. "Plus, he's better."

"How's Plainclothes treating you?" Logan asked Sinead. Harris had a bag of crisps sitting open on the table in front of him. Logan struck like a viper and nicked one for himself.

"Hey!"

"Shut up, I paid for them," Logan said, nudging the boy with an elbow.

Harris grinned, but angled himself so the crisp packet was out of Logan's immediate reach.

"It's good, sir, yeah. Different," Sinead said. "Lot to learn."

"Aye, well, if this Muppet can do it..." Logan said, shooting Tyler a look. "And like I told him, it's just Jack. I'm no' polis, anymore."

A look passed between both detective constables. Tyler tilted his head a fraction in Logan's direction, but a flick of Sinead's eyes bounced it right back at him.

"What do you want to say?" Logan asked. "Spit it out, I'm no' getting any younger."

"It's just... Well, Snecky. He's... He's made it clear he's keen to relocate. There's a CID job in Aberdeen. We think we can get him to go for it."

"Nice one. Sooner you can get shot of that useless bastard, the better," Logan said.

"Aye. Except... Everything's still in a bit of upheaval," Tyler continued. "Now that Hoon's gone. The new Detective Superintendent is settling in, but she's not quite got the lay of the land yet. She wants a safe pair of hands, and she reckons Snecky's reliable. Aye, no' good, obviously, but reliable."

He fired another sideways look in Sinead's direction, and she took over.

"And, well, DI Forde suggested that maybe we might be able to get a replacement for him. For Snecky, I mean."

"A safe pair of hands," Tyler said.

"The safest," Sinead added.

"Oh aye? And who...?" Logan sat up. "Wait. Fuck off. No."

"Come on, boss, it'd be—"

Logan crossed his arms across his barrel-like chest. "Not a fucking chance. No way. I'm done. I'm out."

"Ben checked with the Impaler. She'd be up for it," Tyler said. "Now that all the Petrie stuff has died down, she'd be up for you coming back."

"Well, good for her," Logan said. "But no. Lovely offer, and it's great to see you both, but no."

"But there's a case, sir," Sinead said. She reached down the side of her chair and lifted a briefcase onto her knees.

"She carries a briefcase now," Tyler said with a smirk.

"Not always," Sinead replied, slapping him on the arm. She opened the clasp on the bag and produced a cardboard folder. "We're really struggling on it. We could do with your input."

"It's a belter, boss," Tyler said. "Murder. Blackmail. Infidelity..."

"A guy with a Hitler moustache," Sinead added.

"Guy with a Hitler moustache," Tyler confirmed. "Seriously, it's got the lot."

Sinead slid the folder into the middle of the table, angled in Logan's direction. It sat there between them, unopened, its contents a mystery.

And he always did love a good mystery.

But he had a job here. A life.

Or, not a life, exactly.

An existence. It wasn't bad.

And there was still that second glass to clean.

He looked at the bar, and the newspaper sitting on it.

He looked out the window, and saw the graveyard that lay between him and the shore beyond.

He saw the well-tended grave of Detective Sergeant Caitlyn McQuarrie.

"Ah, bugger it. Wait here," he said, pushing his chair back from the table. "I'll get my coat."

ABOUT THE AUTHOR

JD Kirk is a pen name of multi award-winning Scottish author, Barry Hutchison, who lives in the Highlands with his wife, two children, and a particularly annoying dog.

When not writing, Barry is usually walking said dog, getting rained on, and wishing he lived somewhere sunnier.

He is the author of over 150 books, several screenplays, and an animated series for Dreamworks. Despite all this, his proudest professional achievement is writing *The Bash Street Kids* for *The Beano*.

And who can blame him?

He has no idea what the 'JD' stands for. He just liked the sound of it.

Follow JD Kirk on social media at the links below.

facebook.com/jdkirkbooks
twitter.com/jdkirkbooks
instagram.com/jdkirkbooks

Printed in Great Britain
by Amazon

79155305R00422